DIARY OF AN 8-BIT WARRIOR
FORGING DESTINY

This edition © 2019 by Andrews McMeel Publishing.

All rights reserved. Printed in China. No part of this
book may be used or reproduced in any manner whatsoever without written
permission except in the case of reprints in the context of reviews.

Published in French under the title *Journal d'un Noob (Guerrier Suprême) Tome VI*
© 2018 by 404 éditions, an imprint of Édi8, Paris, France
Text © 2018 by Cube Kid, Illustration © 2018 by Saboten

Minecraft is a Notch Development AB registered trademark. This book is
a work of fiction and not an official Minecraft product, nor approved
by or associated with Mojang. The other names, characters, places, and
plots are either imagined by the author or used fictitiously.

Andrews McMeel Publishing
a division of Andrews McMeel Universal
1130 Walnut Street, Kansas City, Missouri 64106
www.andrewsmcmeel.com

ISBN: 978-1-4494-9446-9 hardback
978-1-4494-9445-2 paperback

Library of Congress Control Number: 2018952004

Made by:
King Yip (Dongguan) Printing & Packaging Factory Ltd.
Address and place of production:
Daning Administrative District, Humen Town
Dongguan Guangdong, China 523930
Box Set 3rd printing-2/28/22

ATTENTION: SCHOOLS AND BUSINESSES
Andrews McMeel books are available at quantity discounts with bulk purchase for
educational, business, or sales promotional use. For information, please e-mail the
Andrews McMeel Publishing Special Sales Department: specialsales@amuniversal.com.

• CUBE KID •

DIARY OF AN 8-BIT WARRIOR

FORGING DESTINY

Illustrations by Saboten

Andrews McMeel
PUBLISHING®

In memory of Lola Salines (1986–2015),
founder of 404 éditions and editor of this series,
who lost her life in the November 2015 attacks on Paris.
Thank you for believing in me.

—Cube Kid

SATURDAY—UPDATE XXI

We set out for **Owl's Reach**—the monsters, mysteries, and musty passages of the **Tomb of the Forgotten King** now behind us. As I fiddled with the squishy **glowmoss,** my mind wandered to **Urf,** to the **advanced crafting table,** and to the bizarre chain of events that had just occurred. Who could have guessed when I left Villagetown that I'd be fighting bosses with Breeze, **Pebble,** and some mysterious human?

Speaking of which, I **bombarded S** with questions during the whole way back to town. He seemed to know **just about everything,** so why **not?** Sadly, this little **interview** didn't go as well as I'd planned. His answers were from a **human's** perspective, which was confusing to a villager like me.

"Why is the sky blue?"

"Because Earth's sky is blue. The original game would have looked **strange** with, say, a **purple** sky."

"Oh. Why do villager boys have **big noses** while villager girls have small ones?"

"**Entity** was responsible for that, I think. He and a few others were working on a **new server mod** to make villagers **more lifelike**. This included villagers with different **personalities,** outfits, and **genders.** But after that, many of the players said the **girl villagers** looked strange, so **Entity** made their noses smaller and gave them hair. Then the **Scribes**—*a handful of players tasked with writing the history of the game world*—added a paragraph about how villager boys shave their heads as a **tradition.** And after the **server crash,** every last word the Scribes originally wrote **became real.**"

"You lost me. What's this about the **crash?** What happened?"

He went on to tell me that, in the Earth year **2039,** their world was facing **imminent destruction.** As the final hour approached, some of them chose to flee into **VR,** or **virtual reality.** Apparently, all they had to do was throw on **a helmet** to be transported to another world. But that was just **imaginary**—an **illusion.** The world they had escaped to was this one—once known as the **Aetheria server.**

After having spent thousands of hours in **this virtual world,** most of them had made **countless friends,** and they wanted to say **goodbye.** They were all the most hardcore of **game addicts,** and they'd spent more time in Aetheria than their own reality. Not many of them even had **friends** in the real world. Some didn't even have **family**. So it was only fitting for them to spend their last moments in a world they cherished, <u>**surrounded by virtual friends**</u>. . . .

"So what happened?" I asked. "Your world **didn't end?** The real one, I mean."

"We have **no way** of knowing. With the countdown approaching zero, those logged in **lost consciousness** and eventually woke up in a different area—still logged in to the game. **And the game was different, somehow. Real.** We couldn't quit or exit. To this day, we're still able to access the original **main menu** system, but it's unresponsive."

"**Oh.**" I stared ahead blankly, until something **caught my eye.** "Hey, look! A coal vein! Let's stop for a bit and mine!"

S looked at me
<u>**and sighed.**</u>

SATURDAY—UPDATE XXII

By the time we hit **Owl's Reach**,
it was <u>dark and cold.</u>

A **chilly wind** blew through the streets. The place would have seemed **abandoned** if not for **those few** scurrying here and there.

Even so, most of the shops were **still open.** Their windows, glowing cheerfully in **the gloom,** flickered every now and then when there was

"Take care out there."

"Breeze. Runt. It's . . . been real. Stay safe."

"Thanks again. Couldn't have done it without you."

"Good luck on your quest. Be sure to visit us, 'kay?"

movement inside. But first we headed to the square with **our new allies.** There, we saw each other off.

I watched them go, **wishing** we'd said more than **simple goodbyes**—wishing we'd never had to say goodbye at all.

But they had **their quest,** and we had **ours.** Wind gnawing at our backs, the two representatives of **Team Runt** walked straight to that blacksmith. Or is it *Team Breeze* after today . . . ?

The blacksmith gave me **750 emeralds** for the glowmoss, as promised. We traded the loot for another ◆**3,572.** That was **unusual,** I think, because it was mostly **Urf's stuff,** not the boss loot. Breeze and I felt it'd be a **good idea** to give those items to our friends back home. Souvenirs from our **first little tour** of the Overworld. And if you were wondering, yes, Breeze **insisted** on keeping **that dumb stick.**

We went to the **Quill & Feather** right after the blacksmith.

After we **sauntered** in, I looked **Feathers** straight in the eye and slammed ◆**2,500** onto her light-blue carpet counter. "I'll take an **advvvvvaeon** forge." *(Not a spelling error. I began to say "advanced crafting table" then smoothly transitioned to the item's **real name.** Because I'm as smooth as an ice block on a warm, sunny day.)*

"That was quick," she said. "You must have found **a quest.**" After glancing downward, and eyeing Breeze with **a knowing smile,** she added: "And by the looks of it, I'd say **your quest went rather well.**"

Huh?!

What'd she mean by that?!

And why does she keep staring at our hands?!

Only then did I realize that Breeze and I were . . . uh . . . **holding hands.**

Well, the wind was **freezing** tonight. It even felt cold **indoors.** So her hands must have gotten cold. These northern biomes, you see . . .

"You've got it **all wrong,**" I said. "She's not **my—**"

Breeze **interrupted** me with a smile. "Our quest **did go well,** but we're rather **exhausted,** so if we could just **get that forge . . .**"

"I'll be right back."

A minute later, I was holding **a cube of raw and unimaginable power.** It was **warm** to the touch, and its emerald-and-diamond grid **pulsed softly.** I found it hard to believe that this item was **thousands of years old.** It looked as though it had been **crafted** only yesterday: shiny, its gray surfaces without a single **scratch** or blemish, the diamond emblems of tools adorning its sides showing **no sign of wear.**

I handed it to Breeze, who began carefully **inspecting it** like the **neophyte historian** she was.

"**Will that be all?**" Feathers asked.

*Like this thing isn't **enough!*** I thought. I gave her a nod.

As Feathers opened her mouth to deliver what I guessed was that **standard shopkeeper line,** I beat her to the punch, saying it **loud** and **fast:** "**PLEASURE** DOIN' BUSINESS WITH YA." *(Boom! She didn't know what to say to that! Only closed her mouth and slowly blinked. When it comes to dealing with these shopkeepers, I'm a **pro**.)*

After I pocketed the forge, Breeze dragged me outside by the hand.

"The mayor will be **thrilled**," she said, as we both approached her horse.

"You don't think he'll be **mad at me** for taking off without speaking to him first?"

"No, **I don't think so.** Once he sees what you're carrying, I'm sure he'll lighten up. **My father, too.**"

"Yeah. You're right."

I felt such a relief.

My mission was complete.

All we had to do was hop into **Shybiss's saddle** and head back home. Well, maybe not right away: It was getting late, and we had more than **enough emeralds** to spare for another night at that inn. If we wanted, we even had enough to buy **a second horse** in the morning, **a breakfast fit for a king,** and about one hundred healing potions—because, like I learned today, you can **never** have **too many** ways to keep up your health.

I mentioned **my plan** to Breeze, who added taking **another hot bath** to the list. So with the forge tucked **safely** away in my inventory, we set out for a warm room, a warmer dinner, and **a sound night's sleep.** Shybiss was also exhausted by now, and the way she puffed with huge frozen breaths resembled **a redstone steam engine.**

SATURDAY—UPDATE XXIII

When we arrived at the **Enchanted Dragon,** Breeze took Shybiss to **the stable** out back.

A few seconds after she left, I heard a loud **knocking.** This was followed by **a shout.** It was coming from **the other side** of the building. So hands in my ~~pockets~~ inventory, I took a little **stroll** in that direction.

This side of the inn, opposite the stable, had a small building attached, with its own door. It must have been **a side entrance** used by the cooks and other staff. When I rounded the corner, the door was **wide open,** and the innkeeper stood just outside with a waitress.

"I thought I told you **not to come back!**" the innkeeper bellowed.

"**Please,**" the waitress said. "I really need the work. Just give me one more chance."

"I've already given you **plenty!** How many times did you show up late? Often **dirty,** no less! **Just as you are now!**"

"I'm sorry, sir. I've been . . . working **a second job.** I need help," she pleaded, voice **trembling with despair.** "Please. It won't happen again. **I promise.**"

"**Enough!** I've already hired someone else. And before you **seek work elsewhere,** little lady, I suggest you learn the difference between a **stormberry roll** and an **enderpuff cake!**"

Upon unleashing this brutal criticism of her serving skills, the portly innkeeper stormed inside and **slammed** the thick spruce door. The waitress **slowly** turned around, head lowered and slight shoulders **sagging.** She **jumped** upon noticing me.

Her **golden hair** was tangled and damp, and her **uniform** *(one of the many elaborate and official outfits worn by servants in the Overworld's larger cities)* was **disheveled** beyond belief.

Her expression was in the same condition. It could only be described as worn. **Exhausted, worried,** and full of doubt. Looking at her, I couldn't imagine she'd spent the previous night anywhere except **out on the street.**

With a slight shiver, she made her way toward the front of the inn, **ignoring me** as she did. **But she didn't make it.** As though **dizzy,** she stumbled and **tripped** on a crack in the mossy cobblestone path, where she fell to her knees with a gasp. She **struggled** to pick herself up.

"Hey . . . are you . . . **are you okay?**" I asked.

"I . . . feel **kinda . . .**"

That was it. **She collapsed to the ground.**

"What happened to her?" Breeze asked. She was **right beside me** now—I hadn't even heard her approach.

"I think she's **sick.**"

The **poor girl** now appeared to be unconscious, mumbling **something about a quest.** As I studied her, I felt more and more as though I'd **seen her before.**

That hair . . . and that voice!
No . . . how is this . . .

Breeze **crouched down** beside her. "**That's strange.** Looks like she recently killed a slime." She pointed to **one section** of the girl's tunic. **A dark green patch.** The dried ichor of **a slime.** "What was a waitress doing **fighting . . ."**

Breeze **suddenly froze** when she realized who it was.

I'd already recognized her. The color must have **drained** from my face. I opened my mouth, but I couldn't make a sound.

Of course, we could have **identified her earlier** using **Analyze,** but we've only had this ability for less than a day, so using it **isn't instinctual** yet. When we did look up, it only **confirmed** what we already knew.

This was a girl **who shouldn't have been here,** let alone in those clothes or **this pitiful state.**

A girl quite famous for her bravery, compassion, honor, discipline, and skill.

A girl praised for graduating at the top of her class.

A girl who hailed from Villagetown.
A girl known as Ophelia.

SATURDAY—UPDATE XXIV

The first thing we needed to do was to **get Ophelia inside.**

Although she wasn't **seriously injured,** she had three status effects: **Exhaustion, Food Poisoning, and Chill.** These were **debuffs,** the same kind as **Mining Fatigue.**

Her **Exhaustion** must have worsened over time, until finally rendering her unconscious. It was a huge stroke of luck that I was there right when it happened. If she'd remained outside, her Chill **would've intensified** in much the same way, until it led to something **far worse** than sleep.

"I've never **carried** someone before," I said.

"**It's easy.** You grab her shoulders, and I'll grab her knees."

"Okay. She's not so heavy, **huh?** Wait. How do we open the door?"

The front door **swung open** just as I said this. **Two dwarves** barged through. One of them eyed the unconscious Ophelia **warily.**

"That's the one who served me mutton instead of a pork chop," he **muttered** to the other. "And my stormberry roll was burnt!"

"**Sounds like a villager,** all right," the other said. "Those NPCs wouldn't know a **crafting table** from a **block of slime**. What's **with** all the villagers lately, anyway? **Where do ya think they're coming from?**"

I wanted to listen **further,** but Ophelia was getting heavy.

Nearly as heavy were **the innkeeper's eyebrows** as he glared at us from the counter.

Upon noticing that we were **carrying Ophelia** like a sack of beetroots, he **started yelling:** "What's she **gotten into** now? Forget it, **I don't care! Take her somewhere else!** I won't lose **any more** of my customers—they can't stand the sight of her!" He **glared** at her. "**Bad** for business, that one. **Never on time!** Always mixing up orders! I've had to give out over twenty **free** potions just this week!"

"We'll take a room," I said politely.

"Maybe you didn't **hear me,** little villager. **There are no rooms avail—**"

I handed off Ophelia to Breeze and *(politely)* slammed a shiny green pile onto the counter. "Like I said, **we'll take a room.**"

I have no idea **how many emeralds** I gave him. I wasn't counting. **Over three hundred,** if I had to guess. For **some** strange reason, **Theor the innkeeper** wasn't so angry anymore.

SATURDAY—UPDATE XXV

Just like the one from **the night before,** our room had only **two beds.**

But that didn't matter: **We had that enchanted bed.** After placing it near the furnace, **we set Ophelia down.**

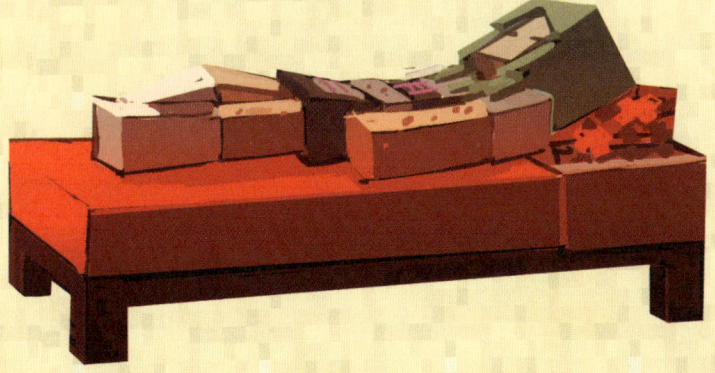

The icon with **the moon behind a bed** is **Exhaustion.** If you stay awake for exactly **twenty-four hours,** you get Exhaustion I. This debuff gives a **small penalty** to most tasks, including **crafting,** movement, and ability use. **Exhaustion II** appears at **thirty-six hours,**

and the penalties are **tripled. Level III** appears after **two whole days without rest,** and the result is the **loss of consciousness.**

The icon resembling **rotten green meat** is **Food Poisoning.** Some monsters, such as **husks,** are capable of inflicting this debuff. It's more likely, however, that Ophelia had consumed a **raw, poisonous,** or **rotten** food item out of sheer desperation. The duration of the debuff was **abnormally long.**

The heart encased in a block of ice is **Chill.** Like Exhaustion, it **hinders** almost every task. Some monsters—and, **according to Breeze,** several abilities—are **also capable** of inflicting this debuff. Yet there was no doubt in my mind that Ophelia got this by staying out **too long in the cold.**

(Note that even though her Exhaustion and Chill had an infinite duration, they could be removed through adequate sleep and warmth.)

Needless to say, this was the **greatest mystery** I'd encountered yet.

What happened to Ophelia? Why was she apparently **homeless?** Had she run away? Why had she been **fighting slimes?**

"We need milk," Breeze said. "**That will treat her poisoning.** The rest will just take time. Two hours, **three at most.**" She paused. "I forgot to bring a bucket."

"I'll go find one," I said. "You just **stay with her.**" It was my turn to pause—much longer than hers. "**Breeze?**"

"**Yes?**"

"Was she still in Villagetown **when you left?**"

"I can't remember," she said. "I was outside with **Emerald** and the others most of the time. I never saw her much after graduation. As far as I know, she was **with her own group.**"

"And you didn't hear anything about her?"

"**No.** Stump did say at one point that he missed her. He hadn't seen her much, either. They **danced together** at the party, remember?"

With a slight nod, I headed back out, **angry at myself** for not having the foresight earlier to buy **three iron bars.** I could have crafted a bucket myself. **Of course,** I'd still need a cow. And then there's the fact that I'm still not the best at crafting. The last time I made a bucket in class, **it had a hole.** I tried to convince the teacher that I'd done it on purpose. . . .

"It's the **Hole I** enchantment," I'd said.

"And what **redeeming quality** does it have?" Ms. Oakenflower had asked.

"Well, um . . . **convenience.** You see, you no longer have to tip the bucket over to empty it."

She'd **smiled coldly.** "Perhaps you could demonstrate this **enchantment** of yours for the rest of the class."

"Of course."

"Sorry, folks! As you can see, this enchantment still needs a little work."

"Our textbooks did need some cleaning, though."

SATURDAY—UPDATE XXVI

Most of the shops were **already closed** at this hour.

On top of that, **the wind** had gotten **even worse.** It practically had a knockback effect, and **its howling** through the alleys is probably what **a ghast** sounds like.

When we were **riding** back earlier, S told us about **a ghost** that **wanders** this city at night. I **laughed** at the time—just another **legend.** But then, as I was walking alone, I totally believed it. There's just something **creepy** about **Owl's Reach** after dark.

I eventually found a general store that had what I needed.

With the bucket like an ice block in my hands, I made my way back **as fast as I could,** hoping I wouldn't **get lost.** And wondering if milk can freeze. **That was when I heard a cry.**

Don't worry—**it wasn't a ghost.** It was three young humans, all of them armored and brandishing swords. Their iron breastplates bore **the sigil of a red sword,** as though painted on. They were running through the streets and **looking down** every passage and alleyway.

"Where'd he go?"

"Curse his invisibility!"

"Look! **Over there! I see him!**"

All of a sudden, one of these men pointed his sword **at me.**

"You can't hide from us, **villager!** Return **that ring** at once, or be forever hunted by the **Solemn Blades!**" As they trudged in my direction, taking their time, I, **um . . .** well, I carefully **stashed the milk.**

What? It took me **forever** to get it, **okay?** I didn't want it to spill!

"**What's your problem?!**" I called out, drawing my swords. "I'm no thief! I didn't steal anything! Can't you see I'm just a **simple villager** doing my nightly milk run? You can't have a stormberry roll without **milk!** You just **can't!**"

One man raised an eyebrow. "What's he babbling on about?"

"Pay no mind," another said, peering into the gloom behind me. "**Just some noob.**"

"It could very well be **a distraction**," said the third. "They often work together. **Don't let your guard down, fools!**"

I had **no idea** what was going on. I backed up against the wall as they drew closer. Then I heard **a voice** less than two blocks to my right:

"Whaaaaat?! Runt, is that you?! What are you doing here?!"

"Oops! Gotta go! See ya later, blockbrain!"

I **barely** caught a glimpse of **who** had just spoken before he disappeared again.

"**There he is!**" shouted one of the knights. "**His invisibility is wearing off!**"

In a symphony of clanking and yelling, the knights **chased after him,** sprinting past me **as if I didn't exist.** The **shouts** and **insults** continued until one last cry echoed in the distance: "**Bat farmers . . . !**"

I stood there for a moment. **Without budging,** only breathing. I forgot about the cold. *Cogboggle. That was Cogboggle!*

What is happening?! Even though it was **dark,** and even though he was only there for a second after I looked, **that voice was unmistakable.** Cog has this **super annoying** voice, scratchy and **shrill.** It's not something you can easily forget.

I sprinted back to the inn with my thoughts swirling in my head.

Ophelia, Cog—why are they here?

One was a waitress. Another's robbing people blind.

Why? To what end?

I had this eerie **feeling.**
And as I ran,
the streets seemed to grow
darker and darker.

SATURDAY—UPDATE XXVII

Breeze was still **tending to Ophelia** when I got back.

Through healing potions and food, she'd nursed the **"waitress"** back to full health.

She'd crafted the potions **herself** using ingredients traded in the dining hall. As for the food, she'd ordered it.

And what splendid food it was! Enderpuff **muffins.** Glazed **moonseed** cupcakes. And, of course, **the most magnificent** of all bread-based food items: **the stormberry roll.**

At the sight of all these **heavenly** pastries, all other thoughts more or less **flew** into an ender portal.

There are many different food items that include **stormberries** in their crafting recipe—biscuits, muffins, scones—but **the stormberry roll** is the easiest to craft, as well as **the most efficient,** since it requires the fewest ingredients per unit of food restored. Further, while cupcakes are best reserved for a sunny afternoon, or perhaps an extravagant party, the stormberry roll—with its **simple, understated elegance**—can be eaten with any meal, in any location, and under any circumstance. Whether you're **crawling** through a dungeon's sewers or attending the **wedding** of a prince, consuming a stormberry roll is **never** deemed inappropriate.

Truly, the stormberry roll is **the workhorse** of the pastry world. With a **subdued,** sweet taste and dark blue berries flickering with yellow swirls like lightning, this **humble pastry** will always be there for you when you need to refill your hunger bar. *(It also provides a slight buff called **Omnessence**, which lasts for one hour and increases experience points gained by 2.5%.)*

After biting into one of these rolls, the icon for **Omnessence** appeared in **my vision** like a little candle glow.

"You haven't eaten in **hours**," Breeze said, handing me another. "I'm **surprised** you could still sprint."

"**Moommmrrrmmeeeemrmrmrrraw.**"

"Uh, what?"

I wiped away some crumbs. "I **said,** you won't **believe** who I saw! **Cogboggle! He's here!** He **stole** something from this group of knights! The **Solemn Blades.**" *(I said this name in a ridiculously deep and heroic voice, because that was how they talked.)*

"Are you sure it was **Cog?**"

"You ever known another villager to call someone a **blockbrain?**"

"Err. **No.**" **She sighed.** "This isn't making any sense. **Why would they be here?** Do you think **Villagetown** could have been attacked?"

"I've been asking myself **the exact same thing.** But if it had been, I'm sure **Cog** would have said something, right? But he just **ran off.**"

"Whatever the case, I'm sure we'll have our answer **once she wakes up,** won't we?"

Breeze took my bucket and gave Ophelia **the milk.** The green icon vanished, and Ophelia's expression, pained up until now, was as **soft** as enchanted wool.

"She'll **recover faster** now," Breeze said. She set the bucket down next to the **Bed of Roses** and then flopped down onto her own bed. "But she still **needs sleep,** and so do we."

"**Yeah.** We're about to hit **Exhaustion I** ourselves. In other news, I'm on my **twenty-seventh** diary entry. What a **day,** huh?"

<u>I turned toward Ophelia.</u>

SUNDAY

I had a **nightmare**.

Villagetown was burning. Everyone was running for their lives.

No, **not everyone.** My friends were still there, **fighting valiantly.**

But it seemed as though they were **losing.** At least, **Kolb's sword** was **broken.**

Was this a **vision of the future?** Or was it already in the past? Or was it just **my own fears** inspired by Faolan's tragic tale?

It was **still dark** when I woke up. My armor slightly clanking, I went over to the window and saw that the moon was on its way down—two or three hours past midnight, roughly.

Breeze was sound asleep, as was **Ophelia.** But the waitress, now at **full health,** was stirring gently in her sleep. She didn't have any more **status effects.** I considered waking her up, but it seemed **a bit cruel,** given that her day yesterday seemed even worse than mine.

I stepped toward my bed but **stopped myself** immediately, because my armor sounded like a bunch of **pots and pans** clanking together. You know the sound an iron golem makes when it walks? **Yep. That sound,** pretty much, which was probably why Ophelia kept moving in her sleep.

All right, you can do this. A **ninja** would have no problem moving *silently* in metal armor, even old rusty armor like this. I did my best creeper impression, more or less **slithering** across the floor without a single clank. **Unfortunately,** Breeze had left that milk bucket in the shadow of Ophelia's bed. So, **of course,** I happened to **step on it.**

Clearly this made me **trip and fall** on it. And **naturally,** this sent the bucket flying into a wall—which **obviously** didn't stop there—and **clattering around the room** with a sound similar to a mine cart on powered rails. **Or two.**

That bucket just wouldn't stop rolling. First, Breeze **shot up** in bed and **scrunched up** against the wall. Then I heard a door creak open in the hall, followed by **muffled shouting.** Only then did Ophelia stir in her bed once more and **rise slowly** with a yawn.

OPHELIA

GOODNIGHT BUFF.

She looked **so confused.**

I mean, imagine: She wakes up in **some random room,** with me, a villager wearing **ridiculous armor** and a hat **covered in mold,** staring at her while a bucket won't stop rolling around on the floor—all of this along with **some dwarf shouting** far away down the hall, whose words are only partially comprehensible but clearly not very nice, stuff like **"slime-loving"** and **"what in the frozen Nether?"** repeated over and over.

Ophelia tilted her head. "**Runt?** Is that you?"

"**It is,**" I said, stopping the bucket with my foot. It made one last little squeak.

The waitress looked down at herself. "**What happened to me?** And . . . **what are you doing here?**"

(What am I doing here?! Like it was totally normal for her to be here?!)

"I suppose **I should be asking the same,**" I said rather calmly, all things considered.

"Well, **I** . . ." She peered over my shoulder. "**Breeze?**"

"Hey, **Ophelia.**" Breeze approached the thoroughly bewildered waitress. "We brought you in. **You fainted** in the street last night."

"**Oh! Did I?** The last thing I remember is talking to **Theor,** the innkeeper. **He fired me** the other day. He said I wasn't cut out for it, and **I'm not,** really. I only took the job because I'd get to **hear all the rumors** and **earn some emeralds** in the process."

"**What rumors?**" Breeze asked.

"Well, the people around here **talk an awful lot** about **quests.** They're like **special jobs,** I guess? Like this farmer I heard about: He was offering a decent stack of emeralds to anyone who could **rid his farm of slimes.** It took me half a day, including travel, but it was well worth it."

"Ophelia," I said. "**Why are you doing this?** Why are you here, in this city, **hoarding emeralds?**"

She **bit her lip,** then gestured at Breeze. "**Her father sent me.** The night of the party. He gave me **a map,** and . . ."

I **glanced at Breeze,** who shrugged helplessly. She seemed **just as stunned** as I was. Then I repeated Ophelia's words absently. "**Her father . . . sent you. . . .**"

"Yes," Ophelia said with a sigh. "And I really **wish he hadn't.** It's been **so hard** for me. Ever since I left, I . . ." She gave us a thoughtful look.

"He sent me on **a mission**. To **save** Villagetown. He wanted me to find an **advanced crafting table**. But **I failed** in the end. I've brought such **dishonor** to my village. . . ."

Her words hit me **like a fist. Breeze, too.**

I'm not sure how to describe what I was feeling at that exact moment. **Angry? Trolled?** But I barely had time to process what I'd heard. Seconds later, **a voice reverberated** throughout the room.

"**There's a reason for all this, you know.**"

Near the window, the air began to **shimmer,** the transparent emptiness slowly taking on **the form of a person.**

And the person who appeared was **Brio**.

Breeze stormed up to him.

"**Father?** What does all of this mean? **What have you done?**"

"All will be **explained.**" He turned to the window. "But first, **I suggest you go downstairs.** Breakfast is waiting, and there are **some travelers** who've come **a long way** to share it with you."

SUNDAY—UPDATE I

If you **don't recognize** these people, don't worry. **I didn't either at first.**

From left to right: Emerald, Lola, Stump, and Max.

"Hey, look! They're finally awake!"

"Dude! Lola! You're hogging the seat!"

"I'm gonna hurgg. I'm gonna hurgg."

"So you started my book yet?"

It seemed like **forever** since I'd last seen them.

And it was **both strange** and **comforting** to see that they looked almost nothing like villagers anymore.

I took a seat next to **Ophelia** and **Breeze**. "**Okay,** I can't even begin to describe **how great** it is to see you guys, **but . . .** will someone **tell me what's going on?!**"

"It's **a test,**" Stump said. "Kolb, Breeze's dad, and the mayor were **the only ones** who knew about it."

"It was **seriously confusing,**" Emerald added. "The council thought it best to **keep everything a secret,** because . . . um . . . villager logic." She **rolled her eyes.** "First, we heard that **you were in trouble.** Then Breeze **disappeared,** and suddenly **she** was in trouble. . . ."

"We wanted to see what **Ophelia, Cogboggle,** and **you** were capable of," Brio said, approaching the table. "In particular, we felt that you had to really **get out there and experience the Overworld** for yourself. If you had left knowing that it was yet **another** test, your experience wouldn't have been the same. Of course, **the forge** is something we **desperately need.** Two bats with one arrow, as the old saying goes."

He then mentioned how the mayor had started **worrying** and sent Breeze to check on me. **Cog** had been sent later to **help Ophelia.**

When I mentioned how I'd seen him earlier being chased by **three angry knights,** Brio nodded sagely. "Seems like he's forgotten all about **his duties,** then. I would like to have a word with him. I'm afraid his **pilfering** from unsuspecting travelers will not bolster the reputation of villagers. . . ."

"**Emerald's been stealing too,**" Stump said casually.

She glared at him. "**Thanks a lot, noobmaster.** I was testing out **my new ability!**"

"Looks like you need to do **a bit more testing,** then. The only thing you managed to steal from that innkeeper was **a block of wood!**"

"**Hurrmmph!** Y'know, we **do** have more important things to be discussing here, like . . . **Runt's little quest.**" She smiled at me. "**So did you manage to find that table thingy?**"

"I did."

I retrieved **the aeon forge** and set it on the table in front of me.

"With this," Max said, "the monsters won't **stand a chance.** Not that they've been attacking. It's been **pretty quiet** back home."

"It seems **the Eyeless One** has been focusing his efforts elsewhere for the time being," Brio said. "A great number of his minions have moved into **the eastern arm of Ravensong Forest,** to the keep known as **Stormgarden.**"

"Some pigman mentioned that," I said. "He wanted to take me there for questioning. **What is that place?**"

"It was **abandoned** by **the Knights of Aetheria** hundreds of years ago," he said. "But the monsters are now occupying the lower levels, where there aren't **too many traps.** At any rate, this means we have **some breathing room.** For now. When they return, they'll be **facing a defense** like no village has ever produced."

Once more, everyone stared down at **the forge.**

In the end, I suppose the mayor's plan **did make sense,** in that **villager** sort of way.

Now that we have this object, our village can be **seriously upgraded.** And in the process, Cog, Ophelia, and I gained **invaluable** experience.

Yet something kept **nagging at me.** "So you **send us outside,**" I said, "to see what we can do, to help us learn more about the Overworld. **Why, though?** Why was it **so important** that we learn of the outside world? I know we'll be **exploring** soon, but sending us out so far, in **secret,** by **ourselves** . . . it's a bit **extreme,** don't you think?"

Brio fell **silent.**

When he finally spoke, **his expression was grave.**

"I didn't want to tell you about this yet. But I suppose the council has **kept this** from you long enough." He retrieved a piece of paper from his robes. "Weeks ago, shortly before **your graduation,** a **messenger** arrived in the middle of the night. A messenger from **the** capital. An **emissary** of the king."

<u>He placed the paper on the table in a gentle way, as though regretful.</u>

ROYAL NOTICE

LET IT BE KNOWN THAT—BY THE THIRD OF DIAMONDSTAR—EVERY CITY, TOWN, AND VILLAGE WITH NO LESS THAN ONE HUNDRED DOORS SHALL SEND EXACTLY FIFTEEN OF THEIR FINEST YOUNG MEN AND WOMEN TO THE CAPITAL. THERE THEY SHALL RECEIVE FURTHER TRAINING AT THE GREATER AETHERIAN ACADEMY, UPON COMPLETION OF WHICH THEY SHALL BE CALLED UPON BY KING RUNEHAMMER II, SEVENTH LANTERNGUARD OF ARDENVELL.

SIGNED UPON THIS FIFTEENTH
DAY OF FROST HARVEST

SUNDAY—UPDATE II

For the longest moment, **overpowering silence** filled the dining hall.

Then Emerald **laughed** nervously. "**Wow**, this is, um . . . **s-some kind of joke**, right?"

"I don't think so," Max said. "That's the **king's seal.** The **Flame of the Eternal Lantern.** Only the **grand magister** knows the crafting recipe."

"**What's today?**" Stump asked. "**The twenty-third?**" He'd hardly touched the **enderpuff scone** *(enderscone for short)* in his hand, which clearly meant he was afraid. "The third of Diamondstar is just ten days away!"

Breeze seemed **really upset.** Her father just **sighed.** "**Aetheria City** is a long way from home," he said. "And we have no idea what **your training** may entail. Therefore, the council felt it **cruel** to send you away without **experiencing the Overworld** first." He turned to his daughter. "Breeze, **I'm sorry.** There's no other way."

"**Really?**" Stump asked. "There's **no way out** of this? We **have** to go?"

"Looks like it." Breeze **sunk** into her chair, arms crossed, and let out a deep breath before **glaring** at her father.

"Well, **I find it marvelous!**" Lola exclaimed. "Such a **delightful little surprise!** To think that we'll actually meet the **king!** Although, I do wonder what sort of outfit I should wear. . . ."

"If this is **what's demanded** of me," Ophelia said, herself once again, "then I'll go. And I'm sure **the members of my team** would say the same." Her **sober** expression darkened with **a hint of sadness.** "I miss them," she said, meaning her friends, the rest of **Team All-Girls.** "Why aren't they here?"

"They wanted to come," Brio said, "but felt they should **remain** in Villagetown in case of **another attack.** You've really instilled a **sense of duty** in them. **Cog's group,** on the other hand, didn't want to bother. It seems they're **not too close** to their captain."

At that exact moment, **the captain in question** decided to show up. Or perhaps I should say **thief.**

Cog looked at us, at the **forge,** at the **king's letter,** and at the mixture of sullen and cheerful expressions—well, except for Ophelia, who was **on one knee** and saying something about **the honor of the village.**

"**Okay,** I'm guessing I missed something." Then he **snickered.** "Oh, and I'm not talking about people's inventories."

A moment later, there were a few **shouts** in the distance.

Breeze's father gave Cog a **smoldering** look. "**Fool!** You will return what you've filched **at once!**"

"Calm down, it was **just a joke!** I only stole a ring!" He held up **an obsidian ring** and examined it. "It's a **lousy item,** anyway. Be right back, guys."

I was too stunned to say anything, but Emerald, looking **more nervous** as she read and reread the letter, asked exactly what I was thinking: "**Um,** h-how many doors does Villagetown have again?"

"**375,**" Max said. "Wait . . . no! **379** after the south tower."

"**Oh.**" She blinked. "**Hey, guys,** I-I was thinking, maybe Villagetown could use a **little remodeling?** Let's be honest—all those doors are a **monster hazard,** y'know? What? Don't look at me like that! **Someone's** gotta look out for our safety!"

The conversation more or less went on like that for quite some time. What that letter said was **simply unbelievable,** and the details weren't exactly clear.

Breeze's father did mention that our training in **the capital** would be **similar** to school back home, except more advanced. Yet we had so many other questions that he simply couldn't answer. **How long** will we be there? **What is life like** in the capital? Will we ever be able to visit our parents?

As the questions dwindled, everyone turned to Max, who'd been **silent** this whole time. **To everyone's surprise,** he moved closer to the **aeon forge,** hunched over it, and carefully arranged a diagonal line of **prismarine crystals.** Suddenly, with **a brilliant green flash,** a column of **pale blue light** sprang forth from each crystal. The crystals then **merged,** forming what I could only guess was **a prismarine staff.**

As soon as this item was formed, however, **a pulsing violet light** began emanating from the forge. There was a weird, **almost sad,** noise, and the staff evaporated with a tiny puff of smoke. The violet light lingered for a moment after **this failed crafting attempt.**

"**Nice job**, ace. Now how about you put that **brilliant mind** of yours to good use, stop messing with that thing, and help think of a way outta **this mess?!**"

The dining hall was not **entirely empty,** even at this early hour, and Max's **little experiment**—along with Emerald's **outburst**—had **drawn the attention** of several people. They mostly **chuckled** to themselves. That's when I noticed Breeze **wasn't there anymore. She'd disappeared without a word.**

I decided to slip away too, and I soon found her on **a balcony upstairs.** She was **alone,** arms crossed, **staring** at the night sky. . . .

SUNDAY—UPDATE III

"Hey."

"Hey."

"So, this training in Aetheria City," I said. "Is it really **so bad?**"

"I don't think it's going to be easy," she said. "**I really don't want to go.** Maybe it's for the best, though. My father says there are **lots of things** we still don't know about ourselves."

"Like what?"

"There are countless unseen **elements** that make up who we are, like **our level, our stats, our experience points.** But even though these elements are invisible, there is a way to see them. It's called a **visual enchantment.** All of the humans have one—**it's easy** for them to use. I'm not sure why it doesn't come **naturally** to us. We have to unlock it through **a special process.** I'm sure those at **the Academy** can show us how."

"**Hope so,**" I said. In truth, I didn't really know what she was talking about. I just wanted to **stay positive.** "Hey . . . back there, when your dad was talking about training in the capital, he mentioned something about **selecting a class?** What did he mean by **classes?**"

"They're like **professions,**" she said. "Only better. It's **hard** to explain. Um . . . **Urf was a Nethermancer,** right? **That's a class.**"

She went on to tell me about some of the classes.

If someone wanted to be a **wizard,** they could gain **the Wizard class.** From there, they could move on to **more specialized spell-casting** classes like **Void Mage, Nethermancer, or Monster Shepherd.** Monster Shepherds sound **really cool,** by the way. You can **summon** and **control** beasts. You start out with animals like bats and rabbits.

"We'll **gain classes** in the capital, too," she said. "Once our training is complete."

"**That reminds me,**" I said. "Sometimes, **you have this troubled look.** Like you know something you're not telling me."

"**Oh.**" She retrieved **a black tome** from her inventory. "Just some things Kolb told me about: **history** again, **legends,** something called **the Prophecy.** It's all in this book. We thought it was **important** at first but . . . **it's rather vague.** Max has been trying to **decipher** some of its more . . . **puzzling** sections. Most of it was written by **this Scribe named Mango** who was apparently **quite the eccentric person.**"

"I haven't even finished the book **Max** gave me." With **a sigh,** I retrieved his book from my inventory and showed her my current place.

THE UNDERWORLD

IT WAS PREVIOUSLY THOUGHT THAT THE BEDROCK LAYER WAS ONLY A SEA OF UNBREAKABLE STONE STRETCHING FOREVER DOWNWARD.

RECENTLY, HOWEVER, TUNNELS HAVE BEEN FOUND TO EXIST WITHIN BEDROCK, LEADING TO A CAVERN SYSTEM RIVALING ANY FOUND IN THE NETHER.

INDEED, BELOW OUR OVERWORLD EXISTS ANOTHER WORLD, WHICH OVERWORLDIAN SAGES HAVE COINED THE UNDERWORLD.

MOOSHROOMS ARE NATIVE TO THIS REALM; ALSO COMMONPLACE ARE VAST LAKES OF WATER, LAVA, AND EVEN FORESTS OF GIANT MUSHROOMS.

OF COURSE, THERE ARE ORES THAT CAN ONLY BE FOUND IN THESE DEPTHS. BUT THEY ARE MUCH HARDER TO MINE, BEING ENCASED IN BEDROCK.

"So. **Anything else you've been hiding from me?**" I asked, closing the book.

"**Nope.** Well, there **is** one more thing . . . but **it's a surprise.**"

"I see. **Do** go on."

She **smiled.** "It wouldn't be **a surprise** if I just told you here, now would it? You'll see when we **get back home.**"

"Okay. Hey, **listen.** I know you're sad that we have to go, but maybe it won't be **so bad?** I read a lot of books too, you know, and **the capital really sounds amazing.**"

"I know. It's just . . . I'm not much of a **city girl.** I like farming, remember?"

"I remember," I said. "And someday, I'll help you **build that farm.**"

"**Promise?**"

Oh no, I thought. *Should I make **this promise?** I'm not the best at building. Truth be told, I came dangerously close to making one of those **building fails.** Oh well. After yesterday, I'm pretty sure I can handle just about anything. So long as **she's** with me . . .*

"Prom—"

The doors behind us **swung open.**

54

The person who'd opened them was **a villager.** But it was hard to tell. In fact, looking at him, it was **impossible to believe** that he had ever seen a place filled with farms and chickens and sheep. Upon his **silver breastplate** was a sigil identical to **the king's seal,** and he was holding a lantern that gave off a cozy glow. He also had **bluish-gray hair.** Clearly, he no longer followed villager **tradition.**

He joined us at the fence rail where we were stargazing.

"**You must be Breeze.** It's **a pleasure** to meet you." He **bowed gracefully.** His accent, though unusual, was just as graceful. "I have been **wanting to speak with you** for quite some time."

Breeze gave him a **strange** look.

"And you are?"

"**Ah!** Yes." He bowed again. "**Please forgive me,** my lady. I have been riding for two days. I am **Sir Elric Darkbane, Knight of Aetheria,** and I have come to ensure your **safe passage** to the capital. I'm afraid you must prepare **without delay,** for we will leave shortly."

I'd stopped listening at Sir Elric. **It's him?! Like, really?!** The guy standing before us was **famous** throughout Ardenvell, a **legendary** knight widely considered to be **the best swordsman in the entire world.** *(I actually have a painting of him in my bedroom. Well, okay, apparently it doesn't look a lot like him.)*

Then I remembered that **the Knights of Aetheria** always carry **lanterns** like that during ceremonies or when meeting **honored** guests. It's just something they do. **A tradition.** For them, the lantern symbolizes light, peace, the melting away of darkness. Even **the king** himself carries one—at all times, no less—though his lantern is unique: **a legendary-tier item** with **eight** different enchantments.

"We will pass **very close** to your home village," he continued, "so **saying goodbye to your loved ones** will not be an inconvenience. Of course, I want to say that I cannot imagine what you must be feeling right now, but I once lived in **Moonglow.** The **very first village** to fall. The one thing I can say with certainty is that, although you will learn **new customs** and an entirely **different way** of life, you will always be a villager at heart. Even as the past fades away, **who you truly are** will never change. And dare I say that you will easily grow accustomed to your new life, as you are one who looks not to the past, or even the present, but **the future.** Face the problems you have not yet had."

That last phrase caught me by surprise. Kolb had said those **exact same words** a few times before. Breeze looked **shocked** as well. "**What? How do you know that?**"

He smiled. "Was this not **a common saying** in your home village of **Shadowbrook?** I know much about you. It could be said that you are rather **famous in the West.** I hope I'm not too **brazen** in asking if what they say is true? **The imprisonment? The experiments?**"

"Yes, **it's true,** but . . ."

"Stories travel far, my lady, and there is **no tale more inspiring** than yours. The girl who escaped **the Eyeless One,** tormented and forever changed, only to rise back up and **fight again.** That is why, in the West, you have many **supporters.** I am among them."

I gave Breeze a look that said: *"On any other day, this would have been a huge surprise. But after yesterday? Nope. Nothing really fazes me anymore."*

Another knight walked through the doorway and saluted **Elric.** "Sir, I bring **excellent news. Etherly Keep** has been reclaimed, and the remaining undead have been **destroyed.** Furthermore, Herobrine's forces have been **driven from Dawnsbloom** entirely. As unbelievable as it may seem, **we are already winning** this war!"

"**So it appears.** Perhaps **Lady Luck** is finally on our side. What of the **initiates?**"

"The rest have just arrived," the knight said. "We are **ready to leave** at a moment's notice."

"Then I guess **it's time.**" Elric smiled at us and bowed once more. "I will go check on **the others.** See you outside?"

After the knights left, I turned to Breeze. "**So what were you saying earlier?** Something about how you didn't want to go? **Huh.**" I shrugged. "The capital doesn't sound **so bad** to me."

"You're still **helping me build that farm** when we get back," she said with a wink. "Don't think I didn't hear you **promise.**"

She took me by the hand again and pulled me back inside. Many knights stood at attention in the hall, a row on each side. The combined glow of their lanterns was **overwhelming:** As we walked past, it seemed as though we'd stepped not into **the hall of an inn** but **a tunnel of brilliant, wavering light.**

SUNDAY—UPDATE IV

It was **still dark** when we gathered outside.

Although it was **hard to tell** without looking up to the sky. **Those lanterns** were everywhere, bathing the streets in a **golden glow,** as well as the knights who held them.

As might be expected, even at this hour, **a lot** of townsfolk were lingering around. They whispered and **giggled,** pointing here and there. Not only at the knights, of course, but also at us: **the nine heroic villagers** who would soon be traveling to **Aetheria City.**

While the onlookers gathered, a rotund man in fancy-looking clothes **rolled** in our direction. Well, he wasn't on wheels or anything—it was just how he walked.

With a wavelike motion of his arm, he shouted at the townsfolk:

"Sound the horns, you peasants! It is a marvelous occasion we witness! **These fine villagers** are going to train in the capital!"

Suddenly, a group of townsfolk with horn-like musical instruments rushed out from the crowd and immediately started playing. I've **never heard** music like it before, and I hope to never hear it again. The deep and rumbling sounds they made were **hideous,** like some giant, **flatulent** cow.

The man **facepalmed.** It seemed things were not going according to plan. Then he waved downward, as if **signaling** them to stop. The horns quieted. Well, not all at once—a few stragglers trailed off **pitifully.**

"**Disgraceful!** Have you not practiced?! You **bring shame** to us all!"

Then this **fancifully dressed** man *(maybe the mayor of Owl's Reach?)* turned to the **Aetherian Knights,** approaching their leader. "**Sir Elric Darkbane.**" He bowed deeply. "It is a pleasure as always. Please forgive them. Not playing **their best,** I'm afraid. It seems they've had a bit too much **stormberry ale** in light of our little celebration. And then, being so far from Aetheria City, surely you can imagine **we don't often play** the capital's anthem."

"**It is nothing,**" Elric said. "These **customs** have never concerned me much. And perhaps I have even grown weary of such music over time. It's played endlessly at **the Academy,** even on the smallest of occasions."

The mayor *(so it was him)* bowed once more. "And with regret, I must say that **our own initiates** already left three days ago. They were **so excited. . . . Oh yes,** so very excited, indeed, to see such a glorious city, and further, I must add that . . ."

He spoke like this for **some time.** No way am I writing all that down. At last, upon wishing us farewell, the mayor left us in peace.

Sir Elric then walked past each villager present, **nodding with respect.** He stopped at **Emerald,** who was sitting on the front steps of the inn, **half-asleep,** elbow on knee, hand propping up one side of her face. Finally, he glanced **at me.**

"Your friends say **you do not have a horse,**" he said quizzically.

"As **crazy** as it sounds," I said, "**you can blame a Nethermancer** named Urf for that."

"Very well." He turned to another knight. "**Zigurd.** The villager Runt no longer has a horse. Would you be so kind as to **find one for him?**"

With a scowl so **intense** it was almost comical, **Zigurd** looked at the other knights as though he couldn't believe what he'd just heard. Then he **glared** at the musicians, who were still holding their horns, then at me, and shook his head in **disgust.**

"This is **noobery,**" he muttered. "**Utter noobery.**"

"**Ye,** it is," another knight said. "How will that lad make it through training if he can't keep track of his own horse?"

"Ye. Almost makes you wonder if—"

"**Enough!**" Elric snapped. "Zigurd. You are a **Knight of Aetheria**, and you will begin **acting** like one, instead of grumbling like a zombie pigman. **Is that understood?**"

". . . Ye, **I'm on it,**" Zigurd said. Still grumbling, he took off to the stables. "I just want to go **home. . . .**"

Elric looked at us once more. "We should replenish **our food bars** before setting out." He raised a hand. A hotbar appeared before him.

"Anyone care for a stormberry roll?"

To a villager, these screens are always **a strange sight.** We can only see our own inventories. It's simply **impossible** to conjure these windows into view for others. The Legionnaires can, of course, but they don't belong to **this reality.** This kind of magic comes **naturally** to them.

Elric, however, was a villager, **born of this world.** An NPC—not a so-called **player. It shouldn't have been possible** for him.

"That's part of your **visual enchantment,**" I said. "Isn't it? How did you **unlock it?**"

"I underwent **special training,**" he said. "In **the Tower Eternal.** Once you begin your studies, **the magisters** there will assist you in his regard."

"How does it work, anyway?" Stump asked. "It's like . . . **magic?**"

"Ye. At least, that is what many believe. But **no one knows** how we came to possess such enchantment. Some say it exists **deep inside us,** infused within our blood long ago. Back when magic was still **commonplace.**" Elric grinned. "Of course, those are the same people who think there are **biomes on the moon.**"

"On the **moon?**" Stump looked up into the cold black sky with an expression of confusion mixed with happiness—as though someone had told him that creepers **were actually vegetables.** "Whoaaaa . . ."

Elric turned to another knight, who was, perhaps, the youngest among the nine knights present. "**Konrad!** Have the horses completely **recovered?**"

"**They have, sir!**" Konrad saluted. "**Full endurance** bars across the board!"

"**Excellent.** And the Swiftness potions?"

"Not too many left, **I'm afraid.** Just under **five saddle chests.**"

"No matter. **That will do.**" Elric flashed **a weary smile.** "All right, everyone. We leave soon. There is another inn to the south, **the Inn of the Laughing Cow,** where we will rest for the night. In the morning, we will ride through **Ravensong Forest** and hit the **moon elf** village of **Glimfrost.** Since their village is so close to **Stormgarden,** we would like to check on them. And, by tomorrow's eve, we will arrive at your home." He turned back to the young knight. "**Oh, Konrad!** Make sure each villager has adequate supplies: **Healing Ills, stormberry rolls.** These initiates are important. **We take no chances today.**"

Konrad saluted. "**At once, sir!**"

Emerald—still half asleep—suddenly stirred. "Huh? **Boats?**"

Stump nudged me. "Hey," he whispered. "What does **'noobery'** mean?"

We were off before sunrise.

At first, I didn't believe we could reach Villagetown in **less than two days.** But as we blazed our way south, the horses were continuously provided with **potions of Swiftness VII**—extended duration. The countless plains biomes **flew by.**

Max figured we were traveling at least **twice the speed** of a mine cart on **powered rails.** To me, it felt like we were going even faster than that. Take a creeper, a slimeball, and a kitten. Attach said kitten to the creeper's behind using the slimeball. Watch as the creeper zooms off super fast.

That's <u>how fast</u> we were traveling.

SUNDAY—UPDATE V

SUNDAY—UPDATE VI

We rode through plains,

We rode through savanna,

We rode through hills and streams,

At times, we rode swiftly,

At times, we rode carefully,

More than a noob ever dreams.

Do you like it?

It's a little poem I wrote called **"We Traveled through the Overworld for Hours and Hours, and It Was Really, Really Boring."**

SUNDAY—UPDATE VII

The Inn of the **Laughing Cow**

We finally came across **something besides grass.**

It was **a massive** structure—looking a bit lonely on the savanna—at least **three times the size of the Enchanted Dragon,** though the design was mostly the same. And the same kind of people occupied it: Imagine a person, **any type of person,** from pirate to fortune-teller. Anyone who came to mind could be found inside.

Needless to say, the entrance of **nine villagers** and **ten knights** drew **little attention.** Well, except for the attention of some waitress in the same outfit Ophelia still had on. She showed us this piece of paper that had a bunch of different **food items** on it.

I ordered an **enchanted moonseed muffin.** It had **little sparkle effects.** Imported straight from the capital, she said.

Let me tell you, that muffin was **perfect.** Whoever crafted it definitely had a Crafting skill that was at least fifty points higher than mine; the one time **I** tried crafting muffins, not only did I burn them but also the **furnace** caught on fire. I took another bite. *Hmm. At least 150 Crafting skill.* Another bite. *Possibly even 175.*

Stump ordered the same thing I did. After his first bite, he said a single word: **"Dude."** The second bite was followed by the same word, only with a little bit more excitement: **"Dude."** Each bite thereafter was another **"dude"** of ever **increasing pitch, volume, excitement,** and/or **confusion.** Once, he even spoke in a different accent.

"Dude."

"DUDE....?!"

"...DEHWD." "Dude."

"DUDE!!!"

After finishing mine, I left the table and stepped outside. The inn's noise had been **getting to me,** which I found **a bit odd.** Noise had never really bothered me before. Villagetown was often **pure chaos:** all the hammering of blacksmiths and bleating of sheep, the **angry shouting** of some trade gone wrong....

Maybe I was growing accustomed to the **silence of the Overworld.**

"Hey."

A familiar voice to my right. **No surprise.**

"Hey." I glanced sidelong in her direction. "**Emerald** said the rooms we'll be staying in are **out of this world.** In the capital, I mean. From the way she spoke, it sounded like even **bedroom slippers** are **enchanted.** And the bathroom cauldrons are **made of gold.**"

71

She smiled at **my lame** attempt at humor. **Slightly.** "You should be **more serious.** We have a lot to think about."

"Does this look like the face of a joking man? We'll be living **like kings,** she says." At last, **I smiled too.** "Oh, I suppose there's no need to cheer you up, is there? You're **Breeze,** she who escaped from the clutches of **the Eyeless One.** It must be **exciting** to know you're going to a place filled with so many **adoring fans.**"

"I still have a hard time believing it," she said. "How do so many people even know about . . . **that.**"

That.

By "that," she meant **her past.**

It definitely is a **curious** story. But even now, I know few details. She's never spoken about being **captured** and **experimented** upon, and I've always found it rude to ask. I've heard **rumors,** sure. Rumors I won't write here. I'd never do that without **her permission.**

As her smile **faded,** my mind raced to think of a good way to change the subject. **Luckily,** the inn's front door creaked open, saving me the effort.

An **old man** in threadbare brown robes hobbled outside. The robe had many dark red patches, the largest of which had white stitching that resembled **the face of a smiling kitten.** Another patch looked like **a green bird.** Both this person and his robes seemed **worn and faded.** If someone had told me that this ancient man lived in an item chest along with five rabbits and two cats, I **totally** would have believed it. Strangely, he displayed **no emotion. None whatsoever.** As I said, that inn held **any** type of person you could **imagine.**

The man **slowly hobbled** up to us.

The whole time he did, **he never took his eyes off Breeze.**

I leaned over to her and said in a low voice, "Seems you have admirers **even here."**

The elderly man continued to stare at her as he crept forward. There was **something off** about him, I felt. Well, okay, an old man with a kitten and a bird on his robes definitely **isn't** normal,

but . . . it was more than that. It was **the complete lack of emotion.** The shambling gait. I was getting some **really creepy** vibes.

Still looking at Breeze, he stopped just outside of sword distance, opened his mouth, and whispered in a **peculiarly hollow** tone:

"Alyss . . ."

An odd-sounding name: **uh-LYSS.**

Breeze looked **shaken.** "Runt. **Get back.**"

Something in her voice—and in the man himself—gave me **the total chills.**

My instincts told me that the figure before us was not some **harmless** old man. Not any kind of person at all.

Suddenly, the **"man"** surged forward. Arms outstretched. **Reaching. Grasping.** Clawing. Movements I'd seen so many times before.

Yet he never reached her. **My swords** reached him first. In less than a second, both **diamond** and **obsidian** were flying at him, removing his health in an instant. Breeze had always been **quick on her feet,** but at this point she hadn't yet drawn her blades. I guess I was **on top of my game** today. What was **in** those muffins?!

With a **low moan,** what appeared to be the elderly man sank to the ground. I don't even know how to describe what happened next, but I'll try. The man's outward appearance was actually **some kind of trick,** like a **magical costume,** that dissolved into **wisps of shadow.** What remained was a **shadowy** figure. It crumbled into **black shreds,** which then also dissolved—leaving behind only a pile of glimmering blue-white dust.

Eerie silence followed.

". . . Breeze."

"**Yeah.**"

"What was that?"

"Don't know."

"I've never heard of **shape-shifting zombies.**"

She shook her head. "No, I think it was more like . . . **an illusion.**"

Illusion, huh . . .

I recalled noticing the **"old man"** in the inn, a while earlier. He was standing by the entrance. Just standing there. I'd never suspected a thing. It wasn't until I really looked closely that I sensed **something was off** about him. The disguise, or illusion, had been quite **convincing.**

Whatever that thing was, it'd been searching for Breeze—and **only** Breeze.

Not once had it looked at me.

Why?

And why did it call her
a completely different name . . . ?

Or had I misheard? Had it **really** whispered a name? Or had it simply made the kind of sound the undead normally make? **A hiss,** maybe? Or perhaps it had been speaking in **an unknown tongue,** and whispering the word **"alyss"** was just **some kind of threat** or curse. As would naturally be expected of a shadowy zombie/ghost.

"I thought I heard it **whisper** something," I said. "It was so quiet, but it . . . it almost sounded like a name. **Alyss.**"

"I . . . **didn't hear anything,**" she said. "Maybe it was **the wind.**"

"**Huh. Yeah.** Maybe it was."

But there wasn't any wind.

The grass was as **still** as a painting.

Whatever. Maybe it said something; maybe it didn't. I was **too tired** for this.

The front door of the inn **creaked** open again. A group of robed humans emerged, heading for the stables. **Breeze's father** appeared behind them. Upon seeing our drawn weapons and the pile of **shimmering dust,** he rushed over, face filled with **alarm.**

"You must **be more careful,**" he said. "Despite his name, **the Eyeless One** has many eyes, and they are everywhere." Crouching down, he scooped up a handful of the brilliant white dust. It sifted through his fingers like sand. "**Ethereal Essence.** There are several forms of undead that leave this residue when slain. But almost never in **such great quantity.** Tell me, what did it look like? Was it **incorporeal?**"

I blinked. "**Incorporeal?**"

"**Spectral.** Ghostlike. A transparent or shadowy form."

"Its true form resembled **a husk made of shadow,**" Breeze said. "Yet, until the moment it fell, it appeared to be an . . ."

As she shared the story, her father nodded sagely.

"I've heard of undead beings that can appear as any of their past victims. In addition, they can **inflict hideous maladies** with only a single touch. They use their illusion to get close to you. By then, it's often too late." He stood. "Consider yourselves **lucky.** And, from now on, don't go wandering off like that." It seemed like he was only speaking to his daughter when he added: "**Nowhere will you be safe.** Not here, not in Villagetown, not even in the heart of the capital. No matter where you are, you must never lower your guard."

"I'm **sorry**," she said. "I'll be more careful."

"Let's go back inside," he said. "I fear we're being watched even now."

When he said this, I noticed someone **over his shoulder,** in the distance. I couldn't make him out clearly. It was getting late, the sun falling red over golden-orange savanna. Even so, I could see that it was some **peasant-like person** in simple earth-tone clothes.

Arms at his sides, he was **staring** at us in much the same way as the creature from earlier. He **slowly** approached. On his belt were **three pouches,** looking like miniature item chests. A **traveling merchant,** then. That was what it **wanted** us to think. Indeed, like the other being, the disguise was rather convincing. Even so, I could see that there was no intelligence in those **dull brown eyes.** I watched this **"humble trader"** creep forward with the mindless, relentless determination of **a zombie.** When it stopped within sword distance, I reached up behind me, resting my right hand upon the pommel of my diamond weapon.

The man **opened** his mouth. **Closed it.**

Just try it, I thought. *Go on. Extend your arms.*

He opened his mouth again: "Milord? Care for **a stormberry roll?**"

". . ."

I **lowered** my arm.

"**Come,**" Brio said. "You two must be exhausted. Let's get you to your rooms."

Breeze pointed at the pile of dust with a boot. "Should we . . . **take that?**"

"I suppose we should," her father said. "It's used in **several advanced recipes.** Mainly for accessories. **One type of amulet,** if I recall."

He should have just said **free cool stuff.** I instantly fell to my knees, gathering as much as I could.

Breeze did the same, though **reluctantly.** "Never thought zombie dust could be **valuable.**"

The merchant gave us the **strangest** look when she said that. . . .

When we went back inside, I paid much more attention to the random people at the tables. **A dark dwarf** in fanciful gold armor, laughing. No, he wasn't one of them. **A human** in basic leather, making a weird face as he took a sip of some potion. No, **he's okay.** A villager wearing a full set of iron armor, with a helmet almost covering his eyes.

Hmm, he looks *a little suspicious*, doesn't he? He's just sitting there staring ahead, no emotion. Now he's slowly turning his head in my direction. **Oh,** now he's staring at me, still no emotion. Could it be? Is it another mysterious shape-shifting <u>zombie entity?!</u>

The villager wiped away some sparkling crumbs. ". . . Dude. Those muffins? **Amazing,** with like five Zs."

It was just Stump.

"By the way," he said, "I got us a room. Don't worry. **I won't snore.**"

The knights were already bidding everyone goodnight or heading to their rooms, as were Breeze and her father, Max, Lola, and Ophelia.

Emerald was at another table, chatting with some guy. He appeared to be **an elf of some kind,** with long ears, longer hair, and a feathered cap just like mine. Only his cap was red and didn't have any mold on it. He also had a **stringed musical instrument** on the table in front of him.

I yawned. Riding at full speed for an entire day is **super tiring.** I went straight to my room and crashed onto my bed, where I am right now. Despite my exhaustion, I haven't been able to sleep. That zombie from earlier was **just too much.** Or ghost. **Or whatever it was.**

Alyss...
What does it mean?!

Hmm. You know, Max has **a dictionary.** Seeing how he **is** my **personal library,** I'm going drag him here right now.

SUNDAY—UPDATE VIII

Correction. Max has **five** dictionaries: *Common*, *Ancient*, *Old Aetherian*, *Enderscript*, and *Netherian*.

Strangely, the word **"alyss"** does not appear to exist in any of these languages. Furthermore, the entity I saw isn't listed in **either** of the two books Max has relating to the undead.

"Whatever you encountered," Max said, "I'm guessing it's almost **never** seen in the Overworld. At any rate, the presence of something like that is **worrying.** It means a lot of things. Of course, **none of them** are **good.**"

"What about that word?"

"Are you sure that's what it said? **'Alyss'?**"

"Could have been a **moan** or something. It **was** a type of zombie, after all. Who knows? Breeze said she didn't hear it, so . . ."

I glanced at the other books piled on the table. The former librarian devoted **at least half** of his inventory space to books. I read some of the many titles.

On Zombies: Monster Hunter's Compendium

From Crypt Slimes to Nightshades: Encyclopedia of Undead

History of Aetheria: Volumes I & II

Coves, Shrines, & Lighthouses: Secret and Forgotten Locales

How to Properly Smelt an Iron Slime

The Divine Weapons

Urg the Barbarian

Moon Elves & Dusk Elves

The Netherian Road: A Traveler's Guide

Calling Your First Familiar

Tome of Wizardry: A Guide to Basic Spells

After **browsing** through this miniature library, I finally spoke up. "So, Max . . . Breeze has been hiding things. Things related to something called **the Prophecy.** Care to **fill me in?** What have I **missed** since I left?"

"Best thing you could do would be to read that book she gave you. I know you don't like reading, **but . . .**"

I gasped. "You know I love books **nearly** as much as you. I proudly boast of having **thousands of pages** under my belt. With just a few thousand more, dare I say my knowledge of the world would rival the **Grand Magister's.**" I looked around before adding: "Whoever he is."

Max **sighed.** "Then why is it you always treat me like your personal library?"

I gasped again. "Personal library? I've never thought of you as anything other than **one of my closest** friends. A friend who . . . just so **happens** to have a very large number of books at his disposal. Oh fine. **You're right.** But aren't you the one always asking me to **help you research?** Aren't you the one who gives me so many books to read?"

"Yeah. **Sorry.** Hey, I don't mind helping out. I've just been kind of busy these days."

"Busy **with what?**"

He ignored my question and asked one himself: "Have you thought about what class you want to become? **Any idea?**"

"I've given it some thought, but Breeze said there are **over one hundred** different classes. I'd like to at least see **a list** before I make any real decisions. What if I decided to become a **Knight,** only to find out there's a **Swashbuckler** class?" I glanced at the *Tome of Wizardry.* "How about you? I take it you want to become **a magician** of some type?"

"I do," he said. "Not sure what, though. Probably start off as a basic Wizard."

The door creaked open. *(Always with the doors creaking open.)*

It was **Emerald.** She peeked in. "What are **you nerds** doing?"

"Nothing your simple mind could fathom," Max said. "**Away with ye, foul noobling.**"

With a *hurrmph*, she pushed the door open and stepped inside. She was holding **the stringed instrument** that was on the table earlier. She held it up. "Look what I **traded** for."

"**Why would you trade for that?**" I asked. "Did those guys with the horns not discourage you from ever wanting to play a musical instrument?"

"**Nope.** In fact, ever since I learned about classes, I've been flirting with the idea of **becoming a Bard.** And you know that guy downstairs with the red hat? He just happens to be one. **His name's Flynn.**

I asked him **a million questions** about his class, and I have to say, being a Bard sounds **really fun.** So it's **official.** I've decided. Once we begin our training, that's what I'm going to be."

I glanced at her. Then at **the lyre.** Then at her again. "And . . . **what does a Bard do,** exactly?"

"**Um . . .** they can play songs with **magical effects.** There's one song that can **heal.** Another song that can **put monsters to sleep.** They're abilities, of course, which I'll need to learn. Oh, they're also kinda **adept** in the shadier skills. For example, you need to have at least some knowledge of **thieving skills** to become a Bard. As well as a decent Music skill, **obviously.**"

As she strummed her lyre, Max winced in **agony.** "On that note," he said, "I'd best be off." He started gathering all his books. "Should be **studying up on spells,** anyway." Before he left, he added: "Make sure to read up on **the Prophecy.**"

"Will do."

"You don't want to do that," Emerald said. "It's **way** too confusing."

"Perhaps you could give me a brief rundown, then. After all, you're quite close with Kolb."

"Sure."

She set her lyre down on the table
and sat across from me.
Little did I know
just what she was going to reveal. . . .

SUNDAY—UPDATE IX

"It's like this," Emerald said. "The Prophecy is **more than just a prophecy.** It involves a **quest,** a massive, **extremely** complicated one. It could take years to finish. Once it's completed, winning the war will be **infinitely easier.** Otherwise, peace will be **impossible.** *For darkness will spread across the land."* She said that last part in a **deep voice,** trying to sound heroic. **Then she smiled** and added in her normal voice: "With me so far?"

I **squinted** at her. "I'm not five."

"**Okay.** Well, some people are **vital** to this quest. There are hundreds of them all across the world—from knights to shopkeepers, dwarves to villagers. Despite their various backgrounds, these people all have **one thing in common.** *They're the descendants of heroes who fought in the Second Great War.* These people are **special.** They're able to do things most people cannot. **It's in their blood.** What's more, some of these people possess **relics** or key information that has been passed down through their family lines." She paused. "Still with me?"

"**I think.** But how is this quest supposedly completed?"

"No one really knows. All the books we have on **the Prophecy** are incomplete. Some are missing a lot of pages, even entire chapters. We do know it involves restoring **a bunch of old weapons.**"

"Old weapons? **No.** You can't be talking about the ones from **that fairy tale. . . .**"

She nodded.

"You mean they're **real?**"

"Yes."

"Real as in, you can touch them? Like with your hands?"

"Dude." She gave me **an exhausted look. "I've seen one myself.**"

". . ."

This is the sound I make when I'm in **total shock.**

Emerald Shadowcroft had just dealt **a critical hit** to my simple mind. What she said next was a **powerful** follow-up strike. Like the second half of a fatal combo that left me totally stunned.

"**Kolb has one,**" she said. "He's had it ever since he arrived in this world. He just didn't tell us. **He's been hiding it** this whole time." She sighed. "I know, right?"

"So **he's some kind of hero,** then?"

Emerald nodded. "Something like that. But he's not a lone hero who will **magically** save the day; there's a lot more to this than just a single person. And honestly, that sword he has is pretty much worthless. **It's broken,** and restoring it will take forever. **Seven other pieces** are scattered across the Overworld."

I sighed. "Well, you were right. This is **a lot** to take in."

"**There's more,**" she said. "Wanna know why he came to Villagetown? Some guy sent him here on **a quest.** He didn't know why, at first. Only recently did he learn he was meant to find you. And Breeze. Pebble, too. **You are all descendants**—you're all linked to that quest. So it's no **coincidence** that you became friends. **You were meant to.** Call it destiny, if you want. **The will of the gods.** Or call it part of the game's code. Whatever it is, **mysterious forces** are at work."

"But why? Why are **we** important?"

"Like I said, we need to learn more in the capital. Guess it's **no coincidence** that we're being sent there, right? There's only one thing I know for sure. You are **bound by blood** to these events. If we think of this world as a game, you'd be called **Quest NPCs.** A step above ordinary NPCs. And it sounds like you have **a bigger role** to play than most."

". . ."

Quest NPCs . . .

So I'm linked by blood to **some major event.**

Like Emerald said, if you're **a Believer,** you call it destiny. Otherwise, you think of it as the laws of a game, countless lines of code. Whatever you choose to believe, in the end, isn't that important. It's as though we're all **tiny gears** in some massive redstone machine.

I heard the lightest footsteps behind me.

"I wanted to tell you," Breeze said. "It's just that . . . you already had so much going on. I didn't want you **to feel overwhelmed. . . .**"

"It's fine," I said. **"Thank you."**

Honestly, I was **glad** she didn't tell me.

Emerald and I have always been **on the same level.** She explained it in a way I could **easily** understand.

The future Bard rose from her seat. "Sorry, Breeze. Didn't mean to **steal a moment** from you. Just thought Runt should know. Y'know?"

"Doesn't matter," Breeze said. "I didn't know where to begin anyway. I've never talked with the Legionnaires much."

Emerald grabbed **her lyre.** "All right, guys, I'm out. Gonna try practicing some more. And Runt, try not to think about it so much. You're **destined** to assist the Overworld in some way, but so are plenty of other people. From shopkeepers to hermits living in mountain caves. You're far from being **the only** descendant. And then, even if you **weren't** destined to help out . . . you would anyway, **right?**" She **winked.** "Night, guys."

After Emerald left, Breeze gave me **a worried look.** "You okay?"

"Yeah. It's a lot to **process,** but . . ."

"When they first read **the Prophecy,** they thought you were one of the only ones tied into this. But as they read more, they learned that there are **hundreds.** But that's all we know for now. We'll find out more in **Aetheria City,** I think. In the **Tower Eternal.**" She suddenly seemed wiped out. "Gonna lie down. **Exhausted.** Night."

"Hey."

". . . ?"

"Is this why **that thing** was after you? Are we being . . . **hunted?**"

She nodded. "If we really are so important in this story, it's in **the Eyeless One's** best interests to . . . **cross us out.**"

I felt **a chill** when she said this, and I remembered how she'd reacted to the old man—how **afraid** she'd sounded. And I recalled what her father had told her: "*Nowhere will you be safe. . . .*"

"**Wait,** this isn't the first time something has attacked you like that," I said. "It's happened **before,** hasn't it? Maybe it wasn't a zombie disguised as an old man, or a ghost, whatever it was, but . . . **other things** have come for **you** in the past, haven't they?"

". . ."

"Well?"

She sighed. "I won't lie to you. **It's true.** After we escaped from our imprisonment, **the Eyeless One** sent his servants after us. They were much different from what we saw today, but . . . always **something terrible.**"

"But nothing seemed to be looking for you in Villagetown."

"We figured out a way to **evade them** before we found your village."

"How?"

"That's . . . a story for **another day.** I don't want to think about it right now."

She looked away with the same **troubled** expression she often had. Today, I finally knew why. **Forever hunted** . . .

"Night."

After she left, I stood there like an iron golem, thinking over and over about what I'd just learned. If everything I heard tonight is true, **dark times** are ahead. For me. For her. Our shoulders bear **the weight** of not only a village but also the **entire world.**

MONDAY

I had all kinds of **nightmares** tonight. And when I woke up from them, I couldn't stop thinking about this **mysterious Prophecy** . . . and what my involvement meant.

Stump was in his bed now, lightly **snoring.** He must have come back to the room after I fell asleep. I still **felt paranoid** after all those dreams, and I went to the window. It was morning, technically, but it was still dark. I didn't see **anyone** outside. I checked the hallway, too. Just to be sure. Then I went back to my bed and sat down to think.

You are bound by blood to these events. . . .

What Emerald had told me was **crazy enough,** but when Breeze confirmed that we're now being stalked by creepy undead things, it really was like an **ultimate combo attack** that slammed me into the ground so hard I bounced then bounced again. Do those girls have no mercy? **None?** They could have at least ordered some tea before telling me all that, right? A nice warm cup of **cocoa-bean tea?** Served in a mug with powdered sugar on top? I saw that on the menu.

With a sigh, I glanced at my snoring friend. He had **a book** in his hands.

> ### STUMP'S JOURNAL
> #### SUNDAY—UPDATE II
> JUST TRADED FOR A NEW SHIELD IN THE MAIN HALL. THE GUY WOULDN'T BUDGE ON THE PRICE. SO FRUSTRATING. I DON'T HAVE A SINGLE EMERALD LEFT. OH WELL. IT'S WORTH IT. I KNOW OUR QUEST WILL BE HARD. I ONLY HOPE I CAN PROTECT MY FRIENDS. THEY'RE EVERYTHING TO ME. . . .

I placed his diary **back in his hands.**

MONDAY—UPDATE I

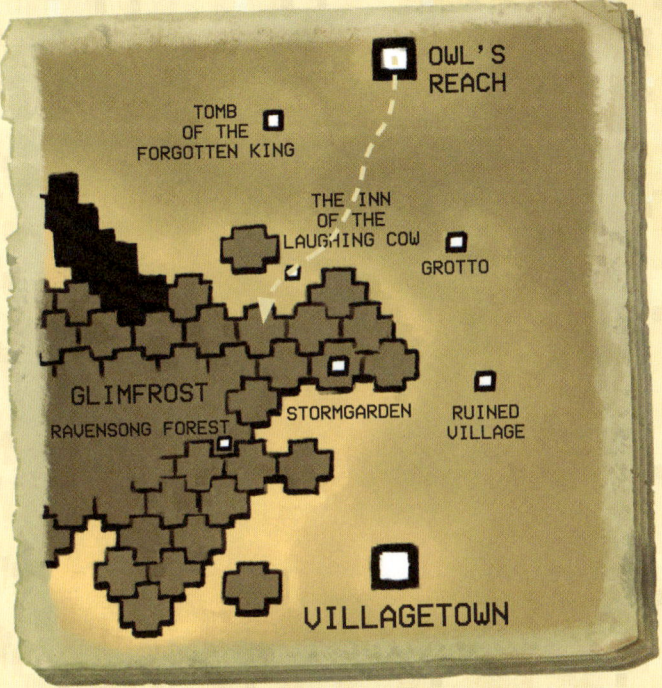

"We quickly ate our breakfast,
And rode to the southwest,
To a dark and creepy forest,
Which Lola mapped her best,
To the south we'll see the moon elves,
In their woods we'll stop to rest,
While there we must act proper,
For Stump it's quite a test."

No, **that's not a poem.** Nor is it mine.

It's a song Emerald sang as we entered northern **Ravensong.**

I can only hope her **singing** is tied to her Music skill, and that her Music skill goes up **very, very fast** once we get to the Academy. . . .

Northern Ravensong Forest

A bat with glowing red eyes watching us . . .

Notice the ruins of ancient fortresses. They fell during the Second Great War.

MONDAY—UPDATE II

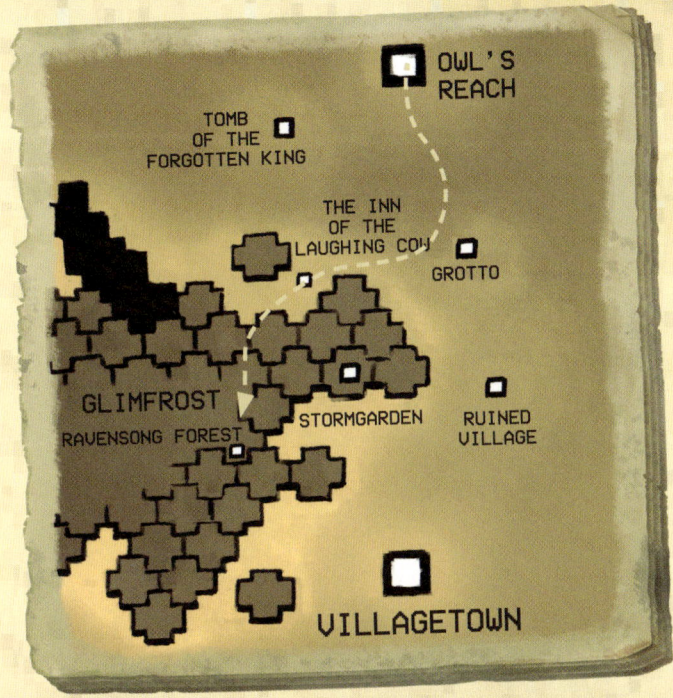

*"We reached the woods before noon,
I thought we'd reached the moon. . . ."*

Before long, the tall pines gave way to **an unbelievable** sight. Upon first seeing **the silverwood,** it really did seem as though we were on **the moon.**

While my thoughts had been dwelling on the ominous Prophecy and on being hunted forever by beings of the night, all of that was **instantly swept away.**

Among a sea of silvery grass stood bushes with **violet leaves,** gossamer white flowers, red and blue spruce, and trees so large they would have even dwarfed **dark oaks.** Far above stretched a canopy almost **the color of ice.** Glowing pools dotted the landscape here and there. Only when I saw these woods did I really understand how **amazing** our world **really** is, how vast and diverse, filled with places that darkness can never reach.

When we stopped to feed the horses more **swiftness** potions, Breeze pointed to what appeared to be a block of green glowstone suspended from the leaves. "That's **a moonstone lantern.** Only **the moon elves** know how to craft them. Their light is **said to be** like lava to the undead. We'll be **safe** here."

"I'm just happy to see **some animals** for a change," Emerald said. "**Here, boy!**" She got off her horse and approached a small red animal. It almost looked like a wolf. As she drew closer, the creature **scampered off** into the ferns.

"I wonder if they can be **tamed?**" Ophelia asked.

Max and Lola were crouching before a wispy white flower. "Hey, is that **meadowsdown?**" Lola asked. "And **morningwhisker! Wow!** I'd say this forest is an alchemist's dream come true!"

Stump was like me: totally **speechless,** looking around in awe. "**D-d-dude.**"

Elric smiled at him. "The first time I saw the silverwood, my face must have looked just like yours." He went back to his horse. "**All right,** everyone. **Glimfrost** lies on the other end of the valley. **Let's ride!**"

And we rode.

MONDAY—UPDATE III

Glimfrost
Moon Elf Village

That's what greeted us.

Although it was **technically** a village, that word seemed inappropriate—if not **insulting.**

As the Aetherian Knights dismounted, the glow of their lanterns had nothing on the moonstone lights. Of course, their lanterns were not held to provide **illumination,** but to signal **respect,** a way to greet honored friends.

The greeting **was not returned**. . . .

The village was certainly **beautiful**, yes. Elegant, **breathtaking**, enchanting. **But it was also empty. Abandoned.** Not a moon elf in sight. The only sounds were **the echoes of our footsteps** on a type of stone I didn't recognize. The silence was **unsettling**.

"They must have left for **Nepheridyll**," Elric said. "That's the largest **elven city**, to the west of here. Although I do not suspect anyone still remains, we must **make sure**." He turned to us. "Would you care to **assist us** in the search?"

Eight villagers nodded in unison.

No. **Seven.** Lola was now studying a light blue flower, its petals embedded with **tiny metallic cubes**. I think it was some kind of ore flower. I've only heard of them. Ore flowers are the **subject of tales** told by old blacksmiths on warm summer nights, their eyes gleaming with not only the light of a nearby furnace **but with hope:** the hope to obtain some of **the legendary metals** such flowers are said to contain. That's all nonsense, though. The only metal **this** flower contained was **iron**.

Breeze's father seemed to be staring at me when he said, "**Remember what I told you.**"

"We'll stay close," Breeze said.

"And behave yourselves." Brio added. "We are guests—**not looters.** Otherwise . . ."

I finished his sentence for him. "You'll make sure the majority of our time training in the capital involves **mushroom stew.**"

He smirked. "Count on it."

Max was already wandering off, book and quill in hand. He seemed to be **taking notes,** jotting something down with every **unusual sight.**

"Figures," Cog muttered, and ran after him. "**Hey!** Egghead! **Wait up!**"

The rest of us trailed after them, looking in **wonder** at the bizarre village filled with **ghostly green light.**

Breeze was lagging behind. Before catching up to us, she turned back again, just for a second. She'd been looking at **one house in particular.**

MONDAY—UPDATE IV

We **ran up** every staircase, across every bridge, and through every house.

Most of the homes were **empty.** The elves had cleared out most of their item chests before leaving.

We stopped in front of an **armor shop,** the only store we'd seen so far. It had a simple design compared to the rest of the buildings. I guess whoever owned it wasn't an elf. A sign outside read:

The Unicorn
Tank in Style

Cog walked up to the door. "There's gotta be some stuff in here. No way the shopkeeper was able to **haul off everything,** eh?"

"Remember what her dad told us," Ophelia said. "We aren't here to **loot.**"

Emerald drew closer to her. "Pretty **honorable** there, Ophelia. Especially for someone who doesn't have **any** armor."

The **former waitress** glanced down at her outfit. She crossed her arms. "I will have **no part** in the **plundering** of an elven village."

"**You sure?**" Emerald drew closer still and all but whispered into her ear: "Bet you could find some **enchanted chain mail** in there. Nice stats. All **shiny. Full** durability."

Ophelia looked at her outfit once more. You could see the conflict in her eyes. The **internal struggle.** Which finally seemed to break as her shoulders sagged. "**Um** . . . I suppose we could see if there are a . . . few spare pieces we might . . . **borrow.** Yes. **Borrow.**" She raised her head. "Whatever we take, we will someday return. Is that **agreed?**"

Emerald nodded. And smiled. "**Yep.** Someday."

As one of the two **captains** present, I should have said something. But **honestly,** looking down at my own pitiful set of armor—armor all **rusted** and full of **negative enchantments** that would embarrass even a **noob**—I found it hard to say anything. In fact, I was the one to open the door. After all, the sign said **"tank in style."** I like tanking in style. Who doesn't? Tanking hordes of zombies is **great and all,** but if you can't **look cool** while doing so, what's the point? I **did** have my reservations about the shop's name, though. **The Unicorn.** And once inside . . . my suspicions were confirmed and **my dreams absolutely crushed.**

Like Cog had guessed, it seemed like the shopkeeper had tried to take everything, but when that proved **impossible,** he'd left some stuff behind. **Scattered across the floor** were many different pieces of armor: tunics, boots, bracelets, bracers, helmets, and leggings, many of which were **enchanted**—with **good enchantments,** I might add. And this would have been **great news** for me, spectacular news, only . . . I'm **not a huge fan** of the color pink. Or violet. Or rainbows. Or pastel shades. Nor am I particularly fond of kittens, baby birds, bunnies, butterflies, unicorns, and seahorses . . .

I've said before that I'd be willing to wear **anything** so long as it had good stats. **I retract that statement now.** Truly, a line **does** exist, and that line was right in front of me. **No way was I going to cross it.**

Uh . . .

Capes with hearts.
Kitten masks.
Unicorn mail.
What's not to like?

In what could be called **pure horror,** each boy present watched as the girls **tested out** different items, **whirling around** and asking **each other's opinions** on color scheme and so on. It was almost **enraging** that they seemed to prioritize each item's appearance over its stats. Didn't they know how to appreciate fine **enchantments?!** I've been hanging out with girls for a while now, and I **still** don't understand them! Breeze seemed to be the only one who had some appreciation for

109

the raw power that these outfits provided, and at least she picked one that didn't look like a costume from a children's play. The rest . . . **well,** to give you an idea, Emerald was wearing bracers that looked like **bunnies.** And a pair of fuzzy boots that **also** resembled bunnies. As for the other two, I . . . **no,** I can't go on. **Words escape me.**

"Well, maybe it's not a **total** loss," Max said. "Maybe we could **dye** some of that stuff."

"Dye or no dye, I'm not wearing something called **Mermaid Veil**," Stump said. "Or **Faerie Rainbow Cloak**, **Butterfly Bracelet** . . ."

"We could **rename** them," Cog said. "All we'd need is an anvil, and . . . **oh**, what am I saying? **It's hopeless.** Most of this stuff can't even be dyed anyway without a **super high** Crafting skill."

"Better luck next time, huh, guys?" Emerald said with a **wink.**

Stump let out a huge sigh. "Yeah, **yeah.** Enjoy your bunny slippers. The monsters will probably go for you first, since only a **noob** would wear something like that."

She walked up to him and **poked him** in the chest. "**Idiot!** They're enchanted with **Echo I!** Know what that does? It'll **slightly increase** the power of any songs I play!"

Stump raised his hands defensively. "Please don't hurt me with your magical songs boosted by magical bunny slippers! Songs you haven't even learned yet! **P-p-please! N-n-no!**"

She poked him again. "There's a song that can **heal,** remember? **You're** the one who wants to become some kind of **tank!** Think your health bar's gonna stay up all on its own? What if you run out of potions? Who's gonna be there to **heal you? Noob!** I was thinking about **you!**"

"Oh . . . well, I feel like a jerk now."

"**Hurrmph!**"

All right, so they weren't totally ignoring the enchantments. Maybe **I'm just bitter.** But it's fine. My time will come. Someday, we'll come across a **real** armor shop. A shop run by an **Underlord.** They're these guys that wear **black felsteel** plate and command the undead. I saw an entry on them in Max's *Encyclopedia of the Undead.* Actually, at this point, I'd settle for any set of armor that isn't sparkly or doesn't resemble **a rainbow fish.** Is that too much to ask?

A potion was lying on the counter, and Cog grabbed it, taking a sip. "**Not bad.**" It was a flavored drink—**moonberry juice.** A white hat was also sitting on the counter, and he grabbed this item as well, throwing it on. "I'll go check on the knights." He headed for the door, turning back one last time and tipping **his new hat** as he did.

After we left the shop, it seemed my luck was only **growing worse:** Emerald found **a bow.** An **OP** one, too. It was just sitting in some random chest. Why couldn't it have been **a greatsword** or something? Upon opening that chest, her eyes **grew wide,** and she let out a small gasp. "**Wow! This is amaz—zzingly useless! Yep!** I'd better carry it, then! Wouldn't want **this** piece of junk **clogging up** anyone's inventory space!"

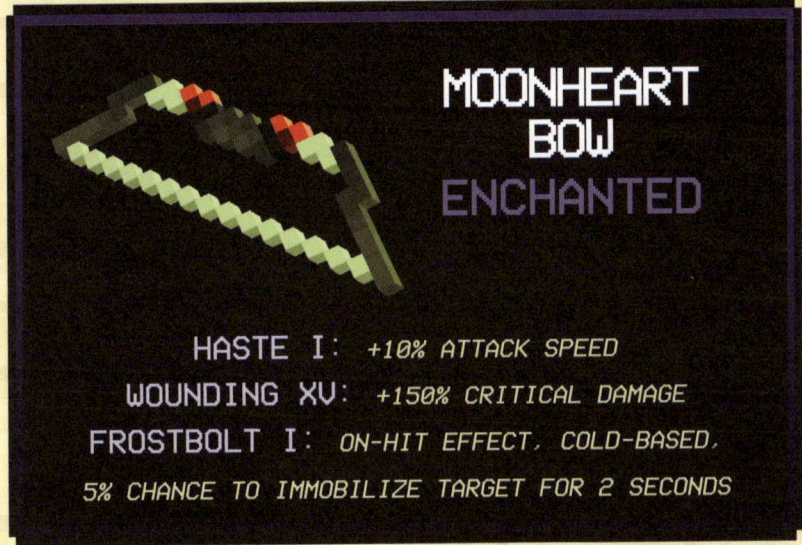

Moonheart? I wouldn't have used it, anyway.

"That should go to **Breeze,**" Max said. He lowered his glasses and gave Emerald the **stern look** a teacher gives an **unruly student.** "It's only **logical.** She's the only one here who's **any good** with a bow."

"Yeah? Well how about **this** logic," Emerald said. "With this **OP bow,** I'll be just as good as her! Why put all of your eggs in **the same inventory?**"

"It's fine," Breeze called out. **"She can keep it."**

She was nearby, in one of the many gazebo-like buildings that were scattered throughout the village, standing on a balcony that overlooked the silverwood.

I wanted to ask why she was being **so glum,** but the scene in front of her made me totally forget. The silverwood stretched far to the west—**unbelievably** far—and from up where we were, with an open view, the tops of the trees looked almost like the ocean. . . .

You could see the mountain range perfectly from here. **The Spines of Ao.** No map could have ever done justice to its size, nor could any view but this one.

Only then I did understand how **truly enormous** that range really is . . . and only then did I realize how **hard** it would be to climb any of those mountains. With vast sheer cliffs whole biomes in height, and windswept valleys packed deep with snow, reaching any of those peaks seemed **impossible.** Suddenly, I remembered **Pebble. . . .**

"That temple must be up there somewhere," I said, joining Breeze on the balcony. "Did he know how hard that climb was going to be? He must have known, right?"

Of course the others gathering around us didn't understand a thing. I'd already told them about **Urf** yesterday. How he'd attacked us. But they hadn't yet heard about **Pebble's quest** to trek to the top of one of these mountains. It was time to tell them.

"I always knew Pebble wasn't such a **bad guy,**" Emerald said. "**Stressed out?** Definitely. **Troubled?** Maybe. But a monster? **No way.**"

"I overheard the knights talking about those mountains," Max said. "According to them, the foothills are **crawling** with undead. The nastier types, too. **Ghouls. Wights.** Even one that can turn you into stone with **a single touch.**"

As if I didn't feel **bad enough.**

Our journey so far has been like **a birthday party** compared to what Pebble must be going through. At least he's with that **S** guy. Surely they wouldn't start climbing without being prepared, and I think I remember some people in **Owl's Reach** talking about a shop that had a sale on **Cold Protection** gear. Or am I just imagining things to make myself **feel better?**

"We could head there now," Stump said. "With us helping out, we could **light** that beacon and be back **in time for enderscones!**"

"I'd love to," I said, "but I doubt the knights would go for it. **Besides,** do you think we'd even be able to get there in time? Well, maybe with Swiftness potions . . ."

"There's no need to **worry about him,**" Max said. "Remember that look he always had during **our exercises** in school? **Such focus.** He's survived this far—I doubt he'll fail now."

Without looking back at us, Breeze nodded. "**I agree.** His main weakness used to be his confidence. It got in his way. **He was careless.** That's how I was able to **defeat him** in our duel way back. But when I saw him a few days ago, he no longer seemed like that. He was . . . less **reckless** than before."

So she noticed that too, I thought, but I said nothing.

Ophelia joined Breeze at the rail. "Just hope he comes back. **Villagetown could use him.**"

"That's something I've been thinking about," I said. "Fifteen of us are going to the capital, right? What if there's **another attack? We won't be there.**"

"I think it'll be fine," Max said. "**Breeze's dad** is staying, as is most of the Legion. And recently, there just haven't been as many attacks. **The Eyeless One** said he'd be back, but so far he hasn't."

"**Yeah.**"

Still at the rail, I looked out at the mountains again. In one **particular** little spot—a shadowy cleft not too far below the tallest peak—I saw a flicker of **golden light.** Almost like that area had been illuminated, **briefly,** by more than a thousand torches. I strained to see another flash but saw nothing else, **only shadow.** . . .

Emerald joined us at the rail. "It is a lovely view," she said. "Look at that river. **Hmm,** no boats by the dock. I wonder if the elves sailed away?" She turned to the rest. "Anyone up for a **swim?** The knights won't care if we leave the village, right?"

Cog was returning as she said this. "Don't think they'll even notice. They're poring over **a journal** some moon elf left behind. Seems like they've **discovered something important.** They wouldn't tell me what it is, though."

"Then we're off!" Emerald said. When no one **followed** her, she turned back. "**What?** The river's just past the wall. **We'll be fine.**"

MONDAY—UPDATE V

In this scene, I'm contemplating my future, Cog is staring at something far away, Ophelia is whispering something to a blushing Stump, Breeze is gazing at her reflection while touching an ear, and . . . Max and Lola are holding hands???

Okay, so we not only **looted** a bunch of stuff but also listened to Emerald and wandered off, **past the wall.**

We **were** in sight of the village, though, and there was nothing else out here besides **a few strange animals.** One was small and gray with

black rings around its eyes, and another was dark brown and larger than any cow, with some **fearsome-looking** horns. For a long time, we just sat on the dock, taking in the beautiful and otherworldly view while chatting. There was nothing else to do but wait. The knights were still reading **those scrolls,** and the horses had hardly recovered **half their endurance.**

"Y'know, guys, I think **I've figured it all out**," Emerald said. "About our world, I mean. Okay, so the Terrarians are always arguing about whether or not our world is **actually real,** right? Well, Kolb said that, on **that game server of theirs,** you used to be able to ride a horse forever. I mean **forever.** Horses had no endurance to speak of. They just **couldn't** get tired. Then the server changed the rules. **An update,** I think it's called. Anyway, after this, the horses suddenly had endurance to make them **more real.**

"And that's not the only thing that suddenly changed in their game world. There were tons of **little modifications** here and there, right? Every month, or every couple of months, a new update **there,** new update **here,** and now **stormberries** exist, with tons of crafting recipes for them. . . ."

Stump seemed very lost. "Emerald? **Please tell me you have a point.**"

"My point is this: Their game was **constantly changing.** One day, there was no endersteel armor. The next day, there was. But our world has never been like that. It's **always been the same.**"

"That's an **interesting** observation," Max said. "Maybe you should become a **philosopher.**"

"**Whatever.** It has to mean **something.**"

"You can say our world isn't changing," Stump said, "but what about Villagetown? **Bumbi** tried making a house of **cake!** Cake, Emerald! **Cake!**"

Emerald **sighed** at him. "That's . . . not what I meant. I meant the **laws,** the **rules,** you know? **Oh,** forget it. . . ."

I was trying to understand what she was talking about, but after Stump mentioned Villagetown, I couldn't stop myself from asking what I'd **missed** back home. He replied so fast and with **such excitement** that I could tell that he'd been waiting for this moment. The words poured out like water from a broken dam. . . .

"**First,** Leaf discovered how to craft **greatswords,**" he said, "and then Winter found an owl, then Drill found a **secret underground** chamber with an iron golem that was trying to **craft pizza** . . . or maybe Winter found the owl first. Oh, and the Legionnaires recruited a new member, **a girl named Rubinia**—she's kinda **weird.** Oh, oh, and the ice cream shop has a new flavor! **Powder keg,** it's called. It's really **delicious!** They called it powder keg because the flavors burst in your mouth! It's gray like a smoke cloud with bits of chocolate cake crumbs. Oh, we also **explored the Overworld** a little bit, and we slept in an underground house. We helped the Legionnaires make some **beacons.** They're like these towers that we can see from far away so we won't get lost. We also traded for some new weapons like **my war hammer** here and **my shield,** because I wanna be **a tank** like Emerald said, maybe a Knight, but maybe starting as a Warrior first, though." He paused only to **take a breath.** "Oh, and **an ocelot** showed up at our village! A **bluuuuuue** one!"

"Nice." Emerald rolled her eyes at him. "Way to **ruin the surprise, nooblet.**"

"Yes, we were hoping to surprise you," Breeze said. "Oh well. Guess I might as well tell you. We ran across him while scouting the Overworld. It sounds like he's **bound to the quest,** too."

I laughed. "**What?** You mean **this ocelot** can talk?"

"**Yeah,**" Emerald said. "I know. Villagetown is apparently a hot spot for craziness."

"You know, I'm not even **that** shocked," I said. "I've already seen and heard so much these days. So there's **a blue ocelot who can talk.**" I shrugged. "**Why not?** I've already seen a shape-shifting zombie-slash-ghost. Oh, and Kolb's **a hero from a fairy tale.** So why not this, too? And maybe Stump is secretly an enderman whose real name is **Eggbert?** Again: **Why not?**"

Everyone turned to Stump, who sputtered: "W-what are you talking about? **What ghost?!**"

I then told them about the thing that **attacked us** yesterday, and Breeze admitted she'd already been **hunted** before. After she and her father escaped, they had **nowhere** to go, because Shadowbrook was in ruins. So they **wandered** the Overworld aimlessly, traveling from inn to inn, village to village, at times sheltering in the wild. No matter where they went, though, **someone** *(or something)* was always on their tail. One time, it was a pigman in black robes; he had a dagger **imbued with Wither XII.** Another time, it was a shadowy form, like a ghost, that **slowly emerged** from a wall, reaching for Breeze while she was on her bed in her nightgown, writing in **her diary.** Not **at all** creepy. No wonder she's always so **withdrawn**—the poor girl must be **traumatized** after all the things she's been through. **I'm** gonna have nightmares just **hearing** about that.

Stump, on the other hand, was more interested in the dagger: "Wither XII?!"

Breeze shrugged. "That's what my father said. He studied that weapon for days. The poison was **so strong** that it had actually eaten away at the blade. It barely looked like the blade of a dagger. And the weapon itself had a **maximum** durability of one."

"So it'd break upon striking anything," Max said. "A kind of **one-use** item with a **serious punch.**" He had **the same look** as when he'd inspected the silverwood's exotic flowers. "Where is it **now?**"

"Think my father still has it," she said. Still sitting on the edge of the dock, she **stared down** into the water. "Anyway, we should assume that **the Eyeless One** has learned what we've learned. Since we're all **close,** it's possible that his servants will come for you, too—if only to **anger us,** to get to us. The capital is a **very large city.** It will be easy for someone to **blend in** there. For an **assassin.** Like my father's told me **again and again** . . . we'll never be **safe,** even at the foot of the king's throne."

They all fell **silent.**

It was **a lot to digest.**

Bound by blood. The **descendants** of heroes. What makes us **so special . . . ?**

Not only do we have to go through **rigorous** training and study up in **the Academy,** we also have to **watch out for** . . . whatever they are.

No one said a word for the longest time. Everyone was **thinking,** staring ahead, watching the clouds roll by or the waves on the river. There was **a slight wind.** Every time the leaves rustled overhead, <u>I looked up.</u>

MONDAY—UPDATE VI

Minutes later, the wind **really picked up,** and the branches above the dock were all but shaking. Just like me. I stared upward, expecting **the worst.** When the wind rushed through the forest again, the **weirdest** sound came from just down the river, almost like a bat or something, **except louder.**

Keee-uuu . . .

I literally **flew up** one block **while sitting down.** No idea how I managed that. I looked around, trying to see what made that noise, and I **jumped again** as that sound rang out once more.

Keee-uuuuuuuu . . .
Kee-kee-kee-kee-kee-kee-kee!

I shot to my feet, as did **everyone else** except Lola and Breeze. Ophelia drew her sword, Emerald **took cover** behind Stump, Max **hid** behind Emerald, and Cog, holding onto his bottle of juice, **crouched** behind Max.

"What's that **sound?**" Lola asked, evidently **unafraid**.

"I think it's **a blockbird**," Breeze said. She pointed at one of the **large violet bushes** not too far away.

Suddenly, **I saw it.** Just down the river, on top of that bush, sat a **reddish, cube-like form.** I ran. I ran with the speed of an enderman who'd just been invited to a pool party. I ran **so fast** that I stumbled into Cog, who cried out in that **screechy voice** of his: "**Runt! You little noob!**" I made him **spill** his moonberry juice. That's how **excited** I was at the thought of seeing a **blockbird**. I had only heard of them until today, and I had to see if they really were just **tiny feathered blocks with wings.** Nothing would have prevented me from reaching this goal. **NOTHIGN.** I know, I spelled "**nothing**" wrong there, but that was on purpose to try and capture **my excitement.**

A blockbird

There it was, **in its nest,** exactly like **I'd imagined.**

All of my friends were running up to me now, and soon they joined me in **staring at** this bizarre animal. Ever seen eight villagers standing on top of a bush? I'm not even **going to try** drawing it.

"It sounds **angry,**" Lola said, petting the bird's head.

Breeze knelt down. "That's because its nest is **almost broken.**"

"**Oh dear.**" For once, Lola **wasn't smiling.** "I suppose we should **craft a new one** then, shouldn't we?"

"And I suppose you know **the crafting recipe** for a **bird's nest,**" I said—having forgotten how **foolish** it is to doubt **the ever-so-talented** Lola Diamondcube.

Her smile **returned.**

Of course her smile returned.

"As a matter of fact," she said, "**I most certainly do.**"

RECIPE FOR BIRD'S NEST

You most certainly have to be kidding me.

In less than a minute, Lola crafted a **brand-new** nest with her own two hands and replaced the blockbird's old nest. Soon, the blockbird was no longer chirping in an **annoying** way, but **singing.** It went something like this:

Kee-kuu-kee-kuu-kuu-kee,
kee-kuu-kuu-kee-kuu . . .

Uh, I think that's pretty much **all of it.** If there was more, I forgot. Only then did it **hit me.**

"Lola, um . . . **how did you craft that nest?**"

"Isn't it **neat?** It's my ability," she said. "**Artisan.** It lets me craft **any 3x3 item without using a crafting table.** I thought it might **come in handy** if we ever need to craft something **in the heat of battle. Rubinia** taught me."

Of course.

While I was out in the Overworld doing my thing, my friends were **doing things too.** Including learning **new abilities.** Basic ones, like mine, but they're all still **requirements** for whatever type of **class** they've thought about becoming.

Stump

SHIELD BASH

THROWING UP A SHIELD AND SMASHING INTO BAD GUYS HAS NEVER BEEN MORE FUN!

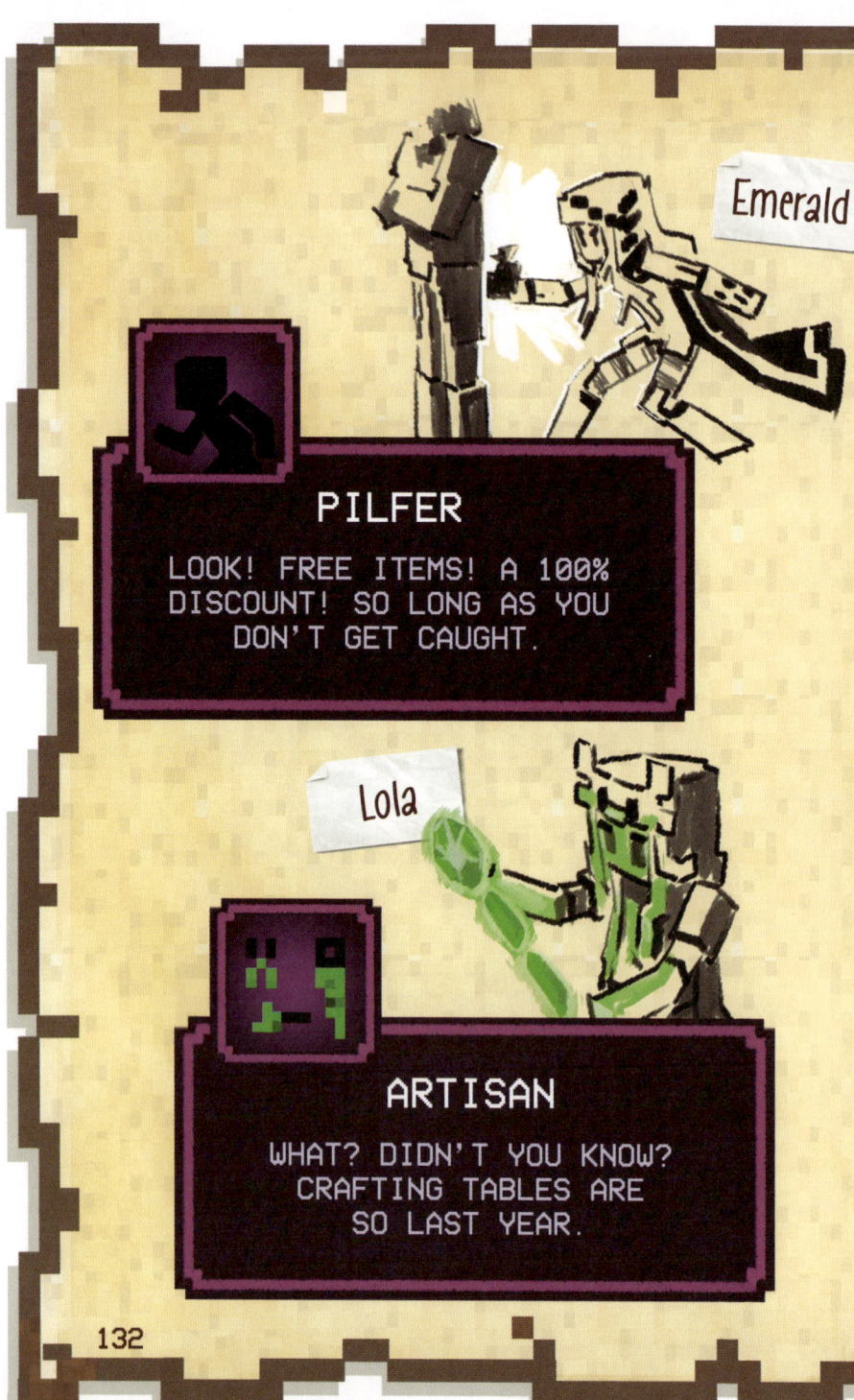

Max

FAMILIAR

IT'S A PET! IT'S A MINION! AND A MOST LOYAL ONE, TOO. AT LEAST, UNTIL YOU FORGET TO FEED IT.

Ophelia

PARRY

SHIELDS? PSH! WITHOUT THE SOUND OF TWO BLADES CLASHING, YOU CAN'T CALL IT A BATTLE!

HIDE

EVER SEEN A THIEF WITHOUT THIS? IF YOU HAVE, YOU SAW A BAD ONE!

"Kolb told me that's what makes someone **elite** or not," Emerald said. "**Abilities,** being able to do **more** than just swing weapons and place blocks. After all, every monster out there has at least **one kind of trick.** It's almost **humiliating,** huh? All this time we've been without any **cool attacks!** In a way, that's like being **beneath a slime. . . .**"

She certainly had a point. **Without abilities,** a person is as simple as **Urg the Barbarian** who—in his words—can only "atak bad things" and "eet good things." That's all Urg does, **atak bad things** and **eet good things.** And truth be told, Urg's not even that great at *eeting* good things—or even *eeting* things at all, for that matter—as evidenced on **page thirty-three** of **volume VII** of his series:

"*Oog!* Me hungy! But where green thing go? **Me want eet!** But where go???"

"Where go???"

·Hungy?· Hmm. I think that ties with **"noobery"** as my **favorite** new word!

At any rate, we need to be less like the **pigman** above and more like the monsters we face. Creepers are feared for their **ability to ruin** your house. Endermen for their **ability to teleport** into your bedroom any time they want. If we really are supposed to help save this world—or even protect our own village—we have to get on their level.

And lately, **we have been.**

Now, we're **duel wielding, sneaking** around and **stealing** stuff, and **crafting items** without the use of any crafting tables.

And that's just the start! So if any of **Herobrine's minion-noobs** just happen to be reading, be warned: Watch your back, **nooblings,** and be **very, very afraid!**

We are **no longer peasants** scared of simple wooden swords! We're on the path to **nobility,** to **perfection** that will make **even the fancy lords jealous!**

"I do say, noble sir, ye have bested me in this duel."

"Thy abilities are most **exquisite**."

WHAT IF I TOLD YOU
ABILITIES ARE REALLY COOL

"**Watch this,**" Stump said.

Along with an **enchanted iron shield,** he was brandishing a **huge war hammer.** He charged at a spruce tree, his shield raised in front, and **slammed** into the trunk. This **special attack** was so **powerful** that the spruce tree actually shook. Such is the power of **Shield Bash.**

As for Max, he has **a pet bat** named **Chompy.** It's a **special** type of pet, controlled through his **Familiar** ability. It has a weak **bite attack** and can be sent flying ahead to **scout** dangerous locations. It can also carry one item with its little clawed feet. The uses for this delivery bat are limited only by one's imagination, **I suppose.** . . . For example, it could carry **healing potions** to wounded allies. Anyway, know that calling a familiar is **the first step** for any aspiring **magician.**

Max raised his hand and sent **Chompy** fluttering into the sky. All it took was the flick of a wrist to change his pet's direction, and before long, the bat was **rolling** and **diving** . . . and nearly **clipping Emerald's hair.**

"**Hurrmph!** You know, I'm still looking for a good reason to try out this **new bow!**"

The bat, returning to Max's shoulder, **squeaked pitifully.**

Having put away his shield and hammer, Stump **rummaged** through his belt pouch. "**Huh.** Thought I still had one of those muffins."

Emerald hastily brushed off a few **sparkling crumbs** from her tunic.

That was about the time Breeze's father came for us. He didn't seem angry; he didn't even seem to **notice** the new outfits. He simply strode up to us with a **grim expression.** More grim than **usual,** at least.

"Come. **We must leave <u>at once.</u>**"

MONDAY—UPDATE VII

No one said much of anything as we **returned** to the horses. Not Elric, not the grumpy knight Zigurd. We just **saddled up** and **left**.

Obviously, they'd learned about **something bad**. I knew it was something to do with **why the elves left**. Maybe it was about **that keep. Stormgarden.** Maybe **an army** was gathering there. Breeze's dad told us it's in **the eastern wing** of Ravensong. We must have passed it this morning. But **we didn't encounter anything**, so I couldn't understand why everyone was **so worried**.

Stars started to appear across **the cold black sky.**

We rode **in silence,** stopping only to feed the horses the very last of the Swiftness potions. Then I saw something else I **couldn't understand.**

It was already morning again: Directly in front us, on the horizon, the sun was trying its best to shine through the heaviest bank of **fog**. That didn't make **any sense,** though, because we were riding **directly south**. Why was the sun rising **in the south** instead of **the east?** And why now? It had set only an hour ago.

But it wasn't the sun.... **I suppose I was in denial.**

My mind was **unwilling to accept the cold truth** in front of me. After we passed that ridge . . .

I **vaguely** recall Emerald screaming, Ophelia shouting.
Everyone shouting.

It was **inconceivable. Villagetown.** Our village. **Burning.**

In places, the flames rose over **fifteen blocks,** stretching toward a sky **filled with ash** that was falling back down like **black snow.**

Every second was an hour as we galloped to **the wall.** I couldn't believe what I was seeing. As we reached the remains of **the north gate,** I spurred my horse inside.

Behind me, everyone was calling out, **telling me to come back.** I almost did. The flames were **sweeping through** the libraries, clouds of thick smoke formed **floating walls,** and the metallic sounds of battle came from **everywhere at once.** How cobblestone was **burning,** I didn't know. And I didn't know it was possible for **sand to smelt into glass** without the use of a furnace. It was **terrifying** to see even iron doors crumble under the **unnaturally red flames.** My horse started whinnying **furiously** and rearing up. I'd never before seen an animal **so terrified** by fire.

"Fine," I said, jumping off. "**Go.**"

With a last whinny, the horse **immediately fled.**

"**Noobery . . .**" I drew **my blades.** "That's what I should have named you."

I was **running** now, sword in each hand, still unable to register the **destruction** around me. Everywhere I looked was a crumbling house. A burning wall. **A pile of debris.** A zombie to my left—I cut it down **without stopping,** just a little spin while running. A familiar hiss to my right, I dashed to the left. The monster exploded **without effect:** I was one block out of range.

As I **ran and ran,** the distant sounds of battle **never** ceased.

Sounds like it's coming from the square, I thought. *I want to help out, of course, but my parents . . . All right. First things first.*

I reached what was left of **Shadow Lane,** encountering **no one.** As I continued on my path, the flames were dancing left and right, and I couldn't see a thing beyond them. **A grayish red haze.** And the faint outlines of buildings wavering in the heat.

Which way? **There,** *I think.*

Although I couldn't see very well, that **didn't matter.** I knew these streets. **Instinct guided me home.**

"Mom?"

"Dad?"

They weren't here.

Jello was gone, too, so I figured they'd taken him and **evacuated** like everyone else.

But where? It was **impossible** to think—I was **just standing** in my burning house, mind **completely frozen.** I turned back to the front door to find there no longer was a front door, only flames.

As I rushed outside, **a zombie** emerged from the smoke to my left, and from the right came **a skeleton in full iron.** Without any effort or thought, I turned each into **piles of experience** that I didn't even bother to collect, leaving them to swirl behind with **the faint ring** of glass. . . .

More emerged from the clouds ahead, vague forms **with outstretched arms.** Whether they were zombies, husks, ghouls, or something worse, I **didn't notice** and **didn't care.** I didn't even look at them; I only saw them **falling** from the corner of my eye, like **puppets** with cut strings. It was as easy as harvesting seeds. But this changed as more emerged . . . **again and again.** Maybe they had been following me and were only now **catching up.** Or maybe they were drawn to the sound of **harvested experience,** which by this point was like continuously shattering glass.

Hopelessly **outnumbered,** my emotions took hold, and I flew into what I can only call **a noob rage**—swinging **wildly, recklessly,** and yeah, I know I'm being a little **melodramatic** right now. **I don't care.**

> Dude, my village was under attack, and <u>my house</u> was on fire.

Then **something happened** that I still **can't explain.** The **diamond sword** in my right hand **swung much harder** than it should have. As though the weapon was **propelled by some external force.** That's the only way I can describe it. At the same time, the blade left behind **a violet trail.** The damage was **crazy. Twenty-five. Triple** the average damage.

A husk's gray form crumpled like **a deflating balloon.**

I took in all of this within **a fraction of a second,** never ceasing to **swing** as the horde trudged **mercilessly** onward. Yet, I was losing ground. There were just **too many.** My back now pressed against a wall, I fought with everything I had . . . hoping **the mysterious** power would return.

Eventually, **it did.**

This time, there was **a sound like wool tearing** as the **obsidian blade** in my offhand swung with the weight of an anvil. Both a zombie and a ghoul fell to either side, like **practice dummies** to me.

As time went on, **these strikes** occurred **more frequently,** until at last I was **pushing them all back.** Whether from **confidence** or the same **mysterious force,** my movements became **faster,** more **graceful,** blades whirling before me. There were times when I delivered **two attacks** on either side **simultaneously.**

In this moment, **I was no longer a swordsman,** but the conductor of some **beautiful** song, controlling the battle's tempo with my swords instead of a baton. With each crescendo came an **arc of brilliant light** that scattered their front line, knocking them all away if not outright **destroying** them; with each **lull** came parries and sidesteps, stringing them all along, **drawing** them all in, and **lining** them all up for yet another **sweeping attack.**

<u>Idiots.</u>
That was too obvious.
Hmm . . . what are they doing over there?

At last, I found that I **no longer** had to drive them away. They began accomplishing this themselves. **They were retreating.**

At first, slight **backward movements** rippled through their ranks. Small waves of **doubt.** With each newly fallen, this turned into more of a blind panic, a . . . **stampede.** The word "stampede" almost seems like the wrong choice, because it brings to mind a herd of animals instead of hideous abominations. But that's what it looked like.

It was unbelievable, but **the horde** of scary undead beings **vanished** into the layers of drifting fog as quickly as it had arrived. The last to leave was **ghostlike.** This spectral entity looked like **tattered black wool,** and it lingered for a moment, **studying me**—its eyes like red coals in a pool of shadow—before **slithering off** through the air.

Just seeing that thing made me **shiver. An actual ghost.** Somehow I could sense that it was **very old and powerful.** I forgot about it when I looked down at **my blades.** Then I **burst into laughter** and **jumped,** practically dancing with joy like a noob probably does upon defeating **his first enderslime.**

What was that?!
What the Nether just happened?!
Whatever, I'll take it!
And when can I do it again?!
Oh, what am I doing wasting time like this?
I have to find Mom and Dad. . . .

A thundering of hooves drove me from my thoughts only moments later. It was Sir Elric, followed by Breeze.

Breeze jumped from her horse and **stormed over** to me, looking **angrier** than Emerald had been that time Stump ate a slice of her cake project in Crafting I.

And she said the same thing Emerald had: "**What** were you **thinking?!**"

"At least you didn't have to **save me**, right?"

"**Your parents are safe**," Elric said. "Come. The square is on the brink of being **overrun**." He glanced down at all of the **crude weapons** and other **random items** lying around. Stuff the undead had dropped. "Might I ask . . . what happened here?"

"**Um . . .**" I wanted to tell them, but how could I explain? "I guess they didn't like **the joke** I told them."

Elric raised an eyebrow. "As you say."

Breeze sighed at me. "**Where's your horse?**"

MONDAY—UPDATE VIII

When we arrived at **the square,** it looked like this.

On one side stood **a valiant line** of **noble heroes.** Knights. Legionnaires. Villagers.

On the other side stood **the enemy.** I couldn't make them out clearly in the fog, but they must have **outnumbered us** at least five to one.

The ones I'd fought were just **a small fraction** of what was found here.

The school was still standing, somehow. What **a miracle** that was, because everything else was . . . **gone.** That beautiful marble fountain?

Gone. The mushroom stand? **All gone.** *(Well that one actually didn't bother me too much.)* And the ice cream stand? Well, I couldn't see it from here as it was about **three hundred blocks to the west**, near the tree garden, but it was probably **gone too.** Oh, and my favorite food stand? The one I wrote about when I first introduced my school? The Lost Legion had turned that thing into **some kind of bunker.** There, people **were crafting** and, above all, brewing. At a time like this, **healing potions** were more **precious** than diamonds. You could trade a whole stack of endercarrots for one. Promise. If endercarrots actually existed, I mean. But **they don't.** Nope. Sorry to crush your dreams like that. And sorry, **this is a huge paragraph,** isn't it? What if I wrote **this whole diary** like this? **Just one big paragraph!** How far could you read without **going crazy,** or at least maybe getting angry? Like, dude, why hasn't Runt **ended the paragraph** yet? Will he? Will it **ever** end? Also why is Runt **the coolest** villager that ever existed? Okay, **I'll stop.** And now that you've read this far, you probably feel as angry as I felt when I realized that . . . **there would never be any more ice cream ever again.**

As I jumped off Breeze's horse, I quickly **wiped away a tear.** Which only made things **worse,** because it reminded me of **ghast-tear swirl.** Oh, the suffering these monsters have caused! **It's just too much . . . !**

"**Runt!**" Stump ran up to me. "Dude! I tried following you, but my horse **panicked!**"

"You shouldn't have taken off like that!" Emerald said. "Do you have any idea what kind of **crazy mobs** are out there right now?!"

I shrugged. "Are you guys not worried about your parents, or . . . ?"

"**They're safe.**" That was Kolb, now approaching. "Well, as safe as it gets, anyway, considering our current situation. Ophelia's friends took everyone **down into the mine tunnels.** We have a new keep there."

Sure enough, besides Ophelia, no one from **Team All-Girls** was present.

I did spot most of **my former classmates,** though. Helmets falling over their eyes, most in **mismatched armor** no doubt hastily thrown on. Many of them **nodded** at me; half as many came up and said something. I don't remember who said what. There were **too many voices** and **questions** flying at me all at once. I **do,** however, remember most of the things that were said. So keep in mind, each of the following lines came from one of my former classmates:

"**Runt?!** Thank Entity **you're here!** Now something crazy is going to happen! **I just know it!**"

"Did you really find **an aeon forge?** Is it . . . going to **save us . . . ?**"

". . . Am I **safe** now?"

"**Dude,** Runt! The mayor was **nearly assassinated!** He's in the mines now, **with our parents.**"

"**Drill?** He's with **Kaeleb,** that **ocelot,** and a few others. They took off after some pigmen **in dark red robes.**"

"We managed to push them back. **For now.**"

". . . D-do you think we'll **m-make it?**"

"Runt, I don't really know what to say at a time like this, so I'll just say . . . **it's been real.**"

"**Nice sword,** Runt. Is that obsidian?"

"Runt! Is that **you?** What's up with that armor? It's all rusty. And that hat. Is that . . . **mold?!**"

"So how was **your quest,** anyway?!"

"Heard you ran into **Pebble.** How is he? Wish he was here. We could **really** use him."

"Stump said you saw **an elf.** Is it true? I hope to see one someday. I heard **moon elves** are found in silverwood biomes. And **dusk elves** are found along the coast."

"Hey man, you've missed some stuff around here. Someone's been planting a new type of tree in the tree garden. **Mossy oak.** I think those trees are normally found in rainforest biomes. I wonder who's been planting them?

"Hello, Runt. Question: Did you happen to encounter any **redstone steam golems** during your travels? I only ask because I heard they have those in **the capital.** Oh. You didn't go to the capital? **Sorry.** My mistake."

"Hey, Runt. Sorry to bother you again, but I just can't stop thinking about **that obsidian sword.** What kind of enchantments does that thing have? Can I see **the stats?**"

"**Runt!** It's been forever! So Stump said you found **a dungeon** that had more than one room? He was joking, right?"

"Um, why is everyone asking him so many questions right now? **I mean, hello?** We're facing imminent destruction, people! **Ready your shields!**"

That's about **all I can remember.**

If you feel **overwhelmed** by that wall of text, imagine how I felt.

(Oh, and that last line was Emerald. But you probably guessed that already.)

"**Enough!**" Kolb said. "Give him some space. He's been through a lot." He **rescued** me from the crowd and gave me a pat on the shoulder. "**Glad to see you,** kid. And hey, good work out there. Heard you managed to obtain **an aeon forge.**" With a smile, he added, "Wish we could have met under different circumstances. We have so much to . . . **discuss.**"

I glanced around, looking for Breeze. She was some ways away, speaking with **Elric** in private. Judging by their expressions, they were discussing **something serious.** No idea what.

I turned back to Kolb. "And what **is** the current situation?"

"Guess they realized it was **the perfect time** to attack, with so many of you gone. **The Nethermancers** burned away part of the wall with **their spells.** We took most of them out, though. Kaeleb **ambushed** several, chased after the rest who fled. Right now, there's **only one** left we really need to worry about. See that one over there? **That's the leader.**"

Across the square, I saw **a figure** that stood several cubes taller than all the rest, encased in black plate adorned with **glowing red runes** and brandishing **a black sword** over two blocks in length. That armor was almost too much, though. Maybe too try-hard? Almost like he wanted the whole world to know that he's the **ultimate bad guy.** Actually, there's a villain in *Urg the Barbarian* who looks like him.

"He's an **Underlord?**" I asked.

"**He is.** Underneath all that plate is **an irontusk** highly trained in **the dark arts.** Most of the undead are **under his control.** He's **our main** target. Once he falls, this battle is **over.** But reaching him **will be difficult.** We'll have to clear a path through his minions. And no, **arrows are useless.**

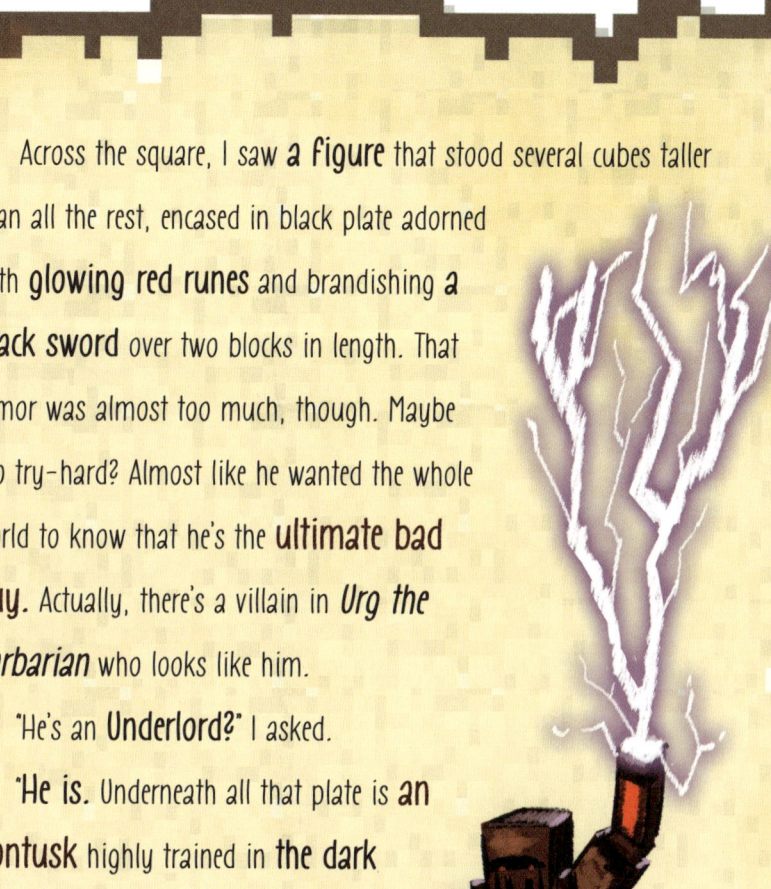

His armor appears to be heavily enchanted against them—they just **bounce off.**"

"What's an **irontusk?**" Stump asked. "Are they like . . . pigmen?"

Zigurd **scowled.** "They're like pigmen, all right, only **twice as strong** and about a **hundred times harder to kill.** Hate those things."

"It seems we've really angered **the Eyeless One,**" Brio said. "As all of his previous attempts **failed,** he has employed some of **his most elite units** to ensure Villagetown's destruction."

Elric returned with Breeze at this point. The knight nodded. "Yet it is no great matter. This village is **still standing** . . . for we are still here." He turned to Kolb. "These are **truly dark times,** but know **the Knights of Aetheria** are honored to stand by your side. It could be said that we are in **great debt** to the Lost Legion. I do not know how many villages in the West were saved thanks to your order, but this number is most certainly great."

Kolb shook the knight's hand. "It is **our honor** as well." He turned to me. "**Hmm,** Runt. Those swords of yours are **almost broken.** You should repair up. There's **an anvil in the bunker.** And grab a few

H-Ills while you're there. Don't forget **milk,** too. There's **a shade** in that army, **high-level, spirit subtype.** Those things can inflict a wide variety of **nasty** debuffs."

H-Ills?

What's he—oh. Healing Ills. Got it.

How'd he notice my swords are almost out of durability, anyway? He never misses anything. . . .

I tried by best to speak **heroically** like the knights around me: "It is **my honor** to assist in the coming battle." I bowed. "Sir."

It was one of those situations where you could either **joke** or **cry,** and I didn't want to be reminded of my favorite ice cream flavor anymore. Before I left to repair, I saw that Kolb wasn't wielding a broken sword. Across his back was **a diamond greatsword**—in **perfect** condition. Emerald claimed **the other one is useless** in its current state. He must have stashed it.

MONDAY—UPDATE IX

Upon seeing this place, I felt kind of sad. The food here used to be SO good.

I pounded away on an anvil in what used to be **a food stand.**

Both of my swords had almost **no durability** left. That's how much I'd fought earlier.

My head was a mess. It had all happened **so fast.** I focused on my items, trying to **take my mind off** everything.

*Hmm. Definitely need to get stronger **Unbreaking enchantments.** Some better armor, too. Something that doesn't slow me down so much.*

*I'm **really glad** Breeze taught me **Dual Wield.** When facing swarms of low-level monsters, dual wielding is far better than using a shield: You need **all the damage you can get.***

*But what was that back there? **The light?** The extra damage? It was almost as if I'd used **some kind of ability.** But the only abilities I have are **Dual Wield** and **Analyze Monster,** right? So how was that possible? It doesn't really matter, I guess. The real question now is . . . how are we going to **pull through?***

I glanced at the other people inside the bunker. Two villagers and three Legionnaires stood on the other side, preparing potions or equipment. They were talking about the first battle. The one I'd heard, earlier. It had been **pretty intense,** according to them. **Many wounded.** They couldn't brew enough potions.

*Wish I'd been there for that. But I had to try finding Mom and Dad. **I hope they're okay.*** I kept hammering on my swords. *They must be scared, down in the mines. They'll be fine, though. **Ophelia's team** is protecting them. . . .*

As **the sparks jumped up** with each blow, Breeze stepped in.

Behind her was **the red-robed wizard girl, Rubinia,** who was, according to Stump, **an Enchanter.** *Or is it **Enchantress?***

The Enchantress opened a nearby **item chest,** retrieved an unusual-looking sword, and handed it to Breeze. "I managed to place **every enchantment** you asked for."

> A sapphire katana?! Seriously, where's mine???

SAPPHIRE KATANA
ENCHANTED

UNDERTOW
ATTACK SPEED 1.35
AVERAGE DAMAGE 11

THIS ITEM CONTAINS THE FOLLOWING ENCHANTMENTS:
HASTE II - WOUNDING II - UNBREAKING III

"It took me **forever** to get the **stats** right," Rubinia said. "I hope you like it. Oh, and here's **a new scabbard,** too."

"Thank you . . . **Rubinia.**" Tears almost welling in her eyes, Breeze fastened the scabbard to her belt and sheathed **her new sword.** She drew it again with **impressive** speed. The blade **sang** as she performed a basic thrust then **parried** an imaginary attack. "**Perfect.**" Upon sheathing this weapon once more, she **gave Rubinia a hug.** "You be careful out there, **okay?**"

Rubinia nodded. "I'm the one who should be saying that. **Take care,** Breeze."

After the Enchantress left, Breeze gave me **a worried look.** "How are you feeling?"

"**Bad,** of course. But we should have expected this, **right?** With us gone, it was **the perfect time** to attack."

"It was, but **we'll be okay.** I know we will. All we have to do is fight, **as we've always fought.**" She drew her new blade. "**Rubinia** found it in **the ruins of Shadowbrook.** We became **friends** when she arrived, and she ended up **giving this to me.** One of the many things you missed while you were away. **All of my armor is from Shadowbrook,** too." She meant the stuff she grabbed from **that shop** earlier, which she was now wearing. "I **wasn't** going to take anything," she said, "but when I saw **all this stuff from my village,** I felt I had to."

I **inspected** her outfit. It had an almost somber appearance, but it reminded me of the ocean. Her gloves, boots, and long tunic were crafted of dyed **shadowmoss** that had been woven and **enchanted,** pretty much like wool. The rest—bracers, armlets, tiara, belt—were of many different materials. **Coral. Seashell. Seastone.** Various types of **opals.** Prismarine. **Dark prismarine.**

Since the people of Shadowbrook lived **by the sea,** their houses and many of the items they used were crafted from such materials. Shadowmoss is usually found in **sea caves.** And opals are commonly found by mining near the coasts. There are **seven different** types of opal, some more common than others. They're like diamonds or emeralds, pretty much, and they're used in a lot of **advanced crafting** recipes. Not like I knew all of that, though. Breeze told me.

She offered **her new sword** to me. "You want it? I almost feel **guilty** with all this new gear. Emerald **also** gave me her **new bow**."

"No, it totally suits you," I said. "**And . . .**" I recalled how my swords had functioned earlier. Even though they weren't anything **special,** they were clearly working. I shook my head. "**Keep it.** I'll be fine with these." I glanced at the item chest. "Let's get some **supplies,** huh?"

I searched through the item chest, which was stocked with **Healing III potions** and **bottled milk.** That's normal milk, contained in a bottle instead of a bucket. It's said that most cows descended from a line of **enchanted cows** that once lived ages ago. Even today's cows have milk capable of **purging our system** of most minor magical effects, good or bad. I didn't have any milk on me, but even if I did, I would've taken some milk bottles anyway. Think about it. I'm supposedly **the descendant** of a villager hero who lived long ago, right? Well, what kind of **hero** drinks from **a bucket?!**

After we stashed several bottles each, **Brio** stepped in. "**Where'd you find that?**" he asked, meaning her armor.

"Some shop."

"I did say **no looting.** But never mind. I'm glad you did." He stepped closer. "**It looks good on you.** It's been so long since I've seen . . ." For the first time ever, he looked **despondent.** He couldn't speak. The armor she wore, of a type commonly seen on **Shadowbrook's female scouts,** was clearly bringing back a lot of **memories.** But her father soon regained his composure—**even smirked.** "Of course, I don't suppose you're going to let your . . . **friend** head off to battle without **something to match.**"

"What do you mean?" she asked.

"Runt has obtained **an aeon forge,** has he not? So let us forge. I still have Shadowbrook's old recipes on hand."

Brio held up **a massive tome.** It was larger than any book I'd ever seen in my life. He set it down on a nearby crafting table, and standing on either side of him, we watched him flip through **countless pages.** Each page contained **an advanced crafting recipe,** and roughly half of the recipes contained ingredients I'd never seen before—some I'd never even **heard** of. It reminded me of the times the Legionnaires talked about how many recipes there are. Over **ten thousand,** according to some.

"What would be **best** for him," Brio asked, "given the ingredients at hand?"

She thought for a moment. "**Hmm.** What about **redsteel?**"

"We don't have much time. It would take **hours** to smelt enough."

"**Oreweave?** No, we need raw ore for that. . . ." Breeze kept thinking. "Wait. How about **gemwrought mail?**"

"Not a bad idea," Brio said. "We certainly have enough opals." He turned to me. "We took **many different types** with us. Yet we haven't been able to use them until now. Every recipe that requires them is of an **advanced** pattern." He held out his hand. "**Forge,** please."

I retrieved the aeon forge from my inventory and handed it to him. I had no idea what gemwrought mail was, but it **sounded cool** and involved an advanced crafting table. I was **totally** on board. He placed the forge on the ground, next to the standard crafting table.

Then he retrieved a set of leather armor from that chest nearby. "What color would you prefer?" he asked.

My time had indeed come: "**Black.**"

He smiled. "Shadowbrook's **main color.** There's a reason why both **my daughter and myself** wear black. You would have fit right in."

He grabbed some black ink from the chest, threw each piece of leather onto the standard crafting table, and dyed the entire set black. He then meticulously placed the tunic on the forge, in the central square, before laying out **several different varieties of opal** in every square surrounding the tunic, all at different—yet specific—angles.

There was a **brilliant green flash,** just like when Max had tried crafting that staff back in the inn. And as before, columns of **pale blue light** sprang forth from each item. This time, however, there was an **iridescent** glow, and the gemstones suddenly **merged** into the armor. What remained **took my breath away.** It looked like a black leather tunic, all right—only, it was **embedded** with diamond-like shards. A suit of diamond or emerald plate is way too flashy for my tastes, but **this . . .**

Breeze's father picked the tunic up carefully, inspecting the result. "Not **my best** work," he said, "but far better than what you're currently wearing. Although it offers a level of protection somewhere between leather and diamond, it is **superior** to diamond overall. **Some abilities** can only be performed in lighter armors such as this, and furthermore, your **mobility** won't be affected, nor will stealth. It's also quite **receptive** to enchantments."

He then crafted the remaining pieces. I **threw everything on,** leaving my old armor in that chest. And for a moment there, clad in a suit of armor that the people of Shadowbrook had proudly wore, I almost felt like **a member of that village.**

Say hello to the **new** Runt!

Brio smiled again. "Now you look like **the hero** you're **destined** to become." His smile faded. "My daughter . . . told me about **the undead** earlier." He stepped closer. "What happened, **exactly?**"

"Don't know," I said with a shrug. "I just . . . **fought way** better **than normal.**"

Breeze stepped closer, too. "Almost like you were using **abilities**, right? The same thing happened to me. Remember **the move** I used to **finish Urf?** Well, when we were **defending** Shadowbrook, I **accidentally** used that for the first time. It just kind of . . . **happened.**"

"Although our libraries indeed had **several tomes** capable of **transferring abilities** to the reader," Brio said, "she'd never read any of them. It seems she was **born with several abilities,** and I suspect the same can be said for you."

"**Huh.** I suppose there's no way I can easily find out what I have?"

"There isn't," Brio said. "Not until you **unlock** your **visual enchantment.** It took Breeze weeks to really understand what abilities she possessed. I—"

The door nearly **flew off its hinges** as Stump barged in, followed by Max and Cog. All of them were carrying **bundles** of crafting ingredients the Legionnaires had given them. Most of this stuff I didn't recognize.

Stump was all **puppy dog eyes.** "Kolb said you might **loan us the forge.** Just for a bit."

Brio **seemed amused.** "Did he now?"

"**He did.** He said the battle's **at a standstill,** and he said it might **make sense** for us to use this time **productively** by crafting some armor. He also said **you would be willing to help us.** Sir."

"It seems like he said **a lot** of things."

Before long, Breeze's father was once more over the forge, crafting away like some **legendary smith:** pounding **endersteel,** sawing aetherwood, shearing moonsilk. He could craft an item with **incredible speed.** He worked each object with such familiarity, without hesitation— as though he'd been crafting for **thousands of years.** When he struck a bar of endersteel with the forge's diamond hammer, the sparks that flew **shimmered** with ghostly hues, as if the sparks themselves were enchanted . . . and I imagined **Entity** must have looked like that, eons ago, when he began crafting **weapons of indescribable power.** . . .

Well actually, it was more like ten minutes. I was just **so** captivated watching him use that forge. I kept thinking about all the weapons I'd seen in that book of his.

"I c-can't **believe** I'm actually wearing **endersteel**," Stump said.

Cog looked at everyone's **rather somber** attire. "Shadowbrook must have been pretty **depressing** if everyone was rolling around in gear like this!"

Brio gave him **an icy look.** "Our village wore black as a way to show our **mourning.** We have battled against **the Eyeless One** for hundreds of years. **Destruction** and **sorrow** were all we knew."

"Didn't know he'd been around for **that long,**" I said.

"He hasn't. **His servants,** however, have. And they are the ones we have faced **through the generations.**" He paused. "**Oh,** I have something else for you. **One more remnant** of our past."

BATWING CLOAK
ACCESSORY—CAPE
ENCHANTED

THIS ITEM CONTAINS THE
FOLLOWING ENCHANTMENTS:
SWIFTNESS I
PROTECTION I
STEALTH I
REGENERATION II
FIRE PROTECTION V

"It's not the most **flattering** thing out there," he said, "but the stats are **much better** than the one you have on. You'll need some **fire resistance** for this battle."

"Some **seriously** depressing people," Cog muttered.

The cloak, designed to look like **a large gray bat wing,** did seem rather **gloomy** when paired with my armor, but I wasn't about to complain. <u>**Those stats!**</u>

Brio then held up **a dark red scarf.** "I almost forgot. **Kolb** wanted me to give you this."

Since I was being **showered** in items, my friends started getting **jealous** and began **pestering** Brio.

". . . G-got **any more** of those cloaks?!"

"Yeah! Where's ours?! **Hurrrg!** So unfair!"

"Hmmmm. I sure could use a **better** cloak myself."

"If you're going to craft anything, I'd like to assist."

I'll leave **you** to decide who said what. **A little game.** You should be able to tell **based on voice.**

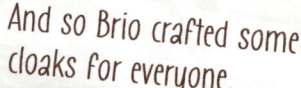

And so Brio crafted some cloaks for everyone. . . .

WINGS OF NIGHT
STEALTH III

MIDNIGHT CLOAK
SPELLFORCE I

CLOAK OF RIME
COLD PROTECTION V

CLOAK OF SECRETS
POCKET III

Stump **whirled** around. "**Dude!** I feel like **a Knight of Aetheria!**"

"Thanks for the forge," Cog said to me. "Here, **buddy.** Have some mushrooms." He stepped **super close** and handed me all sorts of **strange-looking** mushrooms. Some were black with glowing purple spots. Others were white with light red spots, bright orange with black spots, light gray with no spots, or light blue with rainbow spots. Then he handed me some . . . **plants?** They had blue stalks with transparent white bulbs on the end. "Found them in **Glimfrost**," he whispered, **warily glancing** over his shoulder at Brio.

"And just what am I **supposed to do** with all this stuff?" I whispered back.

"**No idea.** But I need to free up some inventory space to stash my old armor."

·Hurgg.·

I put away the mushrooms and plants, and I picked up **the aeon forge.** "Hey, I—"

The door creaked open. **Always!** Every time it's the doors creaking or swinging open, cutting someone off! One of the younger knights, **Drest**, hurriedly stepped in and **bumped into** Breeze. "Oh, I'm sorry, Lady . . . **Breeze**, is it?" There was something **odd** about how he addressed her as **Lady** and **paused** before saying her name. He continued: "The enemy is displaying **unusual movement.** Sir Elric believes they will **soon** attack once more. He wants us to prepare for **the final wave.** And remember, **their leader** must be taken down at all costs."

I could already hear Kolb shouting from somewhere outside, delivering **a speech** to his **clan:**

"**Brothers and sisters,** although we've succumbed to infighting in the past, today we must put our beliefs aside. Today, I ask you to forget who you were and embrace **who you have become.** Regardless of what you believe, you are here, in a reality that cannot be fathomed, whose existence **must be faced.** Isn't that what you **secretly wished for?** There's no doubt in my mind that each of you here has **dreamed of this** in your past life. I know I did. Every time I logged in, I imagined what it would be like to live in **a world of fantasy.** To experience **real** adventure, where every action has meaning and **importance,** where others are truly counting on you. A world that truly does **need to be saved.** And now, that world lies before you. **Darkness** has spread across the land. Countless villages have fallen. The East **lies in ruins** and the West is soon to follow. From what we know, at least fifteen other clans have already **abandoned the idea** of defending this continent. Will you follow them, sailing north as they have? **Or will you follow me today, to victory?**"

At once, every member of his clan drew together and **shouted in unison:**

"We are the Lost Legion! We will **never** retreat!!!"

TUESDAY

Let 'Em Know
Ballad of Villagetown

Written by Emerald

A biome of
desolation . . .

And it feels
like a dream

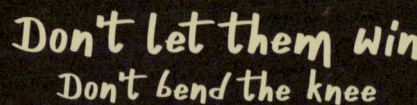

We're OP
and they're going to pay

Let the war wage on

I'd take it over harvesting any day.

It's time for us to **test our skills**

And reach the record for most kills

Let 'em know
Let 'em know

Our damage is quite high

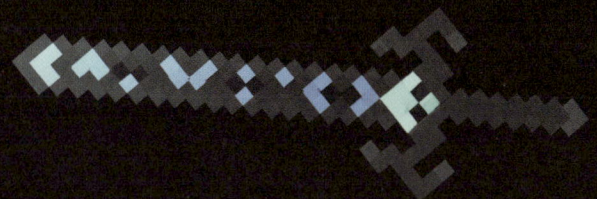

EXCALIBUR BLADE
LEGENDARY GREATSWORD
(NON-UNIQUE)

AVERAGE DAMAGE 25

STORM V
(15% CHANCE OF EXTRA LIGHTNING DAMAGE)

STONE II
(2% CHANCE OF TURNING TARGET INTO STONE)

EMPOWER III
(BOOSTS ALL MELEE ABILITIES BY 30%)

SUNDER VII
(IGNORES 70% OF TARGET'S ARMOR)

WOUNDING X
(INCREASES CRITICAL STRIKE DAMAGE BY 100%)

Here we chug
Our hearts won't stray
Let the war wage on . . .

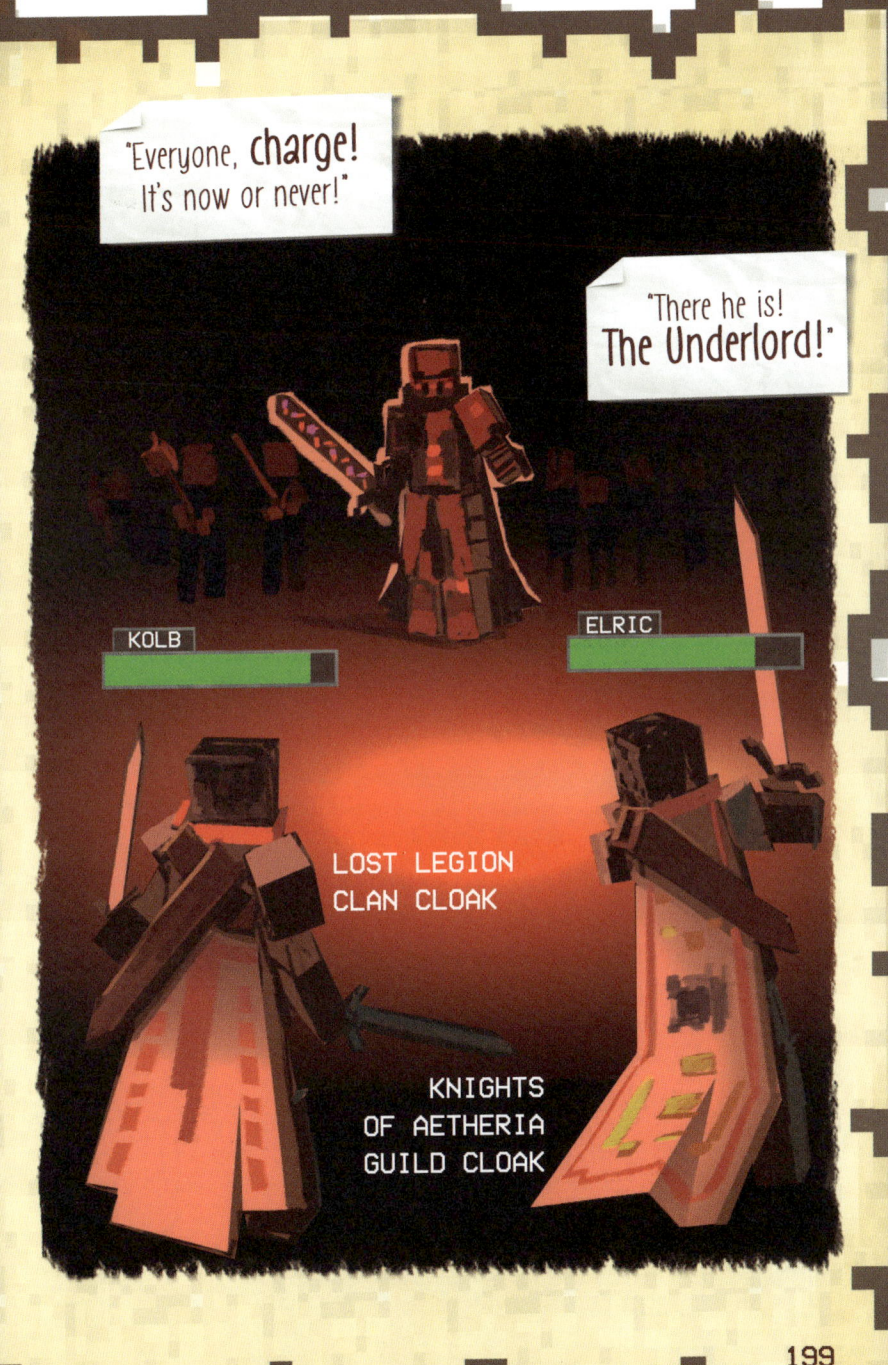

Runt's swords are leaving
Little cube-like wisp
Trails all around

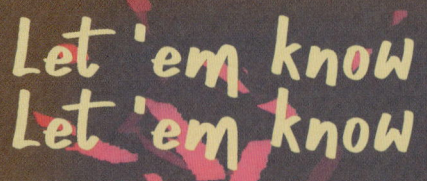

TUESDAY—UPDATE I

As we closed in to **finish off** their leader, he dashed for cover behind his minions and then **ran away.**

Breeze drew **her bow** and chased after him. Elric grabbed her by the elbow, telling her it was **too dangerous,** but she broke free.

"**Go,**" Kolb said to me. After dispatching some more undead, he tossed a **Swiftness III** potion at me. "We'll hold the line."

I ran while chugging and caught up to her by the time **the speed boost** started to fade.

In the light of early morning, we chased **the Underlord** all the way to one of Villagetown's vast meadows, near the tree garden where Breeze and I **first met.**

There wasn't much smoke here, only gray walls far away, like **impending storm clouds.** Across the meadow—at least one hundred blocks away—the Underlord had almost reached the trees.

As Breeze pulled back **an arrow,** I told myself it was **pointless.** The Underlord's armor made him all but immune to arrows. But the arrow she pulled back was **obsidian,** likely picked up from the battlefield earlier. There had been **lots** of skeletal archers lurking out there, their arrows **enchanted with various debuffs.** And this arrow contained **Wither II** along with **Catscratch V.**

Catscratch is nasty. With a successful **critical hit,** it increases the effect of any debuffs the target has—by one point per power level. The Underlord's armor only protected against **physical damage,** not against any debuffs an arrow might bring. It **didn't matter** if that arrow only did one point. As long as she landed a critical hit, the payload would strike—**Wither II** would become **Wither VII.**

Still, it looked like an **impossible** shot. I could barely see him now, just a black speck growing smaller every second.

Breeze took **a deep breath.** Time seemed to freeze completely as I watched her aim. And as it froze, I noted **the scent** of fresh air, the grass sparkling with cubelets of dew, the mud puddles on the surfaces of dirt blocks, shining from last night's rain . . . all of this was at odds with **the devastation** beyond.

"You've got this," I said.

She shrugged. "Maybe."

Just kidding. She didn't shrug, and neither of us said anything.

What kind of **noobs** do you take us for? That would have **thrown off her aim.**

Ziff!

The arrow sped through the sky, **arcing gracefully.** The most beautiful shot I'd ever seen. It vanished into **the shadows of the grove** where the Underlord had just fled.

We ran to the trees, through the flowers and tall grass. The garden had changed since I'd last seen it. Someone really had planted **mossy oak trees.** In places, you couldn't see any bark, only moss.

In the grass, illuminated by rays of sunlight, was **the Underlord's sword,** armor, and an **enormous** pile of experience. As we approached, the armor and sword crumbled into black dust with **a hiss.** The crystal orbs slid across the grass, toward **their rightful owner.** I wondered just **how much experience** she'd gained.

"I guess you **got him,**" I said. "**Nice work.**"

"Yeah. **It was a . . .**" She **shivered.** "Good shot, **huh?** Mostly **luck,** though."

"**Hey? What's wrong?**"

She'd **shivered** like that before. That's when I understood, and time suddenly stopped again. I realized **where she'd found** the arrow. She **hadn't** picked it up off the ground earlier.

She'd pulled it from her own shoulder.

TUESDAY—UPDATE II

Breeze was affected by **Wither II**.

That shouldn't have been **a problem.** We both had a way **to remove this debuff.**

We'd taken a **few bottles of milk** from that chest. All she had to do was chug, and all status effects **would disappear.** But the bottle she now held did not contain milk. She popped the cork on an **H-III** instead. Her health bar **jumped up.**

I didn't understand.

Although the healing potion countered **the damage dealt** by Wither, it didn't **remove the effect** itself. Why didn't she just drink some **milk?**

She **shivered** again.

My thoughts **swirled around** as she drank another. An **H-II**, this time.

"Breeze, **um** . . . maybe it would be best if you tried one of those . . . **other** potions. You know, **the white ones.**"

"**No.** Listen, I've never told you this before, but I . . . um . . . I get **really sick** when I drink milk."

". . . Never heard of **something like that.**" I glanced at her health bar. "**How sick,** exactly?"

". . ."

No reply.

I watched her drink potions of **Healing I, II, and III** for the longest time.

Then she **ran out.** The Wither still remained, endlessly grinding away at her **life force.**

"It has **an extended duration,**" she said. "It has to wear off, though. Another minute at **most** . . ."

With a **sigh**, I handed her **my own healing potions**, which she drank one after another. This, of course, only delayed **the inevitable**.

*What is this **nonsense?***

"Can you just **drink some milk?**"

"I'll be fine," she said. "It'll **wear off**. I'm sure of it."

Finally, every last bit of food we had went toward keeping her health up. **Stormberry rolls. Enderscones.** Then we were down to the basics: bread and a single potato. Actually, I'm not sure how that got into my inventory.

"No muffins?" she asked.

"We're out. **Of everything.**" I paused. "**Hey.** Are you telling me a bottle of milk will make you **more sick** than consuming **all that?**"

". . ."

I held up a milk bottle. "Drink."

"I can't."

"Breeze. **Seriously.** What are you doing?"

She turned away. "**Runt?** Can you do me a favor?"

"What?"

"I need you **to go.**"

"W-what are you talking about?!"

"Can you just give me **some time alone?**"

*Time alone? **What in the Overworld?** She has maybe a minute before . . . !*

"Breeze, this is **insane!** What are you doing?!" I shoved the milk bottle in her direction. "**Just drink,** already! **Drink!**"

"Listen to me. I just . . . need to be alone. **I'll be okay.**"

". . ."

"I'll **force you to drink** if I have to."

She whirled around, **anger flashing across her face.** "You're really **stubborn,** you know that?!"

"When it concerns **the health of my friends,** yes, I am rather stubborn."

Crossing her arms, she turned around again. **"Hmmph!"**

"Well?"

"Can you just go?"

"And leave you here **by yourself** with almost no health. What if something shows up?"

"Fine."

She raised **a gloved hand.**

Suddenly, she was surrounded by **a cloud of smoke.**

I didn't bother waiting for it **to fade.** I knew she'd activated **that ability** of hers and was **running off.** So I ran through the cloud, further into the garden.

Unfortunately, I had no way of knowing which direction she'd gone. That ability turned her **invisible** for a short period of time. **Five seconds,** I think she said. And she barely made **any noise,** even while running. There were three paths through the trees, so I picked one **at random,** depending on **blind luck** to guide me. Maybe I'd be able to spot her once her invisibility wore off.

My mind churned **even faster** than my legs.

Why did she react *so strangely?* Why didn't she want to remove her status effects? She must be *hiding* something. **But what?**

As I sprinted through a section of tall grass, I—

"Oof . . !!"

"Gahhh . . . !!"

—ran **straight into her.**

Both of us went flying in opposite directions and landed on our backs.

A potion was on the ground in front of me, glass sparkling in the sunlight. She'd been holding that. I'd **knocked it out of her hands.** I didn't pay much attention to it, though—I was focused on **her health bar** and felt so relieved when I saw she was no longer affected by Wither. She must have **downed some milk** after she took off. She was still extremely injured, **though.** . . .

She shot up from the ground immediately and **darted** into the shadow of a tree, where she remained.

"**Breeze?** Um, are you okay?"

"I'm fine. **Obviously.** Can you go? **Please . . ."**

I stood up and stepped forward. "**Seriously.** What's going **on** with you? Why are you acting **so weird?!**"

"I need to be alone."

"Yeah, **okay.** Well, we need to get you healed first."

I remembered the potion she'd dropped, turned around, and **reached for it.** As I did, I recalled her stating she didn't have any more healing potions. And truly, **the potion** at my feet wasn't capable of healing **anything.** I picked it up.

Disguise II . . . ?!

. . . ?!

. . . ?!?!

(?!?!?!?!)

I'd only read about **this effect.** We were going to try making some **Disguise I** potions in class, but that was **scrapped.** Someone had taken all of **the required ingredients** from the school's supply chests. . . .

I **tried to remember** what little I knew.

At first power level, it could make you **appear** as a different person, though a person of the same race. At second power level, you could appear as **almost anyone**—from a dwarf to a mushroom man. That depended on the potion's variant, which was set, through use of **extra ingredients,** just before brewing.

And this potion was of <u>the villager variant.</u> . . .

What the **Nether** . . . **?!**

What's she doing with **this** . . . ?!

I whirled around. She was still there, in the shadows.

"You weren't supposed to **find out,**" she said. "Not until later." **She sighed.** "My father's going to be **furious.** . . ."

Peering into the gloom where she was **hidden,** I began to sense there was something **different** about her. Although I couldn't quite tell what. Her hair color was the same, the eyes, the armor . . .

She stepped **into the light.**

Even then, I didn't **notice immediately.**

<u>But once I did . . .</u>

In this instant, so many things **made sense.** Why she **never fit in,** why it had been so hard for her to **make new friends** at school. Why she knew **so much history.** How she recognized the sound of a **blockbird**. And suddenly, I knew who'd been planting **all the saplings**. Enveloped in sunlight, surrounded by **moss-covered trees** only found along the coast, **she looked <u>completely</u>** at home.

TUESDAY—UPDATE III

I couldn't **move**. I couldn't **speak**. I couldn't do anything but **stare**.

It's not like she **turned into a monster**. It was the **smallest** of changes, really. **Long ears**. A face that was **marginally** more slender. A slightly different **skin tone**.

That was it.
But it meant **so much.**

As I **gaped** in total shock, a part of me **feared** that things would never be the same. Another part felt **betrayed**. It's funny how even **the slightest difference** can mean **everything**. . . .

Since **Disguise** was **an illusion**, there had never been an icon to indicate the effect. All illusions are like this. The **zombie-ghost** didn't have an icon either. It'd be **too easy** to see through illusions, otherwise. An ability so basic as **Analyze Monster** would render them **useless**.

"**No more secrets**," I finally said. "No more games, no more lies. **What are you?**"

She lowered her head. "Our **true name,** in the Sylvan language, is **Iaoao E'aeai.** It translates to **children of the cove.** You'd know of us as **dusk elves.** That's what we call ourselves, now."

"**Dusk elves . . .** I thought **Shadowbrook** was a village?"

"**It was.** But as you've seen, **not every** village is inhabited by those like you."

"Why **hide** from us?"

"We didn't want to **endanger** Villagetown. **Alyss** was my name. **My old name.** I changed it thanks to **an enchanted name tag.**"

". . ."

". . ."

". . ."

I'd **suspected** something all along. **Not this,** but something. After all, I'd **never** heard of a villager who didn't know how to joke around. And I've never known one to be so **skilled** in **shooting bows** and **riding horses.**

"**I'll tell you everything,**" she said. "After the battle's **over.**"

I was struggling not to **lose it.** "You're going to return to battle with **health like that?**"

"Um . . . **no.** I guess not."

Looking through my inventory, I retrieved all that stuff Cog gave me. "**What about these?** Can we make stew or something with them?"

"**Hmm . . .** I'm not sure. Let me check. I have **my grandma's craftbook.**"

She held up an **ancient-looking** red book. *Grandma Eo's Craftbook.* It had various crafting recipes for food items, most using a **5x5 pattern.** There was only one recipe that used the ingredients on hand. "**Morel Medley.**" Ghost **morels**—the black mushrooms—were the **main ingredient.** A souped-up version of mushroom stew. **Great.** I gave away all my food earlier, and now I was **starving.**

RECIPE FOR
Morel Medley
FROM THE KITCHEN OF
Grandma Eo

8x ghost morel
4x fire fungus
4x rainbow cap
4x astral toadstool
4x umber stalk
1x bowl (acacia for better flavor)

Arrange all ingredients so that they're facing north, and in the center of each square.

PROVIDES

AND THE FOLLOWING BUFFS:

After I **placed the forge,** Breeze began crafting away, though **more slowly** than her father. And . . . I'm ashamed to admit this, but . . . **a wonderful aroma** filled the air.

She held up a bowl filled with **something that resembled stew.**

"Wanna try?"

"**Uhhhhh . . .**"

It's mushroom stew, I thought. *Don't let the aroma deceive you!*

She took **a sip.** "It's good. **Really.**"

Don't do it. Just don't. But my food bar was about to begin **dancing.** As hard as it is to believe, I took a sip. And it really **was amazing.**

One bowl restores your food bar **completely** and heals **five hearts.** It also provides the **Omnessence** buff, increasing experience gain, along with a buff called **Bounty of the Forest,** which increases strength by one, and finally a third buff, **Savory Hearth,** which makes one immune to the Chill effect. Oh, and all of this lasts for **three hours.**

"**Advanced crafting,** where have you been all my life?!" I said.

After giving me **another sip,** Breeze offered a third, but I declined.

"**Your health** still has a ways to go."

"It's fine. We have enough for **one more**." She smiled. "It's good, **right?** My grandma used to make this when I was little."

"**To be honest,** that stew's **so delicious** that even if I were **completely full,** I'd run laps around the tree garden just to reduce my food bar and eat **some more.**"

She made another, for me this time. And I **almost finished it.** But there was a **slight wind,** and **the shadows** behind her started moving, **changing.** Within them were **two glowing red eyes.**

It was **the shadowy being** from earlier. **Black claws** raked her shoulder, removing **a small fraction of her health.** Then she **fell** to one knee and remained like that, as if pulled to the ground **by intense gravity.** She was affected by **Stun.** With her **out of the fight,** the ghostly apparition turned **to me.**

You know
what <u>happened next.</u>

> They say a picture is worth a thousand words. . . .

Somehow, as I fought this thing, I wasn't stunned. Instead, I was affected by **Slowness II, Weakness, Nausea V, Blindness, Mining Fatigue, Silence, Bad Luck VIII,** and something called **Curse of Icehollow.** Each time the shadowy being struck me, the damage wasn't **all that high,** but it inflicted **one of these status effects.** Seemingly at random.

I don't know **how** I brought that thing down. **A miracle.** In the end, I was affected by nearly **every negative status effect known to villager** . . . and **then** some. I can't even begin to describe how bad I felt, affected by all of this stuff—it took **three bottles of milk** to remove everything. That **Curse of Icehollow** was the last to go.

Breeze was fine. Her **Stun** wore off by the time I reached her. Trying to ignore **those ridiculous ears,** I pulled her to her feet.

"**How'd** you break free?" she asked.

"What?"

"While you were fighting, **you were stunned as well.**"

"Um . . ."

"I saw **the icon.** Although briefly. It vanished in **a fraction** of a second."

"I don't remember."

"And **your slowness** wore off at the same time. I've heard of an ability that can **clear any immobilizing effects.** You must have used that."

"We really need to get to **the capital.**"

"**Definitely.** It's . . . tiring, not knowing anything about ourselves."

I turned to the edge of the garden. The faint **sounds of battle** were still audible. "C'mon. Let's help them **clean up.**"

"Hey! **Wait up!**" As we left, she drank one of those Disguise potions. There was **a puff** of deep red smoke.

When it cleared,
she was back to <u>her normal</u>
villager self.

TUESDAY—UPDATE IV

"Good work, you two."

TUESDAY—UPDATE V

"There they go! After them!"

CRUCIA

KAELEB

FAOLAN

RUBINIA

TUESDAY—UPDATE VI

"The southwest quarter is clear. The remaining undead have been destroyed."

TUESDAY—UPDATE VII

The undead fell **easily** without their master. **The Underlord** had several different aura abilities that **empowered** his minions. **Without him,** they collapsed like **sugarcane.**

According to Sir Elric, that specific Underlord was **sixth in command.** Just five steps below **good ole No Pupils himself.** One of his **dark apprentices.** So today could be called **a major victory. . . .**

As we cleared the last, it started **raining** again. It was enough to put the last of the fires out. With **our village secured,** I ran to the mines. Everyone was there. **Safe and sound.** Including **my parents.** They said a bunch of things I don't want to write in here. You know, the kind of things parents **typically** say to a son who just helped defend their home village from an attack. Oh, all right—I mean stuff like:

"Oh, look at **our little swordsman**—he's leveling up so fast!"

"Actually, I don't think I **have** leveled up," I told them. "We need to learn how to do that in—**oh, whatever.**" I gave them **a hug.**

The mayor **isn't doing so well,** though. He took an arrow coated in **Poison V** and **Frostwisp Venom.** Milk has had no effect on the latter. **The good news** is at least the venom isn't damaging him, but it's put him into a kind of **magical slumber.** Breeze's father claims there's a potion called **Cleansing** that can remove almost any status effect. He just needs **the ingredients.**

Oh, by the way, **Jello** is okay! My parents brought him along to the mine. He's eaten nothing but bread-based food items since I left, so when he saw me, he started jumping around **like a redstone spring toy.** Not that I've ever seen one of those things myself, but Max said he knows how to craft them.

We spent the rest of the day **rebuilding.** The wall, mostly. I was placed on **a different building team** than all of my friends, so I haven't had the chance to ask Breeze any more about . . . **that.** As I threw down block after block of cobblestone, **I couldn't stop thinking about it:** The image of Breeze standing in the tree garden kept **resurfacing.** Now that I know **what she really is,** maybe she'll finally start telling me more about herself. I'm sure the dusk elves have a very interesting story to tell.

Oh.

I finally saw the . . . **blue thing.**

"..."

"Hi."

He was just returning from a **"hunt."** He looks like **an ocelot**, kind of. A **monstrous** one. And his name is **Eeebs**. Yes, **he can talk.** Talking animals just . . . **weird me out.** I've been **avoiding** him ever since he first spoke to me. I'm sure I'll **warm up** to him. Just give me time. So many things have happened lately. I just wanted to come back home and **relax** for a bit, you know? **Oh, Runt!** You're the descendant of some **ancient villager hero!** You're going to be **hunted** by extremely creepy undead things that give you **every debuff** in existence! One of your best friends **is actually an elf!** Oh, and your bedroom?! **Totally blown up!**

Seriously, just leave me alone already . . . !

Finally, I ran into **Faolan,** the **wolf guy** I met in that dungeon. He was there in the battle against the Underlord, using his magic to **freeze the zombie minions** into ice cubes.

He smiled. "**We meet again.**"

I peered at him **suspiciously.** "How'd you get here so fast?!"

"A wise magician never reveals **his greatest tricks.**" He bowed. "Although I wish to speak further, **your leader is ill.** To cure his affliction, the necessary ingredients must be gathered. I wish you **good fortune,** my friend."

He left without waiting for a response. "**Um . . . see ya.**"

TUESDAY—UPDATE VIII

Late this afternoon, Drill asked me to **help Brio** rebuild part of **the village hall.** Since it's a huge building and was mostly undamaged, it's where everyone will be **sleeping** tonight. Rebuilding the outer wall was our top priority. We'll work on the houses tomorrow.

> I couldn't help but wonder what he really looked like under that disguise. . . .

APPELLATE GOWN

Brio slammed down **a block of quartz.** "Hot today," he said, wiping his brow. "By the way . . . **good work** out there."

"**Thanks.** You too." I threw down a block myself. "So the mayor . . . he'll recover?"

"**He'll be fine.** To brew **Cleansing potions,** we only need **aetherspring.** It's a **rare flower.** Typically found in **swamp** biomes.

Faolan and the Legionnaire **Kaeleb** have already set out in search of some." He placed another block. "So . . . my daughter told me **you defeated a shade.**"

"It **followed us.** I think it watched us throughout the battle, lingering, waiting for the perfect time to **strike.**"

"**Indeed.** Shades are **highly** intelligent, a powerful form of undead. Even I wouldn't have an easy time with one. That you defeated one by yourself, well . . . **that's quite a feat.**"

"What does that mean?"

"I suppose it means **the Prophecy** is true after all." He paused. "I also heard that you've . . . **learned of us.**"

"I won't tell anyone."

"It doesn't matter. I'll be revealing **the truth** at tonight's meeting. **No more hiding.** It's time **everyone** knew."

"Sir . . ." *(I wasn't mocking him. I was really trying to show respect.)* "When I fought **that shade,** I was hit with a status effect called **Curse of Icehollow.** The venom affecting the mayor is also related to the cold. Is there **a connection?**"

"There is. **A frostwisp** is . . . like a floating jellyfish.

Extremely dangerous, as all beings native to Icehollow. Icehollow is the common name for **Icerahn, the fourteenth realm."**

"Realm?"

"**Dimension.**" He sat down on one of the blocks that served as a crenellation. That's a fancy word for one of the castle-like things on the edge of the roof. You know what I mean.

I sat down on one next to him, and he continued:

"After he fell during **the final battle,** the **Unseeing Wizard** was not **completely** destroyed. He had a protective enchantment in place that transferred his spirit to **a phylactery,** otherwise called a **soulcrystal.** The location of this crystal was soon discovered after the war ended, in **Icehollow.** The Knights of Aetheria launched **an expedition** to this realm and ultimately found what appeared to be **a violet gemstone** five blocks in height, which was surrounded by **his minions** in the process of performing a ritual that, once completed, would revive their master fully. . . . The knights **defeated** these servants. Yet the crystal **could not be moved or destroyed** by any known means. So they encased it within **layers of bedrock** and built a fortress around it, a remote outpost they continually manned. This was to prevent any of his servants from attempting to **revive him** again. For thousands of years, it worked. Alas, his servants, once **scattered** to the four corners of the Overworld, **regrouped.** They slowly grew in strength and number, and they returned to Icehollow, where they launched an attack upon the outpost. Many knights fell that day. . . . In fact, their order was **nearly dissolved.** Today, the Knights of Aetheria are just a shadow of their former selves. They are **strong,** even now, but they were **so much stronger** then. . . ."

". . ."

And **today** I learned where Breeze gets **her passion** for history. I can see why, too. It **was** a really interesting story.

"At any rate, you can associate the word **'Icehollow'** with the Eyeless One himself, since that is **his home world.** The wisest among my kind was convinced he'd built **a new castle** there, shortly after his revival."

"So we'll have to **go there.**"

"**Someday.** And that is why, when I began to realize that **the Prophecy is indeed true,** I felt only sorrow for **my daughter. And for you.**" For the second time in recent memory, he **looked quite** sad. "You must understand that what you've faced **so far** is just **the beginning.** No matter where you go, they will always be hunting you."

Down below, where the mayor once gave **his speeches,** people were already **gathering.**

"If I may **borrow the forge** again," Brio said. "Village tradition calls for **cake** during any meeting, and today I will craft cake **the likes of which these people have never seen.**"

STORMBERRY

FIREBERRY

MOONBERRY

TUESDAY—UPDATE IX

As the sun fell, Brio, acting as **substitute mayor,** talked about **our victory.** How well everyone did. How the monsters won't **dare** return after the lesson we gave them. How the mayor will **get better** soon. And how fifteen of Villagetown's **finest young cadets** will be heading to **the capital.** A ceremony in our honor will take place in a few days, the night before we leave. As he spoke, **I ate cake** like everyone else, but **not just any** cake. What Brio made earlier **surpassed** even my newfound love for mushroom stew.

The temporary mayor continued:

". . . And I would like to thank **the Legionnaires.** The school caught on fire at one point, but they had the presence of mind to use **Waterburst arrows** to put the fires out." Those are arrows that create **a spring of water** upon contact, like dumping out a bucket. At this news, there was a round of **applause.** "Finally, there's one more thing I'd like to discuss," Brio added. "It will **shock you. I apologize** in advance."

"We never meant to **deceive you,**" Breeze said. "Only **protect you.**"

Together they took out **bottles of milk** and drank them before the crowd.

Before **a stupefied audience,** Brio shared the story of **the dusk elves,** their history, who they were, why they wore black, and where they **really** came from. . . .

"Although we once lived in **Shadowbrook,** that village was not our true home. We originally came from **an island far to the northeast. The Isle of Ioae.** Upon its shores, sheltered within **a vast cove,** was our city of the same name. Alas, our kind was all but **eradicated.** We have always been viewed as **a threat,** and that has never changed. Even now, **the Unseeing Wizard** searches for us. For we carry **relics** and knowledge passed down through the ages, both of which can help **defeat him.**" He paused. "Long ago, I was known as **Ezael Stormblood,** high retainer of **the noble Nightcrest family.**" He gestured to Breeze. "And she . . . was once known as **Lady Alyss Nightcrest. Countess of Ioae.**"

Silence.

So that's why Elric is so polite to her, I thought.

I **staggered** up to Breeze like a heavily damaged iron golem. "You're . . . **some kind of princess?**"

She shook her head. "In our society, **a countess** wasn't very significant. And it doesn't matter, anymore. There's nothing left of **Ioae.** The entire island is **in ruins,** and . . ."

"Although she was once considered **minor nobility,**" Brio said, "I believe she is currently the highest-ranking noble among our kind **still alive** today. Most of us **perished** during the destruction of Ioae, including every last member of **the royal family** and every major house. . . ."

"And that is why she has **supporters** in the West," Elric said. "And why I have been assigned to **personally escort** her to the capital."

"So **you knew**," I said.

"Yes. Just as I knew she was keeping **her identity secret** for a reason. I had no right to reveal it." He smiled. "Although many in the West do not believe in **the Prophecy,** there are a few who feel she can **rally the remaining dusk elves** to our side." His smile faded. He stepped toward her. "Do you think this is **possible?**"

Breeze glanced down, **bit** her lip. "I don't think so."

"It is **unlikely,**" Brio said, "They chose to **abandon** our old ways. They blamed **the royal family** for Ioae's destruction. It was our king who asked many of us to learn of **ancient knowledge,** which ultimately drew the wrath of **the Eyeless One.** I don't believe they want anything to do with **the war.**"

Elric nodded. "Perhaps you are right. But I feel we should **at least** try. If she is willing, of course."

"**Wait,**" Stump said. "So Brio . . . **isn't** . . . your father?"

"Not my real father," Breeze said, "but I've always **thought of him** that way. My real father **fell** in a duel with an **Underlord** shortly after I was born."

*Now I understand why she was **so insistent** on chasing after that Underlord....*

"I swore to **her mother** that I would protect her," Brio said. "And I have. As **Ioae** fell into the sea, I escaped with her in my arms, and we **sailed away,** as others did...."

...

...

So Breeze is **not only an elf,** she's **a noble member of some fallen elf kingdom?** Among the last of a race that has—in Brio's words—only known **destruction** and **sorrow?** Okay, despite everything I learned lately, that was a lot to **take in.** I **actually** leaned against Stump. **My faithful friend** was just as shocked as I was.

"We need **ice cream,**" he said.

I nodded. "We do."

Kolb gripped Brio's shoulder. He talked a bit differently, like the knights. He was totally playing the part: "**A tragic story.** I am sorry for everything that has happened. And I swear on **my sword** that we will put an end to **the Eyeless One.** But regardless of how much you've lost, know that you have **family** here, and not only among the Lost Legion. These villagers are **counting on you.** I'm sure they won't mind following you while the mayor recovers. You've helped so much."

Emerald stepped in between the two of them. "Although I've **never** seen elves before, Brio has never let us down. He was hard on us in school, sure, but he's seen firsthand what **No Eyes** is capable of. He knew what was necessary for **our own survival.** We wouldn't have made it through today without him, **I'm sure of it.**" She flashed **a brilliant smile.** "Besides, he's the person behind **those wonderful cakes!** Eat a slice and tell me he's not every bit a villager as us!"

The villagers needed no real **convincing;** he was already like a second mayor at this point. Within moments, almost all of them were rushing up to him and Breeze to ask **all kinds of questions.** A few were even trying to **touch their ears.**

Puddles emerged from the crowd of villagers, **beaming** at Lola and Ophelia with outstretched arms. "Ready to work on your **gowns?!** Tomorrow night, we're having **another dance** in light of our victory! Think of it as **a final farewell** before all of you . . ." He wiped away a tear. "During your stay in **Aetheria City,** you'll need to dress properly . . . the gowns you'll be wearing are the latest fashion there." He **smiled again.** "Sir Elric himself will be **advising** me on how to craft them!"

"I will also be showing you **a few traditional dances** of the West," Elric said. "You will need to learn them, if you wish to **fit in.**"

Breeze was suddenly whisked away.

When **the elf** returned *(man, it feels weird referring to her as that),* she looked completely **out of this world.**

"I still can't believe you're **an elf,**" Emerald said. "I mean, I knew you were **different,** but not **this** different. Hey, um . . . are **your ears,** like . . . **normal** ears?"

> "If this is what people in the capital dress like, I already feel like Urg the Barbarian."

"Elf countess?" Cog muttered. "**Pah!** What next? Really? **What?!**" He bit into an enchanted stormberry muffin. "**Amazing,**" he said to Stump. "Who cares about elves when stuff like **this** exists?! Can't believe that recipe of yours really worked! **Hurrr!** That silly forge is more useful than I thought it'd be!"

Stump held up a book. **His mom's craftbook.** "Wanna go craft some more?"

"You bet!"

"I'll be **joining** you guys," Max said. The **twinkle** in his eyes made me wonder if he was going to have another go at crafting **a prismarine staff.**

> They didn't even ask
> if I wanted to go.
> Since I had the forge,
> they literally just hauled me away.

TUESDAY—UPDATE X

"It's so good to have you back for at least a few more days. And we're delighted to meet your . . . friend!"

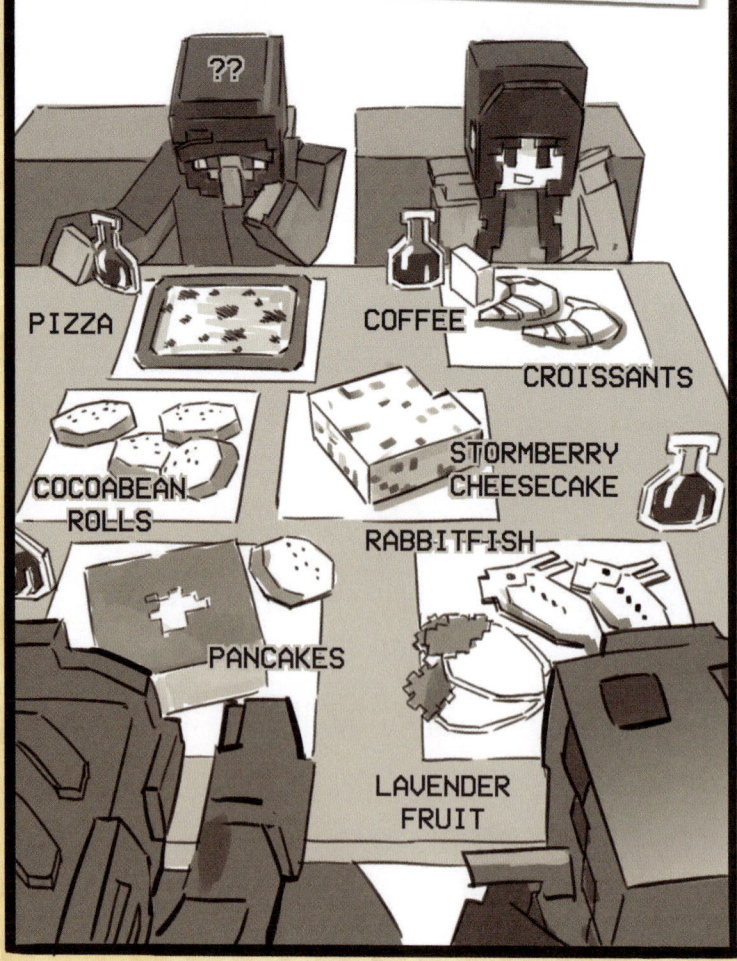

PIZZA

COFFEE

CROISSANTS

COCOABEAN ROLLS

STORMBERRY CHEESECAKE

RABBITFISH

PANCAKES

LAVENDER FRUIT

WEDNESDAY

Drill woke me up this morning. He was standing over my bed, **shouting** about how I'd be **working** with Emerald today. We had to run around the village all day, making sure everyone was building **properly** and helping out **where necessary.** Still in my pajamas—in fact, **still lying down** in bed—I gave him **a salute:**

"Sir! **Yes, sir!**"

I ate a quick breakfast, met up with Emerald, and we ran. As we did, I had this **weird** feeling that we were being followed . . . and yet **I didn't notice anyone. . . .**

WEDNESDAY—UPDATE I

"**Noobery!**
I'm a Knight of Aetheria, not some builder! No, I don't want help! Wait. Got any stormberry rolls?"

WEDNESDAY—UPDATE II

"Told you I saw a zombie rabbit! **Now pay up!** One thousand emeralds! We made a bet, remember? Hey! **Get back here!!!**"

WEDNESDAY—UPDATE III

"Wanna hold him? **Runt?** Hello? Hey! Where are you going?!"

WEDNESDAY—UPDATE IV

"Yes, this is an obsidian farm. No, I don't need any help. **It's dangerous work.** Go bug Emerald. **Oh!** Hey, Emerald."

WEDNESDAY—UPDATE V

WEDNESDAY—UPDATE VI

So our village has survived **yet another attack.** Things started **calming down** by evening, with most of the **important** structures rebuilt. Just after sunset, I went to the observation tower with Breeze. We were **silent** at first, watching **the stars.** I was still having a hard time accepting **who she was.**

"The **Disguise** effect didn't change your hair color? Blue kind of **stands out,** you know."

"I already changed my hair," she said. "**Before.** It wasn't always blue. It was originally . . . **forget it. That was the old me.**"

"How'd you manage to change **your hair?**"

"There's a way to **permanently** alter your appearance," she said. "If you noticed, Sir Elric doesn't have the **typical** eyebrows of a male villager. Things like eyebrows, hair style, and hair color are **easy** to change. We couldn't alter our ears, though. You need so many **rare ingredients** for that. And we were **on the run.** So we decided to use potions. **A quick fix.**"

"Oh. Well, even if you didn't change that much, I don't think I'll **ever** get used to seeing you like that." I sighed. "Okay, what's the deal with the **relics** and **knowledge** your father mentioned?"

"He has **a keystone.** You need one to be able to travel to **the eighth realm** and those above it. And you've seen **that book of his.** It has every **advanced crafting recipe** and almost every **legendary one.**"

"Legendary? As in, more **advanced** than **advanced?**"

"Yes. And as for me, I **inherited** several items. You could call them **family heirlooms.**" She reached into her belt pouch, retrieving **a sword** from the **extradimensional space.** As one might expect, the blade was **black**—or very dark gray—and quite **long,** slightly **curved.** The hilt was made of **bone,** though darker than any type I'd ever seen. I could tell this weapon was **very old,** that it had passed through many hands until ending up in hers.

She handed the sword to me.

"It's a **legendary-tier weapon,**" she said. "One of two." She pulled **another sword** from her belt pouch. It was **similar** to the one I held, except with a hilt made of **grayish crystal.** "Although they're not among the **twelve weapons** Entity crafted, they're still **powerful.**

Or at least they were. They're missing **their gemstones.** Without them, they can't be **correctly** enchanted. I've never wielded either blade. My father said they should be **kept hidden** at all times. To be seen with such a weapon . . . would draw **far too much attention.**"

MORNINGTIDE
GREATEDGE
MATERIAL: BEDROCK, LUNAR CRYSTAL
ATTACK SPEED: 2.5
AVERAGE DAMAGE: 15
DURABILITY: 172 / 7,810

WATER AFFINITY

NEGATE I

[NEGATE CAN TEMPORARILY PREVENT AN OPPOSING WEAPON'S ENCHANTMENTS FROM FUNCTIONING.]

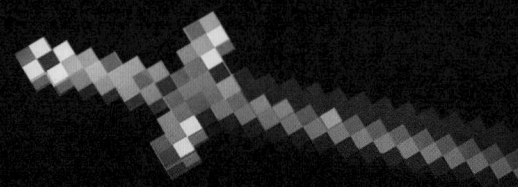

EVENTIDE
GREATEDGE

MATERIAL: BEDROCK, DRAGONBONE
ATTACK SPEED: 2.5
AVERAGE DAMAGE: 15
DURABILITY: 255 / 7,810
SHADOW AFFINITY
LIFESTEAL I

[LIFESTEAL DRAINS A SMALL AMOUNT OF HEALTH WITH EACH STRIKE, WHICH HEALS THE WIELDER.]

"Their durability's **really low**," I said. "Have you ever tried **repairing** them?"

"You mean on **an anvil?** No. **A legendary weapon** can't be repaired that way. Only **re-crafted** on a forge. And we never had access to one. **Lately,** I mean. There were several in **loae,** but they were lost."

"Well, we have one **now.** Although . . . to re-craft, I guess we'd need the **proper materials.**"

"**I have everything.** Both blades are made of **bedrock.** The hilt of yours is **dragonbone.** Mine, **lunar crystal.**"

"**Uhh . . .** The way you said **'yours'** almost made it sound like . . . you're **giving this to me.**"

"**I am.**"

"And here I thought today couldn't get **any weirder.** Wait . . . where did you get **bedrock?** And **dragonbone?** And what's **lunar crystal?** Doesn't lunar mean **moon?** And dude . . . how can bedrock even be **mined?!**"

"We were **once** capable of many things."

"**Clearly.**"

"**Well?** Should we try **re-crafting** them? It should be pretty straightforward. From what I've read, we only have to place each blade on the forge, **overlay the materials,** and . . . I think **that's it.**"

I set down the sword she gave me, grabbed the forge, and placed it on the floor of the sky tower. "Let's **craft.** Err, **re-craft.**"

With a flash of **blue-green** light, both bedrock and dragonbone **merged** with the sword. The weapon now had **full** durability. **Five times that of diamond.** It was slightly smaller than the standard greatsword, and despite the blade being made of bedrock and over one block long, it was **lighter** than I expected.

She **drew closer** and pointed at **the edge** of my blade. "See how the cube pieces are just a bit **smaller** than a normal item? All **legendary weapons** are like that—they're made of slightly **more** cubes. This provides greater **strength** and **flexibility.** From what little I know about them, they were made during the **Second Great War** by our greatest smith, **Oaeo.**"

"Oaeo? What's up with all the **strange names?**"

"Dusk elves from my grandmother's time and before had **Sylvan names,** and Sylvan only uses **vowels.** Anyway, Oaeo became inspired to craft these weapons, like a kind of **madness,** and locked himself up in his tower for weeks to **craft obsessively,** barely sleeping, eating, or drinking. These weapons were **his ultimate expression.** He chose to craft each blade out of bedrock because weapons back then, especially ones made for use in the war, had to be strong enough to withstand **intense punishment.** Monsters were **much stronger** then, and the force that comes with powerful abilities can **destroy** ordinary weapons with ease. . . ."

I raised a hand **defensively.** "Please, no more! I'm **excited enough** as it is. I'm about ready to **charge** outside the village in search of a spider just so I can **try this thing out!**"

We worked on **her sword** next. When she placed the lunar crystals onto the forge, I wanted to ask her again **where she got them.** I **didn't**, though. When someone gives you **an ancestral sword** belonging to dusk elf **nobility**—the "ultimate expression" of some legendary smith—you **don't** ask questions.

"It might be best to keep them **hidden** while we're in the capital," she said. "But we can work on them in **our spare time.** A **side** project. Without the proper gemstones, they won't be able to hold more than one **low-level** enchantment. We'll have to **trade** for new ones."

"What gemstones?"

"Frost opal. Void tesseract. Both aether and ethereal topaz. Fire lattice."

"You lost me at **'void tesseract.'**"

"They're all **extremely** rare. It will take a bit of searching, but maybe we can find some in the capital. It should have more than a few shops that **specialize in gems.**"

"Yeah . . ." I stared down at **my new sword,** then threw it in its scabbard and slung it across my back. "And hey . . . **thanks.** I almost don't want to **accept** this, but . . . I know you'd insist."

"We'll need all the help we can get."

"Suppose we will. I—"

A door didn't interrupt me this time. If one had, I would have **destroyed** it. There are no doors in the observation tower though, only **a tall ladder** going fifty blocks down, and right now came the **clunks** of someone **climbing up.**

Two people, actually. **Kolb and Emerald.**

"Guess we're still going to the capital," Emerald said **glumly.** "I thought maybe we'd get a pass on account of our village being blown up, but **nope.** We'll be staying here for a few days to help rebuild, but then **we're off.** Classes start soon, after all. And get this: Elric says we'll be wearing **uniforms** at the Academy." She **exhaled,** blowing her bangs upward. "**So lame.**"

"I'll be heading there myself," Kolb said. "But I'll be staying behind a bit longer to help out with the **full** rebuild. That'll take weeks." He approached, noting **the new weapons** slung across our backs. "**Interesting** blades. I know dusk elf craftsmanship when I see it. Nothing else **radiates** such sheer gloom." He grinned. "You two have been **holding out** on me, eh?"

"You're one to talk!" I said. "They told me about what you've been hiding."

"Ah. Sorry, Runt. I've been meaning to tell you." He pulled a sword from the extradimensional space of his belt pouch. Only half of its blade remained, ending in a jagged, diagonal fracture. Just like the legend said. Light gray in color, the blade shimmered with a soft, almost rainbow-like shine: the legendary metal known as adamant.

"So that's Critbringer?" I asked.

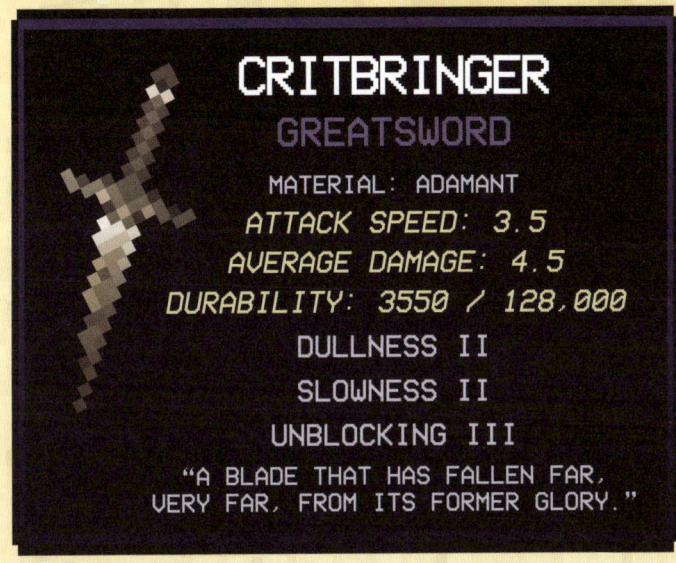

CRITBRINGER
GREATSWORD
MATERIAL: ADAMANT
ATTACK SPEED: 3.5
AVERAGE DAMAGE: 4.5
DURABILITY: 3550 / 128,000
DULLNESS II
SLOWNESS II
UNBLOCKING III
"A BLADE THAT HAS FALLEN FAR,
VERY FAR, FROM ITS FORMER GLORY."

"Originally named **Aeon**," the Legionnaire said, "and renamed by **its former owner,** a Knight of Aetheria. In its current state, its damage is **pathetic.** One of the blade's **fragments** was in **a dungeon** not far from here. Only recently did we obtain it. Maybe I could **borrow** the forge when you're done with it?"

"**Here,**" I said while handing it to him. "**I'm done.** And you can keep it. I won't need it. They say **every crafting room** in the Academy has one."

He nodded. "Once I'm finished, I'll hand it over to **your father,** Breeze. He's already started **an obsidian farm.** Soon, NPCs are going to be walking around **in obsidian plate.**" He laughed. "Never thought I'd see the day!"

"**Aetherians,**" Emerald whispered, elbowing him.

"Sorry. I keep forgetting. **Aetherian,** Terrarian. Aetherian, Ter—"

Clunk, clunk, clunk! Stump climbed up **the ladder.** It's no longer the doors creaking open; now it's the ladders clunking. Next time I pick a spot to **relax,** there won't be any doors or ladders or anything else that makes **a ton of noise.** On the plus side, my friend was looking pretty **dapper** in an exquisite red-and-gold suit. **What a sophisticated young lad!**

"They wanted us to come get you," he said.

Ophelia followed him up, looking **absolutely amazing** in a gown **comparable** to the one Breeze tried on yesterday, only sleeveless and with long white gloves. When she took his arm, **he blushed so hard** his face almost looked like a block of redstone: "Th-the dance will begin in . . . roughly half an hour."

Emerald smirked. "Wow, are you two . . . **an item?**"

"**We are,**" Ophelia said, flashing a smile. "I asked him this evening!"

I looked at the so-called **items,** thoroughly confused. "Can someone explain this item thing to me? This guy named S once asked Breeze if **we were an item.**"

"Then maybe you **are,**" Emerald said with a **wink.** "To be certain, you might want to ask her."

"Ask **what?!** What does it even mean?!"

"We'll see you at the dance," Ophelia said with **a smile,** and the two **"items"** bowed and climbed back down the ladder.

"Same for us," Kolb said, meaning him and Emerald. "Or would you care to **walk with us?**"

Breeze shook her head. "**No.** We'll see you there."

"**Understood,**" he winked.

"**Don't be late,**" Emerald said. "**Tonight, you're the stars of the show!**"

As they went down the ladder, I turned to Breeze. "Why didn't you want to walk **with them?**"

"We still have a few minutes, **don't we?**"

"**We do.**" I approached the edge of the tower. "So . . . this is it. **We'll be off soon. . . .**" I gazed at the countless lights below, all the torches that had been replaced, and all the streets and houses along with the wall, still recognizable despite **the damage.** "I'm going to **miss** this place."

"We'll always come back during the holidays."

"I know."

"After we complete our **training,**" Breeze said, "I'd like to join **a guild.**"

"What's **a guild?**"

"They're kind of like **clans.** There are so many different ones. Maybe we could join one **together** someday. **It'd be fun.**"

Suddenly, **a blue star** appeared on the horizon, much brighter than all the rest, the same pale shade of a sea lantern. It grew **so bright** that it was like a second moon, or the night's version of the sun, nowhere near as bright yet purely **beautiful,** casting soft light on the mountains beneath—a jagged blue outline. It took me a second to realize what it really was.

"Pebble **made it,**" I said. "**He actually lit the beacon.**"

"I always knew he would." She joined me at the edge of the tower. "Once it's lit, **the temple is protected.** Forever. That means it's no longer the biggest priority for **the Eyeless One.** Now **we** are. More monsters will be searching for us. Before we leave, we'll need to **disguise ourselves.** We can use the process I mentioned earlier. And . . . my father still has a few **enchanted name tags.** . . ."

"**A new identity?** Never liked **this name,** anyway." I turned to her. "And no matter who we become, **we will always be an item.**"

When she met my eyes, I was reminded that this world is **so much more** than farms and walls. "I suppose we **are.**" She **smirked.**

"And a **legendary** one."

To everyone who may be reading a copy of my diary: Breeze suggested I **take my journal writing** to the **next level,** in the form of **"archives."** I **agree!** If I'm supposed to record everything that happens in **our world,** I should be a bit more **professional,** right? But don't worry. It won't be **too different**—just a change in **the narration.** On the plus side, there will be some sections that focus more on **my friends.** I'm sure **you're dying** to know more about Breeze and the others, right? And maybe Stump can even share a few of his advanced crafting recipes!

Stay tuned!

ABOUT THE AUTHOR

Cube Kid is the pen name of Erik Gunnar Taylor, a writer who has lived in Alaska his whole life. A big fan of video games—especially Minecraft—he discovered early that he also had a passion for writing fan fiction. Cube Kid's unofficial Minecraft fan fiction series, *Diary of a Wimpy Villager*, came out as e-books in 2015 and immediately met with great success in the Minecraft community. They were published in France by 404 éditions in paperback with illustrations by Saboten and now return in this same format to Cube Kid's native country under the title *Diary of an 8-Bit Warrior*. When not writing, Cube Kid likes to travel, putter with his car, devour fan fiction, and play his favorite video game.

PREVIOUS BOOKS IN THE DIARY OF AN 8-BIT WARRIOR SERIES

Diary of an 8-Bit Warrior

Diary of an 8-Bit Warrior: From Seeds to Swords

Diary of an 8-Bit Warrior: Crafting Alliances

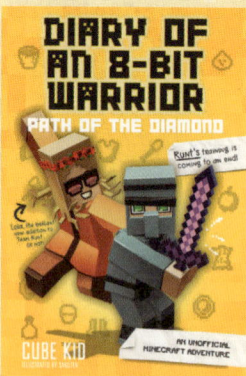

Diary of an 8-Bit Warrior: Path of the Diamond

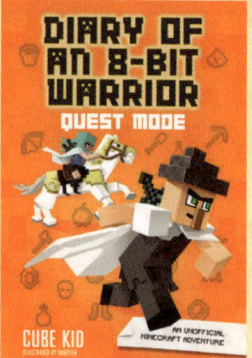

Diary of an 8-Bit Warrior: Quest Mode

Follow your favorite <u>8-Bit Warrior</u> characters in book 1 of the new series, *Tales of an 8-Bit Kitten*.

DIARY OF AN 8-BIT WARRIOR
QUEST MODE

This edition © 2018 by Andrews McMeel Publishing.

All rights reserved. Printed in China. No part of this
book may be used or reproduced in any manner whatsoever without written
permission except in the case of reprints in the context of reviews.

Published in French under the title *Journal d'un Noob (Guerrier Ultime) Tome V*
© 2017 by 404 éditions, an imprint of Édi8, Paris, France
Text © 2015 by Cube Kid, Illustration © 2017 by Saboten

Minecraft is a Notch Development AB registered trademark. This book is a work of fiction
and not an official Minecraft product, nor approved by or associated with Mojang. The other
names, characters, places, and plots are either imagined by the author or used fictitiously.

Andrews McMeel Publishing
a division of Andrews McMeel Universal
1130 Walnut Street, Kansas City, Missouri 64106
www.andrewsmcmeel.com

ISBN: 978-1-4494-9404-9 hardback
978-1-4494-9252-6 paperback

Library of Congress Control Number: 2017958338

Made by:
King Yip (Dongguan) Printing & Packaging Factory Ltd.
Address and place of production:
Daning Administrative District, Humen Town
Dongguan Guangdong, China 523930
Box Set 3rd printing-2/28/22

ATTENTION: SCHOOLS AND BUSINESSES
Andrews McMeel books are available at quantity discounts with bulk purchase for
educational, business, or sales promotional use. For information, please e-mail the
Andrews McMeel Publishing Special Sales Department: specialsales@amuniversal.com.

In memory of Lola Salines (1986–2015),
founder of 404 éditions and editor of this series,
who lost her life in the November 2015 attacks on Paris.
Thank you for believing in me.

—Cube Kid

FRIDAY
UPDATE III—AFTERNOON

I stood **next to Breeze** in a small quartz room. A sea lantern illuminated the room with a **pale blue glow.** Against the center of one wall stood a **mysterious** object. It was **three yards tall, three yards wide,** and flat, like a banner. But instead of dyed wool, it was a surface like the calmest pool of water. Breeze reached out with her right hand and **grazed her reflection.** She lowered her hand, and we continued staring at ourselves in silence. **In awe.** It was the first time we'd seen ourselves this way.

On top of that were <u>our outfits.</u>

Our clothes were sewn of **spider silk. Puddles,** the owner of the Clothing Castle, had worked with the humans for days to craft **perfect re-creations of Earth fashion.** Then, to make us look **even more majestic,** our cloaks had been modified to **fall over our shoulders.**

Poster children. Symbols of hope.
Villagetown's biggest stars.
That's what we've become.

Some would say **it's sweet:** a budding **romance** between two young heroes fighting valiantly against all odds. I'd say **that's an exaggeration.** Although Breeze and I are **close,** we haven't had much time for anything besides battle or preparations for the next. I guess the mayor wants to change that, though. He wants the people to have **something to believe in.** I suppose that's why he whisked us away in the middle of the dance.

And when we return, we're to **smile,**
hold hands, and raise them before a cheering crowd.

"You look so different from when we first met," I said.

"I suppose." Breeze **stared vacantly** ahead. "I wish we could have danced more."

"Me too."

I adjusted the collar of my shirt. We heard a **click,** and the door opened. In the reflection, I saw the mayor step in. As he studied us, particularly our outfits, the faintest trace of a smile appeared beneath his mustache.

"I apologize for taking you away like this," he said, gliding in. "I just wanted to make sure that you two are . . . looking your **very best** for the award ceremony."

"It's fine," Breeze said, still fixed on **her reflection.**

The mayor slid between us and ran his gnarled fingers along the edge of the object's smooth iron frame.

"So, what do you think? **Do you like it?**"

Breeze nodded. "It's . . . **amazing.** What is it called?"

"This is known as **a mirror.** This one is thousands of years old, crafted during the start of the **Second Great War.** As I understand, it came from an ancient temple. **The Tabernacle of Gloomfell Cove.** That's near the sea, beyond a vast mountain range to the northwest, far, far from here."

"I suppose it'd be **impossible to craft such an object ourselves,**" I said. "How did it wind up here, anyway?"

"Our records say a trader brought it here. Traders used to be quite common, back when it was **still safe to travel.** I was just a boy then. So many voyagers and vagabonds constantly visited our village. It seems like yesterday. . . ."

I nodded, vaguely recalling reading something about that in school. Only recently had our village learned of **the Eyeless One's** return, yet our scholars believe he's been gathering his strength and amassing his armies for a long time. The coming war is, perhaps, something he's been planning for at least fifty years. Before that, **monster attacks** were far from common. You could have traveled **the Overworld** for weeks without encountering one. And now . . .

After staring off **into nothingness** for a moment, the mayor raised his head and **smiled** again. Was that a tear in the corner of his eye?

"You two look **so wonderful,**" he finally said. "Yes, you're **exactly** what our village **needs** right now." Another pause. "I . . . hope you can understand why **I'm asking all this of you.**"

I looked his **reflection** in the eye.
"**Of course**, sir."

FRIDAY
UPDATE IV—AFTERNOON

We walked back in silence. Almost everyone was at the party, so the streets were mostly empty. Still, we could see distant **silhouettes** on the wall, spaced evenly—every hundred blocks, more or less. **Humans standing watch,** enchanted bows slung over their shoulders. There was, no doubt, at least one more up in the sky tower—**ready to activate** the note block alarm system should trouble arise—but I couldn't see into the tower's nest from here.

Upon reaching the **village hall,** things were mostly the same as when we left: **posters and banners, jukeboxes and cakes.** And a thousand or so people celebrating Villagetown's success. Even though **the Eyeless One** was still out there, his minions had been driven back.

For us, that was <u>enough.</u>
At this point, we'll take **any victory** we can get,
no matter how small.

I heard some **laughter** to my left: Breeze was already being swept away by a handful of human girls. They couldn't get over **her cloak.** Stump couldn't get over mine. After he slapped me on the back and flashed **a huge grin,** his gaze fell to my shoulders. "What's that about?"

"For the **award ceremony,** I guess." I glanced around at the jovial crowd of villagers and humans. "**So what's new?** Have you heard anything since I left?"

"Yeah. This kid—**Tucker,** I think—said he was playing on the wall the other morning and saw **a rabbit** on the plains. And not just any rabbit. He claims it was **a zombie.**"

Stump made **a spooky face,** then busted out laughing. "The imaginations of kids these days!"

"**Hmmm,**" I said. "Actually, I'd like to look into it. I'll speak to him **later.**"

"Also, I keep seeing **this weird old man,**" Stump said. "Red robes. Red hat. Black sunglasses. Huge white beard. Said his name is **Cocoa. Cocoa Witherbean.**"

"Cocoa Witherbean, huh?"

I **thought** for a moment, but the name didn't ring any bells, and neither did the description. That wasn't all that strange, though. New people have been showing up at our gate almost **every week. Survivors.** Usually, it's a small group of **clueless** villagers who've fled from some tiny, obscure town after being attacked in the middle of the night. Otherwise, it's a lone human who's been **wandering the Overworld** for months. We take them all in, show them around, and assign them some work to do.

"So this **Cocoa**," I said, "is he one of the new arrivals from this morning?"

"Maybe. Whoever he is, **he's creepy.** I've seen him snooping around outside a **library,** too."

"Interesting. . . . ." Once more I thought back but didn't remember seeing anyone who fit Stump's verbal sketch.

"All right, I'll **keep an eye out** for this guy," I said. "Anything else?"

"**Nope.** Not really."

"Well, keep up the **good work**," I said. "And don't let your guard down. Even at a time like this"—I reached up and patted **my diamond sword,** which was now sheathed across my back—"we can't forget who we are."

Stump's smile **faded.** "Yes, **sir!**"

"**Hey!** You don't need to call me that."

"But they said I'm **supposed** to call you that, now that **you're a captain.**"

"**That doesn't matter.** We've been friends since we were just a single block tall. I'm just **Runt,** okay?"

"Sure thing," he said, frowning. "You know, Runt, you . . . you're acting **awfully serious** all of a sudden. What happened? Is anything wrong?"

I lowered my head, unsure what to say. What **could** I say? I couldn't stop thinking about what the mayor had said earlier. *You're a* warrior, Runt—a sworn defender of our village. And today, you must act the part. . . .

Of course, I didn't need to say anything to Stump. He understood. He understood **better than anyone.** He'd been there when hundreds of mobs breached the wall. So as I stood in silence, he didn't say anything, either—just gave me a **slow** nod. Perhaps he was recalling it as well. Several other villagers ran up, **laughing and joking** and handing us slices of **cake** . . . and the images quickly left our minds. For the moment.

For that matter, I was **so wrapped up** in the celebration that I almost failed to notice the villagers' clothes. Many of them were dressed in **human-style outfits** like me. Breeze was right. We really are becoming more and more like the **humans.** Then again, they're becoming more like us, too. One look at their leader was enough to convince you. There he was, **Kolbert21337,** He Who Hails from Earth, **Lord Commander of the Lost Legion** . . . dressed in a **villager's** robe.

"**PLEASE STOP** CALLING ME THAT," he yelled. "**KOLB WILL DO JUST FINE.** I really need to find another one of those enchanted name tags so I can change this silly name. . . . By the way—I have **an important announcement!** My best friend **Kaeleb** recently discovered how to craft **apple pie!** We'd like to **share**

some with you guys! In return, we'd love to try some of **your famous grass stew!** We've heard it's a village delicacy, and we really want to know what it tastes like!"

He went on to explain how there's **a holiday on Earth** that celebrates a time when two vastly different groups of people shared food with each other. The humans wanted to start something like that here. **Unfortunately** for them, they had no idea what they were getting into. **Grass stew** is considered a village delicacy not because it **tastes good,** but because **it's hard to craft.** You need shears **enchanted with Silk Touch** to harvest grass. As for the taste, you're **better off** eating grass raw.

> Poor Kolbert . . . uhh, "Kolb."
> He <u>quickly</u> discovered this.

Finally, the mayor announced that it was **time for the award ceremony.** As we approached, we saw that in his palm he was holding **six tiny objects,** each **no bigger than a single seed.** Two resembled **hearts,** and another two resembled **swords.** The last pair, however, I didn't recognize. They were **gray** in color, **stone,** with flecks of **white-blue diamond** here and there. They almost looked like some kind of . . . um . . . **bird?**

"For this year's **graduates**," the mayor called out, "we've crafted **various emblems** to signify their **achievements**, their chosen professions, and their titles."

He held one of the **birdlike emblems** in his right hand and raised it over his head. The bird's **diamond flecks** caught the setting sun, sparkling brilliantly. "This one specifically," he added, "the **Diamond Blockbird**, is crafted from a single piece of **diamond ore** to demonstrate its **rarity** and value. Thus, each emblem has been crafted to honor those who have **fought so hard to protect our village** in these dark and troubled times. And out of the many brave young graduates here, the two standing beside me have **fought the hardest.** For this reason, we've decided that they may both serve as **captains** and share leadership of **their group.**"

At this, a lot of people began **whispering,** but for Breeze and me, this was **no surprise.** The mayor had mentioned this earlier when he first took us to that room. He had said that he wanted our group to **stand out** above the rest. Since we've proven ourselves and all. . . . But I think there's more to it. He also told us that our group would be the **first** to **explore the Overworld.** When it comes to leading and making the right decisions, he probably trusts Breeze more than me. **That's understandable.** Sometimes I let **my emotions** get the best of me. Breeze, on the other hand, **never** loses her cool. So she'll be serving as, like . . . **my babysitter?** No, that's not how a heroic swordsman would say it. She'll be there to ensure I don't make any mistakes. **That's it.**

The mayor turned and **gave us a knowing nod.** Recalling our instructions, I **fell to one knee,** as did Breeze. Then he began fastening different emblems on the left shoulder of our cloaks, just above our **hearts.** They clung securely, like **sticky pistons.** Then he pulled out **another pair: little blue stars.** The official emblem of **a captain.** He **replaced** my original diamond badge with this.

As he fastened on each pair, one after another, he called out **their meaning** to the crowd. From what I understand, he had borrowed this from the **Lost Legion.** Every member of that clan is required to dedicate themselves to this thing called **role-playing.** Since they're supposed to be an order of **knights,** they have to carry themselves like knights. And whenever a clan member is promoted, it's through this special ceremony known as **knighting.**

"To our noblest of heroes, Breeze and Runt . . . you shall hereby be known as warriors, as well as . . ."

"Defenders of Villagetown..."

"Captains of Night Watch..."

"and Explorers of the Overworld."

I wanted to believe his words, but I **couldn't help feeling** that this whole thing was mostly **just an act** to boost village morale. I don't think of myself as **a hero. Not even close.** In many ways, I'm still **just a kid.** I **still** get scared at times. And I still have so much to learn.

Yet seeing hundreds of faces **light up,** tears being brushed away, it suddenly seemed that our survival **wasn't unimaginable** but likely—even **certain.** It was as if the **Wizard with No Eyes** was just another **low-level monster,** out there somewhere waiting to be farmed.

Below, whispers grew louder and louder, until they finally **erupted into cheers and screams.** But that seemed **so quiet** compared to the pounding in my chest. The more I watched them, the more **I felt this awful weight.** It grew heavier with each smile directed my way. Only then did I begin to fully realize what this all meant, how high the bar was. **The whole village was counting on me.** When I glanced at Breeze, though, that feeling went away.

No, I thought. They're not counting on me. . . .
They're counting on **us.**

What am I worrying about? As long as she's there, Villagetown has nothing to worry about.

"May I have this dance?"

"We found this book in Library Seven the other day. You need to read it."

"We hope you like it! It's got all kinds of useful stuff!"

"Go on— take it."

"Quit laughing! It was a zombie! I saw it, okay?!"

> Without a doubt, today was the best day of my life.

The party was winding down, so I walked Breeze home. Her dad was already there when we arrived. I had noticed that he had **seemed a little off** the entire night . . . **gloomy** . . . but there, seeing him in front of the doorway, his attitude mirrored the **storm clouds** that were gathering above our heads: **somber and unnerving.** Something was bothering him.

Breeze didn't seem to notice, or at least she chose not to bring any attention to it. She turned **with a smile.**

"See you tomorrow, Runt. And make sure you **get some sleep.** We have a big day ahead of us."

Her father made a slight movement, like **a jolt?** I'm not quite sure.

"**Good night**," Breeze said, still smiling.

"Good night."

I was **exhausted** when I got home.

"Good night, **Son!**" my mom said.

"**We're very proud of you**," my dad added.

Yeah, it really was **the best day of my life.** And tomorrow is going to be **even better.** Tomorrow I begin my **first real adventure**, what I've been **dreaming** about for so long. In the morning, we'll start our first exploration outside the walls. We're supposed to head out in our groups, always staying **within sight** of the ramparts. **I can't wait.**

FRIDAY
UPDATE V—LATE

And **strangely**, it seemed like tomorrow couldn't wait for me, either.
Knock! Knock! Knock!

Huh? Who's knocking? It must be Mom. I slept in. I'll be late for school.

I actually thought that, in **my deep sleep,** until my eyes flew open and I **sat straight up** in bed.

But there was no way someone could have been knocking at my door—I'd been so tired earlier that **I forgot to shut it.** That was when I saw the **shadowy figure** standing just outside my window. Okay, so I'm not **the brightest** person upon first waking up, but I knew it wasn't my mom.

No, whoever it was, **it was a human. . . .**

And when I looked closer . . . **yes—**

That human most definitely resembled Kolb.

"Come with me, **hero.**"

He took me to **his house,** to a **small dark room. A secret library.**

There, he told me **everything.**

How **we'd be attacked.**

How we couldn't possibly defend ourselves.

How we needed **better armor, better weapons,** and **better items** than the ones we had. How a standard crafting table **wouldn't be enough.**

He showed me a book, an **ancient** book, and a drawing of something thought to exist only in **legend**. An **aeon forge**—otherwise known as **an advanced crafting table**.

The advanced crafting table.

Weeks ago, **several members of the Lost Legion** went into the wilds in **search** of one. Tonight, they had returned **empty-handed, barely hanging on.** . . .

"I know you will succeed **where they have failed**," Kolb said. "You must go. **Tonight**."

"Alone? What about **Breeze?**"

"She'll **talk you out of it.** You know that. As for the rest . . . they'll only **slow you down.**"

"I assume **there's a reason** you can't just go yourself?"

"**There is.** Members of **the Lost Legion** continue to fight among themselves. If I left now, **the clan would fall apart.** And even if I could leave, **I wouldn't make it** one night out there."

"What makes you so sure?"

"I'm . . . **being hunted.**"

"The Eyeless One's minions have been searching for me ever since I arrived in this world. I was on the run even before I arrived here. I changed my appearance, my armor, and even my name. . . ."

"If they discovered **who I really am**, every last one of them would rush to this area. So **I must stay hidden.**"

"**I don't get it.** Why are they looking for you?"

"They . . . see me as **a threat.** I'll just leave it at that."

"You probably can't read ancient script, huh? This loosely translates to '**Destroy him.**' What can I say? Monsters hate me. A lot."

So Kolb **really** is **a high-level knight?** One so **powerful** that **the Eyeless One's** servants are on his tail? And he's sending me on **a quest** to save my village? What does one say to that?

"**. . . You'll feed my pet slime** while I'm gone?" Kolb's instructions sounded **simple enough:**

"Head north, to the village of **Owl's Reach.** A librarian named **Feathers** has the table we need."

Then he gave me a map. **A map of Ardenvell,** the main continent.

"It isn't very **complete,** but it'll have to do. The other guys lost mine."

On the map, it looked **so close.** I was surprised when he said it would take **days** to get there. . . .

Of course, I should have **consulted** with the others before going on **some crazy quest** alone in the middle of the night . . .

but then, you know me.

SATURDAY

It all happened so **fast.** Before I knew it, I'm on top of **a big white horse,** doing my best to hold on as the animal chugged full speed ahead.

A million questions are running through my mind right now. Was Kolb telling **the truth?** Why is he being hunted? **Who is he?** And this **crafting table . . .** will I really find one in some village called **Owl's Reach?**

Most important, **did I make the right decision?** It feels **so reckless** going out on my own like this. **I'm terrified.** The mayor's going to be **outraged. . . .**

What was I **supposed** to do? If I had talked to Breeze, she would have **stopped me. Anyone** would have stopped me. **Kolb had been right** about that. And if he's right about the upcoming attack, we really will need every advantage we can get.

I glance at **the map** again. Owl's Reach isn't marked, but it's there. **Somewhere. Some fifty thousand blocks away.** Okay, so my quest is pretty clear: all I have to do is head **somewhere,** talk to someone, and try not to get eaten by zombies along the way. **No problem.** But I really wish he'd given me a **better map.** Even if it's the most complete map Villagetown's libraries had to offer, that's not exactly saying much.

Most of the other maps, well...

It's actually not so bad...

compared to this.

ZOMBIE CREEPER

ENDER RABBIT

(He gave me one of those maps, too. I'm . . . not sure why. Yeah, I can't fathom how so much villager knowledge has been lost over the generations, when we have such useful information at our disposal. . . .)

As far as supplies go, **I'm set:** Kolb gave me a stack of carrots, a stack of oak, half a stack of coal, a crafting table, a furnace, a bed. Also **332 emeralds** taken from his clan's **ender chest.** Plus, I have a full set of **stone tools** I crafted earlier and, of course, **my sword.**

There's just one problem. I'm still wearing these clothes. Here's the thing about this outfit: although it makes me seem like a **rich noble**

hailing from some **powerful kingdom**—a kingdom where **golden apples** are served in cafeterias and everyone drinks **healing potions** instead of water—it doesn't provide **any armor or stats** of any kind. And they're rather useful, armor and stats. **I like armor and stats. A lot.** I'd wear a big **beetroot sack** as long as it provided even a bit of armor or maybe increased my **movement speed.**

I'd somehow craft it into a shirt
and <u>wear that thing with pride.</u>

SATURDAY—UPDATE I

As I make my way **north,** I sometimes glance to the **south, toward home.** I decided earlier that if I see **any smoke** after sunrise, I'd head back to the village **as fast as possible.** Of course, by the time I'd make it back, it would already be **too late. . . .**

I can't help but imagine **the mayor's face** upon hearing that I'm gone. It's kind of **ridiculous** when you think about it. Just a few hours after I was **hailed** as one of **Villagetown's heroes,** I vanished without a trace. So much for the mayor's plan of **boosting morale. . . .** I can almost hear **Emerald** cracking **some joke** about it. Something about how I got so wound up over the whole **"Explorer of the Overworld"** thing that I zoomed off without **any instructions.** Okay, I admit it—that's probably something I'd do.

All right. The sun's going down. I'm about to **make camp.** That is, dig an **emergency shelter.** I won't write about the process of **digging** a shelter here. **I've already gone over that.** Besides, I don't feel like dwelling on the fact that I'll be spending **the night in a dirt hole.** I still have a shred of **dignity.**

In a hole . . . next to a horse . . .
a horse whose name I don't even know . . .
a horse who <u>slobbers</u> all over me.

"No!
Those are the carrots;
these are my fingers."

SATURDAY—UPDATE II

<u>I'm having trouble **falling asleep.**</u>

Two blocks of dirt sit between me and fresh air, yet I still hear all kinds of **sounds.** Distant howls, **eerie calls.** Sounds not made by any **zombie,** but that's about all I know.

Back pressed against damp earth, in total darkness, **I wait.** . . . I listen to those cries, **thinking about home.** Family. Friends.

That reminds me—**that very heavy book** Max handed to me before he took off with Lola. I place a torch at my feet and turn the first page.

CHAPTER 1
RARE METALS

We shall begin this tome with an in-depth look at those relatively rare and unknown metals, thought by many to exist in legend only. Let it be known that such fantastic metals do exist. So fantastic are these metals, only a person of godlike power could desire better.

VOIDCRYSTAL   MYTHRIL   FIRE ELEMENTIUM

EARTH ESPER   ADAMANT   ORICAL

SUNDAY

I've come across **a ruined village.** Maybe there was a **fire** here. Only cobblestone foundations remained. After searching around, I didn't find anything. No items. No signs of battle. No rubble, even.

The whole place is just . . . <u>empty.</u>

I actually drew a picture of the place, along with a caption saying: "Actually, it's not so bad. Just put up some flowerpots, some carpet, maybe a painting. . . . Um, never mind."

Obviously, the joke was that **no amount** of decoration could cheer this place up. But **I threw the picture away,** because it felt wrong to joke about other people's **misfortunes.** This has to be one of the villages those survivors came from. **This was their home.** I still remember their faces when they showed up at our gate.

If I ever find out **who** did this . . .

SUNDAY—UPDATE I

The horse is gone. I didn't leash it when I went to check out the village because I don't have a leash. **Why didn't Kolb give me one? Seriously,** that horse was right there, no farther than fifteen or twenty blocks away, just nibbling on grass. I checked a few houses in the village, wrote in here, **came back, and . . . great.** The **weird thing** is that I can see for hundreds of blocks in every direction and there's **no horse** in sight. He must have really booked it. Was I really such a bad master? **As if!** I fed that thing more than I fed myself!

Great. Now Kolb's going to be angry with me, too. And traveling **on foot** is going to consume **way more energy.** I'm not sure if these carrots will last. I might have to **go hunting** at some point.

Oh **wait.** I stashed my bow in one of my **item chests** back home. **So glad I did that. . . .** See, this is where I've failed—a real warrior would have definitely anticipated a human randomly showing up in the middle of the night and sending said warrior to find an item that may or may not **actually exist.**

Okay. Let's stay positive. At least I'm not going to have to deal with **horse slobber** tonight. Horses eat **potatoes,** apparently. And apparently, **my nose** resembles one.

SUNDAY—UPDATE II

I wonder what's **everyone's doing back home.** What happened **after I left?** Kolb could be in **a lot of trouble** for sending me out here **on my own.** It's possible that this whole thing could undo the alliance. What if the humans got **kicked out?** What if the mayor **banished** him?

No, it must have played out differently than that. After all, before I left, Kolb said he would **handle everything.** He must have succeeded, because if **Breeze** found out I left, she would've taken a horse and come looking for me. **She would've caught up to me** by now. So everything must be continuing as **normal.** Everyone's getting their feet wet, exploring the Overworld just outside the wall. **Yeah, that's all.**

Breeze must be leading Max, Stump, Lola, and Emerald on **a field trip.** Finding **caves. Mapping the terrain.** Spending the night in a carefully constructed shelter that would—at least compared to the emergency shelter I just dug—look like **the royal suite in Snark's Tavern.** They must be thinking they're tough, eating stacks of bread and sharing ghost stories in the ruddy glow of a redstone torch placed on the ground. **Oooh, spooky.**

Note: I added the destroyed village to my map. Should I ever discover its name, I'll update it.

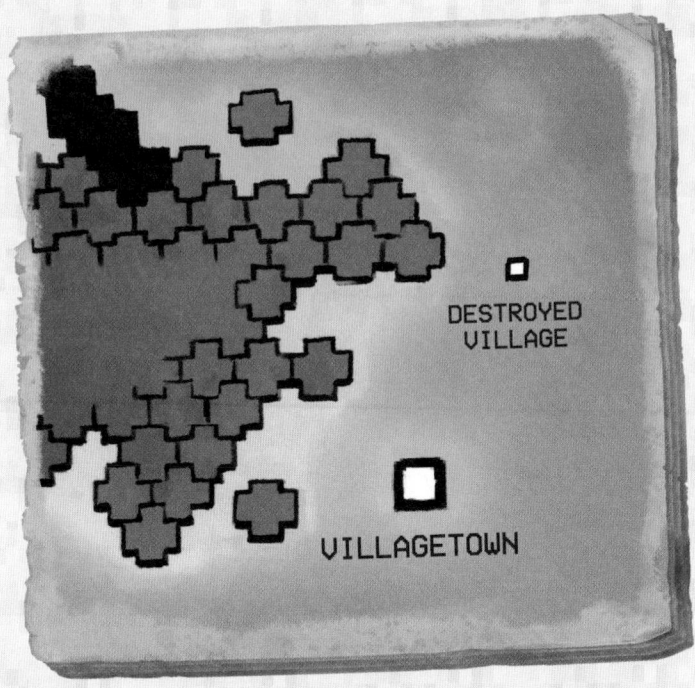

SUNDAY—UPDATE III

"Aetherstone. Adamant. Elementite. Endersteel. Orical. Redsteel. Mythril. Voidcrystal . . ."

In my new underground abode, **I recite these words out loud.** They're the names of some of the **rarest known materials,** or **elements,** of which there are many. Most only exist naturally in the **outer dimensions.** That is, **the dimensions beyond the End.** They're exceedingly **hard** to mine, even with an **obsidian pickax.** Others, such as redsteel and endersteel, don't exist naturally in any known dimension and therefore

cannot be mined. They're created by smelting other materials in an object known as **a crucible**—basically **an advanced furnace.**

I find it confusing that this so-called **elementite** has at least **five different types:** fire, earth, air, water, and shadow. According to the author of this book, a villager named **Theonius** who lived some five hundred years ago, scholars believed there are several more types of elementite. The scholars also argued about what it should be called: elementite or **elementium.**

Huh . . . interesting . . . **Zzzzz.**

Back to reading, even if this book is **slightly boring.** I still can't **sleep.** A zombie has been walking around overhead for the past hour or so. Earlier, I heard this strange sound: *thunk, thunk, thunk.* My imagination went wild. I couldn't picture anything other than some horrible monster, **half tree, half** . . . But no, it was just that zombie, walking into the trunk of an oak tree. **Facepalm.** Some real nice monsters you have there, Herobrine.

What am I even doing out here?
All we have to do is plant trees all around the village and . . .
BINGO! Attack thwarted.

MONDAY

The morning consisted of **walking** and eating carrots. **Mostly. I know. Pretty** thrilling. I like to **start off my mornings** in the Overworld real intense like that.

The highlight of the day was when I came across **an arrow** lodged in the side of a small stone cliff. Okay, so that alone **isn't very interesting,** but it wasn't **a normal arrow.** The tip was made of **obsidian,** with **a creepy ghostlike face.** The face had an odd expression, both **sad and angry,** like someone had just stolen a muffin that he was about to eat. **Which would definitely make me sad and angry.**

Needless to say, I've **never seen** an arrow like that before. I can only assume it's **poisoned.** Or **enchanted** with some horrible debuff that makes Wither look like **slight mining fatigue.** Being **the curious** explorer that I am, I almost wanted to **poke myself** with it just to see what would happen. But I quickly realized that a zombie, a pigman, or perhaps a creeper would be **a much better** test **subject.**

Do you see it? The creepy face? Like, part creeper, part ghast, and both sad and angry at the same time?

Or am I just imagining things again?

"**Nah,** this arrow totally isn't enchanted with **Noob Melting VII**. It was obviously crafted out of **sheer love and happiness.**"

In fact, if it struck a grass block, it would probably sprout <u>thousands of flowers.</u>

TUESDAY

I spotted **a forest** in the middle of the plains. In its very center was a **grotto-like** area with **a cliff** and **a waterfall.**

It was a **beautiful** scene, inviting, with fragrant blossoms and multicolored leaves and mossy stone under streams of **brilliant blue water**—golden sunlight pouring down. *Come on in,* this place seemed to say. *Just go for a little swim. You don't need to worry. There are no creepers here. Promise. Ignore that slight rustling sound behind you. Ignore the hissing. Focus on the water.*

Maybe that was why **I cautiously approached,** expecting **the worst.** But there was nothing. No **giant squid** surging from the depths. No zombies rising from the ground.

Only **tranquility,** loveliness, a gentle breeze . . .
and a most <u>**unusual-looking**</u> girl.

Upon seeing her, I actually gasped.

"Are you . . . **an NPC?**" she asked, stepping back slightly.

"..."

Here we go again, I thought. *As if I haven't already heard enough of that back at the village. Wait, does that mean she's a human?* **No, she can't be.** *She looks nothing like one.*

"My name is **Runt**," I said, approaching.

She **nearly tripped** as she backed up. Then, after another **uneasy glance** in my direction, she **darted into the forest.** Apparently, I'm **the scariest villager** who ever lived.

"Hey! **Wait!** Come back!"

But she was already gone.

I **stood there** for a moment, completely stunned. **Who was she? What was she?** What was up with **her sword?** It was **thin** but **longer** than any sword I'd ever seen.

"Well, she's **definitely** not a human," I muttered. "Not with ears like that."

And suddenly I realized that I'd been talking to myself **an awful lot** lately. Asking myself questions out loud. I never **really** thought about it, but you're **truly alone** when it comes to the Overworld. Sure, I'd heard that it was **barren.** Still, you don't quite understand just how empty it is until you **see it with your own eyes.**

After living in a village my entire life, I find the silence **rather unsettling.**

TUESDAY—UPDATE I

"The Overworld. The Nether. The End. The Void. The Aether. The Cleft. The Shadowlands. The Veil. The Maelstrom. The Abyss. The Channel. The Pinnacle. The Zone. Icerahn . . ."

More self-assigned reading in a temporary underground home. I'm reviewing **dimensions** this time. Before reciting them, I was reading about one in particular: **the Void.** It's this **mysterious** place with **crystalline** plants, pools of water that bestow **magical** effects, and a race of people known as **mycons.** Known for their crafting ability, they are to villagers as **mooshrooms** are to cows.

Maybe I'll visit that place **someday.** There's a path in the Overworld that leads to it; it's **a gigantic chasm** in a forest far to the west. Furthermore, the book says gateways may exist **between the Nether and the Void.** That's pretty useless information for me, since I personally have **no intention** of setting foot in a place where everything **breathes fire.**

All right. Back to studying.

THE AETHER

THE FIFTH DIMENSION, THE AETHER, CONSISTS OF VAST ISLES OF AETHERSTONE SUSPENDED IN A BLACK, STAR-FILLED VOID.

MANY DIFFERENT RACES INHABIT THE LARGER ISLES, MOST NOTABLY THE FISHMEN AND THE BIRDMEN, THE NAMES OF WHICH HAVE BEEN LOST THROUGH THE AGES. ALTHOUGH THESE PEOPLE ARE PEACEFUL, IT SHOULD BE NOTED THAT THEY ARE PERFECTLY CAPABLE OF DEFENDING THEMSELVES.

AS THE DISTANCE BETWEEN EACH ISLE CAN BE VAST, THE MOST EFFICIENT METHOD OF TRAVELING BETWEEN THEM IS THROUGH THE USE OF A FLYING MOUNT, PARTICULARLY A SPECTRAL RAVEN: A BIRD NATIVE TO THIS DIMENSION, FOUND ON MANY OF THE LARGEST ISLES AND QUITE EASILY TAMED WITH BEETROOTS OR SUGAR. THE FASTEST AMONG THEM CAN RIVAL AN ENDER DRAGON IN SPEED.

Uh, giant ghost chickens that you can ride like horses? Why did I have to be born in the Overworld?! Whyyy?!?!

WEDNESDAY

This morning I encountered more people: five humans riding in a V-shaped formation. Both they and their black horses were covered in black armor, and they were riding fast. Those mounts had to be at least twice as quick as Kolb's.

The one in front spotted me, too. Was he their leader? He didn't wave, just turned back as they tore across the plains from the east to the west—from my right to my left—fifty or so blocks up ahead. Wherever they were going, they were in a big hurry. And they were serious. As if the fate of the world rested on their shoulders. The way they dressed almost reminded me of the Legion. Of Kolb. Were they part of that clan?

"Stop! Wait! Seriously, why does everyone keep running away from me?! I . . . just want someone to talk to."

WEDNESDAY—UPDATE I

In other news, I'm running low on carrots. That's the **optimistic** version. . . . In reality, I have **two carrots** left. Something just dawned on me. **It's been what—five days?** But I haven't seen many animals. I spotted **a chicken** on the first day. A **cow** on the second. But I still had a ton of carrots at that point—and a horse.

This is bad. Are animals really this **rare** in the Overworld? Are they like **diamonds** with legs? Now I can't even find 1 chicken. **Not even 1!** I wrote "1" instead of "one" to conserve my food bar. **It's less tiring.**

UPDATE: Never mind, writing in here doesn't appear to be draining my food bar. Or hunger bar. I don't even know what to call it. . . . All I know is that my stomach starts **growling** when I get down to two chicken thighs.

Actually, what was it that Max once said in class? Only **strenuous activities** affect the food bar. Therefore, once starvation creeps up on me, all I have to do is **stop moving.** My food bar won't decrease at all. I can wait days, if needed, until some pig comes along, then **boom**—a nice cooked pork chop sizzling away on an open furnace, sautéed with mushrooms, seasoned with bits of dandelion and possibly some grass torn from a grass block and sprinkled on top the way Stump decorates his cakes at . . .

Oh!
I can taste it now!

Huh? What's that? No, I'm not starving! **How could you even suggest such a thing?** A dashing **gentleswordsman** such as myself would never fall into such a desperate and sad situation! I'm just planning ahead! **Believe me!**

WEDNESDAY—UPDATE II

Tonight I read about **Ardenvell.** The largest city, also known as the **capital,** is called **Aetheria City.** It's far to the west. It sounds like **paradise.** The book speaks of magnificent white towers reaching up to the sky. It's home to some of the greatest blacksmiths in all the land. **The Knights of Aetheria,** too. It's an ancestral order that goes way back, to the time of the **Second Great War.**

Aetheria City

THURSDAY

I saw a chicken. **A chicken!**

On any other day, this wouldn't have made the news. But today, **it was everything.** I literally could have just left this entry like that—*I saw a chicken*—and it still would have been **the single most important** entry in the Overworld, the Nether, the End, the Void, the Aether, the Cleft, the Shadowlands . . . **okay, I forgot the rest.**

But I digress. Back to the chicken. **Without a bow,** I had to chase it down. I ate **my last carrot** to do so—you can't sprint when your food bar is too low. And as the furnace crackled away, with the smell of roast chicken drifting through the air, I heard **a distant cluck,** followed by another. Suddenly, it seemed like chickens were **raining from the sky.** They were fluttering around everywhere, crazily flapping their wings. One even flew into **my face.**

What's their problem? I thought. *Is there a wolf or something?*

I chased after them all, **catching six** in total. And here's where things get **weird.** (Sigh.)

I ran up to the **last one.** Sword held over my head. More than ready to turn that animal into tomorrow's lunch and hopefully one-third of an arrow. Then I . . . well, I noticed **something odd:** the chicken's feathers, instead of being mostly white, were **dark gray, sickly green,** even **yellow-brown. . . .**

I'll have you know that I, being the **thoughtful warrior** that I am, was well aware that this chicken could have been an **unknown** species or could have originated from some special biome, perhaps **the savanna to the west.** . . . Maybe chickens in savanna biomes have different-colored feathers than most—I don't know, do I look like a chicken expert? But the thing was, **this chicken,** it, um . . . well, I mean it, it kind of . . . it had no . . . **you see,** it, um . . . okay, okay, I'll just say it up front, sure, yeah, and **if you get scared,** that's totally not my fault. **Deep breath,** here goes:

This chicken, it . . . it didn't have eyes!

No, whenever someone refers to the "Eyeless One" . . . this is not who they're talking about.

It was a zombie. **A zombie chicken.** So Tucker was right! As **unbelievable** as it may seem, there really **are** zombie animals. But how could **a zombie chicken** survive in the sun? More important, why didn't **anyone** tell us about this in school? Maybe the teachers thought it was best that we didn't know; maybe they figured some of the students would just start **crying** and someone would ask, sobbing, "D-d-does that mean F-Fluffy can turn into a **z-zombie?**"

Or maybe the teachers **don't know.** Is it a new phenomenon? **Caused by what, though? Magic?** Some kind of hideous curse placed by **He Who Never Blinks?** Who could do such a thing to such a poor, **defenseless little animal?** It tried attacking me but moved much slower than an ordinary zombie, its little legs moving awkwardly, **robotically,** like a tiny golem. All I had to do was step back every now and then, no real hurry. A little flap of its wings. One step forward—no, it **stopped. Okay, there it went**—never mind, it stopped **again.** So sad. No, this couldn't go on.

"**Sorry,** chicken."

The chicken's undead state appeared to make it tougher, for it took **two swings** of my diamond sword to bring that thing down. The meat it dropped did not appear to be what one might call . . . **edible.** Besides by **a pigman named Urg,** that is. *(What? Don't look at me like that! He's the hero of this series I came across in the library: Urg the Barbarian. He'll eat anything. In the second book, he survived in the Overworld by eating a zombie's shoes.)*

*But **even Urg** wouldn't eat something like this,* I thought, staring down at the ground. Mind wandering, I left **the rotten food** where it had dropped and moved onward, **onward, forever onward . . .** over highlands and valleys, mounds and hillocks, low outcroppings of stone, and gravel, gravel—dark gray patches that were once, of course, **a very long time ago,** incredibly safe and well-traveled roads.

FRIDAY

A massive wall of cobblestone. I staggered forward, one wobbling foot in front of the other.

Voices. Distant chatter.

My jaw dropped like an anvil.
I wasn't dreaming. **It wasn't a mirage.**

(Look at those little owl banners. How cool is that? What is that, the sigil of this village? I might not know what they are, exactly, but they're cool and I want some. I'll try crafting a few when I get back.)

Owl's Reach.
I'd found it.

Without a word, the three lookouts **waved from above.** Iron blocks gave way to **gravel streets, wooden houses, and so many people**—no two of them the same. Everywhere I looked, **villagers** were bumbling about, building homes, farming crops, and trading with everyone else. **Humans, mostly.** Others **resembled that girl** I saw, with **light-gray skin and the longest ears.** Some looked **even weirder.** There was truly every kind of person imaginable.

They ranged from fairly normal looking, such as this human wizard girl . . .

"Just one more level and I'll have that spell."

From what I gather, **Owl's Reach** serves as a crossroads for **explorers** like myself. Inns and item shops abound, **catering** to all those who wished to rest and **resupply** before heading out on their next epic adventure. And the level of construction here is simply **staggering.** Roaming those streets, I soon **forgot about my quest.** I reeled around in awe, **taking everything in.** . . .

I **wasn't surprised** to hear all kinds of odd names. **ReindeerGirl. Mr. Pasta. EnderLord80000, KraftyKreeper.** As odd and **varied** as their appearances. But some had **normal-sounding** names. Harold. Alex. Jake. Rebecca. Sarah. Emma.

Anyway—seeing all those people made me recall something Kolb once said. **In that game the humans used to play,** there were these things called **skins.** A skin **altered one's appearance.** So a player could become pretty much anything. Knights. Wizards. Elves. Dwarves. Ninjas. Faeries. Princesses. **Even animal-people.** So maybe these strange people **used to be players** from that game. After all, they spoke just like the humans back home. Even so, there were times when I **couldn't quite follow** their conversations. They used **unfamiliar** words, like "**mod**" and "**server.**" Of course, there were many more I did understand. Quest. NPC. Dungeon. Loot. Boss. Armor. Stat. My time **hanging around the Legion** had paid off somewhat.

One conversation in particular caught my attention. A dark dwarf was chatting up a girl with large catlike ears.

"Man, **we really crushed that boss!**" the dwarf exclaimed. "That stone golem **didn't stand a chance!** Honestly, the dungeons around here are **way too easy!**"

"**Yeah,** well, the **patrols** are another story," Cat-Ears said. "Those pigmen are **pretty tough.** What are they looking for, anyway? Why are there so many of them in this area? Maybe we should **head back west.** I'm sick of dealing with them every time we hit **the plains.**"

(Note: She must have been talking about the monsters looking for Kolb. So he wasn't lying. He said they ambushed his clan mates before they even arrived at the Reach. But they probably aren't looking for a villager like me. Maybe that's why he sent me. . . .)

"**Aww, come on!**" the dwarf said. "Just **think of the loot,** huh? Every dungeon we've cleared so far has been **absolutely loaded!**"

I **cleared my throat** and approached the odd duo.

"**Err,** excuse me. I'm a bit lost. Do you know where I could—"

The dwarf glared at me. "What do we look like, the **Lost Legion?!** Go ask **one of them** for help!"

"In fact, **I just saw one,**" said Cat-Ears. She pointed down a sun-filled street. "I thought I saw her go into that library **over there.**" She drew closer and smiled. "**I was a noob once,** too. Don't worry, eh? You'll get the hang of it. **Here's a little tip.** The Lost Legion has **a lot of codes,** and its members must follow them at all times. One is **protecting noobs** from **trolls, griefers,** and aggressive **monsters.**

Another is offering assistance to any player who asks. So whenever you see a Legionnaire, use that to your advantage."

The dwarf laughed. "Ah, what a sight! A high-ranking member of the Boss Wizards, handing out advice like an NPC in a starting zone!"

"It's his lucky day," she said with a shrug. "I'm in a good mood." Then she fixed her gaze toward the sky, toward the dark clouds that warned of a coming storm and the distant lightning that was already flashing above the mountains. "All right," she said, "we are not going out in that. Remember last time?"

"Aye. Let's hit an inn and wait it out." The dwarf patted me on the shoulder. "Good luck, kid."

With that, the pair took off, leaving me even more confused than before. So the Lost Legion had a code of honor, huh? Seems like they forgot all about that when they first showed up at my village. And who were the Boss Wizards, anyway? I decided I'd better hit that library. If someone from the Legion was there, they'd surely help me out. Hmmm. But if they really were in the Legion, why weren't they with Kolb?

A torch lit up above my head. Library. I zoomed down the street, in the direction Cat-Ears had pointed, and spotted it immediately: *The Quill & Feather*.

It really is my lucky day, I thought, glancing at the clouds. But I didn't want to push it. I didn't feel like being turned into a witch just yet. Potion brewing is **so boring.** *Hey! Wait a minute,* I thought. *Why is it called **The Quill & Feather?** Aren't quills and feathers pretty much the same thing?*

The storm was **already raging** by the time I reached the door. That wasn't odd—that's just how it is in the Overworld. One second it's all sunshine, not a cloud in the sky, and **the next** it's pouring rain, the lightning so frequent you can only cower indoors. And **not due to thunder,** or the chance of being struck, but knowing those hills are most likely filled with enough **charged creepers** to blast through **an obsidian** door.

I burst through the library's door **like a human in Villagetown. Unfortunately,** there was only one person inside, and that person was no member of the Legion. Nor was it **Feathers.** It couldn't have been. From what Kolb told me, **Feathers was not only a librarian** also but **a wizard** who specialized in **ancient lore** and **antiquities.** Thus, I expected Feathers to be like the things he studied: ancient and dusty, with a huge white beard, bushy white eyebrows, billowing blue robes, and a gnarled staff. **You know, a cliché wizard or something.** The person who stood before me, however, was <u>**nothing of the sort.**</u>

FRIDAY—UPDATE I

Until yesterday, I thought pigmen looked weird. Upon seeing **a girl with light green skin**, thoughts of **advanced crafting tables** and saving my village once again vanished from my mind. Only **a single question** remained:

"Are you a . . . **zombie?**"

She gave me the **strangest** look. "You've never seen a **limoniad** before?" At my **obvious confusion**, she added: "**Ah.** First time **away**

from home, I take it. Well, you've come to the right place. I have a little something that just might **help you.**" She grabbed **a tome** off a nearby shelf and thrust it forward **violently,** as if she were to **knock me out** with it. "**On the house,**" she said with a smile. "You'd better brush up on your **mythology.**"

Great. As if I needed another book. With a **mental sigh,** I stared down at the red leather cover. *Races of Aetheria.*

"Oh," she said, "**I'm Feathers,** by the way."

She then gave me a lecture on how **a limoniad** is a type of **nymph** with ties to meadows—a natural being similar to elves, dryads, or faeries. Which explained her **skin color,** hair, and bracelets of woven **flower petals.** As for the people with gray skin, they're called **moon elves.** The humanoid wolves are **lupins.** I'd already figured out **dark dwarves** because I heard some people talking about them back there in the street. *(That, and I'm just really, really smart.)*

Okay, enough of this, I thought. *I'm on a quest, not some school trip.*

I glanced at the two **strange-looking** blocks nearby. Feathers had been **fiddling around** with them when I'd first entered. They didn't really look like that crafting table Kolb had shown me, but it was a solid start and **way better** than talking about faeries.

"So, what are those things?" I asked.

"**Command blocks,**" she said, turning to them. "Picked them up at an auction on the cheap. In fact, I was the only one to place a bid. No one wanted them because they seemed worthless, but I think it's only because no one knows **how to operate** them. They're over **three thousand years old!**"

Fearing another lecture, I decided to get straight to the point: "How about **an advanced crafting table?** Do you have one of those?"

"Advanced crafting table? Oh. You mean **aeon forge?**" She smiled again. "Looking to do **some real crafting,** huh? You're in luck, then. I have one for sale. **Only twenty-five hundred emeralds,** too."

My mind **overheated** when she said two things:
1.) **Only.**
2.) **Twenty-five hundred** emeralds.

I almost wanted to **inform her** of proper **trading etiquette:** when stating the price of an item, **1.)** and **2.)** may **never** be used in the same sentence.

"Is there any way you can **lower** the price? **Student discount,** perhaps?" I did my best to **look pitiful.** "It's for a **class project.** Those teachers, they said I'll never pass **Crafting VIII** until I craft **a powder keg."** I wiped away **imaginary tears. Sniffled.** "No, without that table, **I just can't go on!"**

"Sorry," she said. "The price is **not negotiable.** Do you know how in-demand those things are? **No one** knows how to craft them.

Not anymore, at least. It's a **lost art**. Which means there are a limited number of them left in the world. And every time someone carrying one slips and **falls into a pool of lava**, well, that number gets **closer to zero**.

So <u>that's</u> how it's gonna be. . . .

Summoning all my **wit**, I crafted the following response in my mind:

"I see."

That was **all I had**. Seeing all those weird people had **taken a lot out of me**. Nothing would have helped, anyway. She was **clearly proud** of her wares. I had one last idea, though.

Long story short, I **left** and **came back** minutes later with a piece of paper in my hand. I slapped that thing onto the floating carpet that served as a table. *Boom,* **boom**. (I didn't make that sound, although looking back, I should have. For dramatic effect.)

"Nice try. By the way, you spelled 'approve' wrong."

ADVANCED CRAFTING TABLE

90% OFF

REDEEMABLE AT THE QUILL & FEATHER

"MY NAME IS FEATHERS, AND I TOTALLY APROVE OF THIS COUPON."
—FEATHERS

USE SHEERS ON THE DOTTED LINE

FRIDAY—UPDATE II

I roamed the streets after leaving.
Forlorn. Wallowing in self-pity.
Rubbing my chin as I thought about my situation.

Man, my **trading** skills were useless back there! That girl was clearly a pro. **Twenty-five hundred emeralds. . . .** Do people actually walk around with **that many precious stones** in their pocket? And why did Kolb give me so few? **Was that really all he had?**

My food bar was at two. There was a villager **peddling bread** nearby, so I traded twenty-five oak blocks for five loaves. A **bad trade**, but I didn't care. *(Little did that guy know, the joke was on him: I would have traded the entire stack for one.)*

Then I hit up a nearby shop. It specialized in **arms and armor**, judging by the signs.

I don't know why I went in there.
Guess I just **needed** information.

The dwarven blacksmith didn't greet me. Actually, he flat-out **ignored** me. To him, I **didn't exist.** He clearly had a well-trained eye for **low-level emerald-pinchers** such as myself. Which was fine. I just wanted to look at the various **sets,** particularly the leather, **dyed red and enchanted with Fire Protection,** and the two full sets of **diamond.** I'd never seen armor of such quality back home.

Nor these kinds of prices: <u>**8,000 emeralds**</u> for the diamond set . . . gulp!

So it's official, I thought. *Around here, emeralds apparently* ~~grow on trees~~ —*err, drop from leaf blocks like apples.*

That was when I saw an **endersteel** breastplate. It was straight out of that book **Max** gave me. **Diamond has nothing** on armor like that. You could probably **tank an ender dragon** in that thing.

I approached this **wondrous** item, staring at it, gazing at it, studying it . . . it, and its price: **27,000 emeralds.**

This sight . . . the sight of this **masterfully crafted** item, just hanging there on that stand like some ordinary armor despite costing a fortune . . . this sight **undid the fabric of my existence.** It **destroyed** my world. My carefully crafted little universe—so sheltered, **so innocent—shattered,** just like that. I realized that my home village, the place I've lived my entire life . . . is, for lack of a better word, a **noobtown.** There was no doubt in my mind: I knew absolutely nothing of this world and **had nothing, was nothing.**

But that's good, right? Isn't that what I've always looked for, always **wanted?** There I was, a budding adventurer on the open road, surrounded by unknowns, nearly **a hundred thousand blocks** from home, five hundred emeralds to my name, and a newfound desire for more. **I stood up** straighter. Nodded to myself. I had to do this. No moping, **no crying.** My village was counting on me. Just me. **Breeze** was no longer here to hold my hand. But where would I begin? My diamond sword was worth only a small fraction of what I'd need.

<u>How could I possibly get enough to buy that table?</u>

As I stood in the armor shop, **pondering** this question in dismay, I soon found that things often have a strange way of working out. For the answer to my problems **walked right through the door.**

FRIDAY—UPDATE III

A young man, with **tattered** leather armor and **rusted** iron sword, timidly approached the counter, where he threw down **an assortment of flowers.** Blue orchids, daisies, morningcrest. Several others I didn't recognize. The blacksmith beamed **like a glowstone block.**

"**Thank you!** You don't know **how much** this means to me! Oh, it looks like I'll be able to craft that set of armor **in time for the king's birthday** after all! **What a joyous day!**"

Flowers used in a crafting recipe for armor?

I forgot about this immediately when the blacksmith threw down **a pile of emeralds** on the counter.

Whaaaaat?! My jaw weighed **a ton.** That had to be at least one hundred and fifty, or **two hundred,** no . . .

"**Two hundred fifty,**" the blacksmith said. "As promised."

Without a word, the swordsman scooped the emeralds into his belt pouch, turned around, and headed for the door. **He stopped.** Right next to me. Turned **slowly.** Stared at me. Opened his mouth. **Closed it.** Opened it and closed it again. **A cube of sweat** formed upon his brow, and he **exhaled.** If I had to describe him in a single word, it would be **"lost."** That's all I saw in his eyes. Perhaps he had only **recently arrived** in our world, **torn from his own** like all the rest. Or perhaps he hadn't yet come to terms with living here.

"**H-hey,**" he finally said.

"Hey," was my reply. "**Um** . . . I have a question." Fearing **the blacksmith** might overhear me, I glanced over my shoulder before whispering, "Why **so many emeralds** for a bunch of flowers?"

A raised eyebrow. "You . . . don't know? <u>**It was a quest.**</u>"

"Is that **like a job?**"

Another **strange** look. "Quests were one of the things included in the **last server update.**" The more he spoke, the steadier his voice became. "Most NPCs **will give you one** if you talk to them long enough. Especially in this town."

"So I just **ask them about quests?**"

"**Something** like that. Come here. I'll show you."

I trailed behind him as he approached the counter once more.

"This guy's **looking for some work,**" he said to the smith. "Do you have anything he could **help you with?**"

"Why, **yes,**" the blacksmith said. "I'm looking for some **glowmoss.** You'll find some in **a tomb** to the southwest of here. **The Tomb of the Forgotten King.** Retrieve this rare crafting ingredient, and I will pay you most handsomely: **seven hundred fifty emeralds.**"

Upon hearing this, **my heart sank** like a zombie in a waterfall. That was less than **a third** of what I needed. **However . . .**

The swordsman **nudged** me. "**Take it,**" he whispered. "Seven hundred fifty is **pretty good,** and dungeons are usually **loaded with loot.** The items you'd collect could be worth **thousands.**"

Suddenly, the zombie in my chest **chugged a Flying Potion** and was now dancing upon the clouds.

"**I accept,**" I said. "Just show me that dungeon, and **I'll show you** some glowmoss in no time."

"Glad to hear it," the blacksmith said. "**Do you have a map?** I can mark it for you." He took my map and added **the Tomb's location.**

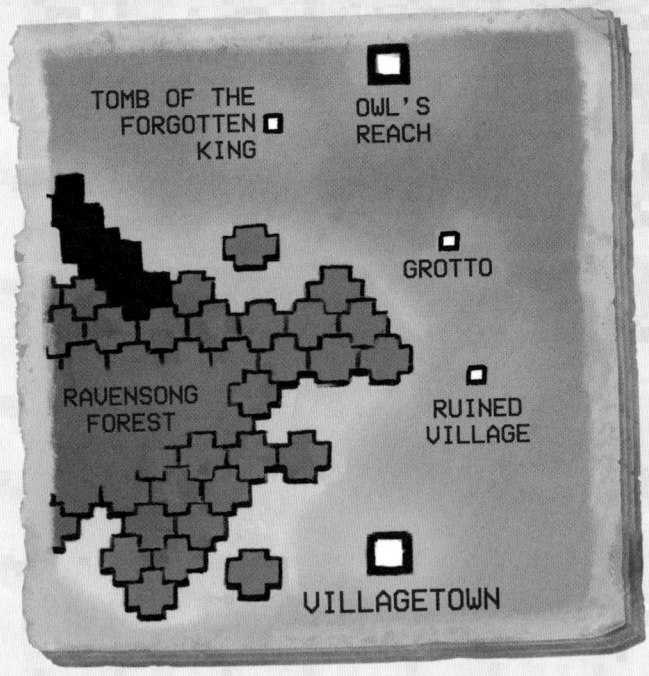

"So I just go there and retrieve **your glowmoss? That's it?**"

The blacksmith smiled. "**That's it!** An easy task for a fine young warrior like yourself! Of course, before you take off, you'll be needing this." He slid **a strange item** across the counter. "Best of luck, young man. Now, if you'll excuse me, I have **a birthday present** to craft. **Armor fit for a king!**"

I stared down at the bizarre object. I'd never seen **anything like it** before.

"What do I do **with this?**" I asked the human, whose name I still didn't know.

"Seriously? You don't know what **a key** is? **Wow.** Never thought I'd meet someone who knew **less** than I do. . . ."

And so I received **another lecture.** This time, about dungeons and keys.

"**Dungeons** were another part of the last update," he said. "They can be anything now, from your typical **underground maze** to a **small castle,** or even an **entire town.** And here's the craziest part. They can't be modified. When you're in a dungeon, **you can't mine or place anything.** Oftentimes, you need to use **a key** to open a dungeon's front door, and these keys are usually provided by NPCs. Beyond that, **monsters** sometimes drop them."

"I don't get it," I said. "**Why can't dungeons be mined?**"

"Because **the Builders** made them," he said. "If you could just run around mining everything, it would **undo** all their hard work. Plus, trolls could place **obsidian blocks** over the front doors to prevent noobs from entering. Or you could just **tunnel your way to the final boss** without first dealing with the minions, puzzles, and traps—what would be **the point?** Dungeons were built for the players to provide **challenges,** places to explore."

<u>**Whoa.**</u> Information overload.
But hey, at least he wasn't calling me an NPC.

Although I didn't understand everything he said, I got the **general idea.** In a dungeon, you have to **play by the rules.** You have to explore it the way the Builders intended. **But who are these so-called Builders?** Why would they go out of their way to create challenges for other people? So mysterious.

I must have seemed **extremely confused,** because the swordsman gave me that **funny look** again.

"I'm guessing you used to play a lot of **single-player,**" he said. "Was it your first time playing on **the Aetheria server?** You were connected, right? When the server **crashed?**"

"**Um,** well, I . . . I mean . . ."

"How'd you even **survive** this long? Have you been hiding in this city the whole time?" When I failed to respond, he followed up with **even more** questions.

"Do you even remember what happened? **The crash? The event?**"

I had **no idea** what he was talking about. It must have had something to do with what the humans back home always argued about. "**Interface**" this, "**MindLink**" that. A virtual world that had **turned real.** He thought I was one of them. A person **from Earth.**

"I kind of don't really, um . . . Err, I'm what some might call **an NPC.**"

"Oh."

What followed were **ten long seconds of silence.**

"**It's the outfit,**" he said. "I've never seen an NPC villager wear something like that, so I just assumed . . . **Yeah.** Feeling a little noob right now. Anyway, I guess it's about time **I made friends with an NPC.**"

He smiled and extended a hand.

"**My name's Eto.**"

"Runt," I said. "**Runt Ironfurnace.**"

We made small talk for a bit after that. Where I came from. Why I'm here. He'd only recently arrived from **the capital,** where he'd accepted **a quest** from some townsperson—a series of errands that had eventually sent him here. He told me how a quest can be **anything.** They're often **mundane,** like his flower-hunting quest. Other times, a single quest could involve traveling to **all four corners of the world.**

Eto stared ahead, as if looking at something **a million blocks away.**

"**Like you,** I haven't explored all that much. I only recently gathered up enough **courage** to leave **the safety** of the capital. But I met this guy a few days ago. Good guy. **Great player.** He's been exploring since day one. While most of us were **still cowering in fear,** he was setting out. The **tales** he had, of the places he's been, things he's seen . . . ships, airships, and an underground city that **puts the capital to shame.** . . . Calls himself **a treasure hunter."**

"When you say ship, you mean **boat,** right?"

"No. I'm talking about real vessels, with sails and cabins and everything. **And this guy has one.** Or so he claimed. He and some villager were eventually going to set sail and explore the ocean. And maybe **the continent to the north."**

"You mean there's **more than one continent?"**

"That's what he said."

Another. Continent. It felt like I'd been **struck by lightning** again. Except I hadn't turned into a witch . . . at least then I could have brewed a potion of some kind that would increase my intelligence enough to understand what this guy was saying. **It took seven days,** on foot, to travel a tiny little distance on that map. There could be thousands of villages on Ardenvell—and just as many towns, cities, and castles. And now some human is telling me there's **more than one continent?!**

"It's pretty **strange,** though," he said. "Despite his **accomplishments,** that guy can't even remember **his own name.** He only knows his name starts with an **S."**

"That is **pretty strange."**

"Yeah. . . ." He glanced at the door. "Speaking of friends, I have to get going. I'm supposed to meet up with someone."

"All right. I guess I should say thanks. **For everything.**"

He nodded. "And hey. If you decide to **try that dungeon,** I suggest getting someone to **tag along. Never go solo. See ya around!**"

And just like that, my new friend **took off,** leaving me with plenty of **unanswered** questions.

I couldn't stop **thinking** about what he had told me. **I envisioned** a ship sailing across **countless ocean biomes,** airships skipping across the clouds, and an underground city filled entirely with **dwarves.**

But none of that was quite **as wonderful** as <u>the small obsidian key</u> in my hand.

FRIDAY—UPDATE IV

The storm had mostly cleared by the time I left the shop. I made my way to the **village square,** since plenty of people seemed to enjoy hanging out there. I soon bumped into the cat-eared girl and loud-mouthed dwarf from earlier. They were replenishing their food bars. When I asked if they could help me out, they **spit out bits of cake.**

"**Let me get this straight,**" the dwarf said. "You want us to join you on a dungeon quest."

"That's right."

"And you've . . . never actually **been in a dungeon.**"

"**I haven't,**" I said, "but I'll do my very best! I'm a **quick learner!** I can **carry** stuff, too! Think of me as an extra inventory. **And** an extra pair of **arms.** Whenever you need a healing potion, **I'll be right there!** Potion support, **at your service!** I'll uncork those potions so fast, those zombies will think you have **ten life bars!**" I sighed. "Basically, I just . . . **really need emeralds.**"

The dwarf **chuckled.** "I'm **sure** you do, but dungeons are **no place** for noobs. I'd feel **guilty** if something happened to ya."

"I'm afraid **he's right,**" the girl with the cat ears said. "Dungeons are full of **powerful monsters.** They're much stronger than what you find in the Overworld. And they're nothing compared to **the traps.** . . . If you set one off, **that's it.** Someone will probably find **your items** on the ground a day or two later, and they'll know exactly where **not** to step."

"**Oh.** Okay. Well, um, thanks. Yeah, see you. **Good luck.**"

After they left, I stood around for a few minutes, looking for a possible companion. Surely I could find someone. But practically **nobody** was alone, and the few I approached avoided eye contact or **politely declined.**

"Dungeon? **Nope.** I'm waiting for someone."

"**Nah.** I don't do dungeons."

"Maybe **some other time.**"

My face must have revealed **a wide variety** of emotions. **Confusion. Frustration. Helplessness. Despair. Doubt.** Imagine a pigman who had been zapped by lightning **eight times** in the same week. Imagine how crazy he felt after that eighth time. Imagine his face. That was **pretty much my face.**

It was beginning to feel like everything I'd learned in school was useless. **At least out here.** The Overworld is totally different from what I'd read about, thought about, and dreamed about all this time. **A noob.** I've really become a noob **all over again.** Which wouldn't be so bad, if I didn't have to be a noob by myself. . . . They say misery loves company; well, noobishness loves company, too.

On top of that, my luck was **running out.** I became acutely aware of this when I heard a deep grunt, like a monstrous pig, directly behind me.

I slowly turned around.

FRIDAY—UPDATE V

"**You!** Villager! **Ogre dare!**"

(Ogre dare? Um, I think he meant over there.)

Far off, past a hundred or so other people chatting away, a **pigman** was approaching. A pigman in **black leather armor** covered in **crude iron spikes.** I knew it must've been one of **the monsters hunting** Kolb, so I turned away and started **walking.** Until I felt **a hand** upon my shoulder. I **whirled around** to face **beady black eyes** and a square pink nose. And breath so **hideous** it probably could have broken though **netherrack.**

"**Hey!**" the pigman said. "**I was talking to you!**"

"You were? **Are you sure?** I thought I heard you calling for some villager."

"Is that not what you are?"

I looked down at myself. "Do I **look** like a villager to you? Do you see a robe?"

"**No,** but your . . ." He pointed to his nose. "**Enough!** I am **Reh,** servant of the **great and powerful god-king** known as **the Eyeless One,** the **Forever Eternal,** the **One True** Wizard, He Who . . ." He **paused,** as though he'd forgotten the rest, then **grunted** angrily. "You are to come with me to **Stormgarden Keep** for questioning!"

God-king? So that's what they call him, huh? Yeah, and what about this guy's name? His name is Reh? That's not a monster name. All things considered, he's lucky I'm such a nice guy. A less composed warrior would have already attacked this ridiculously named pigman as a matter of principle!

"First of all," I said, "**that's an amazing title.** Really. God-king, **One True Wizard** . . . just wow. Admittedly, **'Forever Eternal'** is a bit **redundant,** but still, it does have a certain ring to it. Anyway, I'd love to go with you, **I would,** but . . . it really depends."

"On what?"

"Well . . . during the **interrogation,** will you be serving milk and cookies?"

He grumbled and drew **his obsidian sword.** He didn't like milk and cookies! **What sacrilege!** And here I thought we could be friends!

Suddenly, I heard **Kolb's voice** in my mind. A speech he once gave to his fellow clan members:

You are members of the Lost Legion! **You are OP!** *The* **hardest** *of the hard core! The bravest souls in all the land! Walking tanks destined to* **crush** *the armies of He Who Would Never Wear Sunglasses! Without fear!* **Without mercy!**

I drew my sword with the **glass-like ring** of diamond.

An **epic battle** ensued. All you could hear were the sounds of our swords clashing against each other over and over, along with pig-like grunts and shouts from the surrounding people, more and more of whom were gathering by the second now, asking one another:

"Am I **seeing this right?** Are those **two NPCs** fighting?"

I blocked **so many** of my opponent's attacks. I'd been working on my block moves **for weeks.** Now, one nanosecond after that sword came flying at me, I put up my own to the clash of diamond on obsidian. It was kind of **boring.**

I blocked. He blocked. I blocked. He blocked. Okay, **cool**—he didn't block. I only had to **repeat this** thirty or so times to inch his life bar down, half a heart at a time, until it was nothing but a line of **empty hearts.**

That's right.

I, being the **noble and talented gentleswordsman** that I am—possessing far superior wit and consummate skill at arms—**rid the world** of this foul, netherrack-wilting **stench.**

The humanoid pig sank with a low, sad moan. "**Urggguuu!**"

I returned my sword to its **scabbard** before he hit the ground. *(A total pro move, by the way. I heard a farmer let out a little gasp. At least one person was impressed!)*

Glowing **experience orbs** flew toward me, and I felt the familiar rush of **XP** gain. An eerie silence lingered. The monster **dissolved** into a cloud of smoke. The onlookers begain rambling to one another. Many of them **were armed.** Adventurers, **explorers . . .**

Couldn't they have **helped me out?!**

"What's happening?" someone asked.

"Is this part of a quest event?" asked someone else.

"Maybe it is," said a third. "I say we stick around and find out!"

But they weren't asking the right questions.
Where's the pigman's **armor?**
<u>**And his sword?**</u>

His items had evaporated into nothingness, like the pigman himself. **Pretty rude.** Aspiring evil wizards, **take note:** If you're going to send your **minions** after someone, make sure they don't drop **any items.** This way, if your underlings fail, the person you're after won't have anything to show for it. They'll just be wasting time. So **the Eyeless One** really is as terrible as they say . . . more like **Heartless One!** That pigman could have **at least** dropped an emerald or something!

Moments later, **five more pigmen** charged from the crowd and surrounded me, **swords drawn.** All right, I admit it: at this point, I was definitely contemplating going with them. Even if they weren't serving milk and cookies, surrendering would at least mean **living** to enjoy milk and cookies another day.

"Hey, guys." My gaze swept across so many square pink faces. "**How are you?** About that interrogation. I—"

Suddenly, I heard the **sound of hooves** on gravel. They were approaching **fast.** I struggled to get a better look across the crowd, but I couldn't see past the hats and helmets and ridiculous hairstyles.

At last, I saw her. Breeze rode into view confidently, gracefully, as though she'd been riding **all her life.**

As though she **belonged** out here.
As though there was
no better place for her to be.

"Thought you might need some help."

She leapt from her horse and drew **two blades**, one in each hand. It was then that I noticed the faint, colorful motes **swirling in the air** around her—the visual effects of **multiple potions**. But I was far more **shocked** by her expression: her face showed **anger** instead of its usual **sweetness and innocence.**

The pigmen slowly **turned toward her,** grunting. They had no idea what was in store for them. If they had, they would've thrown down their weapons on the spot and **denounced their beloved "god-king."**

"Herobrine?!" they would've said. "What are you talking about?! Is that **some kind of pickle?!**"

Instead, two of them **pointed at her** and bent over, clutching their stomachs. **They were laughing.**

That's one of Breeze's strengths. **Pebble** once said that, after class. They'd been assigned as dueling partners. The duel started with him turning back to his friends and **smirking.** It ended with him facedown **in the mud.** You'd never think a wooden sword could be **so dangerous** until you saw one in her hands.

All right, I take back what I said about that first battle. **This one was truly** epic. The way we moved **together,** swords **flashing . . .** it was something out of a fairy tale. And it felt just like the old days, when we had fought back to back, uncertain whether we would **survive.** We took them down one by one, until there weren't any monsters left— only gravel and cobblestone. And a sea of people **cheering.**

"After this," someone said, "maybe those pigmen will finally **leave us alone.**"

"**Yeah,**" said another, "but it's strange to see NPCs handling things. It really must be some kind of **quest event.** Maybe **a secret one.** Let's hang around this village for a little longer, huh?"

And in the middle of them all were **two villagers** named **Breeze and Runt.** I still **couldn't believe** she was here.

"How did you **find** me?" I asked.

"The mayor told me **everything,**" she said. "They were keeping it **a secret.**"

So Kolb must have told the council, I thought. And the council decided to **keep the mission a secret?** They probably wanted to avoid widespread chaos. Knowing villagers, they would have definitely **panicked.**

"I'm **really** glad to see you," I said.

"**Me too.**" She gave me a **hug.** "So . . . what happened?"

"**Long story** on that. In short, I'm on **a quest,** and we're going to a dungeon."

"A dungeon?"

"I'll tell you on the way. First, we need to buy **some supplies.** C'mon. Most of the shops are that way."

She grabbed me by the shoulder.

"My horse is over there."

"**Oh.**" I grimaced.

*How **embarrassing**. I hope she doesn't ask about . . .*

"By the way," she said, "**where's Meadow?**"

"Who's Meadow?"

"Um, Kolb's horse? A **rare** charger with an **enchanted saddle?**"

*Charger? Is that a type of horse? Well, that horse didn't look so special to me. And was that saddle really **enchanted**? It had felt really comfortable, like sitting on a block of feathers.*

Another grimace.

. . . Embarrassing.

FRIDAY—UPDATE VI

Atop Breeze's gilded horse, **Shybiss,** we set out to do some trading. I needed **armor** and **potions,** after all, and both of us needed more **food.** At least one shopkeeper was about to have **a good day.**

I went over **everything** I'd experienced and learned so far. My **strange** encounters on the road. **Feathers.** The **absurd** price of an advanced crafting table. **The absurd price of everything.** What that human had told me about quests, dungeons, and keys. As for **Villagetown,** it was just as **I'd thought:** the mayor had told everyone that I was **in trouble** and that I wouldn't be seen again until I was done filling **five double chests** with potato-based food items. Okay, so I didn't expect **that,** exactly, but I did call that he would lie to avoid a **total panic.**

"What am I supposedly **being punished** for?" I asked.

"The paper."

"The paper? **Oh. Yeah.** The paper."

I'd forgotten all about that paper. We were supposed to write **twenty pages** on why we'd chosen our **profession.** It was due the very same morning I'd set out. Of course, I, being **the studious warrior-scholar** that I am, finished writing that paper. The night I left, just before falling asleep, I filled each of those twenty pages with **one single, massive word—or letter.** Well, the last two pages were drawings. One of the monsters' forest **burning,** another of a zombie **crying.** But still, **twenty pages.**

"Of course, I couldn't help feeling that **something** was wrong," Breeze said. "It was **odd.** Why would they **lock you up in a house** for that? I didn't learn **the truth** until two days ago, when I overheard Kolb speaking to **the mayor and my father.** I stormed up to them and demanded the truth. They **told me everything** and sent me to go find you. Said you **should have been back** by now."

"Yeah? How was I supposed to know **horses just run off** like that?" I sighed. "Okay, what about **the others?** Is anyone else coming?"

"**No.** I'm the only one who knows. **They're all training.** Exploring. We've already spent **several nights** outside. Some of the humans made **watchtowers. Beacons,** they call them. Also . . ."

Breeze told me how she'd **traded** for some new items for her journey. **The outfit** she was wearing now. A **black wool** tunic, black wool skirt, and black leather boots. The wool provided as much armor as leather, but it gave **bonuses to stealth and speed.** The boots had similar stats, as well as a bonus to **jump height.** Such bonuses suited her, since Breeze was the type who cherished **mobility.** That was her style, a style she employed **to full effect.**

"I also traded for this," she said, drawing an **emerald sword** from its scabbard. That was one of the swords she'd **wielded earlier,** but I hadn't noticed the **color.** It looked just like a diamond sword, only **brilliant green.**

"It's a bit **better** than diamond," she said. "**Same average damage** but with a slightly **faster** attack speed." She glanced back at me and **smiled**. "After making friends with a few human girls, I found they have **a lot** of interesting items like this."

"How about **those arrows?**" I asked. "Did you trade for those, too?"

"No. **Sophia** and **Talia** gave them to me. I almost **declined** but figured **weakness arrows** could come in handy out here."

"**Huh.** Where'd they find all that stuff?"

"**Dungeons,** I guess. Before they arrived at Villagetown."

"That's **good to know.** Hopefully the one we're going to will be **filled** with items like that. We really need an **equipment upgrade.** Those pigmen were—"

Breeze **stirred** in the saddle. "What's that?"

I followed **her gaze** to a building that resembled **a temple.** It seemed to be constructed entirely of **white quartz.**

At first, I thought it was **a church** of some kind. Breeze did, too. A sign above the door read: **"Temple of Entity."** Another sign read: **"Donation Pit Inside."** I had no idea what a **donation** pit was, but I knew it had something to do with **charity.** As in, giving things away. **Offerings** for the poor. And guess who was currently **the poorest person** in Owl's Reach? Surely they could **spare** a handful of emeralds for this **humble peasant.**

"Should we check it out?" Breeze asked.

"I think that's **an excellent idea,**" I said, glancing at the sign once more.

In my mind, it no longer read "Donation Pit" but <u>**"Free Cool Stuff."**</u>

"Yes, **excellent** idea."

FRIDAY—UPDATE VII

Austere. Majestic. Breathtaking.

The Temple of Entity was all these things **and more.** The double spruce doors gave way to a **vast** chamber filled with sunlight and opalescent stained glass. I couldn't stop asking myself how such a thing could be built, with **chiseled quartz columns** towering far above to a lofty ceiling. What kind of **scaffolding** had been used? Dirt blocks?

Red carpet stretched between countless ancient pews, and far away, on either wall, were **vast murals** of **legendary battles.** One mural depicted an **army of knights** against **monstrous hordes,** rays of light descending from the heavens, and **fires** erupting from below. Farther inside, the windows ended, and redstone torches served as the only light source. Many of these torches surrounded **a black altar,** a **massive slab of obsidian** whose surfaces were sculpted with various reliefs.

Breeze stepped in first, her footsteps **echoing.** Mine were noticeably **louder.** We stared at every mural, every statue, and every etched relief. The farther we ventured inside, the darker it became, until it was **almost gloomy.**

We stopped before **a statue** of a robed man with **two pairs of feathery wings.** There was no face under the hood of the robe, and he held a weapon that I can only describe as a **farming tool,** except **much larger** than any I'd seen.

"The White Shepherd," Breeze said softly, running her fingers across the statue's arm.

"Entity."

". . ."

Entity. . . . He was a character in a **fairy tale,** wasn't he? Yes, my mom used to read me that story when I was **little.** Back when all we had to worry about was our **harvest.** He was a **godlike** figure, an **Immortal,** who lived during the time of the **Second Great War.** The world was nearly torn apart then, and when things grew worse, Entity crafted **twelve weapons of indescribable power** and chose **twelve heroes** to wield them. With them, the world had a fighting **chance.**

"What **happened** during that final battle?" I asked. "I forget how it went. **Both sides** fell, didn't they?"

"The knights managed to **destroy the Eyeless One,**" she said, "although not completely. **They fell** to his minions afterward, vastly outnumbered. They **sacrificed** themselves. Their weapons were then **destroyed**—shattered—yet they survived . . . in some form. **Fragments.** Those knights were to be reborn someday, in order to restore their original weapons and help save the world. **For good,** this time."

"You sure know your **fairy tales.**" I glanced around the temple once more and felt **a little chill.** "Looks like they take them pretty **seriously** around here, huh?"

Her expression suddenly grew **dark.** Or had she been that way ever since we'd approached this statue? Perhaps there was **some truth** to the legend. Maybe a bunch of knights really did end up fighting some **evil** wizard with weapons of **divine** origin. And maybe Entity really did exist, so very long ago. Did any of that matter now?

Hey, what is that?

Eyes **lighting up,** I pointed to a doorway.

"Now there's something I can believe in!"

According to the sign, the door led to **the donation pit.** Call me **disrespectful,** but I practically started **running.** The doorway led to a much smaller chamber, and the donation pit was . . . never mind. **Forget it.** I'm just going to **draw** a picture. Because no words could capture the sheer **amazingness** of what I was seeing.

FRIDAY—UPDATE VIII

Items. **A pool of them,** one block deep. The majority of them **were gold,** but I spotted several pieces of **enchanted leather and iron armor.** A **diamond** sword. Saddles. Potions. Even accessories such as belts, rings, bracelets. . . . I leapt in and **rummaged** around like a dragon wallowing in its **treasure hoard.**

Giddy with delight, I picked up an iron breastplate. **Free!** And an extra diamond sword—**free!** And look at those potions, just waiting to be **chugged!** Why would one go to a shop to trade for items when they could just come **here?!**

Hold on. Hollllllld on. Hold on like a noob holding on to a ladder over a lava pit. This doesn't make any sense. People clearly left all this great stuff here, **but why?**

My smile **faded** bit by bit. Indeed, this piece of armor, shimmering faintly with a soft **violet** light, contained a low-level enchantment. But the enchantment was one I'd never heard of before, and it didn't **sound** like much of an enchantment **at all.**

I turned to Breeze. "**Burden II . . . ?** What is that?"

"It decreases your **attack speed** and **movement speed**," she said. "By 33%, I think."

"Decreases . . . **not increases?**"

She nodded. "A **negative** enchantment. Otherwise known as **a curse.**"

"But who . . . **why** . . . how can such a thing be possible?! I've never heard of **negative enchantments!**"

"That's because you **never spent much time** at an enchanting table," she said, wading up to me. "It happens sometimes. For whatever reason, **an enchanting attempt fails,** and . . ."

No, I thought, *this can't be right.* Then it started to dawn on me, and I examined the items in the **gleaming, glittering** mountain.

Everything here was indeed enchanted, from saddles to horse armor to the most beautiful of golden rings. . . . But each of those enchantments had names like "Dullness," "Breaking," or "**Vulnerability.**"

"Dullness **reduces** a weapon's damage," Breeze said. "Breaking multiplies **durability loss.** And Vulnerability **reduces** an armor's protective value."

"What about this one?" I asked, holding up a diamond sword with **Unblocking V.**

"That reduces the effectiveness of blocking," she said. "I think level V is **100% reduction.** So blocking with it wouldn't reduce damage **at all.**"

"**Whoa!** That definitely doesn't meet my standards of item quality."

I **casually** tossed that sword over my shoulder and retrieved another sword—iron, with **Lifedrain III.**

"And this?" I asked.

"Lifedrain? Let's see . . . I think that **damages you over time.**"

"**Frozen Nether!**" I dropped that sword as if it were a miniature creeper ready to explode.

"And **don't even touch** that one," Breeze said. She pointed at an iron sword with her foot. It had **Binding II.** "If you equip something that has **Binding,** you **can't remove it** unless you use a specific potion."

"Yeah, I get it now," I said, glancing around **in despair.** "That's why everyone **left this stuff** here. We're standing in a **trash pile.**"

"Not exactly," Breeze said. "Many of these items would be of use to someone with nothing at all. An iron sword with Dullness I is **still better** than a normal wooden sword."

"How do you explain all the stuff with Binding and Lifedrain, then? And that dead bush? **Trolls? Griefers?**"

"Most likely." Scanning the items once more, she bent down and picked up a necklace. "**Nice.** I guess **not everything** here is bad."

A necklace, huh. . . .

Like bracelets, necklaces fall under the class of items known as **accessories.** Many different types of accessories can be worn at the same time. It's sort of like **a second set** of armor. It includes one belt, two rings, two bracelets, and one necklace.

FAERIE CHARM
ACCESSORY
REGENERATION I

The effect it gave was **small. Regeneration I,** when applied to a piece of armor or an accessory, doesn't heal **very much** over time, as each level of Regeneration is approximately 10% of a person's natural healing rate. Still, **it was free**—and better than **nothing**. She must have arrived at the same conclusion, because she equipped **the faerie charm**—or rather, wore it around her neck.

At this discovery, and perhaps **a little jealous** of her find, I began sifting through the items again. I **desperately needed** armor. "Breaking III, Slowness VI . . . **oh!** Here's one with every single negative enchantment I've seen so far. Hmm. How about this . . . ? Yeah, this one isn't so bad."

I picked up **an iron breastplate**. Strangely, it had either been **renamed** or had been generated with the following name: **Tarnished Breastplate**. It was covered in spots of brown rust, and **it only had Burden I**, which, according to Breeze, reduced attack speed and movement speed by only **10%**.

I stress "**only**"
because everything else was **worse**.

In the end, I wound up with a **matching** set of **Burden I** armor. Some leggings and a pair of boots, anyway—all **covered in rust**. Next, I examined all the shields. The best had **Unblocking I, a 20% reduction** in blocking effectiveness. That wasn't **the worst** thing in the world. It wasn't even the worst thing about the shield. It had an **owl sigil** on the front that wasn't exactly intimidating. How was I supposed to **scare monsters** with a giant owl on my shield?

"**Whatever,**" I muttered to myself, strapping it on.

Finally, a gray cap with a white feather replaced the outlandish **red-and-purple thing** I'd been wearing. **Moldy Cap.** What a name! But **the look** it gave: the white feather provided a gentle accent to the grays of my armor, a smooth flow of color, **subtle.** And the bits of **green mold** really brought out the color of **my eyes. Just kidding.** What do you think this is, **Celebrity Villager** or something? I only cared about the +1 armor **bonus.**

Wait. What's this **Resilience I** enchantment?

Breeze **noticed** it as well. "**Nice find.** Each level of Resilience reduces damage taken from **critical hits** by 5%."

"You mean the damage **I take?**"

"Yes. It's **not** a negative enchantment."

"Thank you, **teacher.**"

Thoroughly **pleased** at this news, I inspected myself.

I almost felt like **a real warrior.**
A low-level one, surely,
but a **warrior** nonetheless.

TARNISHED BREASTPLATE
+5 ARMOR
BURDEN I

DIAMOND SWORD
ATTACK SPEED 1.6
AVERAGE DAMAGE 7
UNBREAKING I

MOLDY CAP
+1 ARMOR
RESILIENCE I

VEIL OF THE VICTORIOUS
SUREFOOTED II
SAFEGUARD I
(+1 UNKNOWN MODIFIER)

TARNISHED LEGGINGS
+4 ARMOR
BURDEN I

TARNISHED BOOTS
+2 ARMOR
BURDEN I

OWL'S REACH BUCKLER
+1 ARMOR
UNBLOCKING I

Look out, monsters! Momma didn't raise no noob.

Breeze **giggled.** "You know, if you swapped that shield for **a red one,** you could almost pass for **a Legionnaire.**"

"**Yeah?** Too bad I'll never be able to join them."

"**Why not?**"

"I asked Kolb like **five times** already. And Kaeleb. And ObsidianDude. Everyone I asked said **the Legion** has **strict requirements.** You have to be a **human.**"

"**Maybe they'll change** that in the future."

"Maybe."

Scanning the items once more, Breeze picked up a belt made of **iron cubes.** It was the only other **accessory** that had **positive enchantments.** The rest had curses or **nothing at all,** offering no benefit beyond **style.**

She offered **the belt** to me. "You want it?"

"No, **it's fine.** I think I'm set. Besides, you need some armor, too."

With a brief **nod,** she threw the belt around her waist. "**All right,**" she said. "Guess I'm good to go. **Oh, hmm.**" She picked up **a green circlet** and threw it on as well. "**There.** How do I look?"

EMERALD SWORD
ATTACK SPEED 1.5
AVERAGE DAMAGE 7
UNBREAKING I

DIAMOND SWORD
ATTACK SPEED 1.6
AVERAGE DAMAGE 7
UNBREAKING I

ARROWS OF WEAKNESS
DEBUFF 30 SEC
−4 ATTACK DAMAGE

FAERIE CHARM
REGENERATION I

ZEPHYR BOOTS
+2 ARMOR
LEAPING I
STEALTH I
SWIFTNESS II
FEATHER FALLING I

IVY CIRCLET
+1 ARMOR
REGENERATION I

NIGHTSONG TUNIC
+3 ARMOR
STEALTH I
SWIFTNESS I
THORNS II

NIGHTSONG SKIRT
+2 ARMOR
STEALTH I
SWIFTNESS I

OPAL CHAIN BELT
+1 ARMOR
FIRE RESISTANCE I

VEIL OF THE VICTORIOUS
SUREFOOTED II
SAFEGUARD I
1 (UNKNOWN MODIFIER)

> Okay, those boots are OP. I really need to trade with Kaeleb when I get back.

"**Fabulous**," I said. "A true **dungeoneer**."

Of course, looking at the stats of our **many items** might seem **overwhelming**. But to the **experienced**, it was like reading another language, which translated into:

I'd **sacrificed** the ability to move and attack quickly in return for **a strong defense**. With a shield capable of blocking most **frontal** attacks, I could withstand an incredible amount of punishment. In short, I was set up to be a great **frontline combatant. A wall.** Even so, a **10%** reduction to attack speed **didn't mean** my diamond sword was worthless.

Meanwhile, Breeze had chosen **another strategy: high mobility.** If injured, she could easily **retreat**, switch to **her bow**, and attack from a distance while slowly **healing** from her Regeneration effects. And if we encountered a particularly dangerous threat, her **weakness arrows** would reduce its damage. Combined with my high armor, damage could be **cut by half** or more.

"Looks like most of the potions are just **poisons**," Breeze said. "Trolls have been **hard at work** here. They're not entirely **useless**, though. We could turn them into splash potions. All we need is some **gunpowder**."

"**Good idea**," I said, and helped her collect the bottles. "Y'know, if **Emerald** were here right now, I know exactly what she'd say. She'd suggest we haul this stuff to the nearest trader and try selling everything for **one emerald each**."

"I highly doubt anyone would pay even one emerald for half these items," Breeze said. "And who knows what might happen if someone caught us? I'm pretty sure this donation pit isn't meant to be **raided** like this. Besides, that isn't what she'd say."

"**Oh?** What would she say, then?"

"She'd say it's **time to go shopping,** I mean. And she'd show us this." Breeze held up **a stack of emeralds.**

"What?! Where'd you get that?"

"I asked Emerald for **a loan.** Didn't say what for, of course."

"And she agreed, **just like that?** How much did she give you?"

"**One hundred fifty.** And Kolb gave me **another hundred.** I know he had to trade away most of his stuff to do so. Including **his other horse.**"

Whaaaaat?! His other horse?!

Oh, **this is bad! Really bad!** Kolb is going to be so angry. I don't even want to go back home! Okay, there has to be way out of this. Think. **Think!**

Maybe I can just buy him a new horse? **Yeah!** And when he asks why **"Meadow"** looks different, I'll just say that I . . . **um** . . . enchanted her fur? **How genius is that?!**

"Come on," Breeze said. She was standing in the doorway by now. "I know I'm going to sound like Emerald when I say this, but . . . shopping is actually **kinda fun.**"

FRIDAY—UPDATE IX

Moomoo Alpha's **Survival Shop**

A **strange energetic music** came from a jukebox in the corner of the room. There were so many enchanted items behind the counter that **the wall glowed.**

Moomoo, the dwarven shopkeeper, flashed **a wide grin.** He gave us a line that seemed straight out of a **shopkeeper manual:**

"Go on, **treat yourself!**"

Then another:

"See anything **ya like?**"

I swear. . . . Was there anything on that wall someone wouldn't mind having? There was a diamond sword with **Unbreaking V.** A **gold** breastplate with so many enchantments it actually **surpassed diamond** in value. **A leash** for monsters. A bed that gave **a strength buff** for an entire day. Even an **enchanted name tag.**

Yet one of the **most ordinary** items caught my eye. A simple **potion of Healing I.** We needed **as many** as we could get. Sadly, with **582 emeralds** between us, and each healing potion costing **twenty-five** . . .

"Twenty-five emeralds," I muttered. "We could get them for **five** back home."

"Maybe we should go somewhere else," Breeze said.

She said this openly, **so the shopkeeper would hear.** I played along:

"**Oh, that's right.** That other guy was selling them for **fifteen,** wasn't he?"

"**Ten, I think.** Or was it nine?" She tilted her head **thoughtfully,** eyes to the side, one finger on her chin.

Yeah, that **Moomoo** should've been **sweating ghast tears.** But he didn't look **nervous.** Still, I figured that was just an act. Yeah, what do you think about that, bud—two real traders just rolled into your fancy little shop.

Here's the thing, though: **it wasn't an act.**

"I believe **you two are mistaken**," he said with a slight grin, "for every major shop in Owl's Reach follows the **Aetherian Item Index.** This Index is a list compiled in the capital annually and used as **a strict guideline** for determining the base value of an item. Accordingly, you'll find most common items going for the same price **everywhere.** Of course, you are more than welcome to take a look at our town's many other fine establishments. I'm sure you'll find my statement **accurate.**"

Breeze and I exchanged glances. The look on my face was probably a cross between "What did he just say?" and "**That means we can't haggle him down, right?**"

Meanwhile, her face said: "**Don't worry. We've got this.**"

"Then we'll take **fifteen bottles**," she said, winking at me. Those were **one emerald each.**

With a **slight nod,** Moomoo retrieved the bottles from an ender chest and placed them onto the counter. "Anything else, **young lady?**"

"**Nether wart,**" she said. "An equal number."

Three emeralds each. I **realized** where she was going with this. Nether wart was required to craft a **base potion.** A base potion was like the foundation for almost every other potion. We were going to brew **our own healing potions** to save money. Even without haggling, Breeze had found a way around the **absurd** prices of that smug little dwarf.

He realized this as well.

"I guess you'll be needing some **melons** and **gold nuggets**," he said, "as those are the ingredients for a healing potion. **Unfortunately,** I am out of stock for both. I've been receiving **many adventurers** lately who've been looking to do their own brewing. **It's the strangest thing.**"

"Do you know where we might find some?" Breeze asked.

We were treated to **another smile** from Moomoo. "I'd say your best bet would be asking other adventurers. You'll most likely find some with **a surplus** of ingredients to trade. You might try an inn. There's a big one just down the street. **The Enchanted Dragon.** Can't miss it."

"Thanks a lot," Breeze said. "Oh, we need **gunpowder,** too."

She answered my question before I could ask: "We can use gunpowder to make **splash potions,** remember? Splash healing potions are useful because they heal in an **area of effect,** or **AoE.**"

"You mean **a single potion** can heal **both of us** with its splash?" I asked.

She nodded. "**As long as we're close together.** We just throw them at our feet. On top of that, it's **faster** than drinking one. I believe the healing effect would **wound** any nearby undead as well. And all it will take is a pinch of **gunpowder.**"

"**Amazing,**" I said. "Although, I don't recall ever learning this in school. Did **your dad** teach you this stuff?"

"Nope. **Lola.**"

"I might have known."

Thanks, Lola. Even though you aren't here, it's as if . . .

I went over **the numbers** with Breeze. If we wanted to craft **fifteen splash healing potions,** we needed **fifteen bottles** at ◆ 1 each, **fifteen pieces of nether wart** at ◆ 3 each and **fifteen handfuls of gunpowder,** also at ◆ 3.

◆ 15 + ◆ 45 + ◆ 45 – **a total of** ◆ **105.**

The shopkeeper told us that **a gold nugget** goes for around ◆ 2, a **slice of melon** ◆ 1. We needed eight nuggets and one slice of melon per potion.

In short, we determined that it would cost roughly ◆ **360** for fifteen splash healing potions. **The alternative** would be spending ◆ 375 on fifteen **normal** healing potions, without the AoE effect.

"**Booyah!**" I said to Breeze.

The dwarf looked **a little annoyed.**

"**Yes,** you can surely craft your own healing potions," he said, "and you'll save some emeralds. But if you buy from me, you'll save something **far more valuable: time** and **energy.** Both of you are clearly **tired.** Why would you complicate things? Buy my healing potions, and spend **the rest of your night relaxing.**" He patted one of his ender chests. "I have three stacks right in here."

"No thanks," I said. "**We're good.**"

"We'll have **at least two hundred left over,**" Breeze said. "Anything else we need?"

"How about **that bracelet?**" I said. An iron bracelet with **Regeneration I.** "It's only fifty-five."

Breeze pointed at an item frame containing **a stone bracelet.** "**How about that one?** It gives one point of **armor.**"

"**Hmm . . .** It's a bit cheaper, too. I wonder **what's better?** Regeneration I or another point of armor?"

"I'm not sure. . . ."

"Anyway, what about yourself? Check **that ring with Swiftness I.** It's one hundred fifty, but we have plenty to spare, **right?**"

Breeze looked **deep** in thought. "It's good. I like **that one** better, though." She pointed to a **wooden ring** with **Strength I.** It cost seventy-five. With that equipped, she'd do slightly **more damage.** "Oh, wait. Look at that ring. It has both **Swiftness and Strength,** but it costs one hundred fifty."

"That's fine," I said. "I can get the stone bracelet."

"**No,** I couldn't do that," she said. "My items are already **better** than yours."

"Then we'll spend an **equal** amount," I said. "**One hundred each?**" She smiled. "**Yeah.**"

I **realized** you **can't call yourself** an adventurer until you've had **the full** item-shop experience. Count your emeralds. What's the best way **to spend** them? The best **bang for your buck?** Well, this item is good, but is it worth buying over that? Or how about **this** and **this?**

Well, those are the price of this, which is **better** than this, and you could buy **two of those** for the price of this and this. . . .

"Hmmm . . ."

The choice was **difficult.** The eternal search for **the perfect upgrades.** Maybe it's a sword that offers **a slight** increase in damage output, or maybe it's that one last point of armor you so desperately need. Or maybe it's a few potions to give you **an edge** in the next battle. No matter the price, you want **that little bit** extra. . . .

The shopkeeper kept **grinning** at us while Breeze and I debated several more possible buys, arguing and joking and calculating. He kept smiling as he offered to show us **more of his wares,** and the jukebox continually blaring that **strange music**—a style called **8-bit,** I'd later learn.

These kinds of experiences are what any adventurer **cherishes.** The **innocent little moments** of being a carefree **noob.**

Right then, I was fine with being one again.
As long as she was by my side.

"Pleasure doing business with y—"

"We'll take that wooden ring as well."

"Pl—"

"And don't forget our brewing ingredients!"

"... Come back anytime."

"And try **that inn I mentioned**," he said. "It has a few rooms with **brewing stands**."

"Do the rooms have **cauldrons,** too?" Breeze asked. "Buckets? Furnaces? I'd trade anything for a **nice warm bath**."

"**Of course**," he said, taken aback by this question. "**The Enchanted Dragon** is one of **the best** inns in the entire world. Be sure to try the **mutton.** It's practically enchanted with **Tastiness VII**."

"Will do," she said.

With **a single sweep** of her arms, she picked up all three piles of ingredients, then **lost her balance** and almost fell into me.

"Um, can you help me out? My inventory's kinda full."

FRIDAY—UPDATE X

Just after **the sun went down,** we stood before a **massive** building made of oak and dark oak, spruce and cobblestone, and hardened white clay. Panes of **glowstone glass** held the silhouettes of many **jovial** patrons, while **cheery medieval melodies** drifted through the air.

<u>The Enchanted Dragon.</u>

That was the name of this den of noobs, and to its doors **we sauntered** up. **Well,** more like hobbled, really. It had been a long day. Check **the number of updates** today if you don't believe me.

Ah, yes. An inn. How could **anyone** call themselves an adventurer without ever visiting this most **famous** of traveler hangouts? I'll never forget walking into an inn for the very first time.

Woof: The smoke from the torches **hits you** first, followed by the smell of mutton **sizzling** on a furnace, then the sound of **over two hundred voices,** overpowering now that you're inside. People **everywhere,** heads **thrown back** in laughter, with brightly **colored hair** and **long ears,** or with helmets and wizard's caps, or with **huge** beards hanging over mouths filled with **square yellow teeth.**

In the very back, there were several **mysterious figures** quietly sipping their enchanted drinks, faces concealed by the shadows of their hoods, and **one shady-looking man,** probably a rogue or treasure hunter, carving something into a table with a dagger. And even farther back, a human, **an elf,** and another **human-like** girl—except with **fox ears** and a bushy red tail—danced next to a group of **singing pigmen.** One of them was playing **some kind of** stringed musical **instrument,** while to either side a group of knights in iron armor **cheered them on,** mugs raised, **toasting. . . .**

This was what I experienced in **the first few seconds,** and all of it hit me **like a rapidly approaching wall.** Breeze, too. She looked rather **overwhelmed.** We found a table and **sat down** to order some warm food. As if our senses weren't **flooded** enough, our waitress was dressed in **the weirdest-looking outfit** I'd ever seen.

"What'll it be?" she asked.

"**Mutton,**" Breeze said, "and a baked potato. **No.** Two baked potatoes. **And a loaf of bread.**"

The waitress **squeezed** her shoulder. "Wow. Long day, **hun?**" After noticing **our swords,** she continued. "Of course. I know **treasure hunters** when I see them. **Any luck** so far?"

"**Not exactly,**" I said, and nodded at Breeze. "I'll have what she's having and . . ." I looked past her, at two humans in leather. Between bursts of laughter, they were **sipping potions.** "What are **they** having over there?"

"One of the **finest** potions in all the land," the waitress said with a smile. "**The Noob Rager.**"

"Noob Rager?"

"**Best potion** you'll **ever** drink," she said. "Gives a nice burst of **energy,** too. A young man gave us **the recipe.** A treasure hunter, much like yourselves, but **different.** One of those **mysterious** travelers from a faraway land. . . . **Anyway,** he called it **an energy drink,** which is a kind of potion they have in . . . **well,** wherever he came from."

Ah, she must be talking about . . . **of course.** I gave the waitress a knowing smile. "I'll take one."

"**As will I,**" Breeze said.

"Bread's on the house."

Considering she's like half a block tall, Breeze sure can put away a ton of food. She must have two food bars.

And that potion **really was** amazing. It tasted **better than melon juice**—and **the energy!** It was like a potion of Leaping, Swiftness, and Strength all **rolled into one.** I wanted to order another right after I downed the first.

"I wouldn't advise that," the waitress said. "Drink **too many** and you'll go **right to sleep** after the effects wear off! **Buff overload,** they call it."

"I like to live **dangerously,**" I said.

"As you wish, m'lord." The waitress whispered to Breeze, "**Just so you know,** he's going to crash in **exactly** one hour."

After our meal, **the empty bottles** reminded me of how we needed to trade for **ingredients.** Following the shopkeeper's suggestion, we went from table to table to see if anyone had a few melons and gold nuggets to trade. **As luck would have it,** a blue-haired elf girl and one of those wolf people *(another odd couple)* had exactly what we needed.

"Good luck, guys!"

"We'll trade again!"

Another person had **a handful of blaze powder,** which we needed to **fuel** our brewing stand. At this point, we had a total of fifteen emeralds to our name, so we decided to **call it a night.**

On the way upstairs, that **waitress** from earlier approached us. She **glanced around** before speaking to us in a lowered voice. I could **barely hear her** over the noise coming from the dining hall.

"If you **really are** treasure hunters," she said, "could you **do me a favor?**"

"Define '**favor,**'" I said.

"Well, I've **always wanted** a necklace. **A nice one,** you know? I was hoping to craft one myself, but I need **a frost opal.** That's my favorite **gemstone.** If you two happen to find one, could you **bring it to me?** I don't have much in the way of emeralds, but I do have **these.**" In her palm were several **brilliant white coins.** "They're a special type of coin," she said, "crafted **ages ago.** So long ago, in fact, that their original name has been **lost.** Some believe they were once the official currency of the **ancient people.** Now many simply refer to them as **quest tokens,** because this is what **the king** usually gives to someone completing one of his many quests."

"So they're **like money?**" Breeze asked.

"In a way," she said. "**Follow me,** I'll show you."

She took us **downstairs,** into the basement, to a spruce door surrounded by **many signs.**

As we **approached,** two guards **in obsidian armor** immediately **rushed** in front of the door, **without saying anything.**

"This is called the **Quest Store,**" the waitress said. "Several such stores exist throughout Ardenvell. Here, you can find many **unique items** the king has donated as possible **rewards.**"

I was overwhelmed with a sense of **wonder,** almost as much as when I first set foot in Owl's Reach. I had to get in there—**I just had to!** But those guards wouldn't move. I asked them if I could maybe just **take a peek** inside, but they didn't reply.

The waitress **grabbed** my shoulder. "**I wouldn't advise that.** You could get **banned** from entering the Quest Store. **Permanently.** If you want to shop here, you need to show them you have **quest tokens.**"

"So you've offered us **a quest,**" I said.

"**I suppose** you could call it that, but that makes it sound so **serious,** doesn't it? I'm no king, **only** a waitress. . . ."

"**We'll see** what we can do," Breeze said. Finding a quest was definitely **awesome,** but we were both **totally exhausted.** After waving goodbye to the waitress, we went back upstairs and checked out **our room.**

Our room **was nice.** Especially compared to what I'd been sleeping in since I'd left Villagetown.

Before we started **brewing,** we took off to the bathhouse. There, we each found **our own personal** 3x3 cauldron. The block below the cauldrons contained **lava,** so the water was actually **warm.** Since we're farther north, **it's colder**—especially after sunset. **Honestly,** I don't know how the zombies around here **survive.** They must wear clothes enchanted with **Cold Protection.**

Yes, a bathroom **all to myself.** There was a **public** "bathing pool," but it was full of pigmen and dwarves. So we noped out of there and spent **twenty emeralds** for two **private rooms.** And no, the water wasn't **that** hot. I'm not some brewing ingredient, **okay?!**

We **returned** to our room. I asked Breeze a question that had been **on my mind** ever since that battle with the pigmen.

"Breeze? How did you **wield two swords?**"

Silence. That **dark expression** again. She didn't want to let me in on **her little secret.**

"**Your father** must have taught you," I said. "He must have. I saw him do the same thing once. When we were **defending against the wall breach.**"

She turned to the furnace, which was crackling away. "It's . . . **an ability,**" she said.

"**Ability?** What are you talking about?"

"You know how an enderman can **teleport?**" she asked. "How a ghast can **breathe fire** or a spider can **climb walls?** Well, people are capable of **similar feats.** Some are **magical** in nature, like spells, while others, such as duel wield, are **physical.** Their **complexity** varies as well. Some are easy to learn. **Others, nearly impossible.**"

"Does that mean **you can teach me?**"

"I can **train** you," she said. "The same way my father trained me. It would only take **twenty or so** minutes."

"**Twenty minutes?! Seriously?!** Why didn't you tell me about this **before?!**"

She **shrugged.** "Just **slipped my mind.** My father only recently showed me how to do it. And he didn't want me to tell **anyone** about it. He said most of us **aren't ready** yet."

"Well, I'm ready! **Super** ready! I'll be the best student you've ever seen! **Promise!**"

"There's **one thing** you should know," she said. "You can only learn a limited number of abilities over time. If I show you how to duel wield, and you come across **another ability** in the near future, you **may not be able** to learn that one."

"Why not?"

"Because learning an ability **takes experience.**"

"**Got it.** Hmm. But . . . how does that work?"

"If you happened to meet another person who knows a different ability, perhaps something better than duel wield, they could **train you.** According to my father, there are **over a thousand** different abilities. Some are **better** than others. Most are **common** and known by many in the Overworld. The best are **rare, highly sought after,** and can only be learned from some **ancient hermit** living on a mountaintop, **a nymph a faerie** in some secret cove, or **a wizard** in some remote tower. **Like that.** My father said there are even items that can teach abilities. Usually <u>**enchanted tomes.**</u>"

"**Interesting.** . . . Okay, I've thought about it quite a bit, and now **I've made up my mind. Teacher,** please teach me how to duel wield. **Err,** train, I mean."

"Are you sure?"

"**A hundred percent.**"

And so, Breeze began **training me** in the art of duel wielding. **As a precaution,** we wielded sticks in each hand. Before long, and after much **frustration,** I began to effectively wield two sticks at the same time.

I brandished my two "**weapons**" while shouting with excitement.

"Yeahhh!!"

She gave me a little clap. "Oh. You should know that any ability **will improve** the more you use it. You'll be much better by the time we've cleared that dungeon."

"Maybe I should **skip the two swords** and just stick with my shield, **right?**"

"Well, there will be times when you need to do **more damage.** With duel wield, you'll always have that **option.**"

"I guess **you're right.** When I need more defense, I can use my shield, and when I don't, I'll swap the shield out for another sword. Sheer versatility. **Kinda like Batman.**"

"Who's **Batman?**"

"**This guy** Kaeleb was telling me about. He can do all sorts of **cool things** to handle any situation, like . . . throw **smoke bombs** to escape, or use this thing called a **grappling hook** . . . or **deflect** arrows **with his cloak** . . . or **fly** with his cloak, and . . . and . . . why am I still talking when you don't seem interested in this at all?"

"Um . . ." Breeze gave me a blank look. "I know we've been avoiding it, but we really do **need to work** on those healing potions."

"Of course," I said. "**Let's do this thing.** I still feel kinda **energetic** after chugging those potions, so I'm probably going to craft **one million** potions. **At least** one million."

"You mean brew?"

"Yeah. Also, how do we craft those **golden melon things** again?"

Needless to say, **I didn't** brew one million potions. I didn't even brew one. Okay, I **almost** brewed one. I put a base potion on the stand and threw in one of those golden melon things that Breeze had crafted.

But it had been such a <u>long day,
you know?</u>

Yes, **I fell asleep.** No, I'm not proud of it. And yes, Breeze made a total of fifteen healing potions. In her nightgown.

So the waitress **was right** about those energy drinks! Exactly one hour after I drank that second potion, the potion's buffs wore off, and **thunk,** I dropped like an anvil. . . . Anyway, **sorry,** Breeze!

SATURDAY

It was **still dark** when we set out. A **beautiful** sunrise crept behind us as we rode southwest. We had to stop to **admire it.**

Only then did I notice just how many **flowers** there were. A countless number, as far as you could see.

"**Pink roses,**" Breeze said, swinging off her horse. "They're quite **uncommon** this far north. This must be a flower field. It's one of the **rarest** biome types, I think. It has to mean something. A good omen?" She turned to me. "Do you **believe** in that kind of thing?"

"Considering where we're going," I said, "**I'll believe in anything,** so long as it means a better chance of **not getting clobbered** by ten zombies at once."

We walked through the field **together,** then stopped as the sun came into view. **We said nothing.** I think we stayed like that for **a very long time.** I didn't know what was on her mind and couldn't have guessed, but she was clearly **thinking about something.**

"Kolb told me **so many things** before I left," she said at last.

"Like what?"

"He said our world used to be something called a **'server.'** A **Minecraft** server named Aetheria. And the players of that game **dreamt up everything** we see now, their countless ideas added, **over time,** through a series of updates, modifications, with every structure built, by their hands, through **some interface.** Then, one day, that world became this world. A world that's **more** than just a video game. . . ."

"You believe that?"

"I prefer not to, **of course.** It's much more **comforting** to believe they were **summoned** to **our** world."

"Breeze, you and I both know **we're more** than **game** characters. And even if we once were, we aren't any longer. **We exist.** That's all that matters, **right?**"

She said nothing, but I knew from her expression that my words had had **some effect.** I wanted to **believe myself,** too. I felt **lighter,** uplifted, and once more I gazed at the beautiful expanse before us: **the way the light scattered** across what had to be **millions** of petals . . . a game couldn't have created this. Although I didn't understand the **technology** of Earth, I knew no machine was capable of producing a world like this. Even if it was **a thousand times more complicated** than our redstone.

Breeze **held out** a bottle filled with water, which **sparkled** in the sunlight. The bottle's unique design indicated that it was **a splash potion.** A splash **water bottle.**

"**Here,**" she said. "I had some leftover gunpowder, so I made several of these."

"**What are they for?**"

"When thrown, they'll create a **burst of water.** This can put out **fires** or harm creatures with a **vulnerability** to water or affinity to fire. Another thing I learned from Lola."

"I wasn't even going to ask," I said. "**I just assumed.**"

And I thought: *Thanks again, you creative little redstone engineer.*

SATURDAY—UPDATE I

We stood at the edge of a **wide cliff** overlooking the plains below. You could see **forever**: perhaps a thousand blocks away, **the emerald greens** of the plains met the clay browns of **savanna**. That's called **a boundary**, where two biomes merge in a perfectly straight line. Far beyond that, the brown grass turned green again, although a different shade than the plains. Almost **cyan**. That biome was **mountainous**, with the grass turning to foothills rising gradually in steps, leading to **vast gray peaks** capped with snow. All this under a cloudless, **sapphire sky**—a blue so deep I felt lost within it whenever I looked straight up.

But this scene had a flaw. Someone had left **a dark spot** on this painting of sheer perfection. . . . There it was, far away, nestled in the middle of a million grass blocks. **The Tomb of the Forgotten King.**

If that place had once been built by the hands of some human, through some advanced **computer interface**, on some world known as Earth, **you couldn't tell.** Even from here it seemed **ominous**, a dreary slab at odds with the **vibrant** greens surrounding it, all black obsidian and storm-gray bedrock, red torches burning low.

"We're finally here," Breeze said.

I nodded **absently** and stared ahead, feeling a sudden chill run down my back. We were running into **the unknown.** We had no idea what kind of **traps** that tomb contained, how many monsters there were inside, or **how far down** it went. **Truth be told,** I didn't even know what a **puzzle** was. I was **terrified** at the thought of fighting another boss.

But Breeze didn't share my sudden lack of confidence. She turned toward me **with a smile. Nodded.**

"Let's go!"

SATURDAY—UPDATE II

I learned some things **about dungeons** today. Before, I'd always thought they were **single rooms** with a handful of monsters and **one or two treasure chests.** After all, that's what our teachers said. And every book I'd ever read on the subject had said the same exact thing. So **imagine my surprise** upon actually standing before one.

Go ahead—imagine it.

A simple underground room, **they said.** No larger than a 7x7 chamber, **they said.**

Yeah, well, **they were wrong. Just a tad.** Like the ocean has **a tad of water.** . . . *(Seriously—I know I'm supposed to be a brave warrior and all, but can I hurgg now?)*

I'll be honest:
I was terrified.

The little skull next to the doors was a nice touch. It had glowing red eyes. I turned to Breeze.

"Judging by the looks of this place, this must be **the home of a giant wither skeleton.** . . . Neat." A pause. "How about we just **forget about it?** We'll just tell the blacksmith we couldn't find his glowmoss. . . ."

"And maybe he'll send us on **another quest,**" Breeze said. "A **pumpkin pie-eating contest,** perhaps?"

I smiled. "What's **this?** Breeze **joking around?**"

She smiled, too, although it **quickly faded. All business.**

"You said this place is protected somehow?" she asked.

"That's what that one guy told me. Think of it as a biome-wide **enchantment** that **prevents the mining of blocks and the placement of activators.** Actually, the placement of everything."

"If you don't mind, I'd like to see this **for myself.**" Within moments, Breeze crafted **a wooden button.** When she tried placing it against the bedrock to the left of the door, **it fell to the ground,** as if it had been dropped. It failed to cling to the wall the way buttons always do. **This was, of course—**

"**Impossible,**" Breeze said. With a look of **utter disbelief,** she tried placing the button against the dirt with the **same result.** "**What in the Overworld . . . ?**"

I was wielding my stone pickax at this point and swung at those doors with everything I had. One swing, two. **On the tenth,** my pick flashed red . . . and shattered, **crumbling into little gray cubes before my very eyes.** *(There was also a sad little sizzling sound: "p'tweeeeeuu . . .")*

What's interesting here is that my pickax had almost **full durability.** It had gone from approximately **95%** to **zero in an instant.** I glanced at the single brown cube in my hand *(which had once been part of the handle).* "**The Nether?!**"

When Breeze tried **digging** with her iron shovel, she accomplished the very same thing. That is to say, **she accomplished nothing.** After her shovel flashed red and crumbled, she stared down at the iron cubes at her feet, **thoroughly unimpressed.** "**Hurmmph!**" It was the first time I'd ever heard her make that sound, a sound villagers often make when **annoyed.** Indeed, what we were currently experiencing . . . it was simply **unbelievable.** No matter what, a button **always** stuck to whatever surface you placed it against, and a shovel **always** mined dirt in a very short time, but here . . . well, let's just say we didn't go chopping at some grass with our swords to see what might happen. **We knew what would happen.**

"So how far does this extend?" Breeze asked. "The enchantment, I mean. Is it really **biome-wide?**"

"**I think so,**" I said. "Any biome that **contains a dungeon** can't be modified at all. Otherwise, **trolls** and **griefers** could put up **obsidian walls, TNT traps, monster spawners, lava moats** . . . apparently the Builders didn't want anyone **messing** with their creations."

"Got it."

A huge problem, then—**the enderman in the room,** or more appropriately, the iron golem in the room—immediately confronted us. If we really **couldn't place or mine anything** within this biome, that meant:

1.) Without beds, **sleeping would be difficult.**

2.) Old tricks involving the terrain—such as emergency shelters, dirt pillars—were **not an option.**

3.) The **most pressing** issue was something I hadn't yet thought of (but Breeze had, obviously): She tried placing some **fence.** As expected, the single fence post, instead of securing itself to the ground, **fell over.**

"So what are we going to do about Shybiss?" she asked.

Ah, yes. Without any fence, she couldn't **tie up** her horse. If we left Shybiss out here, she could pull a **Meadow** on us and **take off.** I was so close to **hurgging.** So close. **Eto** had mentioned this in the armor shop, but I never really thought about what kind of **problems** it would cause. I almost suggested we **bring Shybiss into the dungeon** with us, but I knew how Breeze would have responded to that. Luckily, she's **way smarter** than I am. She decided to walk around the dungeon and check things out. Guess what was back there? Is your answer "**some fence posts**"? Well, **you're correct!** Congrats, you've won **one million emeralds** and **a stuffed Urg the Barbarian doll!**

Whoever those Builders were, they were very considerate of us adventurers. They left behind some fence posts for people to tie horses to. They forgot the beds, though, and the cauldron full of rabbit stew. . . .

"Well, that's **one problem solved**," she said. "But whose horses are **those?**"

"**Other adventurers,** I guess? Who knows, maybe we'll run into them and we can group up." I showed Breeze **the obsidian key**. "**Ready?**"

Regarding Breeze's response, I could write something **mundane** here, like:

She nodded. *"I'm ready,"* she said.

But even though I'm barely an adult, I'm trying to be a **better writer.** She **nodded?! How boring is that?** Let's cross that one out!

~~She nodded. "I'm ready," she said.~~

Boom! Away with you, **boring** description of Breeze! And now for something **a little more interesting,** such as . . .

***

I didn't have to ask if she was ready. Her expression **said** that she was ready to go in there and **drop zombies** until her résumé no longer read **"warrior"** but **"zombie farmer,"** until so many **dropped items** littered the ground that the items actually **spilled out** like water, until that place was no longer known as the **Tomb of the Forgotten King** but **Item Mountain. Not only that,** but until **so many experience orbs** were swirling through the sky above that explorers **five biomes away** actually got lost because they mistook those orbs for the sun. *(Assuming they don't have a compass . . .)*

> To open a locked door, one only needs to touch it with the proper key. Who knew?

The doors led to a single room **lined with redstone torches.** An **obsidian** staircase led downward, and there was **a large sign** near the doors.

THE TOMB OF THE FORGOTTEN KING
HEAD BUILDER: IONE
APPROVED BY: ENTITY303

We turned back to the staircase and began our descent into **the depths of the dungeon.**

What's that? You're scared?
So imagine how I felt!

SATURDAY—UPDATE III

The hall below was **three blocks wide** and mostly the same as the surface room: **obsidian under bedrock.** The walls had these . . . **alcoves,** I guess. They held what looked like flowerpots, but they weren't flowerpots at all. They contained a **gray gunpowder-like material.**

"Are those **ashes?**" Breeze asked.

"**Looks like it.** As if this place isn't **creepy enough.**"

We had no idea what to expect, so **I went in front,** my shield raised, sword readied. Breeze trailed behind several blocks with her enchanted bow **ready to fire.**

That was when **I heard a scraping sound** coming from the hallway to the right. Moments later, **a zombie** shambled around the corner. **There's no point** in describing this battle in any detail. You know how it played out. **Two arrows** and **a diamond sword** later, the zombie went down. Smoke. Experience orbs. A stone sword, five or so swings from breaking. Leather armor in worse condition. But **here's the thing.** It also dropped **six emeralds.**

I glanced at Breeze. She glanced at me. Silence. The squeak of a bat.

"So . . ." she said, "every time we kill something in here, **it drops emeralds?**"

I looked down at the pile of items.

"I'm not sure. **Eto** said the monsters didn't drop too many. But maybe six **isn't too many** to him."

We heard more scraping around the corner. **Another zombie,** with a sword, shield, and full suit of armor, **all crafted of gold.** We took that one down like the last, **without too much effort.** And like the last, this one dropped every item it carried, the golden breastplate being **enchanted with Protection II . . .** along with **five emeralds.** We exchanged glances again, looked at the pile. More sounds came from around the corner. Three zombies, maybe, **maybe four,** five, six possibly, **no, at least seven.** Well, no, that's way too much noise. Definitely **eight or nine.** We glanced at each other again. It was our first time in a dungeon. What we knew about such places came from outdated books written **hundreds of years ago,** books written by villager librarians who had never even set foot in the Overworld. Even so, after seeing the **gemstones scattered across the floor . . .**

we knew **exactly** what to do.

SATURDAY—UPDATE IV

After that **small battle,** the only direction left to go was forward. The problem was, there was another **iron door** standing in our way. The key didn't work on this one. We had to find a way to open it.

We couldn't find anything, though. We **searched everywhere,** but we couldn't see any buttons, levers, or pressure plates. Before long, I was pressing on **random blocks,** thinking there could be a secret button somewhere. Breeze tried pulling on all the torches, hoping one of them was **a lever in disguise,** to no avail.

Nothing budged, and I was about to **hurgg.** I didn't, though. I managed to **stay calm.** My mind was like a diamond, **clear and sharp, unbreakable** and . . . anyway, I noticed **something different** about the alcove to the right of the door.

It had a small 1x1 shaft
leading down to the floor below.

Two possibilities: either this is how dungeon monsters deal with garbage, or I had found a secret passage.

I whipped out a torch, leaned over the edge, and stuck my head in. Only then did I consider the possibility that this could be a trap. But it wasn't. Nor was it a pigman's trash bin. Thank Notch.

"You've gotta be kidding me. Breeze, come look at this!"

At the bottom of the shaft was **a golden pressure plate**; a line of redstone was **connected** to this **activator,** and it most likely linked to the door. All we had to do was **drop an item on it** and the door would open.

So Breeze tossed in a **beat-up leather helmet.** Nothing happened.

"**That's weird,**" she said. "I thought you could activate pressure plates with items."

"**I thought so, too.** Huh . . ."

I kept staring at the golden tile, thinking back to what little we'd learned in school regarding them. "**Wait,** aren't golden pressure plates **special somehow?**"

Breeze shrugged. "I don't know anything about redstone, remember? If only **Lola** were here. . . ."

At the mention of Lola, I **suddenly recalled** a time when she had been talking about pressure plates with **Max.**

"I remember her saying something about iron pressure plates," I said. "Something about how **they're heavier?** Or heavy?"

"Okay, **iron is heavy,** but so is gold."

"Right, I don't know what she meant by that. Wait." I was starting to remember something. . . . **Wait** . . . **Wait** . . .

"**Weight!**"

The weight of the items on top of it **directly affects** the signal strength of these types of plates! A single item would only send out redstone power for maybe a block. I explained this to Breeze, then tossed in a pair of leather leggings. **Still nothing.** An iron breastplate with Protection I and Breaking III. A wooden sword, a stone sword, a pair of leather boots. An egg. A tulip. A stack of seeds *(we were short on ideas)*.

The door <u>stayed closed.</u>

"Well, the redstone line could extend for **quite a ways** under the floor," I said. "Maybe we just need to throw more stuff in?"

So we did, throwing **pretty much everything** we'd looted from those zombies earlier. And an egg. And a tulip. And a stack of seeds *(yes, I know . . .)*.

That was when I heard **a click** to my left. **The door had finally opened.**

"So I guess this is what Eto meant by **puzzles.**"

"Huh?"

"Never mind."

SATURDAY—UPDATE V

We took down **another group** of zombies, along with some skeletons. We fought **perfectly.** We timed our swings so **nothing** could get close. And when the last skeleton fired at Breeze, I dashed in front of her **with my shield raised.** . . . Beyond **emeralds** and **the usual trash-tier items,** one dropped **an obsidian sword.** I'd **never seen** an obsidian sword and was shocked to learn that its damage is actually **one less** than diamond. And with **half the durability.** Still, it's way better than anything else we've found so far.

    Whenever the situation calls for it, I'll swap my shield out and begin **dual wielding.** According to Breeze, the **Defender enchantment** increases the wielder's armor by its power level. Kind of like **a mini-shield.** So I'll still have better-than-normal defense wielding it in my off hand. As for the pink handguard, or whatever it's called, I'm not sure what that's about. Breeze thinks it could be a type of material known as **"coral,"** but that's just a guess. *(Can more advanced swords be made with three or more different materials?)*

SATURDAY—UPDATE VI

We encountered **another puzzle.** Another pressure plate. It was situated at the end of a horizontal shaft, or tunnel, so there was **no way** we could drop any items onto it.

Do you know how we managed to activate it? **Think about it for a second.** I'll **count to five,** and by the time I'm done counting, you need to come up with the answer.

Ready? One. Two. Three. Four. Five. And?

Is your answer "Runt drank a potion of Shrinking II to become one block tall so he could walk down the tunnel?"

Wrong! First of all, what kind of noob do you take me for?! There is no such thing as a Shrinking potion! *(Item scholars, you're free to correct me if I'm wrong.)*

In truth, the answer was **far simpler.**

Are you ready? Let's test your **knowledge.** You can still think some more, if you'd like. If you didn't come up with an answer and are still thinking, stop reading immediately. Unless you give up, I mean. **And no cheating, eh!** Don't go reading further and then pretend you came up with the answer!

Okay. Anyway. **The answer is: arrows.**

On a golden pressure plate, a single arrow has enough weight to send **a redstone signal** out one block. Since a repeater was placed next to the plate, **boom,** the door was opened. **Of course,** Breeze is the one who handled this. She said **she** should be the one, so we wouldn't **waste resources,** whatever that means. . . .

Wait. Was she suggesting that **I'm a bad shot?!** She was, wasn't she?! **That's it!** Now **I have a bow,** too, you know! One of those skeletons dropped one. Okay, so it might be two or three shots away from breaking, but **that's enough** for me to hit that pressure plate myself and show her who's boss. **She'll see.** Hold on, I'll update in a second. I'll take my time with this, hold my breath, aim carefully and . . .

SATURDAY—UPDATE VII

Okay, clearly that bow had problems. I say "had" because the bowstring snapped on the eighth shot. My aim is normally dead-on.

SATURDAY—UPDATE VIII

The next room was . . . um . . . **interesting.** It was a long hall with **a spruce door** on the end. Oh. And the **obsidian** floor was covered with more of those golden pressure plates.

Hmm . . .
I'm no dungeon expert,
but something isn't
right here. . . .

It's the **color scheme!** Those gold tiles simply do not go with this dungeon's **gloomy aesthetic!** I might even go so far as to say it **clashes,** if I dared to use such a strong word! Just kidding. **I know it's a trap,** okay?

"I know what this is," I said to Breeze. "It's one of those arrow rooms. You **step in the wrong spot,** and **arrows fly everywhere.**" I announced this **proudly.** "Yeah, that's what this is. Urg the Barbarian had to get around one of these things in the last book. It looked similar to this."

"Well, **if this is an arrow trap,**" she said, "shouldn't there be **some of those face things** in the wall?"

"Face things? You mean **dispensers?**"

"**Yeah,** I think so?"

I'm pretty sure that's what she was talking about. A dispenser is a block that can hold other items, and it **releases them** upon activation. Anyway, she was right. If this room was some kind of arrow trap, it would have had dispensers **in the walls.** But the walls here were **just bedrock.** Could it be?! Was it possible that the Builders used some **ancient, mystical** technique to create dispensers that **looked** like bedrock?! No. Not really. It was just **normal bedrock.**

Standing in the doorway, Breeze moved up to the **very edge.**

"I think **it's the ceiling,**" she said. "It's **much lower** than the other rooms and it's made of **cobblestone.** Until now, we've never seen any cobblestone. . . ."

I retrieved **a handful of seeds** from my inventory. "**Let's find out,** shall we?"

I tossed the seeds onto the pressure plate directly in front of the doorway, like I was feeding chickens or something. Nothing happened. The pressure plate sank down, sure, and the seeds clearly activated it, yes, **but that's it.**

"**Try farther out,**" she said.

So I gathered the seeds and tossed them **two blocks** from the door.

Again, this pressure plate **sank in . . .** and **the entire ceiling** flew down with a **deafening** crash—the sound of **over fifty sticky pistons** firing all at once.

Breeze said something, but I couldn't hear her over the noise. She **dashed** in just as the ceiling went up, **grabbed the seeds** and dashed back. I don't know how she moved so fast. It reminded me of the time we first met. *(Was it another ability?)*

The ceiling crashed down **a fraction of a second** after she returned, then went up again and stopped.

We didn't say anything for a moment, just **stared** ahead in silence, our ears ringing. At least, **mine were.** I'd read about trapped rooms, of course, but never in my **wildest** dreams had I imagined **one like this.** I pictured it now: the ceiling of sticky pistons covered in a grid of redstone, the complex trails leading to the floor. Or subfloor. What is that called? You know. A floor under a floor.

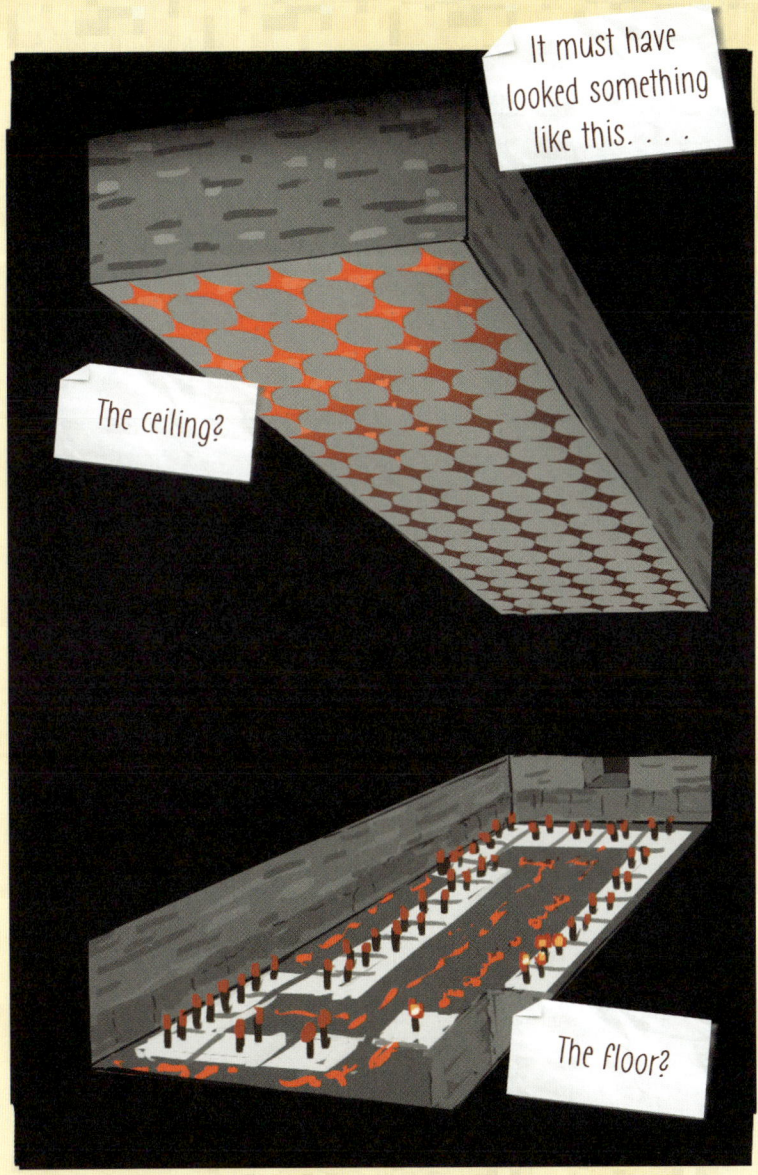

"So this is what the Builders are capable of. . . . Just **what kind of lunatics** are we dealing with here . . . ?"

I didn't **dare** imagine how much damage **a ceiling** would inflict.

In short, we had to figure out **the correct path.** One wrong step, and we'd become **villager pizza.**

Since **the entire ceiling** came down, throwing items in front of us like a reverse trail of bread crumbs wasn't an option.

The answer was right **in Breeze's hands. A fishing pole.** The lure was **heavy enough** to trigger the plates. We could use it to **safely test** which areas were safe and which areas . . . um . . . weren't safe. This was a **time-consuming** process (and deafening). If any nearby monsters weren't **already aware** of our presence, well, they surely were now.

Thirty minutes later, we mapped the safe route. I'm going to include **a drawing of the safe path** here, in case anyone ever visits this dungeon in the future.

By the way, even though we figured out which pressure plates were safe to step on, that didn't make walking through that room **any less terrifying.** After today, setting foot into any building with a low ceiling is going to give me a **serious** panic attack.

STICKY TRAP MAZE

The humans said there's this thing called a wiki that's like a huge book of information on various subjects. If we ever make a wiki about dungeons, this drawing needs to be added.

SATURDAY—UPDATE IX

Another trap. This one was **pretty obvious,** yet there was **no way** to tell what kind of trap it could have been. It was **a long corridor, three blocks wide.** The floor, made from **soul sand,** was completely **covered** in pressure plates. **Cobwebs** filled the remaining space.

We were going to have a **hard time** advancing with all that. <u>Not cool!</u>

Yes, **soul sand** can slow you down, even underneath a pressure plate. **Ask me how I know. Go on.**

Cobwebs **obscured** whatever sat beyond. I turned to Breeze, who was still holding **her fishing pole.**

"Probably **dispensers** on the other end," I said.

"Arrows, you think? Can arrows fly through cobwebs?"

"I guess we'll find out. **Pole it!**"

Breeze sent out her lure, which hit a stone plate. **It didn't activate.**

"**Right.**" I sighed. "These plates aren't weighted."

"What do you mean?"

"I'm not really sure, but . . . I think that kind of pressure plate only works when **a living creature** steps on it. Guess we'll have to test this the hard way, huh?"

I held my shield in front of me. Breeze followed directly behind me. Sure enough, after I stepped onto the first row of pressure plates, **arrows went flying everywhere,** accompanied by blue-gray swirls. "**They're enchanted?** Please tell me those aren't Wither arrows."

"Slowness," Breeze said.

"**Wonderful.**"

While we slowly advanced, and I do mean slowly, **another volley** was unleashed. An arrow struck my shield with a **clang** and bounced off. I was quite happy to have a shield equipped—next to the soul sand and spider webs, the enchanted arrows would have slowed us to a complete stop. We would **never** have gotten out of there.

Approximately nine million arrows later, we reached the end. **All I could taste** at that point were cobwebs. That's not even the worst part. We couldn't loot the dispensers: they were, like everything else, protected. And we couldn't **collect** the arrows themselves. They **crumbled into nothingness** seconds after striking something. (And yes, I tried grabbing one super fast, but the arrow crumbled as soon as I touched it.) **No free arrows** for us. Those Builders, man . . . they really thought of everything, didn't they?

As soon as we were in the clear, Breeze headed for the door, then **stopped.**

"That's **odd**," she said.

"**What?**"

"The door's **open**."

"**Hurmm.** Maybe it's the **same people** who left those horses? **C'mon,** they might be close."

SATURDAY—UPDATE X

We stood before **a vast chamber** with, thankfully, an extremely high ceiling. The style of construction was noticeably different here. Although **still gloomy,** all obsidian and bedrock, it was **beautiful** in a way. I'm no expert, but I had **the impression** that it was the work of a **different** Builder.

They'd somehow engraved portraits into the obsidian. I didn't recognize any of them.

Well, no—I recognized one.

Entity.

Can you believe that this guy was **the nicest wizard who ever lived? Me neither.** With a look like this, you'd never expect him to offer you some cookies and tea. I'd be waiting to be **polymorphed** into a baby rabbit and/or teleported to the **Void.**

"What's the point of this area?" I said. "**Where's the challenge** in walking around giant, empty halls?"

"Looks like someone has already **taken care of it.**" She pointed down a hall. **Countless items** were scattered across the floor. Sword. Axes. Pieces of armor. More common were the **remains of monsters**—bones, spider eyes. . . .

So someone else had **cleared** this area. They must have been in a hurry, because they **didn't bother taking anything.** One of our nicer finds was **a gold ring.** It had a fancy name: **Ancient Band.** That ring was totally mine, because dude, just **look** at that armor bonus.

There was also **a bracelet made of redstone.** Critical Strike means it increases damage dealt through critical hits by **one per power level**—that is to say, **one heart.** Needless to say, **Breeze took that one.**

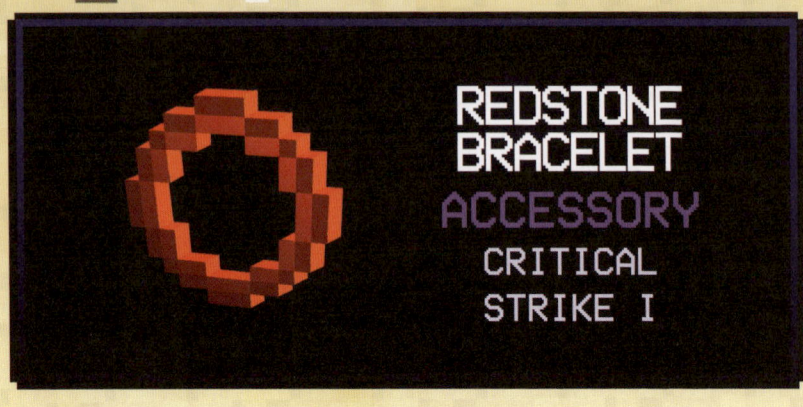

REDSTONE BRACELET
ACCESSORY
CRITICAL STRIKE I

The rest of the stuff was inferior to what we had on. Gold axes, iron swords. Some with **low-level enchantments.** We took everything anyway. We could trade this stuff for **a few hundred emeralds** back in Owl's Reach. A question **popped into my head.**

"Y'know, if someone already cleared this area," I said, "how come the zombies from earlier **were untouched?**"

"I think they'd only **recently spawned,**" Breeze said. "That's one of the things Kolb mentioned, before I came looking for you. Monsters **spawn continually** in dungeons."

"Through **monster spawners?**"

"Yes. Well, something like that. **Except they're invisible.**"

"Then the other people **must be close,** if the monsters here haven't respawned yet."

"Probably."

She said this **absently,** as she was now staring at a nearby wall where there was **a section of iron blocks** instead of bedrock. **Above this** was a massive stone sign. I'd **never seen** a sign like that before.

I could draw **another picture** of this sign, closer up so the words could easily be read, but I'm currently pressed for time. **I'll just write the words down here:**

The Vault of Emerillion
An ancient treasure sealed forever.
Until to our world the light returns.
Emerillion Grayson CharBot Aeonia
Martin Declan335 Robert303 XiangFang
Rainbow_Creeper Creepyguy101

"**Ancient treasure,**" I said. "What's that about? And **who are all those people?**"

"**Builders,**" Breeze said, approaching the vault. "This dungeon **isn't really a tomb** but one of the many **mazes** created, thousands of years ago, **to store things** that pose **a threat** to our world." She paused. "I think."

She had that **dark expression** again, **troubled.** She definitely knew something, and that wall had **made her think about it again.**

She had to know **something,** because she had **never** really talked about this kind of stuff before. Breeze, a history buff?! **That'd be a shocker.** The two go together **like me with bows.** Like Emerald with mud. Like Stump with anything that isn't a cookie or a cake.

"And how do you know all that?" I asked coolly.

"**My father** made me read so many books." Breeze forced a smile. "Let's continue, shall we?"

Oh, nice excuse there, I thought. *She's **definitely** hiding something. Now is the time to confront her.*

Another thought hit me. *(Yep. I totally forgot about confronting her.)*

"**Wait.** Here's a question for you, **Ms. I-Not-Only-Know-How-to-Destroy-Monsters-in-the-Most-Efficient-Way-Possible-but-Am-Also-Secretly-a-Farmer-and-a-Librarian.** If this dungeon contains **dangerous** stuff, things sealed away from the rest of the world in order to protect it . . . well, what things are we talking about, exactly? Like, **giant boss monsters,** or maybe **redstone war machines,** or cursed **legendary-tier** weapons—or possibly a giant boss monster wielding a legendary weapon, or possibly duel wielding two such weapons or riding an aforementioned war machine . . . ?"

My **silly** question failed to elicit any emotional response, only an answer:

"I believe this dungeon holds one of **the Eyeless One's creations,**" she said, "which fought in the final battle of **the Second Great War.** It can never be completely destroyed, only **subdued** for a time. And yes, I suppose that's what the humans might call **a boss monster.**"

"And what about this vault? **How do we open it?** And what does it contain?"

"I . . . well, um, I'm not really sure. I have a guess as to what might be in there, but it would take a long time to explain, and . . . anyway, I don't how it can be opened."

"Hurmm . . ."

*Why is she being like this? She really is **hiding** something from me! Why?! What does she know? Can I trust her? Man . . . what am I thinking? Of course I can trust her. Anyway, it's not a good time. The village is counting on us. Every second matters. **Twenty-five hundred emeralds. Let's go!***

I **studied** the vault again, looking around for some kind of activator. **Sadly,** the only thing being activated around here was **my curiosity.**

Interestingly, there was a horizontal shaft in the wall, **six blocks above the stone sign.** If you look at the previous drawing, you'll see it. It was obviously **the key to this puzzle:** bright flickering **blue light** emanated from within. *(What could that be?!)*

Of course, if this dungeon worked like the rest of the Overworld, it would have been easy to get up there. Just place **a dirt pillar** and you're done. But again, in a place like this, you have to **play by its rules.** So maybe that tunnel contained a button and we needed **a Flying potion.** Who knows . . .

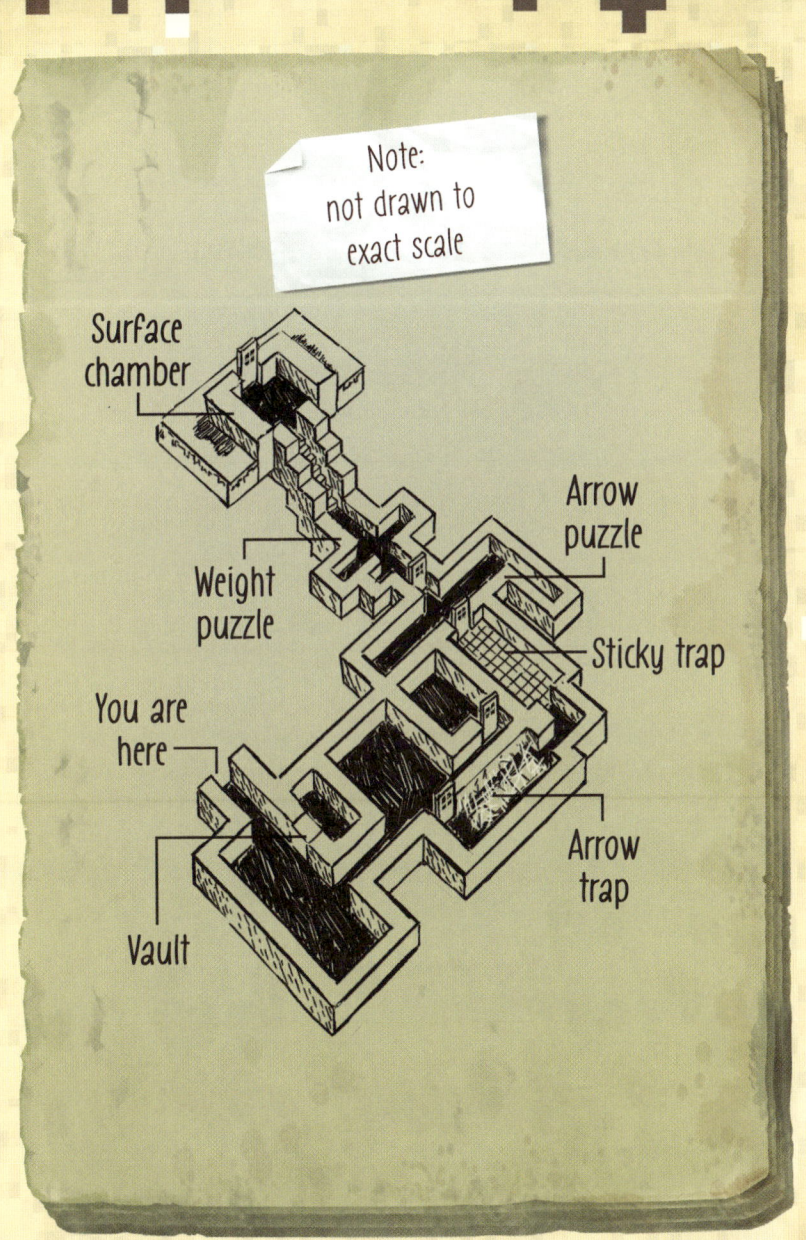

"**Whatever,**" I said. "It doesn't matter, anyway. **We're here to save Villagetown,** right? So let's find more zombies, take down **as many as we can,** collect all the emeralds, find that moss, receive the blacksmith's quest reward, and trade for **an advanced crafting table.** Sound good?"

At this,
Breeze gave me the biggest hug.

Why? I'll never know. I asked her, but **she just shrugged.** Then she mentioned how hugging me was like **hugging an iron golem** because of my armor. And with that, we continued onward down the **silent, empty halls.**

SATURDAY—UPDATE XI

The next hall had **nothing** but wooden doors. Each door led to a small room five blocks wide, five blocks deep, and three blocks high. Most of these rooms held **little of interest: bookshelves,** mostly, and every last book was in **some weird language** neither of us had ever seen. However, in one room we found **not only** bookshelves but also **one of those wolf people** browsing them.

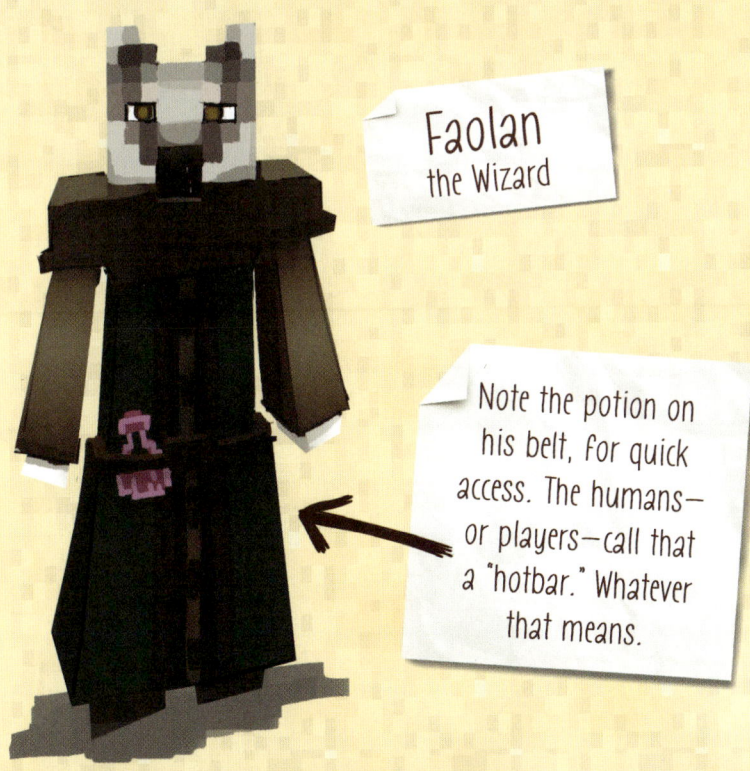

Faolan
the Wizard

Note the potion on his belt, for quick access. The humans—or players—call that a "hotbar." Whatever that means.

He claimed to be not only **a wizard** but also **a scholar** of ancient history and connoisseur of fine potions. More important—far more important—he offered to **teach us a new ability,** magical in nature: **Analyze Monster.** With this, we could see not only **the names of creatures** but also:

1.) A green bar representing **their life force.**
2.) Any and **all status effects,** buffs, and debuffs currently affecting them.
3.) A visual indication of exactly **how much damage they receive** equal to the number of hearts lost.

Interesting, yeah? I consulted with Breeze, who thought it would be **a good idea** for both of us to learn this. **So we did.** It took all of **five minutes.**

Faolan mumbled the words of **some magic spell** and summoned **a transparent blue cube** with eyes. **An ice slime.** I knew it was an ice slime because that was the name **floating over it.**

ICE SLIME

"A golden icon is a **buff**," the wizard said. "A light-blue icon, a **debuff**. As you can see, this slime possesses **one of each**. That is because of the ice slime's cold affinity. It will take **increased damage** from any fire-based attack and less damage from cold. Indeed, **with this knowledge** at your disposal, you can easily exploit **the weaknesses** of monsters."

"Why are there **infinity symbols** underneath the icons?" Breeze asked.

"That's the **duration**," Faolan said. "Normally you would see numbers there, **counting down** by the second. But status effects provided by an affinity are **permanent**."

As I listened, I noticed that the text floating over the ice slime **had disappeared**. "Huh? What happened? Why did it vanish?"

"This ability only works **when you're actively** looking at a monster. For your convenience. Otherwise, larger battles would become quite . . . **busy.**"

"**Oh.**" I stared at the slime again. Sure enough, **the overlay reappeared.** "Cool."

I turned to Breeze. "It's **almost like magic,** huh?! Just wait until we're back home! I'll start teaching everyone how to do this stuff! And we can **trade abilities** with the Legionnaires!"

"**Yeah.**" She was staring at the slime, seemingly lost in thought. She suddenly turned to the wizard. "**What happens if we train** this ability up more? What benefits will it provide?"

"**Additional information,**" the wizard said, "such as a monster's armor, stats, abilities, worn items, and, finally, at the highest level of skill, **their inventory.**"

"**Wow!** That could **really** come in handy," Breeze said. "**Thanks a lot.**"

"Glad I could be of help." **He paused.** It seemed like he wanted to ask something but was too shy to do so. "**Err,** what village do you two hail from, anyway?"

"**Villagetown,**" I said. "You know it?"

"I've heard of it. It has **a wall,** right? **Smart move.**" He looked a little sad. "I wish mine had had **the same. . . .**"

He told us he came not from a village but **a city.**

Diamondhome. The largest port city in the world. It was **attacked** two months ago—**completely destroyed.** Many people made it to the ships, though, and **set sail.** Where they headed, he didn't know. He had stayed behind, **freezing zombies** with blasts of ice until his magic was depleted. **Forced to flee** from his hometown, he returned a day later . . . **to ruins.**

"I'm sorry to hear that," Breeze said. "The same happened to my home village. **Shadowbrook.**"

The wizard **nodded gravely.** "So I've heard. And **not everyone managed to escape,** correct? Some were even **captured. . . .** I'm so sorry. I can't imagine. . . ."

The two **lowered their heads.**

"Maybe **you could come stay** at Villagetown," Breeze finally said.

(I was going to suggest that, actually, but didn't want to interrupt their moment of silence. Gentleswordsman, remember?)

At her suggestion, the wizard's cheeks **turned a little red.** "Oh, **I don't know,**" he said. "Are you sure they wouldn't mind taking in someone like me? My magic **isn't even all that strong** yet. I'm still just a **neophyte,** really. . . ."

"Hey, I'm sure the people of Villagetown would be **more than happy** to have an **actual wizard** around," I said. "Isn't that right, Breeze?"

"**Definitely.**"

Faolan nodded. "**Hmm. Very well.** I shall go there soon."

"Well, you're **more than welcome** to come along with us," Breeze said.

"That's right," I said. "We're heading back **as soon as we finish up** with this quest we're on."

He shook his head. "I'm afraid **I must decline.** I still have much research to do. The libraries here hold **a vast wealth** of knowledge lost through the ages. But I shall make my way there as soon as **I'm finished.**"

"**Great.** Hope to see you around. **Oh,** sorry. I'm Breeze, and this is—"

"Runt."

So yeah, **long story short,** we picked up **a new ability** and recruited Villagetown's first **wizard.** Neophyte or not, he'll be a welcome addition. *(In other news, I learned that "neophyte" is basically the polite version of "noob.")*

Oh! Breeze wants me to include one more thing. Players talk about **buffs** and **debuffs** to describe **the effects of spells.** Buffs are temporary magical effects with a certain duration. For example, **a golden apple provides two buffs** upon being eaten: **Absorption I** for two minutes and **Regeneration II** for five seconds. A **debuff** is the opposite. It's a **negative** effect that you want to **avoid at all costs,** like those slowness arrows from earlier. Pretty simple, **right?**

And that concludes our lesson for the day. Please make sure to leave an enchanted apple on my desk before you leave. **Class dismissed!**

SATURDAY—UPDATE XII

The twelfth update for today. And **what an update** it is! You're **not going to believe** what happened. In fact, I'm so pumped up after what just happened, **I'm shaking,** bouncing around, like a slime wearing boots **enchanted with Leaping II.**

Well, no, that doesn't make a lot of sense, really, because boots would look ridiculous on a slime—especially a baby one. **Here's the real problem:**

Slimes can't wear boots bro

Yes they can this is my diary and slimes can wear boots if they want to

*Note: The above should have had punctuation like commas and exclamation points. That isn't a mistake, however—oh no. I purposefully left them out to achieve a kind of **rushed feeling,** like a little villager kid writing about his first time eating a slice of enchanted cake: DUDE WOW THAT CAKE = AMAZING EPIC LEGENDARY TIER 10/10 WOULD EAT AGAIN #1 FOOD ITEM IN THE OVERWORLD!!!*

Okay, so slimes can't wear boots. **Very well.** So what about a spider, **then?** But spiders have **eight legs** . . . so it would need to enchant like **four different pairs** just to get the effect of one enchantment—and honestly, spiders might climb cacti and do a lot of other silly things, but not even the **noobiest** spider would enchant multiple pairs of boots like that!

Yeah well at least spiders can wear boots, okay???

They can, okay???

Okay???

OKAY NEVER MIND
PLEASE FORGIVE ME I'M SORRY!!!

SATURDAY—UPDATE XIII

Sorry. I got a little carried away there.

Okay, so anyway, **here's what happened** just now. We were wandering the halls again and heard **a shout,** followed by **an eerie howl** and **another shout.**

"Sounds like they're not too far away," Breeze said, meaning **whoever had left those horses tied up** outside earlier. **"C'mon!"** She began sprinting down the hall.

"Hey! **Wait up!** This armor reduces my movement speed, remember?!"

Bedrock walls **blurred past,** along with torches and pillars and the occasional item, **the remains of some monster.** The **shouting** and **howling** grew **louder.** And, upon turning one last corner, we **stopped completely** in our tracks. The hall merged with another **massive room,** and in the center were **two people locked in combat with three wolves.** One person was wielding a large emerald sword and wearing a near-complete suit of leather armor. He was missing the helmet, and we could see **a wave of spiked yellow hair.** The other person was in **a suit of obsidian** and wielded a bright red ax in each hand.

As for the wolves, well, I'd never really seen **wolves like that** before.

> Now was a good time to test Analyze Monster. I almost felt like a wizard.

I'd read about **felhounds** before. They're nothing more than **a scarier version** of wolves. Strangely, I thought I'd read that they didn't exist in the Overworld. **At any rate,** each felhound was affected by **two different buffs**. The gray shield was **Stoneskin,** which provides an armor bonus of five per power level. The little **II** in the bottom right-hand corner meant **its power level was two.** The golden rabbit's foot was **Haste I,** which increased movement speed and attack speed **by 25%.** After Breeze fired a weakness arrow at the wolf I was focusing on, a third icon appeared. **A broken sword.** That was the Weakness I debuff, which reduces attack damage by four.

The young man with yellow *(almost orange)* hair glanced over his shoulder. "**Nice!** We could **really use some** help right about now!"

Without a word, **I charged in** between the two strangers. All three felhounds **immediately focused** on me. I'm not sure if it was **the giant owl** on my shield or what, but they just wouldn't stop **attacking me.** The giant owl often thwarted their efforts with a **clang.** How **humiliating** for them, right?

Meanwhile, Breeze **unleashed more arrows,** and the other two swung their weapons **frantically,** like they were mining the Overworld's **last diamond vein.** I'll skip all the details, but basically felhounds fell one by one in a flurry of arrows and ax swings. (Along with some really graceful sword work from yours truly, I might add. Oh, and that guy with yellow hair.)

After the battle, the **obsidian-clad** warrior bent down, collecting the **emeralds** the wolves had dropped. His swordsman friend turned toward Breeze:

"**Thanks,**" he said. "That would've taken **a lot** longer without you two."

"It took long enough as it is," I said. "So, **um,** are dungeon monsters normally this tough?"

He shook his head. "**Not really.** At least not around here. Actually, I'm not sure what those felhounds were doing here. You usually won't find them in **low-level** dungeons like this. And **those buffs!** Why did they have Stoneskin and Haste? **So weird** . . ."

Breeze moved up to **join us,** slinging her bow across her shoulder. "They could have been **summoned.**"

The swordsman shrugged. "**It's possible.** Not sure why someone would do that, though. . . . I mean, **griefing** used to be a thing back when this was just a game, but now . . ."

At this point, I noticed that the other person, the one in obsidian armor, **was standing still.** Many emeralds were still scattered before him. He hadn't picked them up and wasn't attempting to. In fact, he wasn't moving at all. It was as if he'd been **frozen.**

Well, that's odd, I thought. *What's his problem? He's been like that ever since Breeze and I started talking. . . .*

As **I stared** at this person's back, the usual information appeared above him. **The name. The life bar.** It seemed Analyze Monster worked on people as well. **It took a second** for my mind to process this person's name. **My mind just couldn't accept what I was seeing.**

No. **No, no.**
N-n-nnnnnoooooh!

But the name was there, **real,** and it was spelled correctly.

And it was a weird enough name to possibly be **unique** in all of the Overworld. And it was the name of someone I'd known, someone **I'd hated,** someone I'd **never** expected to see again. . . .

SATURDAY—UPDATE XIV

Pebble. *Pebble!* It was really Pebble!

When he **turned around,** I couldn't believe my eyes. Not only was he **alive** but also he was **in a dungeon** with some human and equipped with **some pretty amazing stuff.** *(Are those redsteel axes I see?!)*

"**Wow!**" he said. "What are you two doing here?"

I approached him, **desperately** searching for words.

"I, **uh** . . . well, we, **um** . . ."

The human, whose name was simply S, flashed **a wry grin**.

"I take it you three **know** one another."

"We do," Breeze said, eyeing Pebble **coldly**. "Unfortunately."

I glared at him as well. "Looks like the Overworld has been **treating you well**. Let me guess. You're no longer the Pebble you used to be. You're a **changed** villager now."

"As a matter of fact, **I am**."

S was still **grinning** when he turned to our former **bully**. "Don't tell me **he's** the one you . . ."

"**He is**," Pebble said.

"So you told him?" I asked, still glaring.

"**Of course** I told him," Pebble said. "I tried blowing up the wall, **tried blowing you up**, and I don't even know why. I could apologize **a million times**. It still wouldn't make me feel any better about it. I . . ."

"**Yeah?!** Well, maybe you should have—"

Breeze **shouted over me**. "You have **a lot of explaining** to do! You nearly—"

I shouted **over her**, and we both began shouting even louder and at the same time.

"People don't just randomly go **crazy** like—"

"Enough!!!"

That shout came from S, and it sounded louder than a TNT blast. **We fell silent** and continued to **glare** at Pebble while S continued.

"**Listen.** He told me the full story, every little detail, and I personally believe he was under the effect of **Confusion III**. It's **a strong debuff** that clouds your judgment. It can even make you believe friends are enemies. The third-level variant can last for **entire days**. Instead of being angry, you should take it up with **the Eyeless One.**"

"Last I heard," Breeze said, "he's been **rather busy** for the past several months."

"**That's right,**" I said. "You're telling us **the Eyeless One** cast a Confusion spell from **a million blocks** away?"

S shook his head. "**It's not like that.** As far as I know, there is no spell that can inflict Confusion III—only **a potion**. It's typically used for crafting **a really powerful arrow.**"

When S said this, I recalled **the battles** that took place in our village. Pebble was always pretty reckless; that was **his style.** He wasn't afraid to take damage, and as a result, he often **chugged healing potions** in the middle of combat. Had someone really **swapped** one of his healing potions for a potion of **Confusion III?**

As if reading my mind, S suggested **this theory** as well. But I **didn't believe it.** Didn't want to. **I wanted to be angry** at Pebble.

I know that's **immature.** If he really had been **brainwashed,** it meant Pebble **wasn't such a bad guy** after all. As much as I didn't like it, this possibility had to be considered. . . .

"Why would someone do that?" I asked.

"More important," Breeze said, "**who** did it?"

"I think these are questions we should deal with later," Pebble said **glumly.**

S nodded. "**He's right.** The monsters around here are going to **respawn** any minute now. Let's move, people."

Pebble was now but a single block away.

"**I'm really sorry,**" he said. "**Really.** I'll do anything to make it up. **A million** emeralds. Anything. Can we just leave all that behind?"

Psh!
As if!
So he tries blowing me up with TNT
then thinks all it takes to make it right is a few apologies?!

I wanted to **shout at him** some more, tell him everything I'd been **bottling up** inside like **a potion of Rage XI,** then leave with Breeze right then and there. But **I had to be better than that,** didn't I? I was bitter about what had happened, but my feelings weren't the most important thing in the world. If **working with** Pebble increased the odds of **Villagetown's survival** by even the slightest bit, how could I refuse?

The past is the past. What was it that Kolb once said? Face the problems you've not yet had? **I extended a hand.**

"**Thank you,**" Pebble said, while giving me the strongest handshake of all time. "You won't regret this. And . . . do you mind telling me **what you guys are doing** here?"

"**Um,** basically . . ."

I told him everything regarding our mission, **summarized**: how Kolb wanted me to retrieve **an aeon forge,** how I needed **twenty-five hundred emeralds,** and how some random blacksmith had sent me on a quest for a handful of so-called *glowmoss.*

"Glowmoss? **The boss drops that,**" S said. "You won't find it anywhere else. C'mon. He's **just past those doors.**"

As S took the lead, Pebble spoke to me **in a low tone:** "Don't worry; this guy really knows what he's doing. I think he might know **everything.** He's already taught me so much. . . ."

And suddenly, after exchanging **uneasy glances** with Breeze, I found myself walking down another corridor with *(I can't believe I'm writing this)* **Pebble the Exile** to my left. Ahead of us, the human named S walked in a casual way, as **confident** as he was **mysterious.**

He stopped before
a pair of __massive__ doors
and turned around.

"He's wrong, you know. I don't know everything. I suppose that's what drives me to keep exploring this insane world. . . ."

"That, and a promise. . . . Where are you, Emerillion . . . ?"

SATURDAY—UPDATE XV

If you look at the **previous drawing,** you'll notice that the doors behind S were **five blocks tall.** That was **no embellishment.** I go for **accuracy,** remember. No, those doors actually were five blocks tall, and they led to an **enormous** chamber. With **an enormous giant zombie.** He was sitting on a golden throne on the other side of the room.

"That's the boss," S said. "Obviously."

"Why is he just sitting there like that?" Breeze asked.

"That's normal," Pebble said. "Most of the bosses wait for you to engage. At least **the lower-level ones.**"

"How many bosses **have you fought** already?" I asked, somewhat **surprised** and more than a little curious.

"**Three.** No, wait." He turned to S. "Does that **Skull Lord** count?"

"**Nah.** Their scripting is pretty **complex,** but I'd classify them as **minibosses.** Quest monsters, really."

Scripting? **Quest monster?** Hurgg . . . I was totally **lost.** And it sounded like Pebble had been on **quite the adventure.** Yeah, I was <u>jealous</u>.

S stepped forward. "Looks like he's also got **Stoneskin II** and **Haste I.** Hmmmmm. You know, there's an item that gives those two **buffs.** And with a duration of **thirty minutes,** no less. What's it called again? **Diamond wafer?** Yeah. First the felhounds, and now this . . . **very strange.**"

It was **extremely** strange. If what S said was true, **someone** was trying to hinder us. Pebble said it best:

"**I don't like this,** guys. Just have a **funny feeling. . . .** Maybe we should leave."

"We **really need** that crystal," S said, and glanced at Breeze and myself. "We're on a quest to **light a beacon** in the mountains to the southwest. We need the enchanted **voidcrystal** this guy drops."

"**Ohh,**" I said, pretending to understand.

Breeze drew her bow. "So **what's the plan,** then?"

S smiled again. "**Simple.** We just wait here until his buffs wear off."

What a great idea, I thought, and peered at the boss from afar to see **how long** we had to wait.

A chill hit me as I did, a horrible realization.

23:53—I hadn't really made the connection until seeing this number.

"If the duration was originally **thirty minutes**," I said, "**then the person behind all this was in this room** just six minutes ago, right?"

S shrugged. "**I guess so.** But there's no one else here."

The four of us **scanned** the room. Especially Pebble. He looked positively **spooked.** But then, he'd looked like that **ever since I first saw him** today. He was like a **completely** different person. Before he was **all bravado,** all the time. Now he gave off **a kind of doubt.** What had made him this way? His time in the Overworld must have been **quite different** from mine.

"Guess we'll just **have to wait** and find out what this is all about," he said.

And so, after **slowly approaching** the center of the room—still twenty blocks from the giant zombie—we waited. For the **looooongest** several minutes, we waited. Silent. **Glancing around. Idle chatter.** I rearranged my inventory. Well, that potion would go better there. . . .

Until finally . . .
precisely five minutes and thirty-seven seconds later . . .

an exact time calculated by observing the duration of the boss monster's buffs . . . Breeze gave **a slight gasp.** She was looking up and far away, near one corner of the ceiling. **I followed her gaze** to a most unbelievable sight. **A potion.**

Mysteriously, it **was floating** fifteen or so blocks above the obsidian floor, **slowly sailing** toward the boss—turning slightly, bobbing up and down—**as though dancing** in the air. . . .

It was **so enchanted** that it had a faint glow, like violet torchlight. **Its destination** was, of course, the zombie's right hand. The potion looked so tiny in that **block-sized fist,** and **the zombie didn't chug,** oh no. It was more like **a little sip.** To the gasps of three villagers and a human, **a third icon** appeared next to the first two. **A golden heart.** That was **Regeneration V,** an **extremely strong** healing buff. Its duration: **three minutes.**

"This is **too weird,**" S said.

Again, Pebble said it best: "S? **Let's get outta here.**"

Suddenly, I heard a faint **crackling** sound from behind me. I glanced over my shoulder. The hallway leading out was now **sealed with a wall of ice,** ice that shimmered almost like it was enchanted.

Shrill laughter resounded from overhead. **Familiar** laughter. A laugh I hadn't heard in **quite some time.** We **slowly turned around.**

Now, perched on top of the throne, was an old man in a deep red robe. Red hat. Black sunglasses. Bushy white beard. It was the same person I'd bumped into earlier in Owl's Reach who had matched Stump's description of a suspicious character named Cocoa Witherbean.

But now, upon hearing that laugh, I knew that this person was none other than . . .

It was the same villager who had **betrayed** us so long ago. Even with his name hovering over his head, **it was hard to accept.** This was a person known for being totally clueless—**incapable of basic combat,** let alone **magic.** But the person now standing before us could apparently **fly, turn invisible,** and **conjure walls of ice.** . . .

"You **seem so surprised,**" he called out. His shrill voice was unnaturally loud. "**So was I,** upon seeing **you three** show up here **together.**" He hopped up and down **like a giddy child.** "Oh, isn't it **wonderful?!** Here you are, **Villagetown's very best,** and I'm going to **erase all of you** in one go!"

"I take it **you know this guy,**" S muttered to Pebble.

"Yeah."

"Might've been good to let me know **you were being hunted** by a crazy old wizard."

"He wasn't a wizard then. **Just some fool.**"

"**Fool?!**" That was Urf. "If anyone's a fool," he shouted, "it's her! She—"

Breeze **fired an arrow with unequaled** speed. I'd never seen an arrow fly so fast or with such **perfect** aim. **A critical hit.** An arrow sticking out of Urf's **forehead.** At least, that's what would have happened, had he not instantly **blinked away**—zip!—like **an enderman.** The arrow struck obsidian instead.

Now Urf was roughly ten blocks away from his original location, **hovering in the air.** "Care to try that ag—"

Breeze **didn't hesitate.** Her second arrow flew **as true** as the first. But Urf was **faster still.** Again he blinked away. Urf appeared on top of **the giant zombie's head.**

"**Are you done?** I can do this all day, m'lady."

I've seen Breeze get **angry** before, but nothing matched her expression right then as she lowered her bow. It was **pointless** to continue. She knew that. She was only wasting arrows.

"Why are you doing this?" Pebble shouted. "**We never did anything to you!**"

"**Wrong!**" Ghostly **flames** erupted around Urf. "You **humiliated** me! You **laughed** behind my back! And then you **replaced** me! Me . . . replaced by a human!"

The flames crackled and **grew brighter.** "Of course, I was going to use my magic on you while you were dealing with **Nethy** here, but I've come up with a much better idea. It's the best way to **end this little story.**" He smiled. "It's true, I didn't know anything before. However, **my master** taught me well. . . ."

Shrouded in flame, Urf closed his eyes and began mumbling, like Faolan had when summoning the ice slime. Then he vanished in a flash of brilliant orange light. No, not quite. He sank downward, into the zombie, in a fraction of a second.

Still seated upon the massive throne, the zombie jerked violently, then closed his eyes and fell completely still. Thankfully, S the All-Knowing explained what had just happened: "I think he just cast Soulshift. It lets you control a monster by occupying its body. It isn't supposed to work on bosses, though. . . ."

I sighed.

So Urf was now in control of a boss monster, one that could easily beat an iron golem at arm wrestling. You know, it's just not my lucky day.

The huge zombie opened his eyes. Then he slowly rose, glanced down at himself and laughed: *hurhh, hurhh, hurhh. . . .* And when he spoke—even though his voice was deep and sounded nothing like Urf's voice—there was no doubt in my mind that it really was the old man.

"You might be wondering how I'm capable of this," he said. "My powers were increased by the master . . . the kind master. So kind is he, in fact, that he asked me to spare your lives if you would only kneel before me. But no, I won't give you that chance. I may have failed to get rid of you before, but I won't fail now. . . ."

As he spoke, I recalled how Stump had seen Urf in Villagetown. He'd been there the whole time, **spying** on us. Doing who knows what. Disguised as **Cocoa Witherbean.**

If S was **right** about that potion, Urf was probably the one behind it. It's a simple task, **renaming a potion.** All you really need is an anvil. I could picture it so clearly now. Urf changed the potion's name, turned **invisible,** crept into Pebble's house while he was sleeping, and slipped the potion into Pebble's inventory. And Pebble, pushed so hard during training, had been too tired to notice the potion's different color. . . .

Thinking about this, **I flew into a rage.** I shouldn't have charged in, **I know.** I should have **waited** for S to give us some command. To be honest, I barely even remember this moment. It was just a blur. I **shouted** something, and before I knew it, I was standing **before the giant zombie** possessed by a **completely** deranged old man.

SATURDAY—UPDATE XVI

I swung my diamond sword at ~~Nethersoul~~ **Boss Urf.** The blade left a crescent in its wake, and **hearts appeared,** indicating the damage dealt—one. A single point. **That is to say, practically nothing.**

Since **Stoneskin II** increased Urf's armor **by ten,** on top of whatever protection the boss monster had naturally, attacking him was like trying to mine obsidian with **a beetroot.**

And he had **Regeneration V . . .** so what little life I'd taken was **immediately** restored. There was, of course, one more problem. **Laughing** at my pitiful display, he struck me with one of his **furnace-sized** fists. Despite the **Surefooted enchantment** on my cloak, I **flew back ten blocks** and landed on my back near the others. I lost three hearts. I'd forgotten to raise my shield. **I was shocked, okay?** It isn't every day you see a **former noob** directly controlling a giant.

Boss Urf once again **laughed** creepily.

"I suppose we shall see who's **the nooblord** now." And he began lumbering forward.

"He can't cast spells right now," S said. "When **Soulshifting,** you only have access to **the monster's abilities,** and **Nethersoul** has none. Only **high melee damage.**" As Breeze **helped me up,** S turned to me. "We need someone to **mitigate that damage.**"

I looked at him suspiciously. "**Mitigate . . .**"

"We need you **to tank,**" Pebble said. "We didn't bring **shields.** Didn't think we'd need any."

"**Oh.**"

I glanced at the approaching boss. **Again:** furnace-sized fists. Then I shrugged.

215

"Yeah. **Sure. No problem.**"

Breeze handed me two potions: **Stoneskin I** and **Regeneration II**. The latter had an **extended** duration. Eight minutes. She **gave me a hug** and said, "**Come back** with your life bar intact, **okay?**"

Then she ~~kis~~

No, I can't write about that in here! **I'm a warrior,** got it?! I have no time for **mushy stuff!** Okay, fine! **She kissed me on the cheek!** That's not so weird, though, **right?** I mean, I heard about this one village where kissing another person on the cheek is **totally normal,** like a **handshake!** So it must have been like that in her old village! **Yeah!** That **must** be it!

Well, for some reason, I **felt more courageous.** Could it be that she's **secretly a wizard** whose kisses give some kind of buff? Whatever it was, **it worked.** I charged back in. Pebble and S were **right there behind me.**

"We'll be on **either side** of you," S said. "If he goes for one of us, make sure to **move over** and **intercept his attack.**"

With Boss Urf now towering before us, I raised my shield. *Intercept. Mitigate.* S made tanking sound **so fancy,** you know? But there's **absolutely nothing** fancy about being **pummeled** by a zombie who most likely wrestles **ender dragons** in his spare time. Oh well. At least with my shield I was only knocked back **half a block.**

SATURDAY—UPDATE XVII

As my shield **absorbed** blow after blow, the amount of damage Pebble, S, and Breeze put out was **simply incredible.** Pebble's axes were **redsteel.** Although their individual attack speed was slow, an ax has **higher damage** than a sword. Duel wielding them almost seemed **unfair.** Breeze cycled between normal arrows and the Weakness variety, using Weakness only when **the debuff** was about to **wear off.** On top of that, she threw a **splash healing potion** at my feet the few times I took damage.

S used a sword ability called **Overblade.** It was **the coolest** thing I'd ever seen. With a loud battle cry, he jumped into the air—**sword raised over his head**—and slammed down into Urf with **such force** that Urf **bent over backward in pain.**

He looked **so ridiculous.**
<u>Urf, I mean.</u>

Twenty-five damage—or **twelve and a half** hearts—with **a single strike!** It was **shocking.** To give you an idea, my maximum health is **twenty-two,** or **eleven hearts.** Even so, Urf's life bar only **shrank slightly**—maybe **10%.** I wasn't sure if that was the monster's life or Urf's, or **a combination of the two.** Either way, he was **nearly indestructible.**

And even though S took away a **significant chunk** of Urf's life, without his Overblade ability, Urf's **regeneration** equaled our damage output. With every one of our attacks, his health bar went down ever so slightly, only to **bounce right back up again.** At some point, Urf actually **stopped attacking** and **laughed.**

"You call that **damage?** You won't even get me to half! This is **so much fun.** I—"

The zombie/wizard/noob **cried out in pain** and bent backward again as S landed another **Overblade**—then he did it **again** before he even landed.

Having lost roughly **30% of his health,** the sound Urf made could only be described as **pitiful.** Naturally, I expected S to follow up with **a fourth** Overblade, because why wouldn't he?! But he went back to **standard-issue** sword swings, the kind we practiced in class. I looked at him **in despair.**

"What are you doing?! **Keep using that jump move!**"

"I can't," he said. "It's on **cooldown.**"

"**Cooldown?**"

"**Time limitation,**" Pebble said. "He can only use it **three times per day.**"

S grinned. "I would be **overpowered** if I could just **spam** it over and over like that, right?"

"..."

It gets **worse. My shield broke** upon blocking Urf's next attack. With my left hand, I **drew my obsidian sword** and joined Pebble and S in swinging away **frantically.**

"Keep at it," S said. "Once that Regeneration buff **wears off,** he'll stop out-healing us, and **it's over** for him! **We're almost there! Fifty-five seconds!**"

Urf offered no response.

Hhmm. What's this? He's not playing around anymore? Seems like he's a little worried.

Now forced to **block** Urf's attacks **with my swords,** I wasn't knocked back very far but still took considerable damage. Breeze threw **splash healing potions** to keep our health up. Our life bars were all somewhere around **50%.** Sometimes, I just couldn't move **fast enough.** We were never going to make it until his Regeneration **ran out.**

53, 52, 51 . . .

Each second felt **so** long. Then, all of a sudden, the arrows stopped. **Breeze was out.** Drawing her swords, she joined us in **the heat of combat,** a blur of emerald and diamond. Then I remembered something—the arrow with the **obsidian point** and the **creepy face**. I had **no idea** what it did. Normally you can see an item's **stats**, but that arrow's properties had been **masked somehow**. Still, by the looks of it, that arrow did **something bad**. And hitting Urf with something bad seemed to be our only shot, seeing as **he was going berserk.**

Blocking another fist with my swords, I turned to Breeze and **handed her** the projectile.

"I'm not sure what this does, **but . . ."**

The look on her face indicated that this arrow did a lot. *(Her face then indicated that I was an elite noob for not telling her about it earlier.)*

"Hurggggaaaaaaaa!!"

Pebble flew past us. He'd glanced over—to see what I was talking about—allowing Urf to catch him off guard.

"Uwwwaaaaaaaaaaaaaaaaaaa!!"

And there went S.

SATURDAY— UPDATE XVIII

There was no **long and detailed discussion** about what the arrow did. Breeze took it and **fired**. Striking Urf **square in the chest,** the arrow didn't do all that much damage *(only three)*, but the **debuff** it *inflicted* . . . it was **such a joyous sight.**

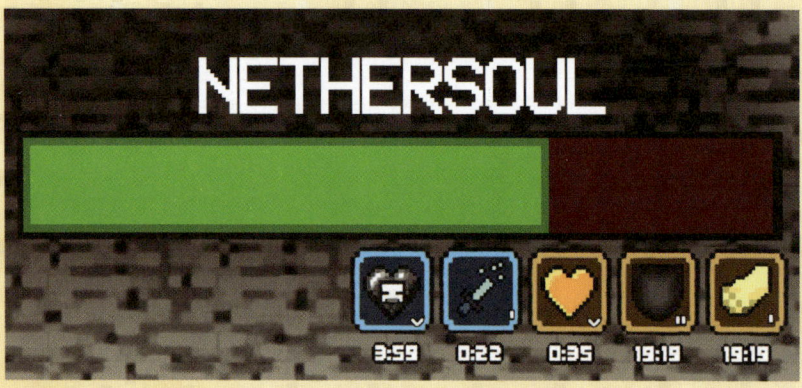

The skull with the gray heart was **Wither**—a **damage-over-time,** or DoT, debuff—**Wither V,** in fact. In this case, Wither V was strong enough to **counteract** Urf's regeneration, and in thirty-five seconds, **when his Regeneration wore off** . . .

"Where'd you get **that?!"** Urf howled. "I can't . . . **I won't** . . ." Like an enormous **baby throwing a tantrum,** he swung wildly and **randomly** at all of us. "I'll take **all of you with me!"**

"**Stay together!**" Breeze shouted over the roars. "**The splash** doesn't reach very far!"

We **drew closer** to one another, and she threw a potion at the ground. The splash hit everyone, healing us somewhat. Then we immediately split up again so he couldn't strike all of us at once.

"**You ruined everything!**" Urf shrieked.

He began **focusing** on Pebble, who couldn't do anything but hold up his axes **in defense**.

"You were supposed **to deal with him!** You were supposed to join us! You drank that potion! I saw you!"

Urf's left arm swung through the air like a tree trunk, and a fist **slammed** into Pebble.

"Why—"

The right arm this time.

"Didn't—"

The left again.

"It—"

Finally, both fists came crashing down, and **sparks** flew from Pebble's axes as Urf **sputtered** in rage.

"**Work?!**"

At the end of this furious assault, above Pebble was a mostly red life bar with **just a sliver** of green. . . .

"**Get back!**" I shouted. When **he didn't,** I pushed him aside and stared up into the wizard's **glowing red eyes.**

"**So it was you! You** made him crazy!"

"**I did!** And I'll do **much worse!** Your little village will come to an end! If—"

From somewhere not too close, I heard a scream. Breeze. She was now **behind Urf, tearing into him,** her swords, like her hair, **a flash** of brilliant green and blue. Urf whirled around in a total frenzy. She never even blocked, trying **to match his damage output.** But there was **no way** she could. Even without his regeneration, he was still at **35%** with an **ample boost to his armor and attack speed.** Looking back, we should have kept our distance and let **the Wither debuff** wear him down further. But everything's so clear **in hindsight.**

Breeze! No!

I sprinted around Urf, **toward her,** each second **an eternity,** and each millisecond accompanied by a beat of my heart, the swing of a weapon, the right-to-left movement of green bars, a shout, or the ring of sharpened emerald through **hard, withered flesh.**

I was only **five blocks away,** and saw that her health was **less than Pebble's.** A thin green line. Three blocks. She **looked up.** So slow. Time had stopped. She was looking up. *What's she looking at?* *Move.*

Get to her. And it seemed like forever until I saw **the shadow,** like that of a cobblestone pillar, quickly moving toward her.

A fist
<u>**slammed down.**</u>

SATURDAY—UPDATE XIX

When the smoke finally **cleared**, all that remained were **scattered items** on the ground, including **two swords** and a pair of black leather boots. All thought **left me. All feeling.** I took a single step forward, **silent.** All four of us stared at **the pile** on the ground without saying a word. **Even Urf.** His expression was almost one of **regret,** if a zombie **could** display such an emotion. But soon, **a deep laugh was welling**

up inside him, which he let escape—at first **slowly** but then **stronger** and **stronger.** All I can remember here was **three loud battle cries,** swords flashing before me, another sword to my right, axes to my left, and Urf staggering back **again and again.** Only later did I realize that **I was wielding her swords.** I must have picked them up.... Breeze had taken him **to 25%,** and we took him **to 7%,** but it **wasn't enough.** He fought back just as crazily, and **we struggled even more** without Breeze and her potions. In the end, he **cornered** us. Backs pressed against the wall, each of us was one hit away from **going out just like—**

Why didn't she dodge . . . ?

I failed her. Didn't make it to her in time.

No, she can't be gone! It's some kind of trick! It has to be!

"This is **so crazy**," S muttered. "What's happening? Why is an **NPC** doing this?!"

"**Runt,**" Pebble said, "I . . . **I'm sorry** for being such a jerk to you before. I don't know what was wrong with me."

"Will you guys **stop that?!**" S hissed. "**Focus!** We need a plan!"

"We can **charge** in," Pebble whispered. "**Flank him.** He'll probably take us out, but . . . **we should do it for Breeze.**"

"**For Breeze!**" I said.

I still **refused** to believe she was gone. There had to be **some other** explanation. She couldn't . . .

"It's a pity, what happened to her," Urf called out.

He was some distance from us, where **he'd been waiting. The Wither** had worn off by now.

"But you should feel **relieved** to know that you will be joining her very soon." A **hideous** smile appeared across his equally hideous face.

"I'm afraid this is the end."

"It is the end . . . **for you!**"

Startled by the voice, the three of us looked around. **It was her voice.** I saw a slight figure appear behind him. **It was her.** As if she could have been **beaten** by a noob like Urf!

Barefoot and **wielding a greatsword,** she was already in the air before he began to turn around. She used **Quietus**—an ability that only works a monster on **who isn't facing you.** The damage it deals is **proportional** to how injured the monster is. With a zombified Urf already **in the red zone,** this ultimate ability **finished him in one go.**

The red flashes of his life bar gave way to **nothing but an empty border.** He **staggered** forward, looking at Breeze, who'd landed a safe distance from him. Then, **trembling with rage,** he bent his head upward and howled.

"Immmmmmmmmmmmmmm—
p–p–posssssssible!!!"

His scream **ended** abruptly; his body **pulsed** bright red, then **flashed,** a slow strobe that illuminated the entire room. With each strobe was a crackling sound like static. At last, **the monster** Urf had possessed crumbled into countless **bright red cubes,** which quickly disintegrated, until all that remained was a **pile of items**—including a **small gray item chest.**

From nowhere and everywhere came **a woman's voice,** as **cold** and **emotionless** as an iron golem's:

The dungeon *Tomb of the Forgotten King* has been **cleared.** All traps and monster spawners have been **deactivated.** Additionally, any remaining hostile monsters have been **purged.** Please note, this dungeon will reset in exactly one week. . . .

She said some other stuff, but I can't remember the rest.

"That's **the announcer,**" S said. "It's part of a **mod.** Never mind. It'd take too long to . . ."

I can't recall what else he said, either, because **I wasn't paying attention** anymore. Not to him, anyway, and not even to the treasure pile. The **real treasure** was right in front of me.

Well, maybe a little to my left.

Putting away her **massive sword**, Breeze ran up and gave **me the biggest hug.** Then **Pebble** gave me **a hug,** followed by S giving Pebble a hug. Breeze and Pebble **almost** hugged but there was **awkwardness** there because of the whole **he-used-to-be-a-bad-guy** thing. Finally, we **broke out laughing** and had a group hug. I just used the word "**hug**" a lot, but what do you expect—we were just **happy to still be alive,** okay?!

"Will you **please** use a healing potion?" I said to Breeze, glancing at her life bar again. "With your health **that low,** I'm afraid to even breathe!"

SATURDAY—UPDATE XX

So you want to know **how Breeze survived.** You also want to know **why** she was **barefoot** and wielding **a greatsword.** Well, dear diary, **don't you worry.** I asked for you. Right after she used up the rest of the splash healing potions on everyone. (We practically bathed in the stuff.)

She explained how she'd **sidestepped** Urf's attack at the very last moment and used an ability called **Smoke Bomb.** It creates **a large smoke cloud** around you, and you **turn invisible** for a short time. To make the illusion of her demise more convincing, she **threw down** her **swords** and the **emeralds** she'd collected, then unequipped her **boots** and **accessories.**

"**Honestly,** I'm surprised I didn't realize that," S said. "That was way too much smoke, and there should have been some **experience orbs.**" He gave her an **approving** nod. "**Nice move,** I have to say. A rather unconventional use of **Smoke Bomb** but **effective** nonetheless."

"Yet **another ability,**" I said. "So you have been holding out on me! **Why all the secrecy, huh?!**"

"**You'll learn more,**" she said. "As soon as we get back."

"And what about **that sword?**" I asked. "Where'd you get that?"

"My father **gave it to me** just before I left. Said I should always carry a backup."

Again, the tone of her voice indicated she was **hiding something.** I narrowed my eyes. Something was definitely **going on** here. Some kind of **secret.** I was almost certain. What was it?!

Luckily for her, Pebble—after glancing around **superstitiously** again—totally changed the subject.

"Hey. Guys. **What happened to Urf?**"

"Good question," S said. "If the monster you've Soulshifted into is **defeated,** you'll **reappear** nearby. But it seems like he really is gone. Those are **his items. Besides that chest, I mean.**"

"We'd better not **take any chances,**" Pebble said. He still had that fearful look. "Let's **grab the loot** and **bounce.**"

Everyone turned to **the pile.** Normally, the boss would have **only dropped that chest.** The items lying around it had **belonged to Urf.** There were books on **ancient history.** Books on **magic, monsters, and dungeons.** That's what S said, anyway. Like those books we'd seen earlier, they were all written in **unknown languages.** *(By the way, knowing a language is an ability. There are many: Common Tongue, Ancient Tongue, Enderscript, etc.)*

We sifted through countless **stacks of blank paper, low-level potions,** and monster parts used in brewing like **spider eyes** and **bat wings.**

Of course, his worn items were also there. While his hat, sunglasses, and shoes had no **enchantments,** his robe—excuse me, **his gown**—had **two.**

NETHERFORGED GOWN
CLOTHING
CONTROLLER I
FLAMEWEAVER I

"I **should have known**," S said. "All **Nethermancers**, upon first starting out, are given such a gown. Those enchantments **boost fire and summoning magic,** which a Nethermancer **specializes** in."

So Urf was a **type of wizard** known as a **Nethermancer.** Wielding **magical fire.** Inflicting hideous plagues. Summoning **undead minions** and controlling them like **slaves.**

Urf had decided to enter **Nethersoul's body**, and that was **a major error** on his part. Had he simply **held back** and summoned an army of skeletons, we **definitely** would have lost. His anger had gotten the best of him.

Anyway, there's **no way** I'd wear that gown. Especially considering the fact that Urf used to **sleep in it.**

"Maybe he was the one behind those **zombified animals**," Pebble said.

"**You've seen them, too?**"

"**Everywhere.** Especially in the forest to the south. Still give me **nightmares.**"

"Only **Nether Rot** could be capable of doing such a thing," S said. "It's a spell—that is, an ability of a magical nature—that inflicts a **horrible debuff** similar to **Wither.** Except when your health hits zero, you don't die. **You turn into a zombie.** Of course, being a **disease,** the debuff will also spread to any nearby life-forms. Works on animals, too."

"It must have been him, then." I sighed. "Guess that's **one mystery solved.**"

Back to the items.

Urf had also been carrying a **most curious** weapon.

FEY CUDGEL
WEAPON (STICK)
ATTACK SPEED 1.5
AVERAGE DAMAGE 2
STUN II

<u>A stick.</u>
An enchanted stick.

I wish I were **joking** here, but alas, I'm as serious as Urf was when he wrote that one handbook. It's not totally **worthless,** though.

I guess. According to Breeze, **Stun II** has a 20% chance of inflicting **paralysis.** According to S, the duration of said paralysis is . . . **one second.** For some strange reason, Breeze seemed **very interested** in this weapon. **Why?** Honestly, I can't see how the **small chance** of stunning a monster for one second makes up for such **pathetic damage.** Not only that, but the item reminds me of Urf's tales of bonking a zombie on the head **with a stick.** Plus, I believe the word "**fey**" has something to do with **faeries.** That means I will **most definitely** pass. Regarding Urf's former inventory, it seemed there was only one item left, which happened to be none other than . . .

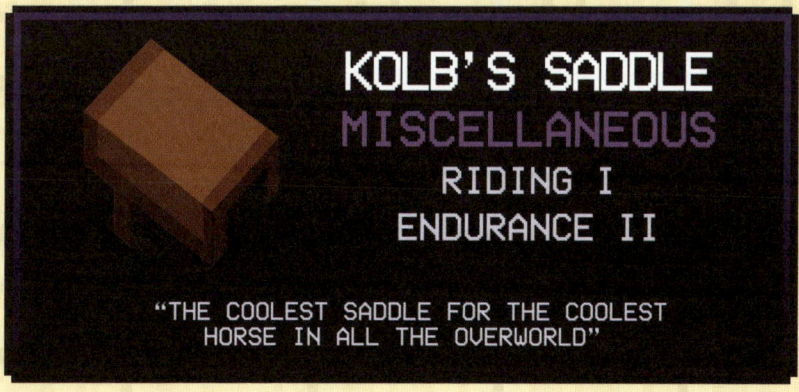

KOLB'S SADDLE
MISCELLANEOUS
RIDING I
ENDURANCE II

"THE COOLEST SADDLE FOR THE COOLEST HORSE IN ALL THE OVERWORLD"

When I saw this, my mind became **a slimeball.**

No.
Nono.
Nononono.
Nuh-ooohh.
NONOPINEAPPLE . . . ?!

Why is this here?! **Why?!** *What does it mean?!* What does it meannnnnnnnnnnnnnnn?!

Think. Think. Logic. **Logic.** Don't panic. Stop breathing like that! *Explanation!* Need! Explanation! Why is everyone looking at me?! Look innocent! *Act casual!* Oh, I don't know how to whistle! Not my fault! Not! My! Faultttttt!!!

"That's strange," Pebble said. "**Kolb's** still in **Villagetown**, right?"

"He is," Breeze said. Then she gave me **the sternest look,** probably the way Stump's parents look whenever he burns the cupcakes.

So what this means is . . . thinking logically here . . . Urf stole Meadow. . . . He took Kolb's horse and . . . Well, maybe Kolb had two enchanted saddles? That's possible, right???

"**I'm not sure why** Urf was carrying that," I said at last.

"So you guys know Kolb?" S asked. "**Small world.** We've been friends since the server launch." He picked up the saddle. "Maybe I should **return this to him.** I'd like to ask him what—"

238

"No, **that's fine!**" I said, **snatching** the saddle out of his hands. "I'll be meeting up with him soon anyway."

Lucky, this whole thing was **quickly** forgotten when S opened **the small gray chest.** It was time for the real loot. **The boss loot.** According to S, most of the items found in a boss chest are **randomly generated.** After opening it, he added, "**Let us pray to the gods of RNG.**"

I'd heard a few **Legionnaires** say this exact phrase several times before. **RNG** has something to do with **random events**—I think it stands for Random Number Generator. So praying to the gods of RNG means hoping you **get lucky?** Is that right? Well, let's just say **his prayers failed. Take the following item,** for instance:

A golden cow. The size of a child's toy. Seriously. I couldn't make this stuff up. Apparently, when placed in a room, this little cow gives off **an aura** called **Prosperity.** At level III, it gives anyone crafting nearby a **3% chance** of crafting **double** the amount of whatever they're trying to craft.

I suppose I can see the uses there, but still, it's **weird**. If the gods above really are the ones who determined this loot, well, they must be laughing right now. I'm not, however. **Next.**

It's official: **the gods really are** laughing.

So it goes like this—there are **several different types** of bed enchantments, and they're all appropriately named: **Goodnight, Sleepwell, Sweetdreams,** and so on. The Goodnight enchantment gives you two extra temporary health, per level, upon waking up the next day. You'll see it in the form of **golden hearts** added to your life bar. This **buff** will last the whole day, only vanishing when you take the appropriate amount of **damage**. Not bad, I guess, but you won't see me sleeping in it. **I do have dignity,** you know. **Next!**

ENDERPOUCH
ACCESSORY
POCKET III

Oooooh, now **this** I like. What is it, you ask? Only **a miniature ender chest** that you wear on your belt. The **Pocket** enchantment is like a small **extradimensional space**. Any item with this enchantment functions as a container. Not only is the size of your inventory effectively **increased** but also you can retrieve items from the container **in record time**. Pocket III means three additional squares, meaning I could put **three different potions** in it. **So Batman**.

I don't yet have a **belt,** but I totally grabbed this. As soon as Breeze explained what it did . . .

DRAGONSKULL HELM
ARMOR
RESILIENCE VI

Hmm. Classic **tank gear** that greatly reduces damage from critical hits. What's not to like?

First of all, it's **kinda cool,** but I dunno. **It's a dragon skull.** Something **Urg the Barbarian** would wear. Or a Nethermancer. Just **not my style.**

But more than that, I'm not so sure about my future as **a tank.** I've tried it out, and I like **protecting** my friends, but dude—**taking damage gets old. Really old.** In fact, if you happen to be an aspiring adventurer, I advise doing anything to not be the tank. Like, **make up a story** about how a zombie in iron armor attacked your village when you were a little kid and **you've had nightmares** about it ever since. Then wipe away **imaginary tears** and say something about how you can't even **look** at a shield without wanting to cry.

Next!

THE SAPPHIRE FLAME
QUEST ITEM

"THE FLAME MUST SHINE ONCE MORE, ELSE ALL OF AETHERIA SHALL PERISH."

"And **there it is**," S said, holding the crystal before us.

Breeze traced her fingers across its surface. "I've heard of **a temple with the same name.** Does this crystal belong there?"

S nodded. "**It does.** It's **required** to **light the beacon** located on the temple's roof."

"**What happens** when you do?" I asked.

"At night, its light will be seen **from anywhere** on the main continent, and even the outlying isles, like **the brightest blue star.**"

"It's an ancient **warning system**," Breeze said. "Those living in remote areas will know to **prepare for war.** Every village should have at least **one librarian** who knows what the blue light means."

"You sure know your **lore**," S said, giving her a **quizzical** glance.

"**I do.** And I know that completing your quest will be **far from easy.** Surely the Eyeless One has already sent a considerable number of **his minions** to that temple."

S clutched his chest. "Wow. I think I'm **in love.**" When Breeze gave him **a cold look** *(me too)*, he raised his hands defensively.

"Joking, **joking.** Wait a sec. Are you two *an item?!*"

Breeze **blinked.** "Item?"

I have **no idea** what he meant by that, either. How can a person **also be an item,** let alone two people?

"**Never mind,**" he said. "Anyway, **yeah.** You're probably right. I'm sure monsters are **guarding** that temple now. The last thing **Herobrine** wants is someone **lighting that beacon**. Good thing I've got **my dark apprentice** here. He won't let me down."

He slapped **Pebble** across the back.

"How about we hit **Owl's Reach** again? I saw a few guys hanging around there who **owe me a favor.** I'm sure they wouldn't mind **coming along.** After seeing what that **Urf** guy was capable of . . ."

"He was such **a noob** before," Pebble said. "I don't get how he became **so powerful.**"

S grinned. "That's **power leveling** for you. Old **Eyeless** probably just kept summoning a bunch of monsters and weakening them for him. It's a **cheap tactic** and one the **Boss Wizards** used to employ a lot back in the day, even though it's **against server rules.** Or **was,** I should say. The rules don't exactly matter now. . . ."

"**The Boss Wizards,**" I said. "I think I met some of them. Who are they?"

"**A clan. One of the foulest.** The complete opposite of the Lost Legion, really. They had no interest in proper player etiquette **before the crash** and infinitely less interest now."

"But the ones I talked to **didn't seem so bad** to me."

S shrugged. "They might **act okay** in the cities, where it's **safe.** But when you're at **the end of the line,** in places like this and in situations like the one we just faced, well, they'd leave you without a second thought. **Don't trust 'em.**"

"We ended up **grouping with some** of them a few days ago," Pebble said gravely. "Didn't . . . **go so well.**"

S made an **annoyed sound** and scratched the side of his face but said nothing.

"Anyway." Pebble looked at me like he'd been **holding in** the most important question of all time. "So, **uh** . . . how's Villagetown doing?"

"Surviving. Barely."

"Kolb seems to think **an advanced crafting table** will help turn the tides," Breeze added.

"**It'll definitely help,**" S said. "With that, you'll be able to **craft obsidian weapons and armor.** About the same as iron, really, but once you make **an obsidian farm,** you'll have **an infinite supply.**"

<u>Obsidian farm?</u>
Sure, I slept **a little** in farming class,
but I don't have a clue what they're talking about.

"Listen, all we really came here for was **the crystal,**" S said. "You guys **take the rest.** Sell whatever you don't want. **Or sell it all.** The boss dropped some **pretty lame** stuff this time around."

"**Appreciate it,**" Breeze said.

"What about **the glowmoss?**" I asked.

"Oh. Sorry. It's in **one of those chests**," S said. "**Minor quest items** load in those."

Yes, you may have been wondering about the **eight ender chests** in the back of this room. **I checked five** of those chests; **all** were empty. However, after I slammed down the fifth lid, Breeze was right there beside me, sticking out her tongue. And also dangling **a soggy green item** in front of my face.

Legendary moss, huh?

How moss can be used to **craft armor,** I don't know, and **I don't really care.** When I looked at this item, which seemed to be little more than phosphorescent slime, I saw not moss but a **pile of emeralds—750,** to be exact. Shortly after I **stuffed** that thing into my inventory, there was **a faint crackling** from behind us. The blocks of magical ice Urf had created were **vanishing.**

(I'm guessing Nethermancers don't use ice spells too often. How can ice exist in the Nether?!)

S returned his **emerald greatsword** to the scabbard on his back. *A bit jumpy.*

"**All right,**" he said. "Since we're both headed to Owl's Reach, I guess we might as well **head there together,** yeah?"

"Yeah, if **Shybiss** can keep up," I said. "That's **her horse.** Not sure what happened to . . . **mine.**" *Quick! Change the subject!* I turned to Pebble. "So **um,** after you've lit that beacon, are you gonna **come back?** Considering how what happened before wasn't your fault, I'm sure the mayor would **pardon you.**"

"**I'm not sure,**" he said. "I already **promised** S that I'd go traveling with him. He's been working on **a ship.** You should see it. We still need to **find several items** to get it up and running, though. One of the items was in this cave. **You wouldn't believe—**"

"Like he said," S **interrupted** with a smile, "it still needs **a lot** of work. But maybe **someday.**"

(There was something strange about the way he cut Pebble off like that. Why all these secrets?!)

The **former bully** looked at me and shrugged. "I'm sure **I'll visit** at some point, Runt. Until then, tell everyone **that I'm . . . sorry.**" He **looked around** again. "**Can we leave now?**"

With that, we left the dungeon. Just as that **mysterious voice** had claimed, the halls were now **devoid** of monsters, and the golden pressure plates only clicked lightly when we stepped on them. Of course, I stared at that vault again as we walked past, wondering what it could possibly **contain. . . .**

PREVIOUS BOOKS

Diary of an 8-Bit Warrior

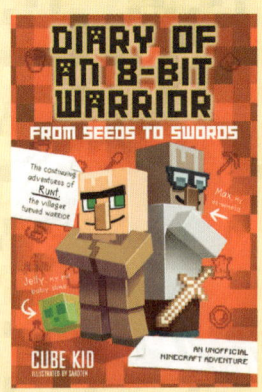

Diary of an 8-Bit Warrior: From Seeds to Swords

Diary of an 8-Bit Warrior: Crafting Alliances

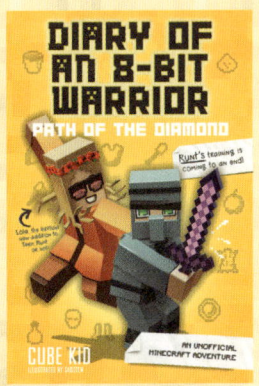

Diary of an 8-Bit Warrior: Path of the Diamond

ABOUT THE AUTHOR

Cube Kid is the pen name of Erik Gunnar Taylor, a writer who has lived in Alaska his whole life. A big fan of video games—especially Minecraft—he discovered early that he also had a passion for writing fan fiction. Cube Kid's unofficial Minecraft fan-fiction series, *Diary of a Wimpy Villager*, came out as e-books in 2015 and immediately met with great success in the Minecraft community. They were published in France by 404 éditions in paperback, with illustrations by Saboten, and now return in this same format to Cube Kid's native country under the series title *Diary of an 8-Bit Warrior*. When not writing, Cube Kid likes to travel, putter with his car, devour fan fiction, and play his favorite video game.

DIARY OF AN 8-BIT WARRIOR
PATH OF THE DIAMOND

This edition © 2017 by Andrews McMeel Publishing.

All rights reserved. Printed in China. No part of this book may be used
or reproduced in any manner whatsoever without written permission
except in the case of reprints in the context of reviews.

Published in French under the title *Journal d'un Noob (Vrai Guerrier) Tome IV*
© 2016 by 404 éditions, an imprint of Édi8, Paris, France
Text © 2015 by Cube Kid, Illustration © 2016 by Saboten

Minecraft is a Notch Development AB registered trademark. This book is a work of fiction
and not an official Minecraft product, nor approved by or associated with Mojang. The other
names, characters, places, and plots are either imagined by the author or used fictitiously.

Andrews McMeel Publishing
a division of Andrews McMeel Universal
1130 Walnut Street, Kansas City, Missouri 64106
www.andrewsmcmeel.com

ISBN: 978-1-4494-8804-8 hardback
978-1-4494-8009-7 paperback

Library of Congress Control Number: 2016934684

Made By:
King Yip (Dongguan) Printing & Packaging Factory Ltd.
Address and place of production:
Daning Administrative District, Humen Town
Dongguan Guangdong, China 523930
Box Set 3rd printing-2/28/22

ATTENTION: SCHOOLS AND BUSINESSES
Andrews McMeel books are available at quantity discounts with bulk purchase for
educational, business, or sales promotional use. For information, please e-mail the
Andrews McMeel Publishing Special Sales Department: specialsales@amuniversal.com.

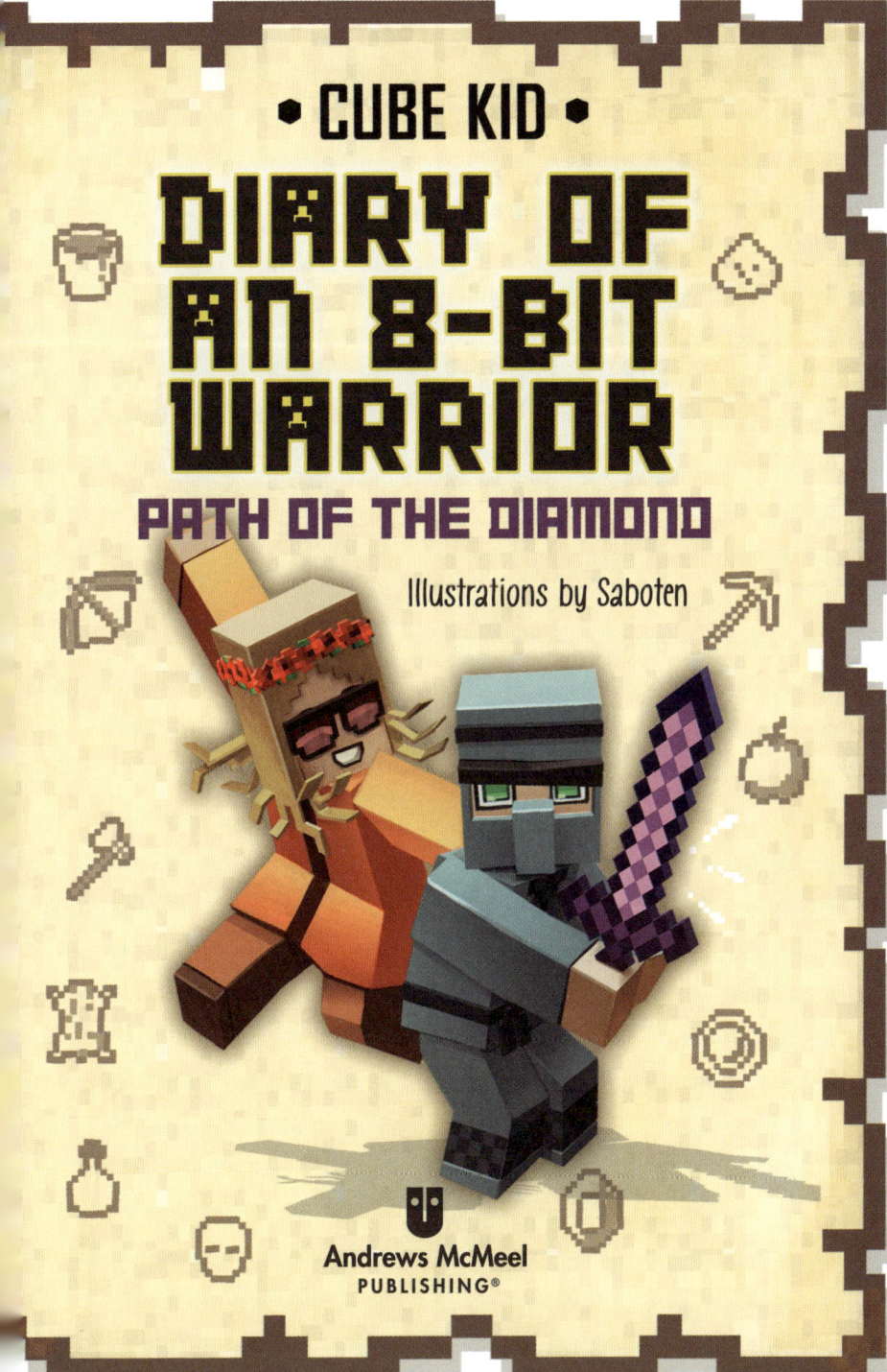

In memory of Lola Salines (1986–2015),
founder of 404 éditions and editor of this series,
who lost her life in the November 2015 attacks on Paris.
Thank you for believing in me.

—Cube Kid

Here's Volume 4!!!
If you haven't read the others, **you'll be like**

O.o

or even

O_O

I also **made this** for you:

<'_"

it's a happy chicken.

SATURDAY—AFTERNOON

My mind was a **water block** in the Nether. One second it was there, and then, with just a little puff of smoke, gone—*poof*—**a little wisp.**

First of all, the five best students would become **captains**, meaning they'd have their own squad to command. As if that wasn't **crazy enough**, Drill admitted that we might someday actually . . . **attack** . . . Herobrine's castle . . . how could we?!
I just don't get it!
Everyone around me was equally **flabbergasted**. Silence grew into murmurs, panicked voices, and questions, questions—**a whole lot of questions.** The most common question being: *"Mayor, sir, is it really true?"*

Alone up on the platform, the mayor **sighed again**. "Yes, it's true. It's something we've been considering, anyway. Now, if you'll all just **quiet down** . . ."

But they didn't quiet down.
Not at all. It was madness.
Madness. Total chaos.

Everyone was **shouting** at once, swarming the platform, asking the mayor an endless stream of questions.

Then an old man got so angry he looked to the sky and started **screaming at the top of his lungs.** *(I have no idea what his problem was.)*

Emerald **said it better** than I ever could *(although I could barely hear her over the constant roar):* "Um, did I hear that right? Not to rain on anyone's **enderman party** here, but, um, this is the **worst** news yet! Clearly Drill was talking about a different Herobrine. I mean, let's face it. There's no way he meant the Herobrine who sends out **streams of lightning** like a dispenser firing arrows, **turns people into rabbits** with the snap of his fingers, and, oh, **has entire legions** of super-powerful mobs under his control."

"**Yeah,** they can't be serious about attacking," Max said. "Knowing Herobrine, his castle probably doesn't even have gates or an entrance of any kind. Come to think of it, do they even know where his castle is located? I've found nothing on this, even after days and days of research." He nudged me. "Speaking of which, are you ready to **help me crack the books** tomorrow, buddy boy?"

Breeze commented with as few words as possible, as usual: "It's like my home village all over again."

Weirdly, Stump seemed a bit happy about this news. "This means I can slack off now! I don't care if I'm a captain, as long as I'm **crushing zombies** with you!"

Kolbert, too, was rather upbeat. "You villagers don't need captains!" He boomed. "**Path of the Diamond?** How about **Path of the Slain Zombies?** For that is what I, Kolbert of **Terraria,** will leave behind on my way to Herobrine's castle!"

A couple other humans looked at him strangely. "**Terraria?**"

He shrugged. "**What?** That's what these people call Earth. **Noobs.**"

(He was telling the truth. I only use "Earth" because I learned that word from Steve.)

Another thing to consider: **What if I somehow fail to become a captain?** If that happens, well . . . knowing my luck, I'd be placed under **Pebble's command.** I'd have to do whatever he tells me to do. I can only imagine how well that might turn out.

"Don't sulk! Carrying lava buckets is super important. You never know when the zombies could attack again, right? Hey! Let's not spill it everywhere, okay?"

If I thought my life at school was bad . . .
FAREWELL . . .

As the crowd grew louder and louder, pressing the mayor for answers, **something happened that nobody expected.** Steve appeared, with Mike at his side. That wasn't so strange in itself, but **. . . they were riding horses.**

I hadn't talked to them in a few days. Last I'd heard, they'd been **working overtime** on redstone contraptions. The sight of those two, as they approached the mayor's platform riding saddled mounts, caused the crowd to quiet down.

"If I may say one thing," Steve said. "Perhaps you should send **messengers** to the other villages. If you really are planning an attack in the future, you'll need all the help you can get."

The mayor nodded, gaze lowered, seemingly deep in thought, **then nodded again. "An excellent plan,** to be sure. But we must assume that Herobrine's forces are everywhere. Such a long journey would be **exceedingly dangerous,** even on horseback."

"Don't worry about us," Mike said. "It's not like we've ever failed you before."

Again, the mayor nodded. **"Indeed,** and I suspect you **never will. Very well.** Shall I send a guide to accompany you?"

"We'll manage," Steve said, and held up a **map and compass**. "Count on it."

Steve was like **my mentor** and **big brother** at the same time. Now he was leaving. Maybe he found this existence **too depressing** and had to try to get away. However, when he rode over to me, I saw only **hope** in his shiny, square eyes.

"I don't know what's happening, Runt. Every day I wake up hoping to find that this is all a dream, just like Herobrine said. **But I know it's not.** We're here for a reason. **I've got to help out.**"

"**But the village needs you!**" I said. "You humans are much more creative than us."

He shook his head. "You may not see it, but you're **just as good** as we are when it comes to defending this place."

"Hurrrm . . ."

"Plus, there's **another reason** why we're going," Mike said. "They might have more **knowledge about crafting.** We'll try to bring back some new toys."

"**Toys?** You mean **new items?** You'll give me one, right?"

"Well, yeah, um . . . sure. Of course."

"Promise?"

"**Super promise.**"

"Hurrr. Okay. **Deal.**"

With that, my **otherworldly friends** took off. They were the ones who had shown us that the mobs could be fought. Without them, we would have suffered the **same fate** as so many other villages out there. I imagined the endless wilderness outside of our walls. Plains and forests and rolling hills as far as the eye can see. **Littered** with the remnants of our kind. They'll be traveling through that for a long time. **Whatever.** That's their decision. Two months ago, I would have dwelt on it, gotten angry and sad. But I'm a new me now. **A future captain,** hopefully. I can't be whining and raging all the time. They can go on their little adventure. Meanwhile, **Team Runt** will be relaxing in the coolest place in Villagetown.

Party at the pool.

SPLASH!!!

For the first time in her life, Breeze was beginning to **have fun.**

After the celebration, we went to **the pool.** The mobs wouldn't be coming back anytime soon, and we totally **needed a break.** The builders made this area **underground.** It used to be a giant cavern the miners had cleared out. The main attraction is the **heated water.** There's a small lava pool bubbling underneath the floor that heats it perpetually. From what the humans have told me, the game version of our world doesn't simulate temperature beyond melting snow and ice. **The real world isn't so forgiving.** Try spending a night in a **tundra biome.** You'll be throwing down a furnace real quick.

We changed into our swimming suits and **jumped in.** We agreed to play **Creeper's Revenge,** one of our favorite games. It's where a single "cat" must avoid the splashes of the many "creepers" as they dive in, over and over. You're probably wondering how we decide teams. After someone shouts "Go," the last one to call out "Boom" is the first to be the cat.

"Go!!"
"Boom."
"Boom!"
"Boom!!"

Breeze glanced at the three of us. "Boom?" *(She'd obviously never played this before.)* We all turned to Emerald.

"Looks like **you're the cat**," Stump said.

However, Emerald didn't respond. She was still standing on the edge of the shallow side, staring **absently** into the water.

> So an enderman from the start? **I knew it!**

So Breeze was happy and Emerald was sad. **What next?!** At this rate, Herobrine will teleport into our village and give everyone **milk and cookies**. I swam over to her. "Something bothering you?"

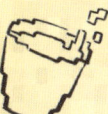

"Yeah. Me." She sat down and dipped her legs into the water. "I've been thinking, and . . . **I just can't forgive myself.**"

"For what?"

"**For running away.** This is the second time I've chickened out."

The other three swam over as well.

"Everyone ran yesterday," Breeze said. "**Myself included.** Don't blame yourself."

"Yeah, but you went back." Emerald exhaled, blowing her bangs upward. "It's funny, y'know? A lot of kids at school look up to me. **They think I'm so brave.**"

I climbed up and sat down next to her. "This reminds me of something. During the second battle, with those zombies . . . **why did you run?**"

"Um, I was **scared?**"

"You came back with iron golems, **didn't you?**"

"Too little, too late."

"But you did **the right thing.** The same can be said for when you ran from **Urkk.** You went to go get the others. Even **set off the fireworks** Drill gave you."

The war heroine looked away. "**So I follow orders. Great.** What's your point?"

"I'll be the first one to say it," I said, glancing at everyone. "**I've been awfully lucky.** When **Urkk** chased me, what would have happened if that **mushroom** hadn't been there? What would I have done? Or what if those skeletons had surrounded me yesterday?"

A slight grin broke out across Max's face. "I see what you're saying. **Good warriors** should know when to run."

I noddded. "**Exactly.** I can't keep being so reckless. My luck will run out eventually. If anything, Emerald, you can teach me a thing or two."

Breeze smirked. "**I hope she does.** Then maybe you'll rescue me someday."

Thankfully, my words seemed to help bring Emerald back to her normal, chipper self. "I did do pretty well during that first battle, huh? I didn't even have good items then! Sara thought she did better, but she had that **enchanted bow!** Just imagine how well I'll do once I have all the best stuff. **Hurmmph!**"

Stump let out a huge sigh. "Guys, why are we talking about this stuff? We're supposed to be **re-lax-ing,** remember? Let's play **Squid War!! Go!!**"

. . .
. . .
. . .
. . .

"Bloop?"
"What . . . ?"
"Uh, isn't that the sound **a squid makes?**"

Seriously?

"I've never played this game before, okay?"

"Never seen a squid before, either, apparently. Squids don't go **bloop!!**"

(Squids don't make noise at all, so the first person to say something gets to be the squid—in this case, Emerald.)

She flashed a huge grin. "So kind of you guys. Really."

(By the way, in this game, you really want to be the squid.)

SATURDAY NIGHT— UPDATE I

After the pool party, we went **shopping.** Although I didn't find any good swords, I traded for a book with **Respiration III** and **enchanted my hood.** *(It was on sale. It's not like anyone in this village has time for ocean diving.)* The next time Pebble tries to well-dunk me, he's going to be in for quite a surprise! **I'll just swim to the bottom and read a book!**

I walked Breeze back to her house just before the sun went down.

"**It's been really fun,**" she said.

"It was even better before the war," I said. "Wish you could've seen the town back then."

"**Yeah. Me, too.** Hey, let's go shopping again, huh?"

She lingered for a moment, until her father came out.

"**See you Monday,**" Brio said. "We've got some new classes. **You'll love them.**"

"What classes?" I asked.

He smirked. "**Wait and see.**"

With a smile, I nodded, **waved,** and shared a good-bye with Breeze—then I took off **under the stars.** The streets weren't entirely empty. These days, they **aren't exactly safe.** Even in the daytime. Even so close to the village center. After the sun goes down, you won't find anyone around. Just closed iron doors and windows with **iron bars.**

Yet I did find someone. **Four people,** in fact. Although I use the term "**people**" loosely.

"You shouldn't be out this late," Pebble said, sneering at me.

"**Yeah,**" Donkey said. "**It's dangerous.**"

Then Rock grabbed me by one shoulder. Sap grabbed me by the other. I tried to break free, of course, but they were **too strong.** It didn't matter. We'd done all of this before. I do something to make Pebble angry, and he and his friends dunk me in a well. It's like a routine now. **What timing, though, huh?** I didn't even have to wait a day to try out **my new hood!**

Maybe that was why I didn't struggle so much. I couldn't wait to see the look on Pebble's face.

I imagined it all in my head. After they **threw me** down the well, I'd swim to the bottom. Minutes later, I'd swim back up and tell them how nice it is down there, **how comfortable, how relaxing,** then swim back down again. **A perfect plan.** A perfect way to make Pebble **even angrier.** And that would have been great . . . if they'd **taken me to a well.**

However...
THAT'S DEFINITELY NOT A WELL.

They took me to an area by **the east wall.** No one lives there. After sunset, it's **a lonely place,** besides the guards standing watch.

No, this place isn't **scary at all.** It's for a surprise party, **right?**

We stopped in front of **a storage room.** Specifically, a **dirt** and **cobblestone** storage room. A lonely little shack that only the miners visit. A building of **low importance,** built against the east wall. I didn't know why they'd brought me here, and I didn't want to find out. I **struggled** again and again, but I might as well have been a rabbit on a **very short leash.**

"We should've taken a lesson from that zombie and made **some weakness potions,**" Donkey said.

Pebble opened the door. The others **shoved** me inside.

"What are you going to do this time?" I asked.

"Make me eat dirt?"

"I guess you could say that. You'll be **flying** first, though."

When they pushed me to the back of the storage room, I . . . suddenly **understood what he meant.**

It's nothing but a normal stockpile. **Yeah . . . that's it!**

Pebble must have **removed** the back of the building. Since the storage room was **connected** to the east wall, they could dig a hole into the wall without anyone noticing. Both of Pebble's parents are **miners.** So today, they probably did something to stop any miner from dumping extra materials here.

"**What are you . . . I don't . . .**" I had to struggle for even these words.

When Pebble turned to me, **his eyes were as black as obsidian.** "**You're a danger** to our village, Runt. You'll be **the end** of us all. My father can see it. I can see it. **This has to end now.**"

"Yeah, so you're gonna help everyone out by **blowing up the wall,** huh?!"

"You really **aren't so bright,** are you? Tonight, I'm dropping **two bats with one arrow.** First, I'll no longer have to worry about you. Second . . ."

I already knew what he was going to say. **It was obvious.** He wanted to reclaim his title as the **hero of this village.** Saturday's celebration took him out of the torchlight, which was now shining directly on me. After that TNT went off, not only would I, **his biggest threat,** be removed from the picture, but . . . monsters could then rush in. Which he'd then take care of. A wimpy villager named Runt would become nothing more than **a distant memory.** A villager punk named

Pebble would clean up and become a hero once more. **A savior. A leader.** A very solid plan.

"**You're totally crazy!**" I snapped, still struggling.

"**Crazy?** After those mobs come pouring in, I'm going to be the best! I'm going to fight them all!! **Every last one!** You'll see!!"

"Actually, he won't," Rock added.

Pebble laughed. "**That's right. Too bad.** You won't get to see any of the changes we're going to make around here."

"Oh, it's so tragic," Sap said. "Poor Runt charged in and **got blown to the Nether and back.** Mayor, sir, we tried to save him, but . . ."

More laughter. Rock stepped into the TNT chamber. "You guys dug the hole **deep enough,** right?"

Hole?
What hole?!

Oh. That hole.

"Get his pickaxe," Rock said. "**Actually, grab all his tools.** He's a **slippery** little noob."

Then Donkey and Sap took my pickaxe, shovel, and both axes, and were about to take more items until Pebble shouted, "**Hurry up!** We still have to **seal up the wall!** And someone check **the redstone line** again!"

Nice. At least I still had cookies.
Then they threw me <u>into the hole.</u>

"**Farewell, nooblord,**" Pebble called out from above me. "I'll make sure to take care of Breeze while you're gone."

As if it couldn't get any worse, Rock placed a **block of explosives** on top of the hole.

19

I was sealed **inside,** three blocks beneath the surface. It reminded me of the emergency shelters they had us dig at school in case we ever got lost outside and couldn't come back before sunset. Except **the blocks surrounding me** were cobblestone, not dirt.

I've been in tight spots before, but this . . .

I could have punched the cobblestone with **my bare hands.** It takes a long time to break a single block that way, though. I heard Pebble's crew sealing up the wall outside, so I guessed I didn't have that long. As always, **I had to think.** Was there a way out of this? **How?**

Well, even if I could **break the TNT** block above me and somehow manage to climb out, I'd still be trapped **within the wall itself.**

Another layer of cobblestone would need to be broken, then, and I no longer had the proper tools. What, was I going to use **a cookie** or something?!

Arrows, pumpkin pie, emeralds, a compass, a water bucket, a bow, some flint and steel. Yeah, that last one was certainly going to help. **It was hopeless.** They were going to **blow me up.** There was nothing I could do about it. I might as well empty my water bucket and **end it** now . . .

Wait.
<u>A water bucket?!</u>

What was it again that old **Professor Snark** said?

Once, we had **a whole class** just on water buckets. He said they were **the best item a warrior could ever have on hand.** Better than an enchanted **obsidian** sword. Better than **Nether dragon-scale armor.** Filled with water, a bucket can save you in a ton of different tricky situations. With it, you could **turn lava into obsidian** . . .

. . . **prevent** falling damage . . .

. . . **hide** from endermen . . .

. . . easily **harvest** seeds . . .

. . . and absorb the damage from **an explosion!**

I emptied that bucket in the space above my head. Water came **rushing** down. The only problem was that I could run out of air, but **my new enchantment** solved that. Actually, I didn't even need it. In less than a minute, explosions tore through the wall.

I still took some damage, in fact.
To tell the truth . . .
I totally blacked out.

SATURDAY NIGHT—UPDATE II

Water. When I came to, the first thing I felt was water. I was lying on my back in a shallow, narrow stream—part of the spring I'd created. As I sat up, I was **awestruck. The damage Team Pebble had caused was unbelievable.**

On the wall above me, a human leaned over **a broken edge.**

"Hey! Villager! **You okay down there?**" It was Sami, the boy I'd mentioned before.

"**It was Pebble!**" I shouted. "Did you see where he went?"

"**Who?**"

Sigh. Never mind. I didn't feel like talking, anyway—too dazed from the health bar drop. I climbed up out of the "**crater**." Only then did I fully grasp the **extent of the damage.** Besides wrecking the wall, the explosions ended up knocking down many of the torches—which created perfect places for monsters to spawn. **Things were not looking good.**

I swam up the spring and refilled my bucket. The spring shrank down to nothing, just soggy ground. Best item indeed. Moments later, **the note-block alarm system** went off. It was located in a short tower near the center of the village. Even though it was some ways away, the noise was easily heard from here. So **the crafters finally got it figured out,** then. They'd been working on it for weeks. Had even modded the note blocks to make **a special noise.** Some of the

humans say it sounds like a **siren**. **Thunder** followed this alarm, followed by **rain**. A flash of lightning illuminated the area beyond the storeroom.

In that split second, through the gloom, a silhouette could be seen: Pebble's **shadowy form** . . .

He stepped into the torchlight, **sword drawn, cloak blowing in the wind,** rain running down his face.

"I had a feeling you'd survive," he said. "Forgot to remove that **stupid cloak** of yours. **That thing is way too good.**"

My cloak? I'd totally forgotten about it.

Still, there was no way it would have helped me survive something like that.

"You mean OP," I said and **drew my sword.** "Just like me."

That did it. He threw himself at me. I met his blade with mine.

A clash of enchanted iron. We traded blocks for a long time, lightning flickering, thunder booming, alarms blaring, heavy rain pouring down. Our health bars shrank slightly every time we did. But mine was **shrinking faster.** There was no way I could beat him one-on-one. He was **too strong, too fast.** On equal footing, I would lose.

Here I was, fighting one of the best students in school—**one filled with insanity and jealous rage**—yet I'd talked about being more careful only hours ago. **I didn't care. I was angry.** He risked our entire village for his own gain. **I had to fight.** Had to do something besides run away. Had to—

Ouch. My vision flashed bright red. At the same time, there was another flash of iron. My health bar shrank from right to left until only **two hearts** remained. A critical hit. He'd also backed me into a corner. So much for knowing when to run.

His sword came down again, **removing the last of my health bar.** At this point, I didn't even feel pain. **Well played, Pebble. Well played.**

His sword came down **a second time.** This time, it removed the last of my health bar.

"What?!" His sword came down **a third time.**

Okay, this time, it removed the last of my health bar. **Wait, no. Hold on.** He swung again.

Okay, okay—the last of my health bar was definitely taken away this time. **Definitely. No, wait. Sorry. It just went back up.**

"Are you **kidding me?!**" Again and again he swung, and each time **my health bar refilled slightly.** Between each swing, I gained about **three hearts,** more or less **negating the damage he'd inflicted.**

Which meant . . . I was **regenerating?!**

The only thing I know of that gives such a powerful regenerative effect is an **enchanted golden apple.** The cloaks the mayor had rewarded us with apparently had this effect. Or something similar.

It was unbelievable. Suddenly filled with confidence, I returned Pebble's aggression. Armed with this buff, I simply **couldn't lose. The end result was Pebble cowering with half a heart remaining.**

"How did you **use it twice?!** I don't see a full moon!! **That's so unfair!!**"

Like the mobs play fair, I wanted to say, but took out my water bucket and waved it before him.

"So it was like that, huh . . ." He turned away.

I threw the bucket onto the ground in front of him.

"Should've **paid attention** in Mob Defense, **noob.**"

"Yeah, yeah, okay. Go on. **Finish me off. I deserve it.** Besides, I can't face my father after this . . ."

"If I couldn't **do it to a slime,** how could I do it to you? Not that you're any better. You'll be way **more useful** alive, anyway. I'm sure they'll assign you **a lot of fun tasks** . . . after they throw you **in jail.**"

Pebble wasn't listening anymore. He was staring at **the massive hole** he'd created, or perhaps staring through it, **at the forest beyond.**

"What have I done?" he said, his voice wavering. "**What have I done . . . ?**"

The sounds of approaching humans grew louder. They were **riding horses** and arrived before anyone else. Of course, Pebble and I received **strange looks**. Kolbert rode up to us. "Someone said that they saw you two **sneaking** into that building just minutes before the explosion! Care to **explain?**"

Pebble shot up. "**I'm sorry, sir!** I tried to stop him, but he **hurt me** so bad!"

All eyes were on me.

That Pebble. And here I just said that he was on the same level as a slime. After this, I'm moving him all the way down—to that of **creeper potato.** By the way, that's not a vegetable. I guess creepers go to the bathroom, too . . .

"**Please,**" Pebble said, "you've got to help me! **He's lost his mind!**"

"What are you talking about?!" Kolbert looked so confused. "Hey! Runt! **What happened here?!**"

I ignored him as well. Beyond the blown-up wall, a chorus of moans could be heard, and they were getting **louder by the second.**

There was no time to explain.

SATURDAY NIGHT— UPDATE III

The rain was straight out of **an enderman's nightmare.** I could barely hear anything through the heavy downpour. Still, when **I listened closely,** I could hear the eerie cries, long and sad. **The shuffling. The scraping.** The endless, **ragged breathing.**

They were coming.

You see, while attracted to torchlight (and, of course, explosions), zombies are particularly fond of **large holes in cobblestone walls.** Only when the lightning flashed did I understand just **how many there were.**

So many, in fact, that describing their count with a single word, number, phrase, or even sentence, just doesn't feel appropriate. For example, I could say there were a lot of them. But then, to a noob or even a level 50 student, "a lot" could mean **three. Instead, I'll provide a little story** to help illustrate what we faced tonight.

Once, in school, we made a **cow farm.** At first, there were only two cows, but their numbers grew and grew. Within a week, **so many cows** were crammed into their little fenced-in area that:

1.) Most cows were **stuck together.**
2.) Many cows were **sticking halfway out** of the fence.
3.) Some cows looked like they had become a **part of the fence.**
4.) Their collective mooing was **so loud** that no one even wanted to go near that farm anymore.
5.) A few cows actually began warping **back and forth,** back and forth, to a spot outside of the fence, **which is just crazy** if you've ever seen that.

Now **imagine a much bigger cow farm**—roughly one-fifth the size of a biome.

Now turn all of those cows into zombies.
Now take away the fence.

That's how many attacked us tonight. What's **stranger** is that they all wore **identical light blue shirts.** Where did they get all that **dye?** Well, some wore mismatched armor, like all gold over a pair of those hideous-looking chain boots. **No class, man. No class.** With gear like that, it was hard **to take them seriously.** *What kind of army is Herobrine sending at us?* I thought. *A bunch of swordless zombies rolling around in chain boots? Really? It's, like, an insult, man!*

ATTACK REPORT:
ONE MINUTE LATER . . .

Hey, zombies! We're warriors in training! Don't even bother!

You can't **block** like us!

You can't **fight** like us!

You can't **run** or **jump** or do **super cool** moves like us!

This made the zombies **very, very angry,** because they totally wanted to sprint and jump and do cool **special attack moves.** They totally did. Luckily, nearly every kid in school had shown up by then. They arrived **so quietly.** There were few words, **no shouts or commands,** and not the slightest trace of fear. They wanted to be here.

Graduation was coming, their ranks weren't high, and what better way **to improve your combat grade** than battling an endless wave of undead?

To the humans, zombies meant items, **experience points,** and perhaps a way to vent the **frustrations** that came with being trapped in a world of one-meter cubes.

Kolbert pointed his sword at the broken section of wall. **"We'll hold them off there!"**

Oh yes, **we would hold them off there.** We would hold that area like a noob clutching **his first diamond.** If we didn't, a countless number of zombies would spill into the streets, and **game over,** thanks for playing. They'd trash everything . . . **including the ice cream stand.**

Ice cream stand

The ice cream stand?!

No! Not the ice cream stand, with its little item frames featuring all eight flavors! **Not that! Anything but that!** Ransack my bedroom, fine! Blow up our fountain, okay! Just don't touch that cute little hut made out of fence and blocks of wood! With it gone, I'd no longer be able to enjoy **diamond ore chunk,** with its perfect texture, its fantastic consistency, and a blend of flavors so utterly amazing it should count as enchanted food! How could they destroy that?! How could they?!

They might be monsters, but **even they have limits, right?** Even they should know where to draw the line!

I bit into a cookie without taking **my eyes off the enemy. No way** were they getting past us tonight.

All we had to do was block this entry point, and their numbers **wouldn't matter.** We also had to pray to Notch that they weren't backed by **endercreepers.** Oh. And we also had to swing.

Experience points swirled through the air in colorful streams. The smoke from **so many dissolving bodies** made it difficult to see.

Arrows, sent from the rooftops, practically outnumbered the raindrops.

Mean = **red**

Nice = **green**

Brio was somehow wielding **two swords at once.** Drill was using **an iron axe enchanted with Smite V.** Breeze only landed critical hits, her feet rarely touching the ground. Emerald and Kolbert were fighting side by side as if they were best friends. And Max and Stump were about to fight the **creepiest zombie ever—it had black skin and glowing green eyes.**

Stump's eyes were almost as **wide** as cookies. "W-what is that?!"

"**A ghoul,** I think." Max adjusted his glasses. "That's what happens when a zombie . . . never mind. **Just don't let it touch you.**"

"In the name of Notch, **you can count on that!**"

The mayor had even drawn his gold sword, **which was unenchanted**—more of a **ceremonial piece** than an actual weapon. That's when you know things are bad. Of course, in the very front fought Pebble. **Of course! And what a hero he was!** There were times when he jumped in front of villagers or humans to save them. There were times when he took out a zombie with a **single, critical hit.** There were times when he nudged someone aside to take out even more.

And all of this was done in a flashy way, to draw more attention to himself.

So brave!
So fearless!
Look at him go!

Every so often, he **glared** at me. I was just glad he kept his distance. Truth be told, part of me secretly **wanted to shove him into the zombies.** How could he blow up the wall? **How could he try to blow me up?** I always knew he was a jerk, but dude . . . is he **Herobrine's kid** or something?!

More important, what was going to happen **after the battle?** Would everyone believe him? **Most likely.** After all, he had his friends to back him up. **But that didn't matter now.** If the mobs forced us back into the streets . . .

You can have any flavor you like . . . as long as it's slime.

My anger only grew. One after **another,** the zombies fell like anvils. Every time I dropped one, though, another stepped in to fill its place.

It went on like this for a long time. My arms got **tired.** It almost felt like I was debuffed with **mining fatigue.**

ATTACK REPORT:
THIRTY MINUTES LATER . . .

"You . . . holding . . . on?"

"Yeah . . ."

Yeah, Stump and I were totally exhausted. My mind wandered at times. I'm not proud of this, but once, I . . . I started wondering if it's possible **to build a house out of cake.**

SATURDAY NIGHT— UPDATE IV

Ninety-four zombies,
ninety-five, ninety-six, ninety-seven . . .
Cake . . . castle . . . ?
Err—ninety-eight, ninety-nine . . .

I was about to hit **one hundred** when another student bumped into me. He dashed forward one block and **finished off the zombie** I'd been working on.

I glared at him. "**Hurrr! You kill stealer!**"

"**Kill stealer?!**" He laughed. "This is my spot, cobblehead! **Go somewhere else!**"

Of course, I knew this kid. **Cogboggle.** Another annoying punk, just like Pebble.

Styled brows and multicolored robes: the latest in villager punk fashion.

For the longest time, his rank wasn't all that high. Somewhere in the middle, **66th or 67th.**

But after he heard about the **Path of the Diamond,** he did anything he could to get ahead. That was why he stole my kill. He was just trying to increase his rank, to break into the top. Some say he only wants to become **a captain** so he can boss others around. **I totally believe it.** He's ruthless, both a scammer and a thief. He cares only about emeralds, items, and ripping off others.

If he was a captain, he could force the students under him to give him all kinds of "**gifts**" and "**donations.**"

With that in mind, I should have been careful around him, but I wasn't going to let him get away with this. He took my zombie, that punk! So I shoved him aside . . . and stole one of his.

"**You little noob,**" he hissed, and shoved me back.

Soon, we were all but wrestling, nudging and shoving and kicking and pushing each other while fighting the zombies before us. Once, I even **stomped on his foot.**

"Dirtface!"
"Noobking!"
"Blockhead!"
"Worthless crafter!"
"Slime nugget!"
"Enderbutt!"

"Bat farmer!"

Bat farmer?! **Now that was just going too far!** I stepped back and let him have his zombie. Then, just as he was about to deal the final blow, **I whipped out my bow and stole his kill.**

LOLoLOL! Trolled, noob!

He actually thought he was going to get that zombie! He thought that! **He did!** The look on his face . . . **WOW.** I tried to draw it but I couldn't stop laughing.

He was super angry. "You know, after my crew passes yours in rank, I'll make sure Breeze gets **placed under my command!** I'll make her do all the dirty work! **I'll put her on a leash!**"

With one last "**Hurrr!**" he stormed off, no doubt to go steal some other kid's mobs.

Why did he have to bring Breeze into this?! I started to go **after him.** Then I felt a hand on my shoulder—**as soft as Silk Touch.**

"Forget about him," Breeze said. "Focus. **We're losing.**"

SATURDAY NIGHT— UPDATE V

At first, **I didn't get what she was saying.**

Stump didn't, either. "**Who's losing?!**" he shouted, a few blocks away.

"The only thing I'm losing is inventory space," Emerald said. "Just wish they'd drop something useful."

Then the realization came, slowly at first, and then faster and faster, like a mine cart gathering speed, until ***boom.***

I glanced down at my sword. **It only had around 50% durability.** In addition, the zombies actually managed to hit us from time to time. Due to **our fatigue,** we'd all grown careless. My own life bar was at eight hearts. This meant our weapons—and our very lives—were slowly wearing down. Throw enough zombies at us, one lifeless body after another, and we'd eventually break.

Everyone else around me seemed to realize this as well. There wasn't much talking before, but now . . . **no one said a word.**

Breeze fought even harder and cut through zombies with **impressive speed**—and **just as quickly,** more shambled up to replace them. Pebble somehow matched her. His speed was insane tonight! Yet in his bravado, he took several hits from the side, and drank a **Healing I** like he was in a potion-chugging contest. Then the mayor's **sword broke**

over a zombie's head. He glanced down at the golden cubes scattered across the ground, as if his sword had been our only hope.

"Oh dear."

Oh dear?

He brought a gold sword into battle and all he could say was, "**Oh dear**"?

Yeah. **It was over.** It seemed that Villagetown would soon come to an end. Our amazing village, the last line of defense for thousands of blocks around, was going to fall.

The **most ridiculous thing** was that the monsters had nothing to do with it. It was all thanks to **one of our top students.**

Then, just when I thought it couldn't get any worse, **Kolbert left the front line.** Without saying a single word, he just turned around and casually walked away. Emerald gave the human a backward glance. You could almost hear her heart shattering like a pink stained-glass block.

"**Wow,**" she said. "I can't believe he just . . . **wait, what's he doing?**"

More of us glanced back at him. The scarf-wearing knight had an **annoyed look** on his face. "**Are you guys noobs or what . . . ?**" he muttered.

Then he did **something legendary.**

Something that no villager will ever forget.

Something epic, amazing, unimaginably cool, and at first, a little bit **confusing.**

Kolbert put away his sword and . . .
from his inventory, retrieved . . .
an <u>enchanted</u> golden shovel.

"Are you guys noobs or what . . . ?"

I know, I know. That doesn't sound **so legendary.** We were just as confused. We gave him the **strangest looks.** A few kids I barely knew even made rude comments:

"A golden shovel?!"

"Um, 'lol'?"

"And he's the one asking if we're noobs?"

"**Hurrr. Poor guy** finally cracked. **He's totally lost it!**"

If it had been anyone else, I'm sure Emerald would have made some comment, but now **she was totally silent.** The sight of Kolbert standing there, golden shovel in hand, rendered me speechless as well. **It was too ridiculous. Too noob.**

Kolbert—the guy who's always talking about how his sword will one day become very close friends with Herobrine—had stopped fighting to . . . **dig?**

I just couldn't **understand.** The thing that baffled me the most was the shovel. A golden shovel. It was enchanted, yeah, okay, okay, sure, but it was still made of gold.

Gold! Not iron or diamond or **elementium** or some other **rare material** we've only read about. Honestly, when it comes to tools, even wood is superior.

In school, we learned that gold has roughly **half the durability** of wood. So it just didn't make any sense. Honestly, maybe the only thing a golden shovel has going for it is . . . Um. **Digging speed?**

Okay, sure. A golden shovel equals or surpasses a diamond one in every known material.

On top of that, I'm guessing his shovel was enchanted with **Efficiency III,** the way it was glowing.

Cool, **so he could dig super fast**—but what was he going to do with all that speed? **Make an underground village?**

As I glanced back at him, wondering what was coming next, Kolbert **tore through the dirt** beneath his enchanted iron boots. And I mean **tore.**

Like **diamond through sand.** Like an enderdragon through . . . anything. Like me with **presents,** which is arguably the fastest known speed in all four dimensions.

A human named **Trevor3419** quickly noticed the dirt flying everywhere. "**Hey guys!**" he called out. "Look! Kolbert's trying out his new strat!"

Huh? New strat?
What's he talking about?
What's he going to do?

I was so **curious,** it was hard paying attention to the zombies in front of me. Hey, zombies, can you guys just stop attacking for a second? **I really want to see what's going on back there!**

Of course, I've been around humans long enough to know that Trevor3419 was referring to a strategy of some kind, but I still didn't fully understand. More humans left the front line, then. **Trevor3419, Alex, Julian, Emmie, AquaCraze, Calla, TreyR9, Ninja Jack, Simone** . . . Wielding their gold shovels, they jumped into the pit Kolbert had created.

As they carved their way through so much grass and dirt, their strategy became clear.

Team Golden Shovel. They dig faster than their own shadows.

They were digging a moat: a wide pit that would prevent the zombies from advancing any farther. Zombies **can't jump,** you see. They can hop up to a higher block, but they can't even **jump across a one-block gap.** There could have been one million zombies out there, but with that moat in place, it wouldn't matter anymore. **It was a brilliant plan**—err, strat.

From the village archives *(top secret document):*

Strategy 11: emergency ditch

This is what the moat would look like, once complete. (The green area represents the bottom of the moat.)

However, there was still one problem: Even with enchanted gold shovels, they needed more **time.** The front line had to hold off the zombies long enough for **Team Golden Shovel** to finish digging.

Drill understood this, and resumed being Drill. "**Protect those humans!!** Hold that line like bedrock!! Swing faster than doors connected to redstone torches!!"

Okay, so he lost me on that last one. I'm guessing doors connected to redstone torches swing pretty fast or something?

Um . . . whatever. **Let's just say we followed our orders.**

"I think even bedrock would crack if a thousand zombies were standing on it."
—Stump

SATURDAY NIGHT— UPDATE VI

All of us were tired. Most of us were wounded and **out of food.** Some were forced to use axes after their swords broke.

The zombies grew **more relentless,** and more of those **creepy-looking things** with black skin and green eyes were showing up. **Ghouls.** They're **very rare** and **powerful,** like the zombie version of a charged creeper. According to legend, they inflict a status effect—**which is worse than that of any wither skeleton.**

GHOUL

LIFE ???
ARMOR ???
SPEED ???
INTELLIGENCE ???

SPECIAL POWERS: WEAKENING, BY TOUCH, EFFECT UNKNOWN

Ghoul data sheet. Notice the complete lack of information. Maybe its status effect hurts you really bad. Maybe it turns you into pumpkin pie. We really need to hit the ancient libraries more often.

Also, well, I don't want to write about this, but . . . a few of the zombies **wore robes. Former villagers.** They must have come from distant villages. **I dropped a few myself . . .**

Even though they were no longer like us, I felt **guilty** every time I did. Once, after one of them fell, the only item he left behind was **a fishing rod.** He must 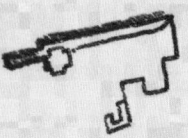 have liked fishing . . . before he became a zombie. I still can't get this memory out of my head. Obviously, some of us in the front line had trouble fighting them after that. It was something that **had to be done,** but at the same time . . .

Whenever I looked into their eyes, I wondered what their village was once like, what their old lives had been like, and how they had come to see living creatures the way I see **pumpkin pie.**

Had they never built walls? **Had they refused to craft weapons?** Had they simply hidden within their houses, praying for an early sunrise?

Their presence even **affected Pebble.** He actually avoided them, and let others take care of them. Every time he encountered one, **he began sweating,** his face became as white as a ghast's, and he shivered, hands trembling, as if a cave spider's debuff were running through his veins.

Maybe it was sinking into that obsidian-thick head of his.

Maybe he realized that, **because of his actions,** the same thing might happen here. Maybe that was why, after about the ninth or tenth green villager arrived, he . . . **suddenly charged in.**

Before anyone could say anything, he was **three blocks ahead of Breeze and me.** My friends rushed in to help him. They weren't exactly rooting for **Team Pebble,** but they didn't know about what had happened earlier, either.

"**What are you doing?!**" Breeze snapped.

Stump cut down a zombie to Pebble's left. "**Are you crazy?! Get back, noob!**"

"W-we can't let them get us!!" he shouted, swinging frantically. "**We won't!! We can't!!**

W-we'll get them all!!"

Zombies swarmed everywhere to our **left and right.** We shouldn't have been this far ahead. **It was too dangerous.** Pebble didn't seem to care. He just waded through them. He cut them down, left and right, left and right, but there were **just so many.**

That was when I noticed the black zombie only one block to Pebble's right. This close, I could see the green particles dripping from its skin, similar to **a slime's ooze,** just like in the ghost stories.

It was reaching for him, **slow and feeble,** and suddenly I recalled some tale about a villager who'd once been touched by one, hundreds of years ago.

It almost got him . . .

I don't know why I saved him. **It didn't involve thinking.** My arms moved automatically. My sword flew as if forced by a piston. **The ghoul flew back.**

I saved him. I saved Pebble without a second thought, without any hesitation, as if I were saving my best friend, despite everything he had done to me . . .

Pebble stared at me over his shoulder,
face twisted in **disbelief**.

·Thanks.·

SATURDAY NIGHT— UPDATE VII

Long story short, **we won.**

The humans **finished digging.** The front line jumped over. Others poured lava in.

Boom, there you have it—the recipe for **sad zombies.** Kolbert's strat worked **perfectly.**

Of course, if this had happened months ago, the zombies would have pushed each other forward until the ones in front fell into the moat. But they are **much, much smarter now.** They stopped immediately.

Then they just stood there, looking at us pitifully, and sometimes moaned. Not one of them dropped into the lava. *(For a zombie, that's really smart, okay?)* I even expected at least one of them to place a **dirt block** to form a bridge, but nope.

They've improved, but apparently they still have a long way to go before graduating from Mob Academy . . .

 Eventually, the zombies shambled off.
Slowly. (For zombies.)

We watched them retreat back into the gloom, into the plains, toward their crummy little forest.

Then the cheers grew louder than a creeper blast. Twenty or so villagers **rushed over to Kolbert** and his friends, praising them, asking tons of questions. Brio even **shook Kolbert's hand.**

Not everyone was so upbeat, though. Many who'd fought in the front line were **too tired to break out their villager dance moves.**

My friends and I regrouped near the **blown-up building** that was once the miner's storeroom.

"**We shouldn't cheer just yet,**" Emerald said. "I mean, moats might work now, but there will probably come a day when zombies can **jump, even fly.**"

Breeze leaned against one of the storeroom's broken walls. "Thankfully, today isn't that day."

"This would have been much easier if we'd just dumped lava **at the entrance points,**" Max said. "I'll make a note of this in my records." *(Yes, Max has a diary now, too.)*

I was one of **the only kids** here who didn't say a word. The other one was **Pebble.** He was staring at the ground, totally still.

Then he approached. Surprisingly, I didn't detect the slightest trace of anger.

"**Runt, uh . . .**" He avoided my gaze as if I were the king of the endermen. "**Can we, um . . . talk?**"

I looked away.

Long ago, I would have **raged hard.** My blood would have been boiling like a potion on a brewing stand. Had I been indoors, I would have shot through a cobblestone roof. But now **I was calm**—as calm as a skeleton in a world without dogs. Which was strange, honestly, because I'd eaten way too many cookies before battle. **Way too many.**

I nodded. "Yeah."

Then Pebble took off. I followed, leaving my friends behind. They were totally speechless. They gave me **the weirdest looks,** like I was trying to craft using my inventory—and not the two-by-two-block grid, mind you, but actual inventory space.

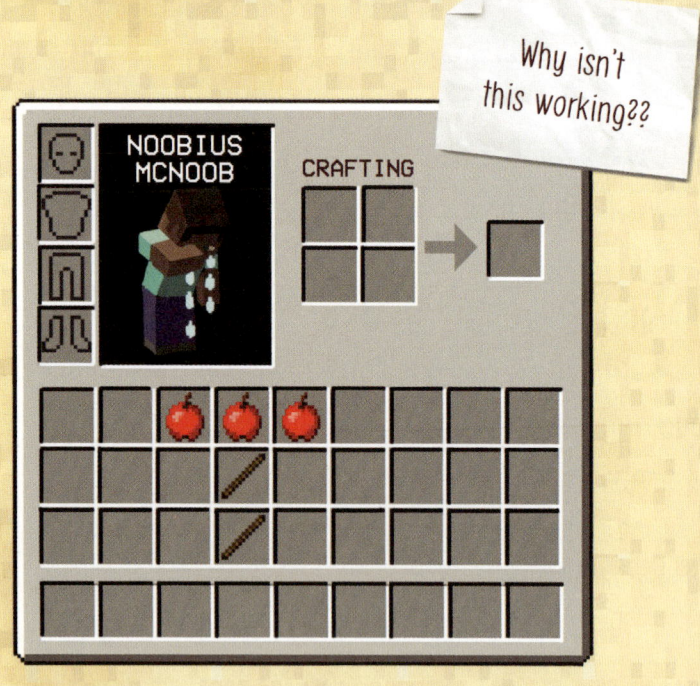

Why isn't this working??

SATURDAY NIGHT— UPDATE VIII

After we gained some distance from the crowd, **Pebble turned to me.**

"I was **wrong** about you," he said. "Totally, **totally wrong.** I know this won't fix anything, and **I know you'll never forgive me,** but . . . I'm . . . **sorry.** You're a good guy."

"Yeah, and I'm sure you're going to say the **exact same thing to the mayor,**" I said.

He gave me a single, slow nod. "I am. Look, I don't know what happened. **I just wasn't myself!** I might've been a **jerk** to you lately, but even you know I'm not like that!"

". . ."

"And I thought you were a spy!" he blurted out. "I saw your pet! **A baby slime!** So I thought you'd turned on us, and when you became a war hero, I just . . . **snapped.**"

"Then you should've talked to me about it," I said. "**Or reported me.** Something. **Anything but THIS!** I mean, do you have any idea what's in store for you once the mayor learns the truth?"

"**I know.** Believe me, I know." He reached into his inventory. "That's why . . . you should take this."

He threw a **stack of emeralds** onto the ground, followed by **five more.** He then emptied out the **rest of his inventory,** including enchanted tools. In utter disbelief, I watched as he threw down each of his items, **one by one.** Finally, he added his armor, sword, and cloak to the mix.

"**All yours,**" he said. "Oh, I have more stuff at home. We can go there now, if you want."

What is this? I gazed down at the **gleaming, glittering, glowing pile of items.** He sure had some real loot. **Three diamonds.** A ton of emeralds. **A golden apple.** Several potions. A fishing rod with **Dredge I.** Even Mobspanker, **his enchanted bow.**

WOW, I thought. *Is this a trick or something? Why is he giving me all his stuff? And what's that Dredge enchantment?!*

I shook my head. "What are you doing?!"

He sighed. "**Come on,** it's not like I'm gonna need them anymore. If you don't take them, they'll just wind up in a storeroom somewhere. **You know that.**"

. . .

Jail, I thought. *He's talking about jail!* Yeah, that's the **standard punishment** around here. But there is a worse punishment, one **reserved for traitors** like him. Maybe Pebble wasn't aware of that, but I was—I've learned a lot from hanging out with Max.

Still, the last time that happened to anyone was over a hundred years ago. Surely the mayor wouldn't . . .

No, I thought, *the mayor isn't that cruel.* I wouldn't wish that fate on anyone, even someone like Pebble.

Pebble shrugged. "Fine, **let someone else have them.** Time to get this over with. Guess this is **good-bye.**"

I didn't say anything, just gave him **the coldest look.** I had to be careful, I felt. I assumed he was going to try **something crazy.**

He turned his back to me. "I just want you to know, I did what I thought was best for the village, and I'm . . . **about to do the same thing, now.**"

Then he took off in the direction of the mayor. **Head low. Face grim.** But his shoulders were still high. His steps came heavy as he walked through the cheerful crowd.

Maybe I should have stopped him.

Did he know what was coming . . . ?

He said he did but . . .

. . . I'm not too sure of it.

SUNDAY

It's hard to believe, but . . .
Pebble is gone.

The mayor's words are still fresh in my mind: "... **destruction** of village property, attempted **murder**, violation of—oh, enough with this mumbo jumbo! **Pebble Graybanner**, you are hereby **banished** from our village **until the Nether freezes over!!**"

The worst part was Pebble had dropped **all of his items.** He was sent out there, totally alone, and **didn't have any items.** Not even a block of wood.

Despite what he had done to me, I almost feel sorry for him. There's no way he'll make it even one day. Five months ago, sure, he would have been fine, but now . . . **he doesn't stand a chance.**

As for Pebble's friends, **they were thrown in jail.** Pebble pleaded, begged, and told the mayor it was all his idea.

I'm not sure how long they'll be locked up. Maybe a month, **maybe longer.**

By the way, Pebble's father was furious about the whole thing. **He disowned Pebble.**

"My son has disgraced our family name," he said. "**I'll never forgive him for what he's done!**"

Many villagers stood on either side of him. Pebble's entire extended family. Most were miners. You could tell by the dark, earth tones of their robes. **Their faces were darker.**

At least a few people have suggested that Pebble's father **isn't exactly a nice guy.** Yet here he was, on the verge of tears. Acting?

<u>Whatever,
I was too **tired** to care.</u>

SUNDAY—UPDATE I

This morning, there was a **celebration**. If you could call it that. No one cheered. The mayor didn't say much about the mobs. He did have some **good news,** however.

"This year, the students have exceeded **our wildest expectations,**" he said. "This may come as a shock, but . . . most of you have **advanced past one hundred** in at least one skill."

The mayor went on to tell us that **we're able to go past 100%** in any given skill. It's always been this way. But the record books were capped before. **They only displayed a maximum of 100%.** The teachers never expected us to do this well. Last year, **the highest level any student attained was 82%.** Due to the war, the students have been pushed hard this year.

It's not that surprising, honestly. Long ago, I wrote about how 100% represents competency. Competency means you're capable of doing the job. It's not the same thing as mastery.

Most blacksmiths are skilled crafters, yes. But what about some **legendary** old blacksmith who lives in the mountains and can forge blades with his beard? His skill might be **500%** or more.

"Your books should be updated by now," the mayor said. "Go on, **take a look.**"

I glanced down at my record book
in shock.

RUNT
STUDENT
LEVEL 106

MINING	99%
COMBAT	107%
TRADING	101%
FARMING	99%
BUILDING	102%
CRAFTING	98%

There were a lot of gasps around me. It sounded like a lot of kids had raised at least **one skill beyond 100%.** Breeze is still ahead of me, **of course.** Not that I expected anything less from a former **test subject of Herobrine's.**

BREEZE
STUDENT
LEVEL 109

MINING	101%
COMBAT	117%
TRADING	101%
FARMING	125%
BUILDING	102%
CRAFTING	106%

How and why is her farming score so high?! What's up with that?! I'll have to ask her . . .

Once the mayor was finished, Drill talked about the **Path of the Sword.** He said students who choose this path will be divided equally among the **five captains.** So if **fifty take up the sword,** each captain will be responsible for **ten warriors.**

The best part about this is that friends will be assigned with friends. Meaning, if I become a captain and Stump chooses warrior, **we'll be working together, no matter what.**

A lot of kids cheered at this news.

Then Brio ruined everyone's mood. He said there will be **four more tests** before graduation:

1) **A mining test.** It was postponed for ages, but now it's finally here.
2.) **A combat test** in the form of a single-elimination tournament known as Ice Cup.
3.) **A redstone test.** I don't know anything about redstone. Stump knows a little, but he's out of ideas after that last test.
4.) **The final.** Students must submit ideas on how to get revenge against the mobs. The teachers will select the best idea. The students will carry it out.

Hurgg.

A redstone test?! Why did they have to pull a trick like this? Redstone hasn't been taught that much in school!

"At least **the final will be easy,**" Emerald said. "Revenge? Hand me that **flint and steel** and follow me to their forest; I'll show you revenge!"

Breeze **giggled.** "The tournament **sounds fun,** too. How will that work?"

"We'll be playing **Skyball,**" Stump said, and then he went over the rules of this villager game.

Skyball **is tough.** You have two teams with six players each, and everyone's **taking snowballs to the face.** Supposedly, there's a huge village far to the west where they take these games way more seriously than we do. They hold an annual tournament there known as **Legendary Cup.** The **best players are like heroes,** respected even more than warriors.

As Stump talked about Skyball's finer points, Max got real close to me. He leaned in right next to my ear and whispered: "**How about you and I take a little walk.**"

SUNDAY—UPDATE II

Max told me something **interesting.** It's something his buddy Razberry came up with. **Operation Snoop,** they're calling it.

Basically, Razberry has been going around school and peeking at other kid's record books.

For the past week, he's spent all of his time snooping around like this. **He's not even studying anymore.**

Why is he doing this? **Because he wants to help us out.** You see, Razberry knows he'll never become a captain. **He's going to be a warrior,** though. So he wants to make sure that at least one member of **Team Runt** is able to choose the **Path of the Diamond.** In return, he'll join us after graduation. A lot of the other potential captains are **jerks.** He doesn't want to get stuck under one of them.

I think it will work because nobody really suspects Razberry of anything. I **feel a little bad** for him, though, since he's sacrificing his grades to do this. But then, when it comes to the **Path of the Sword**, grades no longer matter. Even someone like Bumbi could be a warrior and his combat score is still around 20%.

From now on,
Razberry will give us a little list called a level report, which is pretty much a <u>list of students' levels</u> to show us where we stand in ranking.

SUNDAY—UPDATE III

The "celebration" was finally over. My friends and I trudged off to the ice cream stand. We got our cones and sat around one of the many fence-and-wool tables. Breeze suggested we go here to cheer us up. Didn't work for me. Today, even diamond ore chunk was like **moss-covered cobblestone in my mouth.**

"I still can't believe what Kolbert did!" Stump said. "**What a legend,** cleaning up Pebble's **mess** the way he did! And with a trash-tier item, at that!"

When he mentioned Pebble, I must have appeared **even sadder** than before because Breeze tapped me on the shoulder.

"**Hey, don't let it get to you,**" she said. "Pebble got everything he deserved."

I sighed. "I know, but still . . . I just can't help but **feel bad** for some reason. I don't know."

"Dude, he tried to blow you up!" Stump said. "You almost found out what it's like to be a creeper! And here I was, **trying to protect him!!**"

Max closed a book he'd been reading called *Village Law*. "I have a feeling he'll make it somehow. **Jerk or not,** he was a **top-ranking student.**"

"Which reminds me," Emerald said. "We're wasting time. Graduation is soon, guys. We should really be **focusing on our studies.**"

"She's right." Breeze stared down at her ghast tear swirl. "**There's still a lot of competition out there.**"

"Not that you should be worrying," Emerald added.

Breeze shrugged. "Truth is, **I'm as clueless about redstone as the rest of you.** I'm afraid Stump will have to carry us again."

"We can all try to come up with something," Stump said. "We'd better, because **Cogboggle** is really rising in rank! **Block, too!** We can't let those punks get ahead!"

Hurgg again.

Graduation is coming.

That Cogboggle kid is just a few levels **behind me.** Pretty much every student is around level 90 by now. **Pebble's gang** might be out of the picture, but just like with the zombies, more will step in to fill their place. I'm sure of it.

By the way, I'd say Cogboggle's even worse than Pebble. At least Pebble seemed to care about the village. **At least Pebble was smart.**

Block is just as bad. After hearing about the **Path of the Diamond,** the two of them began stealing ideas from other kids to do better on tests.

They're not the only ones, either. Kids are desperate these days. They'll do anything for better grades. A lot of them want to be a captain. I mean, **how cool would that be?**

So if I lose focus, some of them could pass me by just days before graduation.

With Operation Snoop in place, though, at least I'll have a warning.

Our best agents are on the case!
Our best! Guaranteed!

Breeze **finally tried** her ice cream. Some of it got on her nose. She didn't seem to notice, however.

Everyone else tried to **hide their grins.**

"What's so funny?! **Oh.**" Breeze's face **turned pink** like the horizon just before dawn. "**Oops.**"

Stump laughed. "I don't get you, Breeze. **You're the best student,** yet you can't eat ice cream properly?"

"Don't worry," Max said. "Runt and Stump can help you out. **They have lots of knowledge on the subject.**"

I couldn't help but join in on the **laughter.** But soon, my gaze **returned** to the distant wall.

Even though I couldn't see past it from here, I imagined the **wilderness and the vast emptiness** that stretched beyond. Lately, the wall guards have been **spotting monsters out there in the daytime.** Ones that have no business underneath the sun.

Kolbert said that he had looked out there the other day and seen a group of zombies wearing enchanted helmets. Those helmets were most likely enchanted with **Unbreaking.** If all of them were equipped with helmets like that, they wouldn't even need their little forest anymore. They could roam for hours **without a cloud in the sky.** And then Sami said he saw **a spider chasing a rabbit** faster than a pig chasing a carrot on a stick. In the daytime. If what he said is true, the spider wasn't **blinded** by the sun.

Um . . .
Farewell, Pebble.
Hope you're having fun.

SUNDAY—UPDATE IV

My friends took off. They all had something to do.

Stump had to help his parents. Max wanted to hit the **library**. Emerald was going to **dinner with her father and a few humans**. (Including Kolbert, I'm sure.)

At last, it was just Breeze and me.

"**I want you to take these**," she said. "You should carry at least a few. **Never know when you might need them**."

She can be so sweet sometimes, huh? She must have gotten that from her mother, because she's nothing like Brio.

"**Thanks a lot**," I said. "This human named **Yoonsung** sometimes gets on me to craft or trade for some. **I keep forgetting**, though."

She smiled. "Speaking of humans, I've been wondering . . . why do **so many** of the humans have **numbers after their names?**"

Hurmm.
Good question.

Kolbert's name is really **Kolbert21337**, for example. Then there's **CrafterBot6000, Blaze7381, Meza8, TreyR9,** and **AngryPineapple123**, although they just call him **Pineapple**.

Why do they have numbers in their names? **It's so strange.** If I change my name to **OverlordRunt77777**, will the humans think I'm cool?

"Maybe those numbers are like their **levels** or something," I said with a shrug.

"Wait! So Kolbert is **level 21,337?!**" I added.

"Maybe that's why he's their leader?" She shrugged as well. "Oh, hey, I've been wanting to ask you . . . **have you had any more dreams lately?**"

"Not really. You?"

"Yes. That **wither skeleton** keeps bugging me."

"I'm guessing he asked you to save him," I said.

She nodded. "**Must be the fifth time I've dreamed about him.**"

So strange. Can endermen really control dreams? That wither skeleton must be friends with one.

He's stranded on a block of Netherrack in an ocean of lava. **Whatever.** Not like we can take a trip to the Nether or anything. **Or can we?**

I thought about this for a moment, a **mischievous** grin beginning to form on my face . . .

Breeze's voice tore me from my thoughts. "**Another thing.** I'm . . . the top student, **right?** If that doesn't change, I could **become a captain,** and if I did . . ."

I knew where she was going with this. According to what we heard, a captain will have **a group of students** under his or her command. Maybe they'll be wall guards, maybe scouts, who knows, but they'll work together.

So if **I become a captain,** and Breeze becomes a captain . . . we'll no longer see each other as much. **Worse,** we'll be working with kids we don't know very well. We'll be trusting those kids **with our lives.**

"**We need to make another promise,**" Breeze said. "Otherwise, we might break our first."

I remembered the promise we'd both made.

No matter what, we will always protect each other.

"I don't care if they send me out there," I said, "but . . . not without you, Breeze. **I couldn't do it.**"

And so, we put our hands together. **We made a pact.**

"Even if we both make the cut," she said, "only one of us will choose the **Path of the Diamond. Agreed?**"

"**Agreed.** I don't know if the mayor will get angry at our decision . . . **but it's our decision to make.** Nothing will separate us."

"**Nothing.**"

We went for a walk in the park. Every time I visit that place, I forget about all the stuff going on.

When you're there, **bad memories fade away** as if it were all **really just a bad dream.**

Brilliant sunlight streaming down. Vibrant flowers all around. It's **hard to believe** monsters share a world with a paradise such as this.

SUNDAY—UPDATE V

For the record, **Breeze and I didn't hold hands! We put our hands together,** which is just something you do when making a big promise like that!

Later, she left to speak with her father about something. She wouldn't tell me what, and I didn't pry. It seemed like she—

Huh?
For some reason,
my quill stopped writing.
Let me try again.

Okay, so, Breeze seemed—

Um, wow. My quill is defective or something. **Hurmm.** I see. Its durability is **almost out.** I've been writing way too much lately. Of course, I could **repair it myself,** but why waste the experience points? I can just **trade a potato for a new one.** I have to save every last point so I can enchant a diamond sword. I almost regret not taking **Pebble's diamonds,** that's how bad I want one.

Sometimes, I can't stop thinking about it. **Have you ever seen a diamond sword in real life?** The edge is so **perfect,** the point so **sharp,** all sea blue shades with **a light violet sheen.**

Trust me, you'll find nothing more beautiful in the Overworld. **Well, besides Breeze.**

. . . ?!
Did I just write that?!

No, real warriors don't get all **mushy like that.** Surely it's this quill.

Yeah, that's it. This quill is acting up. It made me write the wrong thing because **it only has a single point of durab—**

SUNDAY—UPDATE VI

I'm back. I went to a library and traded for a **new** quill.

> "Notice that the quills in this world are different from the video game. They aren't very durable in the game. It's almost as if . . . this world were real. Actually, it's Entity303's fault. We would have never had to go to this video game convention. How did he make all this?"

> "After I slipped into that virtual reality gear . . . I found myself here."
> —Kolbert

Sorry, Kolbert added that.

He said there's **too much mystery** behind the humans arriving in this world. They were at some kind of **special event,** I guess, with some **new kind of Earth machines.** At one point they **blacked out,** and . . . woke up here.

Kolbert told me the whole story, **but I didn't understand most of it.** Although he thinks this is real, he also thinks it has something to do with their machines . . . ?

Entity 303 is supposed to be **some guy who helped make the game, or something . . . ?**

Anyway.

I traded for a new quill. And some cookies. And some cake. And some pumpkin pie, **because why not?** All of that trading got me thinking. There's a **redstone test** coming up. Why not pick up some dust? The best place to get redstone is in this massive building that's just two streets from the library. It's called "**the garage.**" It has huge, **piston-operated doors** that are big enough for even an iron golem to enter.

What a mess...
I guess Steve and Mike forgot to clean up before leaving.

It's basically a testing area. Ground zero for redstone **experiments.** Up until they left, Steve and Mike had been working here. Now that they're gone, it's mostly empty. Sometimes, a few humans come in and work on stuff. Not **too many** villagers come here, though. Only a handful.

> Redstone is a new field for us.
> <u>Uncharted</u> territory.

To most of the older villagers, **like my parents,** a circuit is more **mysterious** than a sword.

"Listen up. You connect the trail of powder to . . . things that will . . . make things." "You'll also need another thing to . . . power the things."

That's why we don't have redstone grades, and why we rarely attend redstone class. It's so unknown to us that we don't even have real teachers for it. I glanced at the various items **scattered around. They were so strange.** I didn't know how to craft any of them, let alone use them. Redstone dust is used to make circuits, I thought, but you also need . . . other . . . things, right? **Hurgg!!** I'm such a noob with this stuff! **I sound just like Mr. Glowstone!**

Well, Drill had said something about redstone torches. Actually, I didn't know such an item existed until he mentioned them.

How humiliating. He's older than my parents, but he knows way more about this stuff than I do. Comparators . . . repeaters . . . signal locking . . .

I wouldn't know where to begin! **Man, what am I going to do?**

We made a redstone alarm system earlier, but Stump was behind that. He had to help me explain it when I was writing about it in here. **And that system wasn't very complicated,** by the way. Not nearly as complex as some of the things I've seen the humans make. Stump might be ahead of me in this regard, but compared to the humans **he's a super novice.**

Eyes glazing over, I stood before **a repeater** like a zombie in front of an improperly placed door.

Why are these pistons covered in slime? Are they testing a new monster crusher, or what? This block with the face is creeping me out . . .

I have **two or three days** to turn into a master of redstone science, I thought. **Yeah. That just isn't happening . . . Man!**

. . . I never thought redstone would matter at all . . . **and now look at me . . .**

I'm sweating ghast tears just thinking about that test!

SUNDAY—UPDATE VII

I was ready to give up and go back home when, behind me, **there was a loud clang, clang, clang.**

That's a common sound in my village. **An iron golem** was walking nearby. Then I heard a silvery voice, soft and feminine.

"Strange seeing you here!"

Huh?! I whirled around. The iron golem was standing two blocks away. It wasn't the one speaking, though. **A girl was there, too** . . . riding on the golem's left shoulder. **Pretty cool,** I have to say. Although it didn't look very comfortable up there. She **hopped down** from her giant iron pet and smiled. **Such a strange, <u>strange girl.</u>**

Nessa. Not the shy girl I used to know. Even her hair color is different!

No one **really talks to her** at school. *(Probably because she skips class a lot.)* She spends most of her time **working with redstone,** I guess. From what I've heard, she'd been working on projects with Steve. Beyond that, **she trains her pet iron golem,** experiments with fireworks, **weird stuff like that.** So throughout school this year, her scores haven't been all that high. She's second to last in rank, **just ahead of Bumbi.** The teachers don't assess our skills with redstone, and Nessa doesn't study the other subjects all that much. The only subject she has a decent score in is **crafting,** as she prefers to craft redstone items herself.

I thought about all this in the blink of an enderman. **Nessa's smile only grew.**

"Although I'm not surprised to see you here," she said, "with the upcoming test! **Need some help,** I take it?"

I sighed. "**Yeah.** Connect a lever to my head with redstone dust and turn my brain off, because thinking about this stuff is actually **starting to hurt.**"

She giggled. "**Don't worry!** I was like that when I first started out! Actually, I'm really glad you stopped by! **I've been meaning to ask you something!**"

"Huh? **What's that?**"

"Well, do you have anything **planned for the test?**"

"I was thinking about something involving redstone du—Uhh, **no. Not really.**"

"I see. How about we make a deal, then, hurmm? I can help you out, and you can . . . help me."

There was something about the way she said that last bit—*help me*—that made me pause. Made me cautious, even. *What could I possibly help her with?* I thought. Even if I teach her the basics of combat, going up a few ranks won't matter when you're in second-to-last place . . .

Whatever. I could really use her help. I'm not failing that test. Not for anything. Not when I'm this close . . .

What's the worst thing she could ask for, anyway? Does she want me to be a test subject in some kind of experiment? Maybe to see if a villager can carry a current like redstone dust?

At this point, I'd probably agree. Hook me up and throw that lever! I'm ready!

"Just say it," I said.

"Great!" She flashed a smile brighter than a sea lantern. "First, how about we go get something to eat? Talking requires energy, you see, and my hunger bar is getting pretty low!"

SUNDAY—UPDATE VIII

It was **the first time** I'd ever had ice cream **twice in one day.** No, **technically it's six times.** As we sat at the table, Nessa **kept buying me more.** Who could say no to such skillfully crafted cones, with each scoop a mini arctic biome of milk and sugar instead of snow?

Attention: overheated energy bar!

(In this world, it's possible to consume too much food, which results in a slow debuff: 10% per point over 10. If the humans ever learn how to craft pizza, zombies will be running circles around them.)

So . . . delicious.
Must . . . k–k-keep . . . eating.
Wait a second.
She's being awfully
nice to me . . .

She asked **a ton** of questions, too. **What was Herobrine like? Were you scared? How many zombies did you drop yesterday? Why do you keep writing in that book?**

And finally—

"Well, **about what I wanted to ask** . . . it's about my flying machine. **Have you heard about that?**"

"You bet."

I showed her my diary and the little drawing mentioning **the shy girl and the flying machine.**

"**Ha!** Well, I suppose I was a little shy back then! Back at the start of school, I didn't know anyone!"

Yeah, **she had really changed**, I thought. **Weird.** She was a bit timid before. Now she's **more bubbly** than a pool full of high-diving **magma cubes.**

"Okay," she said, "so I've thought about using my flying machine design for the **upcoming test.**"

Another smile, **radiant**—her eyes became chevrons.

^^

"I've also considered **letting you use it!**" she said. "You and your friends. Then you guys would surely **win first place,** right?"

Hurgg?! Dirt potion?!
Bane of Air III?! Cookie block?! Melon golem?!
<u>Enchanted creeper potato?!</u>

I was so **shocked,** so stunned, that these incomprehensible thoughts flashed through my mind. Had I still been eating right then, the ice cream equivalent of a **firework rocket** would have flown from my mouth.

She's saying that . . . **she's suggesting** . . . she just said that she wants to . . . she'll let us use her flying machine in the redstone test?!

Wait. Waitwaitwait. Wuh-aaaaittttttttt.

That's quite a big favor, no? So that's why she **invited me for ice cream!** Of course! She was totally trying to **butter me up!** She's probably going to ask me to do something **crazy in return!**

What could it be?! What does she want?! **Does it matter?!** Anything, anything!! Ask me how to fight a real zombie, just ask. I'll show you how to turn those things into piles of **moldy beets!**

I don't know what **mold** is, nor do I know how to turn a zombie into anything besides smoke, but if that's what she wants to learn from me, I swear **to Notch I'll manage somehow!!**

That's what I was thinking. Yet **a real warrior** wouldn't freak out in such a situation, oh no.

Like the ice cream in my hand, a warrior's mind should be **cool and calm,** sheer perfection crafted with the most skillful of hands—hands as strong and supple as spider string, forged through countless hours of practice and countless failures—hands that toss aside each imperfect cone until, at last, a legendary-tier item is created, as flawless and smooth as diamond, its icy depths containing a hidden power ready to be harnessed, savored—a **power that is both minty fresh and able to change the world.**

Um.
Yeah.

My mind should be like that.

So, I merely looked at Nessa **in a bored way.**

"Hurmm," I said. "Yes, yes, I see. **Hurmm. Most interesting.**"

"Well? What do you say, Runt? Do you think I have what it takes?"

What is she talking about? I gave her a **blank look,** like a skeleton spawning on a deserted island five sand blocks in size. She leaned forward in her acacia **stair block/chair,** leaned over the fence/carpet table. Once more, **Ms. Noob was smiling** so much that her eyes were like little moons.

"I, **Nessa Diamondcube, would like to join your team!**" She tilted her head slightly. Her smile somehow grew. "My friends call me **Lola,** though! **That's my nickname!**"

Join.
My.
<u>Team . . . ?</u>

"**Whaat.**"

Notice the unusual spelling, here. Notice the lack of a question mark. It wasn't a standard "**What?**" or an excited/shocked "**What?!**" Although similar to **the flat sound made by a sheep,** it meant much more than simply "**I don't understand,**" or even "**I can't believe what I just heard.**" It meant, "*Please place a dirt block above my head, because I'm about to jump so high I'll go past the sky, and if there's bedrock up there, I'll have gained so much momentum that I'll break through it, and I'll then travel through the void at faster than me-opening-presents speed—which is so fast that I'll be able to ignore the damage normally inflicted by this dimension, and that would be cool* since I'd go down in history as the first villager to explore that place, but I'd be without food, which would conflict with my previous goal of being the first villager to eat one hundred cookies in a single sitting."

Yes! I thought. **Yes, yes, yes! Of course, you can join! You can join us like two damaged swords merging together during the repair process!**

Wow, I'm **freaking out** again. I really have to stop that. Okay. Arctic biome. Arctic biome. I am the frozen, windswept plains.

I cleared my throat.

"Yeah. Sure. **I guess you can join.**" A little shrug, real casual. "Yeah. Huh. Why not?"

"**I can't believe this!**" She sniffled. "**Thank you!**" She was so happy, **she was actually fighting back tears.** "Sorry, I'm just . . ."

"Yeah, uh, **don't mention it.**"

(To be honest, I wanted to cry, too. And when I say cry, I mean create a new type of material known as the tear block.)

"One more condition," she said. "We have to hang out every single day!"

"Uh, sure. Okay."

"**Great!** We're going to have so much fun!"

I don't understand **why** she wants to hang out with me so much. That's part of the deal, though. **It might be hard.** I'm not used to being with someone so . . . **cheerful.**

It's going to be even harder training her. **I've seen her at the archery range.** I've seen her use a bow. Remember when Breeze **aimed poorly** on purpose? That's Nessa *(err, Lola, I mean. How confusing.)* on a good day, trying her absolute best.

I'm not trying to **be mean** or anything, just stating the truth. To date, she hasn't participated in a **single battle.** Unless you count hiding on the sidelines . . .

So even if I train her, her scores won't increase that much. Oh, well. If that's what she wants, that's what she's going to get, so long as it means her carrying us through **that test!**

It's official, then.
I've **welcomed** her aboard.
How could I not?
With this girl on our side,
Team Runt simply <u>**cannot lose**</u>!

SUNDAY—UPDATE IX

Nessa/Lola talked for what seemed like forever. Then **Cogboggle** and **Block** walked into the garage. When they saw Lola and I chatting, they looked as if they'd just taken **five hearts' worth of damage.** They quickly recovered, however—and totally ignored me.

"**Hey, Lola!**" Cogboggle said, all smiles. "How's it going?"

Block spread out his arms and approached with the hugest grin. "**It's been such a long time!**"

"Yes, indeed it has!" Lola said. "I haven't heard from either of you since **I helped you with the last test!**"

"Sorry for that," Cogboggle said, following his friend inside. "**We've been really busy.** But we're not busy now, and we were wondering if you wanted to have a . . . **little chat.**"

"We just want to"—Block eyed me **suspiciously,** then smiled at Lola again—"discuss some things."

"Actually, I'm a little busy right now," she said. "**Sorry!** I've just had an amazing idea for something **I've been working on,** so I'll be heading home!"

"**Hey, wait!** We—"

"Let's talk tomorrow, **okay?**"

She waved and bolted **out of the garage.** I looked at the two of them and simply shrugged.

They glared at me. Moments later, they left the garage as well, stopping just outside. It looked like they were talking about something.

So I crouched and **began sneaking up to them.** I was still inside, hiding behind the wall near the edge of the door. It was **close enough** to catch their conversation.

This suit isn't just for show. I really *am* a ninja.

"**Looks like he beat us to her,**" Cogboggle said. "I can't believe that little punk!"

"Maybe **she blew him off,** too?"

"Maybe. But if we find out she is working with him, **we'll have to do something about it.**"

"I have something in mind, actually. **Let's go talk to the others.**"

They ran off after that.

So those guys want her to help them, I thought. **What luck!** I found her at the perfect time!

When they were out of sight, away I went. I must have left **dust clouds** behind as I zoomed through the streets. I quickly forgot about Cogboggle.

Then I went to Stump's house and told him **all about what had happened.** "Dude, we've got **a redstone genius! A redstone genius! A redstone genius!**"

I talked to him so much about **Lola** that he got bored and started reading my diary.

"Dude," he said, "you've been writing an awful lot lately. Yesterday and today **are, like, fifty pages each!**"

"I write a lot when I get **sad.**"

"Look, you need to take a break," he said. "Come on, **let's go fishing.** I ran into Emerald earlier. She said she was going to the lake with her father and a bunch of humans."

Hurrr!

He's right.

I've been writing way too much these past few days, and throwing in way **too many details.**

If I keep doing it like this, soon my diary is going to contain every event that ever happened in the village.

Every event. I said **this.** She said **that.** I was **angry.** She was **happy.** A pig **wandered into the village!** The pig **looked around!** The pig **oinked!** The pig **ate a carrot** that I fed him and both of us became super best friends! The pig is happy! Update—the pig **left! Where is the pig going?!** Why did the pig **leave?!** Why, Oinky, **why?!**

Fine, there's way more stuff to record, like that cloud over there! Yes, a cloud—above my house—**moved!** Get over here, cloud, and prepare to get recorded! Okay, it's moving eastward, I would say, with a speed of roughly **5.7 blocks per second.**

Sorry.

Okay, I won't write any more today. **I'm going fishing.**

Hurrr! Why didn't I at least take
Pebble's enchanted fishing rod?!
What's that Dredge enchantment?!

SUNDAY—UPDATE X

I'm at the lake, now. I was fishing with Emerald, Stump, Kolbert, Alex, Trevor3419 . . .

Then that old blacksmith, **Leaf,** sat down next to me. He asked if I could show him how to use a fishing rod. I didn't mention this before, but . . . **back during the battle,** Leaf tried to help out. He was standing behind the front line, **fishing rod in hand.** He kept sending lures overhead, **snagging zombies randomly.** It did a little bit of damage. It also interrupted their movement slightly.

Sadly, Leaf didn't even know how to use a fishing rod very well, so he sometimes caught villagers and humans on accident.

I remember when his lure had snagged Emerald.

"S-sorry!" Leaf had called out.

Emerald had glared at him. "Hurmph! Maybe you should try aiming that **at yourself** next time!"

Then, **inspired by Leaf,** a little villager boy joined the battle with his own fishing rod. That kid snagged a zombie once, and he reeled it in **as hard as he could,** like he'd just caught a diamond or something.

The zombie flew into Razberry, who was totally confused. Razberry knocked the zombie back with his sword, but the mob flew right back in his face.

"So they can fly now?!"

Good times.

SUNDAY—UPDATE XI

Okay, I know I said **I wouldn't write anything more today,** but . . . The **cloud that was over Stump's house** earlier is now over the lake. **It's a big cloud,** and dark like a rain cloud. Only, it hasn't rained at all. In addition, the cloud lit up a couple of minutes ago, as if from lightning.

However, there hasn't been any thunder.

At one point, the cloud flashed again.

"**Such strange weather,**" I said, sending out my lure again.

Leaf laughed. "Yew think that's a storm over there? **No! That's them! Fightin'!**"

"Who?"

"**The Gods!** Who else?"

After he said that, I stared at the sky for the longest time. Once more, the cloud flickered and sometimes lit up brilliantly **with streaks of red, violet, or blue.**

A lot of people **noticed it,** then. Villagers and humans alike **dropped their fishing rods** and stared up at the strange and colorful display.

Were Notch and Herobrine **really up there,** battling it out? Have they been dueling ever since they first clashed in our village? **How long will they continue? A cold wind picked up.** I saw Emerald draw closer to Kolbert. She looked **scared.** As the rest of us headed home, Emerald remained at the lake with the humans, **watching the cloud in silence.**

SUNDAY—UPDATE XII

The cloud is gone. It drifted away just like any other cloud.

On my way back home, I heard a lot of villagers talking about it. People are **spooked**.

Anyway, I don't have time to think about that.
My rivals are just a level behind me.
I have to study.
Time to crack open this **redstone** book.

MONDAY

This morning I woke up in bed, **facedown** in the redstone book. Last night I'd made it to the **third page.** In my defense, well . . . I'll just include a picture to help you understand.

Redstone textbooks: the reason why you get a good night's sleep.

I sat up in bed and pushed the book away. **A lot** of stuff is going on right now. A *lot* of stuff. Herobrine is out there somewhere, amassing **a big army.** Then you have the humans who **showed up,** arguing with one another.

Pebble goes all "Urf" on us and gets **kicked out of the village.** Meanwhile, that crazy Brio keeps piling on the tests.

And any moment, Herobrine's mobs—which may or may not include **zombie/iron golem/cow hybrids**—could come knocking on our door.

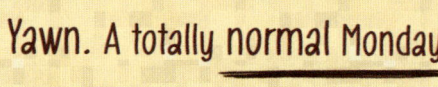

Yawn. A totally **normal** Monday, then.

Better get up and craft some tea and cookies. Well, no. I don't know where Mom **stashed the cocoa beans.** I threw some **wheat** onto the crafting table. Moments later, I wolfed down some bread and chugged a bucket of milk. *(I went back into my room and gave a loaf to Jello. He ate that thing faster than I did. The nerve! How could he show me up like that? Someday, we need to have a competition.)*

Of course, I would have asked my mom to craft breakfast for me, but my parents were still sound asleep. They've been **working harder** and harder in the fields . . . ***They work so hard for our family and never complain,*** I thought. **They're the real heroes. Not me.**

I went out into the gloomy, **rain-filled streets.** The black-robed guys could be found snooping around everywhere. Peering down wells. Creeping through farmland. Searching through villagers' inventories—even stopping the elderly and babies.

School today was the same way. You enter, you get **searched.** Use your inventory too much, you get **searched.** And if you're carrying anything **out of the ordinary,** Notch help you. Stump was one such person. Yesterday he'd crafted some new cookies. He added some stuff to the recipe to make a totally new item. Well, Brio's men spotted those cookies and dragged Stump away to a small, dark room. They **questioned him** for hours in there.

And when he finally returned, he looked **traumatized.** You see, after the questions, they did something horrible to my pal, something **unimaginable, unspeakable.** They . . . **took away** the cookies. Yes, in the interest of village security, the guys in black confiscated **my best friend's food invention.** After all, maybe Stump had added **gunpowder** to the recipe? **They didn't know.**

What a morning. I **couldn't focus** in Brewing II at all. Ms. Sugarcane just kept rambling. We're **low on Nether wart** anyway, so we can't brew much these days. *(Yes, we have a Nether wart farm. How do you think we've been crafting potions all this time? It's really small, though. We only have three blocks of soul sand. More on that later.)*

I spaced out and recalled my **meeting with Lola** yesterday. Sadly, she didn't show up at school this morning. *She probably skipped class to work on her machine,* I thought. And quietly, like a whisper in my mind, came another thought: *Redstone genius.* **My mood immediately lightened.** Classes flew by. During lunch, I showed my friends the last few entries of my diary.

"**Interesting,**" Emerald said. "I don't know if we can train her, **but we'd better try.**"

"It's not **possible,**" Breeze said. "She couldn't hit the broadside of an enderdragon from half a block away. No amount of training can fix that."

(Weird. That doesn't sound like Breeze. For some reason, she seemed irritated after she read my diary.)

I glanced over at Max to see what he thought. **He had his nose in a book.** When I looked at the cover, I cringed. *Village Law.* Again.

"Well, I **like her,**" Stump said. "I mean, I was a **noob** once, too."

Emerald shrugged. "She might be one slip away from stealing the **Noob of the Year** award from Bumbi, but . . . in a way, she is kinda smart, y'know?"

"Quiet down," I whispered, nodding at **the double doors.** "Looks like she **finally showed up.**"

Lola had just entered the lunchroom. She waved at us. Stump and I waved back. A hush fell over the table as **Lola approached.**

"Hey, **Runt!** These are your friends, right? Hi! Oh. Is it okay if I **join you guys?**"

When she said that, it almost felt like we were **the cool kids.** We're not, really, but it felt that way for a second.

Then again, a lot of kids **look up to Breeze** now. They don't talk to her much, but at least they **respect** her . . . or **fear** her.

The same could be said for Max. He's always been somewhat **popular.** Plus, Emerald is still arguably the **most popular** girl in school. Although I can't understand why.

And then there's Stump. Like me, **he's come a long way** from his noobly origins. After staring at Lola, he patted the row of seats. **A true gentleman.** She sat down next to him. "I heard about what happened in Brewing II. **Is everything okay?**"

"Yeah, no one got hurt," Stump said, "but I still **feel bad** for laughing like I did. I couldn't help it. The look on **Ms. Sugarcane's** face when her potion blew up . . ."

"One of your potions **blew up,** too," Max said, never taking his eyes off his book.

Stump blushed. What can I say? **He still has a ways to go** . . .

Anyway, Lola hanging out with us isn't such a bad thing. Even if she wasn't so talented with redstone, we could still use someone like her.

Someone **cheerful. Optimistic.** Forever upbeat. Max can be **negative** at times. Breeze, **withdrawn.** Stump, **mopey.** As for Emerald, well, she's all **over the place.** And I typically **whine** and **rage.**

I'm not sure why, but a **cheerful villager** is a rarity. We're moody. Maybe it's because of all the monsters attacking us over the years. We've endured a lot. So my friends took a liking to our team's **newest addition.** Here's the thing, though. **A few other kids took a liking to her, too.**

Just minutes after Lola sat down, **Cogboggle** and **Block** came over.

"Hey, Lola," Cogboggle said. "**Are you still busy?** We've been wanting to chat."

Block made **a sad face.** "Yeah, **hurrr.** It's been weeks since we've hung out. **Why have you been ignoring us?**"

Maybe you can guess Lola's response: "**Me?** Ignore you? You must be thinking of someone else! Anyway, I'd love to **catch up with you guys!**"

(Facepalm.)

"**Great,**" Cogboggle said. "How about we meet up after class?"

Emerald shot up and wrapped her arm around our new friend. "Sorry, boys. She already agreed **to hang out with me** today!"

Lola blinked. "**Huh?** Did I?"

"Funny," Block said, smirking. "I didn't know you two were friends."

"Yeah, **well, we are**," Emerald snapped, and gave him a look that said, *Back off, this is **our** redstone genius.* Then she squeezed Lola and smiled at her. "**Isn't that right?**"

"Yeah, um, of course!" ^^

MONDAY—UPDATE 1

Remember how I said Emerald is the **most popular girl** in school? **I take that back. I really, really** take that back. Apparently, **that title now goes to Lola.**

After seeing her sitting down with **Team Runt,** every other student realized what we were up to.

Everyone had forgotten about her. I only remembered her after running into her yesterday at the garage. It took us being seen together for that to finally **click** in everyone's heads. And the redstone connection was made.

Suddenly, everyone in school has become **Lola's best friend.** Everyone. **Even Bumbi,** whose life goal is . . . not graduating last.

By the time school was out, she'd become **a superstar.** She left her last class, books bundled in her arms, and kids swarmed around her like cows around the **Overworld's last wheat crop.**

"Hey, Lola, I was just **thinking** about you!"

"**Hurrr!** I brought you a gift!"

"How **long** has it been?"

"You look **so good** in those robes!"

"**I'm your BFF,** remember? Yeah, you remember!"

"Hey! I'm her best friend! **Not you!**"

"Lola, don't listen to any of these guys! I'm the one you want to hang out with! **Me!**"

"Lola, dear, **my bestest best-best friend,** you didn't forget about that favor you owe me, did you?"

Others were a bit more direct:

"We were wondering if you wanted to work with us on a project for the upcoming redstone test. **We're willing to pay. Handsomely.**"

This sparked a huge frenzy of offers:

"Look at my inventory! Anything you want, just take it, **take it!**"

"Carry me through that redstone test and I'll get you through **all the rest!**"

Others had no idea what was going on:

"Who is that girl? Whoever she is, **she's really cute!**"

"Is she a **new student** or what?! Why have I never noticed her before?!"

It was the first time Lola was **anything other than totally upbeat.** She was still smiling, but it was the kind of smile someone makes after hearing **a bad joke.** It was time to act. Team Runt formed **a shield** around her like zombies protecting **a creeper.**

Stump stood in front, ready to take a wither's fireball for his new friend. "Back off, **noobs! She's with us!**"

Their cries only grew louder, their movements more frantic. They tripped over one another as they tried **to hand Lola items,** anything from diamonds to enchanted books. Then I felt a hand on my shoulder. It was Cogboggle. **He shoved me. Hard.** I staggered back and slammed into this kid named Bubbles. Unfortunately, Bubbles was carrying a stack of emeralds in his arms. Those green gemstones went everywhere, and the sounds they made as they hit the cobblestone floor . . . it was like a creeper blowing up a glass house or something. Everyone turned to the three of us.

After that, they just stared **in total silence.** *(Well, an emerald had somehow landed on top of a sign. It finally fell down, causing a tiny bit of noise that echoed down the hall. Tink, tink, tink.)*

Bubbles looked like he was about to, um . . . **burst?**

Cogboggle was glaring at me.

"**Hurrr!** I won't let this slide, Runt! She's **our** friend, **not yours!**"

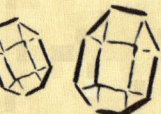

His friends lined up on either side of him. **Block, Porcupine, Twinkle, Soulsand** . . . even **Sara,** since Team Pebble was gone.

"**Everyone calm down,**" Max said. "I think Lola can choose her own friends, right?"

Block looked at her pleadingly. "**Come on, Lola.** Remember the fun times we had? **We made our first circuit together!**"

Lola flashed him a smile so bright, it was like everyone else was staring into the sun.

"Yeah, I remember! **That was great,** I have to say!"

"It was." Block returned her smile with one of his own. "So, why don't we work on another? **We're old buddies!**"

"**Sorry.** I'm afraid I'll be busy until after graduation," she said, "as I've agreed to **work with Runt** here! But after that, certainly! Why not?"

Boom.
<u>*Boom.*</u>

Although most here already knew that, her **confirmation** didn't help any. The rage, man. The rage. Kids started **freaking out,** shouting, shoving, and promising Lola the kind of **loot** only found in dungeons. Cogboggle and Block were **so mad** that they grabbed me and stuffed me into **a nearby school chest.** Judging by the items inside, I'm guessing it was **Bumbi's.**

Who else would use such nooberly items? That kid has no shame! I kinda like those dyed-green leather pants, though.

"**Seriously,** what are you guys doing?" I called out, my voice echoing. "This isn't a **double chest!** I can't fit in here! If you're gonna try to stuff me into a chest, at least do it right, **noobs!**"

Yeah, at least Pebble would have tried throwing me into a double chest. These guys, man. **Total amateurs!**

My friends came to the **rescue** by shoving Block and Cogboggle away. Stump pulled me out by my boots.

"**Get me out of here,**" Lola whispered to us. Her uneasy smile was returning. "I don't want any part of this!"

"**Sure thing,**" Emerald whispered. "We can hang out at my place. They won't be able to bother us there. **Trust me.**"

Breeze slipped Emerald and Lola **potions of Swiftness II.** "We'll see you there later," she whispered to Emerald. She looked at Lola. "Chug."

Lola wasn't about to ask any questions. She chugged, Emerald chugged, and they were gone faster than a cake in Stump's skillful hands. The crowd chased after them **like wolves after rabbits.**

MONDAY—UPDATE II

Soon, the halls of the school were quiet again. **And empty, mostly.**

"My last two swiftness potions," Breeze said. She shrugged. **"Worth it."**

"Totally worth it," Stump said. "That poor girl looked **like a noob exploring the End!**"

Just then, I noticed a few teachers standing farther down the hall, **observing us,** as if taking notes.

Max spotted them, too. "Wonder why none of them bothered to break everything up? Kinda strange, no?"

"My father probably told them not to," Breeze said. "Didn't you guys notice? He was watching the whole time. **He can be a real jerk sometimes.**"

Sure enough, Brio was there, behind the other teachers, arms behind his back as always, eyes hidden behind black sunglasses, with **the biggest smirk on his face.** He approached. His **obsidian boots** tapped slowly and ominously against the newly placed cobblestone floor.

"I'd like to ask you something," he said, clearly looking at me. "It seems you've made **a new** friend, yes?"

"Well, um, yes." I swallowed nervously. "Yes. **Yes, I have.**"

He removed his sunglasses. His eyes are **different** from his daughter's, although similar in color.

When Breeze looks at you, you're reminded of the **soft glow of a low-level enchantment.** Brio's eyes are more like an enderman's.

"You've befriended her because you like her as a person," he said, "not for any . . . **other reason,** such as . . . personal gain. **Is that right?**"

Oh, man.
Why is he asking this?
Well, he's smart. Surely he knows what's going on here.

But then, once I **got to know Lola** more, I actually had started to like her. She's bubblier than a noob mining underwater until his air runs out, **sure,** but at the same time, she's a breath of fresh air in a school full of angry, **competitive kids.**

"**She's my friend,**" I said. "We met at the **garage,** she asked if I needed help, and before I knew it, I realized she's actually a **pretty cool person.** Her skill with redstone is **just a bonus.**"

"Very well," Brio said. "But there's something **you should know,** and I'll only say this once. **Everything has a price.**"

He threw his shades back on and let me **contemplate** what he'd just said. Then he smiled at us, particularly Breeze, and headed back to the other teachers, **whistling** a little tune.

"**What was that?**" Stump said. "**Everything has a price**'? What does that even mean? Could your father have been **a little less vague?**"

Breeze looked annoyed. "Dad's **weird** like that. Those **cryptic** warnings of his . . . I've heard them all my life."

"Then you must know what he meant," I said. "**Are we going to get into trouble or something?**"

She shrugged. "Don't know, don't care. We'll handle things as they come."

"By the way," Stump said, nudging Breeze, "did you ask him about how he was wielding **two swords the other day?**"

"No."

"Well, ask him! **That was totally cool!** I wanna learn how to do that! And where'd he get those **obsidian boots?!**"

Breeze rolled her eyes and sighed.
Hurmm.

So, Breeze seemed **irritated** today. Especially with her father. Yesterday, she said she had to go speak with him about something. I wonder what they talked about. Maybe he didn't agree with something she'd said?

Hurmm, **hurmm,** hurmm.
Once again, <u>Detective Runt</u> is on the job!

By the way, **Detective Razberry** has already gathered some nice information.

OPERATION SNOOP:
REPORT

BREEZE	109
RUNT	106
EMERALD	104
COGBOGGLE	102
OPHELIA	101
BLOCK	99
MAX	97
SOULSAND	96
PORCUPINE	94
TWINKLE	92

Breeze and I are **still at the top.** Looks like Cogboggle really is **catching up** to me, though. How'd he level up so fast?! **I don't know much about Ophelia.** She's **polite** yet strong-minded and very talented. A **model student.**

She wants to become a captain so she and her friends don't have to group up with someone like Cogboggle. She's kind of like the leader of this group of girls. **Team All Girls,** as I call them. They're mostly into **crafting** and **farming.**

Okay, I have to **stop** for now. Stump is **annoyed** at me because I've been taking too long with this entry. We're still at the school, and he wants to head over to **Emerald's house.** I've never been inside Emerald's house before.

I wonder what it's like . . .

MONDAY—UPDATE III

"Good evening, Miss Emerald. **Guests?**"

Meet Charles. He's the head butler. As in, they have **multiple** butlers.

Wahhhhhhh!!!

That's the sound the giant zombie pigman made when he got blown up by TNT. It's also the sound a villager named Runt made upon viewing the inside of Emerald's house. **Quartz** columns. **Quartz** floors. Button-operated iron doors. **An indoor swimming pool.** And, of course, several nannies. The nannies craft breakfast, lunch, and dinner, do all the chest/item organization . . . and take care of Emerald's **baby brother, Pistachio.**

People actually **live like this?!** It's **not fair, man! It's so not fair!** I mean, I saw the outside of Emerald's house a long time ago. Her house looked big then, of course, but on the inside it's way, way bigger. We spent the rest of the evening chatting away in the **church-size chamber** Emerald calls her **bedroom.**

By the way, her bedroom has a bathroom. I wouldn't be surprised if her bathroom has a bathroom. And her bathroom's bathroom has another bathroom. And that bathroom has a bedroom, because dude, why not?

Every **now and then,** the butler came in to check on us, and offer us . . . refreshments.

Needless to say, **Stump took full advantage** of this. "**Ah,** hello, old chap. I've decided that I shall have another glass of melon juice before my nightly swim."

"Is that all, **Sir Stump?**"

"Hurmm. Now that you mention it, after my swim, my sword shall need some repairing, and my inventory shall need some tidying up."

"Of course, Sir Stump," he said with a slight bow.

Max was thrilled upon hearing that this house contains **a library.** With Emerald's permission, he went to go check it out. However, Breeze isn't a **big fan** of this place. She said the house, although beautiful, **felt cold. Clinical.** "Almost like **Herobrine's laboratory,**" she whispered to me.

Lola was, um, well . . . **Lola.** "**Thank you for inviting me!**" she said cheerfully. "It's so **nice** to have met such good friends!"

"It's nothing." Emerald stretched out across **the red wool sofa.** "If anything, we should be **thanking you.**"

"**Yeah,** Runt told us about how you offered to help us out," Stump said. "Strange how you guys just met like that, **right when we needed you.**"

Lola joined me over by the window.

"It's **not strange** at all," she said. "Even if we hadn't run into each other yesterday, I would have gone **looking for him.** I'd been wanting to **ask him** about this."

Breeze stepped between Lola and me. She glanced at me and then gazed out the window. "Why him?"

"Because he can **train** me! My combat score could use a little improvement, that's **no secret!** So I figured an exchange of knowledge would **benefit us both!**"

"An exchange of knowledge, huh." Breeze's voice was a little cold. "**So that's it?** He trains you, you hang with us, and you build your **flying machine** during the test?"

"**That's the plan!** Don't worry, we'll ace that thing! And someday, I'll even get it to fly in **more than one direction!**"

"**One direction?**" Emerald sat up on the sofa. "Wow. You mean, it, um . . . can't go **backward?**"

"It can. I just need **more time!**"

"It's not a **big deal**," Stump said. "Flight alone would be better than anything else Cogboggle's crew comes up with, one directional or not."

Emerald smirked. "Not **arguing** with you there. That kid's a total blockhead. Well, I guess that settles it. **There's really no way we can lose now, huh?**"

We said a bunch of other stuff, but I can't remember it all. Some **stuff about Pebble.** I'm still in Emerald's bedroom, writing this entry while everyone else still chats away . . . **and eats diamonds. Just kidding.** Apparently, her parents don't have inventories **that** deep.

While I was about to finish up this entry, Stump asked the question that was probably on everyone's mind:

"Hey, can't your parents just give us a bunch of **diamonds? Enchanted swords?**"

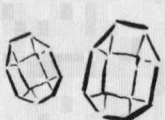

"It's not like that," Emerald said. "We have a big house, but we're not **swimming in loot** or anything. Not anymore. **Blame the war.**"

"I don't understand," Stump said.

"Dude, it's a long story. **Long and boring.** Trust me. You don't want to hear it."

"If your family is so poor now, how do you guys have butlers?" Stump asked. "And security guards?"

"Some are from the group who **fled** from the other village. My father is the one who convinced the mayor to let them stay. They're just **repaying us,** I guess? Dude, I don't know."

"Oh."

Sigh. So no **free** diamonds, then. According to Emerald, **her parents have ten to their name.** Her allowance is even less than mine, too, which seems **hard to believe.** I'm really beginning to regret not taking all of Pebble's loot! **I want a diamond sword!** Well, maybe if I just mine up some of those **quartz blocks . . . I wonder how much they'd go for?**

MONDAY—UPDATE IV

Eventually, Max came back from the library. He didn't say a word when he came in. Something was bothering him. When I asked him about it, his face **grew dark.** "I guess now is as good a time as any."

He reached into his inventory and withdrew a **record book,** which he then placed upon a red wool stool. Like all record books, its surface gleamed brilliantly and held a **list of scores** below the student's name and level. Unlike most of our record books, some of the scores it displayed were **outlandish.**

Pebble's name was on the screen.

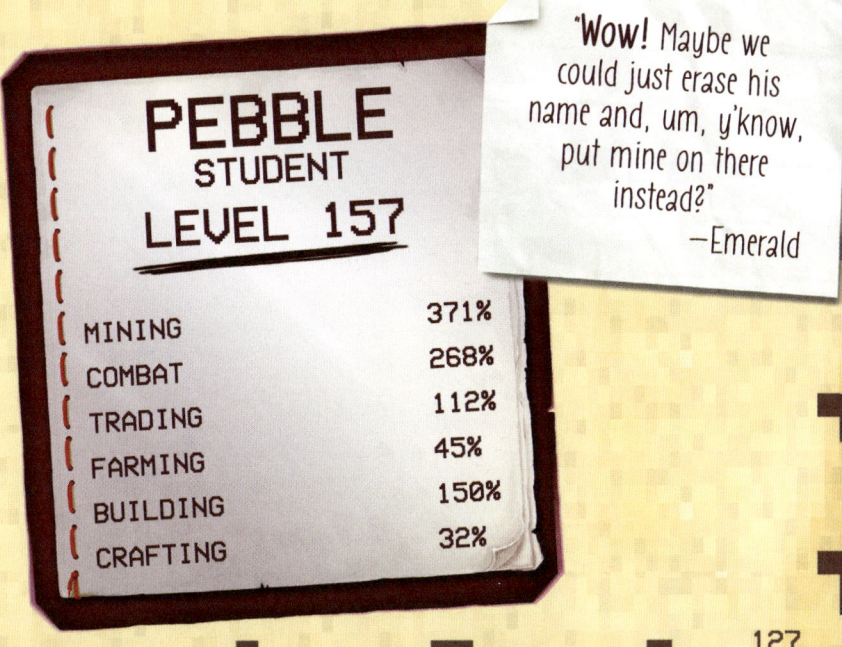

PEBBLE
STUDENT
LEVEL 157

MINING	371%
COMBAT	268%
TRADING	112%
FARMING	45%
BUILDING	150%
CRAFTING	32%

"**Wow!** Maybe we could just erase his name and, um, y'know, put mine on there instead?"
—Emerald

Before Pebble turned himself in, he'd **tossed his record book.** Max had spotted it and secretly **tucked it into his inventory** when no one was looking. How **incredible.** In the days leading up to his banishment, Pebble had somehow retaken the lead.

This made me recall how serious he looked during training the past few weeks. **Yet his mind had been <u>somewhere else.</u>**

So Pebble was some kind of **super guy**, huh? Hmm. I was only able to beat him because of my cloak's ridiculous buff. Once every full moon. I need to craft a calendar.

MONDAY—UPDATE V

We **left** Emerald's house before sundown. Max and Stump walked Lola back to her place. I walked Breeze back to hers. **We chatted** on the way there.

"Do you think Pebble will **join Herobrine?**" she asked.

"How should I know?"

"Out of all of us, you've dealt with Pebble the **most.**"

I thought about this for a minute before answering. "I don't think he will, **no.**"

"Why not?"

"Because of what he said to me just before **he turned himself in,**" I said. "Although a bit crazy, it seemed he really did care about the village. **He thought I was a spy . . .**"

"What about Lola?" she asked. "What do you think about her?"

"She's cool in my book. How about you?"

"She's okay. I don't mind if she tags along. A little strange, though." She smiled and waved. "Have a good night."

"You, too. **See ya tomorrow.**"

What's this? I thought. **No hug?** After glancing back at me **one last time,** Breeze waved again and slipped into her house. I couldn't see him, but I thought I felt Brio **watching me** from somewhere.

Everything has a price, I thought. **What did he mean by that?** I headed home. I felt **a chill** as the sun sank into the horizon.

These days, when you walk the streets this late, you'll notice some **houses without any doors.**

It's not a Building Fail, but the work of a paranoid villager. Some villagers now mine their doors away before sunset and replace them with blocks of stone.

TUESDAY

Today, **school was worse** than yesterday. In Crafting I, **Soulsand** told **Lola** he had a crush on her.

She laughed. "Don't joke around! You certainly can't be serious!"

"**No!** Really, I—" The school's note-block bell **rang**, cutting Soulsand off.

She waved and stepped out into the hall, where she was greeted by two more **admirers.** There was the flash of emeralds, and items formed a pile at her feet—as did **Cogboggle** and **Block**, who groveled on their knees.

"We really need help!" they said. "**Please!**"

"You guys are so **silly!** I'm **not the only one** who knows circuits, you know! What if I introduce you to some of **my friends?**"

"They're **not as good** as you! They don't even come close!"

"He's not kidding! When it comes to redstone, you make that **Steve guy look noob!**"

"I'm **flattered!** And really, I want to help you out! But it will have to wait until after I've completed my **flying machine.**"

Still on their knees, Cogboggle and Block exchanged glances, faces **filled with terror.** Then they turned back to Lola and exclaimed **simultaneously:**

"Flying machine?!"

"Yes! Now, if you'll excuse me!" ^^. She made her way down the hall and found Stump and me. My two new rivals, as if stand-ins for Pebble, glared at me from afar with eyes of **smoldering lava.** Not that I'm worried. I'm not. I'm not. I'm so not.

Seriously,
what can they do? What?

TUESDAY—UPDATE I

Hurrr. It's pretty **dark** in here. So, this is what it's like to **be an item**. Who knew? Speaking of items, I wonder what's in here? Now, where'd I put **that torch?** . . . Figures.

I should have guessed.

Man, what **rotten luck.**

It smells like a **pigman's feet** in here! You know, this is going to backfire on them someday. Maybe tomorrow they'll **shove me** into a chest with **lots of cool stuff.** Wait. They're talking. Their voices are muffled, though. Maybe if I just put my ear up against the . . .

"**Oh,** hi, Breeze. Um, nice to see you."

"**Runt?** Nope, haven't seen him. Wonder where he went?"

"**Us? Oh,** we're just checking this chest to, um, you know, make sure it's still, uh, sturdy."

"Yeah! Creepers can **blow up** chests pretty easily. Can't be **too careful** with so many of them running around."

"Hey, what are you—**OW! That really hurt!**"

"**Crazy girl!** Wait until your father hears about this! Whoa, calm down! **I'm sorry!** I'm sorry! I didn't mean it!"

"Dude, **let's get out of here!**"

. . .

Click.

"Just FYI, I'm still waiting for you to save me someday."

"Yeah. I'm waiting for that day, too. Believe me. This is starting to get embarrassing."

I climbed out. "Lola wants me to check out the machine after school today. **Wanna join us?**"

When I asked this, I could see slight **disappointment** in her eyes. She **bit** her lip, shook her head. "I told Emerald I'd go **mining** with her today. Another practice run."

"**Really?** Oh, okay. That's fine."

"Sorry."

"Yeah."

So they're preparing for tomorrow's test. **The test.** Max had heard that Pebble's family was going to **rig that test** somehow. Although Pebble's no longer around, I can't be sure his father won't try to **get revenge** . . . Of course, if Steve were still here, I'd zoom over to his place and ask for a tip—**a secret little strategy that only a human would know.** What about Kolbert? He's **certainly** been proving himself lately. He's so busy though, trying to get all the whiners **in shape.** A bunch of **pizza-loving crybabies** in iron armor! And some of the humans have formed **a new clan** called the **Creeper Crushers.** They're threatening to leave the village and go do their own thing.

All right.

I guess **that's that.** Time to go see what a flying machine looks like.

TUESDAY—UPDATE II

Our **top-secret** project.

A single slime block hung **in the air.** Around it, Lola placed two more to make a three-by-one-block row. She then connected **two sticky pistons** together, with a third on the opposing side. On this last piston, she placed a sign. Finally, she added **a layer of redstone blocks** on top of the green slime.

She wiped her forehead with the back of her hand. "Well, what do you think?"

"That's . . . it? **You're done?**"

"Yep. It might look simple, but it took me **weeks** to figure out!"

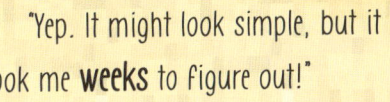

That's **a flying machine**? It looks more like a half-slime monster, half-redstone with piston arms . . .

Um.
I almost laughed.

If that thing's a flying machine, **then so am I.**

All you'd need to do is tell me we won't be having the mining test, and I'd **fly higher** than that thing ever could.

Then the worry set in. **The desperation.** It was now my turn to smile as if I'd just read one of **those ridiculous cow books.** "It's interesting, but . . . where are the **wings?**"

For the first time ever, **she looked slightly hurt.** She took out a stone pickaxe and began chopping at the sign.

"Wait!" I shouted. "Stop! I was **just joking**, huh?!"

She kept mining away. With one final swing, the **sign broke** away from the machine. Suddenly, the sticky pistons **sprang to life,** pushing and pulling the **blocks of green ooze.**

Clattering and **clanging,** the bizarre-looking machine began to **fly** through the garage, **moving** horizontally in the air. Its flight **ceased** when it hit the wall, although the pistons still whirred. Lola ran up, pick in hand, and mined away the three redstone power sources. The pistons **stopped** at once. **Wow.** It didn't look like much, but still. Today I saw **a series of blocks actually move by themselves.** The secret is in the slime blocks, Lola says. They have **unique properties.** They interact with sticky pistons in a special way.

"I'm still working on the **multidirectional version!** It will be **much better!**"

I glanced at the weird array of blocks. "Even in its current state, it's going to **blow away** the competition. No doubt there."

"**Wow!** You really think so?"

"Totally. We're going **to own** that test."

"**This is so great!**" She beamed. "After you become a captain, **we're going to go on all kinds of epic adventures!**"

When she said this, it was as if I'd been zapped by lightning. Her words echoed in my mind. **We're going to go on all kinds of epic adventures . . .**

> EPIC ADVENTURES.

> WE.

> . . .

> . . .

Something was wrong. It hung in the air, **ominous, silent,** like gathering **storm clouds.** I couldn't quite understand what she was saying, although I sensed **the importance of her words,** felt the **horrible weight** they carried. I struggled to collect myself. I tried to grasp what she'd meant.

Meanwhile, Lola's smile **never wavered.**

"**Runt?** What's wrong? I thought you were going to become a captain!"

"Well, I . . . I **don't know about that,**" was all I could say.

"**You will,** of course. **I just know it!** And after graduation, **since we're now friends,** your group is where they'll place me!"

"W-what?"

"**Hey,** now! What's that face for? I thought you **already knew!** Cogboggle's a **real jerk!** As if I would join his group! No, there's **no other choice** but you!"

"Tell me—what are you saying?"

"Oh, come now, you really don't know? During graduation, the **Path of the Sword** is what I'll be choosing! I'm going to be a **warrior,** Runt! And you're **gonna be my captain!**"

Her words petrified me. In that moment, I became an **iron golem.** Made of metal. **Seemingly emotionless.**

A warrior. She wants to be . . . **a warrior.**

"As in, warrior **warrior?**" I trudged forward. "As in, swinging a sword, shooting arrows, taking lots of damage, and avoiding burning zombies as they try to hug you . . . **warrior?**"

She laughed. "**Oh,** don't be so dramatic! Who says warriors need to do all those things!"

Wow, I thought.
Is this girl **serious?**
She can't be! <u>*She can't!*</u>

Oh man, what have I gotten myself into?! For the past two days, I've been **dancing** on the clouds, and now . . . Since we're friends now, if I really do become a **captain**, they'll place her **with me . . . !!**

She doesn't know anything about fighting! Which means I'll have to look out for her. I'll be responsible for her!

"**Everything has a price.**" I get it now, you **crazy old noob!** That's what you meant! She might get me through that test, yeah—**but at what cost?!**

"I can't **agree** to this," I said. "You don't have much real-world experience, and—"

"You needn't worry, that's for sure! **I've been training every day!** I might've been a **noob** before, that's true! But I've improved a lot since you last saw me! Of that I can **surely promise!** ^^"

Her words didn't exactly fill me with **confidence.**

The last time I saw her training was but a week ago . . . She was in the yard, attacking a **dummy.** Her sword flew out of her hands in a way that would have made Urf so very, very proud.

"Show me your **record book**," I said flatly.

"**Certainly!**"

NESSA
STUDENT
LEVEL 41

MINING	7%
COMBAT	5%
TRADING	1%
FARMING	17%
BUILDING	55%
CRAFTING	177%

> Even with a crafting score like that, she still takes noob to a whole new level. At this point, even Bumbi is probably higher.

"See? **Already getting up there!**" ^^

"Yeah, um . . . I can see that. Still, I can't agree. It's for **your own safety.**"

"**Silly boy!** Don't joke with me! **You've already agreed!**" She clasped her hands together. "Oh, this is going to be so much fun! We're going to go on **so many exciting adventures!**"

"**No, we're not!**" I snapped. "You know, this is so unfair! I thought I was only going to train you! **You didn't tell me about this!**"

"I wanted you to train me because I didn't want to let you down!" **She saluted me.** "**Warrior Lola** of the First Scouting Group, **reporting for duty!**" Then she burst out laughing. "**I sound so cool, huh?** Oh, look at this map I crafted! It's mostly **blank** now, but just wait until we get out there!"

She's not only going to be a warrior, but she hopes to go **scouting as well?!** As in, she actually dreams of going out there? As in, beyond the **safety** of the wall?! As in, **is she crazy?!**

And the whole time, I'm going to be the one who has to babysit her! I'll have to watch her every move! And if anything happens to her, it'll be all my fault!

Arctic biome!
Arctic biome!!
Cool, crystalline ice!!
Crisp, refreshing air!!
Yeah, well, even places like that can have bubbling lava pools!!
HuRRrrrggggGGggggggggggggggGGgggggggggg!!

WEDNESDAY

I didn't know how to **fix this situation.** So I avoided Lola today. **Or tried to.** Avoiding her was more or less **impossible.**

"I'll crush these guys with my machine!"

It's not that I don't like her. **I do. She's cool.** She means well. She makes me **laugh** sometimes.

It's just . . . I'm conflicted.
It's complicated.
Let me try to explain.

She's **bored with redstone.** She's going to become a warrior. Apparently, Stump and I had something to do with that. Back when school first started, Stump and I were **the definition of wimpy villagers.** The only thing we were good at then was eating cake. But **we had a dream.** We wanted to pick up swords and **defend** our homeland. So during those first few weeks of class, we tried our best. It was just as hard then as it is now, **sure.**

"Oh! It's not a double chest? No biggie. We can force you back in there."

And we **failed** just as much as we **succeeded. But we changed.** Grew **stronger.** During this time, Lola saw two noobs named Runt and Stump **skyrocket in level.** And she saw us befriend Max, who was considered one of the **smartest** students, then. She even saw me surpass Pebble in the rankings—a kid who everyone thought was **the best.**

A noble hero. Above all else, she heard of our **adventures**. Now she wants to do all those things, too. Even if it means experiencing **as much hardship** as us.

"Carroted"

(I'm here.)

She has a dream now. No one can talk her out of that. No matter what, she's going to open that chest, retrieve that sword, and hold it **proudly** above her head.

Later, she'll be assigned a **captain**. Drill said he will place **friends with friends,** which means she's going to be placed with me. She'll **endanger** our whole group! She could give away our position, do something **foolish** . . . I could be a **jerk,** I guess. Tell her to leave me alone. **Freak out in her face** until she **no longer wants** to be my friend. What then? **What would happen if I did that?**

She'd still pick up that sword. She would. The only difference would be that she'd be under **someone else's command.** Maybe **Cogboggle's.** Maybe **Block's.** Maybe **Soulsand's.**

If that happened, it wouldn't be **good news** for her. Many of the potential captains are almost as bad as Pebble . . . as I've recently discovered.

They'd boss her around. Treat her like a **slave.** Would make her go first into battle. Wouldn't care if she got hurt. If she was grouped up with one of them because I rejected her, how **guilty** would I feel? How could I sleep at night? Furthermore, if I ended **our friendship now,** she might get angry and let others use her design. If that happens, **I could fail** that redstone test. Maybe I wouldn't make captain.

Wow.
My head's starting to hurt again.
And I thought redstone circuits were complicated.
This is ten times worse.

WEDNESDAY—UPDATE I

Team Runt had lunch at the fountain. I told my friends about the situation with Lola. **I'm relieved now.** They don't think it's **that big of a deal.**

"I'll train her," Breeze said. "She won't turn into **Gogar the Destroyer** overnight, but she'll be **all right.**"

Stump: "Remember when we used to attack **grass** with sticks? **Who cares** if she's a noob! Let's give this girl **a chance!**"

Max: "Even if she's all but **useless** in combat, a redstone specialist could come in handy. Plus, from what you've said, she has the **highest crafting** score in school."

Emerald: "I say **we take her.** We can give her a bow and put her **super far back.** Then we can retrieve the arrows from the ground, wave, and shout '**Wow! You're such an amazing shot!**'"

At about that time, I saw Lola **approach.** She had a **proud** look on her face, and she was carrying some strange-looking helmets. "Look what I **crafted!**" she called.

Lola then told us how she had discovered some **new crafting recipes.** The helmets in question looked like the helmets typically worn by miners. They come with a **special enchantmentlike** effect known as **Lamp**. It's almost like wearing a torch on your head. She also crafted human-style clothes for us, and enchanted each piece with **Fire Protection (I or II)** and the boots with **Feather Falling I**. Thanks to outfits like that, lava wouldn't be **as big of a problem** for us, and any falling damage would be greatly reduced. Not only that, but she dyed them bright **orange** for increased visibility in the dark. If we ever got separated, we could find one another easily.

"**Where's your outfit?**" Max asked.

"Oh, I didn't have **enough materials** to make my own set," Lola said. "But that's okay! **I made them for you guys!**"

"Aww, that's **really sweet** of you," Emerald said. She gave Lola a hug. "**Thanks a lot.**"

Stump gave me **a wink**. "You were saying?"

I raised my hands in defeat. What could I say? Here I was, **freaking out**, worrying for no reason at all. I just thought Lola might be a **hindrance. A liability.** More trouble than she's worth. Yet she'd crafted items that will **help us** out on the mining test. The hardest test to date.

Well, lunch is over. The test is about to begin.
We're going to go gear up. <u>Wish me luck.</u>

WEDNESDAY—UPDATE II

In these outfits, we almost **look like** humans. The girls have different pants. Lola said humans call them **shorts,** and human girls often wear them.

Humans, man. It's like they're **invading** our village. First, they charm us with their **wonderful ideas.** Then they talk about crafting their **mysterious** Earth food. Now some of us are even wearing their weird style of clothing? What next? **Maybe Kolbert will run for mayor?** Once someone discovers how to craft pizza, that's it . . . our village will no longer be the same!

These outfits are **kind of cool,** though. Dye the shirt and pants blue, and I'd almost look like Steve. We're also carrying **two pickaxes** each—*one iron, one gold*—along with a gold shovel.

Our iron pickaxes are enchanted with **Efficiency I or II,** meaning our arms will give out long before our tools do. As for the gold tools, well, they need no explanation. We've learned that there are situations in which such items can be useful. **Thanks, Kolbert.**

Then we have **buckets of milk and water,** stacks of **torches** and **food, potions of Healing I . . .**

In other words, we are **totally prepared**. The **ultimate** miners in all of Minertown. If someone trolls you by putting a block of stone in front of your door, just **call us**; we'll take care of it. We'll handle all your **mining-related problems**.

By the way, a few minutes ago, Cogboggle noticed our outfits and called us mining nerds. I think he's just **jealous**. But **it's weird**—he's **no longer being nice** to Lola. In the past hour, he hasn't talked to her at all. I wonder why?

Now we're just waiting for a few other kids to show up. As I write this, Brio and Drill are going on and on about basic safety techniques.

"**Good luck**, you lava splashers!"

"Be **careful!**"

"Careful? Oh, I'll be careful. I'll be careful to make sure I'm not the one going in first."
—Emerald

That's where the test will take place. The **shaft,** they call it. It's the main tunnel that the miners use.

We are actually going down into the mining tunnels. **How scary** is that, right? I can't help thinking about **Tunnel 67,** with its numerous warning signs . . .

As part of the test, some miners put **traps** down there. Nothing serious, I guess, but then, maybe Pebble's father set up some real nasty stuff, like lava. **Who knows?** There could also be cave spiders down there. They typically live in **abandoned mine shafts,** but maybe they're the reason mine shafts are abandoned in the first place. I mean, let's face it—if cave spiders mutated and started living aboveground, there would most likely be such a thing as an **abandoned Overworld.**

If someone saw a cave spider roaming around the plains beyond our wall, I'm pretty sure every last villager would pick up their things and **move to the Nether.** If the zombie pigmen kicked us out, **we'd move to the End.** And if the endermen kicked us out, well, I don't know what would happen, but I'm sure at least half of us would try **the void.**

Don't worry, though. I've already made sure my milk bucket is easily accessible. At the slightest squeak—**whoosh**—I'll swap to that bucket faster than a noob trading an emerald for a **blue-dyed egg** thinking it was a diamond. Yeah, anyone can swap items pretty fast. I have to say, though, I'm even faster than your average kid. While we waited,

I kept swapping between my pickaxe and milk bucket as fast as I could. Every time I did, I whistled, making a little sound—*phwew*—like a sword cutting through air. I did this for dramatic effect.

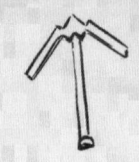

Phwew, milk! *Phwew*, pickaxe! *Phwew*, milk! *Phwew*, pickaxe! And then two swaps at once, super fast, so you could barely see the milk bucket I swapped to. *Phwew-phwew*.

Ninja speed, bro. **I'm not playing around.** No cave spiders are **gonna get me! 0.00001 seconds** after those red eyes appear in the darkness, I'll chug this thing so fast that cave spider will think it actually spawned as a normal spider without **any poison at all!**

Emerald noticed me practicing this. "Dude. Why do you keep switching between your pickaxe and milk bucket? And . . . why are you making those sounds?"

"I'm just, uh, testing a . . . technique. Yes. **A technique.**"

She blinked a few times. "**Um,** whatever."

The rules of this test are pretty **simple,** by the way. The goal is to collect **fifty pieces of . . .** anything remotely valuable. That means any type of ore, including lapis lazuli and coal.

Okay, the last few students are here.
I'll update when I get back.

WEDNESDAY—UPDATE III

After the test began, each team flew down a **different tunnel**. Soon, the distant shouts and shrieks from the other groups faded away **completely.** We **walked** and **walked,** but there wasn't any ore to be found. The miners had really **picked** the tunnels clean.

Then our tunnel **ended** abruptly. Judging by the cobblestone, it had clearly been sealed off. A **sign** sat nearby.

DO NOT ENTER
TUNNEL 77B
RESERVED FOR
THE MINING TEST.

Stump **nudged** the sign with his foot. "Hey, **look at that!** There's something **written** on the back!"

Strangely, on the back of the sign was a single word, inscribed near the bottom.

(Yes, our world has birds. Kolbert freaked out when he first saw one. Blockbirds are basically fluffy blocks with wings. Imagine a chicken without a head—I think you've got the idea.)

"I think it's like **a code word,**" I said. "**Miner slang.** Maybe it means **danger,** or maybe this tunnel is safe. **Pebble probably knew this language.**"

Stump looked around with **wide eyes.** "This place reminds me of **Tunnel 67!** I wonder if Pebble's father really did rig this place. But hey, maybe there's a lot of stuff down there!"

"**I have a bad feeling,**" Breeze said. "Maybe we should try another tunnel."

"**Are you kidding?**" Emerald took a step toward the cobblestone. "We don't know what 'blockbird' means. This tunnel is just as good as any."

"**She's right,**" Max said. "We can't waste time. I say we keep going."

"I know!" Lola said, beaming. "**Let's do a vote!**"

Yeah. Breeze and I were the only ones who voted to turn back. In the end, picks were swung, and the cobblestone wall gave way to . . . **a cave.** It branched in two directions, so we agreed to split up.

"Why don't you go with Emerald and Lola?" Breeze suggested.

Then she gave me **a look** that said,
Make sure they don't do <u>anything too noob</u>, okay?

WEDNESDAY—UPDATE IV

Shortly after we headed down the left branch, Emerald came up with all sorts of reasons for trailing **several blocks** behind Lola and me. At the same time, Lola went **full speed ahead,** all but skipping as she placed torch after torch. She just **wasn't afraid.** When a bat flew up to her, she caught it and **petted it** on the head.

Squeak, squeak.

"So **cute,** huh?"

"**Ew.** Gross." Then Emerald stopped and glanced at the wall. "Hey, **um . . .**"

"I think you need to enchant your glasses."
—Emerald

Wow, Lola really does take **noob** to a whole new level.

"I'll use my pickaxe to **mine** the ore!" Lola said.

Emerald and I exchanged glances. Our faces **were blank.** *Oh, you'll use a pickaxe to mine the ore?* I thought. *Are you sure? I thought you were going to use your forehead! Be right back—I'm going to go walk over here using my legs!*

We mined away **the entire coal vein** in silence, coming up with eight pieces of coal.

Then we **headed deeper and deeper** into the cave. I kept an eye on those two and listened for the **slightest noise.** We soon found another coal vein, and **Lola tore into it.** If it were possible to critically hit an ore block, she would have. As the coal dust settled, Emerald sneezed, which echoed through the cavern. After that, there were no more sounds. The three of us scanned the walls, which were bathed in the ruddy torchlight. We were completely alone, surrounded by crushing **silence** and countless blocks of stone, a **wall of darkness** just **ten blocks** up ahead.

Paranoia hung in the air along with a sense of **confinement,** of being **trapped.** At the same time, there was **freedom** here. Using our simple pickaxes, we could go anywhere we wanted.

There was even a sense of wonder and mystery as three hopeful miners **dug deep into the unknown.** This was the essence of mining.

Nothing captured this better than the sight of Emerald, panting slightly, pickaxe in hand, covered in coal dust, dirt, and sweat as she gazed into the cavern with eyes as bright as gemstones. **Even she'd gotten into the spirit.**

Miner Girl

"Come on," Lola said. "Maybe we'll find emeralds, and we can **trade them for new items!**"

"Trade them for new items?" Emerald called out from behind. "With emeralds? **Are you sure** that's what we use them for?! And here I was saving up for **a house on the beach!**"

WEDNESDAY—UPDATE V

Thirty minutes in, **we found a lot of stuff.** We were off to a pretty good start. We were doing **so good. So good.** I was doing good. Emerald was doing good. We were swinging our picks. We were making some progress. Then Lola really did find **some emeralds.**

"Too pretty, right, guys?"

Mmmmh, it's fishy.

Hmm. Something's off here. In a cave, you don't normally see walls like this. **It was too perfect, too flat,** as if **villager-made,** like the side of a house. And then there were those emeralds, just sitting there. It seemed too easy . . .

So I sensed **a trap of some kind.** A little surprise was waiting for us in that wall. Of course, Lola, being both **a noob** and a villager, just couldn't resist one of the Overworld's **most precious** gemstones. Honestly, I wanted to mine those emeralds, too. They were just winking at us, tempting us. As I gazed at them, **I couldn't stop thinking about it.**

*Come on, there's no danger in a little mining, they seemed to say. That's why you're down here, isn't it? A little swing here, a little swing there. Where's the **harm** in that?*

I tried to **stop** her,
but it happened <u>**so fast**</u> . . .

"I'm on it, guys!"

Emeralds surrounded by a gravel wall . . . nah, it's not a trap.

Well, okay, **it was a trap,** actually.

Once that block **shattered** . . .
the gravel above fell down and water **splashed out.** A water block had been placed behind the gravel block, which created **an endless** torrent.

Normally, even this wouldn't have been all that bad. So my cookies get soggy. As if a little sogginess would stop me from eating them.

Unfortunately, this section of cave had a nice, steep slope. With a slope like that, the water could rush downhill. The current **took all of us**—and any nearby torches—with it. The water pulled us down and down this narrow tunnel until we hit a **waterfall.** And not just a waterfall: a waterfall leading nowhere.

Lola triggered the trap at the block of white wool. The water carried us to the block of obsidian.

It's called **a whirlpool trap.** I read about it once in Mob Defense class. Once the current dunks you, it's really hard to get un-dunked. So this section of cave had been modified. It had been engineered to accomplish this specifically! Pebble's father must have built this trap weeks or months ago. **Seriously,** is everyone in Pebble's family **crazy?!**

Just try to imagine this situation. **Just try.** One second, everything's going good. You've got ore. You're mining away. **You're happy.** The next, *boom.* You're swept away. **Totally without light.** Getting pulled down by the current. Taking gulps of air after being completely submerged. When you aren't submerged, some random bat is fluttering around in your face, squeaking and totally freaking out.

And during all of this, you don't know if monsters are going to spawn nearby to help you reenact a bizarre version of *20,000 Leagues Under the Overworld.*

UNDER THE SEAAAAA!
WATCH HIM BOOGIE!

(It's one of Pistachio's favorite village musicals.)

SWIMMING SO FREELY!
HAPPY ZOMBIE!

WEDNESDAY—UPDATE VI

In first place for the test,
Team All Girls,
led by Ophelia!

In second place,
Team Zombiepunk,
led by Cogboggle!

OPERATION SNOOP:
REPORT

OPHELIA	116
COGBOGGLE	112
BREEZE	111
RUNT	108
BLOCK	108
EMERALD	106
SOULSAND	106
PORCUPINE	104
TWINKLE	102
MAX	99

Cogboggle passed me! I have to hold on to at least fifth rank! This is really, really bad . . .

We had a little **mishap today. A little setback.** We got fifth place in the mining test. **How annoying.** At first, everyone was angry with Lola and even angrier at me. I'm such **a bad babysitter.** Moreover, I was the one who had **agreed** to let her hang out with us. But then Stump said it was their fault, too. After all, Breeze and Emerald could have taken Lola with them when **they went mining yesterday.**

"It's **our job** to look after her," he said. "To make sure she doesn't do anything **too noob.**"

So after school today, we all went out to the park with our **swords drawn.** With the **combat test** scheduled for tomorrow, we were going to turn Lola into an **efficient,** zombie-destroying machine. Or that was the theory. In practice, it didn't work out so well.

We spent hours training her, giving her all kinds of advice. She must have swung **her wooden sword** a thousand times. Somehow, her combat score didn't go up a single point.

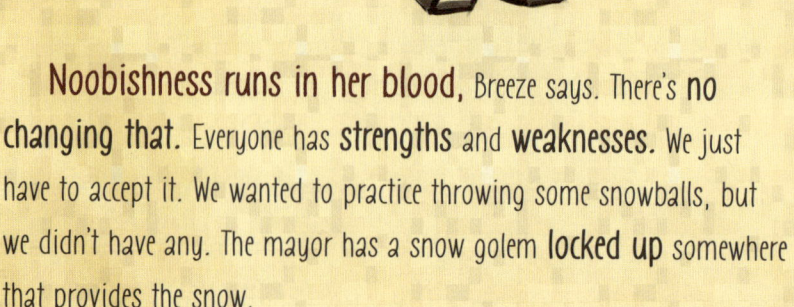

"Oh! So this is the handle! Well, we all make mistakes, don't we?"

Noobishness runs in her blood, Breeze says. There's **no changing that.** Everyone has **strengths** and **weaknesses.** We just have to accept it. We wanted to practice throwing some snowballs, but we didn't have any. The mayor has a snow golem **locked up** somewhere that provides the snow.

THURSDAY

Things are only **getting worse** as time goes on. One of the **reasons** Breeze has been acting **strange** is because of Lola. I realize that now. **Breeze denies it,** of course, because that's just how she is. She always hides herself. Rarely tells me how she's feeling. Still, I know she thinks **something is going on.**

"Hi, Runt! I bought you some cookies!"

Is something going on? Does Lola **like me in . . . that way?** I don't think so. We're just friends, nothing more. **Aren't we?**

 It's funny, you know? Out of all the challenges I've faced so far, this is **the most difficult yet.**

Dealing with monsters is easy compared to this. Grow a giant mushroom. **Dig a trench.** Or simply fire a bunch of arrows. That's it: **problem solved.** But this is **different.** It's too **complex.** There are no easy answers. It would have been so much easier if I'd never gotten to know her. I've felt that way since yesterday, and that feeling only grew stronger today during the first part of **the combat test.**

"Don't worry! I've been training a ton!"

"You're my best buds!"

When Lola had offered to **help me out,** I had been **blinded.** I only saw what I could gain and never really thought about what she could have wanted. I only saw her redstone **talent,** and I never considered the potential **downside** of letting her on my team.

"**Wow!** My sword flew farther than my arrow! Is that a special attack?"

As soon as I agreed to be her friend, **that was it.** She became **my** responsibility, my problem.

And now the first section of the combat test is over.

In less than fifteen minutes,

the Ice Cup tournament will begin.

THURSDAY—UPDATE I

Ice Cup is an **annual** event in my village. As I've mentioned, we play **Skyball** in this single-elimination tournament. Skyball is pretty simple. Each team has a **runner** who stays behind the stone wall on their team's platform. The runner's main job is **to avoid getting knocked into the water.** *(By the other team's snowballs.)* The rest of the team are **guards.** They stand in the front section of the platform. They must **protect the runner** from the opposing team's snowballs while hurling a few of their own. If a team's runner falls into the water below, **that's it. They lose the match.**

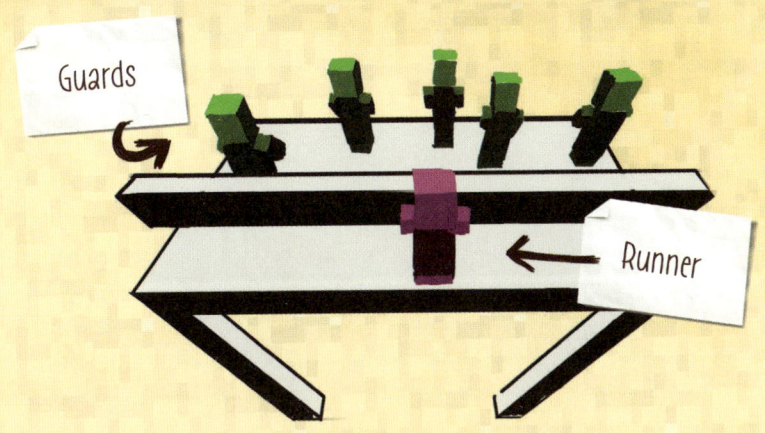

Guards

Runner

Sadly, Brio decided to **change** things up. "This year, I'll be choosing each team's runner," he said.

When he said this, I sensed that he was looking at me specifically. He was **smirking** at me.

Yeah. Who do you think he **chose to be our runner?** Who do you think he chose to be the single most important member on our Skyball team? **Who? Who?**

Lola, that's who. Brio kept **smirking** at me while the teams prepared themselves. He was **enjoying** this. But it's not so bad. We've been matched against a **really noob team** in the opening round. *That team features such legendary all-star greats as Bumbi and Bubbles.*

We'll just have to protect Lola, I guess. I'll **block** snowballs until I turn into **a snow golem,** if that's what it takes. We were each given potions of **Regeneration I.** Snowballs don't deal much damage, but I guess Brio just wants us to be safe. **Our match is about to begin, so . . .**

THURSDAY—UPDATE II

> The match was intense.

As we found out, Bubbles is apparently **a Skyball master.** He might be **ranked 145th** in school, but up there on that platform, he was the king. That kid would jump and weave around in the air to fake us out, and he threw those snowballs **so hard** I swear they went faster than arrows.

This other kid, **Loaf**—well, he didn't do much, but he didn't have to. He's one of the **biggest** kids in school (*over two blocks high and one and a half blocks wide*).

We were totally outmatched. After all, **Lola** was our runner . . . and Breeze had apparently **never thrown** a snowball in her entire life. Still, as long as we stood in front of **Lola**, we'd be okay.

Then Bubbles threw a snowball almost **straight up into the air**. Lola wasn't moving around much, you see, and she certainly didn't notice that snowball coming from **fifty blocks up**.

There was **no way** we could block that snowball. **She had to move.** I wanted to **warn her,** of course, but I took a snowball to the face just after I opened my mouth. When I whirled around, I took two more to the back of the head.

Just in time to see Lola **look up** one second before **the snowball hit her face.**

Oops!
Sorry!

THURSDAY—UPDATE III

... last place goes to
Team Danger Kitty,
led by Runt.

Everyone's **angry** with me now.

OPERATION SNOOP: REPORT

OPHELIA	135
COGBOGGLE	127
BLOCK	123
SOULSAND	121
PORCUPINE	119
TWINKLE	117
BREEZE	111
RUNT	108
EMERALD	106
MAX	99

Ophelia is pulling ahead of everyone **in the rankings.** She's the only one on her team with high-level scores. The rest are around **90%** now, I guess. She's carrying them. And then everyone in Cogboggle's **rotten crew** has passed us up. Breeze is in **seventh** place now, and I'm in **eighth.** One of us needs to be ranked at least **fifth** to become a captain.

I'm so angry that I can't even write. How is this happening? How did we lose to Team Noob in a **Skyball match?!** We got knocked out of the tournament in the first round! Why couldn't those noobs just let us win?!

I'm going to go
<u>**punch a tree.**</u>

FRIDAY

Well, this is it. Lola might have cost us **two tests,** but she'll make up for it with this one. The redstone test is **why she's here.** Even though we fell behind, we'll more than catch up once she unveils her **masterpiece**. Once Brio sees that marvelous invention, his eyes will become **larger** than **enderpearls,** and Team Runt will bounce back to the top like a slime under the effects of **Leaping II,** bouncing on a slime block.

FRIDAY—UPDATE 1

In front of everyone, Lola revealed her **flying machine.** The slime blocks. The redstone blocks. **The sticky pistons.** The sign. **People were amazed,** at first. Kolbert was here with Emerald, and he said Lola's invention reminded him of the **Industrial Revolution.**

"Do you know what this means?!" he said to Alex and Trevor3419. "This thing can **change the world!**"

"We'll begin working on it at once, **sir!**" Alex said.

Trevor3419 gave Kolbert a salute. "We'll put **our best men** on the job!"

Then it was **Team Zombiepunk's** turn to unveil their creation. I wonder what those noobs have come up with, I thought. Whatever it is, they won't beat us. One by one, Brio and several teachers removed the blocks of wool surrounding Team Zombiepunk's redstone creation. Can you guess what it was? **Can you?**

Yeah.
It was a flying machine.

With slime blocks, redstone blocks, **sticky pistons** . . .

They modified it just a little bit to make it look different, **of course.**
And **Team All Girls? Also a flying machine!**

In fact, pretty much every team had a flying machine!

Huh. Imagine that. Seems like everyone else had the **same idea.** How odd. **How mysterious. How coincidental.**

I wonder how they all came up with a **similar design?** Cogboggle and Block totally didn't spy on us when Lola built it in the garage . . .

Of course they did. They're not **dumb.** I'm the one who never even thought to make sure she built her invention in a secret location . . .

We just got counter-snooped. I gained **some levels,** of course, but so did everyone else, so the rankings are still the same.

It's over. It's all over. **My dreams are gone.** The final is on Monday.

I'm sure I'll manage to
mess that up, too.

SATURDAY

I had **bad dreams** the whole night. In every scene, Lola was in **danger**.

"We're going to have so many fun adventures!"

"Poor little guy. I think he needs a hug."

All of this is happening because of **a single decision** I made. I was **selfish**. Greedy. Out for myself. And now **I'm being punished**. There's nothing I can do to fix this. Breeze is **angry** with me, and now I won't even make captain.

Fine.
<u>I give up, okay?</u>
I don't even want to be a warrior anymore . . .

SUNDAY

I had the same **nightmares** tonight. They finally **subsided** and everything went black, until—

"It's been ages, **kid!**"

As if my dreams weren't **bad enough.** Now I get to listen to this **bonehead** talk in that scratchy, **gravelly** voice of his.

"Bonehead?!"

"I'm not the one who just bombed **three tests!** Hey, I'm sorry, all right? **Hey!** Don't shut me out, kid! Look, I'm not going to ask you to save me! **Someone else already did!** Don't look at them like that! **They're not monsters!**

Well, okay, they are monsters, and so am I, but we're good! **We're not like the rest!** We've made a whole city by ourselves! A city of good monsters, **hidden from all the bad ones!** By the way, this is Eeebs. He won't bite. Promise! Oh, and that's Clyde over there. Both of them are really nice!

"Okay, okay, I don't have much time. I just wanted to tell you . . . you think you know a lot, Runt, **but you really don't.** There's a huge world out there, kid. **You can't even imagine.** How could you, **stuck** in that tiny village? You haven't seen a thing!

"When you get a chance, you need to **go out there and explore!** Leave those walls! There's so much you need to learn! So much you need to see! Anyway, that's all I wanted to say. Visit me sometime! Ask around for **Batwing!** That's me! We're gearing up to fight that creepy guy with the glowing white eyes.

"One more thing, Runt . . .

"Even if you don't make captain, who cares? **You're already a warrior, kid!** What counts are your actions and what's inside of you, not a bunch of **silly** tests! Oh, don't look so confused. That Pebble kid might have been a little crazy, **but even he knew that!**"

I woke up covered in **cubes of sweat.**

Was it really just a dream? Or . . . was it real?

Well, Breeze has been dreaming the **exact same thing.** It seems hard to believe, but . . . maybe a monster is actually **communicating** with me.

That's strange though, because Breeze said endermen, not **wither skeletons, control dreams.** Maybe the skeleton was using a magical **item?** Max told me that some endermen are amazing crafters. Even **wizards.** I need to do more research with him. Anyway, I don't want to **leave the village.** How could I? **Batwing** can go bug Lola, and she can go to visit him, and the two of them can become **the bestest best-best friends.**

Does this mean Pebble is still alive?!
Not only is he still alive,
but he has a <u>horse?!</u>

MONDAY

The big day. I'm in the cafeteria. So is every other student. We've all been **working** on the final—writing down our ideas about how to get **revenge** against the mobs. By now, almost everyone has turned their paper in. We're just waiting for the teachers to review our submissions and determine the winners. They sure are taking their time. What's the holdup? As if it's **hard to decide.** We might have worded our papers differently, but the **general idea** is the same.

> I THINK
> WE SHOULD
> BURN THE MOBS'
> FOREST.
> —STUMP GOLDENFEATHER

In my opinion, the best way to take revenge would be: Start a fire in their forest. Wouldn't take much effort on our side, so it's a very effective way to disrupt their plans.
—BREEZE

STEP 1:
WALK UP TO THE FOREST

STEP 2:
USE LIGHTER

STEP 3:
GIVE ME AN A++

-EMERALD SHADOWGROUND

TREE

BUCKET

FIRE

LAVA

HOMELESS ZOMBIE

—RUNT IRONFURNACE

(Yeah, I didn't try very hard. I've pretty much given up.)

CUPCAKES ARE VERY HARD TO MAKE. YOU NEED SUGAR, BREAD, EGGS, MILK, AND FOOD COLORING. I LOVE CUPCAKES. IT'S COOL. EVERY DAY I WAKE UP AND WONDER HOW MANY I'LL BE ABLE TO EAT.

(This is Max's submission. He didn't put his name on it. Looks like he's given up more than I have.)

Of course, Lola is still hanging with us, **as cheerful as ever.** I've decided **to not get angry** with her. As I said, all of this is my fault. **(I don't need to point out that she was the last student to finish writing her paper . . .)**

"I've put **a lot** of thought into my idea!" she said to me. "I think it's really good! **Would you like to hear it?**"

"No, thanks," I said, not even glancing at her paper. I figured her idea probably involved talking with the mobs in a peaceful way. **Maybe some flowers.**

No, I wasn't **curious** in the least. **Neither were my friends.** Breeze didn't say a word to **Ms. Noob** the whole day. Well, **that's that.** BRB, diary—gotta go fail one last test. My life just won't be complete until I do.

Prepare for an update filled with rage,
and **crying**, and **whining**, and *hurgging*,
and **freaking out** in general.

MONDAY—UPDATE I

Cake biome?!
Fermented pickaxe?!
Protection from Pumpkins V?!

Brain . . . malfunctioning.
Bzzzzt. Bzt. Bzzzzzt.
Bzt-bzt. . . .

Bzzzt.

MONDAY—UPDATE II

MONDAY—UPDATE III

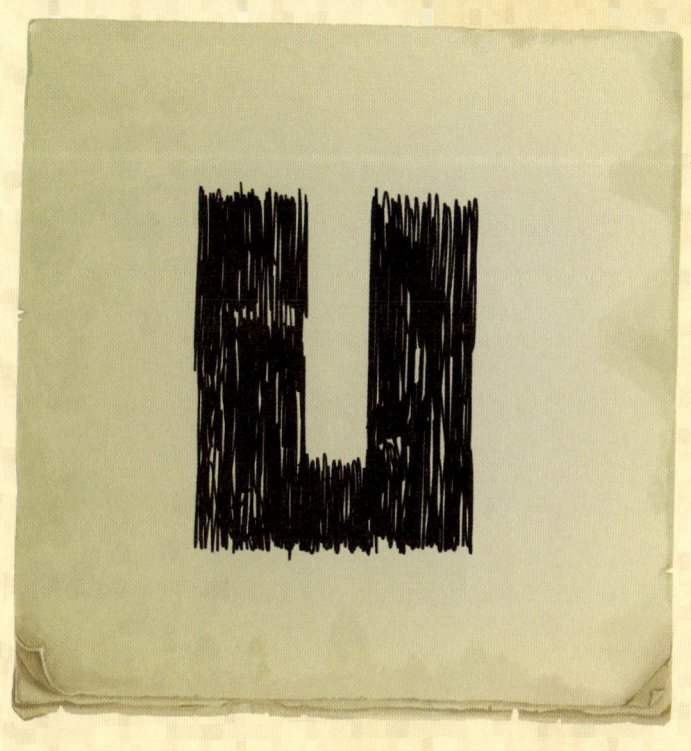

MONDAY—UPDATE IV

MONDAY—UPDATE V

MONDAY—UPDATE VI

MONDAY—UPDATE VII

MONDAY—UPDATE VIII

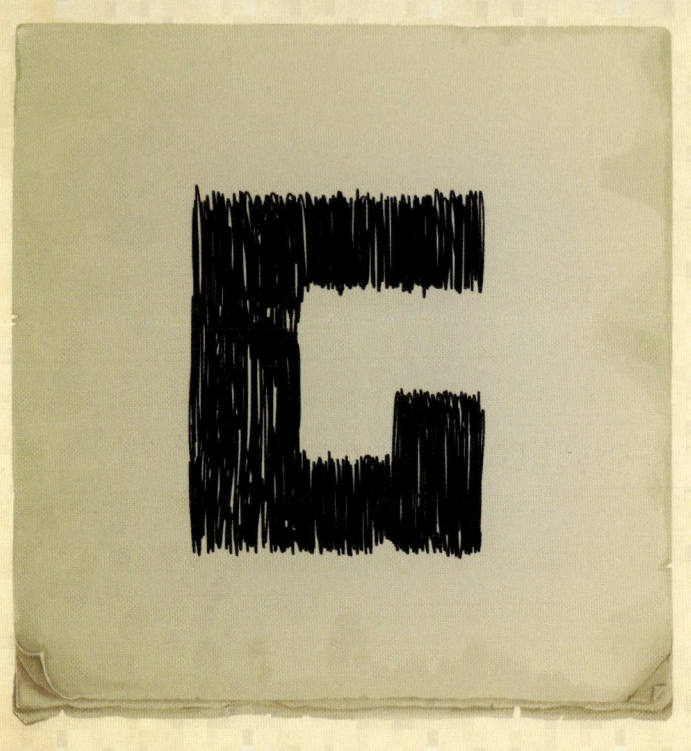

MONDAY—UPDATE IX

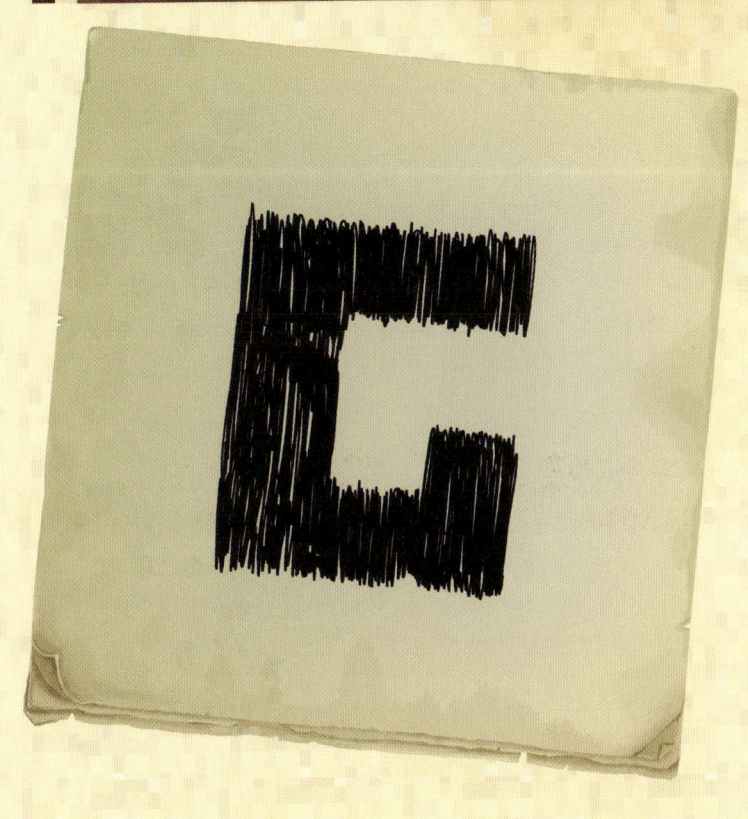

MONDAY—UPDATE X

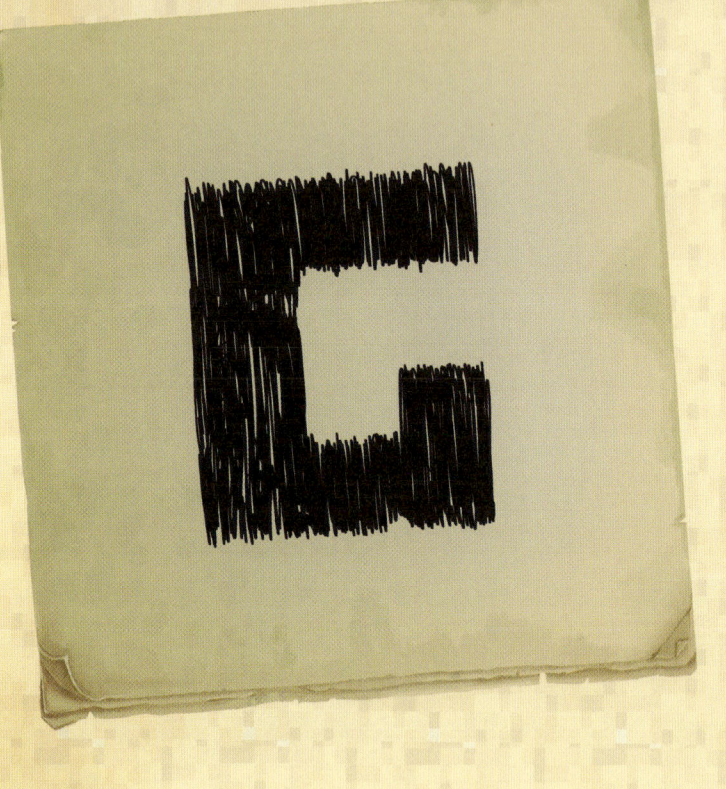

MONDAY—UPDATE XI

P-potato . . . ?
I . . . I-like . . .
p-p . . . p . . . p-p-ppotato?

MONDAY—UPDATE XII

This is Breeze.

Runt is trying to write in his diary, but he **can't**. I suppose he is **too shocked** at what just happened. I could write about that in detail, but I have chosen not to. I am writing in here so he doesn't make any more **strange entries.**

Runt, when you read this . . . I am **sorry,** but I read some of your previous entries. It's true, I've been **jealous of Lola**. You two were spending so much time **together.** I hope you can forgive me. I've been acting childish. Again, **sorry.**

—**Breeze,** who wishes she
knew more about redstone . . .

MONDAY—UPDATE XIII

It's Emerald.

Dude, Runt is like, totally **freaking out.** Honestly, I am, too. I mean, dude—what just happened? **I can't believe it!** Still, though, I'm not **freaking out** the way Runt is freaking out. He's been running laps around the combat yard for the past fifteen minutes and screaming the whole time!

Okay, yeah, um, sorry for writing in here. I saw Breeze doing it and thought it'd be kinda **fun** if I did, too.

Lola is **really cool,** by the way. I know that now. We're gonna go **trading** together as soon as we're not busy. And not just window trading, either. We're totally gonna go on the biggest **trading spree** ever! And she's gonna craft me this thing called a dress and these special boots called **sandals!**

Wow! I can't wait!
Some of that human-style clothing looks so
<u>**super, super cute!**</u>

MONDAY—UPDATE XIV

Meow! Lola here! ^_____^

I'm letting you know that you left your diary in the cafeteria. Silly boy! Breeze, Emerald, and I have been writing stuff in here because it's **really neat! Wow!** I feel like a real warrior recording my thoughts and feelings! **So cool, right?**

And yes, I know I've made a few mistakes these past few days, but that's all part of the learning process, **isn't it?** Anyway, you should now know that I'm **not as noob** as you think! Don't worry, Runt! **We're going to do great things together!**

=<^.^>=
A happy kitty just for you!

~~XOXO, Lola~~

(PS, I don't know what XOXO means! I saw some humans writing that and thought it'd be cool to include!)

MONDAY—UPDATE XV

Dear diary,

Why does everyone keep writing in you? Is this the cool thing to do now? That's fine. I, Stump Goldenfeather, **am officially cool now.**

Yeah. So. Something **ridiculous** happened during the final. I was going to write about it since Runt can't, but Breeze and Emerald are telling me not to.

Hold on.
They're not looking.
Okay, so what happened is—

MONDAY—UPDATE XVI

Runt,

For the record, I have taken your diary **away from Stump.** This is your diary. No one should be writing in here **except for you.**

I will say: **I am as shocked as you** are about what happened during the final.

—Max Whitecloud

MONDAY—UPDATE XVII

Yeahhhhh!!
I stole Runt's diary!
I took it from that **noob**, Max!
I snatched it right out from under his big, blocky nose!

Then I ran through the school halls with it, waving it over my head! **What a rush!** This feels so great, just like that time I stole those **diamonds** from that human!

Oh, great. The **guys in black** are coming. So annoying. Those blockheads are always on my tail . . . What's **their problem,** anyway?! So what if I scammed that kid out of his emeralds the other day!?! That noob didn't need 'em! Time to show these guys why people call me **the sneakiest villager around!**

Until next time,

—**Cogboggle**, everyone's favorite villager

MONDAY—UPDATE XVIII

I'm hiding in the school **supply** room. **I totally gave 'em the slip!** Those cobbleheads walked right past me! All right, I gotta stash this book somewhere. Can't be **caught** with this thing in my inventory. **Oh,** and just so you know, Runt, you might've pulled ahead, but we still have to finish out **the final!** After you mess that up and none of you make captain, your whole crew is gonna be **shining my boots** to a diamond gleam! Especially that **annoying little Emerald!**

Warmest regards,

—**Cogboggle,** the coolest/greatest/sneakiest villager of all time, and **dungeon-looter extraordinaire**

MONDAY—UPDATE XIX

Uh . . . This is **Bumbi.** What is this diary doing in my inventory? Just to let everyone know, **I did not steal this book.** Since I'm writing in here, I'll just say that **I am really sad,** because I am now in last place. I'm rank **150** now. Even Lola is ahead of me. And **Bubbles.** Bubbles! This isn't good. I wonder if they will still let me be a warrior? Maybe I can join **Runt's team.**

Wait, is this Runt's diary? **Wow.** It is! **What luck!** Runt, if you read this, I want to know if I can join your group after we graduate. Pleeze let me know. **Plzplzplz.** I will try my best.

Oops. It looks like everyone took off to finish the final test. I need to be there.

This is Bumbi, by the way.
Bye.

MONDAY—UPDATE XX

Official notice:

This book has been confiscated by the school board. As this item has been modified to such a degree as to fall within the category of strange and unknown items, its threat to village security must be assessed. Furthermore, this item may contain potentially sensitive information, and as such, we cannot risk letting it fall into the hands of the enemy until its contents are deemed safe.

Upon its approval, it will be returned to its owner, Runt Ironfurnace.

—**Brio**, Administrator,
School of Minecraft and Warriory

TUESDAY

Official notice:

Due to the extent of this item's modification, the review process is taking longer than usual. In addition, some entries appear to describe the mayor in a negative fashion, which could be harmful to his image as the brave leader of our village.

Therefore, the school board is now determining whether or not this item should be placed within a lava incinerator for its immediate destruction and its owner appropriately reprimanded.

—**Slab,** Administrative Assistant
(referred to in this diary as one of the "guys in black," "Brio's goons," "creepy weirdos," "thugs," or "blockheads")

TUESDAY—UPDATE I

Official notice:

I, the mayor, hereby declare my intention to designate "Villagetown" as the official name for our village.

Furthermore, I hereby decree that all entries within this diary that portray me in anything other than a stellar light are to be regarded as entirely fictional.

—The Mayor of Villagetown

TUESDAY—UPDATE II

I, Runt Ironfurnace, **officially** acknowledge that any part of this diary that suggests the mayor is a total noob just **isn't true.**

I also agree to **never write** any such imaginary events in the **future,** as they could tarnish the mayor's good name.

Lastly, I will spend Tuesday afternoon in the **school kitchen** crafting various **potato-based food items.**

—Runt Ironfurnace

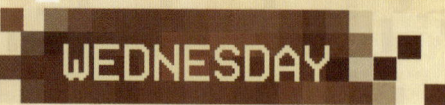

WEDNESDAY

Finally.
Finally!

Brio **gave my diary back to me.** The guys in black studied it for days to make sure its contents were "wholesome" and not a **"threat to village security."** Well, some of my entries do contain a lot of **top-secret** information, but there's no chance the mobs will get their hands on this book. I will eat every last page before that happens. I will. And I could do it, too, believe me. **I get really hungry sometimes.**

Well, enough of that! How about we go over what happened on Monday?! Just remembering it makes me **wanna f-f-freak out, man!**

LAST MONDAY— FLASHBACK I

Okay, so there we were, waiting in the cafeteria. **Lola was bugging me** about her idea, and I just brushed her off. Dude, all of **Team Runt** was fed up with her. And **fed up** with me. Even fed up with themselves! I mean, we came all this way, we studied and practiced and trained and took **all kinds of risks** to do well in school, and then this happens?! **Cogboggle, that punk!** He **stole** Lola's idea! He stole her idea and other kids found out about it, and suddenly **every team** had a flying machine.

I was sitting there, **thinking** along these lines. Then, before the entire school, the mayor held up a **stack** of papers. "We will now announce **the winner of the final test,**" he said.

"**Unfortunately,** almost every entry was identical," Brio said, "resulting in a tie between every team. **Except one.**"

A lot of students **groaned.** So almost everyone had the exact same idea?! **But it was a good idea!** How could the mayor not want to burn that forest down?! One time I saw a zombie standing underneath those trees with this **smug little look** on his face.

Oh, look at me, that zombie was probably thinking. *The sunlight can't touch me! We're so clever! We made a forest right next to this village where we can roam all day!*

No, **we had to burn it down!** There was no better way to get revenge. Yet apparently there was.

Whatever it was, it was something only the sneakiest villager would come up with. **No**, I thought. **No way! It can't be! It just can't be! It's not possible!** Cogboggle's . . . going to win?!

The mayor put away the stack and held up a single paper. "Yes, out of every submission we've reviewed, **only one stood out.** Well, there was one that said something about **cupcakes,** but there was no name, so . . . we threw it out."

He handed the paper to Brio, who shouted: "And the **winning submission** belongs to . . . **Nessa Diamondcube!!** Oh, it says to call you **Lola.** Sorry. Please come up, dear."

Boom!

The crowd **exploded** like a powder keg. *(That's an item Max read about in an ancient book—its blast is stronger than a charged creeper's.)*

Anyway, no one could believe it. **Lola won?!** How could a noob like her come up with such **an amazing idea?!**

With **a shriek,** Ms. Noob clutched her chest and bounced up and down like a slime who'd just consumed an entire stack of sugar. Then she made her way up and stood next to Brio with a smile **so bright** that if anyone here had been a zombie in disguise, they would have burst into flames.

"We really **loved** Ms. Diamondcube's idea," the mayor said. "It's so **elegant,** so **splendid** and **wonderful,** simply bursting with the kind of ingenuity we so desperately need . . ."

And when he said that, I suddenly **remembered** that I used to be like that. I used to be a noob just like her, trying so hard to prove myself. Back then, I never would have asked some stranger for help. Back then, I would have come up with **my own idea.** Have I become lazy? Or am I just stressed out?

Anyway, Lola finally pulled through.

```
           OPERATION SNOOP:
                REPORT
       OPHELIA          137
       COGBOGGLE        128
       BLOCK            124
       SOULSAND         122
       PORCUPINE        120
       BREEZE           119
       TWINKLE          118
       RUNT             116
       EMERALD          114
       MAX              107
```

And since she was on our team... **That was the point when I totally freaked out.**

Our ranks didn't change, I thought, *but we're only a few levels behind! If we do well on the second part of the final, Breeze and I can hit the top five! Even if I don't make captain, and Breeze does, that's enough for me! I'll salute her, craft her breakfast...*

I ran out of the cafeteria and started **running** laps around the combat yard, totally screaming at the top of my lungs. In that time, my friends **wrote a bunch of stuff in my diary**—along with Cogboggle, who wrote a bunch of nonsense. I'm the sneakiest villager, **not him!**

Thirty minutes later,
all 146 students began to carry
out the plan proposed in Lola's submission,
the title of which was . . .

LAST MONDAY— FLASHBACK II

This village is both fun and super happy. Can you tell?

Cakes on top of jukeboxes—the happiest thing ever.

Thirty blocks away, the scariest forest of all time—what better place to dance, play loud music, and eat cake?

Yeah.

We built **a little party area.** So cozy, right? So cute, so lovely, so innocent and girly. But this **happy** little place, smelling of flowers and freshly crafted cake, **had a dark and terrible little secret.**

Hidden beneath all that frosting, beneath the pink glass blocks, the rose bushes, and the seastone lanterns . . .

was our version of
Boom Mountain.

"A-a-**all** right, you guys place the TNT, and I-I-I'll just go wait over here. I mean, someone has to watch the forest, right?"
—Emerald

The **idea** went like this: We were to dance in **Super Happy Fun Town, laughing** and smiling and **joking.** The mobs, who hate **cute** little places like this and super-hate seeing villagers having fun, would rush out. We would then light one block of TNT just before the mobs entered, we'd run back, and the zombies would be given **a free one-way trip to the void.** *(I would then have my cup of tea.)*

And it went like that, **it did.** Emerald threw some music discs into the jukeboxes, and they started **blaring** away. Stump, Max, and a few others climbed up the ladders and did **some jigs** on top of the houses.

"**I'm so happy!**" Stump called out, arms and legs moving wildly. "Good thing the mobs aren't attacking us! **We're having so much fun over here!**"

The rest started dancing down below.

Strangely, Lola still wasn't around—she **disappeared** right after we began building. So Breeze was **happy.**

Breeze approached after the "party" started, and in **a shy way,** asked: "Do you know how to dance?"

"**Not really.** I, uh . . . I never really had the time."

"**Me neither.** Maybe we can learn together?"

"That **sounds like fun.** Sure. We'll have to do that someday."

"Why not **now**?"

> I was zapped by lightning again.
> Dance?! **Right now?!**
> <u>I don't know how to dance!</u>

Thankfully, the mobs—being the **gentlemobs** they are—must have sensed my embarrassment, and saved me in the nick of time. A **huge** army of zombies rushed out of that forest. **Of course,** they were all wearing helmets—like the "helmet squad" Kolbert had seen earlier. Here's where our plans fell apart.

You see, due to school safety regulations, only a few kids had **flint and steel** on them at the time.

Bumbi was one of them, along with Bubbles and Loaf—the teachers gave the flint and steel to these noobs so they had something to do. They were some of the super noobs behind those **Building Fails.** No one wanted them **building**—and who knows how they'd manage to mess up placing TNT.

Okay, so—those kids **ran.** They saw that huge army approaching, the helmets gleaming in the sun, and totally **chickened out.** So the rest of us couldn't light the TNT.

So we had to retreat.

We had to go back **near the real village** and watch helplessly as the mobs began **dismantling Super Happy Fun Town.** The zombies trashed the jukeboxes first, which were all blaring loudly with annoying music. Then they went for the cakes, the pink glass, the seastone lanterns . . .

It looked like Lola's idea was **about to fail.**

Then her voice rang out like a note block set to a high pitch. "Looks like you guys didn't read the **instructions** very well! **But don't worry!** I expected this, so I did the last part myself!"

She was standing at the edge of the crowd, **next to a lever** that had been placed on the ground.

Also next to the lever, forming a long trail across the plains . . . **redstone dust.**

We thought she was the ultimate noob . . .

She didn't think like us, she didn't act like us, she didn't speak like us . . .

But she was hiding strength that no one else had . . .

I judged her just like Pebble had judged me. And at that moment, I knew . . .

. . . I, too, **was wrong.**

WEDNESDAY—UPDATE I

After the explosion, you couldn't see a single block of **Super Happy Fun Town** . . . and there **wasn't a mob in sight.** Since Lola had come up with this idea and was the one who'd laid **the redstone trail**—single-handedly obliterating over **three hundred zombies**—and since she was on **our team** . . .

OPERATION SNOOP: REPORT

OPHELIA	137
BREEZE	129
COGBOGGLE	128
RUNT	126
EMERALD	125
BLOCK	124
SOULSAND	122
PORCUPINE	120
TWINKLE	118
MAX	117

The crater also formed a kind of **no-mob's-land** between our village and the forest.

Man, those explosions were **legendary.** And here I thought we were going to use flint and steel! We were lucky those noobs **ran!**

The first wave of explosions knocked unlit TNT **in every direction.** If someone had lit them by hand, they would have been caught in the **blast area . . .**

It might require planning and lengthy setup time, but redstone does have combat applications. Can I stop being wrong about everything? Please?

THURSDAY

I made good decisions from the beginning.

The wrong choice would have been to throw her off the team before the final exam.

***

The right choice was to believe in her, just like my friends and family believed in me.

If I'd chosen to not save Pebble, he'd definitely be a zombie.

231

There's still one decision left for me to make.

Despite all of the options, I felt like I had only one choice.

FRIDAY

A **long time** ago, I started this diary with a single goal in mind. At the time, it seemed so **impossible,** so unattainable. **A ridiculous little dream.** I was barely a **full-size** villager then, who only knew about gathering seeds and planting crops. Now there's **a diamond pin on my cloak** and a diamond path just up ahead.

Am I **dreaming? Is this real?** I'm so caught up in this, I can barely write. Once more, I'm resisting the urge to create **tear blocks.** However, at the same time, it . . . feels like there is so much more waiting for me.

What about the **humans?** How did they arrive here? How will they **go back?** Are there more of them out there?

Then there are those weird dreams. Who is **Batwing? Clyde? Eeebs?** Is that cat **really a monster?** Do good monsters really exist? Above all else, there's a **man with glowing white eyes.** Is it possible that villagers, humans, and good monsters can work together to **stop him?**

Although the future seems so uncertain right now, I do know one thing for sure.

No matter what happens, **we'll keep fighting.** Somehow, some way, we'll **figure it all out.**

Before long, we will go out there, to a place once filled with people, from villagers to pigmen. Beyond our walls rests the knowledge the ancients left behind, which we must now **reclaim. With this knowledge,** we can craft obsidian swords, advanced redstone machines, enchanted arrows, powder kegs, and armor strong enough to withstand the strongest monsters—monsters thought to exist only in **fairy tales** and ancient times, which now haunt the Overworld **once more.**

The powder keg.

FRIDAY—UPDATE I

This morning, Breeze **asked me to go to the park.** After we sat under a tree, I figured we would craft food and have a **picnic** under the leaves. She pulled out **a diamond sword** instead.

"We **pooled our emeralds** together," she said, offering me the blade. "Even the mayor chipped in."

". . ."

In the sun, the blade had **a slight opalescent sheen,** so faint. Like Breeze, there was something **fragile** about its appearance, **elegant** and **graceful, beautiful.** Yet at the same time, it seemed strong enough to put up with a noob like myself *(also like Breeze).*

"I'm sorry if it seemed like I was **ignoring you,**" I said. "I didn't mean to hang out with Lola so much. I . . . just wanted us **to win.**"

"**It's my fault,**" she said. "When I saw you two spending so much time together, I couldn't control myself. **I was so jealous.** She's so talented in areas most villagers aren't."

"And you **aren't?**"

"No."

"Try telling that to pretty much every monster you've come across."

She smiled, but it **quickly faded.** "I'll . . . tell you **a secret.** Yesterday, when I stood before that chest, I . . . almost didn't **pull out a sword.**"

"What? Why?"

"I thought about **becoming a farmer**," she said. "I seriously considered it."

"I don't understand."

"**I'm tired of fighting,** Runt. It's all I've known. I just want a **peaceful** life, you know? Sunshine. Golden wheat fields. The smell of bread fresh off the crafting table."

"Maybe it's **not too late** to go back. Maybe the mayor will let you choose again."

She shook her head. "**I can't.** Even if I could, I wouldn't. Until this war is over, we'll never have any peace. And besides, there's another reason why I choose the sword."

"What?"

·You.·
(Okay, okay! We did hold hands this time! We did! I admit it!)

·Come on!·
she said, a few minutes later.
·We'll miss the celebration!
I'd really like to try dancing!·

FRIDAY—UPDATE II

"We're going to the hairdresser. We can't go to the party like this! See ya later, Runt!"

"Who's ready to play creeper tag?"

"I'll drag you to the library if I have to, Runt. I found a book about advanced crafting tables."

"Did you learn something about rune chambers? If you've made one, put me inside. I'm going to need to be enchanted with Whiner Protection VII!"

"I heard someone say that Emerald has a weakness for boys with higher levels... It's perfect that Kolbert is level 21337!"

"Good work, villagers!
I trained my men as well!
We'll work together to defeat
this son-of-a-noob Herobrine!"

"And actually, I saw Emerald
leave with Breeze and that redstone girl.
Where'd they go? And why am I always
thinking about her?"

This time, we deserved **a real celebration.** This time, we really did sing and laugh and dance, **even cry,** for we had to say good-bye—to the teachers, the classrooms, and all the times we had as innocent, carefree noobs.

All of which I already miss.

Breeze tapped me on the shoulder. She'd returned from the **salon** with Lola and Emerald.

Now she wore **a sleeveless robe,** and her hair had **the same kind of shimmer** as Lola's.

I'd heard about the salon. It's this place where you can **modify your skin or appearance.** Some of the human girls built it. I'll have to head over there at some point, because I heard you can **customize the appearance of your weapons and armor,** too.

If I really want to become <u>OverlordRunt77777</u>, I'll have to look the part.

"This is called **a dress,**" she said. She whirled around. "Lola crafted it for me. And **the hair,** well . . . Elisa helped me do that."

"What about those things on your feet?"

"**Slippers.**" She glanced down at herself. "So what do you think?"

"**You look amazing,**" I said. "I take back everything I said about human fashion." I paused. "Sure is changing around here, huh . . . ?"

"Yes, **our village is changing** . . . but that's not **a bad thing.**"

"Maybe not."

And suddenly I realized she'd said **our village.** She'd said it so **casually,** without any hesitation, as if she'd lived here all her life. She grabbed my hands and looked into my eyes, and in that moment I sensed that, at last, she was **truly home.**

"Our old way of life is **disappearing,**" she said. "We have to accept that, and look to the future. With the humans helping us, **we can win this war.** But let's forget about all that for today. Just today."

And <u>**her smile**</u>
was like an enchanted diamond.

PREVIOUS BOOKS

Diary of an 8-Bit Warrior

Diary of an 8-Bit Warrior: From Seeds to Swords

Diary of an 8-Bit Warrior: Crafting Alliances

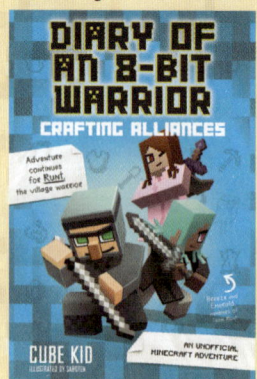

ABOUT THE AUTHOR

Cube Kid is the pen name of Erik Gunnar Taylor, a writer who has lived in Alaska his whole life. A big fan of video games—especially Minecraft—he discovered early that he also had a passion for writing fan fiction.

Cube Kid's unofficial Minecraft fan fiction series, *Diary of a Wimpy Villager*, came out as e-books in 2015 and immediately met with great success in the Minecraft community. They were published in France by 404 éditions in paperback with illustrations by Saboten and now return in this same format to Cube Kid's native country under the title *Diary of an 8-Bit Warrior*.

When not writing, Cube Kid likes to travel, putter with his car, devour fan fiction, and play his favorite video game.

DIARY OF AN 8-BIT WARRIOR

CRAFTING ALLIANCES

This edition © 2017 by Andrews McMeel Publishing.

All rights reserved. Printed in China. No part of this book may be used or reproduced in any manner whatsoever without written permission except in the case of reprints in the context of reviews.

Published in French under the title *Journal d'un Noob (Méga Guerrier) Tome III*
© 2016 by 404 éditions, an imprint of Édi8, Paris, France
Text © 2015 by Cube Kid, Illustration © 2016 by Saboten

Minecraft is a Notch Development AB registered trademark. This book is a work of fiction and not an official Minecraft product, nor approved by or associated with Mojang. The other names, characters, places, and plots are either imagined by the author or used fictitiously.

Andrews McMeel Publishing
a division of Andrews McMeel Universal
1130 Walnut Street, Kansas City, Missouri 64106
www.andrewsmcmeel.com

ISBN: 978-1-4494-8803-1 hardback
978-1-4494-8228-2 paperback

Library of Congress Control Number: 2016948376

Made By:
King Yip (Dongguan) Printing & Packaging Factory Ltd.
Address and place of production:
Daning Administrative District, Humen Town
Dongguan Guangdong, China 523930
Box Set 3rd printing-2/28/22

ATTENTION: SCHOOLS AND BUSINESSES
Andrews McMeel books are available at quantity discounts with bulk purchase for educational, business, or sales promotional use. For information, please e-mail the Andrews McMeel Publishing Special Sales Department: specialsales@amuniversal.com.

• CUBE KID •

DIARY OF AN 8-BIT WARRIOR

CRAFTING ALLIANCES

Illustrations by
Saboten

Andrews McMeel
PUBLISHING®

In memory of Lola Salines (1986-2015),
founder of 404 éditions and editor of this series,
who lost her life in the November 2015 attacks on Paris.
Thank you for believing in me.

- Cube Kid

MONDAY—EARLY MORNING

I woke up **before the sun even rose** and couldn't fall back asleep.

Of course, Mom and Dad didn't have this problem. They'd been working the fields all week.

Maybe that's why they **finally** warmed up to the idea of me becoming a warrior.

These days, **they're just too tired to argue.**

At least they decided to give me a **bigger** allowance.

I recalled the conversation with Mom the other day:

"Use these emeralds to enchant your robe with **Frost Protection II,** okay, **honey?** I don't want you getting sick!"

"I don't think there is such an enchantment, **but thanks anyway.**"

"**Okay, well, be sure to eat more steak!** Cookies won't keep your hunger bar up."

"But cookies are tasty . . ."

"And wear your leather armor underneath your robe today. If you fall again during training, **your health bar won't get so low.**"

"Mom. Armor doesn't protect against falling damage."

"Oh. All right, dear."

Jello was sound asleep as well. From inside his box, he made quiet little sounds—***burble, burble***—the baby slime equivalent of snoring. I put on my boots and grabbed **my sword** on my way out the door. It was still dark. But soon, as I made my way to school, **the square sun crawled** over the gloomy, gray houses and shed pink light upon the gloomy, gray streets. To a villager, this was a precious time. At this hour, the monsters were crawling back to a forest that never knew the sun. In their absence, a sleepy village was now **rustling awake.**

* * *

I went for **a morning jog.** I thought it'd help clear my mind. **It didn't.**

Five minutes in, my anger flared like a redstone torch . . . because I saw the posters. They're everywhere, **those posters.**

Pebble is on most of them . . .

I DON'T ALWAYS KILL MOBS . . .

BUT WHEN I DO, I KILL THEM IN ONE SHOT.

There were nearly as many posters with Emerald, Steve, Mike, the mayor . . . and even Urf. Urf!

He **took off on Sunday,** from what I heard, carrying half **a village supply room with him.** He took two donkeys, each with chests, that he loaded up before stuffing his own pockets—all three inventories filled with **stacks of iron, enchanted books** . . . in short, our **most valuable** items.

Definitely turned traitor!!!
Definitely sided with the mobs.

And definitely offered them more than just piles of **shiny loot.** The right information can **be worth more** than diamonds, and that would explain how the **mobs pinpointed our school so easily.** He left a trail of items on his way out of town. **The heaviest stuff.** Weapons. Armor. He was most likely weighed down. He most likely wanted to escape quickly.

Fear is stronger than greed.

A few posters had **the names of many who fought** on Saturday. The posters didn't have any pictures, but I'm including them in this diary. They fought **just as hard as Pebble** did, after all . . .

Hold on, Weston!!!

WESTON	CHARLIE	GABE
HEATHER	BOSTON	CAMERON
MIA	BECK	RAFI
MARY	GRYFFEN	SAM
EMMA	CASA	BLOOTY
SOPHIA	DYLAN	JAKEY
BRIGID	KHAN	ZAK
LUNA	GABE	NOAH
ALYSSA	DAN	OWEN
ANDREA	MICRO	RHETT
MARISA	MATTHEW	JOEY
RACHEL V	THOMAS	JAMIN
AILEEN	ANTHONY	SIMONE
JOAN	THOM	JOSH
GRACE	SPARROW	CLARK
ZAYNE	PAUL	KYLE
MERIEDI	BRAD	HAYDEN
TOMOYA	LINCOLN	JAY
WILL	ANDREW	OSCAR
BRENNAN	ALEX	SAMUEL
MARCO	JAMES	REMY
TOBI	FINN	JACK
WESTON	ELLIS	CADYN
SCOOEY	FRANKIE	RYAN

Hello, Gabe.

Good luck, Ryan!

Suddenly, **a freezing wind picked up.** I raised the collar on my robe. Then I glanced at the distant houses, wondering whether Breeze **could be out there, somewhere,** at this early hour . . .

Who *is she?*
Was she telling the truth?
Did her father really send
her to spy on me?

When it comes to her, there's **only one thing I know for sure** . . . I glanced down at **my health bar,** at the row of little red hearts, **and remembered** . . .

I entered the school and walked empty halls. I checked every empty classroom. Surprisingly, one room was occupied. **The head teacher's office on the second floor.** *Professor . . .* Brio?

He smirked. "Morning."

I nodded. "Morning."

By the way, we weren't **exchanging greetings**—we were stating a welcome fact. I sat down, either *on some stairs* or *in a chair*, depending on which universe you come from.

"I take it you're **the head teacher** now," I said.

"**Something like that.**" He adjusted his glasses—I caught a glimpse of his purple eyes. "I'll be overseeing everyone's progress from here on out. I suppose you could say it's time **to kick things up a . . . notch.**"

He rose. "Come with me."

I followed him to the tower—**to the very top**—where we looked out at **the eastern wall.**

"I must say," Brio murmured, "I'm **surprised** they were able to **rebuild** that mushroom shop as well as they did." He turned to me. "I believe you caused more damage there than a wither blast."

"Sorry. I just didn't . . ."

"**You survived.** You used what you had and survived. **Honestly, I'm impressed.** Of course, you couldn't have done that **without Breeze's** help. She saved you. Surely you're wondering how she managed that."

"Yes. **How?**"

"**Leaping IV, Swiftness II, Strength III, Stoneskin V.** That last one costs a fortune to craft . . . and has a **very bad taste** from what I understand."

I blinked. "**Potions?**"

"Yes. She chugged so many she **made herself sick.** That's why she's staying home today. **Her father insists.**"

"So, that's it, huh? . . . Potions."

"You were expecting a more interesting explanation. **Special powers. Magic,** perhaps."

"I guess so."

"Cheer up, then. **True magic *does* exist,** beyond enchantments and potion effects . . . and someday, **we will *reclaim it.*"

Reclaim . . . ? As in, get back? As in, **we once *had* magic?!** I couldn't believe what I was hearing. Before I could ask, however, Brio continued: "By the way, I understand **the pigman had a weapon** that found its way into your inventory. I will take that from you now."

"What? Why?"

"You really need to ask?"

"Whatever." I handed him Urkk's hook. "I was never that into fishing, anyway. Besides, knowing my luck, if I tried using that thing, **I'd reel in a creeper by accident.**"

Brio smirked again, stuffed the weapon into a pocket, and turned back to the streets below.

"Beautiful, isn't it? This is the **last remaining village** in all of eastern Minecraftia. For hundreds of thousands of blocks **in every direction**, nothing else remains."

"Nothing?"

He shook his head. "There are **survivors,** I've heard, scattered here and there. But they're all hiding **underground** now. We are, perhaps, **Minecraftia's only hope.**"

". . ."

"As the mobs **evolve,** so too must our village. We will **fortify our walls. Upgrade our defenses. Create new weapons.** Research more efficient farming methods. Push ourselves to the very limit. This is Minecraftia's last stand against Herobrine."

". . ."

He turned to me. **"It's going to be quite a show."**

MONDAY—LATER

Well, **Brio wasn't joking.** Those strange men in black robes **really did** kick things up a notch. They were everywhere at school. They also carried sticks. **No.** Not carried. Wielded. **And threateningly so.**

This one kid, **Rock**—he's not **a bad student:** decent scores, knows how to use a sword. But he was hanging around in the hall for too long after **Mob History II** started, chatting with his friends. Well, one of those guys came up to him **and tapped him on the shoulder with a stick. "What's wrong with you, punk?"** stick guy barked. "The *mobs* don't goof off and skip class. The only thing *they* skip is *lunch*, so they can study *even more!*"

"B-but . . . I'm n-not a m-mob—"

"I'll say! The mobs probably don't talk back to their **superiors!"** He jabbed Rock with his stick. "This is your *second* offense! Don't make a third!"

We heard it all from inside the classroom. We soon found out what happens during a third offense.

After Rock sat down, he started looking around, looking out the window, **anywhere but at the teacher.** Minutes later, two of those guys burst into the room, charged up, and pulled Rock out of his chair so fast they literally yanked him **out of his boots.**

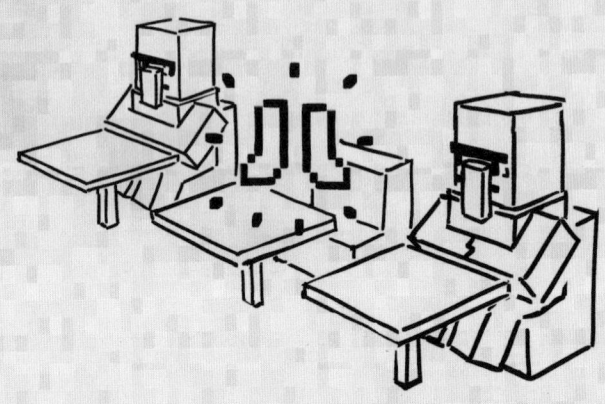

Suddenly, the teacher's **lecture on mob history** became **the most <u>interesting</u> thing in the universe.**

After seeing that, **we took notes.** We paid **attention.** We stared forward and **nodded our heads enthusiastically.** Anything to **prevent a visit from them,** who could be lurking anywhere out there in the hall.

Mr. Beetroot, the history teacher, continued: "After several months of existing in the **Overworld,** a zombie will **turn into** a skeleton. The skeleton will grow **smarter.** The skeleton will run away if injured."

Meanwhile, I thought: *After **thirty minutes** of Mob History II, Runt will turn into a **zombie**. Runt will make **moaning sounds**. Runt will head toward the nearest door and break it down.*

Even Pebble **wasn't immune to their harassment anymore.** After Mob History, he was chatting with **Sara** in the hall. Their backs were to Pebble's locker.

Brio, like a creeper who'd chugged **an invisibility potion,** crept up to the locker and looted it while the two of them talked.

Pebble whirled around. "**Hey!** That's my *stuff*, **endernoob!**"

Brio smiled. "If by '**hey**' you mean '**sir**,' by '**my**' you mean '**your**,' and by '**endernoob**' you mean '**I really hope you enjoy those delicious steaks because you're awesome and amazing**,' then yes, you are absolutely correct."

"Um ... **what?**"

"**First offense.** Don't be late again."

Of course, come lunchtime, the first thing Pebble did was head to the cafeteria. **Guess** who was serving?

I'm joking.

If *he* was serving, the food might have actually been interesting.

Steak wouldn't have been on the menu, but anything a cow might have offered would have been infinitely better than what was available today.

You see, some of Brio's men were behind the counter, and they'd cooked up something **extra special** for all the kids on the "naughty students who must be punished" list.

You want some **mud soup?**

"No? Okay, then. How about some coarse dirt stew? A gravel sandwich? Cooked spider legs? Still no? Then why not skip to dessert? You can try a slice of our nice slime pie."

Look, I get it. I understand what they're doing. They're **toughening us up** for when the real battles begin. They're forcing us to **pay attention**. To remember everything. To never make mistakes. Someday, our lives will depend on it. I know that.

But isn't this going **a little** too far?

The average age of a student is **twelve**, after all. Sure, we're no longer a **single block tall** and golems no longer hand us poppies when they're bored . . . **but we're still kids.**

Aren't we?

It didn't get any **easier** for Pebble. During the daily running drill, they were **screaming at him constantly.** I will say, even though he's a **punk,** he didn't lose his cool. Even when Drill and two others were shouting at him at the same time. **It seemed like his mind was elsewhere.**

The whole time we ran, Brio **walked among us,** arms crossed. His voice was raised in a **dull monotone:** "The mobs have retreated once again . . .

"But they *will* return, and **who knows what they'll try next?**

"Becoming a **good warrior** is why you pay attention in class . . .

"Defending your village is why you spend hours reading about mobs.

"You swing swords at **practice dummies** so future generations can live in peace.

"Someday, we'll all live on **a sandy beach** . . .

"We'll eat cocoa beans.

"We'll drink watermelon juice.

"We'll work on our tans, which is something zombies can never do. Perhaps that's why they **dislike us so much.**"

I have a dream . . .

You'll **love** to do your homework.

You'll **listen** to your teachers.

You will train at least **five hours** per day, you **bedrock-digging** . . .

Pufferfish- **eating** . . .

Enderman- **chasing** . . .

Gold armor-wearing...

Cactus jockeys!!!

At first glance, one might think that this is perhaps **a new type of slime mob.**

Nah. **It's just me,** um... resting.

Yeah. **Resting.**

(Hey, at least I didn't collapse facedown in some dirt.)

It's getting even **more competitive** at school too. In those brief moments when students could actually hang out between classes, everyone stood around in their **little groups.**

- Team Craft;
- Team Noob;
- Team All Girls;
- Team Redstone;
- Team Pebble *(growing in number)*;
- Team Emerald *(good friends with Team Pebble).*

And, of course, **Team Runt,** which everyone seems to be against lately.

Why? What happened to kids asking me for building advice? What happened to the **"green egg kid"?** No one had even **congratulated** me on Saturday. I took down a big boss using a bigger mushroom, and there was almost **no mention of it.**

In fact, I was walking down the hall with my friends today, and **Ariel** gave us what I call **"the look."**

First, **she glared at us.** Tilted her head. Rolled her eyes. Moved her shoulders in a **confrontational** way. Then, she turned back to **Emerald** and **Sara,** said something, and glared at us again while Sara did the same. Whatever they were saying, **it wasn't good.**

Other times, as I passed different groups of kids, I heard stuff like:

"What's his **level** now?"

"I'm *way* better at farming than her."

"She actually *calls* herself a **warrior?**"

"Hey, have you seen her record book?"

"He's *still* wearing those **hideous brown robes.**"

"I totally saw Pebble and Sara *hanging out the other day* . . ."

"I heard Runt and **that weird girl** . . . what's her name again? *Anyway*, Ariel said they took out **a giant pigman.** Not that *I* believe it. **Those two noobs? Pssh. Come on.**"

Before it was time for class, the **"teams"** strolled down the hall together, real **slow.** At one point, **Team Pebble** passed **Team Redstone.** They gave each other **"the look,"** did the whole shoulder thing, the head tilting, and took off to their respective classes.

I'm better than him.

We're better than them.

That girl's trash-tier.

That kid's an übernoob.

What kind of armor do they have?

Even the members of **Team Noob** look down on me now. Including that kid with the **combat score of a door.**

Welcome to my life.

It's always been like this, ever since school started—but lately, things have **gotten way worse**.

I wonder if it's the same way **on Earth?**

Later today, there was a **special after-school activity:** **digging a deadfall field.**

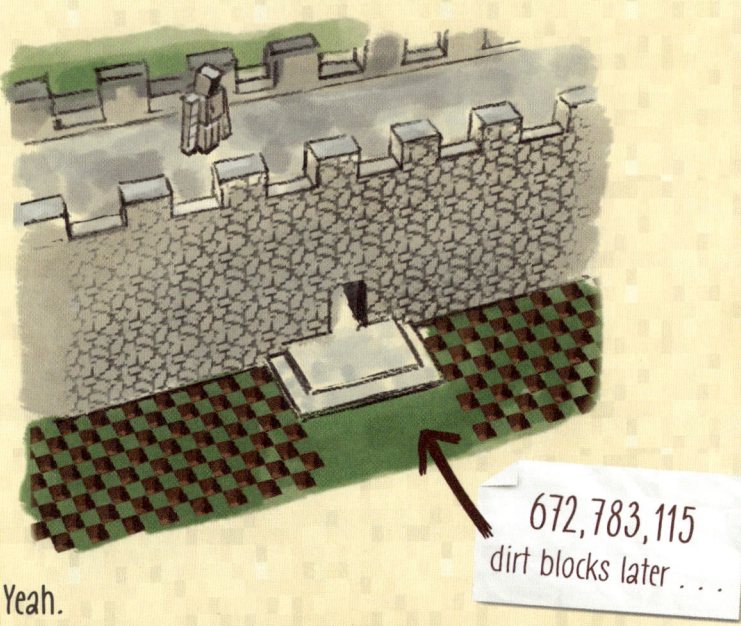

672,783,115 dirt blocks later . . .

Yeah.

After digging about **two hundred holes** myself, it feels as though I've dunked my hands in **lava.** Oh, and don't ask what that golem is doing up there on the wall.

25

No one knows.
It's kind of a **mystery.**

The only way to get up onto the wall is by **climbing a ladder,** and the last time I checked, golems **couldn't do that.** Who knows—maybe the golems are getting **smarter,** too. Just like the mobs. Maybe next year a golem will be **running for mayor.**

I'd vote for him.

Speaking of the mayor, he gave a **speech** just before dinnertime.

"We will build our walls **so high** and **so thick**," he shouted, "any travelers mapping this area will think they've run into an **Extreme Hills Biome!!**"

Everyone cheered at this.

"**Let the mobs attack!!** Let the creepers blow themselves up all night! In the morning, we'll come out and **thank** them for helping us mine dirt and sand!! We'll thank them since we won't have to **wear down our shovels!!**"

More cheers—
it was ten times louder than Drill's shouting.

"The eastern wall . . . **will not fall!!!**"

TUESDAY

Remember everything that happened in school yesterday? **Today was exactly** the same.

Shoot **better!**

I've seen birch doors **hit harder!!!**

If you do not do **your homework**, it will be your turn.

Also, there *was* a new, um, **special activity** today: **Escaping Zombies I.** Drill changed into a dark green robe and painted his face with **lime-green** dye. He was the zombie. He also hid in the **weirdest places.**

Imagine this: One second you're just going to your next class, **on time,** minding your own business. And you think: *I listened in my last class. I wrote things down. I asked some questions. Things are going good.*

Then someone looking very much like a freaky cross between **a zombie, a witch,** and **a creeper** bursts out of a supply room nearby. **Roaring. Slobbering.** Running **straight for you.**

Slobber—**running down his chin**—mixed with **green dye** to resemble watery slime. Cave spiders, please move over. <u>**This is real terror.**</u>

I'm not sure whether the green drool was **intentional** or what, but if Drill's goal was to make the girls **scream louder** than a note block on the highest setting . . .

well, mission <u>**accomplished.**</u>

(the boys screamed too . . .)

I mean, no one had told us about this. Everyone thought he was a **new kind of zombie.** As one might expect, anyone Drill caught was **humiliated:** They had to wear a dark green robe like his for **the rest of the day.** By the way, that was just the start for those poor kids.

Later, **Pebble, Donkey,** and **Rock** took out their anger on such kids by **dunking** them in a well.

I wasn't one of them, though. **Not today.** No, my friends!

When Drill **burst** through that door, I ran so fast I could've passed for **an enderman,** had I been wearing **purple sunglasses** and a black or dark gray robe.

By the way, for the past **three days,** we've had to help repair some damaged areas of the village. That didn't **work out so well.** I mean, *my* building score is pretty good, but . . . let's just say there are some kids who can't say the same. **They made many, many mistakes**—otherwise known as . . . Building Fails. *(For any of my dear readers on Earth, I will point out that building in this world isn't as easy as building in the computer game. Ever tried lugging a block of cobblestone around? Try it sometime.)*

BUILDING FAIL #1

Maybe this is some kind of modern art?

BUILDING FAIL #2

Honestly, who needs stairs? Falling is way faster.

BUILDING FAIL #3

Well, it's only a three-block jump to get to the second floor. It's to keep us in shape, see?

BUILDING FAIL #4

The buttonless iron door. Without a button to press, mobs will never be able to open it! Brilliant!! Oh, wait . . .

BUILDING FAIL #5

This button is reserved for endermen.

BUILDING FAIL #6

Window? Door? What's the difference?

BUILDING FAIL #7

Needless to say, this Building Fail didn't stick around for long. Same goes for the building itself. I guess no one told him that wood and lava do not get along well.

BUILDING FAIL #8

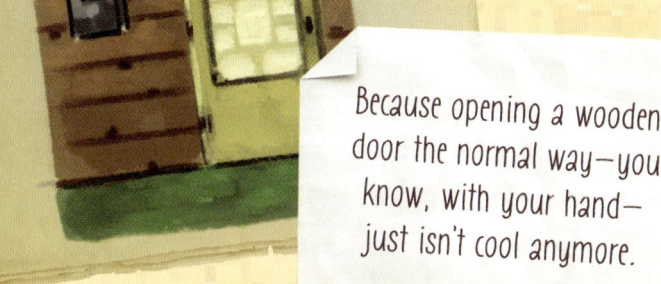

Because opening a wooden door the normal way—you know, with your hand—just isn't cool anymore.

BUILDING FAIL #9

To enter this garden, you have to do a backflip over a fence; obviously, a ninja/farmer built this.

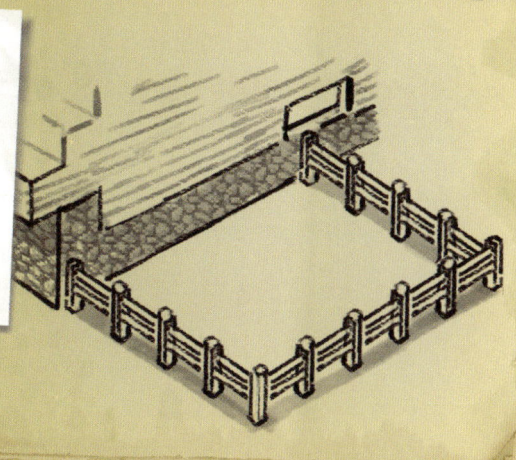

BUILDING FAIL #10

Apparently, an enderman built this house. He doesn't need a door. He just teleports inside.

BUILDING FAIL #11

Ummm, this has to be someone's attempt at trolling. I mean, we've got some real noobs in my village, but no one is this bad . . .

<u>I'm tired.</u>
Going to sleep now.

WEDNESDAY

Did you sleep well? No? Too bad!

Run faster.

Work more.

"There was once a man named **Herobrine**," Brio called out as we **ran** and **ran.** "Sorry. Not once. He's still alive. **Anyway** . . .

"He's lived for a **very long time** . . .

"He's seen this **world's earliest days** . . .

"He lived at a time when there were **towns, castles,** and **vast kingdoms** instead of just **simple villages** . . .

"When **ancient temples** weren't ancient . . .

"When desert temples weren't buried in sand . . .

"When abandoned mine shafts weren't abandoned . . .

"When villagers weren't known as villagers, but another name, long since forgotten . . .

"When there was such a thing as magic.

"This is what we are up against.

"This is the enemy we face.

"We must not let him win."

Just like on Monday, I was so exhausted after training that, again, I collapsed face-first in some grass.

At least nothing bad has happened to me lately, I thought.

I haven't been yelled at too much.

I haven't been singled out.

It's not so bad.

But when I rolled onto my back and opened my eyes . . .

Drill was staring down at me.

"**Congratulations,** Runt. Your unit has been selected for a special role in **Project Squidboat.**"

I rubbed my eyes. "That's, um . . . **great,** sir, but . . . what's Project Squidboat?"

The combat teacher gave me **a toothy grin.** I'm just thankful he wasn't shouting, since his face was a block from mine.

"**Tomorrow,** you and Emerald are **going outside** the wall."

I didn't say anything, but I thought:

Oh, okay. **That's all, then.**

We'll just go outside and **wave to the mobs.**

Maybe go into their **cozy little forest**

and join them for some **tea and cookies.**

THURSDAY

So, today . . . **Project Squidboat** has officially started. Basically, it's a class on, um . . . **"mob psychology."** In other words, the mayor wants to learn more about how the mobs think. For whatever reason, my combat unit was chosen to do the **dirty work.** Since **Breeze** *still* isn't **at school, and since Urf isn't around anymore, that meant . . .** it was just **Emerald** and me.

Hurrr.

Okay, let's go over what **Project Squidboat** is all about.

See that **pile of cobblestone** over there? That was an area Brio called **"the building site,"** or simply **"the site."** Emerald and I were to **leave the safety of the wall** by ourselves and begin **building a house** in this location.

At the same time, the rest of the students were to stand on the wall with **bows and arrows** while they watched us build.

What was **the purpose** of this, you ask?

The idea was we'd build a house in front of the mobs' forest . . . and **see what the mobs did.** Would they **attack** the house? Would they totally destroy it? My guess was that the mobs weren't going to dance around, hold hands, and **sing songs.**

But apparently **Brio** and **Drill** needed us to build a house in order to figure that out. Of course, one might ask *why* grown adults sent **two twelve-year-olds** outside instead of going out themselves.

Real brave, those guys.

"First," said Brio, "we want you two to make an **odd-looking** house."

"The **weirdest** house you can possibly imagine," Drill added.

"**Of course!**" Emerald flashed them a grin. "Leave it to us! Our house will be the strangest house you've ever seen! **Funky** with a **capital** *F* !"

With these words, she **patted me on the back** and gave me a look that said: *Don't say anything to make **them angry, noob,** because I don't feel like doing **one hundred push-ups** right now.*

Then she pushed me forward and said, "I think it's time for someone *strong and brave* to lead this project."

Great.
I took a deep breath,
staring at the gate in front of us.

The gate in the eastern wall is a **dual-lever-operated** iron door system. If one door is **blown up,** there's still **another door** to keep the mobs at bay—another village "**building code.**"

Fun fact: The doors can be opened only **from the inside.** Another fact: When Emerald and I stepped out into the plains, Drill shut the gate **behind us.** And yet another fact: When Drill **shut the gate,** I wanted to **cry.** And dig a hole in the ground. And cover the hole with dirt. And **curl up into a ball.**

Emerald was looking all around. "**Listen,**" she said, "you build the house and I'll uh . . . I'll **watch your back.**"

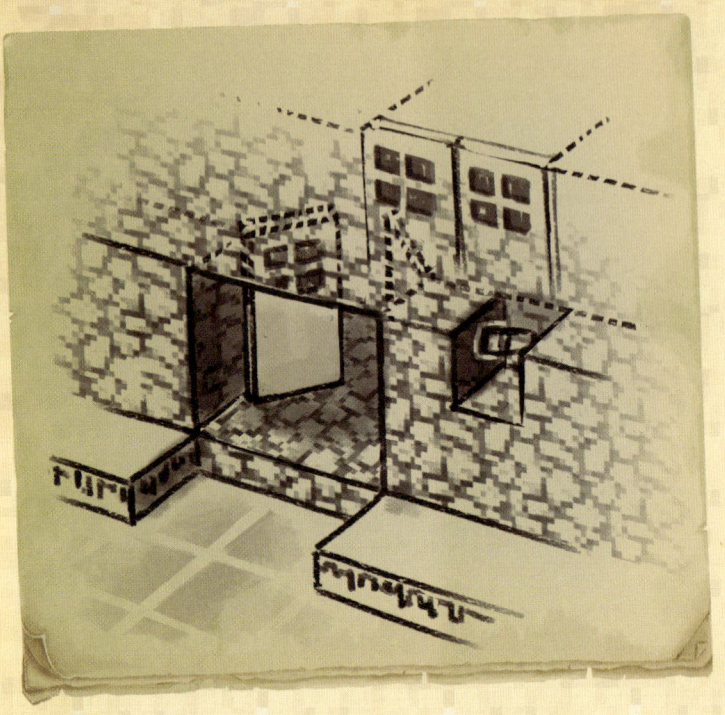

"Why me?"

"C'mon. Screamy wants us to build a weird-looking house, right? That's your thing."

"What's *that* supposed to mean?"

She rolled her eyes. "Dude, you made a furnace house. You defeated a boss with a giant mushroom. You're pretty much the king of weird. Besides, you have absolutely *no* fashion sense. I mean, look at your robe! And that cloak!"

"**Whatever.**" I grabbed a block of sand from my inventory. "As long as it means you'll stop talking."

She crossed her arms and looked away. "Y'know, you can be **such a jerk!**"

But she looked back when I started digging and placing **the foundation-sand.**

"**What are you doing?!**" she hissed. "We're supposed to build a *house*, not **a *sand castle.*"**

I ignored her, keeping **my eye** on the forest . . . just in case the mobs decided to rush us. The slightest movement out there and I was gone. If a cloud looked too strange, or if some bat gave me a funny look—*poof*—even a **mine cart on powered rails** would have nothing on me. **NOTHING.** I didn't see anything moving around, though. Soon, my masterpiece was finished.

"As I said, you're **weird!!!**"

Yeah. A cactus house.
With a roof made of **melon blocks**.

Drill had given us a ton of **building materials**, after all. It was pretty much the **strangest building** I could think of, given the supplies. When we got back, Drill wasn't just smiling—he was beaming like an enderman in a desert . . . he was beaming like a creeper in **a cat-free zone** . . . like a **mooshroom named Binky**. That last one probably doesn't make sense to you.

You see, **Binky** was this mooshroom I met once, and it was, like, **ten times happier** than a normal cow.

So, like . . . smiling like that mooshroom means . . . smiling a lot.

Seriously, um, never mind. I honestly forgot what I was talking about by trying to explain this to you.

Anyway, **Drill was happy,** okay?

"**Well done,**" he said. "Well done . . . **like a noob hugging a blaze!**"

(Wow, that analogy was even worse than my mooshroom one! I feel a lot better now.)

Still looking at my house, Brio **nodded** in approval. Then I took a spot on the wall with **Max** and **Stump,** who **applauded** my new creation. But **Pebble, Donkey,** and **Rock** said it was the **stupidest-looking** house they'd ever seen.

<u>Um, wasn't that the point . . . ?</u>
Noobs!

Then, we **waited,** hidden behind the raised sections of wall.

Before long, a **group of zombies** rushed out of the forest to inspect my **cactus house.** They were speaking in the **ancient tongue** again, so I couldn't understand what they were saying . . . but they were obviously **confused.**

urgaburgauuuguu???
buururrrrguurgurg
gurbu.

Then the zombies **got angry.** They took out some **axes** and began **chopping at my cactus house.** They chopped and chopped until there was almost nothing left except for a few **cactus blocks scattered**

in the sand. They actually took most of it with them. One zombie even **roared** angrily, and then he kicked a mined cactus block as hard as he could. It went sailing off into the plains.

<u>My lovely **cactus** house!</u>
How could they be so disrespectful?!

After the zombies **vanished** into the woods, Drill stood up.

"So the greenies **aren't as bright** as we thought," he said. "Runt's house **confused them** for a second, anyway."

Emerald sighed. "That doesn't mean much. Runt's house had *me* confused."

"It's not very hard to confuse you," Max said.

·Hmmph!·

"**Now, don't fight,**" said Brio. "Because you two are going back out there."

Emerald and I **looked at each other** before exclaiming simultaneously:

·What?!·

It was **Stage II of Project Squidboat.** This time, we had to build **a beautiful house. Princess Whinerella** decided to be the one to build that. Her house was what one might expect . . . **except she added a sign. I forgot to do that.**

I think they will **appreciate** the icing on the cake.

ZOMBIES STINK. TO DEATH.

Again, **we took off back to the wall.** And again, the zombies came to **inspect** the house. A zombie took one look at the sign, **grunted** angrily, and kicked the sign over. Then the zombie shouted something, and **even more zombies came out.**

"They don't seem to **notice us,**" Max whispered.

He was right. We were hiding, but there were over **a hundred** of us. Surely *one* of them should have seen us **peeking** from behind the wall.

"They must have **really poor eyesight,**" I whispered back. "Maybe it's the sunlight."

Stump nodded. "We could use this to our advantage somehow."

Hmm. Maybe **Project Squidboat** wasn't such a bad idea. We've **learned a lot** about the mobs today.

By this time, the zombies were **chattering away** in their low, **guttural** language. Then they totally **trashed Emerald's cute little house.** One zombie stomped on every flower. Another zombie even tried **eating a flower.**

By the way, the zombie was eating a blue orchid, which was roughly the same color as his shirt. So in this picture, it kinda looks like he's eating his own shirt. He wasn't, though. Of course, I could have changed the flower to, say, a pink tulip or something. But I'm going for accuracy here.

As if that **wasn't enough,** a creeper rushed in and exploded.

There was nothing left.

Drill came over to us when the mobs went back into the trees. "Well, **that's it** for today," he said. "I think we've made some real progress today **in understanding** the enemy."

I stood up.

"Wait, sir. I . . . I'd like **to try something else.** I wanna go back out there."

A few students gasped. **Even Brio looked shocked.**

"What is it, Runt?"

"It's hard to explain." I paused. "**Um,** can **I . . . um . . . err . . . have a stack of obsidian?**"

At the mention of **obsidian,** Drill got angry. "**OBSIDIAN?! WHAT ARE YOU—**"

I was already **preparing** myself to do **two hundred push-ups.** Maybe **three hundred.** *(Note: Someday, if I ever become a combat teacher, there will be no push-ups—only pumpkin pie-eating contests.)*

Brio interrupted him. He grabbed Drill and walked down the wall some ways away, and the two of them talked for a **long time.** Drill was making all sorts of gestures—obviously, he thought obsidian would be **wasted** on a project like this.

When they finally came back, Brio said, "We have only **one stack of obsidian** left in the village supply. Urf took the other stack. **Will you make good use of it?**"

I nodded. "I'm sure."

"You're really sure?"

"Really sure."

"You're **really, really, really sure?** You will use this obsidian **wisely?**"

"**Really, really, really** sure with an **endercreeper** on top. I will wisely use this obsidian."

"Okay then. **Here's your obsidian.**"

(It didn't go exactly like that. But I'm just trying to stress how worried they were.)

Here's how worried they were: Brio and Drill worriedly exchanged worried glances of worryfulness. **Enchanted with Worryfulness VII.**

(Worryfulness is probably not an Earth word. If there's something like the **Intergalactic Committee on Proper Spelling,** please don't report me to them. If you don't report me, and you visit me in my village someday, I will have Stump personally bake you either three cookies or one cake. Your choice.)

All right, so Brio gave me **a stack of obsidian.**

By the way, I need to thank the **builder noobs** for this idea—the kids behind all those building mistakes. Within a minute, I was back outside, working on <u>**house number three.**</u> I know I've been talking about mooshrooms and worryfulness and having my best friend bake you stuff.

I'm only twelve, okay?!
<u>My mind wanders.</u>

The important thing here is that I was *building a house made of obsidian.*

Yes. An obsidian house was being built.

Actually, it wasn't so much a house as it was a . . . **uh** . . . **well,** I don't really know *what* you'd call it.

THE CUBE. What does it do?

A simple **five-by-five** box. A **large cube** made entirely of obsidian. It had **no doors, no windows,** and **no mechanisms** of any kind. It could **withstand creeper blasts, TNT blasts,** and any tool **less than diamond.** Remember **Boom Mountain?** The mountain made entirely of **TNT?** This cube could withstand that. **All of that.**

That's how **awesome** a cube made of obsidian is. Not only was it **mysterious,** but the mobs had **no way of destroying it.** Unless they had **diamond pickaxes.** (And let's face it, if the mobs have diamond pickaxes, well, we've already lost this war—wasting a stack of obsidian wouldn't matter.)

The zombies came back **a third time,** thoroughly **confused. They punched** the cube. *(Why?!)* Kicked it. Swung **stone pickaxes** at it. Three creepers even **blew up right next to it.** And when the smoke cleared, **the cube was still there,** unharmed, silently mocking their attempts. After that, the zombies dropped their pickaxes and **ran back into the woods.**

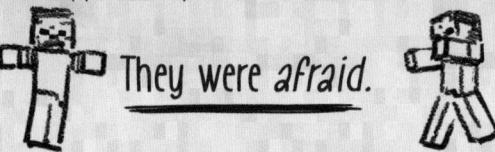

They were *afraid.*

"**Interesting,**" Max said. "**Fear of the unknown** is the strongest type of fear. I read that somewhere."

Stump **patted me on the back.** "**Good work,** dude. They'll spend days trying to figure that thing out. That means we can relax. I really need to get some baking done!!"

Drill didn't know what to make of the cube. He was standing on the edge of the wall, **studying it,** scratching his chin and muttering to himself. When I turned to Brio . . . **he was studying me.** In silence. **Was he angry?** Did I do something **wrong** . . . ?

Maybe I had <u>**wasted**</u> the only obsidian our village had. For nothing . . .

FRIDAY

Yeah, there was **a lot more training** today. But forget the training.

> Dude, complaining about training is so two days ago.

By Friday afternoon, **everyone was talking about the cube.** After school got out, practically everyone in the village was up on the wall, **watching.**

"All we need is **popcorn**," Mike said to Steve.

Steve got the same look he gets when he's talking about *pizza*. "Oh, man. Butter? **Caramel?** I'd pay fifty emeralds for even *plain* popcorn! **What am I saying?!** I'd eat popcorn kernels *raw* without even **cooking** them! Actually, what am I watching this cube for?! **I should be working on recipes!**"

Mike facepalmed. "Why did I mention popcorn? **Why?**"

"Will you two **noobs** be quiet?!" Pebble hissed. "You're gonna **scare off** the mobs!"

Yeah, those mobs sure were **hard at work.** It was interesting watching them **struggle with** that huge obsidian block. You see, the mobs just couldn't stand it. They just *had* to find out what was up with that thing. They wouldn't be able to rest until they **blew it all up**—or destroyed **just a single block** so they could find out what was inside. *(There was nothing inside. Tee-hee. Just a torch.)*

They built **a dirt staircase** alongside it . . .

Then creepers climbed the staircase. **Oh, yeah,** that iron golem was still hanging around.

He looked really sad, too, with his head always lowered like that. Anyway, back to the cube—

CREEPER PARTY
FLINT AND STEEL
NOT SUPPLIED

Also, bring your own armor enchanted with Blast Protection V.

The zombie down below started shouting:
"Urgbo! Jorgbo! Gurggo!"

Emerald: "Uhhh, I'm assuming he was counting to three. Anyone else come to that conclusion?"

I guess the zombie was trying to **make sure** the creepers exploded at **exactly the same time.** Not that it helped. According to Max, it just **didn't matter.**

WELL, ON P. 81 OF **THE PUDDLES BUILDING HANDBOOK**, IT SAYS, "NO AMOUNT OF EXPLOSIVES CAN DAMAGE OBSIDIAN."

MAX—THE WALKING WIKIPEDIA.

Anyway, the mobs tried a lot of stuff.

TNT. Lots of TNT.

Charged creepers.

Enchanted iron pickaxes.

Blocks of <u>TNT</u> **mixed** with charged creepers.

They even tried **digging under** it to see whether there was an obsidian floor.

Pssh. Just LOL @ them.

As if *I* wouldn't have **thought of that!** My building score is **97** now, the **nooblords.** The zombies spent like **fifteen minutes** digging under that thing. And the whole time they were probably thinking, **Ohhhhh, we're gonna dig under it! Ohhhh, we're clever!** Then they discovered—oh, so there *is* an obsidian floor.

LOL

One zombie, after he came back up to the surface, was **so angry** that he kept beating the ground with his shovel, **over** and **over**.

"Dude, that zombie looks really, **really mad.**"

Eventually, it started pouring, and the mobs **called it a day.**

Stump sighed. "Rained away."

"**Show's over,** folks," the mayor called out. "It'll be dark soon. Everyone please go inside."

I said good-bye to Stump and Max. Emerald was looking at me while I did.

It seemed **she wanted to say something to me,** although I couldn't imagine what. I walked past her and took off back home through the wet streets . . .

thinking about Breeze,
and what she might be doing . . .

SATURDAY—MORNING

Well, the mobs **didn't attack the cube** much today. From what I heard, **every hour** or so a new zombie had walked up and swung a pickaxe at it, then retreated back into the forest. He probably heard about the cube from the other zombies and wanted to take the **"obsidian cube challenge."** You're probably not **a cool zombie** unless you do that.

In other news . . . I'm **seriously freaking out** about Breeze. What happened to her? **Where did she go?** She didn't show up to school **the whole week,** and I have no idea where she lives. And since I'm apparently **her only friend,** there's no real way to find out. I'm about to go **door to door** until I find her.

Be back later, Diary.

UPDATE:

I didn't find Breeze. As luck would have it, the third door I knocked on swung open . . . to reveal **Emerald.** And here's the thing: She wanted to talk. **She insisted.**

"I've been, um, wanting to get **something off my chest**," she said. "I realized you're not such **a bad guy.** What you did yesterday was **pretty cool,** actually. So with that being said, I kinda wanna **apologize** for running away last Saturday. I mean, that pigman was **crazy huge,** you know?"

I eyed her cool-looking cloak. "**Happens to the best of us.**"

At this, the so-called war **heroine** poked me in the chest. "Hey! I *did* manage to get some **iron golems!** I'm not a wuss, **okay?!**"

"Sure. You're not a wuss."

Anger **flashed across her face.** She **poked** me again. "You might think you're **hot stuff,** but honestly, your social skills need **a lot of work!** All you do is rage, show off, and **act like a total tryhard!**"

Tryhard? Really . . . ?

Emerald narrowed her eyes. "I don't suppose you heard what my friends **said about you** in the hall the other day?"

"No, and **I don't particularly care.**"

"You should. You're well on your way to becoming **the least popular** boy in school." Suddenly, her anger vanished, and **she smiled.**

"So you should **consider yourself lucky,** because I'm willing to help you out. Let me teach you **how to be cool and likable.** I mean, with the way Pebble's been treating you, you really need **more friends.**"

I peered at her **suspiciously.** "And what would *you* be getting in return?"

"**I wanna join your team.**"

"Um, you *are* on my team. **And what a team it is.** Between **you** and Urf, the mobs pretty much have **no chance.** You know the **giant pigman?** He didn't explode from TNT. He was just thinking *Oh, man, Emerald and Urf are coming for me; I really don't want to have to deal with this,* and then he swallowed a charged creeper."

"**Not funny.** Anyway, I'm not talking about that, silly. I wanna join **Team Runt.** I want to roll with you guys. **You,** that baker kid, the bookworm, and . . . **Breeze.**"

Wait. Wait, wait, wait. So Emerald was saying . . . she actually wants to be a part of *Team Runt?* **Ms. Popularity** actually wants to hang out with a kid who's been dunked in water more times than a farmer's bucket?

"It's **funny,** when you think about it," she said. "They're teaching us all this stuff in school, like advanced **crafting, redstone circuits** . . . but they never teach us anything about **how to make a friend.**"

Her words slowly sank in. Friends **are important.** I had learned that with Stump.

*But **equally important** is not having too many enemies.*

Friends matter! Without Breeze, I'd probably be in **Urkk's** inventory as an item called **"Villager Stew."** If I knew how to make more friends, Pebble and his crew wouldn't be able to harass me so much! Life is **other people,** isn't it?! If there was no one else in this village . . . if it was just me and a **bunch of blocks** . . . how **boring** would that life be? The thing that **matters most** is the people around me.

I go to the bakery to buy cookies so I can eat. I'm trying to become a warrior so I can **protect my family.** Every day I pray that **Pebble** and **Donkey** don't do something horrible to me. And all those things involve . . . speaking to other people. Making friends. Not making enemies. Being **"likable,"** as she puts it. Emerald really has something there.

Why don't they teach us anything about this in school?!

And, honestly, I was such a **jerk** to Breeze. At first, **I totally ignored her!** And, yeah, a lot of kids *did* ask for my help—but I'd ignored them too! No wonder kids at school glare at me in the halls lately . . .

I nodded. Stood up **straighter.**

"**Okay,**" I said. "Let's say I agree with **you.** What then? **Where do we start?**"

Emerald's face **lit up** like a **sea lantern.**

"I know just the thing. **Follow me.**"

SATURDAY—AFTERNOON

Yeah. Emerald took me to the **biggest clothing shop** in the village. **The Clothing Castle.** It's owned by Puddles. Apparently, he's not only **a master builder** but a **fashion designer** as well. As you can see, it's a **huge** place. A bunch of girls from school work as **assistants** here: **Heather, Mia, Mary, Emma.** They love **crafting clothes.**

Oh, and **Sophia** and her brother, **Ryan.** *(Ryan's into combat like I am, so he helps Puddles come up with new types of leather armor.)* Puddles had recently hired **Tomoya,** a kid from school, as a new assistant. Is this information boring you? Stump said I should include **more details** about our village, so . . .

Anyway, Emerald said **the first step** in getting more people to like me is . . . buying **a new robe.** I glanced down at myself.

"Is there **something wrong** with this one?"

She sighed. "Look, I'm not saying you need to buy some **diamond-encrusted outfits** or something, but dude . . . if you want people to respect you, you have to stop walking around in that **ratty old thing.**"

I am not wearing that.

"**Ratty? Come on!** It barely even has any mold spots!"

"**Urggh.** You're seriously **hopeless.**"

Apparently it isn't okay to have mold spots on your robe. **Who knew?** I gave in and looked around at the various garments. Most of the robes were like this.

Emerald held up another robe in front of me. "Why don't you try this one on?"

"**It's bright pink.** Want us to match, do ya?"

"How about bright green?"

"No."

"**Bright purple,** then?"

"No."

"Fine, what about **baby blue?**"

I gave her a look that said: **no**

(That's a "no" without a period. You see, not including a period means you simply don't want to take the time to end the sentence completely. It means you care so little about what was just asked that you can't be bothered with taking the fraction of a second out of your day to add the period in.)

And finally . . . Emerald picked out **the worst robe** in the whole store.

Yellowish-greenish brown.

"This isn't **so bad,** huh?"

". . . It's the color of **baby poo.**"

"**Sigh.** You're so frustrating to shop with."

Then Puddles himself came over. He must have overheard us.

"**Ahh,** vat a strong young mahn! A **fucha warrior, I see! I hev just zi sing for you!**" He turned around. "**Tomoya!** Where's zat **special suit?** Zi dark gray one?"

Tomoya came over and guided us to whatever robe Puddles was talking about. It was slightly hidden in a corner.

Wow !
woWOwOWO
WOwoWOw !

It was the **coolest** outfit I'd **ever seen.**

It even came with some kind of **hood and a special pair of boots** . . . In a robe like that, even *mobs* would **respect you.** If they didn't **break down crying** and beg you not to **crit them.**

Emerald, however, **groaned.** "You **can't go to school** in something like that. Especially not while wearing **the hood.** It's a little **creepy.** You'll become the **boy version of Breeze.**"

Whatever. I bought it **immediately.**

I bought a **second one** for Stump.

(Emerald suggested that.)

Then I asked Emerald to draw me afterward.

CHECK OUT MY NEW GEAR, YO.

Looks pretty cool, right? If you don't think so, it's just Emerald's **drawing ability.** I asked her not to make it **look as cool** as it does in real life. Because you'd probably come to this world, head to my village, and **steal** it from me. By the way, the hood can be removed at any time. That's great, because **we can't wear hats** in school, and the same thing probably goes for **ninja masks** . . . *(Sigh.)*

"By the way," Emerald said, "**you can dye that** just like you can with leather armor. **How about blue?**"

"Okay. I'll think about it."

I felt like someone was
watching me just then.
Breeze? I didn't see her anywhere, though.
Strange.

SUNDAY—MORNING

An **explosion** shook **me** from sleep.

Mom and Dad were peeking out of their room at about the same time I was. Someone ran **by our house** shouting something about how we were **under attack.**

The west wall is **under attack.**
I hate weekends.
Really. I do.

Why does all the **crazy stuff** happen on weekends? I can't even remember the last time I had an **uneventful one.**

My father, of course, tried to **stop me.** Then he just sighed, nodded.

"I've realized by now that **I can't stop you** from going on your **crazy adventures**," he said.

Mom smiled, although there was sadness in her eyes. "**My little warrior** is growing up so fast. Just be careful out there, all right?"

But they didn't have to **worry.** When I got to the west wall, I realized that it wasn't the **mobs** that had caused the explosion.

It was **some humans.** That's a new word I learned recently. *Human.* That's what they call themselves—**the people from Earth.** The west wall wasn't heavily fortified, so **their TNT** blasted through it pretty easily. When I got there, the humans **had already stepped through the hole** they'd created. About one hundred villagers were there, whispering to one another and studying **the two warriors.**

The warrior on the right **pointed in our general direction.** "You! **Villagers!** Is this **Herobrine's** castle?"

The mayor pushed through the crowd. "**Herobrine?!** We have nothing to do with the likes of him! Who are you, exactly?"

"I am **Kolbert** of the **Lost Legion!** I assumed this to be the Kingdom of Herobrine."

"**Real sorry** for that," said the other warrior, a girl, who introduced herself as **Elisa**. "**Our clan is pushing eastward.** We're trying to stop Herobrine's advance."

Lost Legion?
Never heard of them.

And what's a *clan*, anyway? I glanced at Max. **The walking Wikipedia** just shrugged. Moments later, the girl, Elisa, **nudged Kolbert with an elbow.**

"**Right.**" Kolbert cleared his throat. "**Ahem!** This village is now under the control of **the Lost Legion!** As the clan's captain, I demand **food, supplies, and shelter immediately!**"

Murmurs swept through the crowd of villagers:

"What does he mean?"

"Why would we give them our stuff?"

*"Is that guy **crazy** or something?"*

*"He means **give** them things?! For **free?!**"*

"**We will do no such thing!**" the mayor said. "We have enough problems! **Leave us alone!**"

The two humans whispered to each other. Then Kolbert turned back to us. "**You are NPCs!**" he declared. "You will do as I say! You will kneel before us and **show your respect!**"

"Fail to assist us," Elisa said, "and we will lay **siege** to your village **by sundown!**"

The mayor glanced between the two of them.

"You and what army?"

Just then, **more humans** began to appear over a distant hill . . . and more . . . and more. There must have been over a hundred of them, and most of them looked *tough.* I mean, *tough.* Imagine a guy who's **slept in a two-by-one cube** emergency shelter in the ground for months, eating bats and drinking rainwater. *(Two-by-one dimensions mean that you can't move your arms and you're sleeping upright.)* That's the kind of **tough** I'm talking about. Several of them, **like Kolbert, wielded diamond swords** and wore enchanted leather or iron armor.

"Oh," the mayor said. "Okay. **That army.** Well, come right in, then."

He opened the gate and let them all in. **A total of 125 humans, 88 horses, 31 donkeys, 17 cows,** and **11 dogs.** Oh. And **8 cats.** Also **3 chickens.** Also **a sheep. Yeah.** I am *not* drawing all of that.

So things are **even worse** in our village now. Now we can't even **walk** the streets without being harassed or bossed around in some way by a multitude of different people.

"**Hey! Villager!** Help me with this!"

"**Hey! Villager!** Help me with *that!*"

"**You! NPC!** Get over here and give us a hand!"

"You don't even know what **NPC** *means?!* That stands for **non-player character!**"

"NPC, that's what you are!"

"Sorry to break it to you kid, but you're just a **game** character! A bunch of computer data! **Oh,** don't cry! It's impossible for you to have feelings! **Hey!** I said **stop crying,** kid!"

"You exist only to **trade** with us!"

"We will **eat** your food!"

"We will **sleep** in your beds!"

"We will **barge into your house** whenever we want to, **open** your chests, mine part of your house, and possibly take your door."

"And also your **crafting table.**"

"And possibly your **furnace.**"

"And maybe the **carpet.**"

"Especially if it's white. I just love white carpeting."

"Blue's also **nice,** though."

SUNDAY—AFTERNOON

Emerald **didn't like being told what to do.** Kolbert demanded that she **clean** his new house for him. She **demanded** that he go **jump down a well** until his **air meter ran out. Surely you can see the problem here.** Call it a **personality clash.** The end result was . . . Emerald's **hands being tied behind her back** with **spider string.** She was then led to **Kolbert's** house, where she was untied and **forced to scrub the floors** on her hands and knees. **At swordpoint.** Here's another problem: Emerald is now a member of **Team Runt.**

I marched up to Kolbert. "I want you to **release my friend.**"

"Who? The **mouthy** one?"

"That's right."

Kolbert turned to Elisa. "**What's up with this village?** Seriously. It's **weird. Five-block-high** cobblestone walls, **hundreds of houses.** One of them's even referring to himself as the **mayor!** And now we have villagers **talking back** and giving us **orders.**"

The captain turned to me and pushed me back.

"Since you want to be with your friend so bad, how about you **help her out?**"

Just then, I saw **Breeze** drop down from a house into an **alley** to my right. She stepped out of the shadows.

"**Release her,**" Breeze said.

Kolbert whirled around. "**And who are you?** Whatever. Looks like we'll have three workers, then." He took out some spider string and **reached for Breeze.**

"**You really don't want to do that,**" I said.

The captain ignored my warning . . . and promptly found himself **facedown** in the grass.

Breeze had thrown **three punches** in **less than a second**— and these unarmed attacks **hit hard**, from what I could tell.

Kolbert rose, rubbing his cheek. "That girl," he said. "**She's . . . OP!!**" Breeze strode past him and stepped **into the house** that held Emerald.

"These villagers are **crazy!!**" Kolbert said.

"It could be **another player**," Elisa said. "Maybe using some kind of **hack**."

"Maybe . . . but if that's the case, we're talking **extensive skin hacks** here! I mean, what's up with the villager girls having **long hair** and **small noses?!**" He looked up to the sky. "**What is this place?!**"

"This is **Minecraftia**," Max said, approaching. "It's **not a game**. And **we are not NPCs.**"

Stump stepped out from behind Max. "We will **treat you with respect**," he said, "but you must do the same. **Got it?**"

Kolbert **nodded weakly.**

"**Well, good, then.**" Stump held out a cake. "Want a slice? Just made it."

And so this was **the first step—one of many**—toward getting the **humans off our backs.** At the end of the day, **all five members of Team Runt** went down to **Snark's Tavern.**

While we drank our tea, Breeze told me why she **hadn't been in school** last week.

"**I was grounded,**" she said. "My father was really **angry** at me for joining the battle on Saturday. He said I shouldn't have **risked my life** like that . . ."

"Well, I owe you a **big thanks,**" I said, "for that battle and today's. And . . . I'm super sorry for ignoring you before. Even if you really were the biggest noob, **I'd still be your friend. Welcome to Team Runt!!**"

She smiled. "Thanks."

"By the way," I said, "today, when you beat up Kolbert, I didn't see you drinking any potions."

"Whatever. Let's have a feast, huh?"

The five of us ate and chatted for hours. The way we joked around, it was as if the angry teachers, the mob attacks, the rude humans, and the constant threat of Herobrine . . .

it was as if all that wasn't actually happening.

ONE WEEK LATER—
SUNDAY, PART I

Oh, no.

Not this dream *again*.

What's up with that redstone machine, *anyway?*

Wait. What's an **enderman** doing in this dream?

"I . . . h-help you."

What? How can you help me?

"Another useless dream. Just your . . . fear."

I suppose you're controlling my dreams somehow? Endermen can do that?

"Oh, yes. Wait. Give you . . . g-good dream."

What's your name, anyway?

SAVE ME!!

C'mon, **kid!**
Get me **out of here** already!

You can't just ignore me forever, y'know! What, you are afraid of the Nether? The pigmen don't bite! Unless you bite them first . . . Say, tell ya what. You help me, and I'll tell ya where the secret treasure room is. I know where it is! I saw it! That'll serve 'em for abandoning me here . . . Besides, there's this kitten you really need to meet.

"By the way, you'd better wake up right now. Trust me on this one."

I **woke up** from the nightmare and **climbed out** of bed. When I looked out the window, **the sky was bright red. Deep laughter** echoed overhead. It was not unlike **thunder.**

Was I **still dreaming?**

"**Dear?**" My mom was in the living room, looking out the window. "What is that?"

"I don't know," I murmured.

I left my house after giving Mom **a worried glance.** It had to have been night still, or at least before sunrise, yet the red sky was so bright that it cast a fiery glow brighter than a full moon.

When I made my way to the fountain, **I spotted Max.** "What is this?"

He shrugged. Of course, there was no way he could explain what was going on. The **deep laughter** continued overhead as more and more villagers gathered at the square. **Members of the Legion** showed up as well. Kolbert looked **more** terrified than we were.

"Um . . . I'm guessing this isn't good," he said.

"Yeah," Emerald said. "I have to say, you guys kinda came at a **really bad time.**"

"**Stay calm,** everyone!" The mayor weaved through the crowd and stood at the base of the fountain. "Go back inside! **Seek shelter immediately!**"

But everyone was staring at the sky. There was an **eerie ringing sound,** almost inaudible. More and more people, **villagers** and **humans** alike, moved closer to one another.

Mia and **Mary** embraced, their robes fanciful, their faces **mournful.**

"I'm gonna miss you, my **BFF** . . ."

"**Hey!** Don't talk like that, okay?! We're gonna be fine!!"

Moments later, Elisa tapped Kolbert on the shoulder. "You know, **it's probably him.**"

The captain **drew his sword.** "Yeah, you're right. **Man,** he just won't leave us **alone!**"

"Who are you guys talking about?" Emerald asked.

"**Herobrine,** who else?"

"**What?** You mean he's *attacked you before?!*"

"**Well, yeah.** That's one of the reasons we're here."

Emerald approached him until she stood nose-to-nose with the captain. "Y'know, you might have *warned* us about that *before* we let you into our village!" She paused. "**Wait.** Where were you guys staying *before*?"

"Oh, well, we built **a castle**," Kolbert said.

"And what happened to it?"

"Well, um, basically . . . it was **utterly destroyed.**"

Emerald grabbed him by the collar of his undershirt. "**You . . .**"

"**D-don't worry!**" Kolbert said. "Surely the same thing won't happen here! Your village is **much, much bigger!**"

Emerald sighed and pushed him away. "**Jerk.**" Then she joined the rest of Team Runt. All five of us drew closer. Together, we gazed at the red sky.

Soon, **a figure** could be seen up there. It soared just below the clouds. More and more people noticed.

"**Look!**"

"Up there!"

"It's . . . **a human!**"

Then this person **landed** near the fountain. Indeed, it was **a human.** Or human-ish. An aura of **godlike power** emanated from him.

Even the **toughest-looking** Legion members—**in full iron armor, enchanted, with enchanted diamond swords**—**cowered** in fear.

It was the man I'd seen before **in a dream.** It was the **most powerful** wizard in this **world,** perhaps the very last. It was the wizard who went by the name of . . .

"Herobrine!!"

"It's **Herobrine!!**"

As some villagers **turned to run,** Herobrine raised a hand. A **chain of bluish-purple lightning** leaped from his fingertips and arced through the crowd. **I couldn't move.** I couldn't even speak. I **slumped** to one knee, **totally weak.** Everyone seemed to be affected in this way.

Then **Herobrine's voice** swept through the square:

"No matter how many mobs I send, you just... won't... die!!"

This time, waves of red lightning flew from his hands and zapped everyone in the crowd.

I watched my health bar **inch its way down.** *So Herobrine came to take care of us **himself**. Maybe it's because humans and villagers began cooperating.*

Maybe that scared him.

I was barely able to turn my head to see Breeze, Brio, Drill, Stump, Max, or Kolbert... they were all in **a similar condition.** Herobrine raised his hand again, which would no doubt finish most of us off.

Just then,
another person
landed behind him—
fwump!

Like Herobrine, he had **a powerful aura.** Unlike Herobrine, however, there was **something good** about him, something peaceful and kind.

There was no doubt in my mind. **It was Notch.**

Herobrine whirled around. **"It's been a while, old man. You've been spending way too much time on Earth."**

Notch stepped forward. "Herobrine, you will stop this madness **at once!"**

"I'm afraid that's no longer possible," Herobrine said. **"This is beyond my control now."**

"So it's true? This world really is . . ." Notch looked down at his outstretched palms. "Tell me; **how did you do it?"**

"Even if I explained, you wouldn't understand."

"And why not?"

Herobrine turned away. **"You always were one step behind . . ."**

"Enough." Notch drew his sword—obsidian. "I don't know what you've done, but this will soon **come to an end!"**

There was a **metallic whine** as Herobrine drew his own sword, made of a **metal I didn't recognize.**

A thin **smirk** spread across his face.

"I'm not so sure of that."

When you looked at the two wizards facing off, all you could imagine was the most epic battle of all time. After all, if someone were to refer to them as the **gods of this world,** well . . . it wouldn't be an **exaggeration.**

Humans and **villagers** alike simply stood there in awe.

"Why do I get the feeling we're going to be repairing the village for **weeks** after this?" Emerald whispered.

How strange. I had that same feeling.

But the two wizards didn't fight. Not for very long, anyway. And at first they just kept talking.

"**Put your sword away,**" Herobrine said. "We might be at war, but we're still gentlemen."

"That's **funny,** coming from you!" Notch said. "How many villages have you **destroyed** so far?"

"**Only a few.**" Herobrine glanced around at the buildings. "I must say: they could have learned from these guys. At least they have walls."

At this, Notch growled and **swung his sword.** And that was it. The battle was on. **Obsidian** met **glowing red metal.** Sparks flew from Herobrine's blade.

By the way, these kinds of weapons were **common** ages ago. In ancient times, the mobs were a lot **stronger, different** from what we see now. You needed weapons like that just to **fight** some of them. Anything less and you **didn't stand a chance.** If we had weapons like that, we could cut through zombies like shears through cobwebs. **Sadly,** the crafting recipes have long since been forgotten . . .

"I believe Herobrine's sword is **elemental** in nature," Max said. "**Lava is one of the ingredients.**"

"Can we make one?" I asked.

"I doubt it. We'd need a **special crafting table.**"

Special crafting table? That was the first time I'd heard about something like that. But now was not the time for a crafting discussion.

Their blades **clashed** over and over again. At one point, Herobrine **hurled a green** fireball, which Notch deflected with his blade as one would deflect a ghast's.

"I see you've grown **stronger**," Notch said. "Or maybe you've become **soft**." Their blades met once more. Their faces were inches apart. Herobrine smiled. "**Yes, I think you've been spending way too much time on Earth!**"

"Say what you want!" Notch said. "You won't be speaking much longer!"

"**No, I'm afraid it is you who won't be speaking. I tire of this.**"

Suddenly, **Herobrine stepped back,** and pink lightning flew out from his free hand.

It zapped Notch . . . and the wizard became . . . **a black rabbit.**

For a moment, it was as if time itself had **stopped**. At least for me. I just couldn't believe what I was seeing. One of the **greatest wizards** of all time—**a legendary** hero—defeated, just like that.

We'd learned in school that **Notch** was the only one capable of stopping this madman. The only one **powerful** enough. But Herobrine had turned him into a helpless animal with **no effort** at all. Which meant . . . **this war was over.**

We were **history**.

Behind me, a girl **screamed.** There were a few gasps here and there. The humans talked excitedly among themselves:

"He . . . **polymorphed** Notch?!"

"Was that some kind of **admin command?**"

"So, like, we have to fight him ourselves or something?"

"A **boss battle?!** I'm in!!"

"I wonder how much **life** he has . . ."

"**Who cares?!** Imagine the experience!!"

"And the **loot!** I hope he **drops** that sword . . . !!"

There were a lot of comments like these. It seemed most of the humans had no idea how much **danger** they were in . . . It was almost as if they were expecting Herobrine to say,

"Just kidding! Trolled ya!
This is a **new version** of the game!
The latest in virtual reality! Pretty amazing, right?"

Herobrine **picked up the rabbit** and stroked its neck. He did so with a **slight grin.** He was obviously proud of his work. When he turned to the crowd, you couldn't help but stare into his **glowing** white eyes . . .

"People of Earth," he said, his voice impossibly loud, *"welcome . . . to Minecraftia. Please understand: I'm not the one who brought you here. Thank him for that."* He looked down at his **new pet.** *"He summoned you in one last, pathetic attempt to stop me."*

The mayor emerged from the crowd. *"If I may ask . . . why did you come here?"*

"I came to make an offer. For the humans, I'm willing to send you all back. You will return to Earth, safe and sound, with almost no memory of this world. You will wake up thinking that this was all . . . just a dream. As for the villagers, your lives will be spared. You'll be able to go on farming and building, just like you always have. Of course, in return, you must do something for me."

Kolbert, the **leader of the humans**, joined the mayor up front.

"**Forget it!**" He drew his sword. "The Legion does not negotiate with boss monsters! You are a **walking pile of experience orbs** to us! **Nothing more!**"

Herobrine **chuckled**. "**Oh? You must think you're still in his little game.** How sad. **He never told you anything, did he?**"

Kolbert opened his mouth again.

But before he replied, **Brio's men** grabbed him.

"**What is this?!**" the knight shouted. "The players should be making the decisions!! **Not you NPCs!!**"

"**Forgive this human!**" the mayor said. "He's a bit confused, you see. Anyway, **we're willing to cooperate! What do you want from us?!**"

A lot of people, both humans and villagers, gave the mayor a **confused** look. I was one of them.

There was a **long silence**. Herobrine's gaze swept across the crowd. Then a banner appeared in his other hand. **It was white** with a strange **black symbol** in the middle. Herobrine tossed it onto the street.

"I . . . want you to surrender."

Surrender.

It took a second for me to **understand** what he just said. Everyone around me was equally shocked. Breeze moved closer to me. **Even she was scared.** Although Herobrine didn't smile, I somehow knew that he was enjoying **watching us squirm.**

"Place this banner in a **visible location,**" he said, "and my mobs will not harm you. Some will live in your village. You will supply them with the **materials they need.** In addition, you will help them improve their farming and building techniques."

"And how do we know you'll keep your word?" the mayor asked.

"You can ask **Urf.** I'll tell him to pay a little visit. As a **general in my army,** he has everything he's ever wanted. **Power. Money. Respect.** All these things can be yours as well, if you just kneel before me . . . and accept me as your king. You have two weeks to decide. That is when my main army will arrive at your gates. If they do not see that banner, believe me when I say that there will be nothing left of this place—**and nothing left of you.**"

The more he talked, **the quieter we became.** But there were still a few whispers here and there.

"Urf!"

"That **traitor!**"

"So he's some kind of **boss monster,** now?"

So Herobrine wanted us to **give up.** Not only that, he wanted us to **join him?!** It was unimaginable. Humans and villagers **working with mobs.** Kolbert was right—how could we do **such a thing?** How could the mayor agree? But then, the mayor was only looking out for us. He would do anything he could to protect us. Even if that meant . . .

No!
We can't do that!

I **pushed** to the front and shouted:

"If you're asking for our help, that means you're afraid of the **villages to the west!** Some of them are even **bigger** than this one! You've realized you haven't been able to defeat us, and you'll have an **even harder time** dropping them!"

I honestly don't know what came over me. When I said all that, I . . . felt like a **different** person. Someone **strong** and **brave.**

This seemed to get Herobrine's **attention**. He stared at me. He seemed to be **thinking** about something.

"How **interesting**," he said. "Tell me: **who are you?**"

"I am **Runt Ironfurnace**," I said.

"And I'm asking you to surrender."

Yeah. I actually said that. Seriously, what was I thinking? I wasn't thinking, I guess—**just angry.**

"Shut up! **Shut up!**" The mayor said this through clenched teeth.

Herobrine made the most **ridiculous face.** Imagine a creeper smiling as if it had just heard that cats had become **extinct**—it was something like that. Then **he laughed so hard** that if he really had been a creeper, he probably would have **exploded.** But then the laughter abruptly stopped. His smile faded, replaced by an expression of **extreme irritation,** as if the street beneath his feet was made of slime blocks instead of cobblestone.

"You will join me!" he cried. *"You will help me restore this world to its—"*

The rabbit jumped out of Herobrine's arms. Then it began **shaking** on the ground until a **puff of smoke** obscured it. The smoke faded, revealing a **very angry Notch.**

"**Don't listen to him!**" he shouted. "If he ruled the **Overworld,** it would make the Nether look like a mushroom island!"

Herobrine glared at him. *"How did you break out of my spell?!"*

But Notch was no longer **in the mood** for conversation. There was a sharp ringing sound as their blades met once more. This time, Notch moved with the **strength of an iron golem** and the speed of a mine cart on powered rails.

Herobrine struggled to keep up. He dashed back. *"No matter what you do, you can't stop me! In two weeks, unless they join me, this place will be in ruins! The west will crumble next!"*

With that, **he suddenly flew up into the sky.**

This world is **mine.**

Notch **turned** to us. He didn't say anything for a **second or two.** Even though it wasn't a very long time, it felt like **forever.** When he finally spoke, the expression on his face could have made **a ghast look happy.**

"Build, you fools!"

That was it. That was all he said. It meant **fortify the village.** It meant **prepare for the next attack.** Without another word, **he took off into the sky.** He was **chasing** Herobrine. Before long, the two of them had vanished into the clouds.

Everyone just stared **upward.** The humans were too confused about what had just happened. Some had the most **clueless expressions.** Some of them might have been great players back home, but here, they didn't understand a thing. As for us villagers . . . well, most of us were **too scared** to speak or even move. Finally, Elisa, the Legion sub-leader, joined Kolbert and the mayor.

"So, um, **now what?**" she asked.

"What do you mean?!" the mayor snapped. "We **build,** just like he said!"

Kolbert nodded. "I never thought I'd ever **agree with an NPC,** but yes—we won't give in to the likes of him!"

"We will fight to the last noob and villager!!"

Another human named Minsur raised his sword. "Yeahhhh!! The Legion doesn't know defeat!!"

Steve and Mike looked at each other in a **glum way.**

"**Everyone meet at the city hall!**" the mayor shouted. "We can't just stand around! Notch is up there fighting for us at this very moment!

"We are at war!"

SUNDAY—PART II

At city hall, while we waited for the **mayor** to start speaking, **everyone was talking about what had happened.**

Notch this.

Herobrine that.

Their magic was so *cool*!

Are we really going to surrender?

Does anyone know how to **craft the sword** Herobrine was using?

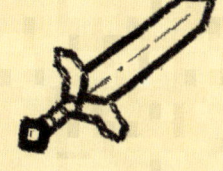

(That last question was mine. Tee-hee. Of course, no one knew how.)

My heart had **stopped pounding** by then. I expected more to happen, honestly . . . but seeing Notch break out of the **polymorph spell** had been pretty cool. (Herobrine's lightning, ehhhhhh, not so cool. It hurt. A lot. If that's what charged creepers have to go through, I almost feel sorry for them.)

The mayor finally spoke. "First, let me say that I don't believe we should **surrender**. I just didn't want him to hurt anyone."

"You mean we're actually going to **fight back?**" a girl asked. That was **Sophia,** someone on **Team All Girls.**

"Herobrine seems so **strong**," her friend Emma said. "How can we possibly **defeat him?**"

"We've faced many **hardships** before," the mayor said. "Humans in the form of **griefers, trolls,** and **noobs.** Mobs who have grown **ever smarter**—who use tactics like **creeper bombs** and **zombie ladders.** But soon we will face our biggest threat: **Herobrine himself.** As we understand, his main army is **stronger** than anything we've seen so far."

"How do you know, sir?" That was Pebble. He was in the front row. **The mayor's little pet.**

His buddy, **Rock,** joined in: "**Your excellency,** have you seen his army?"

"**I haven't,**" the mayor said. "But . . . there are some who have."

The mayor turned to Brio and then stepped away from the wooden block he'd been standing behind. Brio took his place and **gazed into the crowd.**

"**Please come up,**" Brio said. At first I thought he was **speaking to me.** But then I realized, no . . . he was talking to someone right next to me. **Breeze.**

She glanced at Stump, Max, Emerald, and me, then pushed her way through the crowd. Stump and I looked at each other with expressions that said, "What in the Nether is going on?!"

"For those of you who **don't know me,**" Brio said, "I am the mayor's **head assistant.** I haven't **lived in your village** for very long. I come from a village to the east of here, **near Herobrine's castle.** And this—"

He put his arm around Breeze.

"—is **my daughter.**"

Wow.

Wowowowow.

So that **explains a lot**. Everyone around me was totally **freaking out,** but they stopped as soon as Brio continued. "Over a year ago, our village was **attacked**," he said. "Many lives were lost that day. However, my daughter and I, we . . . we were **captured**. Even then, the mobs were **under Herobrine's control**. They took us to his castle, where we were **held prisoner**. And Herobrine, he . . ."

Brio looked downward.

"He **experimented** on us."

When I heard this, his words were flint and steel and my mind was a block of **TNT—my mind was BLOWN**. Breeze, **the silent girl. The weird girl.** The girl a lot of kids whispered about.

Herobrine had **tried** to turn her into some kind of super-soldier?! What kind of **experiments** did he do?!

I was **so curious** . . . but Brio answered before I could even ask.

"He **infused us with magic**," he said. "The same way one enchants a tool or a piece of armor, he . . . **enchanted** us."

To my right, Stump gasped. "So that **explains their purple eyes**. That's why Brio wears **sunglasses**! That's why Breeze hides her face with her **hair**!"

"**Man**," Emerald said, "what did Herobrine do? Throw them onto **an enchanting table** like they were items or something?"

"I remember reading something about that in the **ancient texts**," Max said.

As Breeze stood next to her father, she **lowered her head** as well.

I felt so sorry for her. She must have felt like **an outsider**. **A freak.** It explained so much. Why she was so quiet and . . . why she was **so strong**.

"While we were **held prisoner**, we overheard many things," Brio said. "We learned that the purpose of his **experiments** was to create an army stronger than anything this world has ever seen. But villagers are good at heart. No matter how much he tried, **he couldn't control our minds.** Before long, we managed to **escape.** Our village was in ruins by then, so we moved west . . . **and found yours.**"

I noticed a **tear** running down Breeze's cheek—it looked like **a small glass square.** Whatever she had experienced back then, it must **have been horrible.**

"And there you have it," the mayor said. "This is what we're dealing with, folks. **An army** of magically enhanced mobs—we're not talking about a random group of **potion-chugging, helmet-wearing zombies** this time. Please forgive me for not telling you sooner. I simply didn't want to **cause a panic.** In the end, you can feel safe knowing that we have people here who have actually seen **Herobrine's castle** with their own eyes. They know what we're dealing with."

Many villagers nodded to each other.

There were many *hurrrs* and *hurms* and *rhurrrggs.*

"So everyone put your **tryhard** pants on," Brio said. "We all have to do our part. We all have to do extra chores now. Even you, students. No more games on the weekends. No more hanging out at the fountain after school. This village is going to become an **efficient, mob-slaying, redstone machine.** And you are just one of its many redstone circuits."

Many students groaned.

"Aw, man. **Wars are so lame.**"

"**This isn't fair!** I was supposed to go fishing this afternoon!"

"If this village is **a redstone machine**," Emerald said, "I'm a **repeater**, not a circuit."

"**Extra chores?!** I already have so much homework!" The girl who shouted this glanced back up at the sky. "**I really hate you, Herobrine!!**"

An old man simply asked, "**Ehh?** What are **'tryhard pants'?**"

*(For the record, my tryhard pants are **ALWAYS** on. I **NEVER** take them off.)*

SUNDAY—PART III

So like the mayor said, everyone must **work constantly.** With the threat of a **huge mob invasion,** there's simply no more time for anything else. That includes getting ice cream, which is something my friends and I almost **always** do on Sunday afternoons.

So annoying.

Herobrine, you're **messing up** my schedule, **man!**

School, school, school.
Chores, chores, chores.

Will there ever be a time when it's just **play, play, play?** I should look at the bright side, though; after this, Pebble will probably be **way too tired** to harass me much.

Speaking of Pebble . . .

I was standing in line with Stump, Emerald, and Max. We were waiting to get our assigned **chores.** And Team Pebble was a little ways behind us in line. I heard Pebble say, "If a bunch of endermen attack, **all** we need to do is send Runt at them. He cries so much he's like a **walking fountain!** No enderman would get **within twenty blocks of him!"**

A bunch of kids **laughed. It got worse,** though. Soon after that, the mayor approached Pebble. "I want you to make some **more posters.** You are **excused** from doing chores. Have you and your friends come to my house."

"Nice! Thank you, your **excellency!"**
Wow.

I guess being a war hero really has its perks. Pebble shoved me out of the way as he passed me. "**Later, noobling,**" he said. "**Work hard** for me, huh?"

Sap, Donkey, and Sara **smirked** as they walked by.

Rock winked at me. "**Enjoy your chores."**

Then the mayor called Emerald and Breeze over. They were going to make their own posters, the mayor said. After all, in her own way, Breeze is an **actual war hero.** She **survived** whatever Herobrine had done to her.

"**What about our friends?"** Emerald asked, pointing to the rest of Team Runt.

Breeze glanced at me. **"Can they come with us,** too?"

"Afraid not," the mayor said. "Girls only. I want the other girls to see that they can be strong too!"

Emerald and Breeze nodded and waved good-bye to us.

"Sorry, guys," Emerald said. "I tried."

Breeze looked **sad.** "I'll come **help you** when I can."

Watching them go, **I felt so jealous.** Especially when I listened to the chores Drill and Brio were giving the rest of us kids. They all sounded so **terrible**...

First, there was the **slopper.** That's someone who has to **craft mushroom stew,** over and over. Our village has a lot of extra mushrooms. They're not really used for anything except **stew.** So the mayor said that we should all try to eat mushroom stew as much as possible and save all the other food for when things get really bad. **I don't understand the logic behind this.** *(Remember that villagers are strange sometimes. Before Steve showed up, we hadn't even thought about building a wall. A WALL. How sad is that?)*

Then there were the **sorters.** They have to **organize** the contents of chests in the village supply rooms. That doesn't sound bad, until you think about what kind of items they handle. **Spider eyes. Rotten zombie flesh. Slimeballs. Bones.** Oh, and **gunpowder,** which is basically a **creeper's innards.**

The **repairers** work with the sorters. They go around the village finding two of the same item with low durability and combine them to take advantage of the **5% repair bonus.** Some of the most common items that need repairing are leather boots—I'm guessing most of these unlucky kids will end up **smelling like feet.**

Hurrggg.

There were a lot of **chores** like that. That was why, when it was finally my turn to be assigned, I was **silently praying** to Notch: *Please don't let my chores have anything to do with **mushroom stew**.*

It didn't look good, though. Drill was the one **assigning** me.

He grinned. "**Hello, Runt.** Ya wanna hear the **good news** or the **bad news** first?"

"**Good news,** please."

"All right. You'll be working **with Stump.**"

Wow.

That was good news.

Ridiculously good news.

The best possible news ever.

(Well, maybe not the best. He could have said something like, "Your job will be tasting cookies to ensure their quality and freshness.")

Still, I wasn't complaining at all. In fact, I cheered and gave my best friend a **high-five.** *(By the way, Steve said that in the original game the villagers didn't have fingers. But here they do. They're blocky, though. Steve said our fingers look like big French fries. I'm not sure if that's good or bad. And hey, if it's bad, well . . . in this world, his fingers look just the same!)*

I looked at Drill **fearfully.** ". . . and **the bad news?**" I asked.

(No mushroom stew. No mushroom stew. No mushroom stew. Please, please, **please, please, please** *. . .)*

The combat teacher grinned **even more.** "In three hours, your arms will know the true meaning of the word **'pain.'**"

He handed each of us **a stone axe.**

At least it wasn't some <u>wooden bowls.</u>

SUNDAY—PART IV

Before, when I thought about fighting mobs in a war, I imagined dropping **a mountain of zombies.**

I imagined **diamond swords** and high-level enchantments. I imagined people **cheering my name.**
<u>Not this.</u>

I hate this job . . . uh . . . **birches**.

Yeah. **We're choppers.** That's a fancy word for **lumberjack.** You see, the village needs **more arrows.** Enough to fill **five double chests.** That was why Drill ordered Stump and me to go to the **tree farm.** *(The place where I first met Breeze.)*

So starting today, we go to school **every morning.** Then, when school's over, we don't head home. We **must chop trees. So many trees.**

"Why do birch trees have to be **so tall?**" I asked.

That's the **annoying** part of harvesting wood. There's always that **last block** you can't quite reach. So you need to throw down a wood block from your inventory and jump on top of it. Then after harvesting the once unreachable block, you have to harvest the other block **a second time.**

I almost wished I was an **enderman.** Stump finished chopping his own block and **wiped sweat** from his brow. "It could be worse," he said.

"Yeah? **How?**"

"We could be doing this on **Earth.** Mike once said the trees there **fall over** after being chopped."

"Seriously?"

"That's what he said. And when they do, the lumberjacks shout, **'Timber!'**"

"What does that mean?"

"**I have no idea.** Anyway, let's be thankful we're here, huh? At least the trees won't **squash us.**"

"Good point."

Man, Earth really is **a strange place.** Some of the people in my village say that Earth is just a **myth.** When I hear about things like trees that fall to the ground, **I almost want to agree with them.** I mean, come on. **Falling trees?** Who could believe that? **There's no way that could possibly be true** . . .

I soon finished chopping another block. I let out **a huge breath.** "You know, it really is **quiet** out here."

"Yeah . . ." Stump glanced at the surrounding trees. "It's almost like we really are . . . **out there.**"

Out there. He meant **beyond the wall.** Even though the tree farm looks like **wilderness,** it's near the center of the village. I picked up an oak sapling that had fallen from the leaves overhead.

"This is what it would be like." I planted the sapling in the grass at my feet. "**To be a warrior,** I mean. **A real one,** like Steve. All alone. No one around for **thousands of blocks.** No one else to rely on but **yourself.**"

"I dreamed **I was outside** once," Stump said. "I had a log house in the woods. I went out to **explore** and **got lost.** The sun was going down, and I couldn't find the way back. I panicked after that. I started running. The forest was getting darker and darker and my house was nowhere in sight. I couldn't even see torchlight. And I wasn't sure if I was getting closer or moving farther away . . ."

After he told me this, the forest suddenly seemed **so scary.** We drew **closer to each other.** Both of us looked around with wide eyes.

"Sounds more like **a nightmare.**" I paused. "You know, someday, if we ever become **warriors,** the mayor might actually send us . . . **out there.**"

My friend swallowed nervously. **"You mean, like scouts?"**

"Maybe. I heard the elders talking about it the other day."

"I guess that makes sense. We need to know what's going on out there."

"Exactly."

We chatted like this for a while. It was honestly like the **good old days,** back before I started this diary. Back when I thought Herobrine was just **a fairy tale.** Back when the mobs weren't **so clever.** Back then, Stump and I often went to places like this and just talked and talked about **anything and everything**. So even though today came with a lot of hard work, **it wasn't all bad.**

For at least **an hour** today, we totally forgot about **the war.** The mobs. The two wizards. The possibility of our village being **utterly destroyed.** While we swung our axes and talked about random stuff, it was like we were innocent kids again. But eventually we had to come back to reality. **It was something that couldn't be ignored.** You just couldn't avoid it. These days, you can't get a **cup of tea** in my village without hearing about Herobrine at least **fifty times.** He's trying to **take over the world** . . . with a huge **army** of mobs . . . and there's almost no one left to fight him. There's **Notch,** sure. A handful of villages in the west, **yeah.** And then there's this village . . . with **tryhard noobs** like myself . . . and **a bunch of clueless humans.**

"I wonder if the wars in the past were **the same** as this one," I said.

Stump shook his head. "There were **a lot more people** back then."

"I guess you're right."

I thought back, recalling what **Mr. Beetroot** had taught us in history class the other day . . .

Long ago, this world was once filled with **all kinds** of people. There were people who were **part wolf** . . . others who were **half pig** . . . even people who looked **like the humans** from Earth.

There were **kings** and **princesses, valiant knights** who slew the fiercest mobs . . . merchants, scholars, wizards, thieves, and everything in between.

But now,
there is nothing.

When you look at **my world** now, it's mostly wilderness—**an endless amount** of grass blocks, dirt blocks, stone, sand, and water blocks. These **simple cubes** form hills, mountains, deserts, valleys, rivers, lakes, forests, swamps, plains, chasms. But when it comes to civilization, my world doesn't have much to offer. Every **now and then,** you might spot a village. That's all that remains. It's hard to imagine that those lands once contained towns and cities, castles—**vast kingdoms.** Knowing that, one must ask . . . where did all the people go?

Simple. They **vanished** in **puffs of smoke** long ago. Back then there was **a huge war** led by Herobrine. In this first war, the various races joined together and drove the mobs back. **They even defeated Herobrine.** But he **didn't die.** He retreated into some **underground lair** where he plotted his revenge for many, many years.

Much later, he launched **a second war.** It was way worse than the first. He still **lost** that war . . . but every kingdom, city, and castle was **destroyed.** So many lives were **lost defending them.** Entire races were wiped out. Remember when I said one of those wolf people visited our village once? He's the only wolf man we've ever seen. We believe he's **the last one left.** He hasn't shown up in months. Maybe the mobs **got him,** too.

Stump and I talked about this, but we found it depressing and a **little boring.** We soon changed the topic to something far more interesting. **Magic.**

"How **cool** would it be to actually cast a spell?" I said.

Stump nodded. "Shoot **fireballs** like a blaze . . ."

"**Teleport** like an enderman."

"**Summon** a kitten just before a creeper gets close to you . . ."

"**Whoa.** Can wizards actually do that?"

He shrugged. "Why not? If they can bring humans here, they can surely **summon kittens.**"

"Hurmmm. I never considered that."

"I wonder whether a wizard can **create food,** then?"

"Well, if they can summon kittens, maybe they can summon cake, too?"

"I wish I could do that." He sighed. **"Would make my life so much easier."**

When he said this, I **thought** of something. All this time, I've wanted to **become a warrior . . .** But what about becoming **a wizard?** How crazy would that be, huh?

I pushed this **ridiculous idea** away. As far as I knew, no village had ever had wizards before. I'd heard **stories** of some who turned evil and became **witches**—but even then, they just dabbled in potions, not actual spells.

Stump gave me a funny look. **"Hey,** you're awfully **quiet** all of a sudden," he said. "What are you thinking about?"

I smiled and shook my head.
I chopped at some more wood.

"Nothing, dude. Nothing."

SUNDAY—PART V

After chopping for **over an hour,** our inventories were nearly filled up. I felt like an **expert lumberjack.** Swing **this way** and **that way**—I know how to **chop!** Pebble had better **pray** that the village doesn't have a wood-chopping competition!

> I'll be there for that!
> I'll be the <u>first</u> one to sign up!

With all of that chopping, our **hunger bars** had gotten pretty low. So we took a **break.** As usual, Stump had brought some cake. Steve once said eating in this world is just like **in the game.** No matter how carefully you eat, crumbs go flying. But then, I'm never careful. Why should I be? A warrior should **eat quickly.** If I'm ever in battle and need to top off my hunger bar, do you think I can just **call time out?!**

Ahem. Excuse me, my dear zombies. May we take a break from all this fighting? **My hunger bar,** you see . . . allow me to set a dinner table so that I may replenish it. You're most welcome to join me. We shall have an appetizer followed by a main course and then a most elegant dessert.

As if.

No, that food needs to be eaten as quickly as possible so my health bar can **regenerate** in combat! Sword in one hand, half-eaten cookie in the other—that's a **real warrior!** So today, during our break, when I jammed a whole slice of cake in my mouth, I wasn't being a pig—no, no, no. I was just . . . **training.** Yeah. Training. **That's it.**

"**Oh,** I almost forgot," I said. "I bought you **some robes** just like mine. They've been in my inventory the whole time."

I handed him the robes, **the special boots,** and **the mask.** He slipped into them immediately, then looked down at himself.

"**Hurrmmm.** These robes are **really cool** and all, but . . . we look kind of similar now, **don't we?**"

He was right. Our robes were the same **dark gray color.**

"Emerald did mention that these robes can be dyed," I said.

"**Oh.**" Stump turned his gaze to the woods. "I guess we're in luck, then."

Yes, we were in luck. The tree farm has just as many flowers as it does trees. All we had to do was go around and pick whatever color we needed.

"I wanna dye my robes **black**," Stump said. "I wanna **look just like Notch!!** All black with an **obsidian** sword. Even a **big hat!**"

"You need **ink,** then. Not flowers. We can go squid hunting in the pond. **Wait.** Maybe we should think about this carefully."

"Why?"

"Well, Emerald came up to me the other day . . ."

I told Stump about what Emerald had said about **popularity** and how we're not exactly on many people's **friend lists.**

"**Tomorrow** at school, let's ask all the other kids what their favorite color is," I said. "We'll dye our robes the two **most popular** colors. That's sure to boost our popularity, **right?**"

Stump looked unsure about this idea. "I dunno . . . what if most of them like **rust brown** or something?"

"That's **the risk we take!**" I said. "Our team needs more allies!"

"All right." His uncertainty seemed to fade. "**Let's do this.**"

MONDAY—PART I

Remember that time Razberry distracted me by asking **a bunch of random questions?** At school I kinda felt like him today. We just went up to kids and asked, **"What's your favorite color?"**

Or, "What color do you like most?"

And also, "If you were stuck on a deserted island **with just one color,** what color would that be?"

As you can imagine, we got a lot of **weird looks.** Still, when we show up at school in our dyed robes, it'll be <u>**totally worth it.**</u>

Here are the totals.

- Gray: 2
- Obsidian: 3
- Blue: 29
- Red: 23
- Orange: 4
- Purple: 3
- Black: 20
- Green: 17
- Yellow: 1
- Pink: 1
- White: 2
- Greenish-yellowish brown: 1

We lumped **similar colors** into one category. For example, a few said **lapis lazuli** was their favorite color—we counted that as **blue.**

Obviously, blue was the clear winner, followed by **red.** We dyed the robes after school on the tree farm. It took us only about **five minutes** to gather enough **blue orchids** and **poppies**. We didn't even need a crafting table. *(Not that we were short on wood or anything.)*

Well, what do you think?

Watch out, Herobrine! This will be the last thing you see.

The **first person** I showed off my new robes to was Breeze. I ran into her after I came back from the tree farm.

"**I like that color,**" she said. "It's somehow **peaceful.**"

Of course, I asked her what it was like being a **prisoner** in Herobrine's castle. She shared her **experiences** there but made me promise not to write about it. I wouldn't have written about it even if she hadn't. You'd probably start **crying** if you knew what the mobs did to her. **I almost did.** The thought of eating grass stew for weeks and weeks . . . how could the mobs be **so cruel?!**

Oops.
Please forget I wrote that.
(Breeze would get angry, and I'd rather face Herobrine than her.)

In the end, I **reassured** her that we're good friends—and that she'll always be a part of **Team Runt.** I also said, since we're such good friends, she should tell me how Herobrine managed to make her **so strong.**

She wouldn't tell me.
She claimed she didn't know.

Whatever. I'm about to go to an enchanting house and sleep on an enchanting table myself.

Wish me luck.

MONDAY—PART II

Well, I just took a **nap** on an enchanting table. And when I did, I learned something very **important.**

Enchanting tables are **very, very uncomfortable.** In other words, **nothing happened.** I feel like I've been scammed! I just want to be able to kick a zombie **so hard** it flies back **thirty blocks.** At least thirty. Is that too much to ask?!

Hurrmmmph!

After **my chores** were done, I visited Max at the library. He'd been assigned to **rearrange all the books.** At least this suited him.

"Did you say that you've read something about **people** being enchanted?" I asked.

He **closed** some random book.

"Yes. It's done through something called **a rune chamber.**"

"What's that?"

"It's like an enchanting table for **pets.** Let's say you had a pet wolf. You could place the wolf in this chamber and give it **special powers.**"

"Like what?"

"**Like,** you could give its bite a **knockback effect** or a **flame effect** or **increase its armor.** I guess you could do this with any pet, even baby ones."

"So maybe **Herobrine** figured out a way for this table to enchant people?"

"**Maybe.** I need to keep researching."

"Good. Let me know what you **find out.**"

I know, I know. So many bad things are happening in my village. All you really need to know is . . . **Herobrine is a punk.** Take Pebble. Multiply his bad attitude by ten. Give him the ability **to cast crazy spells.** Now you have Herobrine, the <u>**Ultimate Bad Guy.**</u>

To think, **I actually mouthed off to him!** He's gonna be looking out for me now! I may have to **change my name.**

I shouldn't have shared my problems with you. If you weren't crying before, you must be **crying** now. "**Oh, those poor, poor villagers,**" you're probably saying between sobs. "**Won't they ever get a break?!**"

If you're reading this and you're **a ghast,** please come to my house!

Your tears will go for a **fortune** here!
We can start a very profitable business
together!

TUESDAY—SCHOOL

Well, our **idea** paid off. It could just be my imagination, but the other kids treated me **better** at school today. At least I'm not getting so many dirty looks.

But having **nice robes** is just one part of the equation. When I get a chance, I need to ask **Emerald** more about that.

Before classes even started, Brio informed us that there are **two tests** coming up. One is the **mining test.** It had been delayed for some reason. So we're having that next week. The other test is **a building test.** Each group must come up with a new way to protect our village. **Cactus** pits. **Lava** moats. **Piston** traps that crush mobs into goo. Yeah! We're finally getting to the **cool stuff!** After school, I'm gonna spend all day dreaming up such things.

Oh. Wait. I have no time to think about all that! I have way **too many trees** to chop after school! I've already crafted **an iron axe.** And now I'm thinking about using up some of my experience points to enchant it. That's how **serious** I am about my chores. In fact, I'm so serious **about harvesting wood** I'm even thinking about putting two axes on my hotbar. First, there will be the iron axe—the basic axe I normally use. Then there will be a gold axe—for when I need to chop **really, really fast.** As I said, you will never see a more serious harvester of wood. After I'm done harvesting a block, I will immediately turn to the next block and begin chopping all over again. After school, so many trees will be chopped. After school, we will be the most professional woodchoppers in the **Overworld**, the **Nether**, the **End**, and even **the Void**.

After school,
there will be absolutely no <u>**goofing around**</u>.

TUESDAY—AFTER SCHOOL

Stump tried to chop the oak tree with his **stone sword**.
It didn't **really work**.

"**Overlord** Runt!" he shouted. "This oak golem is way too tough!"

"Then we must **surround** it!" I shouted back.

"Of course, **my lord!**"

We were standing next to each other, so there was no reason for us to be shouting. We were just doing that for **dramatic effect.** We were also trying to sound like **courageous knights.** However, our dialogue was **a little cheesy** . . .

Stump dashed to the other side of the "**oak golem.**" "Take this, **foul tree mob!!**"

Meanwhile, I stabbed the golem from the front. "You're right, **Commander Stump!** This golem's bark is like **enchanted bedrock armor!**"

"Perhaps we should use **magic!**" Stump took out a water bucket from his inventory. "**Frost II!**"

He dumped the bucket of water next to the oak tree—err, the oak golem.

"**Great work!**" I said. "The frost has frozen its feet! **Now it can't move!**"

"Do oak golems even have feet?"

"Who cares? **Attack,** Commander Stump! **Attack!!**"

"At once, sir!"

We began clobbering the tree from both sides with our swords.

"**Hurrggg!!** You'll never take our village!!"

"We are wizards and warriors, **leaf head!!**"

"There will be nothing left of you but **planks!!**"

So we weren't really fighting an oak golem. We were just making the best of our lumberjack situation. Can you blame us? As we finished off the **legendary** tree monster . . . there was a laugh in the distance. A girl's laugh.

It was Emerald.

"What are you guys doing?" she called out.

Stump and I froze in place. We slowly turned our heads to her, then back at each other, then back to Emerald again.

I lowered my sword. "Umm . . ."

"**Well,** we were just, **uh** . . . testing out how fast stone swords can **harvest wood**," Stump said.

"**Yeah?** And why is there water everywhere?"

Oh. Right. We were standing knee-deep in water from Stump's bucket. Stump scooped the spring back up, but the damage was already done. **Soggy boots are no fun.**

Emerald rolled her eyes. "You guys are such **noobs.**"

I decided to change the topic quickly. "What are you doing out here, **anyway?**"

She looked at me as if I'd just asked whether **ender dragons** really fly.

"Drill wanted me to check on you guys," she said. "I mean, **hello?** The sun's going down in **an hour.**"

She was right. The blue sky was already beginning to take on a golden tinge just above the trees. It would be night soon. Even so, we would be **safe** out here at night. Torches covered every block of this tree farm with light. There was no chance that any mobs could spawn even in this secluded area. But when Herobrine's influence can be felt everywhere . . . even your own bedroom **seems scary,** let alone a place like this.

We headed back. I hadn't seen Breeze at all today, so I asked how she was doing.

"She's all right," Emerald said. "I've been trying to get her to be a little more **outgoing.**"

I turned to her and said something boring and lame, like, "**That's good.**"

That was when I **noticed** it.
In the distance, past Emerald, there was a
<u>hole in the ground.</u>

This hole was about as hard to find as Breeze. At night. During heavy rain.

"What are you **staring at?**" Then Emerald saw it too. "**Um,** were you guys **trying to test** how well swords dig holes?"

Stump and I **shook our heads** wordlessly. It was a **terrifying** discovery. A hole had been **dug** in the tree farm. Grass grew around it, helping to **hide it from view.** I only spotted it by chance when I'd glanced at Emerald.

We soon **learned** that it
was more than just a hole.

It had **a ladder** along one side that went down several blocks.

It was . . . a tunnel.

What's the big deal?
It's probably just
some guy's house.
A guy with
blue skin, eight
legs, and super
venomous fangs.

"**I don't believe this,**" Stump said. "The mobs have been digging right under our village?"

I looked both of my friends in the eye. "Either that, or **Urf** made this. Or maybe there's another **traitor** we don't know about."

"Well, we've gotta go tell the mayor," Emerald said.

I carefully **approached the edge of the hole** and peered in. "How about we solve this **mystery** on our own? I mean, if there really is another **spy** in our village, they could be close to the mayor. So if we do the right thing and report it . . . maybe the spy will come and **cover it all up.**"

"**I agree,**" Stump said. "Besides, I don't want someone else taking credit for our discovery."

"Maybe we're getting ahead of ourselves," Emerald said. "This could be something that **Steve guy made.**"

"Then maybe we should check," I said.

"**'We'?**"

As Emerald said this, Stump gave me **a pitiful look.** Of course. I didn't **even bother arguing.**

Torch in one hand, I climbed down the **ladder.** The shaft ended after five blocks. **The floor was cobblestone.** As I'd expected, it didn't lead to a **storeroom** or anything like that.

144

The tunnel went straight for as far as the eye could see ... which, um, wasn't very far.

A small part of me wanted to **explore,** just to see how far it went. (The rest of me was trembling and sweating uncontrollably.) I climbed **back up** and told my friends about it and how it was **heading east.**

"Of course it's heading east," Stump said. "It probably leads to the mob's forest."

"**Great,**" Emerald said. "So the **mobs made a tunnel.** If we're not gonna report it, **then what?**"

"I say we wait," said Stump. "Maybe we can find out who's using it."

"And how are we gonna do that?" Emerald demanded.

Stump glanced upward.
I followed his gaze
to the top of a tree.

Oh, look! There isn't a ladder on this tree! Good, well, we tried. There's nothing else to do.

TUESDAY—NIGHT

"**Move over!** You guys are such tree hogs!"

Yeah. We totally climbed a tree. We also removed some of the leaves to make a nice, **little hiding** spot. If **spies** were using that tunnel, they would probably use it at night, right? All we had to do was wait and listen. **Eventually, the spy would come.** That was Stump's **thinking,** anyway. It made **sense.**

Emerald's stomach **grumbled.** "Man . . . I really need to remember to keep some food in my inventory."

Stump handed her a slice of cake. She almost took a **bite,** then stopped. "**Eww.** It smells like wood."

"Awfully **picky** for a war hero," I said with a **smirk**.

"**HurrMmph!**"

"Will you guys **be quiet?**" Stump hissed.

"**Whatever**," Emerald whispered. "It's not like we're not gonna . . ."

Just then, there was a distant sound. Beyond the trees, beyond the tall grass and flowers, came **a slight rustling.** All three of us ducked down in a sneaking position and froze. We didn't even breathe. The rustling **grew louder.** Soon it seemed as if it was almost beneath our tree. Yet I didn't see **anything.** I looked and looked through the leaves and couldn't tell what was making that noise.

Then it **filtered into view**. It had been invisible, and its invisibility had just worn off. Although the torches provided ample light, it was still hard to see through the leaves. Actually, it would have been hard to see even in plain view. It **blended in** with the surrounding greenery.

A creeper.

There it was, slithering toward the hole. It looked quite ordinary, but it had to be a **special** type. Perhaps this monster was another one of Herobrine's **experiments**. Or perhaps it had simply been given **Potions of Invisibility**.

The creeper looked around before **descending** into the hole. It did this in a **calm way,** as if it had done this many times before.

My friends and I **sat there.**

When we finally opened our mouths, the only things that came out were broken sentences.

Stump: "Did you guys just see . . ."

Emerald: "How was it . . . I mean, it was . . ."

Me: "Invisible. I don't . . . um, how could it . . . so, it's actually . . ."

. . . **Real. The village creeper is real.** Not only is it real, but it had been **invisible. A scout.** It had been watching us this whole time. Every day it slunk through our streets, **observing.** And every night it went back and **reported** everything it saw.

Our village was just now talking about having scouts . . . but the mobs have had them for **who knows how long.**

"How can it drink potions, though?" Emerald asked. "And how did it climb down the ladder? **It doesn't even have arms!**"

"**It doesn't matter.**" I stood up. "This is the biggest **discovery** yet."

"We have to tell someone about this."

As we **talked,** I heard a voice call out, "What are you guys doing up there?"

Max and Breeze were not too far away, looking up at us. They had obviously come to see whether we were okay. Breeze **glanced at the hole,** then at the three of us standing in a tree.

She blinked in **confusion.**

"Did we . . . **miss something?**"

WEDNESDAY—SCHOOL

Last night, we told Max and Breeze **what we saw.** But it was so late—we weren't able to go into **extreme detail.** So during lunchtime at school today, **we talked so much** we didn't even eat.

Even though I was **starving,** you could have put an **enchanted golden apple** in front of me and I would have ignored it. Every second was spent going over **the events** of last night. **Every little** detail. We did this quietly, though. We couldn't let someone like Pebble **overhear** us. If he found out about the village creeper, he might get his friends and go **capture** it himself . . . we'd see his posters on every village block. **As if I would let that happen.** Tomorrow, the village is going to explode with the news: **Team Runt not only found the village creeper, but captured it as well.**

"There's just **one problem** with this idea," Max said. "How do we hold it **prisoner?**"

"Right," Stump said. "**It can just blow itself up.**"

Hurrmmm.

There were a lot of these sounds as all five of us brainstormed. Max brought up water. Creepers are filled with gunpowder, so maybe if we **drenched** it, it couldn't **explode**.

But we didn't know for sure. As far as I knew, creepers were still able to blow up even while **swimming**.

Breeze offered another solution.

"**We scare it,**" she said. "We make it so **afraid** it won't even think about exploding."

"But how do we . . ."

Of course, **I already knew the answer.**

PROJECT DANGER KITTY II

Meet **Fluffles.** He's a **nice kitten.**

His **favorite hobbies** include:

1) eating **pufferfish;**

2) resembling **a block of wool;**

3) **scratching** the chairs in our house.

He also has a best friend named Sprinkles.

— This is what a creeper's **nightmares** look like.

Despite his name, Sprinkles is quite **large.** In fact, Sprinkles has the distinction of being the only kitten often confused for **a baby cow.** I guess a diet of bread, cookies, cakes, and pumpkin pie does that to a kitten.

As you can guess, the name of his owner is Stump.

(If I ever go on vacation, I will not let Stump take care of Jello. Will not. Will not.)

Breeze has a kitten named **Dandelion.** She named him that because of his **bright yellow fur.** Emerald and Max's kittens have **no names,** however, as they had only recently traded for them.

Anyway, I understand that **scratching chairs** can get boring after a while. It's time for these kittens to try out something new. Besides, when it comes to sharpening claws, what better surface is there than **a creeper's face?**

Max handed everyone **leather jerkins** that were enchanted with **Blast Protection III**—just in case. We all equipped them underneath our robes.

Project Danger Kitty II **has begun.**

WEDNESDAY—NIGHT

We blocked off the tunnel. Then every member of Team Runt **hid** behind trees surrounding the hole. **We waited.** With kittens **on leashes,** we waited. We waited and waited for **a very long time.** Then the rustling came. The grass swayed. **The creeper emerged into view.** It neared the edge of the hole and whirled around. **It was intelligent**—it knew that something was wrong. Surely it sensed the trap. But it was too late. My heart was pounding in my chest at the thought of getting so close to such a **dangerous** creature. Even so, I jumped out from behind the tree, **leash in hand.**

"Out for a **stroll?**" I asked.

"**Ehhgbzzt!**"

It spoke in that **strange language** . . . but stopped once my friends stepped out.

Five villagers with five kittens (with one being very large for a kitten and quite angry looking because it hadn't had anything sugary to eat in at least five minutes).

Max stepped forward. "**Slowly,** guys."

We all converged on the green plant monster. It didn't move at all. Well, besides **a slight trembling.** *(It was shaking like a zombie villager who'd just been given a golden apple. It was absolutely, totally afraid.)*

I **pushed** Fluffles ahead one more block. My heart was beating so fast. Fluffles didn't have any **protective armor,** and his life was but a fraction of mine. If the creeper decided to **explode** . . . I'd have to dive back and yank on the leash as fast as I could . . . or my kitten **would be history.** But this had to be done. This green mass of living vegetation was why the mobs seemed to **know so much** about our village.

Even if it blew up, we could **call that a victory.** Still, it would be better if we could **capture** it, study it, learn from it . . . *(Also, if we captured it, we could walk up to the mayor with it and get medals and diamonds and have posters with us on it and be called awesome and amazing. Or just awesome. I'm not greedy!)*

Summoning the **last of my courage,** I got within one block. Breeze did **the same.** She picked up **Dandelion** and held the kitten in front of the creeper. She had that **don't-mess-with-me** look again, like when she took out those zombies during the first battle. **The creeper leaned away from her.**

She moved even closer. "Can you . . . **understand me?"**

The monster moved in a way that could be called a nod. "Y-yes. I can. Please, don't hurt me . . ." Its voice sounded like sugarcane rustling in the wind. "I don't want to blow up . . ."

I relaxed the grip on my leash. Max, Stump, and Emerald cautiously joined Breeze and me. We **formed a tight ring** around the monster.

Monster.

We had <u>captured</u> a monster.

A live one. Real. **Much stronger** than a baby slime.

"Put those animals away," it begged. "Please . . . the sounds they make . . ."

"We will," Emerald said, "but only after you promise **to cooperate.** Otherwise, you'll no longer need to imagine what **a kitten's claws** feel like."

It promised.

Oh, did it <u>promise</u>.

Surrounded by mewing **kittens**, it promised **more than anyone had ever promised before.**

THURSDAY—MORNING

Captured Creeper!!!

STUDENTS HAVE CAPTURED THE
"EYE OF HEROBRINE"
LEGENDARY MOB NOW IN CUSTODY

Eat that, Pebble. We captured the **Eye of Herobrine.** That's the name of the creeper that once stalked our streets. Brio and his men took the monster away. Probably to the same building where Brio had once taken me. There, they will figure out exactly how it manages **to turn invisible.**

"Believe me," Brio said, "**we'll make it talk.**"

Interrogation under way!

My parents were **in the crowd.** I could see that they were **so proud** of me. The mayor **praised** us in front of the whole village:

"**Thanks to the efforts** of these fine young villagers, we've learned of a **new threat.** In the past, the mobs have climbed over our wall and even blasted through it, but we never imagined that they might actually dig under it."

"**To be honest,**" Kolbert said, "the Legion never thought about this, either. In the original game, the mobs never used **tools!** Their AI is **really advanced** here, I must say."

"This new game is **so cool!!**" Minsur said. "I always thought the original was a bit **too easy.** I beat it on **hardcore mode** like five or six times!"

A lot of villagers looked at them and sighed. Steve and Mike did, too. They hung out at the back of the crowd.

Anyway, the mayor was so **pleased** he decided we didn't have to go to school today or **even do chores.** And like back in the good old days—*like when I aced that building test*—other kids have been coming up to me, **congratulating** me. On top of that, Brio gave me another **payment.**

"This is for the **obsidian cube.** The mobs are still confused by it. Last night, they **covered it in dirt** to hide it from view." He handed me a

stack of emeralds. Then the mayor himself handed me **five more.**

"Those are to be split among you and your friends," the mayor said. "**Good work!**"

A **glittering** green pile. All you could hear was the sound of emeralds falling into my inventory like so much broken glass.

I'd never seen so many.
128 of them belonged to me.

Pebble, of course, was **annoyed.** He approached after Brio and the mayor left my presence.

"**Hey, Runt.**"

"Hello, good sir." I patted the pocket of my robes. You could hear the emeralds shifting. "Are you here for a **loan?**"

"**Please**. You might have a lot of money, but you can't buy **skill**. My scores still walk all over yours."

"Someone's a sore loser," I said.

Pebble **glared at me** with a look that reminded me of Herobrine himself. "**You're smiling now,**" he said, "but you won't be after that mining test. You won't be doing **anything** at all."

He shoved me.

I shoved him back. "What's your problem?"

"**You're** my problem," he said. "**You're a noob.** If you're ever tasked with defending this village, you'll be **endangering** us all!"

He **stormed off.** His words lingered in my head. Especially what he said about the **mining test.** That was next week. Max had mentioned something about how Pebble's father was going to **rig that test.**

Whatever. I'm not afraid. Lava pools, gravel traps . . . no matter what he tries, **I'll avoid them all!** Anyway, I'm not going to think about it right now. With no school, no homework, and no chores, **it's time to relax.** I'm gonna go get ice cream with **my friends,** and then we'll all head down to the pond. I know; I've said that before—and soon after, **the village erupted into flames and smoke.**

But that won't happen this time. **Not today.**
No way. Today is mine. <u>**Mine.**</u>

THURSDAY—AFTERNOON

I cast my line. The lure of my **fishing rod** went flying. You thought the mobs were gonna attack again, **huh?**

As did I.
As did I.

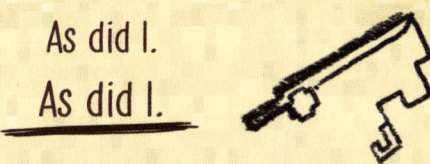

This pond is located on the south edge of the tree farm. It's more like **a small lake,** really. It was built to give us a place to **practice** swimming . . . and it serves as another source of food. Yes, **we'd gone fishing.**

We might be in the **beginning** stages of a war—a huge army of mobs will soon be knocking on our door—but even warriors in training need to rest. **Every now and then.**

The fishing lure **bobbed** slightly. I reeled in my line. A **pufferfish. Surprise, surprise.** *I'll save it for* **Fluffles,** I thought. After last night, it's the least I can do. Beside me, Breeze was still **fumbling** around with her fishing rod. She seemed a little embarrassed.

"Haven't fished much, **I take it?**" I asked.

"No, not really," she said. "Can you show me?"

"Sure. It's pretty simple, really. All you have to do is . . ."

It was strange, teaching her how to fish. She was the top student by far, and it was fishing rods that confused her. When she managed to send out her line all by herself, I'd never seen her so happy.

"Not too many lakes where you come from?" I asked.

"Actually, there were many. But since we lived so close to Herobrine's castle, our village was more focused on fighting."

"A warrior village, then."

I wasn't being serious when I said this. Yet she didn't return my grin.

"It was."

"Wait," I said. "You're saying your village actually had warriors?"

"Is it so hard to believe?"

"A little."

She looked away. "What you're experiencing now is nothing new to me. My life has always been like this. We began training at a very young age."

I didn't know what to say. She'd been a warrior even before being captured. Then whatever Herobrine did had only made her stronger.

Breeze and her father were more like **super-villagers,** then. If normal villagers were rabbits, the ones from her place were **killer bunnies.**

Pebble was right about one thing, though. **His scores are better.** To be honest, mine **haven't improved** much lately. Then again, the same can be said for everyone else. The higher our skills rise, the **harder** it becomes to improve them. For example, when my building score was low, all I had to do was place a few blocks to see an **increase.** Now it feels like I'd need to build a castle for it to jump up a single point. I think I'm hovering between **fifth** and **sixth** place. If I can just **ace** that next building test . . . Groups are allowed. Up to seven, they said. Or a student can roll solo, if he or she prefers.

"I keep having these **weird dreams,**" I said.

Breeze nodded knowingly. "Did see you **an enderman?**"

"**You've been having them, too?!**"

"Yes. Endermen can do a lot more than just **teleport** around. They're like **wizards,** in a way."

"**Controlling dreams,** huh . . ." I recalled the dream with **the strange redstone machine.**

"So that enderman is trying to help us?"

"**I think so.** My father has had those dreams, too. He thinks the enderman is **working for Notch.**"

"**Mobs? Helping Notch?**"

"Not all mobs are **bad,** Runt."

I nodded, immediately **thinking of Jello.** I haven't spent much time with him lately.

On the other side of the pond, Emerald was talking to Stump and Max. They were arguing about whether the mayor was **really serious** about surrendering. It seems like some villagers actually think we should. **I'm proud** to say that none of my friends think that way. If Brio and Breeze are **really so strong,** maybe they can teach us how to **fight.** More than the humans already have, anyway.

Suddenly, Breeze's lure bobbed in the water. **Her face lit up.**

"**Hey, Runt!** I think I've caught something!"

"**Reel it in!**"

And she pulled in her line like **Urkk** himself. Her catch landed in the grass nearby. **It was a book.** Not only was it a book—it was **a fake version of my diary.** I burst out laughing. "It looks almost **exactly** like my diary!"

The more I inspected the cover, though, the more I saw the errors. **A noob had obviously crafted this forgery.** The writing inside was of the same poor quality. It was so **bad,** in fact, I almost wondered if a zombie wrote it. Or perhaps **a magma cube.**

"I wonder who the author is," Breeze said.

"**Pebble,** most likely. Or some random noob. Who knows. If I ever find out . . . !!"

Breeze tossed **the fake diary** back into the pond where it belonged.

Two hours before sunset, the other three headed over to our side of the pond.

"We've been trying to come up with something to build for the test tomorrow," Max said, "**and we're failing.**"

"It's like my mind **isn't working,**" Emerald said. "**Too much stress,** you know?"

Stump mentioned a few things—**TNT traps,** stuff like that—but he admitted that they were all pretty stale.

"**We need something fresh,**" he said.

"What if we think of a way to stop the mobs from tunneling under the wall?" Breeze asked.

Of course, this was something the village **desperately** needed. But I couldn't come up with anything besides **an underground obsidian wall.** We chatted for at least an hour, and nothing. At the end, Stump was strangely quiet. He was looking at something in the distance.

That was where, weeks ago, I'd **dug** up a bunch of sand to make **bottles.**

"That's it!" Stump said. "**Sand!**"

All eyes were on him. He put his hands on my shoulders.

"This time, I'm the one with the **crazy** idea."

FRIDAY

The big day.
Building Test III.

Students had come up with all kinds of **defensive concepts.** Let's go over a few of them, shall we?

First, **Team Pebble** made a **lava trap.** There were a few people who said they just **copied Mike's house.** Still, the teachers had never seen Mike's house, and Mike wasn't around to defend himself. **So Pebble's crew made out well today.**

Team All Girls, with Emma, Mia, Sophia, and the rest, came up with something way cooler. They called it the **lava water door.** Basically, you put some **lava** over a **door** and **water** in front of it, like this: ➡

(It can protect against the biggest explosions. The girls did a demonstration using two blocks of TNT. **What a show!**)

169

Before

After

"Like **a frozen burrito** cooked too long in a **microwave**," Steve said. The lava and water combined **to form stone**. Additional explosions could **remove** the stone, and the lava and water would continue to **make** more. A **regenerating** shield. There were a lot of **neat concepts** like this.

There were even a bunch of new item concepts that I will go over later. *(They're classified right now. Top secret.)*

Still—and I'm not trying to brag here—nothing was as cool as what **Team Runt had come up with.** You see, there's no good way to prevent mobs from **digging under the city.** However, the village can at least make **a system** that warns us when they do.

Allow me to explain the
Tunnel Warning System.

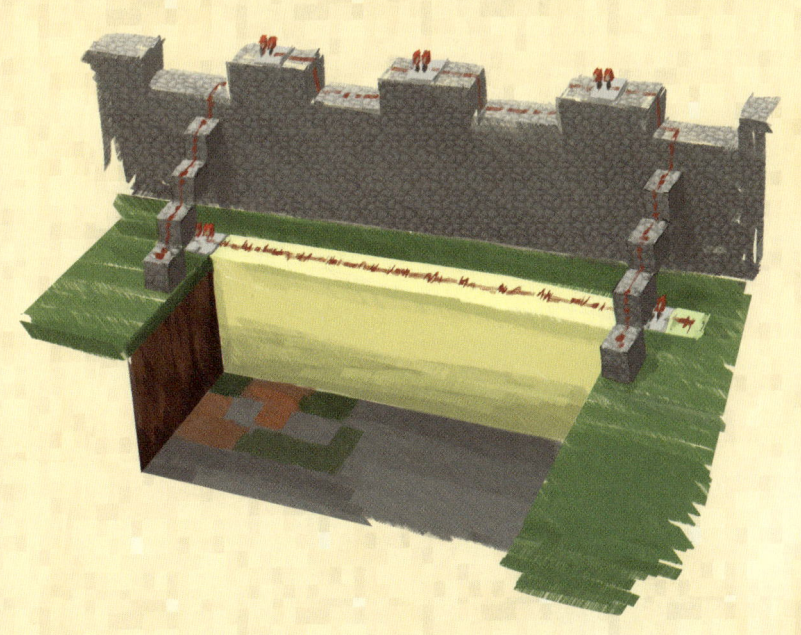

Here's how it works:

The ground in this world comes **in layers.** There's the **grass layer**, which is grass-covered dirt—that's a single block thick. Then there's the **dirt layer** underneath that. It goes down for five or so blocks, roughly. After that, it's all **stone** until you reach **bedrock** deep down.

In short, the mobs **dug a tunnel** in the dirt layer because it's way easier. Tunneling through stone takes a **very** long time. So all we'd need to do is place a wall of sand around the village in the dirt layer. Then whenever the mobs **dig through the sand,** it will collapse. This will **break** the redstone circuit on top of the sand. As a result, the redstone repeaters in that area will **no longer glow.** So the guys guarding the wall at night—**Brio's men, humans**—will at least have **some kind of warning.**

Yes, Team Runt came in **first place.** The teachers really **loved** this idea because we have a ton of **extra redstone** lying around.

Team All Girls came in **second,** and
Team Pebble came in **third.**

I have no idea what **rank** I am. **I guess I'll find out.**

Teachers and students were **scattered** all around. Everyone was chatting about the **new inventions** on display. Everyone except Breeze and me.

"Runt?"

"Yeah?"

"Are you afraid?"

"**Always.** If my dreams don't involve endermen, it's the **mobs attacking.**"

"Me too. I always have **nightmares** about getting captured again . . . and returning to his **dungeon.**"

"I won't let that happen," I said.

"Promise?"

"**Promise.**"

This weekend, we're getting **another** break. I've decided to spend all Saturday and Sunday in the **libraries** with Max.

Long ago, during that second war, a lot of information was **lost.** Wizards' towers, the biggest libraries . . . all burned, **all blown up.** But if even a shred of that **ancient knowledge** still exists somewhere in our old, dusty books, we have to find it. The stuff we build now is noob-tier compared to what the ancients once made. The rocket potion I crafted earlier is an example. Max thinks the advanced crafting table has a **five-by-five** grid instead of **three-by-three.** Crafting on a table like that would be much harder. In addition, there's an even better crafting table that has seven layers of **seven-by-seven** grids. In other words, **3-D crafting.** That's crazy. But then, what am I doing thinking about all this stuff? I don't even have **a diamond sword** yet! A diamond sword . . . It seems hard to believe, but I can actually afford one now. My friends have a sizable amount of emeralds as well.

I turned to Breeze. "Let's go find the others, huh?"

"Why? What's up?"

I reached into my inventory and gave her a **stack of emeralds. "We're going shopping,** that's why."

"I don't think Stump will want to join us," she said. "He keeps talking about how he wants **an obsidian sword,** just like Notch."

"I'm working on that." I winked. "This year, I plan on giving him an **early** birthday present."

"Speaking of Notch," she said, "**it's strange** that he hasn't said anything to us about the lost information. But then, maybe we're not very important . . ."

"**Don't think like that.**" I gazed at the cloudy sky. "He's just . . . **busy.**"

Just then, I thought I heard faint **thunder** coming from up there. But it **wasn't stormy** out. Just a layer of white clouds. Nah. It must have been **my imagination.**

We took off in search of our friends. I started thinking about what items I was going to buy. If I actually do buy **a diamond sword,** I'm gonna use all my experience points **enchanting** it. That thing is gonna **glow so bright** that if **I ever meet skeletons at night,** they'll start looking for trees to hide under! When Pebble sees me wielding that, can you imagine the look on his face? He took off with a **scowl** after he found out his team got third place.

He **probably** went to go work on another **fake** diary.

FRIDAY—LATER

Today was one of the best days of my life. So I'm going to warn you now: I'm including a lot of details.

Details on how
I've become the—

Oops.
I almost ruined the surprise.

FRIDAY—EVEN LATER

Emerald has **a crush** on Kolbert. At least **I think she does.** She's really secretive about it, though. I figured it out from her **reaction** to the picture I drew of him earlier. She insisted that I redraw him. In her words, to **"do him justice."** According to her, he looks way more **dashing** than my original drawing suggests. I've also been asked to point out that Kolbert doesn't actually have a beard. He just turned **fifteen.**

Wahhhhhh!
So I'd given him a beard! <u>**So what?**</u>

I think beards look funny, so I put one on him. **What's the big deal?** Also, I've apparently misspelled his name. Also, the **color** of his armor is all wrong. **Oh no!** Also, the armor itself is all wrong. He never wears a helmet. Dear **Mr. Diary,** what have I done?! The truth is I never put much time or effort into including Kolbert in my diary. Why would I? For the longest time, **the guy was a total jerk. Ordering me around.** Telling me to do this and that. I'm not your pack animal, bud. Do you see a chest **strapped** to my back?

All things considered, I should have made Kolbert look like a cross between an **enderman** and a **mine cart!** Lately, however, **he's come around.** He's been **a lot nicer** to us. Courteous. Respectful. The longer he stays here, the more he involves himself with our kind. He swore to protect us, no matter what. He even saved the village from a creeper attack the other night. **All by himself.** Maybe that's why Emerald forgave him. She bought him a gift today while we were shopping at the **Clothing Castle.**

"**What?** My parents told me to buy him something," she said with a shrug. "After all, he, um, did kinda **save** us and all."

Yeah . . .

If there's one thing I learned today, it's to never let Emerald buy armor for me.

She bought him **a scarf.** Not a helmet. Not a cap or a hood. Not anything a knight might typically wear. **A black wool scarf.** I told her that Kolbert would probably go diving in the Nether before putting that thing on. Puddles, **the shopkeeper,** thought otherwise.

"But it's the same color as his armor," she said. "Don't worry, **sugar block. He'll love it!**"

Yes, Puddles is a she, not a he. She has a deep voice for a woman and wears a **witch-style hat** so low that you can't really see her face.

I need to start paying more attention.

"He'll like it," Emerald said. "After all, this scarf is enchanted with **Protection III.**"

Stump spit out bits of pumpkin pie. "**Protection III?!** How much did you spend on that?"

"**Two stacks.**"

Two stacks of emeralds. **Sure,** that sounds about right. That's about what **a diamond goes for** these days. To our shocked expressions, she rolled her eyes.

"Those came out of my father's inventory. Not mine. He says we need to **strengthen our alliance** with the humans."

When she said that, our eyes grew even **wider.** Puddles made **a slight gasp.** She didn't know much about the humans and thought their **taste in fashion was terrible.**

"Side with them? Now, why would we do that?"

AN ALLIANCE?

It's not **unthinkable.** We **need** them and they **need** us. But first, the humans will have to come to terms with their issues. Right now, there are **a lot** of humans in our village. New ones wander in every day. **Strangely enough,** they've become divided into **two factions,** each with entirely **different beliefs.** One group believes that this world isn't real. They're known as **the Seekers—seekers of the truth.** If you ask them, this is all some kind of elaborate **virtual reality show.** Alternatively, it's the result of some accident involving their Earth **technology.** That group throws around many **theories,** attempting to explain this world in human terms. In their way of thinking, it doesn't matter how they treat us, because **NPCs don't have real feelings.** To them, even if we display **emotions,** that's the result of programming, **scripting,** AI—stuff I don't understand.

The other group **disagrees.** They call themselves **the Believers.** They believe in the **impossible:** that the game has somehow **come to life.** At the very least, they've given up trying to understand and have come to accept this world for what it is. The two groups often have heated discussions over this. They discuss it more than they do **pizza,** which is saying something. Their biggest quarrel occurred when **Kolbert,** their leader, suddenly changed his mind. He's a **Believer** now.

"These people are real," he said the other day. "As such, they should be **treated** accordingly."

I only hope he can **sway** some more humans to his side . . . Call me picky, but I like it better when they **don't treat us** like slaves.

Kolbert talks about that stuff in his diary. **I read most of the entries.** I even copied **one section** down. It's from a few days ago, when Emerald tried speaking to him.

That villager girl talked to me again. It was eerie. Seeing her sent chills down my spine. There was emotion in her voice. Warmth in her smile. A soul behind her eyes. I had once assumed that these people were NPCs. But right then, the truth became so clear. Standing before me, a girl who was once just polygons was now real live flesh and blood. Although I couldn't understand how this had happened . . . I understood that it had happened.

A world made of cubes—once so many countless pixels—had inexplicably sprung to life.

Hurmmm. I want to get a full copy of his diary now. By the way, we ran into him after we left the **Clothing Castle.** Emerald gave him the scarf—**and crazily enough,** he actually **liked** it.

DESPITE WHAT RUNT SAID, I'M NOT A <u>**WIMP**</u>.

I WEAR THIS SCARF BECAUSE IT GREATLY STRENGTHENS MY DEFENSE.

IT IS A MERE COINCIDENCE THAT IT ALSO HIGHLIGHTS MY PERFECT HAIRSTYLE.

A lot of kids at school joke about how he acts like a **wuss** sometimes. A little girly. Come Monday, after they spot him walking around with that thing on, that's all we're gonna hear.

Not every human is like Kolbert, **though.** Many are still **rude** to us, making comments. My friends and I passed some of them on the street.

"What are they wearing?! **Ninja outfits?!**"

"**Forget the robes!** It's still strange to see villagers wielding swords!"

"**Hey!** That's the kid who's always running around being weird! What's his name again? **Grunt?**"

"You mean they actually **have names?**"

"Let's go see what they have to trade."

Villagers wielding swords?!
Villagers having names and being weird?!

Those things just aren't supposed to happen, I guess. We're supposed to just walk around randomly, make strange noises, and sometimes . . . if we're feeling **adventurous** . . . **plant** new vegetables.

Big adventures in a little village: Part 1

Will Grunt manage to plant the carrot?!?

Oh no, be careful— you're planting it next to the potatoes!!!

The humans **continued talking** as if we weren't even there.

"I don't want to trade with them. **They're creepy.** Besides, it's not like they have **macaroni** or something."

"Oh, man. **Macaroni.** I'd pay fifty emeralds for a single bowl!"

"Or some **spaghetti** . . ."

"With some **garlic bread** . . ."

"Topped with **sprinkle cheese** . . ."

The last two lines were said by **human boys** whose eyes started watering.

Hurggg!!

Stop crying already and eat some pumpkin pie, **you noobs!!!**

Stump gave the humans **a tired look.** "Maybe I should figure out how to craft **a large pepperoni,**" he said in a low tone.

"If you did," Breeze said, "villagers everywhere would **rejoice.** You'd probably get voted in as **the new mayor.**"

Yeah, don't even get them **started on pizza.** They have heated arguments over it. "**Supreme**" this. "**Stuffed crust**" that. "**Ham and pineapple all the way.**"

Suddenly, I had a great idea. Maybe I could try to make a few emeralds off their **pizza craze.** You see, this world already has pizza. **Kind of.** In a way. So I'll sell it to them and **profit!** Here's a poster I'm thinking about using for **my future pizza shop:**

CRISPY
PUMPKIN
PIZZA

WITH SAUCE AND TOPPINGS
MADE FROM
MASHED PUMPKIN

Pumpkin pizza?!
How crazy is that?!
You think you're hardcore with pineapple on your pizza?! I don't even know what pineapple is, but honestly, you're not a **REAL** pizza fan until you've tried a pizza topped with glorious, glorious pumpkin!! *(Diamond armor, here I come!!)*

The five of us eventually arrived at **Leaf's shop.** In case you forgot, he's **the cranky old blacksmith** I scammed a long time ago.

Yeah. That guy. I can't say **why** we chose to visit him. Maybe we were too busy thinking about **trading** for more cool stuff. Come on, how could anyone not get excited at the thought of trading for **cool stuff?!** Max likes trading for cool stuff. Stump likes trading for cool stuff. Drill, the mayor, this one human named **Sami**—

<u>everyone likes trading for cool stuff!</u>

I classify **cookies** as cool stuff, but when I get one, I immediately eat it and have to trade for another all over again.

Also, Breeze has **never traded** for cool stuff before because she used to live in a village where she couldn't trade for cool stuff. Still, when I asked her if she wanted to trade for cool stuff, her face totally **lit up** like a firework rocket enhanced with a fire charge. Even cows would like trading for cool stuff, probably, except they don't have **hands** with which to hold emeralds.

> Unfortunately, for a cow, "cool stuff" just means "grass."

If cows could trade, grass farming would be a thing—and tools with Silk Touch would be even more valuable.

So we had **a plan,** then. We still had **a bunch** of emeralds and wanted to keep shopping. There was **one problem.** We were about to buy new weapons. We had to do it in a cool way. We had to do it like warriors, **you know?** In my opinion, *real* warriors would probably do the following:

1) Go into a **blacksmith's** shop.

2) Slam the **emeralds** onto the table.

3) Ask to buy **weapons** that would make an obsidian golem cry.

4) Give the blacksmith **a mean look**. I mean, **mean.** The kind of look that says, "Don't mess with me. **I'm tough.** In fact, I'm **so tough** I have an item called Noob-On-A-Stick which allows me to ride ender dragons as if they were giant winged pigs."

Yeah, that's what <u>real warriors would do</u>.

So we did. Of course, considering what happened last time, Leaf just **laughed.**

"You call those **emeralds**, kids? I know yer **tricks**.
Just a bunch of dyed green glass."

He actually **bit into** one just to see whether it was real. *(I'm not sure why his biting an emerald would prove anything though, because he doesn't even have teeth.)*

When he realized our emeralds were—**unbelievably–real emeralds,** his face lit up like a firework-rocket explosion enhanced not by a fire charge but a creeper head instead—**which is just crazy.** Don't try to imagine that, okay?! **I'm still trying to forget.**

So anyway, at least now we had Leaf's attention. "Make an obsidian golem cry, huh?" he said. He pointed at an iron pickaxe. "**What about that?** I bet that would do the job."

We gave him blank looks.

"You need **diamonds to mine obsidian**," Breeze said calmly.

"**Oh.** Of course, **of course.** I was just, um, testing you. No noobs allowed in my shop, see."

Awkward silence.
More blank stares.

The blacksmith glanced around his shop.

"**How about this?**" he asked, holding up an iron sword.

The sword **wasn't enchanted** and had low durability on top of that. *(Actually, it looked like it was only a few swings away from breaking.)*

He looked at our **still-blank faces** and shrugged. "**Well,** it will definitely make a ghast cry. Guaranteed! **Or yer emeralds back.**"

"Dude," Stump said, "**are you joking?** A pink tulip would make a ghast cry!"

Max sighed. "Imagine a sword that was so bad it actually **healed** whatever it struck. It would still make a ghast cry."

"**Hurmpph!**" Emerald whirled around. "That piece of **junk** would make *me* cry . . . if I **traded** for it."

Breeze just shook her head and left.

Everyone else was **quick** to follow her out the door, but I took one last glance around at Leaf's items. **Something caught my eye.** It was round and slightly shiny, bluish-green in color. **An ender pearl.** They're quite rare around here. It was only **five emeralds,** too. I'd been wanting to buy Breeze **a gift** anyway and thought she might like to have one.

Wow.

Breeze used to **annoy** me,
and now I'm **buying** her stuff?!
What's going on here?!

Without another word, I joined my friends in search of another place to spend our **hard-earned gemstones.**

As we made our way to another blacksmith, there was **a distant shout.** Far away, some humans were standing **on the wall.** Christina and Sami were among them—two humans **I actually like.** They were shouting, although I couldn't hear what they were saying from this distance. Also, I couldn't see what they were looking at. The wall was totally blocking my view. **It didn't matter.** If there's one thing I've learned from **growing up** in my village, it's that shouting is bad. Is there any kind of shout around here that isn't followed by **a wave of zombies,** people running in **terror,** explosions, and/or burning houses? Usually, no.

So we ran **to the east wall.** Gone were my dreams of **spending** some serious gemstones. Gone were my dreams of enchanted boots, a new sword, and more gifts for my friends. As we got closer to the wall, the only thing filling **my head was what the terrified humans kept screaming.**

"Slimes!"

"There're SO many!"

"Why don't we surrender already?!"

So the village was <u>**under attack.**</u>

It was going to be **a totally normal weekend,** then. I mean, this village can't possibly have a weekend without a random mob attack! It's **tradition** around here! Apparently, the mobs in **Mob City** have classes in Mob School only during the weekdays, and during Mob Weekend, **it's something like this:**

> Your homework for the weekend . . . **terrorize the village.**

> The enderman hung his head. It was supposed to rain all weekend.

Still, from what the humans were saying, it was just **some slimes out there.**

Slimes usually aren't **a very big deal.** It's not like they can wield pickaxes, unless Herobrine found a way to give them **arms.**

They were probably going to **creeperbomb** us. Have the humans never seen a creeperbomb before? There's a lot of **commotion** after one, sure. Baby villagers **crying.** Young girls **screaming.** Tiny slimes **bouncing everywhere.** But these days, it's not exactly what we could consider **an emergency.** The little slimes don't deal any damage—they're just really annoying. And we've come to realize that a creeperbomb is an excellent source of slimeballs. If anything, we're now **thankful** for such attacks, because slimeballs **can be used to craft cool stuff.**

And let me tell you **right now**—to a villager, there's only one thing better than cool stuff, and that's free cool stuff. So I hadn't even climbed up the ladder yet to see what all the fuss was about. **I didn't have to.** My plan was I'd just wait for the green cubes to come **raining down,** play **Whack-a-Slime,** and profit.

(I only wished they could have attacked after I'd bought a new sword so that I could test it out on them right away. Those mobs are so inconsiderate!)

I told my friends about the plan. Max, Stump, and Emerald thought it was **a great idea.** Breeze, however, made **no comment.** Instead, she climbed up the ladder. (I'm guessing that was her way of saying my plan stunk worse than zombie breath.) What is she doing?! I thought. The slimes will rain down in the city, **not on the wall!** The streets will be filled with slimeballs! We have to be the first ones **to collect** them! Slimeballs sell for, like, **one emerald each!** Emeralds might as well be **falling from the sky!**

Hurmmmph.

I went up the wooden rungs after her. By the time I reached the top, everyone had **stopped shouting.** A bunch of humans and a few villagers were just **staring** at the forest without a word. **I quickly understood why. A huge row of slimes** stood out there, in front of their forest. Now, everyone knows that slimes hop around constantly. They never stop bouncing. Not these, though. No, **they didn't move at all.**

To the right is the **obsidian cube**. (The mobs really did **cover it up** with dirt. I plan to uncover it soon just to **mess with them**.)

It was **unsettling** to say the least. A row of slimes, just sitting there, **motionless**. It was like **watching** a skeleton hug a wolf—

totally unnatural.

I really hope **Jello** doesn't get as fat as these guys.
He's totally going on a diet.

After Emerald joined us up top, she made **a slight gasp.**

"Well, this is new."

Max slowly stepped toward the edge of the wall. "They must be . . . **practicing.**"

"**Practicing?** Practicing **what?**"

"Formations, I think."

I suddenly had a horrible idea. Maybe our village is just like a **practice dummy** to the mobs. Maybe they've been **studying** us. **Learning** from us. Using us to **improve their techniques.**

Which means . . . when they finally **destroy us,** they'll be experienced enough to handle the **real villages to the west.** Could it be? Is that all we are to them? **A training ground?**

A tutorial?

A hands-on test called

How to Properly Destroy Walled Villages?

Before long, the slimes began **advancing.**
That **Herobrine . . .** he sure has those <u>**mobs trained.**</u>

They all hopped **at the same time.** They looked like a bouncing wall of goo. Naturally, this caused **a lot of commotion.** Perhaps one-third of the village had gathered on the wall. **A small army** of villagers and humans—mixed together, bows ready, faces grim—**studying the approaching enemy.**

"What are they doing?"

"Why are they all lined up like that?"

"Are they about to have a race or something?"

Soon, everyone realized the purpose of **today's attack.** Slimes are somewhat **transparent.** You can see through them. As they inched closer, I started to make out more mobs **behind them.**

You could also see their feet whenever the slimes jumped up. **Nice try, mobs.** You are NOT that sneaky.

It was a **solid strategy**, though.
After today, we're calling it the **slime wall**.
The slimes were acting as **shields** to protect the creepers.

They were testing whether slimes would be **enough** to bring creepers **close to the wall.** If the troops made a large hole, it would take too long to repair. A huge army of zombies could then **pour** in. It would take a huge **amount of arrows** just to break through those meat shields.

Their little plan had one major flaw, of course:

Me and the small mountain of arrows that I now haul around at all times.

← Me!

Well, **not just me. There were a lot of us.** These days, everyone carries two stacks of arrows in his or her inventory. At least **two stacks.** My grandfather carries around three. **And TNT.** And a **lava** bucket. And a water bucket, **because why not?**

Did I ever mention that my grandfather **doesn't like** mobs? Maybe it just runs in the family. Some zombies **trashed** his flowerpots a long time ago. **He's sworn vengeance ever since.** I haven't talked to him much since I started school, **but he taught me a lot.**

Actually. I didn't speak much at all before I started school. **Maybe it's a family thing.**

Anyway, we had **enough arrows** to turn every last slime out there into **a huge supply of leashes,** slime blocks, and sticky pistons.

Then, once the slimes fell, **the creepers** could be easily picked off before they could cause any real damage. Simple, **right?**

There's **two steps** in the plan:

It's not exactly redstone science. Until today, though, that was our plan for pretty much **any mob attack.** Almost any mob-related problem can be solved with a **ridiculous amount of arrows.** Almost any. But today, that strategy didn't work out so well . . .

Breeze was standing on the very edge of the wall, next to Brio. **At her father's command,** she pulled back her bowstring all the way. *(The only other student strong enough to do that is Pebble.)*

Then there was **a loud twang**. Her arrow made the sharpest sound as it cut through the air. And even though the slimes were still some ways away, I heard a **wet slap** as the projectile **sank** into one of them.

Strangely,
nothing happened.

The slime quivered slightly, but that was it. It was as if the slime hadn't taken any damage at all. Beside her, Pebble drew **Sir Mobspanker II, his enchanted bow.** "Let me **show you** how to shoot," he said to Breeze. "Then you can go back to your **wool crafting.**"

Calm as always, she only smirked and said in a cold way, "Weren't you the one asking me for **archery lessons** the other day?"

There were a few gasps. Behind him, Mia and Emma **laughed.** Also, Priyanka, Nadia, Kaylee, Ben, Bekah . . . yeah. **A lot of kids laughed.**

Pebble's cheeks turned **red.** "Like I need archery lessons from a nooblord like—"

"**Enough!**" Brio shouted.

All laughter **ceased immediately.** Then Pebble **scowled** and turned back to the slimes. Like Breeze, he unleashed an arrow that had enough force to one-shot a zombie **in leather.**

No effect.

Face reflecting both anger and confusion, the **"war hero"** sent out another arrow. Again, it was as if the slime had been struck by **a snowball, not an arrow driven with Punch I.** Immune. It was like they were somehow **immune to arrows.** If watching the motionless slimes earlier was like seeing a skeleton hugging a wolf, well . . . this was like a skeleton and a wolf being bred to create something **I don't even want to imagine.** It was **the craziest** thing we'd seen yet.

There were a few seconds of total silence. Then everyone exploded into blind **panic** all at once.

"What is this?!"

"Their arrows had **no effect?!**"

"Pebble and Breeze are **the very best!** How is this even possible?!"

The mayor looked **super scared,** like a noob who'd built a small base but forgot to light one small section, and a creeper spawned there, and the base had a hole in the roof, so lightning struck the creeper, turning it into a **charged creeper,** which blew up **the noob's entire . . . base.**

Um. Never mind.
The mayor looked **really scared.**

"Are you two using **those things** correctly?!" he asked, meaning their bows.

Yeah. **Sounds about right.** A wall of slimes, backed by creepers, was slowly crawling toward Villagetown, and everyone around me was freaking out. **No, not everyone.** Breeze and Pebble had both fired shots, so I thought it'd be a good idea if **I did, too.** With **sudden anger,** I almost pulled my bowstring back all the way. **Almost.** That arrow went soaring. **There was so much power behind it.**

So much.

Huge. Huge power.

Whatever, dude. I was just trying to see if it'd flinch. Scare tactics, bro. Scare tactics. Get on my level.

Max **nudged me.**

"I think those slimes are **enhanced** somehow. Remember what I told you about **rune chambers?**"

"You mean they're enchanted?"

"Something like that."

I recalled what little Max had told me about the so-called **rune chambers.** They're extremely **advanced**—about ten times harder to construct than an enchanting table with a full set of bookshelves.

Today, everything changed.
Today, we finally realized
just what we were up against.

Everything we villagers had **learned in school** . . . everything the humans had learned in **the computer game** . . . all that was just **the basics. Baby mode.**

At the basic level, you know that a slime is **difficult to drop** because it **splits** into smaller slimes. Past that, we've learned that mobs work together—zombies and slimes stand in front of more important mobs **to protect them,** for example. But today, things were taken to **a whole new level** and training for the real stuff began. Up on that wall, we were **noobs** all over again. A few kids around me looked at the slime formation with actual tears in their eyes.

It was Drill who pulled us to our senses.

"They may be able to protect against our arrows, but **anti-sword protection** does not exist!!!" Drill shouted.

Look at Stump staring at Drill's diamond sword. We can only dream . . .

He was right. We had to go **down there.** We had to go down there and show those mobs **a few good swords.** No longer could we stand upon a wall and **fire a small forest's worth of projectiles** until nothing moved. **We had to climb down those ladders,** open that gate, and come **pouring out,** screaming, ready to defend our biome village. There were about **twenty slimes** out there, though . . . big slimes, too. **Just over two and a half blocks in size.**

I'd heard stories about how large slimes can **swallow a rabbit,** a chicken, or even a block of dirt whole. Well, I'm not that small, but then . . . **I'm not that big, either!!**

Suddenly, my legs felt **too heavy** to move. Suddenly, it was like I'd **forgotten** how to climb down ladders. I wasn't scared, though. I was probably under the effects of **some kind of magic.** Yeah.

It's the strangest thing, too. Everyone else around me was suffering from the same mysterious spell. Brio, of course, helped Drill in removing this debuff.

"**This is it,**" he said. "**This is the day we drive back the enemy. The day we've all been waiting for.**"

"**Yeah,**" Emerald muttered to Breeze. "I've been **waiting** for today . . . and would be happy to continue waiting for at least five thousand years. Possibly six. I'm patient."

The mayor **joined** Brio and Drill with his own little speech.

"If we fail today . . . we will all **become slaves.**"

You'll salute creepers.

You'll lick zombie boots.

You'll eat slimeball stew every day.

Slimeballs are used in lots of their recipes. They raise them like cows or pigs.

"Now they're telling us kids' stories to make us scared? There's no such thing as slimeball stew."

No, they're telling the truth.

"My dad knew the recipe. Right up there with slimeball stew is herb stew. **Nothing like ice cream.** Ice cream with cookie pieces . . . and bits of cake."

Protect!!! The village!!!
AHHHHHHHHHGGGGG!!!

Why is this guy still fighting with a wooden sword?!

You can't really see our mouths because of our ninja masks, but believe me, we were screaming.

EPIC BATTLE. We charged out of that **gate. Angry. Scared. Desperate.** *(Some of us were also kind of hungry.)* No one wanted to **imagine** a future in which mobs ruled. No one wanted to imagine a day when eating things like slimeball stew was **totally okay,** even fashionable. Drill surged past me, uttering the loudest battle cry, and repeated what he said earlier about how our swords would **tear through them.**

Boy, **was he wrong.** After those first few swings, we realized that our swords were doing **almost** no damage. It was like trying to drop **an ender dragon** with your **bare hands**—possible, sure, and brag-worthy to your friends, okay, but very, <u>**very time-consuming.**</u>

"It's their armor," Max said. He took another swing. "**It's the only explanation for this.**"

That was certainly **possible.** If the slimes were resistant to both arrows and melee weapons, an increase in armor was most likely the reason.

"**Hurmm.** Are they under some kind of potion effect? **Stoneskin?**"

I remembered that **battle with the zombies.** Their armor was **so high** that my sword more or less bounced off them. **It was just like this.** Still, even large slimes don't deal that much damage. All we had to do was **stay away** from the hungry-looking ones.

(For anyone who says slimes don't eat things, just come to my world. After one looks at you like you're a giant cookie with legs, you will cry. CRY.)

It would have taken time, but we could have chipped away at their life until they eventually dropped. Together, Breeze and Pebble had already removed **half** of a slime's health bar.

We were making progress!

By the way, you might be thinking to yourself, "If they wanted to reach the creepers, why didn't they just run around the slimes?"

I might go down in battle someday, but not like that.

Herobrine must have **known** that we'd try this. So he told the mobs to bring backup . . . **just in case.** Behind trees, **hidden in shadow,** they'd been waiting there the whole time. As soon as we tried moving around the slimes, they charged out. **There were so many of them.**

That Herobrine . . .

what a guy.

I hate to say this, **but he really is a genius,** you know?

He rounded up these mobs, **trained** them, and buffed them somehow. **These mobs were so noob before, you know?!** Back when I was a **little kid,** you could confuse a zombie with a dirt block. **A dirt block!**

Then they start planting trees, **spying** on us, chugging down ten potions before battle . . . **now this?!**

At that point, I understood that our strength **didn't matter at all.** Brute force wasn't the answer here. No. **We needed something else.**

A flaw. **A weakness.**
A hole in their defenses.

Something that Herobrine had **never imagined.**

We needed to think. Unfortunately, **the only thing** anyone was thinking of right then was **survival.**

"**Back inside!!**" Drill shouted. "Retreat!! **Retreat, you bedrock jockeys!!** You're moving like mine carts off rails!!"

"**The Legion never retreats!!**" Kolbert stepped forward, surveying the approaching swarm. "Actually, in this case, **I think we can make an exception.**"

Within seconds, everyone was running.

Everyone.

If a Nether portal had been around, some of us probably would have **jumped** in just to escape; we were that **terrified.**

I'll be completely up-front here: I also ran. Yes, that's right. Runt, the kid who dreams of someday becoming **Overlord Runt, ran away.**

But I stopped. For some strange reason, I just stopped running and watched everyone go. The mayor's words echoed in my head. **If we are defeated today, we will all become slaves.**

What are we doing? I thought. *We can't give up so easily. So we can't deal with the slimes, but we can still **take out the creepers**, right? With the creepers gone, those slimes won't matter at all. Of course.*

Still, I was alone. No one even looked back. No one had any second thoughts. I can't blame them. They were just **following Drill's orders.** Besides, we hadn't trained for this kind of situation. **We were totally disorganized.**

Even as the mobs **approached,** I stared at the wall. Behind me, I heard the **slimes crawling, the zombies breathing . . .**

Suddenly, I pictured all the kids who lived in my village. **Every last one.** Some I barely knew. Regardless, I knew at least one thing about each of them.

They all had **dreams.**
Hopes. Secret little wishes.
Just like me.

A kid named Tucker dreamed of having a **rabbit farm**.

A somewhat shy girl named Nessa dreamed of constructing a flying **machine**.

There must have been over **one hundred** of them, each with their own dream. Thrasher, who hoped to **improve the combat cave.** Olivine, Shelby, and Anna, who wanted to **become expert horse riders.** Enderstorm, whose goal in life was someday **mapping the End.** There was even a human named **Bobbyzilla** who hoped to **start a human city near us.** One after another, they flashed across my mind, clear, like **paintings** on a wall. If those mobs reached our village, their dreams and ideas would never turn into reality. Drago's lavaspring trap. Flamewolf's note block music machine. Skyler's restaurant featuring legendary, hard-to-craft food.

All that would be gone.
<u>**I turned around for them.**</u>

They were **the reason** I reached into my inventory. After remembering all of them, **I had come up with an answer.** For this, both sword and bow went into the extra-dimensional space of my inventory.

My bow was too bulky. I needed something **easier to handle.**

My iron sword was too heavy. I needed to replace it with **something lighter.**

Watch out, mobs! Welcome to the crash course, "**How to Destoy a Village.**" You'd better sit down, because I have some bad news. **I will be your teacher today.**

> . . . and you all get a
> **zero !!!**

I started **running** at the slime wall. As I neared it, **I threw that ender pearl high into the air.** I'd never thrown one before and had no idea just **how far up it would go.**

It felt like
forever.

I reached the slimes while the pearl was still **high in the air.** They looked at me; I looked at them. Then I started running back to the village.

At last, like an arrow that had been shot almost straight up, the ender pearl came **crashing down.** **Behind them.** And suddenly, **I was behind them,** too.

The ender pearl. 9 out of 10 ninjas recommend that you carry at least 3 at all times, whatever happens.

The ninja who doesn't agree is obviously an undercover enderman.

The slimes and creepers were **totally confused.** I had been running away from them, **and then I'd vanished.** Surely I had teleported in the direction I was running, **right?** They had no idea that I was close, just three blocks behind them. The zombies spotted me, though, since they were facing me, and swarmed in my direction. **That was right where I wanted them.** Everything was falling exactly into place. You see, I'd learned in Mob Defense that **flint and steel** could cause creepers to begin their detonation sequence. **It takes only a single hit**—against them, flint and steel might as well be **an obsidian sword** with **Bane of Plants XXVIII**. Of course, they still blow up, which is usually an undesired effect.

In this situation, though, well . . . that was more like a bonus.

Thank you, Professor Snark. (He's the new Mob Defense teacher. Former owner of that tavern the mobs blew up. Yeah. He wants revenge.)

I sprinted away just as the **first blast** went off. Unable to **react in time, the zombies were obliterated.** The large slimes broke down into **medium ones.** They were trapped in the **trench the blasts had created.** The skeletons retreated back into the woods. I'm not sure why. **They could have finished me off.** There must have been a reason . . .

I took a step back. My ears were **ringing.** My heart was **pounding.** Worse, my vision was **flashing red.** I was in so much pain. I hadn't moved entirely out of the blast radius, **so I'd taken a lot of damage.**

Before that, I'd suffered falling damage from **the ender pearl.** I'd forgotten all about that. **I was in a state of shock.** Despite this, my mind was still functioning: **There were three things left to do.**

1) Eat a **cookie.**
2) Eat **another cookie.**
3) Eat **another cookie.**

Crumbs **flying,** my hunger bar was finally topped off. **My health bar** slowly began to fill back up. I know. **Facepalm.** Not only had I forgotten about the ender pearl's damage, but I hadn't thought to **eat** before the battle. **Go ahead, laugh at me.** I'm not a noob, however. I'm only **slightly** noob—technically not a full one. No, scratch that. I'm just not **Steve level** yet, okay?

Life no longer **in the red,** I gazed at the **smoking chasm.** The slimes tried hopping out, but there was no place to climb up.

No one messes with Villagetown on my watch, **I thought.** *No one.* Well, except **ender cave spiders,** I mean. If those things start attacking us, I'm becoming a cow farmer and/or milk bucket salesman. **My shop will also be in the sky.** In a rain cloud.

For a second there, I felt **so cool.** Blown-up zombies **strewn all around.** A smoking crater full of **defeated** slimes. The wind caught the smoke just then, making it drift across me. All I needed was **the steely gaze of a warrior.**

Oh, and a cool one-liner.

"Guess you guys didn't have **Blast Protection.**"

(Wait a second. Doesn't armor protect against explosions?)

I walked over to the **edge of the pit.** A **countless** number of slimes **trembled helplessly.** Then I retrieved the lava bucket from my inventory. Due to the **incredible heat,** it was uncomfortable to hold for any length of time. A **weird** feeling came over me. It felt like I was beginning to change in some way. Yet I wasn't sure if that **change** was entirely . . . good. **The bucket trembled in my hands.** No, I wouldn't be pouring lava on those slimes. If a zombie comes charging at me, I'll give it arrows until it resembles **a guardian fish,** but this—**not for anything.**

What was my problem?
Was I getting <u>soft</u> or something?

Pebble would have done it **without a second thought,** like he was **watering** crops. I really can't explain what came over me. **It just felt wrong somehow.** Even if they were mobs. Or maybe I just thought of Jello. **Who knows?**

As the smoke **cleared,** I noticed some people standing on the wall. They were waving, shouting, pointing. They were cheering for me. **Or so I thought.**

Then I heard a crunching sound behind me . . . *tch, tch, tch* . . .

BOSS BATTLE?!

One of the things we've been learning in Mob Defense is how to identify a monster by **the sound of its footsteps.** Well, from behind me came the sound of **iron boots** across grass.

I was certain. I whirled around.

Oh.

Okay.

Not iron.

Gold, enchanted to the brim.

A zombie in a full suit, with a sword to match. **So shiny.** Apparently, that's the fashion over there in **Mob City.**

He was probably their commander. It wasn't fair. I was way too tired for **a boss fight.** Judging by the look on his face, I doubted he'd wait around for my health bar to refill. Not even if I said **"pretty please with a charged creeper head on top."** After he got within **stinky-breath** distance, the zombie spoke:

At night, when he's not harassing villagers, **Angryface McSparklebutt** stands on Mob City's tallest tower so lost mobs can find their way home.

"Ten creepers. **Not bad.** I hope that was worth **the pain** you're about to experience."

With **impossible speed,** the zombie threw a potion using his left hand. It happened so fast. In my tired state, there was **no way** I could have avoided it.

It struck me right in the chest. The glass bottle shattered against my body. Liquid splashed out and evaporated into a cloud of **grayish-blue swirls.** Surprisingly, there was no pain. **I took a step back.** It was the slowest step I'd ever taken. I might as well have been walking underwater. On top of that, my whole body felt weighed down, like I was wearing **armor made of anvils** or something.

The truth immediately became clear. The zombie had hurled a **Slowness Potion.** It must have had some kind of **enhanced** effect, too. Normally, that kind of **potion reduces your speed** to that of a crawl. This, however, was more like moving through cobwebs over soul sand over ice. Slower than that, even.

> To quote Drill,
> "like a mine cart off the rails."
> Hurggg.

Who would have expected a zombie to throw **a splash potion?** I opened my mouth to shout for help, then closed it. It'd only make me look like a **wuss.** It was pointless anyway. No doubt everyone was already charging back here. **As if that would help.** By the time they arrived, they'd find only a pile of items on the ground . . .

If he doesn't loot me first, I thought. And he probably will, if I know funky-looking zombies.

Huh?
What's that?

Something was moving slightly in the corner of my eye. It was past the zombie, past the **dirt-covered** obsidian cube. Yes, hiding behind the dirt mound was a familiar thin black form . . .

Figures.

I turned my back to the zombie.

Well, at least I can relax now.

A gentle wind drifted through the plains. In addition, the flowers around here were **quite lovely.** I closed my eyes and **took in** their fragrance. Thankfully, the zombie was **upwind.**

"**Turn around and face me,**" the mob said from behind. "You have no chance of running."

"**Running . . .**" I caught the flowery scent once more. "No, I'm afraid **you're the one who should be doing that.**"

"**Oh?**" Deep laughter erupted at my back. "**And why is that?**"

"**You'll find out soon enough.**"

To the casual observer, **I should have been afraid.** At the very least, I shouldn't have turned my back on him. This zombie was quite **powerful,** deserving of the title **"mini boss."**

Alone, the only way I could have defeated him was through superior footwork, which, given this current debuff, was **impossible.** Yet it no longer mattered. I knew who was out here. I'd caught her movements. After today, only one thing is for certain. No matter where I go or how much danger I'm in . . . **she will always be there.**

And since I had **promised to protect her** . . .

She made me
a promise
in return . . .

It was something she would **never say** in words.

But she had **always been there for me.**

SATURDAY—MORNING

Yesterday, **Breeze gave me a hug.** This morning, we actually **held hands.** Um, technically, I guess. It's really not what you're thinking.

I'm hanging this in my bedroom—and some day, I'll craft a **gold frame.**

We had a **huge** celebration.

The mayor joined us up there, along with Brio, Drill, and many other teachers. **Rose petals** were flying everywhere.

"Herobrine's forces are constantly **improving**," the mayor said, "and yesterday, their attack caught us all **off guard**. Yet two brave young villagers stood up to them. **Aspiring warriors everywhere should take notes.**"

Unbelievable, right?

You never thought you'd see the day, huh, Mr. Diary?

As of today,
Breeze and I are officially <u>**war heroes.**</u>

We received **special cloaks,** too. Wanna know what's **super amazing** about that? Our cloaks are actually **better** than the ones Pebble and Emerald have.

THE VICTORY
CLOAK
SUREFOOTED II
SAFEGUARD I

Free cool stuff. Free cool stuff. Free cool . . . **control yourself,** Runt. **Control yourself.**

The cloak comes with not one but two really amazing enchantments. **Surefooted** is for **knockback** resistance. The **usefulness** of that goes without saying.

As for **Safeguard** . . . if I have very low life, a **protective effect** will kick in. It only can do this once per full moon, **but it's still amazing.**

Kolbert was also **praised** for his defense of the village the other night. I wasn't surprised to hear Pebble's friends making jokes about his **new scarf.** Notice how I said, "**Pebble's friends,**" not "**Pebble and his friends.**" Pebble didn't say anything. He was like that since the start of the celebration. He took off with Rock when the speeches were over and it was time to eat. He seemed **angry,** although I could tell he was trying to hide it. Who cares. No need to dwell on someone like him. Good food was everywhere, and everyone else was **so happy.**

It was the biggest party we'd ever had.

Even Breeze smiled. **A rare moment.** Once more, she ran her fingers across her new cloak. She's never really had a **good item** before. Now I feel guilty for using that **ender pearl** . . .

I was thinking about what to buy as a replacement gift when Drill **came up to me.**

"**Good work out there,** Runt. Keep it up. Some day you might be calling me **endermite.**"

He shook my hand. **Thankfully** I was still wearing my hood because my cheeks must have been as **red** as a redstone block. The combat teacher raised a bottle of melon juice. A flavored drink. **The village's very first.** Something Tails and Maya had come up with.

"I don't know if you'll manage to become a **captain,** though." He took a glug. "Tough competition this year. **Pebble sure has it out for you.**"

My **mind** totally froze.

Captain?!
Why had I never heard
anything about this?!

At my obvious confusion, Drill's smile **faded.** "Never mind," he said.

He took off in a hurry after that, before I could ask any questions. Breeze turned to me as Drill vanished into the crowd. "Why do I get the **feeling** the mayor's going to make a big announcement today?" she asked.

Indeed. Even before Drill had come over, I'd sensed something **different** about the teachers today. You could see it in their expressions. Hear it in their laughter as they chatted together in small groups. **Nervousness.** Yesterday was the biggest **victory** our village has seen. Yet, at the same time, the monsters surprised us, as they always have . . . I thought about this for a moment, but yeah—you know how my mind **wanders.** Besides, Brio came over not too long after that.

"It's time," he said, in an extremely serious tone.

I blinked. "Time for what?"

Then he smiled—**but ever so slightly.**

"Time to make posters, <u>of course.</u>"

OUR WALL
WILL NEVER FALL.

So cute!

Even now it feels **unreal** to me, like this is all just a dream.

Here's another thing I thought I'd **never** actually see.

RUNT
STUDENT
LEVEL 95

MINING	87%
COMBAT	100%
TRADING	100%
FARMING	89%
BUILDING	98%
CRAFTING	97%

BOOM!!!

(Like the noise of a row of creepers thinking they're tough hiding behind slimes then getting ignited by flint and steel.)

After yesterday's battle, I've become the **second-highest student.** I passed everyone **but Breeze.** Graduation is right around the corner, too.

All I have to do is hold onto my ranking. Make sure no one **sabotages** me.

Pebble, I'm watching you . . . !!

In less than thirty minutes, Breeze and I finished **our posters.** We rejoined the **celebration** to open arms and cheers. Stump gave me a **high five.** He'd heard from the other teachers about my rank in school. He wasn't doing bad himself—**seventh place.**

I promised to help get him **up there.** How could I not? How could I fight hordes of monsters without my **BFF,** my buddy, my pal? The friend in question retrieved a **strange,** box-like item from his inventory.

"Look what I **crafted,**" he said.

I stared at the curious-looking item. I'd **never** seen anything like it before.

"The humans were telling me about how they have these things called **birthday parties,** where they eat **cake** and open **presents.** And this . . . is a **present.**" He shoved the box into my hands.

"Um, **thanks.**" I stared at the colorful item again. "So what am I supposed to do with it, exactly?"

"Well, it's like a gift—"

Gift . . . ?
As in, free cool stuff?

I immediately knew what I was supposed to do with this item.

Literally **0.0000000001** seconds after that word came out of his mouth . . .

> I knew what to do.

No, I'm not eating it—those pieces are flying from my excited little hands. By the way, you can't see my hands because **they're moving that fast.**

As **quickly** as I'd opened it, the wrapping faded to reveal . . .
a diamond.

A diamond!!!

I don't need to tell you how **super mega rare** diamonds are in my village. Even so, I'd like to share a little story to help you fully understand. There had been **a bunch of diamonds** in a **storeroom** somewhere, including the ones from that double ore vein we'd found. The mayor had been saving them for the **right time.** Before that time had come, though, **Urf** decided to **betray** us. Now there are **zero diamonds.**

The miners have been digging deeper and deeper in recent days, trying to find more. So far, **nothing.** Not a single new vein. Actually, even iron ore is rare now. In the countless layers of stone beneath our village, we've already mined up almost everything.

Even stone. We extracted a great deal of stone for our constant building, leaving huge, dark tunnels. Now those mine tunnels extend far and wide, in confusing twists, like a **giant maze** with many levels. Endless corridors of stone and gravel entirely picked clean.

In short, we're running out of **resources.** We have a continual supply of wood from the tree farm, but you can't grow new ore. For this reason, the miners grew **frantic.** The mayor has been pushing them to find more.

So they started working harder and faster. Deep down, in **Tunnel 67,** one of them opened up a hole into a **dungeon** of some kind. The chamber they broke into was **massive.** Their torchlight barely reached the ceiling. The opposite walls couldn't be seen. Just inky darkness. Whatever that place was, it was huge—and most likely filled with **treasure chests, gold, emeralds, weapons, armor, and the relics of a forgotten time.**

At first, the miners were too excited. After all, there were probably diamonds in there as well. Yet as soon as they entered, they heard this **horrible hissing.** Heard something moving in the darkness beyond their torchlight. Whatever it was, it was big. **Really big.** An enormous spider, perhaps. Or something not found in any of our books on ancient monsters.

Well, those miners aren't **noobs.** There's a reason why they're still alive after working down there for so long. They climbed right back out, sealed up that hole, and sealed off the mine tunnel leading to it—with **five layers of cobblestone,** no less.

Later, they put numerous **signs** around the area, warning everyone not to enter. **They even made a fence.**

I just hope humans don't wander by some day. They might whip out their pickaxes thinking they've found our secret stash.

I gazed down at the **diamond** resting gently in my hands. Considering all of that, I had to wonder how many emeralds Stump had to trade for it. My friend just shrugged, like he'd given me a loaf of bread instead of an **amazingly awesome** gemstone.

"I know you've been wanting **a better sword**," he said, "so I thought I'd try to help out. We should find a good crafter."

". . ."

I was so **overwhelmed** that I didn't know **what to say**. Stump seemed to understand what I was thinking, though.

"Don't worry about **repaying** me," he said. "You already have. By being **my best friend**."

"**Thanks**," I said. "I want to say—"

I paused mid-sentence. Around me, everyone else had stopped talking. One by one, their heads were slowly turning to—

THE MAYOR.

He was standing on the raised platform again. He had that **gloomy** expression he was famous for, which meant it was time to listen.

"I have one more **announcement** today," he said. "I've discussed our mob situation with the rest of the leaders, and . . ."

There was a long silence.

". . . we've decided that any student graduating this year may choose the **Path of the Sword.**"

Path.

That's what many of the older villagers call **professions.** There's the **Path of the Seed, Path of the Fishing Rod, Path of the Book and Quill,** and so on. Every year, the village holds a ceremony in which those graduating must choose one **item** from a special chest. They then hold it proudly above their head, in front of everyone, to show what **Path (and profession) they have chosen.** It's a **permanent** decision. **No looking back.** Like always, that chest will be filled with items like fishing rods, pickaxes, cobblestone, books, anvils, crafting tables, wool, leather . . .

But this year, it's also going to contain **swords.**

In other words, everyone can **become a warrior,** regardless of his or her rank. Although I was **shocked** by this big reveal, in a way, I'd always been expecting it.

With so many mobs running around now, how could five villagers keep things under control? At this point, we need a small **army.**

Maybe the humans will eventually shape up and all start fighting. Even if they did, it wouldn't be enough, and we couldn't expect them to stick around and protect us forever. No, this was something that had to happen. **It was inevitable,** really. The only real question is—what about the **top five?**

Was all of my hard work for nothing? All of my studying and constant risk-taking? A few students voiced the same **concern.** In response, the mayor nodded in a knowing way, perhaps expecting this reaction.

"Of course, those graduating with the **highest rank** will not go **unrewarded.** They'll have the option of choosing a special path.

·The Path of the Diamond.·

Now beside him, Brio spoke up.

"Diamonds are valued for their **purity, rarity, brilliance,** and **durability** . . . just like anyone who follows this Path. You will lead our warriors into battle. **You will devise combat strategies.** You will lead us to victory as **captains. Our fighting elite.**"

"And someday," Drill added, "you will lead our warriors to the **very gates of Herobrine's castle itself!**"

The mayor turned to him angrily. **"Fool!"** He glanced down at the **bottle of melon juice** Drill was holding. Then he leaned over to the combat teacher, took a sniff, and **slapped** the bottle out of his hand. **"Fermented!** I should have known!"

"Fermented?" Drill glanced at the bottle as it rolled away across the cobblestones. "What are you talking about?"

Fermented melon juice. Sure. That explained a lot. After the girls' discovery of this recipe, they'd found that adding a fermented **spider eye** would change normal melon juice into a fermented variety.

Upon drinking it, a person is affected by a debuff. The debuff makes it **hard to walk** in addition to other weird side effects, like being **extremely forgetful,** having **difficulty concentrating, slurred speech . . .**

So strange. Since this is a newly discovered recipe, and since Drill doesn't know much about **brewing or crafting,** he wouldn't have been able to tell the difference.

He could have noticed the distinctive **sour smell**, sure, but maybe he hadn't been paying attention. Of course, even Drill knew that this was **no accident.** Someone must have served him that juice on purpose.

"If I ever find out which one of you did this," he roared at the students, "after you're done doing push-ups, **you're gonna resemble a creeper!!"**

(I'm guessing he meant their arms were going to fall off?)

With how many students were **giggling** right then, there was no way to tell who the **trickster** was. But the mischievous grin Max was trying to conceal told me all **I needed to know.** I doubt he'd expected **his prank** to cause so much **chaos,** however. Anyway, it didn't matter. **The truth was already out.** The mayor **sighed** and hung his head. Brio ushered the angry combat teacher away, and **the students' laughter soon faded.**

Then there was only eerie **silence.** Perhaps all one hundred and fifty students were contemplating what Drill had blurted out.

The gates of Herobrine's castle.

The end . . . For now!!

Read the dramatic conclusion in book 4:

Diary of an 8-Bit Warrior:
Path of the Diamond

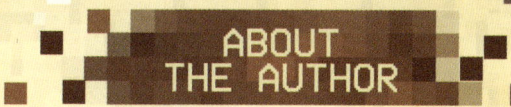

ABOUT THE AUTHOR

Cube Kid is the pen name of Erik Gunnar Taylor, a writer who has lived in Alaska his whole life. A big fan of video games—especially Minecraft—he discovered early that he also had a passion for writing fan fiction.

Cube Kid's unofficial Minecraft fan fiction series, *Diary of a Wimpy Villager*, came out as e-books in 2015 and immediately met with great success in the Minecraft community. They were published in France by 404 éditions in paperback with illustrations by Saboten and now return in this same format to Cube Kid's native country under the title *Diary of an 8-Bit Warrior*.

When not writing, Cube Kid likes to travel, putter with his car, devour fan fiction, and play his favorite video game.

DIARY OF AN 8-BIT WARRIOR

FROM SEEDS TO SWORDS

This edition © 2016 by Andrews McMeel Publishing.

All rights reserved. Printed in China. No part of this book may be used or reproduced in any manner whatsoever without written permission except in the case of reprints in the context of reviews.

Published in French under the title *Journal d'un Noob (Super-Guerrier) Tome II*
© 2016 by 404 éditions, an imprint of Édi8, Paris, France
Text © 2015 by Cube Kid, Illustration © 2016 by Saboten

Minecraft is a Notch Development AB registered trademark. This book is a work of fiction and not an official Minecraft product, nor approved by or associated with Mojang. The other names, characters, places, and plots are either imagined by the author or used fictitiously.

Andrews McMeel Publishing
a division of Andrews McMeel Universal
1130 Walnut Street, Kansas City, Missouri 64106
www.andrewsmcmeel.com

ISBN: 978-1-4494-8802-4 hardback
978-1-4494-8008-0 paperback

Library of Congress Control Number: 2016934073

Made By:
King Yip (Dongguan) Printing & Packaging Factory Ltd.
Address and place of production:
Daning Administrative District, Humen Town
Dongguan Guangdong, China 523930
Box Set 3rd printing-2/28/22

ATTENTION: SCHOOLS AND BUSINESSES
Andrews McMeel books are available at quantity discounts with bulk purchase for educational, business, or sales promotional use. For information, please e-mail the Andrews McMeel Publishing Special Sales Department: specialsales@amuniversal.com.

In memory of Lola Salines (1986-2015),
founder of 404 éditions and editor of this series,
who lost her life in the November 2015 attacks on Paris.
Thank you for believing in me.

– Cube Kid

TUESDAY

I really ended that last entry on a cliff-hanger.

I was basically like, "ZOMG! I heard a noise coming from my monster box! What am I going to do?!" and then nothing.

The end.

Boom!!!

Just like that.

Sorry.

There was a **pretty good reason**, though. After I heard that sound, I dropped my diary and dropped my quill . . . Wait. First, let me show you the blueprints of my house.

My house plan

I made this illustration so you'll have a better idea of what happened last night. **I'm such a nice villager, huh?** Let's zoom in on my bedroom.

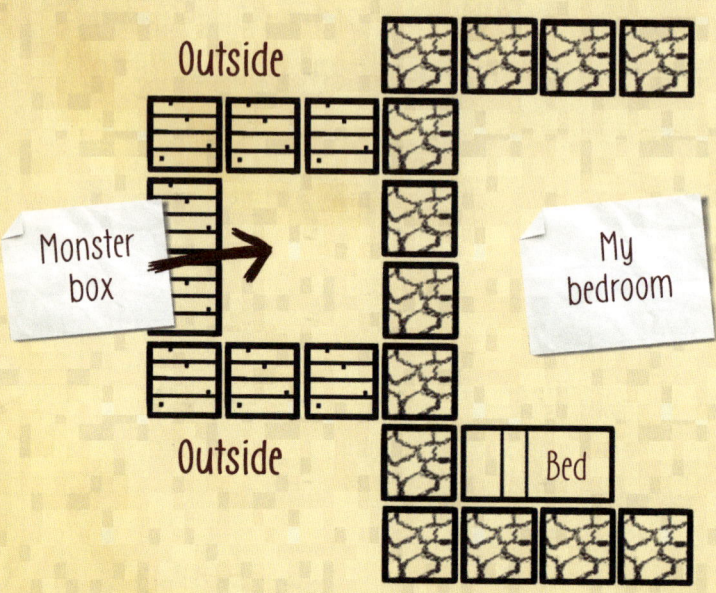

Now, I was sitting on my bed last night, and for the first time, I heard some kind of noise coming from the direction of the box. **It wasn't too loud.**

It was like a little squeaking sound. At first, I just wanted the noise to go away. Then I realized . . . **it wouldn't go away.** Whatever it was, that mob was going to *stay* in that little room **forever and ever.**

Or at least until someone let it out. I decided that *someone* should be **Steve**. It was time to tell him about . . .

my plan of getting
us students
some **real** mobs.

I ran over to his house, but he didn't want to talk.

"I can't say anything more about those trees," he said. "**Mayor's orders.**"

"I'm not here for that," I said. "Will you please come look at something? It's really—"

"Not tonight," he replied. "I'm starving. Not only do I have a growling stomach, but also my hunger bar is low. I'm still trying to accept this hunger bar, floating in the bottom of my vision as if it were part of a HUD in a computer game, as reality."

"You mean **people on Earth don't have hunger bars?**"

"**No**, Runt. People on Earth don't have hunger bars. They don't have anything floating in their vision. Speaking of hunger bars . . . would you like to join me for dinner?"

I glanced at the mushroom stew on his table.

"NiiuuuUUuu."

"Really? You sure?"

"**NNNNNooooo. Nonono.**"

I ran out of Steve's house before I grew more **nauseated**. I didn't even say good-bye.

So,
Steve wouldn't be any help.

Mike was busy at his **castle-house**, working on some new lava trap he called **"The Burninator."** His face was covered in **redstone dust**.

Stump was baking with his parents. His face was covered with the various ingredients required to craft a cake. How that had happened, I don't know, and I didn't ask.

I could've begged **Max** for help, maybe, but . . . **no. Just no.** Someone had to open that room, all right, and

I guess that someone was going to be me.

Well, I could have asked my dad for help, but what kind of warrior would do that?

No, *I* was responsible for this. I had to deal with it on my own.

I'm brave, I told myself. Dealing with an actual mob all by myself? No problem.

It's my first quest.

But how could I talk it into cooperating? "0, hai, mob. Thanks for spawning. Can you please just be a good mob and let a bunch of villager kids beat on you with wooden swords like a training dummy? It's a good job. It pays a lot. We'll even give you healing potions to heal up all the damage so we can beat on you again."

Sigh.

Scratch that: asking nicely **wouldn't work.** I'd have to scare the mob into helping out.

I went back to my house, back to my bedroom, and made my best warrior face. When that mob finally saw me, I wanted it to know that I meant business.

I never laugh.

ALL BUSINESS. ALL THE TIME.

Now, someone looking at the above picture might think I was totally scared.

Nah.

My eyebrows were like that to help block any sunlight that might have come through the window and blinded me—**an advanced warrior technique**, see?

The sweat on my brow? I was just sweating in advance, simply **forcing my body** to cool itself for the possible heated battle ahead. My face was pale because it was trying to blend in with the cobblestone wall behind me. **That's ninja stuff right there.** As for my scrunched-up mouth, um . . . I was about to make a really scary battle cry. No scared villager here.

I walked toward the wall of my room, wielding my pickaxe.

I didn't want to mine from the outside because I didn't want anyone to see what I was up to. If anyone saw me swinging away at **my own house**, they'd certainly watch, and then they'd see whatever mob was in there, and there'd be a new **"incident."**

The funny thing was . . . my hands were shaking a lot.

I began swinging at the cobblestone wall.

Each swing seemed to take forever.

My heart was pounding in my chest. That was because I was so . . . excited? **Yes, excited.**

What kind of mob will it be? I wondered. By the sound of it, I thought it might have been a **baby ghast.** Still, I'd never seen a ghast before, only read about them. As far as I knew, they could only be found in the **Nether.** Also, there was no such thing as a baby ghast, and a normal ghast wouldn't fit in a room like that.

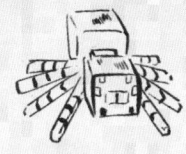

Hmm. It could have been a spider. It didn't sound like any spider I'd ever heard, though.

Then I thought, **maybe it's a CAVE spider?**

Wait, Mike was saying something about cave spiders. Something about how, upon seeing one, it's a good idea to run away, screaming like an enderman in an ocean biome. **Something about how cave spiders are about as dangerous as a charged creeper.** And how you should have a bucket of milk with you if you're crazy enough to face one, since milk cures poison . . . and cave spiders are

super . . .
Super . . .
Poisonous.

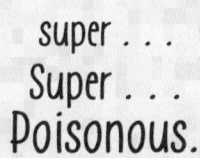

I immediately stopped swinging my pickaxe. Again—not that I was afraid. **Come on,** who's afraid of a little poison? Poison that makes your health bar tick all the way down until you have only half a heart left and you're so low that **even a chicken** could finish you off and the whole time you're writhing in pain, shivering? **Who's afraid of that? Not me.**

I was just thirsty. For some reason, I had a huge craving for milk right about then. I went and got a bucketful.

Actually, I came back with **two** buckets of milk. I set one down next to me on the bedroom floor. I held the second bucket in my other hand. My reasoning was: after I was done mining away at the wall of my bedroom to get to the box, I could pause real quick and drink some milk if I was still thirsty.

I began mining again.

While I mined, I held the milk bucket up **close to my lips**—how could anyone *not* want a big glug at a time like that?!

Not even afraid

Soon, the first block was mined. **I took out my sword,** but the squeaking had already stopped. **No sounds** came from within the box.

Whatever it was, it was waiting.

Hefting the pickaxe again, I mined away the block below **and switched back to my sword.**

Still nothing.

But after the second block, still nothing. **I waited:** sword ready, milk ready—nothing. Then, I ~~slowly crept toward~~ **charged into the box** and finally discovered what kind of mob was in there. Secretly, I had been hoping for something **epic. A poo screamer. Mungo the Overlord.** Something crazy like that.

Maybe even a **zombie cow**.
A zombie cow would have been **really cool**.

Sadly, there was no zombie cow in there.
It was . . .

. . .

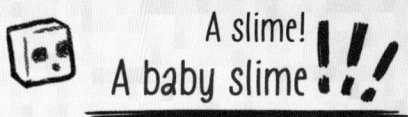
A slime! A baby slime!!!

The smallest slime I'd ever seen. It squeaked again when it saw me. **How sad!**

Here I was, hoping it'd *at least* be a **zombie, a skeleton**, something we could practice on. I thought about smashing the slime **with my pickaxe.** That way, I wouldn't get into trouble for bringing a mob into the village, my parents wouldn't freak out, no old men would scream and get the mayor, and it'd be like nothing had ever happened. No one would know.

I could just cut my losses right then and there. **Boom.** The end of **Project Mob Spawn.** **Plus,** I'd get a **slimeball** as a bonus.

I raised my pickaxe, but something **stopped** me. There was something **weird** about this slime. **It wasn't hostile.** It didn't try leaping at me. It just sat there, quivering, occasionally squeaking.

Considering that, how could I just end this creature's life?

And hey, wasn't capturing a real mob for combat class the whole reason for this in the first place?! Sure, it wasn't a zombie, but maybe this little slime had a use. We could study it, you know?

Long story short, **I have a pet now.**

I fed it a **piece of bread**, which it devoured in less than a second, and it became **my friend** immediately. *(Well, technically, it let out a huge belch and then became my friend, but yeah.)*

Actually, maybe I should refer to it as my "**test subject.**" That sounds way cooler than "**pet**," right? My bedroom could become a **laboratory.** Stump could be my assistant, and we could conduct many secret experiments on this poor mob.

Can it **laugh?** Does it sleep? Will it cry if we make scary faces at it? Will it begin writing its own diary titled *Diary of a Heroic Baby Slime?*

His future portrait

No! No! Niuuuuuuuuuuuuu!

My pet slime **won't** be attending slime school, thank you very much. He's gonna grow up to be polite and sophisticated and an all-around good citizen. **Minecraftia's first gentleman slime.**

This will be him.

By the way, I named my pet slime Jello.

I heard Steve talking about Jell-O the other day. Apparently, it's an Earth food that resembles slime. I figured it'd be a good name.

Of course, I have to tell Steve about Jello at some point. I know that. Until then, I emptied out my double chest, and it now serves as Jello's, uh, **bed, or house, or cage,** or whatever. Jello **calmed down** a few minutes after I picked it up. Now it doesn't even mind staying in the chest with the lid closed.

Sit! Stand! Roll over! Good boy!
Now, split into a bunch of smaller slimes!

Wait. Baby slimes can't do that, can they?

WEDNESDAY

So I have a pet baby slime, and there are more and more trees. **Yay.**

Fascinating. Yes, everyone's still freaking out and talking about them nonstop.

Steve still won't tell me what's going on.

Hmm. Actually, it is kind of weird, huh?

Why are the trees so important?!

Why do they matter so much?!

If anything, that forest is just **a huge source of wood** that's steadily moving closer to our village.

What's so bad about that?!

I mean, the lumberjacks in our village should rejoice. They don't even have to **move** to get their lumber anymore! They can **just sit around all day** eating pumpkin pie until the trees get close enough for them to chop.

It's like **the easiest profession** ever now!

In other news, a lot of people were talking at school today. Even though there's no official **ranking** of the students—as far as we know, anyway—everyone has a general idea of the **top ten** students because we're constantly peeking at other students' record books and sharing the information. Ask any student and they'll tell you:

- Max, obviously.
- Yours truly.
- ???
- **Pebble** *(the guy Max warned me about)*.
- **Donkey** *(Pebble's friend)*.
- **Sap** *(another member of Pebble's crew)*.
- **Stump** *(my BFF!)*.
- **Porcupine** *(haven't seen him much)*.
- **Sarabella** *(another member of my crew)*.

- **Twinkle** *(I don't know anything about him—he's really good at crafting, supposedly).*

Now, here's where the **mystery** begins. For the past week or so, everyone had assumed Pebble was the third-highest-level student. However, someone overheard a few teachers talking after school, and one of the teachers said **Pebble** was ranked *fourth*, **not third**. But no other student has scores better than Pebble, Max, and myself. **It's weird.** Of course, there are many students out there who are **very secretive** about their scores and never give anyone the chance to peek at their record book.

I really wonder who it is? Razberry?

Nah. According to Max, he's near the bottom.

So who is this **mystery guy** with scores nearly as high as my own? And why have I never noticed him before?

As for Jello, **he's sick.** I showed my secret pet to Stump, who gave him **a slice of cake.** Jello devoured it instantly, as he does with bread, then the poor slime turned bright green and became even slimier for about an hour.

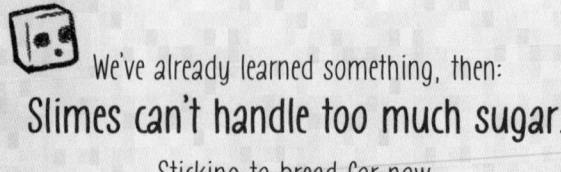 We've already learned something, then:

Slimes can't handle too much sugar.

Sticking to bread for now.

THURSDAY

Today in school, the teachers handed out **an official textbook.** It's a new book, apparently, called the **Golden Rules Handbook.** The inside cover says:

This collection of masterful secret tips and hints was brought to you by Urf, the masterful talented swordsman and combat guru.

Two diamond swords strapped across his back? **A bit much.** Yes, that's the guy who **almost** killed a zombie once. **With a stick.**

His handbook contains, without a doubt, **some of the noobiest information imaginable.** Still, it's required reading for all students. The elders figured it might have some stuff we missed. Here are a few of the handbook's more groan-inducing pearls of wisdom. *(Each "Golden Rule" comes with a mini fairy tale to teach us students a "valuable lesson.")*

GOLDEN RULE #1
ALWAYS BUILD A DOOR FOR YOUR HOUSE.

Once upon a time, a noob named Lenny never liked doors.

They got in his way.

They slowed him down.

He had to open them and close them.

Without a door for his dirt house, Lenny was free to run inside and outside without any delay.

Then one night, Lenny couldn't understand why so many zombies were approaching his house with their arms outstretched.

THE ZOMBIES AREN'T COMING IN FOR TEA, LENNY. OMG, THE ZOMBIES AREN'T COMING IN FOR TEA.

Seriously?
Who doesn't build doors?

It's interesting to note that this **Lenny** guy looks *exactly* like **Steve**. If you ask me, this is **Urf's** way of getting back at Steve for taking Urf's place as **combat teacher**.

GOLDEN RULE #3
MANAGE YOUR INVENTORY AT ALL TIMES.

There was once a fierce and powerful warrior named AxeNoob. Despite his name, he was not a noob but the greatest warrior in all the land. No one could chop like him. No one. But as he ventured through the land, he chopped and swung at every bush and flower he could. Eventually, his inventory, clogged with flowers, seeds, and other random items, drove this fearsome warrior insane.

THE GREATEST WARRIOR MINECRAFTIA HAD EVER KNOWN—ABLE TO CUT A SPIDER IN HALF WITH A SINGLE CHOP—AND YET, IT WAS THE FLOWERS THAT GOT HIM.

Looks like Urf tried to disguise Steve in this one. Anyway, I actually agree with the advice given. I used to gather seeds for my family, remember? Still do sometimes. After five hours of that, managing your inventory is like playing some kind of **puzzle game.**

GOLDEN RULE #5
DON'T MAKE A MUSHROOM FARM WITHOUT RECESSED TORCHES IN THE CEILING.

In a land far, far away, a noob named JonBo checked on his mushroom farm. When he opened the door, he saw not only red mushrooms growing on the floor, but also bright red glowing lights in the darkness beyond. The noob assumed those were special, glow-in-the-dark mushrooms. Overjoyed, he stepped into his mushroom farm to begin harvesting.

DUDE, MINECRAFTIA DOESN'T HAVE GLOW-IN-THE-DARK MUSHROOMS. THOSE ARE REDSTONE ORE VEINS, NOOB!!

GOLDEN RULE #17
DON'T MINE STONE WITH YOUR BARE HANDS.

Long, long ago, there was a noob named Steven.

He harvested wood with his bare hands because he thought using tools was a waste of resources.

Why reduce tool durability? Why bother crafting axes at all? Steven's hands had no durability, as far as he knew. Even if it took him longer to chop down trees this way, he could save materials. He could punch and punch all day and never waste any crafting tools. Steven was the kind of guy who, after loaning his best friend a wooden sword six months earlier, would ask for exactly one stick and two oak planks to be returned.

Once, Steven and two friends bought a cake together. The cake cost six emeralds and was cut into six slices. That meant each person had to pay two emeralds. However, one of Steven's cake slices was slightly smaller than the rest, so he argued that he should have to pay only 1.75 emeralds instead.

In this one, the Steve look-alike is named "Steven." **Coincidence? I don't think so.**

At this point, the elder stopped trying to disguise his obvious jealousy:

In other words, Steven was stingy. A cheapskate. A miser. The Scrooge McDuck of Minecraftia. Minus the huge pile of gold, the black top hat, and the general appearance of a cranky, humanoid duck.

Unfortunately for Steven, he began mining stone with the same miserly logic. Why build a pickaxe? He could just mine the stone with his bare hands. And so he did.

"IT'S BEEN THIRTY MINUTES, BUT I'VE ALMOST MINED THIS STONE BLOCK! BOOM! GOT IT! WAIT, WHAT?! WHERE'S MY COBBLESTONE?!"

We get it, Urf. You're angry at Steve **for taking your job.**

GOLDEN RULE #22
YOUR FISHING POLE HAS SECRET USES.

Once upon a time, in a land far, far away, oh, yes, very far indeed—approximately 18,972 blocks—Bob liked fishing.

Bob really liked fishing.

Bob really, really, really, really (really really really really really really really really really) liked fishing.

Bob was so crazy about fishing he even tried to fish in the Nether.

There were lava lakes, so why not? Maybe the Nether had some kind of fiery fish monster. Who knows? Bob sure didn't know!

Because Bob was just that crazy.
It was a
secret technique!

Bob didn't know much of anything. But he **did** know he really loved fishing. Even if he knew for a fact that there weren't any fish in those lava lakes, he'd fish in them anyway, because Bob was just that crazy.

Well, Bob fished and fished, without any luck.

He was so sad he tried reeling in a ghast just so he could say he caught something.

IT SEEMED LIKE A GOOD IDEA. ONCE HE REELED IN THE GHAST, HE COULD CHOP IT WITH HIS SWORD.

Right. A secret technique. When the ghast was only two blocks away, it spit a fireball at Bob that Bob couldn't dodge. Bob made farting/gurgling sounds as he melted into goo.

THE END.

Seriously,
this is the level of advice Urf's book contains.

Golden Rule #31 was **the worst,** though.

There wasn't a fairy tale with this one. No text at all, in fact.
Just a picture of a lily pad.

I'm . . . not sure what to make of it.

Today wasn't all bad, though. In combat class, **Steve** showed us how to never fall off a ladder. He said it's possible to dig straight down using this method. You'll never fall off. All you have to do **is crouch while holding onto the ladder.**

Actually, Steve didn't appear to be holding on to ANYTHING. The guy's a master.

FRIDAY

Today was bad.
Really bad.

After Crafting Basics, I saw **Pebble and Max** talking in the hall. At some point, Pebble took Max's record book, **tore** it into pieces, and threw the pieces **on the ground.**

"I thought you were the **top student**," Pebble said to Max, "the best of the best. What happened there, **ace**?"

Pebble's friends **Sap and Donkey stepped** on the fragments of Max's record books.

All three of them are high-level students, **just under Max and me.** They're all very skilled in combat and mining.

Strangely, Max didn't respond.

He simply stood there, **seemingly calm.**

"Aren't you gonna say something?" asked Pebble.

Donkey snickered.

"Too bad about your record book. Maybe you can tell a story about it."

I watched the whole thing in disbelief. For the longest time, I had considered Max a bully—but these guys were, like, **super bullies.**

I hadn't even noticed them before, but now they were acting like total punks.

It's just like Max said. They know graduation is coming soon **and want to finish in the top five.** The competition this year is getting **really insane . . .**

Pebble rammed his shoulder into Max and said something. He kept his voice low. I had to strain to hear it:

"Better not participate in the next mining test, ace," Pebble said. "Wouldn't want you to get **hurt.**"

Max still said nothing, looking down at the pieces of his record book. **I had to step up and say something.**

I walked up next to Max and nudged him with my elbow. "You know, the elders said the rising ocean levels were due to the melting ice plains biomes. But as it turns out, it was because of Pebble's river of tears after he **bombed** the last test."

Pebble's face momentarily resembled **a creeper's**.

Yeah. Saying that was a bad idea.

"**Well, look at that,**" he said. "Just who I wanted to see next!"

Sap and Donkey sprinted over to me, lifted me up by the robes, and took **my record book out.**

Pebble grabbed it and **tore it into tiny little pieces.**

It happened so fast!

It was as if part of my **body had been torn up.** I'll admit **I nearly cried** staring down at my shattered record book. All that hard work . . . Gone. *(At least, until I coughed up the emeralds for a new one. Those punks.)*

The three **laughed** and walked off.

I glanced down at the **purple fragments**.

The pieces crumbled into bright violet dust—the magical energy of the book's enchantment. The dust soon faded away . . .

I approached Max. He was picking up the pieces of his own book. Not that it mattered. **The book was no longer functioning.**

"So you were telling the truth," I said. "Those guys really have it out for us."

"Yeah. Told you this is bad."

"So, what are you gonna do?" I asked.

"Nothing."

"What about our record books? We can get new ones. Let's go to the **head teacher** and pay up. Tomorrow, **we'll flash them in Pebble's face** and thank him for making us get new, shiny record books. And then we can argue with each other about how low our scores are."

Max shook his head. "Didn't you hear? They raised the price on them. They're **fifty emeralds** now. Why do you think those guys did that?"

What?!

Fifty emeralds?!
Wow, I thought, this is bad.
Where am I gonna get fifty emeralds?

"What about your parents?" I asked. "I thought your family was **wealthy.** Say, can I . . . **get a loan?**"

"Sorry, Runt, but after the pickaxe incident, **they cut me off. I'm broke. They aren't even giving me lunch emeralds. Razberry's been sharing his with me.**"

"**We've gotta get back at them,**" I said.

"No, I think I'm out." Max slipped the pieces of his record book into a pocket of his robe.

"I'm just gonna tread water from now on. After all, I wanted to be a librarian, remember? Striving to be a warrior . . . **honestly,** it's not worth dying over. Didn't you hear what he said about the mining test? Pebble's father is gonna rig the test somehow."

"How would his father manage to rig the test like that, though?"

Max gave me that cold look again.

"**You really don't get it, buddy boy.** Pebble's family goes way back. They've got connections. **His father is best friends with the mayor and most of the elders.** He's also the **head miner.** So, when the school holds that mining test, who do you think the teachers are going to ask for advice?"

"Pebble's father."

"**Right.** He'll probably suggest an area with a lot of sand and gravel. **A dangerous area.** An area he knows. And he'll fill Pebble in on where to go."

I recalled what Max had said earlier . . . Something about **a cave-in.**
Gravel or sand from up above could come down and **crush someone** . . . **Hurrrrrrg.**

Things were getting **so serious.**

Bullies tearing up record books.

Powerful families **pulling strings** behind the scenes.

The mayor and the elders, who won't tell us anything about the trees.

The mobs, who never came back after Steve and Mike kicked their behinds. Suddenly, **I opened my mouth** . . . and said something I never thought I'd say.

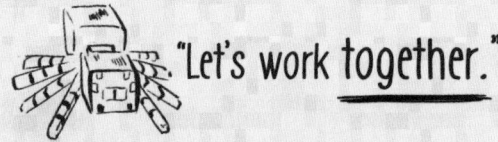

"Let's work <u>**together.**</u>"

It seemed my words **shocked** Max as much as they did me.
He lowered his glasses.

"W-what did you say?!"

"You might've **pulled a lot of pranks on me,**" I said, "but those guys . . . if they become warriors, I'll never feel safe. In some ways, **they're worse than the mobs!** Anyway, it's just like you said. If they're out to get us, then we've gotta stick together."

"You sure about this?"

"**Yeah.** But if you pull any tricks, Stump and I are gonna harass you until you're rank 150. **Got it?**"

"Don't worry about that," he said. "**No tricks. I promise.**"

He paused, as if thinking about something, then said, "I have an idea."

"What idea, **hurrrrr?**"

"I need some time. I'm still not sure how well it'll work. Over the weekend, **gather as much sand as you can.** We'll discuss it next Friday."

"Sand?"

"Just trust me."

Hmm.
Trusting Max . . . It seems difficult.
But I suppose I need him.
And then, **he needs me**, too.

SATURDAY

I needed to clear my head after yesterday. So this morning, I took off for the park. **Alone. Yes, our village has a park.** It's pretty much like a forest near the middle of our village. People go there to relax, but **it's actually a tree farm so we can harvest wood safely** without ever stepping outside the walls. There are also lots of flowers for dyes.

An outsider noob came out here long ago, wanting to dye his armor red. But I guess this world is different from the game he used to play . . . **because his armor turned pink** instead.

"Don't worry, bro. You look cool. You look cool."

So there I was deep inside the park, enjoying the **beautiful scenery.** At one point, I had the urge to check my record book—an instinct by now—but it wasn't there. **Fifty emeralds . . .** Would I ever be able to earn that many? Maybe I could **sell Jello** to some old rich guy who likes exotic pets . . . Then I had a weird feeling—you know, that creepy feeling, like you're being watched? **Yeah. That one.**

Moments later, I caught sight of something out of the corner of my eye. Like a shadow. **So weird.**

It vanished as quickly as it had appeared.

Of course, I immediately thought of the **"Village Creeper"** that supposedly sneaks around in our village. **Great.** Things sure were getting better. Yesterday, **I was mugged by a bunch of punks.** Today, I was all alone in the park, with a creeper hunting me.

Not good!!!

I heard the rustle of grass behind me. **I whirled around** . . . but there was nothing. Just the beautiful, flowery forest.

Was I seeing things? **Hearing things?** Maybe I was too stressed out. I shook my head, rubbed my eyes. And when I reopened them . . . **a girl was standing before me.**

I knew her. **Breeze.** She was a student. I'd seen her from time to time, although we didn't have many of the same classes and she usually kept to herself. She was pretty **shy.** Even so, she was one of those students who asked me questions after I aced a building or trading test. She **smiled.** I couldn't return the expression. Not today. What did she want, anyway? Why was she following me?

Honestly, it was a <u>little creepy.</u>

"I haven't seen you in a few days," she said. "What have you been up to?"

Um . . . yeah. She was acting like we were **old friends** or something.

"I'm **busy**," I said.

"You always say that," she said, her voice cool. "Anyway, you don't seem busy. Let's hang out."

"No, thanks."

Her smile faded. "What happened? **You seem so upset.**"

There was no way I was going to tell her about yesterday. I'd only talked to her a few times before, and it was mostly just stuff like, **"I can't teach you; uh, I'm sick tomorrow."**

Then again, from what I know, she comes from a **wealthy family**, like Max.

Her parents are miners. Supposedly, they once **found a cave loaded with diamonds.**

I could have asked her for a loan, perhaps, but . . . **no.** I didn't want to be in debt to a stranger.

"I just wanna be left alone," I said. **"Okay? Is that possible?"**

She nodded and **zoomed off into the trees.** She ran so fast. In her black outfit, she looked like a blurred shadow. I thought I saw tears in the corners of her eyes. Or did I imagine that? What's with that strange girl? I thought. Come to think of it, I've seen her a lot recently. At the blacksmith. Near the well. In the hallways at school. But always from a distance. **Watching me. Seriously weird.** Why was she following me like that?

Whatever.
I whipped out my shovel and within
thirty minutes had gathered half a stack of sand.

SUNDAY

I had my Sunday all **planned out.**
   Step 1: Feed the slime.
   Step 2: Go bug Steve and Mike on their day off!

I tossed Jello a bread loaf, grabbed my shovel, and ran out the door. *(Hopefully, my parents wouldn't discover my new pet.)*

Within minutes, I was at **Steve's** house. He and Mike were both there. Mike was seated at the table, **looking a little angry,** or **at least not happy.**

Steve was hunched over a furnace, his face blank, as if he was thinking very hard about something.

I decided to break the silence with a friendly greeting:

"Hey, guys. **How's the forest?"**

Before, villagers often asked something like "How's the weather?" but lately it's **"How's the forest?"** Meaning that **weird** forest in the east. Now, I didn't ask this to try to get Mike and Steve to tell me about their secret. It was just a greeting, **I swear!** But the two outsiders **glared at me.**

"We still can't tell you anything," Mike said. "So stop asking, buddy boy."

"That's fine," I said. "I have **a secret of my own.**"

Steve looked up from the furnace.

"What secret?"

"**Ohhhhhhh nothing.** But I bet it's more interesting than a bunch of trees."

Mike smirked.

"You'd be surprised."

Suddenly, Steve **pounded** the furnace with his fist.

"I can't stop thinking about **pizza! Pepperoni. Cheese.** Oh, I'd give anything for some black **olives!**"

"I'm not a fan of olives, myself," said Mike.

I stared at both of them.

"What are you guys talking about, **hurrrr?**"

Mike gave me a pitying look, as if I wouldn't understand a thing, even if he explained. Steve ignored me. **There was a feverish gleam in his eyes.**

"Those mobs, they're so **smart**," he said. "This is how they get you . . . they made us afraid . . . holed us up in this village . . . limited our food supply . . ."

There was an **awkward silence,** then Steve spoke up again.

"Every day it's bread, bread, bread . . . and if you're lucky, steak and potatoes. **I'm sick of it!**"

"I'm sick of you talking about it," Mike said.

Steve stepped over to the crafting table. A huge amount of food items had been piled onto that massive chunk of wood.

"**Pizza**," he said. "What about **pizza**? Is it possible? Maybe if we just arrange these bread loaves like so . . ."

Mike **rolled his eyes**.

"Dude. No tomatoes. No tomato sauce."

"**Burritos?**"

"No flour. No **tortillas**."

As they talked—naming an exhaustive list of foods I'd never heard of—I said nothing, totally confused.

"How about an **omelet?**" Steve asked. "We've got eggs! We've got mushrooms!"

Mike closed his eyes this time.

"Again, I've already tried that, man. Every possible configuration. Eggs with more eggs. Eggs with milk. Eggs with mushrooms. Even eggs with a potato."

Steve gasped. "Omelets with diced potato chunks?! Who does that?! **Wait,** what am I saying?! I'd settle for that!"

"You're really freaking out, dude. **Chill.**"

"How about cheese?"

"Nope."

"Butter?"

"Went through five buckets of milk trying to figure that one out."

The desperation in Steve's voice was heavy as he said,
"Apple . . . pie?"

Mike shrugged. "It should be possible, considering the fact that this world has apples, pumpkins, and pumpkin pie. However . . ."

"No apple pie?! And we can't even have toast! **Not even dry toast without any butter!** We have loaves of bread, right? But the furnaces won't toast the bread, and swords won't cut the loaves! No matter how many times I try, the bread just **crumbles!**"

More silence.
Mike and I exchanged **worried glances**.

Steve **scratched** his chin.

"And yet, they have **ice cream**, these villagers. Many flavors, too. But not the ones I like! **What kind of world is this?!**"

Mike rose up from his chair and looked out the window.

"A Minecraft world."

"You know, I've been thinking about quitting," Steve said. "Quitting teaching and building a **redstone** robot."

"And what would the purpose of this . . . **redstone robot** be, Steve?"

"A food-crafting robot. **Night and day**, it'd set random types of food on the crafting table, until it finally found a new recipe."

"That's the **most ridiculous** thing I've ever heard you say," Mike said, turning back to the window. "Not even **Marky** could build something like that! **And the guy's a crafting master!**"

Steve's eyes lit up.

"Marky! Yes! If only **Marky** was here! He'd know **how to craft pizza!**"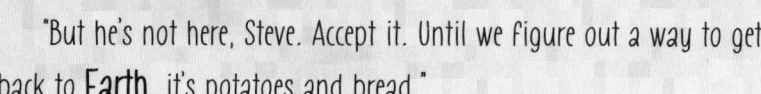

"But he's not here, Steve. Accept it. Until we figure out a way to get back to **Earth**, it's potatoes and bread."

"I'll teach a golem to craft food for me!"

"**No, you won't.**"

"Yes, I will! It will craft while I sleep!"

Mike groaned, but Steve just laughed.

"Supreme pizza, **here I come!!**"

Yeah.

Needless to say, I didn't hang around there much longer. I understood what was going on, though. Steve missed **Earth food**, stuff like **pizza** and **hamburgers**, things I've never eaten before. **I guess they must taste amazing.**

Still, I don't get it—what's wrong with our ice cream? Maybe he tried that **nasty Creeper Crunch?**

 It is really **gross.**

Later, I went back to the park with Stump. That's where the ice cream shop is.

While Stump and I got ice cream,
I felt like someone was watching me again.
I didn't see anyone, though.

MONDAY

Dear Diary,

I like you, diary, I really do. But I can only assume you're going to suffer the same fate as my **record book.** Torn to pieces, crumbling into nothingness. You see, Pebble and his friends shook me down today. Took everything I had, from my **sword** to my **lunch emeralds.** Well, **almost everything.** Thankfully, **Urf** arrived just before they grabbed you, diary. But it's only a matter of time.

What can I do?
There are three of them, and they're
a lot bigger than I am.

Stump tried to **help out.** I warned him not to. He's probably next on their list. Even though Stump is the **seventh-highest-level student,** he's still a threat.

Worse yet, that Porcupine guy has apparently joined Pebble's crew. Porcupine saw Pebble pushing me around and figured he'd be better off with **the punks.**

So all the top students . . . they're taking sides. You're either on **my crew** or on **Pebble's** . . . and it's easy to see which crew is the strongest.

I saw **Sarabella** hanging out with **Donkey.** She gave me a **guilty** look.

"I'm sorry," she said later. "It's just . . . if I keep talking to you, they'll **harass** me, too, you know? I just wanna graduate with good scores."

I looked away.

"Yeah. **It's fine.**"

"We're still friends, right?"

"Sure."

I totally understand, though. I'm not bitter. <u>Team Runt</u> is a sinking ship.

TUESDAY

Didn't bring the diary to school today. **Didn't bring anything.** Except a **carrot.** My lunch.

A single carrot. Not two carrots, not a carrot and an apple. A single carrot. THAT'S POOR, OKAY?!

So go ahead. Beat me up. Take everything in my inventory. **Well, today,** Team Pebble tried just that.

"GIMME THAT CARROT!!!"

But when they grabbed me, I immediately whipped out my carrot and ate it as fast as I could. They struggled to take **my only food item** away from me. I chomped down faster. Little pieces of carrot went flying everywhere.

OM-NOM-NOM-**NOM**-NOM.

"Get that carrot!"

"**Grab it!**"

But I managed to eat it before they took it from me.

"**You little noob!**" shouted Pebble.

Even as they roughed me up, **I smiled.**

It was a **small little victory** today. They couldn't do anything to me. The only item they could have taken I ate right in front of them.

Good game. Noobs.

WEDNESDAY

OOF!
OOF!

Those sounds came from me. Team Pebble walked up and said they weren't going to steal anything today; they were going to *give* me something. They gave me a **pumpkin**, all right— jammed it down over my head and began punching me. "Don't just stand there!! **You're a pumpkin zombie, little noob!!** It's combat training!!"

OOF!!
OOF!!
OOF!!

I don't want to write much today.

I . . . will . . . get . . . my . . . **revenge.**

But I can't feel sorry for myself. The things they did to Max were even worse.

Really wish he'd hurry up
with that <u>big idea of his.</u>

THURSDAY

"You like eating things, **do you?!** Let's see if you can eat this **whole cake!!**"

That about describes my day. By the way, that wasn't their cake. It was Stump's. Something he'd made in Crafting Basics.

Max.
Please.
Hurry. Up.

FRIDAY

Pebble **didn't try** anything today. It's because a new **rumor** has been spreading through the school—in fact, spreading through the **entire village**. Supposedly, someone spotted **an enderman** in the village. A friendly enderman who only wanted to **trade**. He was looking for a potion. And not just any potion, but a **Potion of Water Resistance**. This isn't something that prevents drowning damage but . . . damage from water. I've never heard of such a potion, and neither has anyone I've talked to. Yet . . . that doesn't mean such a potion doesn't exist.

Now, here's the thing.

The enderman is willing to pay **five hundred emeralds** for a stack of such potions. **Five hundred emeralds.** This enderman is rich, apparently. **Of course,** everyone in the village started freaking out. Especially the kids at school.

"We've **gotta find out** how to craft that potion!!"

"We've gotta make some before that enderman returns to the village!!"

"With that many emeralds, I can buy an **enchanted diamond sword!!**"

Like that. Forget the **trees**—the enderman was all anyone was talking about. As the rumor goes, the enderman is a world traveler and has a dream of becoming a **professional swimmer. The problem** with that, obviously, is that water is like **acid** to endermen. They can't even be out in the rain, much less swim for any length of time. But this Potion of Water Resistance would fix that, **I guess.**

"Finally! My dream will come true!!"
GLUGGLUG GLUGGLUGGLUG.

SATURDAY

The rumors were flying even more today.

People kept talking about what they were going to do with their massive pile of emeralds once they discovered how to brew that potion. That girl **Breeze** came up and asked me about it. She keeps talking to me every chance she gets. **What is her problem?!**

Later, I ran into Max. He apologized for being late. While we stood there in the streets, we heard kids nearby talking about the enderman. Max gave me **an evil grin.**

Suddenly, **I understood—he** was the one responsible for those rumors. That meant the rumors weren't true. The enderman didn't actually exist. The world-traveling enderman was just another one of **Max's creations,**

like the **poo screamer.**

Yes, Max was at it again with his crazy tales—and this time, I didn't mind them at all. It's like this: Everyone's gonna be crafting potions for at least the next few days, experimenting, trying to figure out how to make that special potion. And what do you need when crafting a bunch of potions? **Empty glass bottles.**

"Supply and demand, buddy boy. Supply and demand."

Max went around the village and **dug up every sandy area** he could. I dug up a bunch myself in the park. We figure we probably have at least **75% of the village's available sand.** At least, the easy-to-find stuff.

When people run out of bottles, they'll have no option but to come crawling to us. **We'll be able to charge anything we want for them.**

I have to admit, this plan of Max's is pretty brilliant.

SUNDAY

This morning, I finished reading Urf's *Golden Rules Handbook*. At the end, there was an advertisement for his next book . . .

The Ultimate Legendary Handbook.

MOBS HATE HIM!

THIS TOP WARRIOR HAS DISCOVERED ONE WEIRD TRICK TO BEAT ANY MOB.

LEARN THE SECRET TECHNIQUE THAT NINJAS AND THE GOVERNMENT DON'T WANT YOU TO KNOW ABOUT.

THIS HANDBOOK HAS ALREADY BEEN BANNED IN SEVEN VILLAGES.

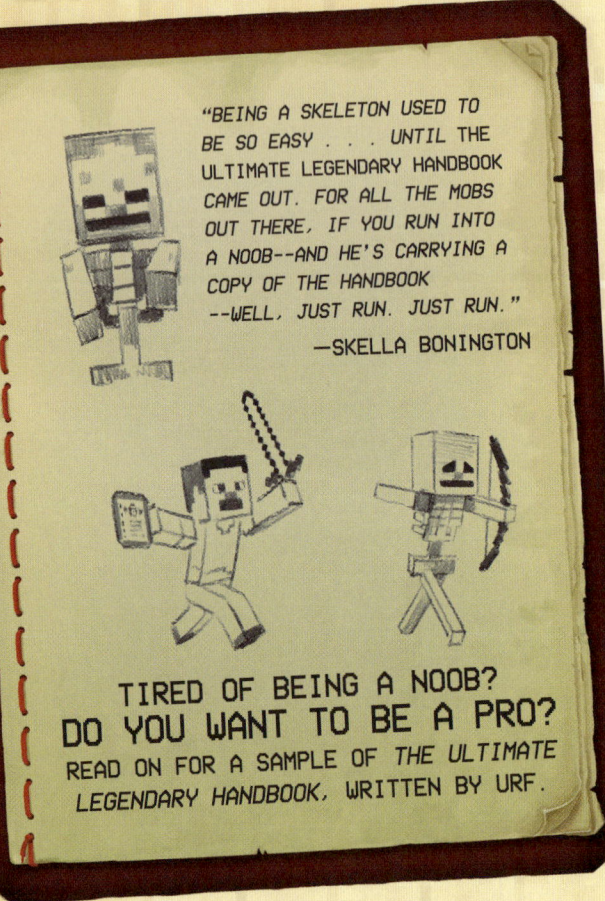

"BEING A SKELETON USED TO BE SO EASY . . . UNTIL THE ULTIMATE LEGENDARY HANDBOOK CAME OUT. FOR ALL THE MOBS OUT THERE, IF YOU RUN INTO A NOOB--AND HE'S CARRYING A COPY OF THE HANDBOOK --WELL, JUST RUN. JUST RUN."

—SKELLA BONINGTON

TIRED OF BEING A NOOB?
DO YOU WANT TO BE A PRO?
READ ON FOR A SAMPLE OF *THE ULTIMATE LEGENDARY HANDBOOK*, WRITTEN BY URF.

ULTIMATE LEGENDARY SECRET #1:
USE A SWORD TO ATTACK MOBS.

Once upon a time, a noob named Mike was a total noob. He was almost as noob as Steve the Noob, who was the mayor of Noobtown. Mike was so noob that he didn't use a sword. He thought using a stick as a weapon would be almost as good.

"HMM. I GUESS THIS SWORD COULD USE SOME ENCHANTING."

ULTIMATE LEGENDARY SECRET #2:

EVEN MUNGO IS AFRAID OF *THE ULTIMATE LEGENDARY HANDBOOK*.

"MUNGO SCARED.

URF BOOK MAKE TINY MAN TOO STRONG.
SO, MUNGO BECOME FARM MAN.

MUNGO SAD NOW.

MUNGO NO LIKE FARM WORK.
MUNGO NO LIKE EAT ORANGE THINGS.
AND BROWN THINGS NO TASTE GOOD!!
BUT EASIER THAN EAT TINY MAN. URF
BOOK MAKE TINY MAN TOO SMART.
OK, BYE. MUNGO GO EAT PIE-PIE NOW."

ULTIMATE LEGENDARY SECRET #3:
URF IS WAY COOLER THAN STEVE.

"I used to be a bad warrior . . . For example, I once hugged a creeper because it looked sad and I thought it needed a hug.

"But not any longer. After reading *The Ultimate Legendary Handbook*, I'm now a combat teacher.

"Urf taught me everything I know and I'm so thankful for that.

"Someday, I hope to be as amazing as Urf. It's not possible, but I still try."

—STEVE

Ahem. Runt here.

My first thought upon reading this advertisement was:

What?! Steve wouldn't say something like that! **Urf clearly made that up!**

Hurrrr. Urf better be careful. When Steve finds out about this—and he will—he's gonna **explode** like a **mountain made of TNT**—and not just *any* mountain made of TNT, but one inhabited **by creepers.**

Boom Mountain. It makes the Nether look like a Flower Forest.

Anyway, what am I doing thinking about **Urf** and **Boom Mountain**?! Today was a **big day!** Max came up with a **clever plan** to earn the emeralds we need to buy new record books. It was pretty simple.

1) Max cooked up a story about an **enderman** who wants to be a professional swimmer and is willing to pay **five hundred emeralds** for a Potion of Water Resistance *(so he doesn't burn while in the water).*

2) After hearing about the enderman, kids at school **freaked out.** They wanted to **brew that potion.** Kids kept bugging the brewing teacher about it. *"How do I craft one?" "What's the secret recipe?"* And so on.

3) Max and I dug up **most of the sand** around the village. *(You need sand to make glass, glass to craft bottles, and bottles to brew potions.)*

4) Yesterday, we spent hours **crafting bottles** and set up a stand to sell them:

BOTTLES
SEVEN EMERALDS
PER STACK

Stump wasn't interested in selling bottles, but he brought a **bunch of cakes**. He didn't sell many . . . and I'm *so glad he didn't*.

Because an hour after we set up our stand, we were so **swamped** with customers there was no way we could take a **lunch break**.

Stump's cakes were the only food we had. *(Even if we had remembered to bring lunches, our inventories were too clogged with bottles.)*

Within an hour, we made **twenty-one emeralds!** A bunch of other kids just stood around, though, asking us to lower our price.

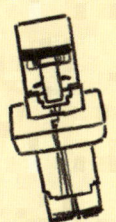 What can I say?
Villagers will be villagers.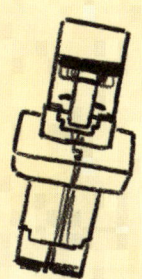

I had that creepy feeling that someone was **watching me** again. Which was **strange**, because obviously, a lot of people were watching me. I wonder why I had that feeling?

Anyway, it seemed we were going to make the **hundred emeralds** we needed. Sadly, things never come easy for me, and today was no exception.

There was a shout nearby.

You've got to be kidding me . . .

It was Pebble. "**Finest-quality** bottles!" he called out. "Only **six emeralds** per stack! Get 'em while ya can, folks!"

People rushed over to his little stand—a flood of **cries, shouts,** and **elbows.** Through the crowd, I saw Pebble give me a wink.

Urg!!!

What a copycat. His bottle stand was like a smaller version of ours. All he did was copy us . . . and offer a **slightly lower price.**

What a poo screamer. I put up a new sign:

> BOTTLES
> FIVE EMERALDS
> PER STACK

Boom!!!

That'll fix him, I thought.

In response, Pebble dropped his price to **four.**

So, we went to **three.**
Then *he* went to **two** . . .

It was a price war—**Bottle Mart versus Dork Depot.** Finally, I dropped our price to **one emerald per stack.** There was no way he could go any lower, right? He'd have to match our price, and we'd get half the customers. **Right?**

I . . . **couldn't believe** what that punk did next.

Free?!
Seriously?!

I'm gonna **hurgg,** I thought.
Yeah. I can definitely feel **a big one coming on.**
Okay.
Calm down.
Calm down.

I stood there until I no longer had the urge to **hurgg**.

Then an idea suddenly hit me, like lightning **hitting** a pig and turning it into a **zombie pigman.** Except, uh . . . I'm not a zombie pigman. I'm not a pig, either. **Gah.** Never mind.

Anyway . . . **My idea was this:** I had managed to peek at **Pebble's record book** earlier. By doing that, **I learned his weakness**. You see, his crafting score is his lowest score. Brewing is a subskill of crafting, which means he doesn't know how to brew very well.

Why does that matter?

It will become clear **soon enough.**

I turned to my friends: "Max, go to school and grab a brewing stand. Stump, go to my room and grab **two nether warts, two rabbit's feet,** and **a water bucket. Oh,** and **a pinch of glowstone dust.**"

Looking at their faces, you would have thought I'd just invited them to a slumber party in the Nether or something.

"Huh?! Why?!"

"Because it's time to **humiliate** our competition," I said. "And don't forget the glowstone!!"

Away they went. **I left our bottle stand** and walked into the crowd.

"Everyone, if I may have your attention," I called out. "It seems there's only one way to determine who has the highest-quality bottles: **a brew-off!!!**"

People turned to me with confused looks.

"A brew-off?"

"Hurrr? What's that?"

"It's like a dance-off," I said, "except with brewing, not dancing. **A competition.**" The crowd broke into low murmurs. Hushed excitement. **Laughter.** Even a few **cheers.**

Pebble scowled and pushed through the crowd. "So, it's a brew-off you want, eh, **buddy boy?!** You don't have a brewing stand!"

Then someone cleared his throat. "Ahem." Max was standing behind Pebble, brewing stand in hand. He must have **sprinted** the whole way. He set it down between Pebble and me.

I smirked. **"You were saying?"**

Beads of sweat formed across Pebble's brow.

"Err . . . **ahh** . . . **well, y-you** need more than just a brewing stand! You need **ingredients** too! Wanna brew Air Potions, **do ya?**"

Grrrrrrr. He can laugh all he wants, I thought, but if my idea works, he's gonna be **the laughingstock of the whole school.**

Thankfully, Stump showed up moments later with **all the ingredients** and a water bucket in hand. "Here you go, cap'n."

"Looks like we have **everything** we need," I said, looking Pebble **in the eye.**

Pebble **swallowed** nervously and **wiped his brow.**

"W-well, yes," he said, "but I w-wouldn't wanna **embarrass** you in front of a-all these kids! You sure you want that?"

"**Oh, I'm sure,**" I said, with a nod.

I gave Pebble one nether wart and one rabbit's foot. Then Stump **dug a hole** and emptied the bucket into it.

From left to right: Stump, Runt, Max, and Pebble. Hurrm. Again, it felt like someone was watching me . . .

I addressed the crowd.
"**The brew-off has officially begun!**"

Everyone backed up to watch the show. The chatter grew louder. I raised **an empty bottle.**

"We will test the quality of our bottles by brewing Potions of Leaping," I said. "We'll then **drink our potions,** and the one who **jumps the highest . . .**"

Of course, even if the glass I'd used had somehow been of higher quality, it wouldn't have affected the potion at all. You needed **extra ingredients** for that, like **redstone or glowstone dust.**

I was just **bluffing.**

A lot of the people in the crowd didn't seem to catch on to this. Probably most of them hadn't paid too much attention in brewing class. Or perhaps they questioned it but weren't sure enough to say anything. After all, Stump was nearby, and his crafting score was **really high.**

Pebble stepped up to the brewing stand.

"I'll show you how it's done, kid."

He whipped out one of his bottles, filled it with water, brewed an Awkward Potion with nether wart, and finally, a **Potion of Leaping** using a **rabbit's foot.**

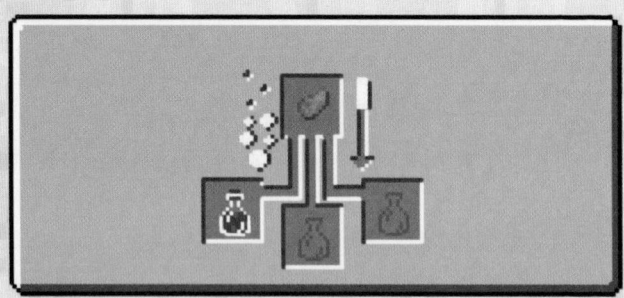

Ta-daaa

The brewing stand bubbled away. After Pebble's potion finished brewing, he held it up **triumphantly.**

There were a few **cheers**—and gasps—from some of the younger kids. It might have been the **first time** they'd ever seen a potion.

"Wow!"

"Cool!"

"It's so shiny!"

I nudged Stump.

"Hey!" I whispered. "**Dust me!**"

"Oh. Right."

Stump slipped me some **glowstone** dust. Luckily, Pebble kept showing off his potion to the crowd.

"**See that?** The **best** bottles in the village! Forget those **noobs!** Use my bottles or don't brew anything!!"

All eyes were on him at that point, which allowed me to add some glowstone to my Potion of Leaping without anyone noticing.

Within ten or so seconds, I brewed . . .

. . . a Potion of Leaping II:

for when you absolutely, positively need to **bounce around** like a slime.

This would allow me to jump higher than Pebble, since he'd only brewed **a standard Potion of Leaping.**

Yeah, **I cheated.**

But you know what? **That guy deserved it.** Besides, when the mobs come knocking on our iron doors again, I highly doubt they're going to **play fair** . . .

As soon as I brewed my potion, the crowd grew noisier. **They wanted us to chug.** Pebble slammed down his potion, then tossed the bottle aside and glared at me.

"Bottoms up, noob."

I did the same. Immediately after, I felt **sick,** as if I'd eaten too much ice cream or something.

Pebble jumped up into the air. He jumped maybe **half a block** higher than normal, landed, and jumped again.

"What's up, kid?!"

I grinned and said, "About to set **a new record,** that's what's up."

"Yeah, yeah. Let's see it."

"On three," I said. "One, two, thr— eeeeeEEEEEEEEEEEEEEEEEEEEE EEEeeeeeeeeee . . ." (As I jumped, the word "three" turned into a thin, catlike scream.)

You see, I jumped kinda high. Like, **really high** . . . Honestly, there were better words than **"jump"** to describe what I was doing, really. Like **"fly."**

I'll admit it—**I was terrified**. Terrified and **confused**.

Why did I leap so high? **A Potion of Leaping II** should have made me jump one and a half blocks higher . . . **not one hundred.**

"STUMP!! I SAID A PINCH OF GLOWSTONE!! A PINCH!!"

That was when I saw it. **The forest.**

Of course, **it had grown** over the past few days. From up here, I could see how **massive** it really was. Dark oak trees, tall and thick, stretching forever into the horizon.

I thought I saw **something moving there.** Whatever it was, **it was big,** but I saw it for only a second—then the clouds blocked my view.

Had I **imagined** it?

I **tore** my gaze away.

I didn't have time to dwell on anything except trying to **survive**. I realized I had no **Feather Falling** effect, which was required to survive landing after such a jump.

I glanced around, looking for a nearby pool, a canal. **Anything.** As luck would have it, the roof on one of our wells had been taken down. Maybe the builders were about to repair it, or maybe some **noob** had come into the village and taken it. It seemed like a better spot to land than in the middle of some **farmer's crop**.

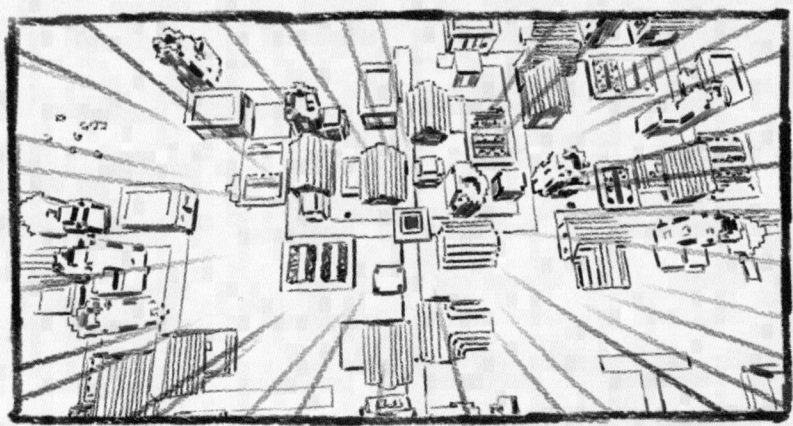

Falling, **falling, falling.** This is how it feels to be a raindrop.

Falling, falling, falling.

Faster than the prices at my bottle shop.

I'd never been **this afraid** before.

The kind of terror where time seems to **slow down** and the color drains from your vision. The whole thing **had a dream-like quality.** One moment, I'm about to show a punk from school why I'm the **number-two student.** The next, I'm flying through the clouds, where even bats won't go . . .

I suppose
these things happen.

MONDAY

First, the good news:
I survived.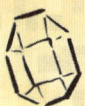

Didn't take **a single heart's worth of damage**. On top of that, I got **a new record book** and still have **seventeen emeralds left over.** Apparently, after I jumped **over eighty blocks up**, the rest of our bottles sold out in less than a minute.

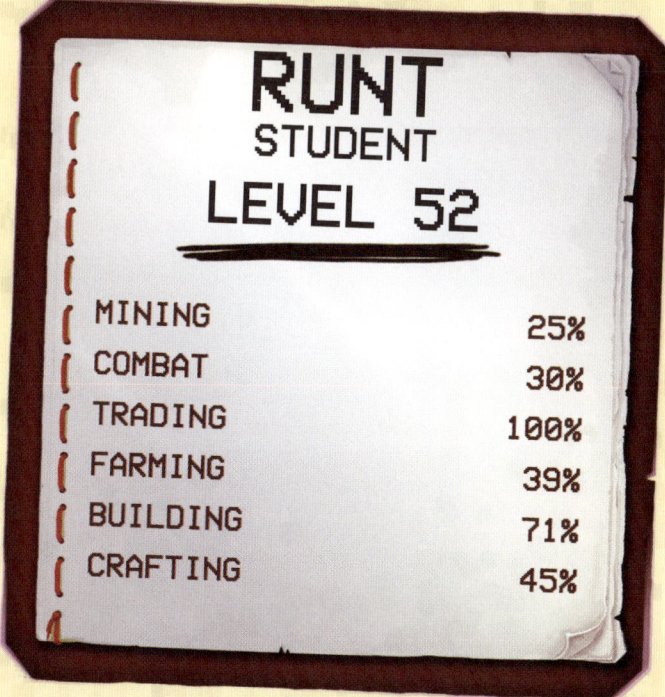

RUNT
STUDENT
LEVEL 52

MINING	25%
COMBAT	30%
TRADING	100%
FARMING	39%
BUILDING	71%
CRAFTING	45%

I felt whole again, and I breathed a **sigh of relief.**

How long has it been since I'd last seen this? **Eight days? Nine?** Well, it felt like **forever.** I was **happy** to see that my level had jumped almost as high as I had jumped last night.

On to the bad news. I had just arrived at school, right?

Went to the head teacher, plunked down **fifty emeralds** for the book, and was on my way to class, right?

Then I noticed some **creepy-looking** guy following me.

He was trying to act **all normal,** but come on—how many older guys in <u>**black robes and sunglasses**</u> do you see walking around a school like mine? I whistled merrily to myself, trying to look **innocent.** Didn't help. He kept following me down the hall. **I walked faster.** So did he, until he caught up.

"A bit windy today," he said. "**The clouds** sure are . . . *zooming across the sky.*"

"**Hurrn.** That's interesting. **Excuse me.**"

I zoomed off down a hallway, through a few doors.

Lost him, I thought. So, what is this? He's an elder, certainly. Does he want to talk to me about yesterday?

Another one soon approached.

"Good day, Runt. I've heard your **scores** are . . . really up there. Why, yes, why I'd say you're . . . **flying high.**"

"Thanks," I said. "Really. **It's nice of you to say that.**"

I turned around to make another run for it, but the first guy was there, **blocking my way.**

"**Come with us,**" said the guy without glasses. "**Immediately.**"

Thirty minutes later, I was on the other side of the village—in a cobblestone building with iron doors and iron bars for windows. This place was not a **jail,** however. It was like a hangout spot for a **bunch of old, cranky guys** who called themselves **elders.** They led me to a small, featureless room and . . . **offered me some pumpkin pie.**

And so began my **wonderful** day. I guess soaring through the sky has its downsides. **Mostly,** these guys wanted to know how I had managed to do it. *(Actually, everyone in the village wants to know that, including Steve and Mike.)* As if I could tell them.

"I crafted a **Potion of Leaping II**," was all I could say.

"Sounds like you crafted a **Potion of Leaping One Billion**," the guy with black sunglasses said.

"Look, Runt. **My name is Brio**, and I simply want to ask you a few questions about yesterday's . . . **incident**."

By "**a few questions**," he meant **over one thousand questions.**

Stuff like,

"So how *exactly* did you put the **glowstone dust** into the brewing stand?"

"Which hand did you **grab** the potion with?"

"Did the glowstone dust have a **funny smell**?"

"What was the weather like during that exact moment?"

"Can you remember the specific pattern of clouds?"

"Was the sun behind a cloud?"

"Would you like some more pumpkin pie?"

"Were there any **chickens** around?"

"How about some cookies?"

"Can you show us, **precisely,** how you crafted the potion? Re-create your exact movements?"

I blinked.

"We'd . . . need a brewing stand for that."

Brio pointed to the other guy.

"Pretend he's the brewing stand."

Right. After they were done asking questions, I had one of my own.

"Brio. Yesterday, I thought I saw **something walking** in that strange forest."

"Oh?"

"Yeah. The thing **was huge.** Almost as tall as the trees."

"Probably **shadows** playing tricks on your eyes," he said.

"But . . ."

"Or maybe it was a zombie?" He patted me on the head.

"Who knows?"

Yeah. He totally brushed me off. It only got **worse** from there. When Brio finally let me go, he gave me a book. It's **the second schoolbook** for this year.

The teachers had handed it out today, but since I wasn't at school . . .

"Finish it by tonight," Brio said. "You might find some good tips in there."

This is **cruel** and **unusual** punishment, man, I thought.

After today, I'm never going to drink a potion again.

TUESDAY

Well, Steve went <u>boom</u> today.

I guess he finally saw **Urf's books.** The whole front cover with him **riding a pig,** in a mine cart, on his way to **"Noobtown"** *(of which he is supposedly the mayor)* was just too much for him.

So he **quit.** He's been wanting to experiment with **redstone** anyway, he said. The mayor will have him working on that stuff from now on. Of course, Urf was overjoyed. He figured he was going to get his old job back.

Sadly, the head teacher wanted to try someone new.

I say **sadly** because . . . I'd rather have Urf than this new combat teacher. **Drill** is his name.

He's an elder, like Urf. But one hundred times **grumpier.** The first part of his combat class was sprinting **fifteen laps** around the field. That wouldn't have been too bad, but he dug holes all around the edge of the combat field and filled them with water.

Seriously,
this guy is crazy.

"MOVE, YOU ENDERMITES!! I'VE SEEN ZOMBIES SWIM FASTER UP WATERFALLS!!"

It was **the most intense** combat class I've ever had. After running, we had to swing at practice dummies **five hundred times.** Stump, Max, and I started beating away at the same dummy. Drill rushed over.

"I SAID GROUPS OF TWO!!" he screamed, and glared at me. "YOU!! WITH HER!!" Then he pointed at her. **Breeze.** She'd chosen a practice dummy near mine, of course—and of course, she was all by herself.

I could tell it was going to be **one of those weeks.**

"But they're my friends," I said.

"WHAT DID YOU JUST SAY, YOU SQUID-BRAINED POTATO JOCKEY?!"

Potato jockey?! That's like a chicken jockey, except . . . riding a potato.

I tried to **imagine** someone riding a pig-size potato and couldn't. **Just couldn't.** The very attempt **hurt my brain.** Then I got **angry.**

Who's he calling a potato jockey?!

"I *said*, they're my—"

Let me just make this clear: That was a bad choice of words.

No, let me be more clear: **Any** choice of words would have been a bad choice of words.

Drill got **so angry** he couldn't even speak in full sentences, just single words that sputtered out of his mouth:

"GIVE!! ME!! F-FIFTY!!"

Sigh. After the push-ups, I gave my friends a shrug and joined Breeze.

"Hey."

"Hey."

Whatever. It could have been worse. I could have gotten paired with one of Pebble's friends, or that **Bumbi** kid.

So Breeze and I swung our swords **in silence.** My arms already felt like anvils from all the push-ups, so I **slowed down** whenever Drill left our area and **sped up** when he came back.

Breeze was different. She swung at **a steady rate,** whether Drill was there or not. In fact, come to think of it, she was one of the **few students** Drill never shouted at. Even though she never did anything **amazing** in class, she never drew the anger of the teachers, either. Even this teacher, who freaked out over the tiniest thing.

In other words, Breeze was invisible —neither good nor bad— a **completely average** student.

That was why I'd never really noticed her until she started **following me around.** I mean, I've never seen her use any **fancy** moves—like that time I landed that huge critical hit and made the dummy's head fly off and roll on the ground with Steve clapping and telling me **good job** afterward. *(I'm proud of that one. Can you tell?)*

Later on, everyone moved to the **archery range.**

I'll just be up front: I'm a terrible shot with a bow. Give me a big sword and I'll show you bigger crits. Give me a bow, however, and you're endangering your own life, and everyone else's, including mine. How does someone hit themselves with their own arrows? I don't know, but I'm sure **I could do it.**

Here's some proof:

This was my shot while standing **still**, with a motionless target, from **thirty blocks away.**

Basically, if you need someone to hit a fully grown ghast at a range of ten blocks, well, **I'm your guy.** I'm totally your guy. *As long as the ghast isn't moving.* Outside of that, all I can really do with a bow is **scare mobs** with the whistling noise the arrows make.

Oh, now it's eleven blocks away. Aim carefully.

Breeze did great, though. **At first,** anyway. The first five arrows she shot were all **dead center**. Two were so close, the second arrow **split the first in half.** That's something I've only seen in storybooks at the library, with **some crazy villager dressed all in green.**

"Wow." I glanced at her, at the wool target, then back to her. "You're amazing."

"Not really," she said, shaking her head. Her cheeks were pink. "Just luck."

Maybe it **was** just luck.

Because after that, she never managed to hit red again.

So strange.
Maybe I made her nervous.

With ten minutes left until the end of class, we had to do another **fifteen laps** around the field. It started pouring rain. A few kids complained. A streak of anger flashed across Drill's face, and his voice boomed like thunder:

"YOU THINK THE MOBS ARE GONNA CARE ABOUT YOUR FEELINGS?! MOVE, YOU CREEPER-FACED ENDERBABIES!! MOVE!!"

Nice.
Just think—tomorrow,
I get to do this all over again.

TUESDAY NIGHT

I just **woke up** in the middle of the night from a **crazy dream.** I'm going to write down everything I can remember:

In the dream, Steve had built some **huge redstone contraption.**

"It's **a vending machine,**" he said. "We have them back on Earth."

"And what does it do?" I asked.

"In this case, you **drop an emerald into the hopper** here, select which **potion** you want, and the potion comes out of the dispenser there."

"What kind of potions?"

"**Well,** they're not really potions so much as **flavored drinks.**"

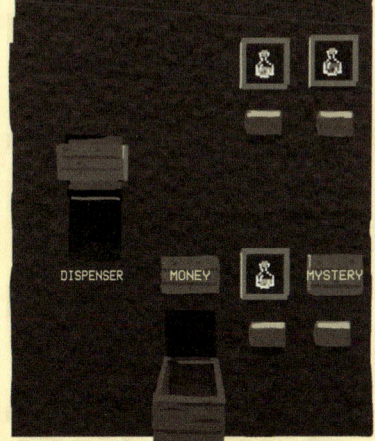

"Flavored drinks?"

"Never mind."

I studied the strange machine.

"What happens if you put in something **besides an emerald?**"

"It **rejects** it. Or **eats** it, but that only happens sometimes. It's a work in progress."

"It can recognize what kind of item you put into it? Is that even possible with redstone?"

For a second, Steve's eyes had an almost **opalescent** shimmer.

"With enough hard work, **anything is possible,** Runt."

I glanced at the button on the lower right:

Mystery . . .

"What does this button do?"

"Maybe you should find out."

Hurrrn. I pressed the button. The scene faded. **Darkness.**

"Please help me," the **wither skeleton** said. "I'm stranded on a lava island."

"Why would I help you? You're a mob. **You're a noob mob,** too. Wither skeletons are immune to lava, **aren't they?** So just swim to shore."

"**But not all of us are bad.** Surely you know that. Also, I can't swim. Please build a bridge for me. If you help me, I'll . . . help you."

"Help me how?"

"There's someone you need to meet."

"**Whatever.** This is *my* dream. Go away."

"Right now, I might be just a part of your dream . . . but we will meet in the future."

". . ."

"By the way," the wither skeleton said, "**tell Jello I said, 'Hi.'**"

Darkness. Then I was in an unfamiliar house.

Three kids—two girls and a boy—were sitting at a table.

"Who are you guys?" I asked.

"I'm **Skyler**," said one girl.

"**Katie**," said the other.

The boy smiled. "**Ben**."

The girl named Skyler **stood up**. "Notch sent us into your dream to give you a message," she said. She pointed out the window.

"**They'll be here soon.**

"You must warn the mayor. He doesn't realize how much danger the village is really in. **No one does.**"

I glanced out the window again.

"So . . . **the trees are coming for us?**"

Ben approached the window, too.

"No, not the *trees*. **Them.** Isn't it obvious?"

"Who?!"

"You aren't too bright, are you, Runt?"

That came from Katie, who was behind me, now. All three began pointing out the window. **"Look again!"**

The grass under the trees began rustling. Yet . . . everything else was **absolutely still.** Not even the clouds moved. There was an **eerie** feeling. It made me sick to my stomach. Then the whole world **shook** slightly. There was **a horrible roaring** sound far in the distance.

"It's him!" said Ben.

"Yes! He's here!"

"Who?!" I shouted.

Skyler turned to face me.

"Runt! Listen! **Remember** what you saw when you were—"

The scene cut away. Again, darkness. A man appeared in the inky gloom. He looked like Steve, yet there was something **creepy** about him. He . . . **had no eyes.** Or, rather, his eyes were white. And glowing. White light emerged behind him, and smoke, as if from a massive fire. Something was **burning.**

"I'm . . . coming for you . . ."

The **roaring** sound came back again, deafening this time. The man's eyes grew **brighter and brighter** until everything was white.

"Wuah!!!"

I sat up in bed, wide-awake, and remained like that for a while. An **eerie feeling** lingered on the edge of my mind. Those three kids said Notch sent them into my dream . . . Is something like that possible? Are they from Earth? Maybe they play that *Minecraft* game, like Steve and Mike used to. Is our village really in so much **danger?** We haven't had a mob attack in quite some time.

And who was that guy with the glowing white eyes? He didn't seem very friendly.

After I brushed off the fear, I opened up **Jello's item chest** and fed him some bread.

"You don't happen to know a wither skeleton, do you, Jello?"

I petted him. He was **cool to the touch**.

"No, of course you don't. **It was just a dream.**"

WEDNESDAY MORNING

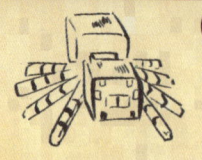 

There was a **huge meeting** this morning. The mayor **finally** talked to everyone about the **ever-encroaching forest.**

"As you are all aware, a vast number of **dark oak trees** have been growing in the east," he said. "This area is considered **dangerous.** Sunlight won't reach the mobs there, which means they **can travel around during the day.** We're currently experimenting with ways to deal with this problem, should the trees grow too **close to the village.**

"**Don't be alarmed.** We've survived many attacks in the past, and we'll survive so many more. This is simply the next step in the mobs' strategy, and it's **a very obvious one.**"

Brio—*the guy with black sunglasses*—**joined** the mayor at the oak block.

"From now on, the students will face **more and more difficult classes,** harsher training, and . . . each student must **submit an idea** to help protect our village. This will be your **final test** before you graduate."

The mayor nodded.

"Students, you must **train your hardest.** The mobs are improving quickly, it seems. So must we. I've noticed **petty squabbles** between some of you, and I suggest you end them today. The real enemy lies beyond those walls, **not within.**"

That was pretty much it. So, the trees allow mobs to **hide** from the sunlight. Zombies and skeletons can **move around during the day**, as long as they stay within that forest.

But is there more to it than that?
Skyler, Ben, and Katie
seemed to think so.

Hmm.

Later, in combat class, I had to be **partners with Breeze *again*.**

I got to enjoy another hour of being screamed at by Drill, crawling through mud, and **a weird girl** as my partner. Max and Stump have been having a blast in comparison.

Needless to say, it's been the **worst week of my life.**

It soon got worse. Brio and the mayor observed the combat class today, from a distance. After class, Drill **spoke** with the mayor.

Drill said that Breeze and I are **such good partners,** we should work together *every* class . . .

That teacher is too **mean**.
<u>Too mean.</u>

Call me a potato jockey: okay, that's fine, I can roll with that. But working with Breeze every day until I graduate?! **What is this?! Such cruelty! Such pain!**

I complained to the head teacher, but that was **useless.** He likes Breeze. He thinks she's a great student. When I mentioned how weird she is, he didn't believe me—in fact, he gave me the **"Runt just invited me to a slumber party in the Nether"** look.

Why does **everyone** give me that look?!

Why**!!!**

"Come on, it'll be fun!! Bring your own beds!!"

WEDNESDAY NIGHT: ANOTHER DREAM

The weird dreams came back tonight. This time, it was the events of Sunday—**in reverse.** So, in a way, it wasn't so much a *dream* as it was me **remembering** things. There wasn't much sound while the scenes played out, just an eerie static or buzzing noise.

Creepy, right?

I tried **my best** to remember what I saw that day.

It was like a zombie, or a skeleton . . . something standing upright . . . **except it was huge.**

It was almost as **tall as the dark oaks.** Not even endermen are that tall. What was it? I couldn't make it out **clearly.** It was too far away, and my **eyes were all watery** from the wind. I soon began **dreaming for real:**

Nonono.
NNNNNNo.

This dream is **not** turning into a nightmare. **Come on, Runt.** This is **your dream.** You're the boss in here. Control this thing.

There we go! Now this is a dream!

Yeeeeahhh!!

I don't wanna wake up!

THURSDAY

Breeze was such a noob today.

My new **"partner"** did almost everything wrong. One of her potions even **exploded** in brewing class. Afterward, she just blinked, sneezed, and said, **"Oops."**

"Wow," Pebble said, "looks like you **two noobs** are made for each other." Almost everyone in class **laughed.**

Max and Stump gave me a guilty look. At least **they** were having fun . . .

Anyway, I had to **get away** from her. So, during lunch, I took off to the school library. I couldn't stop thinking about what I had seen in the forest, anyway, and wanted to do some research.

Mungo the Overlord was the **biggest mob** I'd read about. Thinking back, the thing I had spotted on Sunday could have been a huge zombie. I remember reading about giant zombies. **They were super rare.**

Fast-forward an hour: I didn't find any mobs, even **legendary** ones, in the library's books that fit what I had seen. Afternoon classes went by in a blur. I didn't even pay attention to Drill's shouts; I just did my push-ups, ran my laps. He was a bit hard to ignore, though.

"I'VE SEEN SILVERFISH CRAWL THROUGH COBBLESTONE FASTER THAN YOU!!"

After school, I told Steve about my sighting. **He laughed it off.**

"Probably just a **cow.** There might be a few zombies out there, but that's it."

The mayor said the same thing.

"You want me to **modify my plans** because you think you saw something?"

Stump also blew me off.

"**Lay off the potions**, dude. Really." His blue eyes, normally cheerful, were filled with **worry.**

"Can't you just be a normal kid and stop getting into trouble? What happened to just studying hard and becoming warriors?"

Hurrrg.

(I haven't had a good old-fashioned hurrrg in a while.)

However, when I mentioned my dream to Max, he nodded slowly.

"**I saw something, too,**" he said. "Heard something, rather. The other night. My dad and I had an argument, so I stepped outside and went for a walk. Went to the east wall. Something **moaned so loud** out there I had trouble sleeping when I went back home."

"So I'm not the only one, then."

"How about we go find out?"

"What are you talking about?"

"I say we head over there tomorrow night," Max said. "Just sneak out of the village and go find out what's in there."

"Are you crazy?!"

"Maybe. After all, what **sane** person would ever want to fight mobs for a living?"

Stump's words came back to haunt me: *(Can't you just be a normal kid and stop getting into trouble? What happened to just studying hard and becoming warriors?)*

I told Max that I didn't want to do anything **crazy** anymore.

"Besides," I said, "if the mayor ever found out about this . . ."

"He won't find out," Max said. He clapped his hands together. "**It's like this, Runt.** Let's say the mayor's right, and there's nothing out there except some zombies. Maybe a skeleton or two. Then we  won't be in any danger at all. I've got some **Potions of Invisibility.** We'll be totally fine. However, if the mayor's wrong and we're right, then **the village really <u>needs to know</u>.**"

I couldn't believe this kind of stuff was coming from Max . . .

But what came next—

"**I love my village,**" he said, "and I'm prepared to take **minor risks** to help the people I love.

My family.
My friends.

"The little kids that play in the street near my house. I'm not gonna let the mobs get them."

He had **a kind of strength** when he said this, a confidence I'd never seen in anyone else, not even Steve—it was **impossible** not to feel moved. And at that point, I understood: **these are the words of a warrior.**

I stood up straighter.
Nodded.
<u>Even smiled.</u>

FRIDAY NIGHT, JUST AFTER SUNSET

We **crept** out of the village after the sun went down.

The east wall of the village didn't have a gate, but there was a **secret trapdoor** that allowed easy passage. We crept through the tunnel and exited into the plains.

Max **wasn't kidding** when he said he had **Potions of Invisibility.** He'd been stockpiling them. I didn't ask where he'd gotten **so many golden nuggets.** Even **a single potion** had a **pretty steep price**—eight per potion, plus a fermented spider eye—yet Max handed me **five** without batting an eye.

"How long do these potions last?" I asked.

"They're extended," Max said. **"Eight-minute duration."**

At **five** potions each, we had **forty minutes** to snoop around. We chugged a bottle each. At first, it **was difficult walking** without seeing our legs or hands. The closer we got to the dark forest, the more my heart sank into my stomach. **There was no sound** beyond the soft crunching of grass underneath our feet.

"This way," Max said. **"The valley.** See it?"

"Yeah."

We crept forward, **slowly, slowly.**

I could hear him breathing, and he could no doubt hear me.

Both of us were afraid.

"At least this place still has animals," I whispered, pointing. "Maybe it's **not so bad** here?"

"Quiet."
"What is it?"
"Listen."

We stood there for a long time—*at least a minute, although it seemed like forever*—**invisible, barely breathing.**

Then Max's footsteps **broke** the silence.

"Let's go."

We stepped into the forest. It was gloomy, hard to see, and I regretted not bringing some potions of my own—**Night Vision.**

"Saplings," I said.

"Let's keep going."

We **crept** forward, **waited, listened, looked around**, and when we felt we had two minutes left on our invisibility, we drank another potion each—**just to be safe.**

At one point, I thought I heard a crunching sound.

I bumped into Max, almost knocking him over.

"Forward," he said. **"Real slow."**

We moved forward, past some big trees . . .

And then—

I almost screamed—

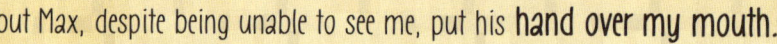

but Max, despite being unable to see me, put his **hand over my mouth.**

He grabbed me, and we both **backed up,** until the mobs were out of sight and only the crunching **sounds of the shovel** could still be heard. **"This is insane,"** Max whispered.

"The mobs . . . they . . ."

I was thinking the same thing.

I . . . can't believe it. The **mobs** made **this forest?** A skeleton was holding a shovel. A zombie was holding a sapling. But . . . they're **mobs! Not villagers! Not Earth kids!** Not noobs, or warriors, or even iron golems, who often hold flowers the same way that zombie was holding that baby tree—**so delicately,** with the utmost care.

That zombie was acting like he didn't want to damage the sapling's roots. **He probably had a respectable Farming score.**

Mobs!!

With Farming scores?!?!

Mobs that know how to farm?!

How can they . . . how did they . . . **they've been planting trees?!**

How?! How is that even possible?!

What, they've got farming classes over there in **Mob City,** *do they?!*

I mean, I assumed this forest would be crawling with them, but to think that they actually created—

Boom!
Boom!!
Boom!!!

The ground was **shaking** slightly. **A massive creature** shambled toward the skeleton and the zombie.

It must have stood at least **six blocks high.** Its fists were **one block across;** its head was slightly bigger than that.

My scientific calculations concluded that this could mean only one thing:

105

RUNRUNRUNRUN
RUNRUNRUNRUN.

SATURDAY

Max and I made it back in one piece. None of the mobs **noticed us**. Not even **the big guy** with tree trunks for arms. We found Stump and told him everything. Of course, none of us had seen or heard of a mob like that. **We wanted to know what it was.**

Max suggested we try to find more information in a library. The three of us headed to the biggest library in the village and began looking through a bunch of ancient, **dusty** books.

Breeze slipped into the library shortly thereafter. She entered when two other kids were leaving to prevent me from noticing her. But I saw her thin form—*like a blurred shadow in the dim corner of the library*—just as she zoomed behind an aisle of books.

Max eventually **found** what we were looking for. A librarian can come in handy, after all. It was a book with a simple green cover and an even simpler name:

Legendary Mobs of Minecraftia.

Despite its **boring** outward appearance, this book was filled with a lot of **crazy stuff**. It's an encyclopedia of legendary mobs—**boss monsters,** as they're referred to on Earth. Well, the three of us sat around and **flipped through its chapters.**

By the way, all of the mobs in this book were **100% real.** Some of them sounded downright **terrifying,** such as **the screaming cow** *(all living things close enough to hear its cries get the wither debuff).*

Or **the obsidian giant** *(it's nearly twenty blocks tall and the only weapon that can harm it is a diamond pickaxe).*

Then I found one that sent **a chill** down my spine.

URKK DOOMWHIP

"That's our mob," I said.

Stump seemed **skeptical.**

"You're sure? Maybe it was an enderman?"

"**No,** this thing was no enderman," Max said. "Every time it walked, it created a **mini earthquake.**"

"Well, if this guy's really out there," Stump said, "**then this village is in big trouble.** Says here **Urkk** is a **midlevel boss mob.** Can take out iron golems without even trying and **hurl creepers up to fifteen blocks** for a ranged explosive attack. This ability has earned him the nickname

'The Creeper Express.'"

". . ."
". . ."
". . ."

Everyone fell **silent** for a moment, considering these words. Max then read aloud from the book.

First, Urkk **is seven blocks tall.** He's got special bone armor made from the bones of **wither skeletons.**

(The book estimates that this guy has maybe **three times the life-force of an iron golem.**) That's a lot of hearts. But the **craziest** thing about him is **his weapon:** a modified fishing rod—**a special, unique item.** How he crafted it is still a mystery to Minecraftian sages.

It has a longer reach than a normal fishing rod with a fast-flying hook. But what makes this fishing rod truly deadly are the **Pulling II**

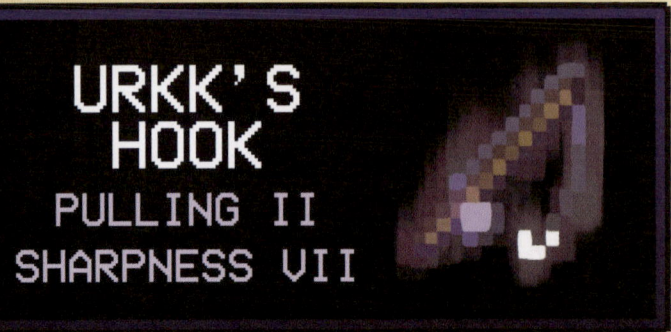

URKK'S HOOK
PULLING II
SHARPNESS VII

and **Sharpness VII** enchantments, meaning it pulls hooked targets **closer** and deals an **incredible amount of damage** when it does.

"I didn't even know a **seventh level** of Sharpness **existed**," Breeze said. All three of us looked up at her in **surprise**. *(Even though I had seen her enter, I'd already forgotten about her.)*

Max shrugged. "Boss mobs like this tend to have **crazy items and abilities**."

The **fear** snuck up on my heart like a creeper that had drunk a Potion of Invisibility. "How can we **defend** ourselves against this guy?" I asked.

Max shrugged again. "Don't get hooked?"

"Come on," I said. "There has to be something else."

Stump pointed at the bottom of the right page. **"He has a phobia."**

"Huh?" I said.

"What's that?" Max asked.

"It's another word for **fear**," Stump said. "You know how creepers are **afraid of cats?** Skeletons, dogs? Well, he's got one, too.

"He's afraid of heights."

"**Interesting.**" Max read some more. "So, he's terrified of any vertical drop greater than **five blocks.**"

Suddenly, Stump rose from his chair. "What are we doing here?! We're just sitting around talking! We've gotta go **warn the mayor!**"

I figured the mayor would just brush us off, but we had to try. Max grabbed the *Legendary Mobs* book and off we went to the mayor's house.

The sound of a distant explosion echoed through the streets— and then there was a distant roar, which could have only come from that **gigantic pigman, Urkk.**

I drew my wooden sword, remembering Max's words.

Friends. Family. The little kids who play in the street. No mobs are going to get them.

This giant noob named Urkk is going down.

SATURDAY: BATTLE—PART ONE

Ever been in a big village **just before sunset?**

Ever watched all the villagers **scrambling around,** desperately trying to get home before the sun went down? Well, after the **explosions,** our village was like that. **Only in reverse.**

And with a lot of screaming.

Despite weeks of **intense training,** we just weren't prepared.

It was **total chaos.**

Smoke was rising in the east, and almost no one wanted to stick around for the mobs' little surprise party.

Well, some did. Some were actually running *toward* the smoke, like fish swimming upstream. My friends and I fell into that last category. **Call us brave. Call us foolish, or foolhardy, or simply fools.**

Call us whatever you want to, but we were determined to crash that party. The thing is our anger toward the mobs goes back a long way— *way* before the slime bombings. All those years of living in fear, unable to sleep, listening to the spiders shrieking, the skeletons rattling . . .

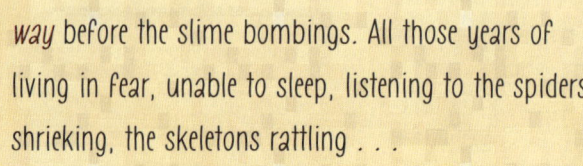

We'd had **enough.**

We'd decided that we just weren't going to **put up with it** anymore.

I won't provide a detailed narrative for this battle—not too many *he saids, she saids, I did this, he did that.*

To be **honest,** I can't remember much. It was just a blur.

In those first moments, I, like everyone else, was struggling to accept the cold, hard reality: **In broad daylight,** with barely a cloud in the sky, the mobs had launched the biggest attack in the history of the village.

SATURDAY: BATTLE—PART TWO

The first thing I noticed was . . . **the zombies weren't burning in the sunlight.** There they were, shambling in the distance, without so much as a spark emitting from them. It was their **armor.** Some were **fully suited in leather;** a few were even in **iron.**

Regardless of what they wore, though, every single one was equipped with *at least* **a helmet.**

(Some zombies wore a helmet and a pair of boots without a tunic or leggings, which was just bizarre.)

Not scary—just bad fashion sense

Anyway, amidst the terror and confusion, I remembered hearing about how a helmet can protect a zombie from the sun.

Which brings us to our first interesting point: A zombie wearing *any* sort of armor is **quite rare, let alone an *army* of zombies wearing armor.**

Consider how much work it must have taken to outfit them all. I mean, have you ever tried crafting a full suit of leather armor? It's **an epic quest.** You need, like, **fifty cows,** which means feeding cows over and over for what seems like forever—and the whole time, you're listening to that endless **mooing** and wondering if you have enough wheat: you're going out to check your crops at night, thinking, *Are those torches close enough, should I use bone meal, should I gather more seeds, should I go to those plains over there and take out some horses for* **extra** *leather*—until finally, you stop farming for leather altogether and go into a cave, because why not? The truth is you could get **iron faster.**

By the way, that's just for *one* **set of leather armor.** How about **one *hundred*?** That's the estimated number of zombies, in full leather, **that attacked our village today.**

Knowing that, one must ask: **Where did they get the materials?** It meant they were farming cows. It meant, somewhere in Minecraftia, there was a cow farm—a farm quite possibly the size of our entire village—tended by various mobs. It also meant they were **mining** and **smelting iron.** Not only did they have the resources for such a massive number of items, but they knew how to craft them as well. So—they probably have zombie **blacksmiths.** Zombie **miners.** Zombie **butchers.** Zombie **armorers.** Zombie **crafters.** Zombie **builders.** Zombie **cooks.** Zombie **bakers.** Zombie advanced **redstone engineers.** Zombie every possible profession <u>**you could possibly ever think of.**</u>

And why stop at zombies? Somewhere out there, there's probably a **charged creeper lumberjack.**

Meet **Creepojack.** He's so manly he swings his axe with his teeth. HIS TEETH. And when his axe finally breaks, he just explodes, providing easy harvesting for the next guy.

Nothing would surprise me anymore. But hey, all this is just preparing me for **the real world,** you know? At least this way, if I ever see a slime fisherman, I won't freak out, or be shocked, or offend him by asking how a slime could possibly be a fisherman since he has no arms. Instead, I'll just plunk down next to him, whip out my own fishing rod, and ask if he's had any bites. **Skeleton librarians. Enderman shepherds.** I could accept all that.

There was one possibility I couldn't, though: What if some of those zombies have **a better combat score than I do?**

Zombie . . . warriors?

No way!!

I refuse to believe it!!

With sudden anger,
I cut into a zombie with my wooden sword.

SATURDAY: BATTLE—PART THREE

This, of course, brings us to our next point.
You see, after I **attacked that zombie,**
well, it attacked *me.*
Who knew?

Let me tell you, that single moment was **worth more** than two or three days' worth of Intro to Combat. Steve is a **great teacher,** don't get me wrong, and that Drill guy scares me to no end, but that zombie gave me a hands-on lesson in just how **strong** zombies actually are. My vision flashed bright **red.** A wave of pain flooded my senses. **The life bar in the bottom of my vision reduced by two hearts.**

The **courage** I'd felt just moments ago **vanished** like an enderman in the rain, like water in **the Nether,** like mushrooms in sunlight, like a waterfall after someone scooped up the spring block with a bucket.

(Actually, that last example is a bit slow, isn't it? Gah. Never mind.)

Anyway, I was **knocked back** from the sheer force of the zombie's attack.

Just then, a **horrifying** thought hit me: **Real.** This is real. I'm **20%** closer to vanishing in a **puff** of smoke. If I make too many mistakes—if I let Mr. Stinkypants remove every last heart from my life bar—**that's it.**

After that, I felt impossibly **heavy** and **cold.** An anvil in my stomach and ice blocks in my veins. For a moment, **Intro to Combat** went right out the window. So did Sir Runt, the word **warrior,** and everything in between. <u>I forgot everything.</u>

Everything I'd ever learned, everything that Steve had ever taught me, and everything Drill had ever drilled into my head—gone, like **an enchanted diamond** sword accidentally dropped into lava.

In fact, I . . . <u>almost ran</u>.

In my defense, the number of mobs out there was enough to make an iron golem cry.

In the words of Urf: "**This is baadddd.**" He said this in a deep, **terrified voice.** (In addition, he made a deep grunting sound before saying this, which I cannot replicate with words or letters. Perhaps something similar to what a pigman might sound like when struck in the butt by lightning.) Then he ran into a nearby house and peeked out a window with **the most ridiculous expression** on his face. He reminded me of a creeper that had to go to the bathroom really bad.

In contrast, Drill was at his **angriest.** Somewhere in the distance, he was **shouting so loud** my ears hurt even from where I was standing.
"HOLD THE LINE, YOU RABBIT JOCKEYS!!
GET IN FORMATION!!"

Whatever. No one was listening to him. Everyone was too shaken, too confused, and way too **preoccupied.**

It was like this **everywhere** you looked. Kids from school, the **best of friends,** fighting back to back as zombies trudged endlessly forward.

Chris and Kevin.

Joanne and Jamie, twin sisters.

And fighting in one big group: **Kristen, Brennan, Marco, Beth, Jackson, Jenn, Tanesha**, and a kid nicknamed **CamouflageBoy.** They all fought **valiantly,** oblivious to Drill's shouts. Besides, no matter how many times he ordered us to **"hold the line,"** there was simply no line to hold. Zombies were **everywhere.**

Things looked really grim. Until Stump **freaked out,** that is.

"I hope you brought **an anvil,**" he said to a zombie, "because you're gonna need it to repair your face ten times after this!!"

With a loud cry, he slammed the zombie back **again and again.**

The zombie actually tried to run . . . before it crumbled into **light gray dust.**

Experience orbs flew from the pile, into my friend, who then **swung** his sword around slowly in the air.

Kids cheered as if he'd just slain **the ender dragon** itself. It was enough to bring me to my senses and **respawn** several weeks of combat classes in my mind. This time, when a zombie lunged for me, I stepped back and swung my blade. When he staggered back, **I dashed forward and swung again.**

<u>**Three** swings later, I defeated my **first** mob.</u>

After the zombie fell, I felt a **slight surge of energy** from the experience flying into me.

Max dropped his own zombie at about the same time. He **muttered something** about how slaying his first mob wasn't as cool as it had sounded in the adventure books he'd read.

All around me, more and more villagers were doing the same. We were pushing them back. *(Well, technically, we were chopping them or slashing them.)* Morale only increased when **Mike showed up.** "I saw that," he said to Stump. "**Nice work,** kid, but don't get too reckless, huh? Same goes for you two."

"Okay, hurrr."

"You got it, Mike."

"Don't worry. We'll be **careful.**"

The warrior gave us **the strangest** look.

"Man, what *are* you guys? **The Three Muskanoobs?**"

I returned the expression.

"Um, what?"

"Never mind."

Hurrrgg.

I was still trying to remember all **the weird words** Steve had taught me, and now *Mike* was using them, too. Max seemed equally annoyed.

"Honestly," he said, "if any more of you guys show up in our village, we're gonna need **a class on Earth slang.**"

SATURDAY: BATTLE—PART FOUR

The third point I'll bring up is perhaps the most **interesting** *(to me, at least)*.

Tactics. Not ours, mind you. Our tactics mostly consisted of **screaming, trembling, shaking,** and randomly **freaking out.**

But the mobs had it down. As a **warrior-in-training**, I'll admit it: the way they moved was beautiful. Even Drill was **impressed,** shouting something about how he wanted to switch sides instead of commanding a bunch of **no-good, carrot-brained** dirt farmers.

Here's the most common trick the mobs pulled. We're calling it the **"zombie shuffle."** Basically, the zombies seemed to realize that they were **the least valuable**, the most worthless. So they'd make a formation in front of the skeletons. They were shielding the skeletons with their own bodies.

The technical term here is <u>meat shields.</u>

But it didn't end there. Sometimes, the skeletons **hissed** in an unknown language. *(That language is the ancient tongue, by the way, like the words found on enchanting tables.)* Then the zombies **moved** to the side slightly, giving the skeletons enough room to **shoot** arrows at us.

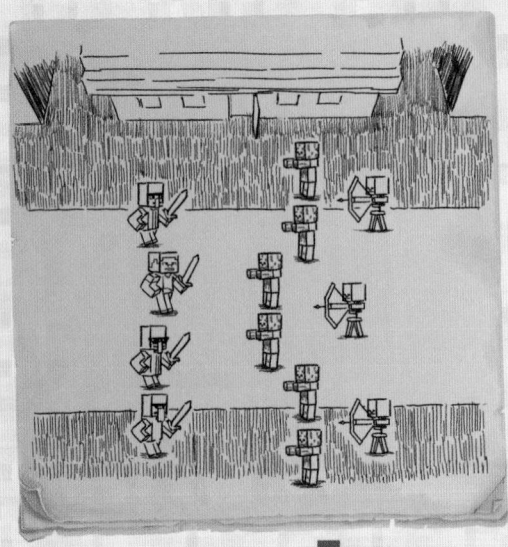

If anyone tried to **close in on a skeleton**, the zombies moved back, **blocking** their path.

Unbelievable, right? At least, **Mike couldn't believe it:** "So they're using formations now?! Is this even *Minecraft?!*"

Max **blocked** an arrow with his sword.

"Welcome to our world, **buddy boy."**

Of course, the mobs had many more tricks up their sleeves.

Once, a single spider carried **five skeletons** up a house, one by one.

A few zombies carried **axes** and chopped holes in walls to launch **surprise attacks.**

One zombie even had **flint** and **steel** and set fire to everything he could. A lot of houses were lost today.

The craziest mob trick, however, was the "**zombie sandwich.**" When we first saw it, we didn't know what to think.

What *is* a zombie sandwich, you ask?

How can you make one? What are the ingredients?

Here's **the recipe:**
   Step 1: Take **three to five** creepers.
   Step 2: Surround those creepers with **eight to eleven zombies.**
   Step 3: **Just cry.**

They moved together as **a single unit,** which meant that we had a hard time taking down the creepers before they **blew up.** When those creepers started **hissing** and **flashing,** all we could do was move back. They pulled this off a few times, whenever they wanted to blow up a certain building . . . or take out a group of iron golems.

Incredibly, the zombies **moved away** before the creepers went off, **minimizing** their losses.

Meanwhile, a few of us had trouble *holding a sword.*

We're never gonna hear the end of this in Intro to Combat. **The Nether will likely freeze over** before Drill's done **scolding** us.

SATURDAY: BATTLE—PART FIVE

That's not to say we didn't have **tactics** of our own. For example, once, **two zombies** lunged for me at the same time. I managed to knock one back but didn't have time to deal with the second. Then **an arrow** cut through the air, above my right shoulder, and **nailed** the zombie in the arm. It wasn't the **best shot**—*not that I could criticize someone's bow skill*—but it did **knock** the zombie back. I finished the second off before it could recover, then dropped the first and looked around.

Who shot that arrow?
They must be perched **on top** of a house.

Of course.

Even at a time like this, she's still following me around . . .
No matter where I go, **she's there,** somewhere in the background . . .

A crazy fangirl. A creepy stalker. Well, she did **help me out.** Am I being too harsh? **No. No way.**

If she wants to **be friends**, she can talk to me like a **normal person** instead of lurking around like that! Besides, combat class has become **so lame** because of her! If she wasn't always hanging around, Drill would have just let me keep training with **my friends!**

I wish she'd leave me alone!!
I don't need her help!!
Hurrrgg!!

My anger returning, **I cut through a new zombie.**

SATURDAY: BATTLE—PART SIX

While we were fighting, **some girl showed up** and made some flashy moves. Well, she wasn't just **some girl** . . . Her name's **Emerald,** and she's one of **the most popular girls** in school. I've never really talked to her much. **She's kind of annoying. She's** *never* **humble,** occasionally **snide,** often cowardly, and always getting into and out of **jams.**

Despite her somewhat girly appearance, her **bad temper** can be legendary. Max said she outshouted Drill a couple of days ago when he scolded her about something in the street.

After taking out a few mobs, she turned and **bumped into me.**

"Sorry." She smirked. "You, **um** . . . kinda got in my way."

"Sure thing, **hurrr.**"

She glanced at the piles of dust.

"So, are you guys holding up?"

"We're getting by."

She nodded.

"By the way, have you seen **Pebble?**"

"No. Here's hoping an iron golem mistook him for a zombie."

At my response, she made an expression like a cat left out in the rain. "**Hmmph!** Y'know, he's not so bad."

She **took off** after that. So another one has joined **Team Pebble.** Anger level: **off the charts.** A zombie approached with a clueless look on his face. He had no idea what was in store for him. No idea.

<u>I almost felt sorry.</u>

SATURDAY: BATTLE—PART SEVEN

Still, **as angry** as I'd become, I soon cheered up. You see, one of my dreams is to someday wield **a diamond sword.** Diamonds are **super expensive,** right? Well, today was a wonderful opportunity to save up. There were a few **iron golems** roaming around, smacking mobs high into the air. At one point, I just started following a golem around and picking up all the **dropped items.**

Why not? The golem didn't need them. Besides, it was better those items went to *me* instead of **some noob.**

But then, the golem was a bit slow. **Rusty,** perhaps. It would knock a zombie into the air, and I'd have to wait for it to come back down . . . and then wait even longer for the golem to trudge over and do it all again.

Eventually, the golem knocked a zombie onto the roof of a house. The zombie **didn't jump back** down, either. He just glanced around, decided that was that, and sat down. **Urg.** After that, I started following **Mike.** With the way Mike dropped zombies, he was a much more **time-efficient source** of items.

I figured he already had enough **emeralds** and wouldn't mind if I took a few things.

Just a few.

Man,
was I wrong.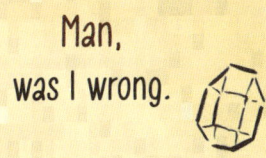

He glared at me as if I'd just looted every last item in his **secret ender chest.**

"Why are you giggling over there, Runt? **It's not funny!** Stop **stealing** my items, noob!!"

Tee hee hee.

SATURDAY: BATTLE—PART EIGHT

At some point, **Breeze** jumped down from a house.

She must have **run out of arrows.** But she was **afraid** down here. She didn't even draw her sword. In fact, I don't even think she *had* one. **What a noob . . .**

Several zombies went for her then—*Steve once said they can sense weakness*—and that was when I **lost it.** I glanced to the right and shouted:

"What are you doing?! Get back!!"

She **tumbled** back before the zombies closed in and hid in an alley. Since I was distracted, a zombie nearly **struck me.** Claws swiped inches from my face. I dashed back and shook my head.

What is this?

I was thinking about **her safety** before my own. Am I starting **to care about her** or something?

SATURDAY: BATTLE—PART NINE

Near **the end of the battle,** I noticed something **strange.** I spotted Brio—the guy in all black, with the **black sunglasses.**

He was in **a church tower,** far in the distance.

He was . . . **observing us.** Watching us fight for our lives. Of course, with all the zombies running around, I wasn't able to keep my eyes on him for very long. A few minutes later, **I spotted him again,** on top of the same tower. He jumped down onto the roof of an armory and then into a street, where he slowly walked away. **It gets weirder.**

He went in a direction that was, to my knowledge, totally **overrun** with mobs. A bunch of kids had fled from that area minutes earlier and had warned us **not to go there.** It must have been bad in there, because their faces were so white, as if they'd seen **a ghast.**

Yet I watched as a distant Brio **calmly** strode toward that place, seemingly unafraid—*and without any weapons*—until he vanished behind a house.

Seriously **weird**.

What was he doing? Where was he going? I was so **curious** I almost went in there after him. But then I turned back to the battle as a few shouts rose up over the chaos:

"Hey! Look!"

"The mobs are breaking **formation!**"

Drill started screaming at the top of his lungs.

"ALL IN!! NO MERCY!!"

Everyone else screamed just as loudly.

"CHARRRRRRRRRRRRRRRRRGE!!"

A wave of angry villagers,
led by **an even angrier combat teacher,**
rushed after a **fleeing enemy.**

SATURDAY: BATTLE—PART TEN

Twenty minutes later, the mobs were totally **wiped out.**

An **eerie** silence swept through the streets. Stump sat down and offered me some bread. It was enough to **refill my life bar.**

"Thanks," I said, glancing at him. "You know, you were **amazing** back there."

He shrugged.

"I'm just glad **Urkk** didn't show up."

"Right."

Just then, **Steve walked around a corner**—shambled, really. He was **covered in slime** and dust, his leather armor hung in **tatters,** and he was moving slower than a zombie over soul sand—soul sand with cobwebs placed on top and ice blocks underneath. With a sigh, he tossed his iron sword onto the cobblestone street.

"I'm so done with these mobs."

I rose up.

"Where *were* you?"

"At the square," he said. "They almost pushed through Sunset Lane. You wouldn't believe **how many."** He slid down a wall, eyes closed. "Looks like they were trying to take the school."

The school?

That didn't make sense to me. Why not the city hall, or the farms, or the storerooms? But I didn't ask any more questions. We were **too tired** to even talk.

The silence was interrupted as a chorus of **shouts** and **cheers** gradually grew louder. At first, I assumed some villagers, and perhaps the mayor, were coming to congratulate us on our victory . . . until I realized what they were shouting. Actually, they were *chanting*. A single word—or rather, **a single name.**

"... Peh-bull!! Peh-bull!! Peh-bull!!
Peh-bull! Peh-bull!! ..."

About one **hundred** people then came into view. They were hoisting **Pebble** up over their heads, carrying him down the road, along with that girl **Emerald**.

. . .

There was a wooden clatter as
I threw my own sword <u>**onto the street.**</u>

SUNDAY

By Sunday morning, **posters like this** were all you could see:

15 ZOMBIES
8 SKELETONS
5 CREEPERS
1 HERO

Pebble the war hero. The poster boy of the war on mobs. He had apparently killed a total of **fifteen zombies, eight skeletons, five creepers, two spiders, an enderman, and a chicken** *(the chicken was an accident, or so he says).*

An **impressive** number, more than my own, and backed by praise from the mayor, who'd seen it all happen. That girl **Emerald** was praised **even more,** probably because it isn't everyday that you see a horde of zombies taken down by a girl in a light pink robe. **What can I say?** The right place at the right time **and all that.**

In the afternoon, there was a **ceremony** to congratulate all those who had risen up to **defend the village** during the horrible attack.

My friends and I were included in the praise, **of course,** but the two "**heroes**" stole the show. I'm not bitter about that, however. What burns me is how Pebble and Emerald were awarded special cloaks. **Honestly,** they're **the coolest** cloaks I've ever seen, and they're **enchanted** on top of that, granting **protection from fire.**

HERO SHROUD
CLOAK
FIRE
PROTECTION II

Everyone else who **took part in** the battle was given a **cloak,** but these items were **trash-tier**—*the kind of item only a noob would get worked up about.*

When I **tried** mine on, Steve said it could have been a **"bib"** . . . whatever *that* is. When I asked him, he said he didn't want to tell me, because I've already been **humiliated** enough today.

On top of that, **Pebble** is now **rank one,** and Emerald is **rank two** . . . Meaning, Max is **third** and I'm **fourth.** Maybe. No one has discovered the identity of that other **high-ranked student,** so who knows. Why can't the teachers just come out with an official ranking system instead of forcing us to guess and peek at one another's record books?

In other news, we told the mayor about **Urkk.** Here's the thing, though. He asked how we **knew about Urkk.**

None of us wanted to get in trouble by admitting we had left the village at night, so we just said we had seen Urkk while we were standing on the wall at night.

"**Probably just a cow,**" the mayor said. "They get pretty big in these parts." He sighed. "**Urkk is a legend,** boys. Nothing more. Mobs like that simply don't exist anymore."

Why did I even try?

(Insert something about the mayor being a noob here.)

I'm so tired of this kind of stuff; I'm currently lacking the **energy** to even come up with a good way to **insult** him. I'll come back to this entry later and fill it in . . .

Lastly,
I'm a little shy to ask, but . . .
what do you think of
my cloak?

It looks **crooked** because it keeps bunching up on the left side and no matter what I do, I can't fix it.
What's that? You said it looks cool?

Okay. Thanks.
I'll keep wearing it, then.
(By the way, what's a bib?)

MONDAY

There was **no school** today. Due to **the attack,** the mayor thought it would be a good time to establish village **"building codes."** The building codes include various **anti-mob** upgrades. The mayor encouraged every family to add these upgrades to their homes.

Of course, since it's not yet required to do this, most families didn't bother . . . but if you recall how I had to walk Fluffles during the creeper scare, then you know my mom.

Besides, after hearing *anti-mob upgrades*, I envisioned **lava moats, piston traps**—you know, **crazy stuff** like that.

Yeah.
Right.

In reality, upgrading our house involved tearing up the wooden planks that served as the floor and replacing them with **cobblestone slabs.**

Then I had to dig up dirt in a five-block radius around the house and put **slabs** there.

"Slabs are resistant to **explosions,**" page seven of the building code manual states. "Slabs are heavy and annoying to properly place," *says twelve-year-old villager Runt.*

A house should have eaves so spiders can't climb onto the ceiling.

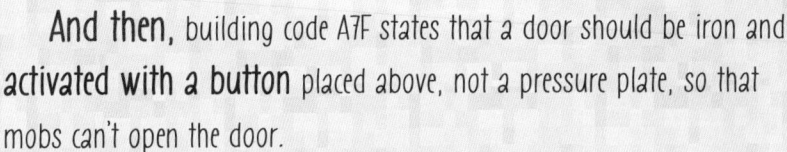

A fence should be made out of cobblestone to resist fire and explosions.

And then, building code A7F states that a door should be iron and **activated with a button** placed above, not a pressure plate, so that mobs can't open the door.

As if mobs **can't press buttons.**

That's how ridiculous the mayor is, you know?

Doesn't he understand how smart the **mobs** are?

The mobs are brilliant. Astoundingly, preposterously, ridiculously, improbably, absurdly, fantastically, wonderfully, unbelievably, amazingly, impossibly, **astonishingly brilliant.** If the mobs can come up with such tactics as zombie sandwiches, then surely they can press a button with a finger. And if they don't have fingers, then they'll just jump up and headbutt the buttons.

And if they don't have heads, well, I'm not sure *what* they'll do, but I'm willing to put one hundred emeralds on them figuring it out somehow.

There is one more thing **I didn't like** about all this additional iron and stone. After I performed all the necessary upgrades, our house looked . . . **colorless.** Emotionless. Devoid of warmth and feeling.

Gray walls.
Gray floors.
Gray fence.
Gray doors.

I'd include a picture of our new house, but **honestly,** it's extremely **depressing.** You'd probably start **crying.**

Even Steve commented on this. "If every house ends up like yours, this village will be straight out of a **dystopian film.**"

Dystopian?

I didn't know what that meant, but by the look on his face, I knew **it wasn't a good thing.**

Also . . . Pebble drew on my cloak with **red dye.**

I totally saw this coming.

TUESDAY

After school, **Brio kidnapped** me again. As before, the **special building** was full of guys in **black robes**. And as before, Brio offered me a wide variety of snacks after we sat down in a small cobblestone room. In fact, he was **generally pleasant and happy,** until:

"By the way, Runt . . . have you seen **any slimes?**"
I began to sweat profusely.
"**Er,** once," I said. "The slime **incident.** If you remember."
"I mean **recently.**"
"**N-no,** of course not."
"Well, we've managed to re-create the potion you made earlier," he said. "It's called a **Rocket Potion.** Interestingly, the key ingredient— that is, the extra ingredient used to augment a Potion of Leaping—is **fermented glowstone.** This is made by combining regular glowstone with **a slimeball.**"

Of course. I can't remember how long it's been, but one day, I came home from school completely **exhausted**. The brewing teacher had given us some supplies—including glowstone—for us to do our homework with. But I was **so tired** I put the glowstone into **the wrong chest** in my bedroom. Perhaps my pet slime tried eating the glowstone, then spit it out?

As I thought about this, **awkward silence** filled the room. My mind raced as I considered what I could possibly say to **Brio**. Finally, I offered a **carefully crafted response:**

"Oh."

To be fair, it was a *bubbly* sounding "**oh.**" Naive. Innocent. *Full of* **innocence.** The most innocent "oh" that ever was. After hearing that "**oh,**" there should have been no doubt in anyone's mind that the only slime *I'd* seen in the past year was **the stuff** the school serves for **lunch** on Thursdays.

Brio removed his sunglasses. **Slowly.** Set them down upon the table in a **gentle** way. However, there was nothing gentle about his expression. Or the quiet tone of his voice:

"We . . . are . . . **at war** . . . if we are not careful, the mobs **will** destroy us . . . do **you** . . . **understand?**"

I held the sides of my seat. Arms locked straight. An effort to either hold myself upright or keep myself from **shaking** too much.

"Yes."

"**Good.** So, if you're **harboring** a mob . . . even something so innocent as, say, **a baby slime** . . . you will **report** it. **Immediately.**"

Wow. What a tough decision. What was he saying, anyway? **That Jello could be a spy?** No, I just **couldn't believe it.** Jello is a **nice slime.** A true gentleman, remember? In fact, someday, he's going to run for president. He wouldn't do a thing like that.

I didn't want to **betray** my village—but at the same time, I didn't want to turn in my pet, either. Besides, I felt my pet slime had a purpose . . . and it *wasn't* providing other mobs with **information.**

"Sir," I said, "I **do not have** any mobs in my possession."

Brio glanced down at the table, hands together, perhaps considering my words. When he spoke again, it was in his usual, **cheery tone:**

"**Very well. That's good news.** And there's *more* good news. Since you are directly responsible for the discovery of that potion recipe, you will be rewarded. Expect a payment of **fifty emeralds.** Within a few days."

More awkward silence, until:

"**Brio?** Can I ask what you were doing out there?"

"Out where?"

"**During the battle on Saturday.**"

"You are dismissed."

Brio rose up from his chair. I did the same.

"Oh, and look out for anything **strange,**" he said. "We have reason to believe there's **a spy** in the village."

"**A spy?**"

"Yes. You see, our data indicates the mobs wanted to destroy the school. How else could they have known where the school was located? Surely there must be a spy hiding somewhere within the periphery of the village. Or, possibly, **a traitor.** Understand?"

"Yes, sir."

I bowed before him and took off out of that place *(grabbing a few cookies as I did).*

As I ran back home, **my mind was racing.**

A spy in our village. **A traitor.**

Is it **Jello?** No, how can he spy on anything? All he does is eat bread. He never even leaves his box!

What about Breeze? She's **very weird,** after all.

Hurrrmm . . .

After I got back to my house, I went into my bedroom and opened the chest. Jello was there, sleeping. He woke up moments later and began **hopping around.**

I picked him up.

"You're not a spy, are you, Jello?"

I petted his flat head.

"No, of course not. **You're a good boy.**"

144

WEDNESDAY

I've been mentioning my school for weeks but I've never shown it. I suppose now would be a good time. After all, if the mobs really *do* want to destroy it, then I should make a few pictures while I still can.

And so, say hello to the **Villager School of Minecraft and Warriory.** (Steve said warriory isn't an actual word. Yeah, Steve, I get it: our vocabulary is different from yours on Earth.)

With more than twenty classrooms, our school is without a doubt the biggest school in all of Minecraftia.

The combat yard

By the way, an incident occurred in the combat yard today. Drill was **screaming at Max**, so Max put a **sign** up on one of the dummies.

Ten minutes later, Drill came over, wondering why so many students were attacking **the same dummy.**

Anyone who attacked that sign had to do **two hundred laps.** By the time we finished running, lunch was already over. Still, **the look on Drill's face** when he saw that sign was priceless. I'd give up **ten lunches** to see that again.

The front entrance

Obviously, the school hasn't seen the necessary **safety upgrades** yet. Glass windows for walls probably aren't the safest way to guard against zombies. **Just a guess, though.**

The cafeteria

You're probably wondering how **150 students** manage to sit down in this place. They don't. The food here makes mushroom stew look tasty.

> And this is why I always
> bring my own lunch.

See that **green potato?** That's a **fermented** potato. It's a village specialty. Made using **a secret crafting recipe.** Most adults consider it **a delicacy,** and it's supposed to be healthy. That's why it's on the menu, I guess.

By the way, I wasn't joking about **the slime** they serve on Thursdays. It's that bowl of **green stew** on the right. It isn't really slime, of course, although it looks just like it. **Grass stew.** Another villager "**delicacy.**" My grandfather loves the stuff.

Okay, I'm just gonna rush through the rest of the tour because it's **not very interesting,** and honestly, I'm getting a bit hungry.

The Mobs Defense classroom

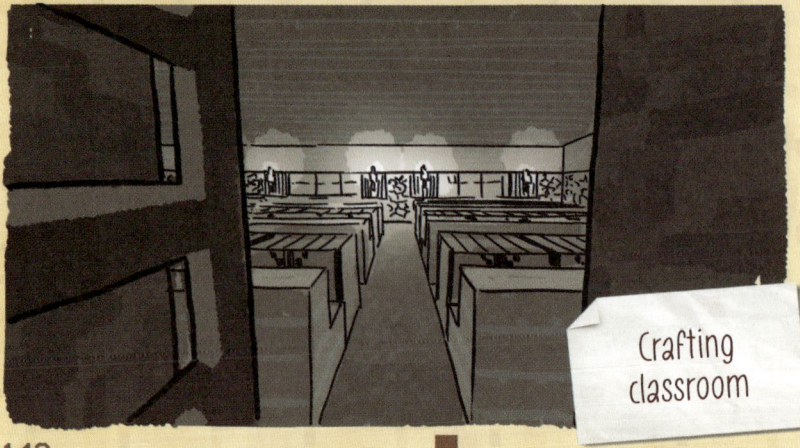

Crafting classroom

The Tower

I've never been to the second and third floors.
I think the teachers do **weird experiments** up there.

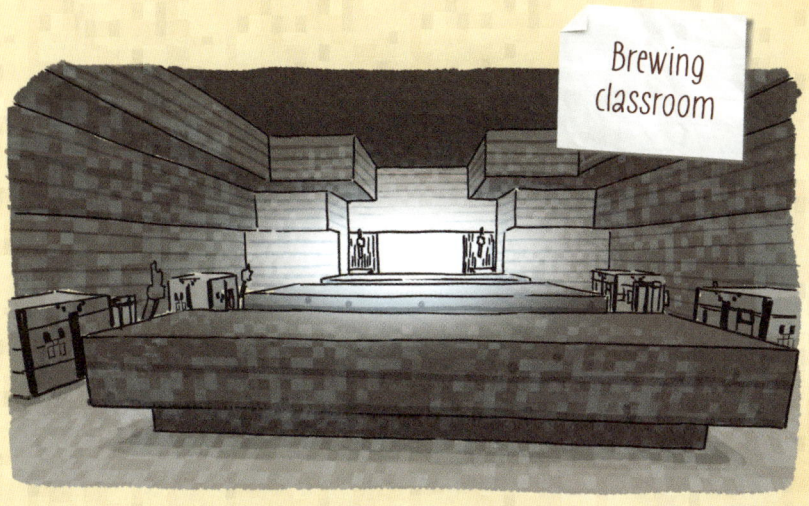

Brewing classroom

Near the school is the village square. It's a trading zone, full of merchant stands.

The fountain. The mayor ordered **its construction** years ago. After it was built, that old blacksmith, Leaf, took off his shoes and began **washing his feet.** Many people have **avoided its waters** since.

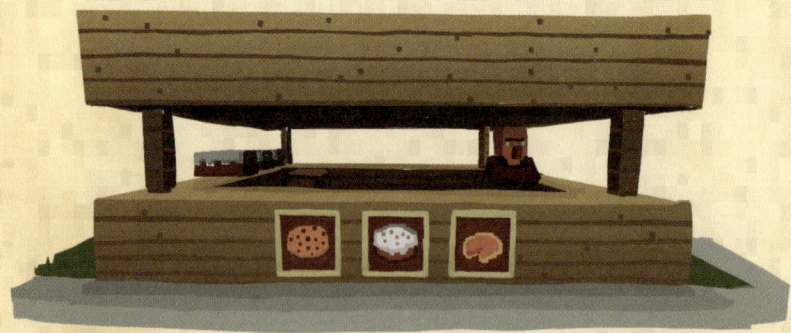

The square's food stand. My **favorite stand. Obviously.** If I had saved up all my emeralds instead of buying junk food at this place, I'd probably have enough for **a full set of diamond armor** by now. Kids who forgot to bring their own lunch and can't stomach grass stew go here.

The stand that shall not be mentioned—although I will say the roof, made out of acacia and birch to resemble a giant red mushroom, is **kinda neat.**

That was a **ton** of pictures. Sorry. Wait, what am I apologizing for?! **It took me forever to draw those pictures!**

Anyway, there you have it. To be honest, that was only about *half* the places I could have shown you, but I didn't want you **to fall asleep.**

Oh. I received that payment from Brio. So I went **shopping** today and ended up buying a **full set of leather armor** *(except for a helmet)* along with **an iron sword** and **two enchanted books.**

Then . . . In the street just outside the blacksmith . . . I ran into **Pebble.** He eyed me, eyed my sword, then **smirked** and stepped closer.

"I see you've brought me **a gift.**"

"**Don't even try it,**" I said, raising the blade for the first time. "This thing's enchanted with **Bane of Noobs V** and **Wuss Slaying VII.**"

He put his hands in the air and backed up slowly.

"Oh, dear! **No! Please!**" He dropped to one knee and clasped his hands together. "Please spare a humble noob such as myself!" Two of his friends came around the corner then, glanced at us, and **snickered.** Then the three of them took off.

Sigh. I'd been trying to **avoid** him, but I guess that's impossible now. At least he didn't dunk me in the well again. I should be thankful for that. He did that yesterday, but I didn't put it into my diary. It was just **too humiliating.** I wish there was a **Bane of Noobs** enchantment, though.

<u>Pebble would have been totally shaking in his boots.</u>

THURSDAY

This morning, **Brio and company** showed up at school. They set up **an office** on the second floor. And the whole day, they observed everyone. They also randomly searched **through kids' inventories** in the hallways and dug through our school chests . . .

It was eerie. You couldn't go anywhere without being **watched**, without being searched, followed, or endlessly questioned.

Then, during Intro to Combat, a few of those black-robed guys stepped in. They made us run in place for a **long time** and shouted in our faces while we did it. A guy in black was yelling at Stump so loud that spit was flying from his mouth. **Poor Stump** was moving as fast as he could, arms swinging, knees moving up and down like pistons, with the most **scared yet serious** look upon his face.

(I refer to them as "guys in black" because I really don't know who they are. They're **elders**, certainly, but I don't know any of their names. The only thing I do know about them is that they're not **complete noobs** like Urf.)

Annoyingly, Pebble and Emerald seemed immune to their **harassment.** Neither of them have received a question, an inventory search, or even an angry look.

I want out.

Lightning, please **strike me** and turn me into a **witch**.

Or an enderpumpkin.
Or a <u>**creeperman**</u>.

I don't even know what a **creeperman** is or what a creeperman's life would be like, but **I don't care.** I'll take it. Anything is better than this.

FRIDAY

If my life hit **bedrock** yesterday, then today, it somehow broke through that **bedrock** and vanished deep down into the **void**.

Today, they assigned every student to a **"combat unit."** Should the mobs **attack again**, we must stay with the other members of our **unit** and follow Drill's orders. Sounds good, **right? Yeah.** Here are the other three members of my unit:

It's almost like the mayor spent a whole night **calculating** how to annoy me the most.

Emerald didn't seem **too happy** about it, either.

"**You can't do this,**" she said to Drill.

When the teacher chuckled but said nothing, she **continued**:

"**Hey!** I *refuse* to group up with them. **Especially him.** The **weirdest stuff** always happens to him! He's like a lightning rod for trouble! **A magnet for craziness!**"

She was referring to me, obviously. *(Do I really get into that much trouble? It's not like I ever asked for it. Stuff happens, you know?)* Besides, I didn't do anything crazy during **the battle on Saturday.** I stuck with my friends. **Protected** them. Even resisted the urge to **follow Brio.** Emerald's **silvery voice** tore me from my thoughts.

"**How about that creepy girl?** What are you *thinking* putting the two of them together? And don't get me started on Urf. He's totally—"

She fell silent when Brio walked up.

"**There is a reason for everything,**" he said. "Trust me."

The "**war heroine**" lowered her head, fists clenched—but she waited for Brio to take off before letting out **a big sigh.**

Hurrrmm.
This is gonna be fun.

I'm stuck with **Weirdostalkergirl, The Great Bearded Noob,** and **Princess Hissyfit McCrybaby.** Good thing I like **a challenge,** eh? Stump arguably has it **worse,** however. He's grouped with Bumbi, who is currently the lowest-level student in the whole school. Apparently, he still has a **combat score of 1.** How is that even possible? A door has more than that.

Anyway, **I'll be okay.** Tomorrow, there's no school and no chance of another attack. I mean, the mobs attacked *last* Saturday, **right?** The mobs would *never* attack on *another* Saturday because that would be too predictable. **Yeah.** I'm totally safe. Tomorrow, I'm going fishing. And I'm getting some ice cream. And I'm hanging out with my friends.

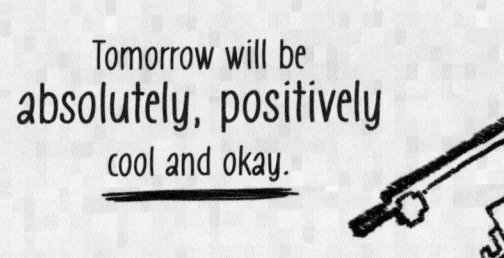

Tomorrow will be **absolutely, positively** cool and okay.

SATURDAY: BOSS BATTLE—PART ONE

"YOU'RE FACING THE WRONG WAY YOU SU——"
BOOM!!!

An **explosion** drowned out whatever insult Drill was about to **hurl**. Beyond him, the streets might have passed for one of the nicer parts of **the Nether**.

As Emerald said when we first arrived,

"You know, this would make a good ad for promoting those village building codes."

Fires were **blazing**, the ground was occasionally trembling, and **the smoke**, drifting across the ground on its little gray feet, made it impossible to see just how many mobs there were out there. A lot, I guessed.

"FIRE!!"

Arrows flew from **rooftops** in endless streams, vanishing into the gray mist. Earlier, we'd cut down almost every tree in the park to make a countless number of shafts. Those who were the best shots with a bow had been put into the same unit. Minutes ago, they'd been sent to the tops of houses. **It was nice having archers.**

Our unit was assigned to the ground to fight the **enemy with swords**, and with **so many arrows** flying, we didn't have to do that much. The sheer number of arrows the archers sent out caught the mobs by surprise. Some sections of wall could barely be seen due to the amount of arrows sticking in them.

It was **intense**.

Then, like the last battle, the mobs started **to run**. **Ridiculously,** a zombie broke out into a really funny dance before it took off.

"GET!! THAT!! **ZOMBIE!!**"

At Drill's command, over one hundred screaming villagers charged forward . . . along with Steve, Mike, and my two best friends. At last, the archers **jumped down** and followed at a safe distance.

But my unit wouldn't be joining them. We were on **guard duty**. Our job was to protect the school, just in case the mobs pulled **any tricks**.

We had to prevent **any creeper** from getting within five blocks. Drill turned to us. Surprisingly, he didn't shout or even raise his voice:

"**Remain near the school** until further notice."

I nodded. Then Breeze nodded. Then Emerald nodded. But Urf was nowhere nearby. He was walking down the road, **trying to sneak away.**

"And where might *you* be going?" Drill called out.

The elder slowly turned around.

"Well, **uh**, you know, I just thought I might, um, go check on something—"

The current combat teacher smiled, beckoning him closer with a finger.

Urf finally nodded—*but glumly, glumly. Then he trudged back into the blazing street.*

"**Now,**" said Drill, "if you guys get into any trouble, just set these off." He handed Emerald some **blue fireworks** along with a flint and steel. "And don't leave the school." With that, he sprinted off through the smoke, which was only swirling at knee level now. The four of us silently watched him go.

In the distance, an occasional explosion or shout could be heard.

We were alone.

I wanted to **be out there**, of course, **next to my friends**, but we had to obey our orders.

There were no mobs here, and it seemed like there never would be, but maybe Drill **was right.**

I sighed and glanced behind me, **at the school.**

The sounds of combat faded. And then—

SATURDAY: BOSS BATTLE—PART TWO

To the right, distant footsteps could be heard.
It was more like scraping, shuffling.

Zombies.

"I heard that!" Urf jerked his head every which way. There was another scraping sound. Then the elder made the same **ridiculous creeper** face, the same pigman grunt.

"Mobs! **They're around the corner!** I heard them!"

"Will you *shut up*," I hissed.

The school was across the square, which meant that if we ran there now, the mobs would **surely see us.** So I motioned for everyone to hide. All four of us crept into the alley to the right. Urf latched on to Emerald, **trembling.**

"Don't let them get me!"

"**Go away!**" She pushed him back and glared at him. "Dude, you're such a—"

Just then, **several zombies** walked into view and stopped in front of the fountain. Their **deep, guttural** voices drifted through the air. They were speaking in the **ancient tongue.**

It took me a moment to realize **what one of them was holding.**

"You forgot zombie demolitions expert. Punk."

Emerald drew her sword.

"I call dibs on **Explody** there."

"He's mine."

With a loud scream, I charged, sword held in both hands. I don't know why I was being so reckless. Just . . . when I saw that zombie holding a block of TNT, **something snapped inside of me.**

I mean, who did they think they were? **They were zombies.**

They were supposed to **moan.** Burn in the sun.

Get **confused** by improperly set doors.

My sword sliced through the air. However . . . after connecting with its target, it was as if the blade had **struck cobblestone** instead of rotten flesh. **The zombie didn't moan,** stumble back, or even flinch—instead, it punched me so hard I flew five blocks backward and landed on my back. Despite my armor, the attack reduced my life **by four hearts.** That was a **huge amount of damage** from a single attack. Yet it couldn't match the amount of pain I felt.

Ten blocks to my right, Emerald had **skidded** to a halt and was now slowly backpedaling into the ruined street. Urf, of course, had already fled the scene. I thought I was a **goner.** Then **Breeze** yanked me to my feet.

Silly girl . . . What is she doing?

We just **stood** there, while more zombies trickled in from **every direction**.

Within moments, at least ten had surrounded us.

We were cut off. We couldn't run.

Yet . . . they didn't close in. Instead, several of them laughed, chests heaving, heads raised back, faces somehow **jovial.** Their deep laughter echoed across the square.

That was when I noticed the **swirls emanating from their bodies.**

Red swirls.

That meant the zombies were under the effect of **strength potions**—maybe **Strength III**, considering how much damage I had taken from one punch. There were **faint gray swirls**, too, although I had no idea what kind of effect they signified.

After another round of **laughter**, the zombies moved in, one step at a time, **impossibly slow**, as if they were trying to draw this moment out and **prolong our suffering.**

Then a zombie began speaking, its voice screechy yet deep. It was gibberish, **unintelligible**, the language of **enchanting tables and wizards** long since forgotten. Still, even though I couldn't understand the words, I knew what was being said: **We were doomed**. There was no way out of this.

There was just no way.

Then, behind me, ringing out above the zombie's frightening speech, was **a metallic cling.**

Breeze.

It was the first time she'd drawn her sword in battle. When I glanced behind me, I noticed she **wasn't trembling** like before. On the contrary—she stood **perfectly still.** It was as if she had suddenly **grown stronger** while I had **grown weak.**

I found her courage **inspiring,** yet it ultimately wouldn't matter. The zombies were **impossibly strong, impossibly resilient.**

She's fighting even though there's **no way we can win.**

And **I ignored** her this whole time . . .

"**Run,**" I said. "I'll distract them, huh? **Just run.**"

SATURDAY: BOSS BATTLE—PART THREE

I . . . don't know what happened. There's . . . really **no way to explain it.** In less than ten seconds, **piles of dust were scattered everywhere** . . . I stood there for a long time, my mind a malfunctioning **redstone machine.** A light breeze scattered the dust.

Breeze was staring at the ground, her expression **dark**.

"You can't tell anyone."

"So . . . you've been **hiding yourself?**"

No response.

She turned away.

I studied her for a moment—then, after realizing she wasn't going **to talk anymore**, I surveyed the destruction in her wake. **Tons of items** lay within the zombie's remains. Armor, swords. Bows. Arrows. Flint and steel. Tools of all kinds and **a great deal of potions**. Even a **bone**. Those zombies were really packing. Especially the zombie Emerald had dubbed **"Explody."** TNT had **spilled out everywhere** after Breeze took him out. Had we not been sent here on guard duty, the school would be **ten times worse** than that street over there.

Good job, Drill. *When this is all over, I'm gonna buy you a pie.*

I picked up all the items, wondering **how many emeralds** I could get for all of it.

Speaking of emeralds, Emerald eventually came back with two iron golems. Not a bad idea. She met the **square** with wide eyes.

"What *happened?*"

"It's **complicated.**"

Then, the ground trembled. Again, **deep laughter** boomed in the distance—**but this time, it wasn't** from any <u>zombie.</u>

SATURDAY: BOSS BATTLE—PART FOUR

To the south, down another ruined street, perhaps a little more than **fifty blocks** away, stood the **legend** himself: **Urkk Doomwhip.**

Two creepers slithered around at his feet, like baby chickens in comparison. *(Important note: One of them was glowing a brilliant shade of blue.)*

Needless to say, Emerald did more **backpedaling.**

"**Wow,**" she said. "They **really, really** want the school. I say we **compromise.** We could let them take out the combat yard. Then we'd all shake hands and call it a day. I mean, they'd be **doing us a favor anyway,** y'know?"

The two iron golems charged. Breeze sagged her shoulders and followed them in. Emerald and I ran after her.

"**Wait!**" I called out. "He's gonna—"

And yes. It can really do this.

Yeah. He's gonna do that.

Even though I'd already read about Urkk's ability to **throw other mobs,** it still came as a shock, seeing that **creeper** fly, its sad little face growing bigger and bigger . . .

We had to **take cover. Snark's Tavern** was the closest place.

There used to be a sign here that said something about Steve owing Snark sixty-seven emeralds. I guess he lost a bet during an **iron golem race.**

We **burst through** the door.

What a cozy little place. Stump and I often went to Snark's when we were kids. The tea is pretty good. **Sadly,** there was no time for tea now. On the plus side, **we were safe.**

Snark said his tavern is the only original building still standing after the **creeper rush of 1511.** Little did I know, Breeze, Emerald, and I were nothing more than the **Three Little Pigs,** with the incoming charged creeper as the Big Bad Wolf.

And Snark's Tavern?
Just so <u>much straw</u>.

I guess Snark **failed to mention** that the only other homes around in 1511 were made of dirt and/or grass.

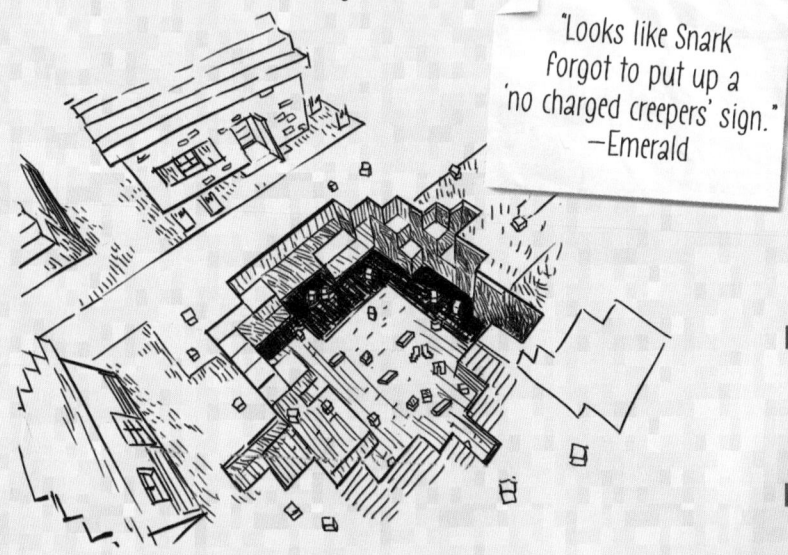

"Looks like Snark forgot to put up a 'no charged creepers' sign."
—Emerald

When the smoke cleared, I spotted **several iron ingots** down in the crater. The remains of the iron golems. They must have taken a direct hit. **Poor things.**

(There was also some leather armor, which I can only guess was from a zombie that tried running after us.)

After **glancing** at the crater, Breeze **left the building** without a word. She ran so fast I couldn't keep up. Then she jumped—a height of five blocks, impossible—and struck Urkk square in the face. From what I'd read, Urkk had an **incredible amount of life,** yet her attack not only **forced him back,** but **shattered** his black helmet as well.

However . . . When she landed, the pigman sent out his **chained hook.** I only had time to see Urkk's hook **snag Breeze** and pull her within arm's reach . . . Then he smashed her with one of his **huge, block-sized fists,** like an iron golem hitting a baby rabbit. Breeze went flying. Somewhere over a house. **She vanished beyond the roof.**

She's okay, I thought. For all I know, she **probably has more life than Urkk does**.

Emerald glanced at the **smoldering crater,** at the melted remains of the iron golems, at the sky where Breeze had flown, and at the **enormous** zombie pigman with glowing **red eyes** and a crazy-looking fishing rod who'd just thrown a creeper roughly **twenty-five blocks.**

There was a brief silence as she reflected upon the situation, then: "*That's* it. **I'm outta here."**

After she took off, I did some glancing around, too. A little glance here, a little glance there. Real innocent. Casual. **Unfortunately,** Urkk was glancing, too. At me.

Hurrrmm . . .
This is baddd.

SATURDAY: BOSS BATTLE—PART FIVE

For a second, I actually **took out my shovel.**

Okay, think. What did Max say about Urkk's fear of **heights?** Something about a height of **five blocks?** But it's all stone down here.

Just my luck! I have no time to **dig a pit** wide and deep enough to scare him. I'd need **an enchanted diamond pickaxe.**

(I guess your plans can't all be brilliant, eh, Max?)

Okay.
Run for now.

I **climbed** out of the hole and took off to the square.

Urkk ran, too—and let me tell you, I'd never really thought about just **how fast a giant pigman can run,** but believe me, it's fast.

He had **nearly** caught up to me by the time I reached the square. I looked behind me, saw him **sending out his chain** . . .

. . . **and dashed** to the right just before it caught me.

The chain made a **high-pitched whine** as it cut through the air inches from my left ear. **Urkk roared.** His voice was so loud and deep.

"You quick one! Like **big rabbit!** Me love rabbit stew! Hur, hur, hur."

I couldn't **run** from him, so I had to hide.

If I can hide, and **survive** long enough, maybe someone will come over and **help me out.**

Actually, on that note, **where is everyone else?!** Preoccupied, I guess. There are still more iron golems, though.

Step 1: Dig a hole.
Step 2: Hide from Urkk.
Step 3: Wait until iron golems save me.

172

Impressed? Neither am I. **Neither am I.** But it was all I had. Yet . . . if I tried digging out in the open, the pigman would hook me, and that would be that.

I had to find cover. The closest thing was . . . **the mushroom stew stand.** Today was definitely *not* my day. It had a **low roof**, though, so I knew it would be hard for Urkk to see me. The huge pigman sent out his hook, and I dodged again. Then I dove into the stand.

A **brown mushroom** was growing on the grass floor. Still holding my shovel, I dug **down into the grass.**

From there, I could only see Urkk's legs. The **ground shook** as the pigman took a step forward.

Then the second creeper caught up to him, and Urkk grabbed it . . .

A second later, **I heard a thud.** Above me. **And a hiss.** Yes, Urkk had tossed the creeper onto the roof of the mushroom stew stand.

(Can these mobs get any more annoying?)

The scientific and technical term used to describe the roof would be *splinters.* **Splinters everywhere.** The smoke cleared, exposing Urkk's huge face, **staring down at me.** He raised his huge fist back to send out his chained hook.

It was over. He was going to eat me. *At least Max and Stump aren't here to see this,* I thought. *I hope* **Breeze is okay** *. . .*

Then something **amazing** happened . . .

 Jello appeared.

He bounced over the counter of the mushroom stand and **hopped up** and down in front of me. The giant pigman **scowled and shook with rage.**

"Move!!"

Jello hopped again and made some **weird noises.**

He's . . . protecting me?!

"I said **scram,** slime!! **This one's mine!!**"

More hopping. More squeaking. **Well,** it was nice that my pet slime had come to my rescue, but even *I* knew there was nothing Jello could do except buy me some time.

Then the following words echoed in my mind:

"... *height* of *five blocks* ..."

An idea began forming. There was a way to defeat Urkk. It was **complicated,** I realized, but maybe ...

I looked at the oak planks scattered around me. At the brown mushroom growing on the ground. Then I glanced at the bone, the flint and steel, and the TNT in my inventory. **Yes,** piece by piece, I was formulating a **ridiculous plan** ... I had no idea if it would work, honestly.

"Distract him, Jello! Okay?!"

"Squerk!" *(Maybe that's how slimes say "okay"?)*

With shaking hands, I grabbed four oak planks and crafted a crafting table. Urkk kept yelling at my pet.

"Just a few more seconds, Jello!"

Squerk!! Squerk!!

Finally, I turned the bone into a few **handfuls of bone meal.** Of course, the whole time, Urkk was shouting.

"So you've sided with them?! **Traitor!!** Time to join your friend!!"

The pigman raised his weapon again.

"Jello!! Run!!"

I **pushed the baby slime** out of the way, then dove backward over the counter, away from Urkk.

There was a **crackling** sound as the hook drove into the oak wood between us. Another roar, followed by **his footsteps.**

Boom, boom.

He was standing on top of the mushroom stand's front counter, now. He looked down at me, his face visible again, and **licked his lips . . .**

I ran away, knowing that hook would be coming for me. It cut through the air. **A horrifying sound.** Yet I turned around and let it hook me. . .

***

Ooof. Urkk pulled that chain with all his **might.** Even though it was just a special type of fishing rod, it dealt a huge amount of damage when it reeled me in. Still, I grasped the end and unhooked myself before his massive fist grabbed me.

I **dropped** to the ground, taking slight falling damage. But the brown mushroom now sat before me. More important, the mushroom sat **under Urkk's legs.** As Urkk raised a foot to stomp me into villager stew, another arrow whistled through the air, **striking** Urkk in the face.

Breeze?
She's alive!

The arrow didn't do much to the pigman, but he put his foot down and looked up for a second. **Another distraction.** It bought just enough time for me to dump a handful of bone meal onto the mushroom. Green motes of light flew forth . . . and the mushroom **instantly** grew . . . . . . pushing Urkk up high into the air.

Uwaaaaahhhhh!!!

It was amazing.

The giant brown mushroom **not only forced Urkk upward**, but also somehow supported his weight. Up that high, with Urkk's fear of heights, he must have felt like a skeleton surrounded by fifty dogs, or an enderman on a tiny island in the middle of the ocean . . .

You get the idea.

"You will pay for this!! **Herobrine is coming!!**"

I **ignored** his cries, grabbing all the **TNT** from my inventory. There was only one thing left to do.

Once I lit a TNT block, I grabbed Jello and ran. I guess Urkk was too scared to even try to do anything to me. He just cowered up there on top of the giant mushroom, as I sprinted to safety.

"You . . . little . . . runt!! Uwaaaag!!"

Cloudy, with a chance of mushroom-and-pigman stew . . .

A slight wind rustled the grass nearby. **Experience orbs** flowed through the sky. The wind calmed down. Urkk's fishing rod had landed **five blocks away.** I **petted** Jello, wondering how he'd gotten out of his chest.

"Good boy."
Squeak.

Only then did I **feel the pain.** My vision kept flashing bright red, and my life bar was flickering the same color. **I had half a heart left.** I slid down against the wall, **my vision growing blurry,** dim.

Within moments,
everything went black.

SUNDAY

Don't worry. **Everything's okay.**

I didn't get much recognition for **dropping Urkk**, since Breeze was the only one to witness it, but hey, how can I complain? **I'm alive.**

By the way, one of the first things I did after waking up was ask Breeze if I could see her record book. **She actually showed me.**

BREEZE
STUDENT
LEVEL 98

MINING	97%
COMBAT	100%
TRADING	91%
FARMING	100%
BUILDING	100%
CRAFTING	100%

Turns out **everyone at school was wrong**. Breeze has been **rank one** almost the entire time. Which means Pebble is rank two, Emerald rank three, and so on. Whoever was rank three a couple of weeks ago is **still a mystery.**

My own level is getting up there.

```
         RUNT
        STUDENT
       LEVEL 81

   MINING          57%
   COMBAT          89%
   TRADING         100%
   FARMING         79%
   BUILDING        95%
   CRAFTING        68%
```

I'm currently rank five. Breeze, Pebble, Emerald, and Max are ahead of me. If I slip up, maybe **I won't become a warrior after all.** But at this rate, the mayor's gonna have to let everyone become warriors, so maybe it doesn't matter. No. It will matter. I'm sure of it.

Breeze and I went to get ice cream this afternoon, and she told me more about herself.

"When I saw **everyone competing** and showing off," Breeze said, "I knew I shouldn't try to draw attention to myself. That way, I wouldn't receive any **harassment** from someone like Pebble."

"Why didn't I think of that?" I paused. "Wait a second. Remember the archery range? Your shooting wasn't too great then."

"I wasn't actually trying," she said. "After the first five shots, you noticed, so I . . ."

Right. Anyway, I think there's even more to this weird girl than she's letting on—she's obviously not ordinary—but **she won't tell me anything** about her family, where she comes from, or anything like that.

"I've been following you because my dad asked me to," she said. "My dad has been **watching you.** He thinks the village needs you."

"Needs me? **Why?**"

She gazed at the endless blue sky, **lost in thought.**

"Maybe you're not the best student, but my dad thinks you have **great potential.**"

"**Really . . . ?**"

(I think this was the first compliment I've ever received in my life.)

". . . and who's your dad?" I asked.

. . .

"Well?"

"You'll find out **soon enough.**"

Hurrgg.

I really wonder who her father is . . . Someone told me he was some **wealthy miner** type or something like that, but who knows.

I also found out *she* had let Jello out. After Urkk knocked her away, she ran to my house and grabbed him. She thought that maybe he could talk to the pigman, since he's a **mob** and all. It was worth a shot and bought me enough time to **blow up the pigman.**

Of course, I was wondering **how she knew about Jello,** since I'd never told her about him.

"It was Stump, **wasn't it?!**"

"No, no. Um, I . . . saw you **playing with him once.** Through your bedroom window."

As for the village, things are **getting grim.** This second mob attack has sent the **mayor into a panic** and prompted him to rigidly enforce the building codes, among other things. The village is becoming more and more **gray** . . . stone and iron everywhere . . .

And the guys in black robes harass us in school every day.

"Study **harder!** Run **faster!** What do you think the mobs are doing?! They're training sixteen hours a day!"

"Spies and traitors will be **imprisoned without question.**"

If you have reason to believe someone you know is providing the mobs with information, please **contact** . . ."

"We are **searching your inventories** and school chests for the **safety** of the village . . ."

"Anyone who goes outside after sunset will be **detained for questioning** . . ."

The last thing I have to add is . . . a lot of **huge building projects** are underway. Deadfall fields are to be dug outside—a huge project, considering how big the wall is. Then guards will be placed on the walls at night. In addition, a new tower will be built, **an extremely tall one,** to detect incoming attacks.

From here on out, we can't have **any more mobs breaking any more walls.** The crazier the mobs get, the crazier our defenses will get. **It's that simple.**

Herobrine can eat
a fermented potato.

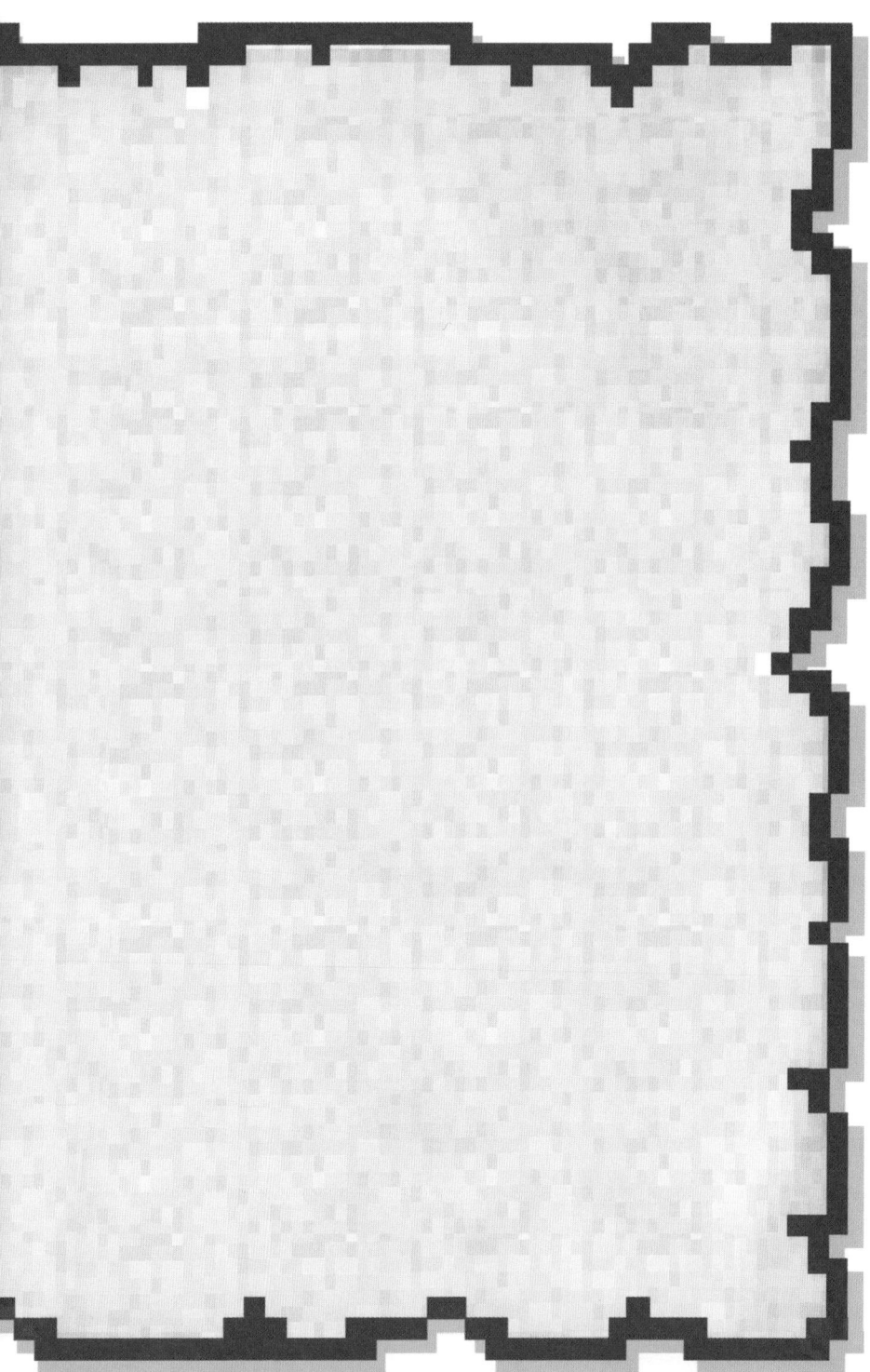

YOU KNOW
the drill by now.

I had to stop somewhere!
The story picks right up in book 3:

ABOUT THE AUTHOR

Cube Kid is the pen name of Erik Gunnar Taylor, a writer who has lived in Alaska his whole life. A big fan of video games—especially Minecraft—he discovered early that he also had a passion for writing fan fiction.

Cube Kid's unofficial Minecraft fan fiction series, *Diary of a Wimpy Villager*, came out as e-books in 2015 and immediately met with great success in the Minecraft community. They were published in France by 404 éditions in paperback with illustrations by Saboten and now return in this same format to Cube Kid's native country under the title *Diary of an 8-Bit Warrior*.

When not writing, Cube Kid likes to travel, putter with his car, devour fan fiction, and play his favorite video game.

TALES OF AN 8-BIT KITTEN
LOST IN THE NETHER

This edition © 2018 by Andrews McMeel Publishing.

All rights reserved. Printed in China. No part of this book may be used or reproduced in any manner whatsoever without written permission except in the case of reprints in the context of reviews.

Published in French under the title *Un Chaton Qui S'est Perdu dans le Nether Tome I* © 2017 by 404 éditions, an imprint of Édi8, Paris, France
Text © 2015 by Cube Kid, Illustration © 2016 by Vladimir "ZloyXP" Subbotin

Minecraft is a Notch Development AB registered trademark. This book is a work of fiction and not an official Minecraft product, nor approved by or associated with Mojang. The other names, characters, places, and plots are either imagined by the author or used fictitiously.

Andrews McMeel Publishing
a division of Andrews McMeel Universal
1130 Walnut Street, Kansas City, Missouri 64106
www.andrewsmcmeel.com

20 21 22 23 24 SDB 10 9 8 7 6 5 4 3

ISBN: 978-1-4494-9447-6
Library of Congress Control Number: 2018932587

Made by:
King Yip (Dongguan) Printing & Packaging Factory Ltd.
Address and location of manufacturer:
Daning Administrative District, Humen Town
Dongguan Guangdong, China 523930
3rd printing—6/29/20

ATTENTION: SCHOOLS AND BUSINESSES
Andrews McMeel books are available at quantity discounts with bulk purchase for educational, business, or sales promotional use. For information, please e-mail the Andrews McMeel Publishing Special Sales Department: specialsales@amuniversal.com.

TALES OF AN 8-BIT KITTEN

LOST IN THE NETHER

Illustrations by
Vladimir "ZloyXP" Subbotin

Andrews McMeel
PUBLISHING®

In memory of Lola Salines (1986–2015),
founder of 404 éditions and editor of this series,
who lost her life in the November 2015 attacks on Paris.
Thank you for believing in me.

—Cube Kid

CHAPTER 1

Eeebs was a **naughty little kitten. Very naughty,** in fact. He **never** listened to his mother.

    She always told him: "Don't go too far into the forest, Son. It's **dangerous.** And if you ever see a purple light . . . run away. **Run** as fast as you can."

But Eeebs **loved** exploring the woods. He didn't think the forest was **dangerous at all.** No, it was an **interesting** place. Interesting and **mysterious.** He went there at least once a week—like today—along with his closest friends, **Tufty** and **Meowz.** The three of them had found a new meadow to play in. The meadow was filled with all kinds of **beautiful flowers.** They were **racing** to see who could pick the most.

Eeebs watched Meowz and Tufty **fight** over a lovely blue orchid. At last, Meowz **tripped Tufty,** who went tumbling into the grass. Then, she **hurried** to pick the orchid before he could get back up.

"**Hey!**" Tufty hissed. "**Not fair!**"

"Well, you **never said** no tripping," she said.

Tufty only flattened his ears and **glared** at her.

She presented **her colorful collection,** fanned out like a rainbow. "Look at all these flowers," she said, beaming like the square sun. "I guess that means **I win,** huh?"

"**Whatever,**" said Tufty. He threw his clump of dandelions onto the ground. "It was a **stupid** game, anyway."

"I agree," said Eeebs. "**I'm bored.** Maybe we should just head back?"

"**You can't be serious,**" said Meowz.

Tufty stepped forward. "We're not gonna get caught again, okay?"

"I know," said Eeebs. "**But—**"

"Look," said Tufty. "The **only reason** our parents don't want us playing here is because they're **jealous.** They can't stand us kittens having **so much fun.**"

"He's right," said Meowz. "I mean, **have you ever seen any zombies** around here? The truth is they just **cooked up** that story to keep us closer to home. Easier to **make us do chores** that way."

Eeebs **sighed.** Maybe they were right. And anyway, the forest really was **the best place** to play in. There were so many **mysteries** just waiting to be discovered.

"Fine," he said. "How about we go play some **hide-and-seek?**" The other two patted him on the back.

3

"Now you're talking!"

"**Yeah!** That's the Eeebs I know!"

But Eeebs had no idea **how much** this suggestion was going to affect him. He could have seen those dark rain clouds in the distance as **a sign of things to come.** Or the chilly breeze that blew through the meadow just then . . .

He didn't, though. Eeebs was just thinking about **how fun** this day was going to be. A day of playing and exploring. And **misbehaving.**

The three kittens began their new game.

"I think you should go first," Tufty said.

"**Why me?**" Eeebs asked.

"Because this was **your idea,** silly."

Eeebs nodded. He didn't mind. He liked being it way more than he liked hiding. And he knew the **real reason** why Tufty wanted to hide: he liked sitting around, doing nothing. He was a bit out of shape and already out of breath after all of that flower collecting.

As Tufty lumbered off into the bushes, Meowz **smirked** at Eeebs.

"I almost feel sorry for you," she purred. "I know the **ultimate hiding spot.** You're gonna be searching **forever.**"

Eeebs flicked his tail. "I like a challenge."

A **real** challenge. He wasn't going to be disappointed. . . .

He waited for Meowz to scamper off before **starting to count.**

He reached twenty, called out, and began the hunt. Eeebs bounded through the hills, through the trees. He peeked in every crevice, every clump of tall grass. He raced up and down **all the nearby valleys.**

But he **never found them,** not even Tufty, who was normally easy to find. Were they **hiding together?**

Yes, Eeebs thought. *Meowz must have felt sorry for him and taken him into her **fantastic** hiding spot.*

He searched and searched **to no avail.** Perhaps twenty minutes passed, then thirty. The first **drop of rain** hit Eeebs square on the nose. It started **pouring** soon after.

Grandpa said it was just going to sprinkle, he thought. *This is some sprinkle! At this rate, I'll need a boat!* What happened next sent a shiver down his spine. He walked through some tall ferns . . . and found himself standing at the edge of a **mountainous biome.**

I'm . . .
*on the **other side** of the forest.*

He had **never** been this far away from home before. He was so focused on finding them that he hadn't paid attention to his surroundings. **He was lost.**

"**Hey!**" he called out. "**I give up!** Guys?"

His thin voice was **drowned out** by the torrential rain. Even if his friends were nearby, they wouldn't have been able to hear him. **And they weren't nearby.** Eeebs was sure of that. **They were smart.** They never would have gone this far.

I'm smart too, Eeebs thought. *I'll figure **something** out. I can just follow the edge of the forest. Yeah, as long as I stick to the edge, I'll end up home on the other side. Right?*

He paused. *But what about Tufty and Meowz? Are they **looking for me** right now? Or are they still **waiting** for me? I can't just **leave them.** What should I do?*

The rain grew **heavier.** Eeebs began **shivering.** He decided to go back into the forest and look for them. It was **the right thing** to do. With a **sinking feeling** in his heart, he turned back to the mountains one last time. **A flash of lightning** suddenly lit up the gray expanse, revealing . . . **wolves.**

They were **moving slowly** toward him. His heart sank **even deeper.** If he had seen them, they **must've seen him,** too. Then he heard a **howl.**

His heart was no longer sinking. It was **pounding wildly,** jumping into his throat.

So he started running. He ran fast, very fast. Eeebs had always been good at running, but he'd **never run faster** in his life. Trees blurred past. **Blind panic** set in. He had **no idea** where he was going and didn't care, as long as it was away from those **howls** and **snarls.** Yet **no matter** how fast he went, the sounds stayed behind him.

Wolves could run fast, too.
Very fast.

Eebs dashed **into a thicket.** Cries echoed through the trees. He could hear the wolves snuffling, **sniffing,** searching for his **scent.** That was when he noticed **a purple glow** coming from farther in the thicket. He **turned away** and **crept closer to the light.**

To a **kitten** like him, it looked like **a screen of violet water . . . floating** in the air . . . framed in **black stone.** For a moment, he **forgot about the wolves** completely. He didn't understand what he was looking at. He had **never seen anything like this** before. Well, the humans made things that resembled it called . . . **doors,** but this was something **different.** Whatever it was, it was **very old.** It seemed as if the forest had grown up **around** the strange object.

Was this **the purple light** his mother had warned him of? It didn't **seem that dangerous.** The light glowed in a **calm** way. **Gentle,** even. For some reason, Eeebs felt he should **approach** it. It was almost as if the doorway was calling to him, **inviting him** to come closer.

And why shouldn't he? By now, those **mangy mutts** were just outside the thicket. **Anything** was better than facing them. And the light was **so warm. Warmer** than any sunlight. Warmer than the furnace he had slept on that time he snuck into a farmer's house. As Eeebs drew closer, **the heat washed over him,** removing the rain's **damp chill.**

Then, **three wolves burst** through the undergrowth.

They **stopped** upon noticing the light. Their snarls turned to whimpers, **soft whines.** After some hesitation, they began growling again, their red eyes fixed on Eeebs as they **slunk slowly forward.** He was an **easy dinner,** after all. Those wolves must've seen far worse than a **violet glow.** . . .

Eeebs **backed up,** right next to the light. Heat waves **blurred his vision.** He felt the light behind him, **pulling him closer.** He thought about **his friends.** He hoped they'd make it back **safely.** He was sure they would. Meowz **always knew** how to find her way home.

That was his **last thought** before
<u>**diving into the screen of light.**</u>

His vision became **blurry,** and suddenly he saw **only darkness.**

Eeebs would **never be a normal cat again.** His days of **climbing trees** and **swatting at butterflies** were over. Stories would spread among the villages, stories of a **strange kitten** with **blue fur** and **violet eyes.**

He hadn't listened to his mom.
He'd ventured into the Nether.

CHAPTER 2

Eeebs **felt nothing** for several seconds. **Nothing** except **his pounding heart.** Bit by bit, the darkness gave way to a **deep red expanse.** It was like an **enormous cave.** Eeebs couldn't see the sky anymore, and **everything was gloomy.** Pillars of **twisted stone** surrounded him. He'd never seen anything like it. Far away, **bright orange streams** flowed down into **a sea** of the same color.

He recognized **this orange stuff.** There was a pool of it in the plains not too far from his home. It was **very hot,** like **liquid fire.** On cold days, the kittens sometimes went near that pool to **warm up.** Of course, his mother had scolded him for hours after finding him there.

*That must be why it's **so warm** here,* Eeebs thought. He turned around, back to **the violet screen.** He had moved **a great distance** by crossing it. Even if he didn't know how, he was certain of this. So that meant he could **head back** at any time. But those **flea scratchers** were probably still waiting for him. If he went back through now, they would **tear him to shreds.**

No, he thought. *I'll stay for now. I'm **safe** here. I only need to **wait** for a while, and . . .*

Just then, **a single wolf emerged from the portal.** It was very close. Eeebs could smell its **rotten breath** and the musky scent of its damp fur. At first he only stared **into the wolf's red eyes,** and it stared back. Neither of them moved. **Total silence.** Then its **confusion** wore off. **Jagged fangs** and a **low growl** shook the kitten into action.

That action, of course, was **bolting across the dark red stones.**

He must be really hungry, Eeebs thought as he jumped across a shallow chasm. *Why **follow** me here? Why couldn't he have just **forgotten about me** and gone after a rabbit?* He zoomed around a column of glowing **yellow rock.** *Rabbits taste better, **don't they?***

Eeebs's path soon came to **an end.** He skidded to a halt on a vast ledge. On each side was a **dizzying** drop. He wasn't afraid of heights, obviously. He was a cat. From countless days of tumbling and tussling in the forest, falling from the **tallest trees,** he could survive **any drop.** He **always** fell feetfirst, but landing on his feet in an **ocean of lava** wouldn't do much good. . . . And that was all he could see down there.

A fiery orange sea.

The wolf **scrambled** onto the ledge and stopped, knowing it had **cornered its prey.** Eeebs **backed up** against the edge of the abyss. His future seemed **grim. Burned? Or eaten?** If he died now, though, he couldn't **explore** this place. And it **had to be explored!** To a **curious little fuzzball** like him, it was the most **fascinating** place he had ever seen. Forget the forest. Forget the swamp and the ravine. This world would become **their new playground.** Still, he had to deal with this **tail-chaser,** first. . . .

Suddenly, he remembered something that **Tufty** had taught him. When chasing prey, a wolf could get pretty **careless.** The hound surged forward, and Eeebs waited for **the right moment.** Then he dashed to the side with unnatural speed—even for a cat. The wolf's fangs chomped down on **thin air.** That was also the only thing supporting it now: **thin air.** The wolf had leapt **right off the cliff.** It yelped and turned as it fell, **disappearing** over the edge. When Eeebs approached and looked down into the lava far below, there was **nothing.** *Poor wolf,* he thought. **Sadness** washed over him. He had only wanted **to get away.** . . .

Which reminded him: How had he **moved so fast?**

He realized he was **trembling.** His heart was **beating furiously,** and he was suddenly **exhausted.** Eeebs moved away from the edge and sank down onto the ground with **a sigh.** Only an hour ago, he was gathering flowers. **And now** . . .

*What **rotten luck**,* he thought. *This is the **worst** day of my life.* An **icy chill** danced up and down his back. *And it's **not over yet.** I still have to find my way home.*

That portal would be **easy to spot,** of course, but it **wasn't in sight.** Eeebs had run fast, for a long time, and lost his sense of direction. All of a sudden this new world seemed **much, much** larger and **much** more ominous. Despite the waves of heat, he couldn't help but feel a little **cold.** He curled up into a little ball, pulled his paws in, and wrapped his tail around him.

*What should I do? I'm **trapped** in this **gigantic cavern,** and I have no idea where to go. But* . . . *I'm smart. Right? I'll figure something out.* **Right?**

The kitten looked around with big, **fearful eyes,** eyes that shimmered like pools of deep green water.

What will I do now . . . ?
What will I do now?

CHAPTER 3

While Eeebs **trembled in fear,** he started to hear **mysterious noises.** They seemed far away. **In the shadows.**

He could hear piglike **grunts,** horrible **slithering** noises, and something that almost sounded like **crying.** With each new sound, his eyes grew wider and wider. He **shrank back** against the side of a small cliff, his back arched.

Whatever I do, thought Eeebs, *I can't panic anymore. I'll only get more lost. I have to think back, retrace my steps. That's my only way out.*

Suddenly, the crying seemed **very close.** He slowly turned his head, **afraid** of what he might see. That was when he noticed it: **a kind of small white cloud,** floating in the air. Floating directly toward him.

No, it wasn't a cloud. It had a . . . **face!** Whatever it was, it looked **very sad.** It really was **crying.** A few **light blue tears** were streaming down its cheeks.

"Eeeek!"

The **ghostlike creature shrieked** when it noticed the kitten. Eeebs **sprang back,** tail straight up and fur raised, as if **electrified.** "Leave me alone!" he hissed.

The creature paused and gazed down at itself. "Do I really look **so terrifying?**" The creature sniffled. "I must. Even **this poor little magma cube** can't stand the sight of a monster like me."

It started **crying** again—fountains of sparkling **blue tears,** this time.

"**Magma cube?**" Eeebs peered cautiously at the bizarre creature. "I'm a **kitten.**"

"A . . . **kitten?**" Its closed eyes shifted with suspicion, ever so slightly. "I don't think I've ever seen a kitten before. You must have come from **a nether fortress,** yes?"

"A forest, actually."

"I don't quite understand." Another sniffle. New tears formed in the corners of its eyes. "Oh, that's why I don't have **any** friends! I never understand **anything** about **anything!**"

Eeebs stepped forward. **His curiosity** had taken hold. He had so many questions. Besides, it didn't seem like this thing had any intention of **eating him.**

"Why are you crying? It's **a little strange,** isn't it? I thought ghosts liked to **scare people.**"

"Ghost?" The white being floated down to the kitten's level. "**I'm a ghast.** And I'm **not strange! Every** ghast is sad about **something.** Some of us cry because there are no flowers here. Others, because it's too hot . . ."

"Well, why are **you** sad?"

The ghast turned away. "Because I . . . **I have no friends.** My whole life, that's all I've ever wanted."

The puzzled kitten **fixed his eyes** on the ghast. Surely, this was the most **interesting** creature he had ever met. Why couldn't he have found that portal **sooner?**

"I'll be your friend," Eeebs said.

"What? Oh . . . I get it. **A joke,** yes?"

"**Not at all,**" Eeebs said. "To be honest, **I don't have any friends either.** At least, not **here** . . ."

The ghast turned back to face him. **"Really? You mean it?"**

"Of course! Why wouldn't I? I'll introduce you to my other friends back home, too."

The ghast **spun around** in midair. "How can this be? Am I **dreaming?"**

"I doubt it," said Eeebs, glancing again at this strange new world. "Dreams are never **this** crazy."

The ghast nodded. **He even smiled.**

Although neither of them had any idea, this was **a special moment.** It was the first time **in the history of Minecraftia** that a ghast had experienced **happiness.** Their friendship would be **documented** in books and discussed by scholars and sages **for generations** to come.

CHAPTER 4

The ghast *(whose name was Clyde)* floated near a chunk of glowing yellow stone. "This is **glowstone,**" he said. "It lights up areas that don't have any lava."

"**Lava,**" said Eeebs. "That's **the orange stuff,** right?"

"Correct."

For the past **hour or two,** the ghast had explained his world to Eeebs. A guided tour of the **Nether.** The kitten absorbed all of this information, from the **zombie pigmen** to the **blazes** that soared above their heads.

"I wonder if I could bring some glowstone back home with me," said Eeebs. "**It's pretty.** I think my friend—"

"**Ornk-ornk.**" A zombie pigman **bumped into him** with a grunt. Eeebs gasped and **darted** behind the ghast.

"Don't worry," said Clyde. "**He won't hurt you,** remember?"

"Right."

The undead pigman stared at the strange companions before **wandering away.** Clyde went back to the tour. Of course, the kitten's **curiosity** seemed infinite. Every time the ghast answered one of Eeebs's questions, the kitten asked **another.**

Why is there so much lava?
Why are zombie pigmen **zombies**?
Is there such a thing as a normal pigman?

Only stuff like that. But those endless questions **never annoyed** Clyde. The kitten could have gone on **forever,** and he wouldn't have cared. For the first time in his life, the ghast was helping someone. He was making a difference. **He had a real friend.**

At some point, **a chorus of grunts** and shouts became audible. Far away, across the lava lake, an army of creatures had gathered: zombie pigmen, magma cubes, blazes, wither skeletons—**even an enderman.**

"**Wow!**" said Eeebs. "I've never seen **so many monsters** before! What are they doing?"

"**Causing trouble**," said the ghast. "You see that tall one? The one with the purple eyes?"

Eeebs nodded. "That's **an enderman,** right? I've seen one before."

"Well, endermen **never** come here," said the ghast. "Except for **him.** His name is **EnderStar.**"

"So why is he here?"

"From what I understand, he was **exiled from his homeworld.** Even the other endermen grew **tired** of his **crazy ideas.**"

The kitten's ears perked up. *Wow. This is way better than playing hide-and-seek,* he thought. *An army of monsters! An enderman who got kicked out of his own world! What next?*

"Can we get **closer?**"

Clyde paused. "I'm not so sure that would be such **a good idea,** Eeebs."

"**Why not?** Don't you want to **hear** what they're talking about?"

"Well, **all right.** But don't let them see you, okay? They won't care about me, **but if they notice you . . .**"

Eeebs nodded. "How about we **hide on that ledge** over there?"

With that, **the unlikely duo** snuck closer, up a hill that overlooked **the army.** Eeebs peeked out from behind a single block of netherrack.

Clyde **floated** nearby. The monsters below could no doubt see him, but none of them **paid any attention.** He **was** a monster, after all.

Beyond that, everyone was too busy listening to **EnderStar's** speech. All eyes were focused upon that **enderman,** who stood in the middle of the crowd.

"We must take back **what is rightfully ours!**" he shouted, before **pacing back and forth.** He waved a fist in the air. "**We will crush them all!**"

"Rarg!" A zombie pigman raised his golden sword. "Crush dem awl!"

The other monsters joined in. The air erupted into an angry chant.

"Crush dem arl!"

"Crush dem awl!"

"Crush dem ull!"

The monsters fell silent when EnderStar waved a hand.

"There's **a portal** not too far from here," he rumbled. "Our **first attack** will commence from there. This is **a practice run**, nothing more. Once you see **how easily their town crumbles,** you will understand the speed with which we can **reclaim our world!**"

A huge **wither skeleton** stepped forward and cut the air with his massive sword. "**Blah, blah, blah!** Talk boring! When me get to **chop things?**"

Another zombie pigman raised his head and screamed. "**Urggrgagrrgr!** Me want smash!"

"**Rargragr!**" One of the blazes trembled with rage. "**Gragragagzzzt!**"

EnderStar **chuckled**—a slow, **smoldering sound** that echoed across the Nether. "**Yes!**" he boomed. "That's the spirit! **Follow me, my brothers!** Let us show them **our might!** Let them bow before us!"

A chorus of shouts shattered the air. The army took off at once, **slithering** and **staggering** across the dark red ground. Their cries faded bit by bit.

"**I don't understand,**" said Eeebs. "What's going on? They're attacking? **Attacking who?**"

Clyde looked away. "Well, **um** . . ."

"**Tell me!**" Eeebs shouted. "I'm **your friend,** aren't I?"

"I . . . I'm afraid they're on their way **to your world.**"

No, Eeebs thought, blood freezing in his veins. *No way. Why would those monsters want to **live there**? Don't they like this place?* Another **frightening** question spawned in a dark area of his mind.

"Wait," he said. "He mentioned **a portal.** Was he talking about the thing I came through?"

"**Most likely,**" said Clyde.

"So, they're attacking **a city nearby?**"

"**A human** city. Your kind will be safe."

"But what if they **burn** everything?" Eeebs suddenly felt **weak.** His head spun. He **stumbled.** "I have to **get back! I have to warn them!**"

Clyde sighed. "It's **dangerous,** Eeebs. Your mother would want you **to be safe.** You know that."

Eeebs leapt forward, his eyes **filled with anger.** "What if it was **your family,** huh? Would you just sit here? **You want me to . . .**"

As his voice **trailed off,** Eeebs collapsed. He felt so **weak, drained, helpless.** His limbs were like jelly. What was happening to him?

Clyde zoomed down. "Hey! **Eeebs! What's wrong?**"

"I . . . don't know. It's like **I'm . . .**"

"Climb onto me," said the ghast. "I know someone who might be able to help."

"I . . . can't."

"If you want to **help your family and friends,** you will."

Eeebs **took a deep breath.** An image of his mother flashed through his mind. And Tufty. Meowz. All of them. With **the last of his strength,** he pushed himself up and climbed up onto the ghast.

Seconds later,
everything went black.

CHAPTER 5

In her tiny stone hut, Eldra the witch was hard at work.

She hovered over **a brewing stand,** deep in concentration. With one **bottle of water** and one **nether wart,** she created an **Awkward Potion.** Blub, **blub, blub.** The potion burbled to life on the stand. After adding **a dollop of magma cream,** she made a **Potion of Fire Resistance.**

Of course, Eldra **didn't stop there.** It would take only a **pinch of redstone dust** to increase the potion's duration from **three minutes** to **eight.** She did just that, carefully measuring the amount. More bubbles and smoke this time—even **a little flash of fire.** But the extra effort was worth it.

That will do nicely, she thought. *Now I can go hunting for more* **blaze powder** *in the fortress nearby. Those silly blazes won't lay a spark on me. Afterward, I could even take* **a lava bath.** The witch giggled to herself. *Just for fun.*

Then she frowned. *But I shouldn't go without at least one* **Potion of Regeneration.** *Who knows what else I might run into?*

She opened up her ingredient chest and rummaged around. Spider eyes . . . pufferfish . . . blaze powder . . . *no, this won't do at all,* she thought. *Now, where did I put that* **ghast tear?**

Sometimes, when a ghast **cries,** one of its tears will **harden** and **crystallize;** this is an **essential** ingredient to make a **Potion of Regeneration.** Unfortunately, this is a **rare** event, so such tears are **highly prized** by witches like Eldra.

And she was **totally out.**

By some **fabulous** twist of fate, however, the answer to her problem arrived right at her iron door.

Clang, clang!

"Who is it?" the witch called out, still searching through her storage container.

"**Me.** Who else?"

Odd, she thought. *Clyde sounds **less drooping** than usual.*

In her **excitement,** Eldra whirled around, zoomed over to the door, and peered through the window. **Sure enough,** it was him. Was that **the hint of a smile** on his face? He **almost looked . . . happy.** The witch **blinked,** as if she had just seen **a flying cow.**

She hit **the button** to open the door then stepped outside. "You couldn't have come at **a better time,**" she said. "**I need to make a—**"

"Listen, **I really need your help,**" Clyde **gushed.**

Eldra sighed. "Oh, how many times must we go over this, Clyde? Let's stick to our **original deal.** After you've given me **a thousand of your tears,** I will be **your friend.** You only have **eight hundred and eighty-eight** tears to go! See? You're almost there."

What the witch had done was indeed **a little cruel.** The ghast was so **desperate** to make a friend that he'd agreed one year ago to give Eldra **one thousand** of his **crystalized tears.** In return, she would **officially** be his friend. But not really. Not in **her heart.** How could she befriend **a monster like that?**

On the other hand, was it really **so bad** to trick the ghast like this? It was **nicer** than **killing him.** Since their tears were **so valued,** ghasts were close to becoming **an endangered species.** So the witch wasn't **completely** bad. Especially compared to the likes of **EnderStar.**

"It's not about that," said Clyde. "**It's about my friend.**"

Eldra **burst out laughing**. "**You?**" She giggled again at the thought. "**Have a friend?**"

"As **unbelievable** as it may seem, **yes**. And he's . . . **hurt**. Or **sick**. I don't know."

"Where is he?"

The ghost touched down on the ground. "**Right here.**"

The witch approached. She **laughed** again upon seeing the unconscious kitten resting on top of him.

"I won't even ask how you two **met**," she said. "And what exactly is wrong **with—**"

She froze. Her eyes grew wide all of a sudden. "It **can't be!** This kitten . . . has **the mark!**"

"Mark? **What mark?**"

Eldra shook her head. "Oh, you **foolish ghast!** Why didn't you bring him to me sooner? **Hurry!** Give him to me! There's **no time to waste!**"

She **cradled** the limp kitten in her arms then **dashed** inside her hut.

Clyde floated over to the window and watched Eldra set the kitten down on her **blue wool mattress.** The witch performed a series of **gestures** over his motionless body.

That was when he noticed **Eeebs's size.** He had **grown** slightly—**his claws,** too. His fur now had **a blue sheen.** Was he **changing?** Why? Was that **normal?** Did kittens really grow **so fast?**

"It must have something to do with **his illness,**" the ghast sighed. He felt so **helpless.** He could only float by the window while the witch **performed her magic.**

Eeebs will be okay, he thought. *She'll know what to do. I don't know what happened to my friend, but **she'll know what to do.***

CHAPTER 6

Eeebs **slowly** opened his eyes.

He was lying on a **soft** surface. He had slept on something like this a while ago: **the farmer's house.** Eeebs liked houses. **Real houses,** anyway. There were so many comfortable things to sleep on in a real house. Stoves. **Beds.** Carpets. Much better than the **hollowed-out log** that served as his home.

No, he was wrong. How could he think **something like that?** His home was a **real house,** too. He remembered the smell of salmon, a smell you'd never find in a house like the farmer's—and **suddenly,** he thought of **his mother,** of **his friends. His home.**

He had to get back. Had to **warn them. Save them.**

Eeebs sprang up. He was in **a stone hut** made of . . . he couldn't remember the word. He tried to recall what Clyde had taught him. Netherrock? Netherstone? No, quartz. **Nether quartz.** That was it. Where was Clyde, anyway?

Just then, he heard **a voice** coming from somewhere outside. **A woman's voice.**

"Don't take this **the wrong way,** but I'm delighted **to see you crying** again," the woman said. "What would I do without your tears? Only **eight hundred and eighty-seven** left, by the way."

"I just hope he'll be **okay.**"

The kitten's ears perked up. *Clyde?*

Eeebs leapt off the bed and through the window. The ghast was just outside, facing **a strange woman** he had never seen before. Both turned to face him.

"**No way!**" said Clyde. "*You're already awake!*"

"Nearly." Eeebs rubbed his face with his paws. "So . . . **what happened?**"

"Something **extraordinary**," said the witch.

The kitten gave her a confused look. "And who are you?"

"This is **Eldra**," said Clyde. "She's **a witch**. She's the only one I could think of who could help you. **And she did.**"

"**Honestly,** I didn't do much," she said. "All it took was **a bit of milk,** that's all."

"**I don't understand,**" said Eeebs. "Will someone just tell me what's going on?"

Eldra nodded. "You've been . . . **chosen.**"

"**Chosen?** By who?"

"The Nether."

Clyde floated closer. "The Nether found you, Eeebs. **It called you!** Your arrival here was **no accident.**"

What? That just doesn't make sense, thought the kitten. *Am I dreaming?*

He shook his head. "What would this world want from a kitten like me?"

"**Purity,**" said the witch. "**Innocence. Courage. Love.** You must understand that the Nether isn't an **evil** place. It's filled with **darkness,** but it isn't evil. However, **many of its denizens are.** The Nether needed **a champion,** and when it couldn't find one here, well . . . it looked elsewhere. **It found you.**"

Eeebs **staggered.** It felt like his body was . . . **different.** Well, maybe he was just drowsy—still **a little weak.** He **ignored** these thoughts.

"**A champion** for what?"

But as he asked this, Eeebs realized that this was the one question **he could already answer** himself.

"EnderStar wants to **rule the Overworld,**" said Clyde. "**He's terrible!**"

"And if that happens," Eldra continued, "the **Nether** will be in a **great deal** of trouble. **The End, too.** You see, EnderStar won't stop until **he gains control of all three worlds.**"

"I think I get it." Eeebs **paused.** Was he getting **smarter?** He normally wouldn't have been able to grasp this kind of stuff. "The Nether wants to **stop him** before he gets **too powerful,** right?"

The witch smiled. "**Exactly.**"

"But . . . even if I want to help," said Eeebs, "what can I do? **I'm just a kitten.**"

As Eeebs said this, Clyde got **that look** again. It was the *"I don't want my friend to **freak out,** so I'm not going to say **anything**"* look.

Eldra wasn't as considerate. She smirked, looking him up and down. "**Not anymore.**"

Eeebs followed her gaze.

His black fur had **a vibrant blue sheen.** His claws were a bit **larger,** thick and black. And **sharp.** He was also **bigger** and **stronger**—nearly as big as an **adult ocelot.**

Eeebs held out his paws, examining them, moving each digit. They were almost like **human hands.** "What . . . **happened to me . . . ?**"

"It's not like it's a **bad** change," said Clyde defensively. "I mean, think of it this way: At least you'll **never** have to worry about wolves again."

The witch placed a hand upon his shoulder. "**The Nether changed you. Strengthened** you. And granted you . . . **powers,** you could say. Once you **learn to control them,** the minions of EnderStar will fall before you like **turnips** during a harvest."

The ghost managed a **slight grin.** "I think '**nether kitten**' has a nice ring to it, don't you?"

Eeebs stared down in **horror.** His mind spun and spun. It was just **too much** for him. What would his mother think? His friends?

He would be an **outcast.**
He would become an exile . . .
just like EnderStar.

Again, Eeebs thought of home. His vision **blurred** as **tears** filled his eyes. He wiped them away with a clawed paw and **nodded** at his two friends. "**Thank you, Clyde. Thank you, Eldra.**"

Then, **he took off.** The Nether's **dull** red terrain streaked past him.

"**Wait!**" Clyde called out. "**Eeebs!** There's still a lot **you need to know!**" Eeebs **ignored** his friend's cries. He had wasted **enough time.**

A crazy **nightmare***,* he thought, leaping over a narrow lava stream. *A hallucination brought on by too much stress. Or, maybe this is really happening; maybe the Nether really did turn me into some kind of* **weird** *monster.* He **tore across** a ruddy stone plain.

It must have, because he could **sense** the portal's location across all that twisted stone. He pounced up from ledge to ledge and raced through every plateau, until the **glowing violet door** was directly in sight.

He didn't know much about the Nether, what it was capable of, or **what kind of magic** it had placed upon him.

Was it **a curse? A miracle?**

Right now, there was only **one thing** he knew for sure. He was now **a pawn** in a deadly game . . . and he had no choice but to "**play.**"

Armed with this **sole truth,** he cut away his fears and doubts—cut away as if they were just cobwebs in a mineshaft.

Just hold on, he thought, sprinting toward the portal.

Mom . . . Meowz . . . Tufty . . .

I'm coming!

CHAPTER 7

The lava. The inky gloom. The hot netherrack underneath his paws. All of these things the kitten ignored as he ran toward the portal.

He was too busy trying to make sense of it all. **The Nether:** a **dark** world, a **fiery** world, a world that should have **nothing to do with** kittens. But for some reason **this world chose** a kitten to **protect** it. Perhaps a kitten was **a better choice** than a zombie pigman.

Then this world **called** that kitten, **pulling** him from his own world—the bright and tree-filled **Overworld.** Later, the Nether granted him **special abilities** to help him fight the hordes of darkness.

That kitten's name was <u>**Eeebs.**</u>

He's now a **funky-looking** cat.

And Eeebs was trying to **escape the Nether.**

The **intense** heat no longer gave him any trouble. The clouds of smoke, which once **made his eyes water,** were nothing to him. Instead, those eyes were now fixed on the warm light radiating from the portal.

Portal.

His friend Clyde had taught him that word. This portal was a **doorway,** linking two worlds. It looked like a screen of **violet energy,** surrounded by a great ring of black stone.

Eeebs couldn't help but think about Clyde.

I'm sorry, he thought. *Please* **forgive me,** *Clyde, for running away without listening to you. I'll* **come back.** *I have to, because I have to thank you. And* **that witch,** *too. She removed whatever* **illness** *I had.*

Eeebs forced himself to **stop thinking** about his new friends.

I'm sure they understand.

Eeebs had to **go through that portal.** He had to leave this world and **return to his own.** Suddenly, it was the **only** real thought in his mind.

No.

There was **another** thought.

Monsters, from this world, were headed to **his own** world. **To attack, to destroy.** To **claim the Overworld** as their own.

Of course, Eeebs had to **warn** his family and friends before that happened.

He slowed down as he neared the portal. Its **enormous** obsidian frame towered before him. All he had to do was step through, as he had before, and **he'd be back**.

His heart **froze**.

He **feared** what he might see upon returning to **the Overworld**. Maybe the monsters had **already** . . .

A frightening image spawned in his mind. . . .

No! There's no way something like that could happen! Those pigmen are **too slow!**

He pushed such thoughts away, but another **replaced** them.

Enough, he told himself. *I can't waste any more time.*

He leapt through **the purple mist.**

As expected, everything **went black.** He nearly closed his eyes. He was **so afraid** of seeing **something horrible.** But **the darkness** became . . .

Shades of **green, brown. No fire, no ashes.** Nothing was burning. He stepped out of the portal into the thicket where the wolves had almost caught him.

The trees were **still there,** along with the grass and the flowers, and suddenly he realized just how **nice** the forest smelled. He had never thought about it, until now. Actually, **even the swamp** smelled better than the Nether. That place was **horrible** for a kitten's nose.

That was when he caught **another scent.** A familiar scent, like **rotten** mushrooms.

That was the stench of **a zombie pigman. Yuck.**

He sniffed and sniffed, detecting more scents in the air. That ashen smell was from a **blaze,** and that bitter smell no doubt came from one of those **magma cubes.**

They were . . . here.
Somewhere. Somewhere close.
Maybe just beyond that large hill.

Relief washed over him. The monsters were stupid and slow—they **hadn't yet** reached his home. It was far from this area, on **the other side of the forest.**

His mind was working **like never** before. The monsters also hadn't reached the village, where the villagers lived. It was **even farther away,** in the plains past the forest.

So since Eeebs was **so fast** now, he could reach his home before the monsters.

Of course, he **did** want to know what those monsters **were up to.** Why were they still here, in the forest?

Shouldn't they have **attacked the village** by now? What could they be **doing?** He hadn't the slightest idea, which meant . . . he **had to find out. He nodded** to himself.

No matter how much the Nether had changed him, it couldn't remove his curiosity.

With **his nose** as a guide, Eeebs began heading in the direction of the monsters. **Slowly,** at first, until soon he was **bounding** over mushrooms and **zooming** through tall grass.

CHAPTER 8

Eeebs **climbed** up a hill. With every step, **the stench of monsters** grew stronger, and their snarls became **louder.** When Eeebs finally reached the top, he crept low through the grass and peered down the other side.

His pulse quickened. **There they were.**

All of them.

From **blazes** to **wither skeletons**. A snarling, **growling** mass of undead and **fiery beasts.**

And in the middle of them all . . . **EnderStar.** The kitten's fear, however, soon **evaporated.** In fact, he had to keep himself from **laughing.**

He **crept closer** to get a better view.

The monsters, they were . . . **staggering around, stumbling** into one another. At one point, a zombie pigman fell over into the grass.

Then a second pigman **tripped over him,** went flying, and **knocked over** a third.

It was **a ridiculous sight**: an army of **fearsome-looking** mobs, **bumbling around** in a daisy field.

Their distant screams **caught his attention**. Eeebs **perked his ears** up to catch what they were saying.

"It **hurts!**" screamed a zombie pigman.
"Mee **eyes!**"

A blaze **hissed** and **sparked**.
"Massssshter . . . me no see!"

"**Urgggg!!!**" A wither skeleton **fell over,** dropping his stone sword. He **pointed a bony finger** toward the **sun.** "Yellow square thing! Up there! **Too** . . . **bright!**"

Another wither skeleton was **chopping at a tree.**

"Mee do good, **mashter?** Look! **Mee chop!**"
A zombie pigman **joined** the skeleton.

"Mee too, **mashter!**"

The wither skeleton's sword seemed to be **stuck** in the tree. "BoSssH, mee sword! The enemy is **so strong!**"

The **huge** enderman let out a long sigh. "That's a tree, **you idiots!!**"

The wither skeleton glanced at **EnderStar** and then back at the tree.

"How can me know, **bossh?** Mee eyes don't work right now!"

The zombie pigman kept chopping at the tree. "**Mee want chop things!** So . . . **mee chop!!**"

A great many zombie pigmen **writhed** on the ground, hands covering their eyes as they **screamed.**

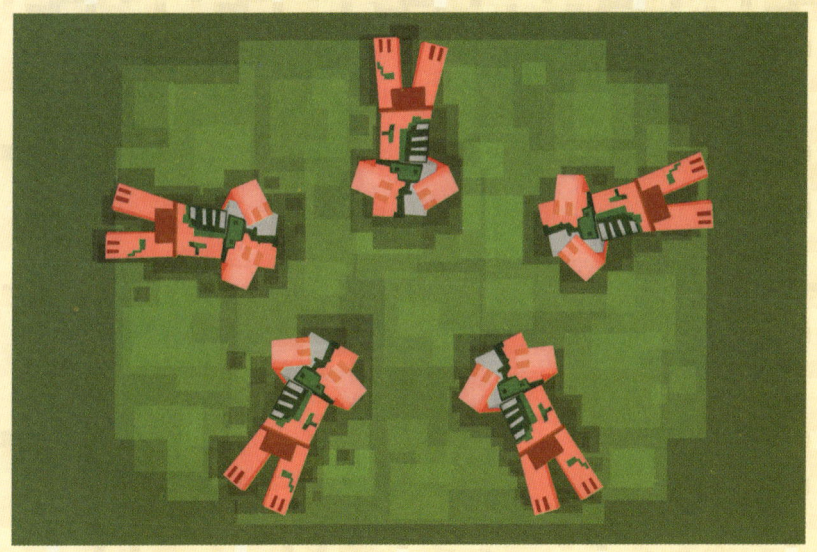

"Urggh! **Mashter!!** Make yellow square go away!"

"It burn! It burn! **Rarrrggg!!**"

"Bossh! You say attack village very easy! **Holp mee!!**"

"**Arggg!!** Villagers use magikk on us!"

"Mashter, mee cannot chop if **mee cannot see!**"

There were lots of shouts like these.

Eeebs only watched **in disbelief.**

It reminded Eeebs of **a scary time,** when he'd gone playing in a cave. There had been a big spider in there, and it had **chased him** for a long time. The spider had run **fast,** Eeebs remembered. Faster than him. So fast, the spider had caught up to Eeebs by the time he exited the cave. Eeebs had thought he was **a goner.** All he could hear was that **horrible squeak.** And then there were those **glowing** red eyes.

However, when the spider **stepped out into the sun, it froze.** The spider just sat there, **right in front of Eeebs,** fangs dripping and eyes gleaming. It **couldn't do a thing,** because it couldn't see.

That was how Eeebs had learned that spiders were **blinded** by sunlight. Spiders lived in caves. Their eyes were **used to the darkness.**

With that in mind, Eeebs now understood why these **Nether mobs** couldn't see. They shared **the same weakness.**

The Nether was, in **many ways,** similar to a cave. When he first arrived there, Eeebs assumed it was just one **gigantic** cavern.

Even though the Nether had areas **filled with lava,** it was still pretty dark in most places. So these monsters had lived their whole lives in that **gloomy** place. Their eyes were **used to the darkness.** Just like the spiders.

Wow, he thought. *I never could have understood that so easily before. I'm getting* **smarter,** *huh? Maybe that's one of the things the Nether did to me?* **Made me more intelligent?**

Concealed in the tall grass, Eeebs kept **spying**. EnderStar seemed angrier and **angrier**.

The enderman looked up and **shook a fist** at the sky. "I can't **believe this!** All of my planning . . . **ruined** by the **stupid sun!!**"

A zombie pigman **walked up** to the enderman. He was wearing **a golden object** on his head.

"**Mee lord?** Maybe **we go now** . . . and come back . . . when **no yellow square thing.**"

EnderStar **patted** the pigman on the head.

"**You're a clever one,**" he said. "That's why I've made you **a captain.**"

"So . . ." The zombie pigman paused. "We go back **now?**"

"Of course." EnderStar's voice **crackled** like lava. "**Gather the troops.** Take them back. This was only meant to be **practice,** anyway. I wanted you all to get some training before we . . . attack **the real village. . . .**"

The pigman **nodded.** "**Yesh,** mee lord."

Eeebs **squinted,** focusing on the zombie pigman. He seemed **different** from the others. He wasn't **completely** stupid, at least.

So that pigman was EnderStar's **assistant?** Also . . . what was that **thing on his head?** Eeebs continued observing the mobs from his hiding spot. His ears were raised up in the direction of the army.

"**Anyway,** today was not **a total waste,**" said EnderStar. "We've learned **something useful.** Next time, we'll come right **after the sun sets.**"

"Of coursh, mee lord. So . . . **you go?** I take pigmen and fire things back now? **We go home?**"

"Yes," said the enderman. "See you back at **the fortress.**"

With that, **EnderStar vanished** into thin air.

POOF!

Eeebs had encountered endermen before. He knew they had **this ability,** so he wasn't too surprised.

EnderStar also said something about a . . . **fortress.**

Fortress.

Clyde had mentioned **that word** before. He thought Eeebs had come from a "**nether fortress.**" So that must be **the monsters'** . . . **home?**

Eeebs needed to **speak with Clyde** about this. After he talked to his friends and family, he had to **return** to the Nether.

Shaking himself from his thoughts, Eeebs looked at the mobs again.

Now **in charge of the other mobs,** the smart pigman turned to his comrades. "**Hey!** All you! **Shut up!** Stop crying! **We go home!**"

Loud grunts and snorts filled the air. "**Home better** anyway," said a wither skeleton. "**Mee no like this place.**"

"**Bzzztrg** . . . t-too **c-c-cold** here," a blaze sputtered. "G-go h-home w-w-warm. **Mee happy!** Argg! **Bzzzt!**"

A magma cube **shivered** and hopped in **agreement.**

"But **we no see**," said a wither skeleton. "We no see! So . . . **how we know where go?**"

"I can see," said the smart zombie pigman. He pointed to **the golden object** he wore on his head.

Eeebs had seen humans wearing such things to **protect themselves** in battle. So did that allow the pigman captain to see in the **sunlight?** He really was **smarter** than most zombie pigmen.

"Follow me," he said. "I take you home. All you. Use ears. Me sing song. Okay?"

"Thanks, Rarg! Mee so cold!!"

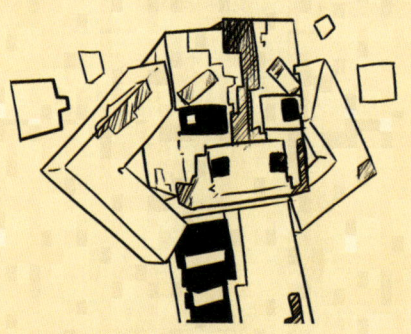

"Okay! We follow you, Rarg!"

"Yes!! Lead the way! Get mee out of here!"

With that, the captain pigman (*whose name was apparently Rarg*) began singing.

"Ninety-nine villager noobs in da town! **Ninety-nine villager noobs! Smash one down!** Into **da ground!!** Ninety-eight villager noobs in da town! Ninety-eight villager noobs in da town! Ninety-eight villager noobs . . ."

As he bellowed, the captain **trudged off** in the direction of the portal. The other monsters **followed.** Some began **singing along**:

"Ninety-seven villager noobs in da town! **Ninety-seven villager noobs! Smash one down!** Into—" Rarg **stopped,** turned around.

"**Shut up!** Only I sing! If others sing, how you know **who to follow?**"

"Rarg so **smart!**"

"Okay! **We shut up!**"

Rarg turned back around and began singing and marching again. Eeebs watched them go.

Their little attack **failed,** he thought. *They must have arrived very early in the morning, just before sunrise. Then the sun came up and blinded them all.*

And they were **stranded**. Helpless. Helpless underneath that **overpowering light**. That means . . . **the Overworld** still has time. Maybe **a lot of time**.

But . . . when they do come back, they'll be more **prepared**.

Maybe, when they return, they'll all have **those golden things** on their heads, like Rarg.

Eeebs didn't realize, of course, **just how well hidden** he was. In fact, as he remained **motionless** in the grass, he had become **nearly invisible**. Without another thought, the kitten **jumped down** the hill. After he moved, **he became fully visible** again.

CHAPTER 9

Fifteen minutes later . . .

Eeebs was standing outside of **the grove.**

It was where **all of the cats** lived. He could hear playful **meows** in the distance.

Was that . . . **Tufty? Meowz?** He crept through the grass.

He couldn't believe it. He was actually **home?** And . . . he could **see them** now, in the distance.

His friends.
They were playing some kind of game.

"Hey, **not fair!**" hissed Tufty, glaring at Meowz. "You **always** cheat."

"**I didn't cheat,**" she said. "You **never said** no peeking."

"It's always like that," said Tufty. "**You never said this. You never said that.** I miss Eeebs. At least **he played fair. . . .**"

Meowz looked down at the ground, her eyes **full of tears.** "Me too."

Eeebs froze. They were still thinking about him. They were **worried** about him. But what would they think when they saw him? **His fur was blue** now. . . .

He stepped forward anyway.

"I wonder where he is . . . if he's **still alive. . . .**" said Meowz.

"If you ask me," said Tufty, "he went into **that thing.**"

"**Hmm.** Let's go looking for him again."

"Sure, but do you have any idea where **that black thing** is?"

"It's called **a nether portal,**" said Eeebs.

Tufty and Meowz turned to him. The **look** on their faces was **indescribable.**

A piercing sound came from Meowz. "**Eeeeeee . . .**"

Tufty stepped back. "Who . . . **is** . . ." **Then,** the two seemed to recognize him. "**Eeebs?**"

"Eeebs?" Meowz **cautiously** stepped forward. "**Is that . . . really you?**"

Eeebs nodded.

"What . . . **happened** to you?"

"I'm the one who should ask," Eeebs said.

"You went **in**," said Tufty. "**Didn't you?** You actually . . . **went into** that place?"

The kittens knew **stories** of the Nether, although they didn't call it by that name. Stories about **the black door.** The glowing **purple light.** Old stories. Legends telling how the **bravest** and **strongest** cats once went through that door. And **never came back.**

Eeebs, however, had come back.

Maybe he had been **lucky** to meet Clyde, who taught him **all about** that world. Or maybe it wasn't luck. Eeebs had thought nothing of talking to Clyde. But an older, wiser cat probably wouldn't have **tried** talking to a ghost. An older, wiser cat would have **simply run.**

Just as Eeebs had **ignored** the legends and the warnings from his mother, he'd also ignored his **common sense**—which generally encouraged **running away** from giant white flying things that **cried** and **shot balls of fire** from their mouths.

Who knew there could be a ghost who was actually **kind?** That was why Eeebs had survived.

As Tufty and Meowz stood before him, **in awe,** Eeebs told them about all his adventures. What happened to him. How he **changed.** How the Nether had **chosen** him.

"**Chose you for what?**" asked Tufty.

"To help **fight** against that army," said Eeebs. "I guess."

Then, Eeebs told them about how an enderman was **planning to take over their own world.**

"So let me get this straight," said Meowz. "That place, the Nether, chose you? To be some kind of **warrior?** And you have like . . . **special powers** and stuff?"

Eeebs nodded again. "Basically, **yeah.**"

"**Wow,**" said Tufty. "That's **too cool,** huh? **Special powers?** Fighting **bad guys?** And honestly, Eeebs, you don't even look that **scary!** Where do I sign up? **I wanna help you!**"

"By the way, what kind of powers do you have, anyway?" asked Meowz.

"Well, **I don't know,**" said Eeebs. "I mean, Clyde and his friend were about to tell me more about **the change,** but . . . I ran off before they could. I just wanted to **find you guys.**"

"**Awww.**" Meowz's eyes grew even more tearful. "**Thanks.**"

"A **good friend,**" said Tufty. "Us too. We looked for you everywhere, you know? We haven't really slept since you disappeared. Anyway . . . I'm just **glad** you're back."

Eeebs sighed. "Me too, but . . . at some point, I'll have to go . . . back there."

All three of them looked down at the ground. Then, **a cry broke the silence.**

"Eeebs?"

It was <u>his mother.</u>

CHAPTER 10

Eeebs's mother **carefully** approached the three kittens. She looked like Eeebs *(the old Eeebs, anyway)*, only bigger.

Eeebs only **swallowed,** his eyes **wide.**

"Oh boy," whispered Tufty. "Things are gonna **get crazy.**"

Meowz joined him in cowering.

"This isn't good," she murmured. "She scolded Eeebs **for days** just for going too close to the **fire lake,** over in the plains. How do you think she'll react to **this?**"

His mother was now quite close, and as she noticed her son, she couldn't hide her **astonishment.** "Eeebs Cottonpaw Thistlewhiskers, what on Earth happened to you?!"

"Mom, **I can explain,**" said Eeebs, his ears **lowered,** tail **between his legs.** "You see, **there's this—**"

"**Enough!**" she hissed. "You'll explain this to **your father!**"

She picked him up by **the scruff of his neck** and hauled him off to their **cat burrow.**

Tufty and Meowz exchanged **worried glances.**

CHAPTER 11

For half an hour, Eeebs **stared at the floor** as his mother **scolded** him. Of course, he tried telling her about what had happened. But she **wasn't hearing any of it.**

"I told you not to go near **that door!**" she said. "Cats have no business in there!"

"**I'm okay,** Mom. **Really.** Maybe what happened to me is a **good** thing."

"**Good?**" She turned away. "How can it be good? You look so **different** now. Your fur, it's . . . it's . . . **it's blue!**"

Eeebs rubbed up against his mom.

"**Hey.** I'm sorry for going in there, but . . . monsters really **are** going to **attack our world.**"

"Well, what can we do about it?" she said. "Let the humans deal with it. And those . . . villagers."

"I don't think it's that simple," Eeebs said. "I mean, the mob army is **huge.** I've seen it with **my own eyes.**"

This made his mother even **more worried.** "And what exactly are **you** supposed to do?"

Eeebs sighed. "**I don't know,** Mom. But there must be **a reason.** That's what Clyde said. **He's a ghast.** Oh, and his friend, Eldra. **She's a witch.** She said—"

"**Ghast?!**" his mother yelled. "**Witch?!** Young man, you won't go near those things again! **Do you understand?**"

"But they're **my friends.**"

"**Friends?!** No, you won't be making friends with **monsters!**"

"Not all monsters are **bad,** Mom. . . . Clyde is really, **really nice.**"

His mother was **really upset** now. "Just wait until your father hears about this! You're lucky he's **out hunting** right now!"

"Mom, please just **calm down.** . . ."

It went on like this for some time. Like most mothers, she was <u>a bit **overprotective.**</u>

His father eventually **came back,** carrying some salmon. He was a good hunter.

When his father noticed Eeebs, he dropped the salmon on to the grass floor of their house.

"**Son?** What . . . **happened?**"

And so, Eeebs explained **all over again.** Thankfully, his father **wasn't as upset.** He almost seemed **proud** of Eeebs.

"The Nether **chose** you?" he said. "I don't like it, but . . . this must be **important.**"

"**What are you saying?**" said his mother.

His father flicked his tail, **thinking** for a moment. "I just think we should **try** to learn more about this."

"I can't believe you're saying this!" His mom circled back and forth.

"Honey, we can't do anything about it. What happened . . . happened."

His mother sighed. Then, there were **several cries** outside.

"Monster! Run!!"

Eeebs glanced at his mom and dad then dashed outside.

CHAPTER 12

A crowd of cats and kittens **scattered** in **terror.**

A **witch** walked out from behind a massive oak tree.

"**Eeebs!**" she shouted. "Eeebs! **Are you there?** Oh, there are so many kittens, but none of them are the one I'm looking for! At least, I don't think any of you are Eeebs. . . . **Blue fur? Purple eyes?** No, no, **no!** Where is he?!"

The few remaining kittens **squealed** and ran off to their parents. But one kitten remained.

Eeebs **slowly** walked toward the witch.

The other felines **crouched** in their hiding places, watching Eeebs approach what appeared to be **a hideous monster.** *(Actually, to them, Eeebs appeared like a monster as well.)*

"**Eldra!**" Eeebs said. "How did you get here?!"

"Same as you. I simply **went through the portal,**" Eldra said. "I'm from **the Overworld** too, you know!"

Suddenly, Eeebs's mother and father ran up to him. "**Get away** from that thing, Son! It's **dangerous!**"

"**Dangerous?**" The witch giggled. "Yes, I suppose I am dangerous! But only when I have **potions,** and I'm all out."

"**Enough!**" said Eeebs's father. "Leave our son **alone!** He will not associate with the likes of **you!**"

The witch **cackled**—an eerie, high-pitched sound. This caused some other kittens in the distance to begin **crying**. After the witch stopped laughing, Eeebs **sighed**.

"Mom, Dad, **meet Eldra.** Eldra's a witch. But she's **really, really nice.** She helped me when I got sick. I wouldn't be **alive** if it weren't for her. So you should **thank her.**"

His parents peered at Eldra.

"You don't have to praise me," said Eldra.

A bat flew past her. She **grabbed** it. "**Ooooo! How lucky!** I need bat wings!" The witch stuffed the **squeaking** creature into her belt pouch.

His parents backed away, **making low growling sounds,** pulling Eeebs along with them.

Eldra continued. "Actually, your son is **special.** I'm certain he would have survived, even **without my help!**"

"**No way,**" said Eeebs. "I was so sick. My stomach was roiling, and I passed out, and—"

"**Stop it, Eeebs!** Just stop!" His mother was beginning to weep again. Then she wiped her face with a paw and turned to Eldra. "Is it true? You . . . **helped our son?**"

Eldra nodded.

"Who wouldn't help a lost kitten? Besides, he's got **the mark!**"

"**Mark?** What do you mean?" asked Eeebs's father.

"I can tell you what I know," said Eldra. "But first . . . let the rest of your kind know: I wish you no harm. In fact, if you want to **survive** . . . you'd best listen to me."

And so Eeebs's parents finally **calmed down.**

The rest of the felines eventually crept back—but **cautiously, slowly, very slowly.**

At last Eldra began to tell everyone the history of **Minecraftia.** . . . How an **innocent** kitten came to befriend a nice ghast named Clyde . . . And how an **evil** enderman, exiled from the End, **rose to power** in the Nether . . .

CHAPTER 13

After perhaps an hour of talking, Eeebs said his goodbyes to everyone he knew. His mother and father were in tears.

"In case we get attacked," said his father, "we'll dig **a small cave** nearby. That way we'll have a place to run and hide."

Eeebs nodded.

"**Good idea.** And don't cry, huh? I'll be back soon! **I promise!**"

Then Eeebs turned to his **two best friends.** Strangely, Tufty and Meowz didn't seem upset. In fact, they seemed a bit **happy.**

Am I just imagining things? Eeebs thought. *How can they not be sad?* **Even I** *want to cry right now!*

"I wish you didn't have to go, Eeebs," said Meowz. "**I'll miss you.**"

"**Same here,**" said Tufty. "I'm **so sad. So sad.** But hey, you've gotta do what you've gotta do."

Eldra the witch smiled at Eeebs's mother and **patted** her head.

"Don't worry," Eldra said. "Your son just needs **some training.** I'll do my best. He'll be back soon. I **promise.**"

With that, Eldra and Eeebs took off, back to **the portal.**

CHAPTER 14

Five minutes later, Eeebs already missed his parents. And his friends. He hadn't even been home for more than two hours.

But then, his heart **grew lighter** at the thought of seeing Clyde again. Upon entering the Nether, Eldra led Eeebs back to her **stone hut.**

"I've been meaning to ask," said Eeebs. "As you said, **you come from the Overworld.** So why do you have a house in the Nether?"

The witch **sighed.** "Well first, it's called **a hut.**"

The kitten looked up at her, waiting for her answer. The witch continued.

"Brewing," she said. "**Nether wart. Blaze powder.** The Nether has a lot of things I need. So, I decided to build **a second hut** here."

She opened the door. "Now, **let's begin.**"

Eeebs followed Eldra inside. She walked over to the cauldron. **The purple liquid** bubbling within it smelled **strange** yet **delicious** at the same time.

"**Mushroom-bat stew,**" she said. "Care for some?" Eeebs's stomach **grumbled** as the witch said this.

How sad, Eeebs thought. *I didn't even eat anything while I was at home. I should have grabbed some* **salmon** *. . . or a* **pufferfish.** *I'm not picky!*

"**Sure,**" he said at last.

The witch set a steaming bowl of stew on to the floor. The kitten **lapped it up** hungrily. Actually, it **wasn't that bad.**

"Now," said Eldra. "Before we start, let me tell you: You're not the only **strange creature** walking around Minecraftia."

The kitten's ears **perked up.**

"You mean there are **others like me?**"

Eldra shrugged. "In a way."

"Like what?"

"Well, during **a full moon,** one out of a hundred spiders that spawn are granted special powers **similar** to yours. **The Dark Blessing,** it's called. Some can **heal** their wounds **quickly.** Others are **impossible to see** or possess **incredible strength.** And then there are creepers, who become **much stronger** when struck by **lightning.** Pigs struck by lightning turn into **zombie pigmen.** And where do you think I came from? I used to be **a villager,** you know . . . until I went out in **that thunderstorm. . . .**"

Eeebs **scratched** his chin. "Is all that related to the **Nether,** like me?"

"Not exactly. Still, there are many unusual creatures wandering around. **So don't feel alone.**"

"Thank you."

Eldra smiled. "As for **your powers . . .**"

"Yes," said Eeebs. "You've mentioned that before. What are they?"

"Well, first, you're probably already aware that you can **think** more clearly."

Eeebs nodded. "I've been able to **figure stuff out** on my own way easier than before."

"And your senses are **sharper,** correct?"

The kitten nodded again. "I can **sense nether portals** and even see in the dark better than before."

"Of course." The witch gazed into his **purple eyes.** "From what I've read, the spider's **Dark Blessing** also affects you, in limited form. If you **stand still,** you'll be nearly **invisible.** I'm not sure what you have to do to **heal** faster, though. Beyond that, you'll find that you have **the powers of every mob** native to the Nether."

"What does that mean?" asked Eeebs.

"For one, you're all but **immune to fire.** Including lava."

Lava, Eeebs thought. *That's that fiery orange stuff!*

"You mean I **won't be hurt** by it?!"

"Not at all," said the witch. "You can **swim around in it** all day if you want, and it won't even singe your whiskers."

At this point, the kitten's **curiosity** was overflowing. He didn't have to fear the Nether anymore! He could **explore** as much as he wanted!

Wait, he thought, *how can I think about exploring at a time like this?!*

"What else?" he asked.

"**Hmm.** You can **spit fireballs** the same way a ghast can, and I'm guessing you have a **Wither** effect, like all wither skeletons. And a zombie pigman's **strength.** Perhaps you can even **fly** like a blaze? But you'll have to learn how to do all of that **from the mobs** themselves. Of course, I believe you have **even more** special powers, but I must research more. I haven't had much time, since I had to go looking for you."

"This is **so great!**" said Eeebs.

"Indeed. When you come to understand your strengths, you'll basically be **a boss** monster, like the **ender dragon** or the **wither**. Cool, huh?"

"What are those?" Eeebs asked.

"Oh, **never mind**."

The kitten sighed. "Whatever. I **can't wait** until Clyde teaches me how to shoot fireballs. Where is he, anyway?"

The witch looked down at the floor. "**Um** . . ."

"What?" The kitten crept forward. "What is it? **Where is he?**"

"Well, it really hurts to say this, **but** . . ." The witch turned around. "Shortly after you left, Clyde . . . joined **EnderStar's army**."

Eeebs stepped back, slowly. The words repeated in his head, **over and over**.

Clyde. Joined EnderStar's army.
Clyde.
A happy ghast.
A nice guy. **Helpful.** *Cries at the slightest hint of bad news.*
And he joined . . . **those monsters?!**

"I . . . I don't get it. . . . **Why?**"

"I don't know," said Eldra. "He tried **following you,** but ghasts can't fly very fast, you know. He couldn't even find the portal. I've never seen a ghast **shed so many tears.** He kept asking me where the portal was, how to find you. I'm not a tour guide! Then **he just floated away.**"

A single tear ran down the kitten's cheek. "I . . . **can't** . . . believe this. . . ."

"**Be strong,**" said Eldra. "There must be a good reason why he did something like that. **Believe in** your friend."

Eeebs looked up at Eldra again. "I have to go **find him!**"

"**Of course you do.** You should stay here first, though, and **train** with me . . . but you're not going to do that, are you?"

"**Not a chance,**" said Eeebs, shaking his head. "**I owe him.**"

"Then you'll want to head to **the nether fortress.** It's **that way.**" She pointed out the window. "You can't miss it."

Eeebs glanced out the window, then back at Eldra. The witch gave him a **blank look.**

"**What?** Are you expecting me to ask you to stay here? I know you by now, Eeebs. You'll go. You'll do anything to save your friend. There's simply nothing I can do."

"You're right, just . . ."

"**What?**"

"Do you have **any advice** for me? It's not like I've ever been to a nether fortress."

Eldra took out **a book** from her item chest.

"The best piece of advice I can give you is to **write in this** every day. It's called **a diary.** Within its pages, you can record your experiences and any important information."

"But I don't even know how to write! Or spell. Or read. **I'm a kitten.**"

"**Wrong,**" Eldra said. "That's another one of your abilities. I forgot to mention that."

"But even if I know how to write, I can't **hold a quill!**"

Eldra handed the kitten a quill. "Haven't you noticed your paws are a little **different?**"

Eeebs glanced down at his paws, held each one in front of him, and then grabbed the quill.

"**Unbelievable.**"

"What's so hard to believe?" asked Eldra. "This is **Minecraftia.**"

"**Right.** So . . . book, quill, anything else?"

"You're **smart.** You'll figure out the rest. And do bring Clyde back. He owes me more tears."

"**Count on it.**"

Once again, Eeebs took off **without much hesitation.** He had an inventory, a diary, a quill, and **a whole lot of courage.**

But how am I going to sneak into a nether fortress? he thought. What's Clyde doing, anyway?

Why did he join that **crazy army?** Was he **angry** because I took off? **What happened?**

CHAPTER 15

Eldra watched the kitten zoom off into the Nether.

"He's sure got **spirit**," she said to herself. "I think he'll be just fine."

She went back into her hut, glanced at the bubbling cauldron, at the brewing stand, and finally . . . her mat on the floor. It was just **carpet**, but it was the best she could do. **Beds exploded** in the Nether, for whatever reason.

She **suddenly** felt **exhausted**. She yawned, headed over to her mat, and . . . heard **a mewing** sound coming from just outside her hut.

What's that noise? she thought. *It almost sounds like a kitten! But . . . what's Eeebs doing back so soon?*

The witch, **thoroughly confused**, went outside and glanced around. Lying nearby, on the reddish netherrack, was **not just one** kitten, **but two**.

They looked **sickly**, barely conscious, as Eeebs had been after he'd **first entered** the Nether.

However, they didn't look like Eeebs at all. One had **tan fur with orange stripes**. The other, **light gray and brown** with **bright blue eyes**.

Both kittens soon stopped moving, having lost consciousness.

Eldra **carefully** approached them. She realized she wouldn't be getting sleep anytime soon. She needed **two buckets of milk** to cure their illness, and she was **fresh out**.

I wonder, she thought. *Can I bring a cow into the Nether?*

She bent down and picked up the two kittens, one in each arm, then took them into her hut and laid them on her mat.

Of course, she wasn't **surprised** when she examined them.

Like Eeebs, both kittens had the mark.

SUNDAY

SUNDAY—UPDATE 11

Meow?

Okay. There we go. I **finally** figured it out. Apparently, I needed to use **a chicken feather,** not my paws.

So, where do I begin? **My name is Eeebs.** I'm a kitten. Well, sort of. I'm a little **different,** nowadays.

What happened? I still don't know completely. I was just trying to get away from those **wolves.** Then I found that **nether portal.** . . .

After I stepped through, **I began changing.** I found that I could run **faster,** jump **higher.** Even turn slightly **invisible.** This witch I met said I could even gain **the abilities of monsters.**

Plus, I'm **way smarter** than I used to be. After all, kittens don't typically have diaries.

The witch said there's a reason why all of this happened. I've been **"chosen"** to help save the world. There's this **huge army** of monsters, and they want to take over **all three** dimensions.

Of course, I'm supposed to **help stop** them. Me. **A kitten.** I find that **hard to believe.**

The only thing I've ever been good at is **chasing bats around.** I'm pretty sure there's **a lot more** to saving the world than that.

Anyway, for now I'm putting all that aside. You see, during my time in the Nether, I also made **a friend: Clyde.**

He's a ghast. He taught me a lot of things about his world. But then, the witch said he took off to **join that army.**

My best buddy, siding with the **enemy?** Clyde would never do that! And if he did, it must have been for a very good reason. Maybe he's **spying** on them. Or maybe they **forced him.**

In the end, it doesn't matter **why** he left. I have to go **find** him.

The witch said that Clyde took off to this place called **a nether forest.** Was she **joking** around with me? I don't think the Nether even **has** forests.

I've been searching for **hours** and haven't found <u>a **single tree.**</u>

SUNDAY—UPDATE III

I **searched around the Nether** some more.

At first, all I found were **mushrooms, glowstone,** and a lot of zombie pigmen.

Then I saw **a weird creature.** He was stranded in the middle of a lava lake, **balancing** on a single block of netherrack.

The Nether is full of **strange stuff,** but I've never seen anything like it before. I just had to see what he was doing there.

But as I got closer, I noticed that this creature **looked unfriendly. Dangerous,** even. He was made of bones and was carrying **one of those sharp things** the pigmen always have on them.

Just as I turned away, he shouted:

"Hey! Don't **leave,** huh?! I really need some **help** over here!"

My **curiosity** got the best of me. I turned back and approached the lava.

"How can I **help?**" I called out, stepping to the lake's edge. "**I can't swim in lava.**"

"**Sure you can,**" he said. "You won't **burn up!** Just hop in, float over here, and **give me a ride!** Wait . . . you **are** a magma cube, aren't you?"

"Actually, **I'm not.**"

The creature leaned forward slightly, as if taking a better look. "**Oh, sorry!** My vision's not the best these days. Well, if you're not a magma cube, what **are** you, then?"

His question totally **threw me off guard.**

How could someone **not** know **a kitten** when they see one? Even one such as myself . . .

"What do you mean, **what am I?!**" I hissed. "**What are you?!**"

The bony figure whirled around, apparently just as **shocked.**

"**What?** Haven't you ever seen **a wither skeleton** before?!"

"I have," I said. "But only a few times, and I never knew what you guys were called. I'm from the **Overworld. Long story.**"

"Right. Some other time." The **so-called** skeleton paused. "**Got a name?**"

"**Eeebs.** You?"

"**Batwing.**" He glanced around. "Well, Eeebs from the Overworld, how about we **help each other out?**"

"Assuming I even **could** get you out of there," I said, "what would you do for me?"

The skeleton **laughed.** "**Simple.** You need **a guide.** You're **clearly lost.** I mean, if you knew **anything** about this place, you **wouldn't** be going that way. No, **anywhere** but **that** way."

I glanced in the direction I'd been heading earlier.

All I could see were netherrack hills, nether quartz veins, and lavafalls.

"**It doesn't look so bad,**" I said, **pretending** not to care. But again, my curiosity soon took hold. "What's over **there,** anyway?"

"**More of my kind,**" Batwing said, "plus a whole lot of **blazes.** And none of them are as **nice** as me. Believe me, **fuzz block,** the **last place** you want to be going to is a nether fortress."

My ears perked up. **Nether fortress . . . ?**

So that explained why I never found any trees. I thought the witch had said **nether forest,** but I must have **misheard.**

This whole **language** thing is still new to me. I could speak with **other cats** before, yes, but my conversations with other creatures were . . . **very limited.** The only non-cat word I knew before this change was "**grr,**" which is **wolf** for "**I'm going to eat you now.**"

After realizing what the skeleton had said, I was **so excited** that I stepped to the very edge of the lake and **nearly slipped off**.

"**A nether fortress?!** That's exactly where I need to go! **My friend went there!** I need to **save** him!"

"You've got to be **kidding** me. . . ." The wither skeleton lowered his head. "And here I thought it was **my lucky day**. . . ."

"The deal's still on, right?"

The skeleton shook his head. "**No. No deal. No way** am I going there."

"Fine." I turned around. "Then I'll just have to go there myself. **See you around!**"

"**N-no, w-wait!**" the skeleton called out. "Okay! **You win!** Just get me off this rock, and I'll take you **anywhere you want** to go."

I nodded. "What do I do?"

"**That's easy.** Since you can't swim, you're going to be **building** a bridge."

Bridge? Another word I didn't know. Clyde had taught me a lot of words, but he'd **never mentioned** anything about bridges.

"A what?"

"**Seriously?** They don't have bridges in the Overworld, either?"

"Maybe they do, but I've never heard of them. Also, what's **'building'?**"

Batwing **grumbled** to himself. "**Never mind.** I'll walk you through it. You don't happen to have any tools, do you?"

My confusion only grew. "Tools?"

More grumbling from **my new friend**. He glanced downward, particularly at my paws. Then he **chuckled**.

"Y'know, actually, I think **we can make this work**."

SUNDAY—UPDATE IV

"Come on! **Punch!**"

A skeleton named **Batwing,** surrounded by lava, shouted these words at me. It's been a weird couple of days.

Still near the shore, I stared down at **the reddish netherrack** beneath my paws. "So, **I just hit it?** Like this?"

"**Exactly! But harder!**"

I threw a real punch this time.

Cracks formed where my paw struck the ground. Only, they vanished as quickly as they had appeared.

"**Don't stop!**" Batwing called out. "Just **keep punching!**"

"Seems a little **weird.**"

"**It's not!** It's what you have to do when you don't have any tools!"

"Right." More punching.

My paws hammered away at a block of netherrack.

I didn't let up this time—just kept punching away. The cracks grew **larger and larger,** until finally the block **came loose.** I pulled it out without too much effort.

It **wasn't as heavy** as I'd expected.

Batwing seemed **pleased.** "**That's it!** Now, just place it over by the edge there!"

I did as he instructed. Since I was holding the block with my front paws, I had to stand upward on my hind legs.

I was walking. Just like a zombie pigman. Only **not as fast.** Hobbling over, I shoved the block against the edge of the shore. Strangely, **as if by magic,** the block snapped into place.

I'd **never known** that it was possible to change the environment like this. Truly, I understood nothing about **the rules of this world.** *(Even if I am smarter than the average kitten, I still have a lot to learn.)*

"**Great work** so far!" Batwing said. "Now, do it **five more times!**"

I glanced at the lava between us. Suddenly, **it all made sense.**

If I placed enough blocks, a row of netherrack would be formed across the lava, a so-called **"bridge."** *(Gosh, these monsters and their fancy words!)*

Punch, punch.

I moved a **second** block. **A third.**

Finally, after I placed the **sixth,** Batwing jumped **so high** it was almost as if he could have cleared the lava without a bridge at all.

Then he **zoomed** to safety, stopped, spun around, and **jumped again.** "Oh, man! I can't believe this! You don't know how **thankful** I am, kitten! I was **trapped** there for **weeks!**"

"Now that you mention it," I said, walking up to him, "exactly **how** did you wind up there?"

Batwing looked away. "**Those animals! They** put me there! After I told them we shouldn't be attacking the Overworld!"

"Who's **'they'?**"

Then it hit me. "You mean you were part of **that army?**"

"**Yes. Was.** I couldn't go along with everything they were doing. That enderman is **crazy.**"

I knew he must have been talking about **EnderStar**—an enderman **so bad** his own kind actually **kicked him out of the End.**

"**By the way,**" Batwing went on, "you should know that **not everyone** in the Nether is bad. Like my friends. I'd like to **introduce you** to them."

"**That's fine,**" I said. "But first . . ."

"Yeah, **yeah, I know.** We'll find your friend. But let's get **one thing** straight first."

"**What's that?**"

"**I'll do all the talking.**"

91

SUNDAY—UPDATE V

We finally reached **the fortress.**

I'd never seen anything **so big**—just **block after block** of nether brick.

Another so-called **"bridge"** spanned a wide chasm filled with more orange fire water. A wither skeleton was **standing guard** there.

"That's **Wishbone**," Batwing whispered. "Not too smart, but an **all right** kind of guy. Just follow me and don't say anything. Actually, wait. Make **a hissing sound.** Can you do that?"

I hissed. "**Like this?**"

"Kind of. But more like **smoldering magma** or something."

"**Magma?**"

Batwing **facepalmed.** "Dude. You **have** seen a **magma cube** before, right?"

"Maybe? **I don't know?**"

"**Whatever.** After we go up to him, just start **hissing.**"

"Okay."

Batwing walked up to the wither skeleton, and I followed.

"I never thought you'd **make it off** that block," Wishbone said, "with your **fear of swimming** and all. Anyway, the boss said you aren't exactly **welcome** here anymore."

"That's fine." Batwing pointed at me. "I just wanted to show the boss this, and then I'll be on my way."

"Huh? What's that?"

"A **very rare** type of magma cube," Batwing said. "Might be useful for the army."

Wishbone approached me. "Doesn't look like any magma cube **I've** ever seen. Aren't they supposed to look like, **um,** you know, magma?"

Batwing **shook his head.** "As I said, this is an **extremely** rare type. And **very powerful,** I might add." He glanced at me. "Plus, it **hisses,** just like any magma cube."

Oh. **Right.**

I hissed **as loud** as I could.

"What kind of sound is **that?!**" Wishbone said. "Listen, it doesn't sound like a magma cube at all, and why is it **blue?**"

Batwing sighed. "You're **making fun** of a poor little magma cube because he's **blue,** are you? You know the boss doesn't like such **discrimination!**"

"**N-no,**" Wishbone said. "I—"

Batwing shook his fist, seemingly **angry.** "So **he's blue!** So what?! Do you know how many monsters have **made fun of him** for this?"

"I was just **joking!**"

"**Clearly!** A joke at **his** expense!"

"**I'm sorry!** Please **come in!** Don't tell anyone I said that!"

"Fine. And don't tell **anyone** we're here," Batwing said. "I want EnderStar to be **surprised** when he sees his new **gift.**"

"Y-yeah, okay, okay." Wishbone looked at me. "Sorry, man. Blue magma cubes are **totally cool,** all right? Even blue magma cubes with **legs!**"

"**Hissss?! Hisss!** Hiss-**hiss**-hiss!!"

"I said I'm sorry!" He stepped backward and made a wide gesture. "**Come on in.**"

With that, we walked past him and stepped inside the fortress.

"You're probably wondering why that guy was **so afraid,**" Batwing said once we were out of earshot. "From what I've heard, EnderStar was **picked on** as a kid because his eyes glowed **too brightly.**"

"I certainly know how it feels," I said. "So, any monster under his command who makes fun of another's **appearance** is **punished?**"

"**Yeah.** Something like that."

As we wandered farther inside, I began to realize just how **huge** the nether fortress was: Endless halls stretched for **hundreds** of blocks.

There were **so many monsters** here, too. I'd seen most of them before. Batwing told me the **angry fire things,** floating in the air, were called blazes. More wither skeletons **marched in groups,** along with zombie pigmen. I even saw a few ghasts **floating around** in the larger chambers. **Sadly,** none of them were Clyde.

Another wither skeleton soon **stopped** and questioned me:

"**Hey! You there!** What are you, exactly? You're the **strangest-looking monster** I've ever seen!"

"I am **Lord Sizzleblock**," I said, "**Royal** Magma Cube from the Overworld. EnderStar has asked me to pay him a visit. **And you are?**"

"Yes, let us know **your name**," Batwing said, "so that **the noble Lord Sizzleblock** can inform the **great** and **powerful** EnderStar of such **discrimination** and—"

The skeleton fell to his knees and **bowed** so deeply he all but kissed the nether brick floor. "Forgive me at once, **Your Majesty!** I simply didn't know that your kind came in such **lovely shades** of blue! How many times do you want me **to bow?**"

"**Fifty** should be enough," I said.

"Of course, **my lord!**"

Every time a monster **questioned us,** it went pretty much like that.

Once, a zombie pigman grunted at us. "**Urg!** Who you? Why you here?" He looked closer. "**Urguu?!** What you are?!"

Batwing pointed his sharp stick at the **zombified** pigman. "How **dare** you address the **grand** and **majestic King Flamepixel** with such insolence! He visits upon EnderStar's request, who shall be **notified** of your—"

The zombie pigman **didn't apologize.**

Instead, he **ran off** the nearby edge of the fortress—**without jumping,** just kind of **tipping** over—and fell into the lava far below. The way he dropped off instead of jumping . . . it was like he wanted to reach the lava **as fast** as zombie pigman-ly possible, to the millisecond.

(*In case you were wondering, we were in an open section of the fortress at this time.*)

"**Wow**," I said. "Um . . . that was a **pretty extreme** reaction, no? They must **really** fear EnderStar."

Seconds later, a blaze appeared. "**Gzzzzt?!** Www-w-what?! Bgzzzt!! **A-a-are?!** Gzrrg!! Y-y-ou . . . ?!"

I stepped forward, **about to say something**. I didn't need to, though. Not this time. The blaze was **very confused** by the sight of me. So bewildered, in fact, that it began **trembling** in the air, made a weird **sputtering** noise, and flew off while spinning around and **gurgling**—its direction and angle changing **randomly** as it did.

I watched the blaze **disappear** into the gloom overhead. "Do I really look **that weird?**" The sputtering sound eventually faded completely.

Then I heard a voice in the distance.

"**Eeebs?!**"

There he was, gliding through the air.

"**Clyde!** What are you doing here?! **I've been looking everywhere for you!**"

"Oh, Eeebs. **I'm so sorry.** I . . ."

"Did you really **join their army?**"

"**Yes,**" he said. "But I only joined because I was looking for you, too! I didn't know how to **go to the Overworld** and was too scared to go there alone."

I felt **so relieved.** Of course. I knew Clyde wouldn't **actually** join them.

"We have to **get out of here,**" I said. "Everyone keeps **freaking out** when they see me."

Clyde nodded. "**I'll say!** A blaze just flew past me, **upside down!**"

We heard a faint boom off in the distance, as though the blaze had **crashed into a wall** and **exploded.**

Batwing **winced.** "**Poor guy.** Anyway, let's get out of here. More monsters will show up **any minute.**"

"He's right," Clyde said. "**Let's go.**"

Long story short, I finally **caught up** with Clyde again. We made it out of the nether fortress **without much trouble.**

"The Overworld is in **danger**," Clyde said, once we were **in the clear**. "EnderStar is gearing up for something **big**. Much bigger than we thought. **Not even the Nether will be safe**."

"About that," Batwing said. "You two seem like **cool** mobs. I'd like to **introduce you** to my friends."

"**Fine by me**," I said. "As long as they won't do something crazy upon seeing me like turn into **a baby slime**."

I didn't know it then, but Batwing was about to show us what I now consider to be **the coolest place** in the Nether.

SUNDAY—UPDATE VI

During our trip to see Batwing's friends, the wither skeleton did something **strange.** He retrieved **a purple rock** from somewhere I couldn't see.

"That's **a strange-looking rock**," I said.

"It's not a rock. **It's a crystal.** And it's called a **tellstone.**"

"What does it do?"

"It can be used to **send messages** to other people. Even people who are **far away.** Even people you don't really know. You can speak with them **in their dreams.**"

"How is that possible?"

"I don't know. **Magic.** Anyway, it isn't working properly. I was only able to **contact two villagers.**"

"Can we speak to them now?" I asked.

"Hmm . . . maybe. **Let's try.**"

Batwing held the crystal closer so that I could see.

"**Nah.** Maybe they're not sleeping right now. . . . **Oh, wait!** Guess they are."

The face of **a villager boy** appeared in the crystal. It was **the strangest thing** I'd ever seen.

The villager's voice seemed to resound from **within** the tellstone:

"As if **my dreams** aren't bad enough. Now I get to listen to **this bonehead** talk in that scratchy, gravelly voice of his."

Batwing moved the crystal closer and began speaking into it.

"**Bonehead?** I'm not the one who just bombed **three tests!** Hey, I'm sorry, **all right?** Hey! Don't shut me out, kid! Look, I'm not going to ask you to save me! **Someone else already did!**"

Then the wither skeleton extended his arm to move the crystal farther away from us.

When he did, the villager boy seemed **shocked.** It was like he really could **see me** somehow.

"Don't look at them like **that!**" Batwing said, speaking into the crystal once more. "They're not monsters! Well, **okay,** they **are** monsters, and so am I, but **we're good!** We're not like the rest! We've made **a whole city** by ourselves! A city of good monsters, hidden from all **the bad ones!** By the way, this is **Eeebs.** He won't bite. **Promise!** Oh, and that's Clyde over there. **Both of them are really nice!**"

He said a lot more to the villager *(advice of some kind)*, but I've already forgotten it.

SUNDAY—UPDATE VII

After walking across **countless** hills and following Batwing through an enormous cave, I finally saw it:

Lavacrest.

The city of **good monsters,** hidden **deep** within a netherrack mountain.

Vast streets of nether brick **stretched endlessly.** Blocks of **glowstone** sat upon posts of nether-brick fence. Countless **iron doors** led to **shops,** homes, and even **schools** where monsters could study **various crafts,** like mining and **enchanting.**

Every monster **imaginable** could be seen here, even some not native to **this dimension,** such as **endermen** and **witches.** They had traveled here to learn more about **magic.** Magic . . . that was something I was totally unaware of, **until today.**

Witches, **huddled in groups** outside, were uttering strange words. **White glyphs** hovered in the air before them.

"What are they doing?" I asked.

"Casting a **protective spell,**" Batwing said. "I forgot the name."

"**Reinforce,**" Clyde said. "They're enchanting the city's blocks to be **more resistant** to explosions."

"There's even a spell that can make a block **impossible to mine,**" Batwing said. "It's pretty **high-level,** though, and consumes **a diamond** upon casting."

As we **wandered** the streets, with me staring in awe, Clyde and Batwing went on about the many **block enchantment spells.** One spell, **Spike Growth,** caused a block to grow spikes on each of its sides, **damaging** anyone touching it or walking across its surface—much like **cactus. First Burst** acted like **a trap:** Anyone stepping on it **caught fire.** There was also a lightning-based version, known simply as **Zap.** Another, **Frost Aura,** provided a **slowing effect.**

"Kind of like **soul sand,**" Clyde said. "Except it also makes you attack slower."

"Soul sand?"

Batwing sighed. "That **sand** you saw in the nether fortress."

In addition to block enchantment spells there were spells that created new types of blocks, such as **Shadow Block.** After casting this spell, you chose a **material**—sand, cobblestone, netherrack, anything—and **a block of that type** would appear. This block, although **appearing real** in every way, was something called an **"illusion."** You could **walk through it** as easily as walking through air.

"We're about to place these blocks across **the cave entrance** leading to this city," Batwing said. "That way, EnderStar's **soldiers** will **never find** this place."

"Don't you need **a bat's wing** to cast that one?" Clyde asked.

Batwing nodded. **"Yeah.** We really need to head to the Overworld and go **bat hunting.**"

Another spell was called **"Light Block."** It created a block of **intense** white light, which could be walked through. However, standing within such a block was like standing in **sunlight.**

A more powerful version of the spell, **Concentrated Light Block,** was **twice the normal strength** of sunlight, meaning it would burn monsters to **a crisp.**

"We figure a wall of light blocks might be **useful** against a zombie horde," Batwing said. "Sadly, both versions of Light Block require **emeralds** to cast."

And then there was **Mud Aspect,** which gave a block **mud-like consistency.** Anyone stepping into it would slowly **sink down.** Their movement speed would be **decreased** as well, although not as much as the effect Frost Aura provided.

Needless to say, **Slime Aspect** gave any block the properties of **slime,** meaning it could be used to **bounce upward.**

But the **most interesting,** in my opinion, was **Teleporter Cube.** I didn't understand how it worked, but Clyde said it could be used to **travel** vast distances **instantaneously.**

"Not a single monster in the city knows that spell," Batwing said. "**Not even Greyfellow.**"

I blinked. "**Greyfellow?**"

For once, Batwing **wasn't annoyed** at my cluelessness. "He's the guy who **runs** this place."

"He's also the guy we're **going to see,**" Clyde added. "I'm sure he must know more about your . . . **current state.**"

Perhaps ten minutes later, we reached **Greyfellow's** home: a huge hut made of **nether quartz.** Batwing increased his pace, muttering something to himself.

<u>Clyde and I exchanged glances and followed him in.</u>

SUNDAY—UPDATE VIII

Greyfellow was an enderman.

He wasn't black, however, but **light gray** in color with bright **sky-blue eyes.** In addition, he wore a fancy-looking **white hat,** not unlike those typically worn by witches. He's known as an **"endermage,"** one of the last **enderman wizards** in all of Minecraftia.

"**Where have you been?**" he said to Batwing.

"Yeah, about that," Batwing said.

"**Those bums** stranded me out there."

"Oh?"

Batwing withdrew **the brilliant purple tellstone** from his inventory. "And your little **crystal** didn't work."

"What do you mean **it didn't work?**"

"Well, I tried telling **those villagers** that the Overworld is in danger. I **begged** them to set me free. **The girl** just **ignored** me, and **this little punk, Runt,** kept telling me to go away."

"My apologies," Greyfellow said. "Villagers are a **crude** folk. They can sometimes be . . . **uncouth.** Interesting that you weren't able to contact **anyone else,** though. Hmm . . . Give me **the tellstone.**"

"**Gladly.** Take it."

"I shall craft you **a new one** later tonight," the endermage said. He glanced at Clyde and me. "And who are **your new friends?**"

Batwing introduced us, and the endermage noticed **my mark.** "**Interesting.** You come from the Overworld, then? Yes. You were once **a kitten.** I can see that now."

"Do you know what happened to me?" I asked.

"**I believe so.** Although, I must consult the **ancient texts.** Go now. **Eat. Sleep.** In the morning, we shall speak again."

Before long, I'd eaten **three cooked salmon** and was **curled up** next to a burning block of netherrack. How these monsters got ahold of **salmon,** I didn't know and didn't ask.

Magic, **probably.**

Yawn. Maybe they can conjure food as well as blocks?

As I dozed off,
I started **purring.**

MONDAY

That morning, I met up with the **gray enderman** again. He told me a lot of stuff and showed me this **huge, ancient book**.

He let me **borrow it,** so I'm going to copy some of it down.

***

THE PROPHECY OF MINECRAFTIA, VOLUME I

And so shall it be: In these perilous times, two Saviors shall descend from the Sacred Light and drive the Veil of Darkness to each corner of the world.

One Savior shall take the form of a young Human man—KOLB. He represents all that is Earthly and Known. The other shall arrive in the form of a young Sylph woman of most enchanting beauty—IONE. She represents the Unearthly, the Unknown.

Alas, our Saviors walk a difficult path, for their Divine Weapons, forged by the White Shepherd and blessed with Sacred Light, were all but destroyed during the Second War. Only when their shards have been reunited can each Weapon be fully re-forged.

In addition to our Saviors, five Beings shall be Chosen by the Light:

1.) A villager displaying incredible creativity and insight, with compassion for all life. He shall take up the sword and become not only a Warrior but a supreme Tactician without equal. Although his power comes from within, the Sacred Light shall assist him in the form of Luck. He is a champion of the Overworld.

2.) Three animals displaying the highest bravery in the face of great danger and loyalty to their friends. The gender and form of each animal are Unknown. They shall be blessed with higher intelligence and begin to take on the aspects of monsters. The first of these Chosen Animals shall seek to meet and serve the first Chosen Being. These animals are champions of the Nether.

3.) The third Chosen Being is entirely Unknown, although it is Known that this Being shall be most bizarre in nature. He serves as a champion of the End.

Know this: As the Darkness continues to spread across our World, our Saviors must seek to reclaim the fragments of their Divine Weapons, for these blades are the only two Divine Weapons remaining after the Second War. The rest, destroyed by the Eyeless One, are lost for eternity.

Before all else, our Saviors shall head to the Capital of our World, known as Aetheria City, where they shall learn of past knowledge and train themselves, for their energy will have diminished during their journey.

Soon thereafter, the Great War shall begin between the forces of Light and Darkness.

***

Okay. There's **much more** to that book, but my head hurts. *(My paw, too.)*

In dark times, heroes from **"another world"** will arrive to **fight** against evil. Five beings from this world have been **selected** as well.

I'm **one of the animals** mentioned. I'm supposed to find and serve the first **"Chosen Being."** A villager. That means I need to return to **the Overworld.**

But that enderman wizard, **Greyfellow,** doesn't want me to. Not yet. He says I must learn more about **my abilities** before I leave. I must become **stronger.**

We talked about this stuff **all day.** I'm really **tired,** now. Talking in **a non-cat language** I've just learned is still difficult for me, remember?

By the way, some of the monsters here **really can** conjure food with magic. **It's so cool. All I have to do is ask** some witch or enderman for raw salmon. I can **cook it** myself because I've been blessed with **higher intelligence,** according to that old book. **How cool is that?! Meow!**

Time for sleep.
My <u>"training"</u> starts tomorrow.

TUESDAY

"They've found us! They've **found us!**"

I woke up to **a creeper wizard** shouting these words. I was still at **Greyfellow's** house. When I walked outside, I saw so many different monsters **running around** and shouting.

From this crowd, Greyfellow and Batwing **emerged.** They were holding on to a zombie pigman by each arm. He seemed familiar somehow. But where could I have **seen him before?**

"We found him **sneaking around** just outside the city!" Batwing said. "**Little snoop!**"

Clyde floated down to our level. "What are we going to do with him?"

"We'll have to **imprison him,**" Greyfellow said. "If we let him go, he'll give EnderStar **the location** of our city."

"N-no," the pigman said. "**Me. Want. T-to—**"

"**Shut it!**" Batwing said. "You'll say anything to get away!"

A creeper shouted: "**Hisssss, me blow him up!**"

"I say we **throw him** into the **pit!**" a nearby witch shouted. "That's the **best way!**"

"**Yesh!** Duh pit! **Duh pit!**" After uttering these noises, several zombie pigmen *(good ones, apparently?)* began chanting: "**Duh pit! Duh pit! Duh pit!**"

Soon, hundreds of monsters joined in.

(However, most were shouting/chanting "the pit" as opposed to "duh pit." Why do some speak differently?)

"They're **right**," Batwing said. "There's only one way we **deal with** our enemies, and that's tossing them in **the pit**. A good dropkick from behind—not too hard, eh, a little encouraging tap in the rear—and **boom,** one-way ticket to another dimension. Suddenly, our problem is **no longer our problem,** just **breakfast** for some hungry **Void beast.**"

A tear ran down Clyde's cheek. He spun around. "**No!** What are you saying?! **We can't do that!** If we do, we'll be just as bad as EnderStar!" He paused. "Wait. **Um . . . guys?** What's **the pit?**"

TUESDAY—UPDATE 1

"**Oh. Okay.** So that's the pit."

Some say it goes on **forever**, but Greyfellow told me the truth: **It actually reaches the Void.**

When you fall in, you'll fall for **quite a long way**. But after some **6,570 blocks,** you'll eventually arrive in **a bizarre world**. A world of **eternal night** containing **crystalline** plants, lakes of **glowing blue ooze, invisible** things brushing past you and **whispering** into your ear, and, yes, **horrifying** monsters.

At least, that's what **Greyfellow** told me when I asked him about it. Maybe he's just **trying to scare me?**

He also said **a race of peaceful mushroom people** live there, who know about such things as "**advanced crafting**" and "**advanced brewing.**" Whatever **that** means.

Anyway, **thirty minutes** later, over one thousand monsters were standing around this seemingly **bottomless hole** that may or may not have led to a place **one thousand times crazier** than the Nether.

The **prisoner** was standing on the very edge, his back turned to us. Batwing was right behind him.

"Just **say the word,** Greyfellow, and I'll dropkick this **punk** into a **brand-new dimension!**"

"**P-please,**" the pigman said. "Me. No. **B-b-b . . . b . . . b-bad.**"

The endermage closed his eyes for what must have been **several minutes.**

Ghast tears were **running down** Clyde's cheeks, and two witches were now trying to **collect them.**

I stared at the pigman the whole time. *Now where have I seen him before? That thing on his head.* I saw a pigman wearing one of those before.

Wait a second! He was the guy leading all the other monsters in the Overworld after EnderStar teleported away. He was the **smart one**, the zombie pigman who could actually talk.

What's his name again?

Rarg? Yes! **Rarg,** *the zombie pigman captain!*

"Very well," Greyfellow said at last. "I have decided that—"

"**No!**" I shouted. I walked up to Rarg and turned to the other monsters. "**Wait!** I've seen this pigman before!"

"**What?** In the nether fortress?" Batwing said. "So what?"

"In **the Overworld**," I said. "I watched from a distance as EnderStar's army **panicked, blinded** by sunlight. They had no idea **how bright** the sun can be."

"What's your point?" Greyfellow said.

"Well, while I was watching them, I sensed **something good** in this pigman. Since he was wearing **that thing** on his head, he was **the only one** who wasn't blinded. He helped his fellow monsters return to the Nether by **singing a song** so that they could follow him."

The endermage nodded. "I see, I see. **Hmm . . .** wearing a helmet, **yes.** So, he's quite **smart.** Hmm."

"Not only that," I said, "I could somehow **sense** that he didn't **want** to be there. Didn't want any part of attacking the Overworld. He kept **hesitating** whenever EnderStar spoke to him."

"**C'mon!**" Batwing said. "You know we can't do anything but give this guy **a good kick!** He'll give away our **location** if we don't!"

"**Quiet,**" Greyfellow said. He walked up to Rarg. "Pigman. **Is it true?** Do you really wish to **abandon** EnderStar's army and join us?"

"**Y-yes,**" Rarg said. "Me **tired** of **boss man.** And me have many friends also tired of boss man. Boss man **always screaming.** Always want us do **bad thing.** We don't want do bad thing."

"Then why didn't you leave **before?**" Greyfellow asked.

"**We scared.** Boss man **make fire** from no fire. Boss man make **white zap light** from no white zap light. Boss man also turn three me friend into **flying black squeaky thing.** Then he **eat** flying black squeaky thing. **Me so sad.** Me so **angry.** When me see flying black squeaky thing . . . **me remember. Me cry.** Me want help beat him."

"Flying black squeaky thing?" Batwing facepalmed. "This is like talking to that kitten! **Can you make sense, please?**"

"He means **bats,**" I said.

"Oh. Right."

"I'm no wizard, but I believe there's only one spell that can **turn someone into a bat,**" Clyde said.

"Yes." Greyfellow's expression grew even **more serious**. **Polymorph III.** This is **bad news** indeed. He's **much more powerful** than we thought."

"Why don't we let Rarg **join us,** then?" Clyde asked. "If he really does **want out** of EnderStar's army, he can tell us **everything** he knows!"

"**Not a bad idea,**" Greyfellow said. "He may also **convince** his friends to switch sides and join us."

Batwing **facepalmed** again. "Man, don't you guys know **anything?** We can't take **any chances!** Listen, I'm a wither skeleton, okay? I grew up in that nether fortress. I used to be a **bad mob.** I know what bad mobs think. And here's what bad mobs think: **bad things.** EnderStar probably sent him here and told him to **say all of that stuff.** And, once we finally start **trusting** him and let him stay here and feed him **mushrooms** and **slimeball stew** and the many other **nasty** things his kind eats, he'll learn everything about us, go back to the nether fortress, and **squeal** like a . . . um . . . pigman?"

The other monsters seemed **divided.** Some nodded their heads in agreement with Greyfellow and Clyde, and others were thinking along the same lines as Batwing. It was a situation **stickier** than any slime.

Then Rarg held out **a stack of ender pearls.** "Me. G-g-g . . . g-g . . ."

"**Give?**" I asked.

"Y-yes. **Me g-give.**"

"W-where did you get those?!" Batwing cried out.

"Me grab **green things**. From big red house. Me g-g . . . give you. Okay?"

"**Interesting**," Greyfellow said, taking the stack of ender pearls. "First the kitten, and now **this**."

Rarg then held out a stack of **gold bars**. "**Shiny thing**. Me also take these. Boss man shiny pile. Boss man have **many shiny things** in shiny pile."

He dropped the stack on to the ground, then he retrieved a stack of **shiny green rocks** from his inventory and threw them onto the ground as well. Many monsters **gasped**.

"So many emeralds!"

This was followed by at least fifty different glass things filled with water. Although, the water inside wasn't blue but **purple, red, and green. . . .**

"Potions, too?!"

"Boss man tell me, **always watch** bottle things. Make sure no monster take bottle things. Why bottle things so important? Me wonder. But secret. Me try drinking bottle thing once. Me **jump very high**." He chuckled. "Me **like** bottle things."

An **unbelievable** amount of items formed a pile at Rarg's big boots.

There were several books, like the one I'm currently writing in. Except, they **shimmered purple**. Was that due to magic?

"**Enchanting books?!**" a few monsters exclaimed.

Rarg also threw down a pile of **shiny whitish-blue rocks.** Those are called **diamonds,** apparently.

"Boss man say shiny rock **most good,**" Rarg said. "No eat shiny rock. Shiny rock hard. But shiny rock make good stab thing. Shiny rock also make good **body thing,** like on head or feet."

Around me, **the excitement** of the other monsters **filled the air.** They kept chattering away about emeralds, diamonds, enchanted books, potions. . . .

"Okay. Very last thing. **Shiny metal.** I find in wood box. Boss man say this **junk.** But me think **so pretty.**"

Rarg the zombie pigman withdrew another rock from his inventory. Wait, **no?** It wasn't a rock. **It was a piece of metal?** It was **bright silver** and shimmered **many different colors.** It was **so beautiful.** The most common color by far was this **dazzling shade of green.**

"**Unbelievable,**" Greyfellow said. "I don't believe . . . **this is . . .** quite surely, **it can't be.** . . . My fellow monsters, we are looking at **a shard. One of the seven shards of Critbringer.**"

Everyone fell **silent,** and then:

"Huh?"

"Shard?"

"**Critbringer?**"

"What are you talking about, Greyfellow?"

"It looks like **a piece of metal** to me."

"It is a piece of metal," Greyfellow said. "But not iron. **That is adamant,** a metal **so rare** in our time that it was thought to exist **only in legend.**"

I remembered the old book Greyfellow had let me borrow.

. . . Divine Weapons . . . all but destroyed during the Second War. Only when their shards have been reunited can each Weapon be fully re-forged. . . .

"You mean, this is from one of the sharp sticks mentioned in the book?" I said. "**The swords,** I mean."

"**Exactly!**" Greyfellow said.

The other monsters didn't seem to **understand.** They looked at each other with total **confusion** in their square eyes.

The gray enderman scowled at them. "**Fools!** Have none of you read of **the Prophecy?!** This piece of metal is **a fragment from the legendary sword Critbringer!** A sword forged in ancient times, when monsters **far more powerful** than any of you roamed in great number! Back then, weapons had to be strong enough for **land wyrms, lurkers,** and other **horrific** beasts you cannot possibly imagine! This is one of the only weapons still in existence **powerful enough to harm the Eyeless One,** whose real name I shall not utter here!"

"**Lurkers?**" Batwing sighed. "Are those the giant black squid-like things with **one thousand tentacles** and a single huge purple eye? The ones that live deep underground? The reason why certain mineshafts are abandoned? The monsters that reduce the **durability** of your items with a single glance? I thought those things were just **a legend.**" He shrugged. "Huh. Who knew?"

"**Fool!**" Greyfellow grabbed **the shard** and turned to Rarg. "I can see now that **destiny** has brought you to us."

The enderman addressed the entire crowd: "No harm shall come to this pigman! **Free him at once** and see to it that he is **introduced** to our city!" He sighed. "I **must go** now. I have much work to do. **Kitten, come.**"

Rarg turned to me. "Thank you, **blue fuzz thing.** You help me. **Me so happy.** You me **friend** now?"

"Yes," I said to Rarg. "**Me you friend now.**"

TUESDAY—UPDATE II

"Breathe!" the endermage shouted. "**Breathe!!**"

"I'm **breathing**," I said. "I'm **breathing!** But as you can see, **your Grand High Endermage-ness,** no fireballs are coming out!"

"Try harder!"

Breathe, breathe, breathe.

Nothing. Just little puffs of air.

We were back at Greyfellow's place. The endermage was trying to teach me how to use **monster abilities.**

As I exhaled **over and over,** a non-zombified pigman who stood nearby saw me and started doing the same. Moments later: "**O'gorg!** Me pants-pants **heavy** now. I go **bathroom** now-now."

"**Leave us at once!**" the endermage shouted. The pigman left. "Clyde! **Clyde!** Oh, where did that silly ghast run off to?!"

"**I'm here!**" the ghast called out. "What's **the problem?**"

"Do you see that **wall of obsidian?**" Greyfellow asked. "Breathe **a fireball** on it!"

"Can you stop shouting?"

"**Now!!**"

As commanded, the ghast drew in a deep breath, and—**whoosh!**—spit out a large **fireball.** It hit the obsidian wall nearby without any real effect.

"Now do it **again! Keep doing it!**"

One after another, I watched Clyde spit fireballs at the obsidian wall.

"**Good!**" the enderman said. "Now, kitten. **You try.**"

"Sure thing."

Breathe! **Breathe! Breathe!**

Pretty pathetic. Not even a **puff** of smoke.

"You aren't trying hard enough!" Greyfellow shouted. "**Try!!**"

"I **am** trying!" I shouted.

"**Try harder!!**"

"**I am!!**"

"There's a large chance your homeworld is going to be **destroyed,** kitten! **Do you understand?!**"

I hissed. "Hey! Stop freaking out, okay?! For the past hour it's been '**Jump here!** Swim in that lava **over there!** Go **invisible!** Magically **spit out fireballs** as if you're a—'"

Suddenly, my whole body shook.

Cough, hack.
Ahackckahackahack.
Hackhackhackackackkkkkkkkk.

What's wrong with me? **This is so painful!** It's like coughing up **a hairball** but ten times worse!

123

I coughed up **a fireball** instead. It was a **tiny** thing, maybe ten times the size of a spark. It flew out of my mouth and **wobbled** through the air. There was a sad little sound as it did: **p'tweeeeeeeeee....**

This tiny fireball, flying **so slowly** *(slower than a zombie pigman walking)* slowed down even more the more it flew toward the wall. It continued making that little noise: **eeeee....**

We **all watched** as it continued to fly forward **pathetically**. It **literally** took twenty seconds to travel a distance of **nine blocks**. Finally, there was a slight sputtering sound as it hit the wall and vanished.

I coughed **again**. A little puff of smoke came out. For a long time afterward: **silence**.

I looked at **Clyde**. Clyde looked at **the enderman**. The enderman looked at **me**. I looked at **the enderman**. The enderman looked at **Clyde**. Clyde looked at **me**. Then we **all** looked at the small obsidian wall **my tiny little fireball** had struck.

"I don't believe it," Greyfellow said. "**The Prophecy! It really is true!**"

Clyde started spinning around **frantically**. "**So cool**, Eeebs! **Wow!** I knew you could do it!"

"Yeah, yeah, **not bad, kid!**" Batwing was standing in the doorway, now. "So, you're **some kind of mutant**, huh?"

Moments later, I heard **a familiar voice.** A **girl's** voice. Most of all, it was **the voice of a kitten.** "Hey?! **Eeebs?!** What was **that?!**"

Tufty and **Meowz** were also standing in the doorway. **My friends from the Overworld.** Strangely, although I recognized them, they no longer looked like kittens. **Not really.**

Big claws.
Ridiculously long ears.
As a matter of fact, and, as **strange** as it sounds,
well . . . **they almost kind of looked like me.**

WEDNESDAY

Yesterday, **I breathed fire.**

At the same time, my friends **showed up, Tufty** and **Meowz.** They were pretty much in **the same boat** as I was several days ago: **clueless.**

They still **resembled** their former selves. Tufty was still **orange-ish.** Meowz was still mostly **white.** However, they **looked scary** now. Like an-enderman-staring-at-you-in-a-totally-dark-room-making-weird-little-noises-with-only-its-glowing-purple-eyes-being-visible scary. Actually, **worse than that.** Like my-mom-calling-me-by-my-full-name-and-threatening-to-make-me-eat-pufferfish-casserole-for-a-week scary or human-trying-to-tame-me-with-a-pumpkin-instead-of-a-fish scary.

Meowz **crept** into the house. "**Eeebs?**"

Tufty followed her in with his tail between his legs.

The endermage, **Greyfellow,** nearly **fainted** upon seeing them. He turned to Batwing. "I can't . . . **I don't** . . . what is happening, Batwing? Yesterday, everything was so **normal.** I was drinking some **redstone tea,** thinking about what to **craft.** Then this kitten shows up with **the mark.** Then a zombie pigman not only joins our side but **hands over EnderStar's treasure horde.** Then, the kitten actually **breathes fire.** I'd never believed in **the Prophecy** myself!

Did you? And now two of his friends arrive, apparently **Chosen** as well. . . ."

He **trailed off** and appeared to be looking at something far away.

Batwing sighed. "Three kittens as **Chosen Animals.** Why couldn't it have been something way **more crazy,** like a chicken and a donkey? A bat and a cow?"

"I was hoping for a squid and a pig!" Clyde said. "I read about **squids,** once."

"Anything but **three kittens.**" The wither skeleton nudged **Greyfellow.**

The endermage mumbled absently, still **staring** ahead: "I like redstone tea . . . and . . . **kittens** . . . **three** kittens . . . what does it **mean** . . . ?"

"So, these are **your friends,** Eeebs?" Clyde **smiled.** Well, he didn't, really, but he **didn't sniffle** or anything like that, and his frown vanished. That's **pretty much** like smiling for a ghost.

"**Yes,**" I said, approaching Tufty and Meowz.

"We came across **the witch,**" Meowz said. "She told us everything."

"We didn't believe her when she said we could use **the abilities of monsters,**" Tufty said. "**It's true,** though. This is so **cool!** How can I breathe fire like that?"

"You guys really shouldn't have followed me," I said. "**Really.** You don't know what you've gotten yourselves **into.**"

Meowz looked like she was about to cry. "**Eebs?**"

"Yeah."

"What's happening?"

"**About that,** purrrr . . ."

I tried telling them about **the Prophecy,** and I showed them Greyfellow's book. It was **hard** for me to explain everything to them, and the endermage wouldn't chime in and **help me out.** He just kept **babbling** on about redstone tea: how he liked it warm although not too warm, how he added some crushed **flower petals** like blue orchids to the recipe to make it taste better, how he thought it further improved the taste and added **"more kick"** when he made it using a brewing stand instead of **a crafting table.** . . .

I turned to the endermage. "**Hey? Greyfellow?** Who wrote this book, anyway?"

". . . it's the **bubbling** process," he mumbled. "A brewing stand **aerates** the tea, providing a more **crisp** and **refreshing** flavor. . . ."

My ears and tail lowered, I started thinking that after learning how to spit fireballs, my next **power** was going to be to **shoot smoke** out of my ears.

"**Right,**" I said. "Forget about who wrote it, then. What I really mean to ask is, how did they know all of this stuff was going to happen? How did they know **three animals** would be **changed?**"

Greyfellow nodded. "Why, yes . . . **pink tulip** certainly tastes better than **oxeye daisy,** yes . . . yes, indeed. . . ."

"**Um,** what's wrong with him?" Batwing said.

Clyde **shrugged.** Well, Clyde has no shoulders—he's just a giant white block with a face, really—but, anyway, for some reason **I felt** that he shrugged. "**Too much** has happened today."

"You could say that." The wither skeleton glanced out the window. "I'll go check on **Rarg** and see if he's okay. Listen, Eeebs. Why don't you hold off on telling your friends about **the Prophecy** till our endermage friend here isn't **bumbling around** like a **land squid?** In the meantime, you can show your friends **around the city.** Cool?"

"**Sure,**" I said, glancing at the two nether kittens. "Shall we?"

The three of us left Greyfellow's hut. I didn't **freak out** at the sight of my friends, not even then. I was still **so shocked** by everything. I was about to join the endermage. If just **one more** crazy thing had happened, I'd have started mumbling about **pufferfish cookies:** how to align the eggs, milk, and sugar **pixel** by **pixel** on the crafting table in a purrfect way to achieve a five-star rating from the **International Minecraftian Baker's Society,** in not only **consistency** but also **form** and texture, the **lightness** of the bread, **crisp** yet never crumbling, with each tiny cube of sugar and baked pufferfish spread evenly throughout the biscuits to achieve a pastry both **magnificent** to the eye and simply **bursting with flavor.**

But then I wasn't sure if the **International Minecraftian Baker's Society** had such a **refined** taste as a nether kitten's, and soon I began to wonder whether any of them would appreciate the **elegance** of a cookie made of equal parts sugar and fish.

Speaking of **Greyfellow**.

(Wait . . . I wasn't speaking of him. Whatever.)

Anyway, here are a few drawings of **his house**.

Easy to guess that an enderman lives here.

WEDNESDAY—UPDATE 1

Well, I showed my friends around **Good Mob City**. We didn't **talk** much, though. They were **just as silent** as me.

I mean, all of this stuff has happened **so** fast. Just a week ago, we were playing **hide-and-seek**. Now, we're nothing like our former selves. We're supposed to help **save the world**.

An hour or so later we headed back to the gray enderman. He'd **finally calmed down** a little.

"Sorry about that," he said. "I just couldn't believe it. Still can't. **The Prophecy** really is **true?!** Which means . . . our world is going to suffer through yet **another Great War**."

"What are we supposed to do?" I asked, getting **straight to the point**.

"**Hmm.** First, let's try something. Kittens, I want you to think about the word **'ability.'** Or just **imagine** your abilities in general. Picture them in your **mind**."

Tufty must have thought of his abilities first.

Seconds after the endermage spoke, **a gray screen** appeared before the orange nether kitten. This screen was **completely flat**, two-dimensional, and seemed to be made out of **colored light**.

"**Wow!**" Meowz waved a paw through Tufty's screen, and it **passed through** without any resistance. "What **is** that thing?"

"Those screens are called **visual enchantments**," the enderman said. "They can be used to **interact** with objects or your **inventory**, or they can simply **display data**."

"And what are **abilities?**" Tufty asked.

"All monsters have abilities," Greyfellow said. "Creepers **move silently**. Endermen **teleport**. Zombies **break down doors**. Of course, you kittens have **more abilities** than any normal mob."

I tried to concentrate on the word "ability."
A screen appeared before me as well.

ABILITIES

OBSIDIAN FUR
HIGHER INTELLIGENCE
PIGMAN FRENZY
ASPECT OF THE SPIDER
GHAST FIREBALL
CREEP
FIRE AFFINITY
PACK BEAST

The enderman then **told us** that we could either **touch** an ability's name on the screen or **focus on it** with our mind to access **another screen.** This screen would tell us more about **that specific ability.**

When I batted at the words "Obsidian Fur" with a paw, the words upon the screen **changed** to:

> # ABILITY:
> ## OBSIDIAN FUR
> LEVEL: ■□□□□□□□□
> TYPE: MONSTER, PASSIVE
>
> Your fur has become exceedingly dense and tough, making you more resistant to damage. For each level of this ability, your armor is increased slightly and all critical hits will deal 5% less damage (50% maximum).

"If you want to go back to the **first screen**," Greyfellow said, "just concentrate on that word. '**Back.**' Or you could speak it **out loud.**"

I tried the latter. "**Back.**"

The visual enchantment screen returned to its former state.

"**Interesting.**" Touching the screen with her paws, Meowz began **browsing through** all of her abilities.

I did the same, pawing down the list, accessing each **sub-menu**, reading it, and saying the word **"back"** in my mind each time.

Here's a **full list** of my abilities:

ABILITY:
HIGHER INTELLIGENCE
LEVEL: ■■■■■☐☐☐☐
TYPE: MONSTER, PASSIVE

This skill increases your INT as well as the effectiveness of your AI in many regards, such as orientation, positioning in combat, target priority, preservation of life, item use, spell use, communication, energy management, memory, and adaptive learning. Decision time is also reduced slightly with each level.

(I'm guessing **"INT"** means **intelligence?** I have no idea what **"AI"** means and neither does Greyfellow.)

ABILITY:
PIGMAN FRENZY
LEVEL: ■■■☐☐☐☐☐☐☐
TYPE: MONSTER, PASSIVE, ACTIVATED

Passively increases your base movement, sprinting, crouching, and swimming speeds. Additionally, you may activate this ability to ignore any slow debuff for a short amount of time (1 second/level), such as that caused by walking through cobwebs or soul sand.

ABILITY:
ASPECT OF THE SPIDER
LEVEL: ■☐☐☐☐☐☐☐☐
TYPE: MONSTER, PASSIVE

You can move vertically up and down walls as though they were ladders.

ABILITY: GHAST FIREBALL

LEVEL: ■□□□□□□□□□
TYPE: MONSTER, ACTIVE (75 ENERGY)

You can breathe fire! Each level increases the fireball's damage and velocity and reduces the energy cost by 2.

ABILITY: CREEP

LEVEL: ■■□□□□□□□□
TYPE: MONSTER, PASSIVE

You move as silently as a creeper. While standing still, you will gain camouflage, which increases with level, resulting in almost complete invisibility once mastered.

ABILITY:
FIRE AFFINITY
LEVEL: ■■■■■■■■■■
TYPE: MONSTER, PASSIVE

You've mastered this skill!
You are immune to the effects
of both fire and lava.

ABILITY:
PACK BEAST
LEVEL: ■■☐☐☐☐☐☐☐☐
TYPE: MONSTER, PASSIVE

You gain one additional inventory
slot with each level of this skill.

The endermage said an ability's **level** is a measure of how **powerful** it is. So, most of my abilities are still **pretty weak.** But they won't be like that **forever!**

"By the way, **energy is used** for abilities," the enderman said. "Spells, too. Using abilities and casting spells **drain your energy bar.** That's why Eeebs could breathe **only one** fireball yesterday and only puffs of smoke afterward. Energy **slowly recharges** over time. So it's best to use your abilities **only** when you **absolutely need them.** Like most monsters, you have a maximum of **100 energy.**"

"How do we know how much energy we currently have?" Tufty asked.

"That's **the yellow bar** in your **HUD**, or **heads-up display.** Simply concentrate upon the word 'HUD' in your mind, and it will appear across the bottom of **your vision.** If you are injured, hungry, drained of energy, or debuffed in any way, your HUD will **automatically** appear, as a kind of reminder, until your condition **improves.**"

Okay, let's try it: HUD.

As soon as I thought this, a **bunch of stuff** appeared across the bottom of my vision, just like the enderman had described.

"The hearts are a measure of your **life force**," Greyfellow said. "Each heart represents **two hit points**. By the way, I'm curious. How many hearts do you have?"

Each of us replied with the same number:

"**Ten!**"

"**Twenty hit points**, then. **Not much.** You'll gain much more as you **grow stronger**, though."

"What about the **gray shirt things?**" I asked, not wanting to think about what would happen if all of my hearts were **removed**.

"That's a visual indicator of your **protection**, otherwise known as **armor**. The more armor you have, the **less damage** you will take. Some forms of damage bypass armor, however."

"How about **the boxes?**"

"Your **hotbar**. You can secure items to your body—with the help of a **belt**, for example—or in an easy-to-reach location in your **inventory**. You may then access those items **quickly**."

All three nether kittens exchanged glances: "**Inventory?**"

The enderman then explained how we each have an **"extra-dimensional space"** that lets us carry many items. We only have to say **"inventory"** in our minds for the inventory screen to appear. That must be how Batwing withdrew **the tellstone** from what looked like thin air: He accessed his inventory.

"Your inventories are currently **quite small**," Greyfellow said. "You can increase the size of your inventory by wearing a container, like **a belt pouch**. There are even **enchanted** containers that **dramatically** increase your inventory space. Sadly, such items, enchanted or not, **won't be easy** for kittens to wear. They aren't normally designed for animals. An easy way around that, if you felt the need to carry many items, would be to level-up your **Pack Beast** ability."

Tufty **blinked**. "Um, can you repeat that? I'm **totally confused**."

"**Same here**," I said. "I guess that means we **really** need to level-up our Higher Intelligence ability, huh?"

WEDNESDAY—UPDATE II

After we **played around** with our **visual enchantment screens**, a question spawned in my mind. "Say, how do we **get stronger**, anyway? And how can our abilities gain **levels?**"

The enderman gave me a **strange** look. All of his expressions were strange, really, but his expression then was as if I'd just asked why zombie pigmen are purple and have **ice cream cones** for heads.

"By doing **your job**," he said.

"And that is?"

"Turning **Herobrine's** and **EnderStar's minions** into clouds of smoke. Every time you **defeat** one, you'll absorb some of its power. Of course, you'll also grow stronger by **questing**."

Questing . . . ?

Before anyone could even ask for clarification, **more screens** appeared before us.

Like with the ability screens, simply thinking about the word **"quest"** conjured what could be called a **"quest screen"**:

> ## ACTIVE QUEST:
> ## SERVING YOUR MASTERS
>
> Your destiny awaits! Go now, nether kitten, and find the villager you are meant to serve!

Sadly, Tufty and Meowz had different messages on their quest screens.

> ## ACTIVE QUEST:
> ## SURPRISE ATTACK!
>
> You must remain in the city of Lavacrest. Here, you will further improve your abilities and take part in a siege upon the nether fortress!

"What does all of this **mean?!**" Tufty said. "**It's so weird!**"

"I have to agree," Meowz said. "I'm **so confused** I could **hiss!** It's not fair, you know? We've been chosen to help **save the world,** and all this new stuff is being thrown at us, and we don't even get **classes** or something?"

"It does seem **an awful lot** has been thrust upon you kittens," Greyfellow said. "**A heavy burden,** indeed. I am doing my best to **teach you,** but there are many things I do not know. Eeebs, I do suggest returning to **the Overworld** as soon as you can. Once there, the first place you should head to is **the capital.** Ask around for the **Library.** One of **my colleagues** there knows much about **the Prophecy** and may be able to help you locate that **villager.**"

As he said this, I tried **piecing everything together** in my mind.

1.) We're supposed to help fight against **the Eyeless One,** otherwise known as **Herobrine.**

2.) We've been given **abilities,** and we have these things called **quests**—tasks we're supposed to complete.

3.) My first quest is meeting up with that **villager.** A villager I don't know anything about. Is it a boy or a girl? **What's his or her name?** Why do I have to serve that villager, anyway? What, am I just a **pack kitten** or something? I thought **my role** in all this would be a bit more glamorous than that.

"My friends really have to **stay here?**" I asked.

"I believe so. Your quests were **given to you** by **the Immortals** themselves. It would be wise to **follow them.**"

"**That's not fair!**" Meowz said. "I don't want to stay here anymore!"

"**You can't be serious,**" Tufty said. "We can learn more about our powers! How **cool** is that? Besides, don't you want to help save the world?"

"Yeah, it's just . . . I already **miss** my family."

"At least you don't have to go into the Overworld alone," I said, "**looking like this.**" I turned to the enderman. "What about Clyde? Can he **go with me?**"

The endermage avoided my gaze. "Well, I . . . **um** . . . it's not exactly written in **the Prophecy.** Plus, I'm not sure whether a ghast could even **survive** in the Overworld for any length of time."

Oh, man.

I didn't want to be **a hero** anymore. **Not without him.**

How could I leave **my best buddy** behind? I'd just caught up with him again!

"There has to be **a way,**" I said. "I really want Clyde to go with me. He's **so smart.** Besides, I know he'll want to."

"It's up to him," Greyfellow said. "I will warn you that **constant exposure** to sunlight could weaken him, possibly even **kill him.**"

"Maybe he's **right**," Meowz said. "Once you return to the Overworld, you're going to **scare** enough people as it is. A huge ghast floating behind you certainly won't **help** any."

*What will Clyde do once I tell him he **can't go** with me?* I thought. *Maybe it's for **the best**. The witches seem to like ghast tears, and after I tell Clyde that he can't tag along, their inventories will be **overflowing** with them.*

WEDNESDAY—UPDATE III

"There's **one more thing** I'd like to try," the enderman said. "**Please follow me.**"

To our **complete amazement,** Greyfellow then whirled around . . . and stepped **into the back wall** of his house!

"Come on! Don't just stand there!"

Tufty and Meowz had **no idea** what was going on. But I'd heard about **shadow blocks** and remembered how you could **walk through them.** In other words, the endermage was taking us to **his secret** chamber.

Now, I'd never really met a **wizard** before. At this point, I had no idea that most wizards even had something called **"secret chambers,"** much less how **cool** secret chambers might actually be.

I saw a lot of new stuff today and learned a lot of new words. Such as **"brewing stand."** And **"anvil."** And **"crafting table."** And **"enchantment table."**

and **"rune chamber."**

"This is called **a rune chamber**," the enderman said. "Do you know what it does?"

I glanced at the **giant silvery box**. Even though it didn't look all that scary, it **scared me** all the same. "**Errr**, no?"

Tufty wasn't scared, though. He immediately zoomed inside. "Is this like **a house?**" he asked, sniffing the silvery material.

Meowz ran inside as well. "**WOW**," she said, lifting up her paws, as if the silver material *("iron," I learned later)* was **painful** to the touch.

She left the box as quickly as she'd entered. "It's **freezing** in there!"

"Indeed it is," the enderman said. "It contains a most **powerful** form of magic. Only **three wizards** in all of **Minecraftia** know how to **create** such a device."

"What does it do?" I asked.

"It makes you **stronger**," he said. "Stronger than you already are, I mean."

Stronger than I already am? Even if I didn't know **how** it made me stronger, it sounded **good** to me. Is there any **downside** to having more super powers? **Basically no.**

"A rune chamber can **permanently** enchant an animal or monster," he said, "granting them additional **strength, defense,** and so on."

"What's **'enchant'?**" Meowz asked.

The enderman shook his head. "Sorry. Not **'enchant.'** Enchanting is more for items, physical objects. The technical term is **'enhance.'** A rune chamber can be used to enhance you. But let's just call it enchanting to make things easier."

Tufty stepped out of the rune chamber, **shivering**. "S-so, it m-makes us more **p-powerful?**"

"Yes. And I would like to see whether it's possible to affect **Chosen Animals**." Greyfellow's eyes **glowed** more brightly as he glanced at us. "Are any of you willing to serve as my . . . **test subject?**"

Three little paws flew into the air at the same time.

"Me!"

"Me!"

"Me!"

Tufty lumbered toward the chamber again, but Meowz grabbed his tail. "I called it **first!**" she hissed.

He grumbled. "Whatever. Don't **freeze** your tail off, huh?"

With a smirk, **the white nether kitten** zoomed into the rune chamber. "How long do I have to wait in here?"

"**Not too long.**" As the enderman said this, a **gray window** appeared in the air before him. It contained many boxes. In one box was **an image of Meowz**.

He placed a blue cube into one of the boxes. "That's called **lapis lazuli**," he said. "It's used for this type of thing." The cube disappeared, and a flat image of the cube appeared in the box.

"Almost **done**," he said. "The process should take only a few seconds."

Suddenly, there was **a bright white flash** from inside the chamber. Meowz made the biggest and most terrified-sounding screech before jumping out.

"Mreeeeeeeeeew! What was that?!"

Greyfellow **smiled.** "That was you being **enchanted**."

"**Really?** I don't feel any different." A screen appeared before her moments later.

```
ENHANCEMENT:
REND I
TYPE: RUNE CHAMBER,
PERMANENT

Your claws have been strengthened
with runic power. Your unarmed
attacks deal 10% more damage.
```

"Look," Tufty said. "**Your claws** are kind of **purple** now."

Meowz held out one of her paws. Indeed, her black claws had a **faint violet glow,** just like the books **Rarg** had dropped earlier.

In addition, **faint little shapes,** almost like weird-looking letters, could be seen upon the surface of her claws. They were also violet, slightly **brighter** than the glow itself.

"This means I can do **more damage?**" she asked.

"**A little,**" Greyfellow said. "**Rend I** isn't very powerful. Sadly, you're not strong enough for anything beyond that."

Greyfellow turned back to the chamber.
"**Okay. Who's next?**"

WEDNESDAY—UPDATE IV

(10 minutes later . . .)

Check out **my claws.** *(I almost cried.)*

So, I've been modified with Rend I.
Every bit helps, right?

It feels kind of **girly** having glowing purple claws, but whatever. I don't care **if my entire body turns bright pink,** so long as it means I no longer have to **run from wolves.**

The rest of the day was spent **training.** After Tufty and Meowz **coughed up** their own ghast fireballs, we **inched silently** across soul sand like **creepers, climbed up** netherrack walls like **spiders,** sprinted like **zombie pigmen,** placed a few items in our inventories, and then

swam in that orange fire stuff—**err**, lava—for over an hour. . . .

There's a huge lake of that stuff in the center of the city. The mobs often go swimming there. They call it a **"pool."**

And today, that lava pool was filled with hundreds of monsters—a **"pool party."**

Swimming in lava was **so terrifying** at first! It took me **ten minutes** before I could dip one of my paws in. But it didn't **burn.** Didn't even hurt! Lava is like warm water to me now.

(I still haven't tried drinking it yet. That's on my to-do list.)

By the way, Batwing is **immune** to lava, too! So, I didn't even need to save him! But he's **terrified** of swimming . . . Greyfellow actually had to **push him in.**

Clyde was swimming, too.

Yeah, **I haven't told him yet.** I keep thinking about how I can say it without **hurting** his feelings.

I know he'll want to go with me, and **I want him to come** too, but . . . I don't want him to get **hurt.** I remember what **the sun** did to the zombie pigmen and the blazes.

Maybe Clyde could wear **a helmet?** No, probably not.

Greyfellow could **sense** how I was feeling. He waded over to me. "Still thinking about **your friend,** Eeebs?"

"**Yes.** I'll miss him. I'll miss **all** of them. I'll even miss you. **Thanks** for teaching us."

"I'm **glad** I could help," the enderman said. "Listen. Your friend, Clyde. There **is a way** he could go with you."

"**There is?**"

The enderman nodded. "One of the **enhancements** that rune chambers offer is **Sunlight Protection.** Shall we ask him about this?"

"**I suppose,**" I said. "But I want it to be **his** choice."

"**Of course.** Also, I have something you'll need for your return to the Overworld."

"What is it?"

"I'll show you tomorrow. **I think you'll like it.**"

THURSDAY

The following morning, I was holding one of those bottle things: a **"potion."**

"That's a **Potion of Disguise I,**" Greyfellow said. "Villager variant. Simply drink it and it will **seem** as though you are an **ordinary** villager."

Clyde stared at the **red liquid** contained within the glass. "Will Eeebs **still be able** to use his abilities?"

"Yes. **Disguise** is merely an **illusion.** Regardless of which form you take, you'll still be able to do everything you could before. Go on, Eeebs. **Don't be afraid. Drink up.**"

"Whatever," I said. "**Here goes.**"

I chugged the potion. The taste . . . yuck! It was like grass mixed with cobblestone. *(Don't ask how I know what those taste like.)*

Thin **white smoke** appeared all around me. To the **gasps** of my friends, I glanced down at myself and found **pale skin** and **brown robes** instead of dark blue fur.

The endermage smirked. "Of course, you'll need to practice standing on **your hind legs** for the illusion to be effective."

"Right."

I tried **standing up** but fell to all fours again.

Meowz began rolling around on the floor: "Ha**haha . . .** that's just . . . **wow,** I can't. . . ."

Soon, what appeared to be a very real and **ordinary villager** *(me)* stood before everyone. Although I was **wobbling** around on my feet.

"That potion has a duration of only **one hour**," the endermage said, "so I'll brew **half a stack** for you. Make sure to drink one before going into any town or village. If you must **remain there** for any length of time, drink another before the effects wear off."

"How will I know how much time I have left?" I asked.

"See **that icon** in the lower left corner of your vision?"

"**Got it.** Hey, what about Clyde?"

"**What about me?**" Clyde asked.

"Oh, **man**." Batwing lowered his head. "You mean, you guys didn't tell him yet?!"

"Well, **um** . . ."

The ghast sniffled. "**Tell me what**, Eeebs?"

"I'm going to the Overworld," I said. "It's part of **my quest**."

A single tear fell down the ghast's cheek. "**I see.** So, you'll be gone for good?"

"**No way**," I said. "Come on, Clyde. I'll come back. The Nether is just as much **my home** now as the Overworld is."

"**All right.** Then I guess there's no reason to be sad, right?"

"If you want, you can **come with me.**"

"I can? **How?**"

The enderman then chimed in with how it was possible to **protect** him from sunlight. "It won't make you **immune**," he said, "but you'll be **all right**."

"But it's your choice," I said. "You have to **decide for yourself**."

"Then **I'm staying**," Clyde said. "You know the Overworld, Eeebs. It's best for you to go **alone**. I'll stay here and **help protect** the city in case EnderStar finds us."

<u>Purrrrrr.</u>

That was **way easier** than I thought.

And Clyde was right. He would be **way more useful** here. "You're sure?" I asked.

"**Definitely.** I know we'll meet again."

And the ghast actually smiled. I mean **actually smiled**. It was like seeing **a flower growing in the Nether**.

I nodded.
"We will."

THURSDAY—UPDATE 1

And so it seemed I was **finally ready** to venture into the Overworld.

With **Rarg's** assistance, the mobs here will try **recruiting** mobs from the nether fortress and work on **defeating** EnderStar.

I want to help with that, of course, but **my destiny** lies elsewhere. Still, Greyfellow **suggested** that it might be possible for the mobs here to join forces with villagers in the Overworld. Together, we could **take out** EnderStar first then deal with **Herobrine** later.

"That really depends on whether anyone in the Overworld is willing to help," Batwing said. "Seems **unlikely.** But then, those villagers **I spoke to** were different from normal villagers."

"In what way?" Greyfellow asked.

"Seems like they're **training** to be **warriors.** They know how to wield swords, at least. In fact, they appear to have helped fight off **several large attacks.**"

"**Coordinated** attacks?"

Batwing shrugged. "If your **little crystal** was **accurate,** then yes. The mobs were clearly working together."

"So, **the Eyeless One** has already begun to amass his army."

The endermage nodded. "**This is no surprise.** We already know that the Prophecy is true. **The Great War** will soon begin."

"Do you think it's possible that one of those villagers is the one **mentioned in that book?**" Batwing asked.

"Perhaps. **Perhaps** that is why you were able to speak with them."

"Why **two,** though? I thought there was only one **Chosen Villager?** Well, actually, no. **Three.** I spoke with a third villager once. What was his name, again? **Pebble?**"

"I don't have any answer for that," the enderman said. "In fact, there is **much I do not know.** The tome I have regarding the Prophecy is **incomplete.** Many pages have been removed."

"One more thing," Batwing said. "Does **the Eyeless One** know about **tellstones?**"

"I'm not sure," the endermage said. "Why do you ask?"

"Because that one villager, Pebble, said **the Eyeless One** was speaking to him in **his dreams.** Told him that **Runt** was a spy. **A traitor.** He appeared in Pebble's dreams **at least ten times.**"

"Why would **Herobr—the Eyeless One** take such an interest in their village?"

The wither skeleton shrugged. "**Beats me.** My only guess is he's aware of **the Prophecy** as well and discovered the identity of the **Chosen Villager.**"

"Yes, I suppose you are correct. **Hmm.**"

A villager, two kittens, and a ghast remained silent before Batwing and Greyfellow, trying to understand **these mysteries.**

Batwing seems to know a lot about what's going on, I thought. *And he's always talking to Greyfellow. He must be really important?*

As I **listened,** a realization suddenly hit me. If Batwing is correct, then one of the villagers he spoke with is **the same** villager I'm supposed to meet.

Breeze. Runt. Pebble. I'm writing these names down here so I don't forget them. I should try to **locate them** in the Overworld as soon as possible. **It's my quest,** after all.

"I have **a question,**" I said.

The endermage turned to me. "What is it, Eeebs?"

"Well, you said that I should head to **the capital city** first. But I'm supposed to meet up with that villager, **right?** What if he's not in the capital?"

"**Hmm.** Batwing, do you recall seeing any buildings when using the tellstone?"

"A few times," the skeleton said. "**Runt** had a nightmare, once. His village had been **overrun.**"

"So, he **is** in a village, then?"

"I believe so."

"Did you see any buildings made of **quartz or clay?**"

"None. **Wood** and **cobblestone,** mostly. There was a wall in the distance. Their village was surrounded by **a huge cobblestone wall.**"

"**Interesting.**" The endermage closed his eyes for a moment. "That sounds more like a town, not a village. You're sure they were **villagers?**"

"**Hey,** I'm sure," Batwing said. "Both **Runt** and **Pebble** had **shaved heads** and **huge noses,** while that girl had **super long hair** and a **little nose.** Sound like villagers to you, bud?"

"**Certainly.** I've just never heard of a village **with a wall** before."

"Maybe they're **smarter** than the average villagers?"

"Maybe. **Hmm.**" The enderman closed his eyes again. "**Warriors,** you said. Training to be warriors. Why does that **remind me** of something?"

"Same here," Batwing said. "Wait a second. I thought there was a village in the east like that? **Real serious** folk. Kids start training for combat at the age of **six.**"

"That almost sounds like **Shadowbrook,**" the enderman said. "A village of proud warriors. **Hmm.** Batwing, join me in my library. We have much research to do."

The enderman turned to me. "I'll give you **your answer** soon, Eeebs. For now, rest. Spend time with **your friends.** After today, **you won't have much time for either.**"

THURSDAY—UPDATE II

After wandering around the streets, I finally found **Rarg**. He was in the center of the city, at the edge of the lava pool, **staring off into space**.

"Hey, Rarg."

"**Hi-lo**. Me friend. Me again want say. **Thank**."

"No problem. Somehow I just knew you were a **good** guy. I'm glad you **joined us**."

"Me too. **Boss man crazy**. But **boss man** now-**now** no boss man me. Now-now boss man me **tall gray blink man**. Tall gray blink man no **angry-say** make me black flying **squeaky** thing."

Um . . . What's he talking about?

Oh. He's saying EnderStar is **no longer his boss**. He now takes orders from the endermage. He doesn't mind, because Greyfellow doesn't **threaten** to **turn him into** a bat.

I'm guessing "**angry-say**" means **yell**? And "**blink**" must mean **teleport**. . . .

What's "**now-now**," though? Why is it **repeated?!** Why do zombie pigmen talk so strangely?!

"**Yes**," I said. "**Tall gray blink man** no **angry-say** you. But angry-say me, me no know **breathe fire**. But. Tall gray blink man **happy man**. Most time."

"He **smart** also."

"Yes."

"You. **Name**. Eee . . . **bu?**"

"**Eeebs**," I said.

"Eee . . . **buzz**."

"Close enough."

"**Eeebuzz?** Me want know."

He wants to ask me a question? Hmm, I'm getting better at this.

"You **what** want know?" I asked.

"You go? You go **where-where?**"

"I go **big light**." I pointed at **the cavernous ceiling** far above. "Big blue. **Yellow square.** You know?"

"Me know. Me no like big blue. Big blue **scare me.** And me eyes hurt me look big yellow square thing. **Eeebuzz?** Me also want know."

"**Yeah?**"

"You. **No feel real?**"

"What you say me **no feel real?**"

"No know. No know. Me no know **how say.**"

"What you say you no know how say? **Me no know.**"

"Me think some time **me no real.** No know how say. But me **no-no feel real.** You?"

*He's saying he **doesn't feel real?** What does he mean by that? Actually, sometimes, **I kind of get that feeling.** . . . I just assumed it's from all the **stress lately?***

"**Some time,**" I said. "Yes. Me also no-no feel real."

"Why you me no-no feel real?"

"Me **no know.**"

"**Me also no know.**"

Rarg held up a fish. I'd never seen that kind of fish before. It was dark red in color.

"Me use **wood string thing,**" he said. "Me know how use **wood string thing.** Wood string thing get red swim-swim. **You want eat?**"

"Me no want eat. Me eat, you no eat."

"**No.** Me many red swim-swim."

"**Okay.**"

He handed me the red fish, and I **bit into it.** It was the best fish I'd ever tasted.

He then pulled another red fish from **his inventory** and ate it in seconds. He grinned. "**Hee hee!** You like?"

"It's **delicious,**" I said, taking another bite.

"Delishi . . . ?"

A blank look, until I clarified: "Me think red swim-swim **yum-yum.**"

Wait a second. Where exactly did he get a fish like that?! There's no water in the Nether!

"Rarg. Where you **get** red swim-swim huh?"

He pointed to the lava pool. "There-there. **Orange fire water.**"

Seriously? He caught a fish in the lava?! There's such a thing as *lava fish?!*

"**How** you get? Can show me **wood string thing** now-now huh?"

"Okay."

He pulled **a strange-looking item** from his inventory. It appeared to be a stick with some **spider string** attached. At the end of the string was something I didn't recognize.

"**You want try?** I try now-now. **You see me try. Okay?**"

"Okay."

For the next hour or so, Rarg showed me **how to fish.** As a cat, we usually just **dived** into the water, but this **wood string thing** made things **way** easier.

Still, using that tool was **difficult** for me at first, as I had to stand up on **my hind legs.** Standing was something I still needed to practice.

And Rarg **wasn't lying.** I eventually caught a **lava fish** of my own, to my complete **surprise.**

I'd originally wanted to find Rarg to see whether maybe Batwing had been right about him being **a spy.** But as we sat down at the edge of the pool, **eating** lava fish in silence, I knew that he was **just as innocent** as me—another **little piece** in what at times felt like some kind of **weird game.**

THURSDAY—UPDATE III

I **curled up** next to my friends on the pink carpeting of the endermage's house.

Still, I couldn't **sleep.** I just kept thinking and thinking and thinking. About the upcoming **war.** About my abilities. About **my quest.** Plus I could hear Greyfellow and Batwing chatting, although **I couldn't make out** what they were saying.

They were in **the secret chamber,** I guess.

At last, I crept over to Greyfellow's **huge bookshelf** and glanced at a few books on the very bottom. This section was labeled **"junk."** When I grabbed several of the books, I quickly understood **why.**

DIARY OF AN ANGRY ENDER EGG
VOLUME 2,152,557

YO, THAT HEROBRINE MAKES ME SO ANGRY. LIKE SO ANGRY. SO TODAY, I SAID TO HIM. "HEROBRINE, U MAKE ME SO ANGRY."

THEN I PLACED A GRASS BLOCK NEARBY. WHY? I DUN KNOW. I JUS DID.

THEN I ATE AN APPLE.

THE END.

WHAT HAPPENS NEXT IN DIARY OF AN ANGRY EGG 2,152,558?!?!

DOES ANGRY EGG EAT A STEAK?

DOES HE?!?!?!

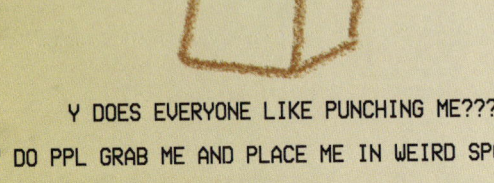

DIARY OF A MINECRAFT GRASS BLOCK

Y DOES EVERYONE LIKE PUNCHING ME???
Y DO PPL GRAB ME AND PLACE ME IN WEIRD SPOTS????
Y CANT I JUS GO TO MINECRAFT GRASS BLOCK SCHOOL AND LEARN HOW TO BE A MINECRAFT GRASS BLOCK LIKE ALL THE OTHER MINECRAFT GRASS BLOCKS?????

I'm not sure **why,** but I decided to check out *Diary of a Minecraft Grass Block.* There was an introduction, and it read:

There was once a Minecraft grass block named Minecraft Grass Block. Minecraft Grass Block liked doing the things most Minecraft grass block children did. Minecraft Grass Block wanted to learn how to be a better Minecraft grass block, but how would Minecraft Grass Block become a better Minecraft grass block than the other Minecraft grass blocks who hoped to become better Minecraft grass blocks, or at least better Minecraft grass blocks than Minecraft Grass Block was at being a Minecraft grass block and hopefully even the best Minecraft grass blocks a Minecraft grass block could possibly become?

Just turn the page, and follow the adventures of Minecraft Grass Block in this Minecraft Grass Block Diary of a twelve-year-old Minecraft grass block named Minecraft Grass Block, a Minecraft grass block boy who hopes to become a true Minecraft grass block or at least a better Minecraft grass block than the other Minecraft grass blocks.

<u>Wow.</u>

I had no trouble
sleeping afterward.

FRIDAY

This morning, I said **my goodbyes.** To Tufty and Meowz. To Clyde, Greyfellow, and Batwing.

Greyfellow gave me more **Disguise potions** and an item called a "**compass.**"

"Remember, you'll want to **keep heading east.**"

Batwing gave me **a tellstone.** "Maybe you'll be able to reach them at some point. **Who knows?**"

Clyde was **crying,** Meowz was about to join him, and Tufty was trying his hardest to be **brave:** "Gonna miss you, man. **Stay safe,** all right?"

"You know me."

"Goodbye, Eeebs," Clyde said. "Thanks for **finding me.**"

"Thanks for **saving my life.**"

"Come back soon, all right?"

"**I will.**"

And that was it. The endermage took me to **the edge of the city,** where he'd built **a nether portal.**

"I will be traveling to the Overworld **as well,**" he said. "Yet, I won't be **joining you.** I'll be traveling to the capital, **Aetheria City.** If you should journey there, ask around for **the Library.** I'll be conducting my research there."

I nodded.

"Now, do you remember **what you must do?**" he asked.

"After I arrive in the Overworld," I said, "I must head **east** and find the village of **Shadowbrook**. It lies on **the east coast** of the main continent. If instead I reach the ocean, I should head **north** until I find it."

"Good. What will you do if you find **this village?**"

"I'll ask to see a girl named **Breeze**," I said.

"Who else?"

"**Runt. Pebble.**"

"Good. And what will you do if you **cannot locate them?**"

"I'll head **west,** to **Aetheria City,** and find you."

"And if you do come across them?"

"I will tell them they need to **abandon their village**," I said, "and seek refuge in the capital."

"Why?"

I **crept** forward, trying to recall what he'd told me earlier. "Because according to **the Prophecy, a dragon** is going to burn it to the ground."

"**Excellent.** It seems your **Higher Intelligence** ability really does work."

". . ."

I remembered **the first time** I'd stepped into a nether portal. The **uncertainty** I'd felt, then. **The fear.** The hesitation.

Now, it was much like that, only **ten times worse.** I was **afraid** of what I'd see and what I might have to face. At last, I stepped in.

My vision **wavered.**
All grew dark.

SATURDAY

As soon as I arrived in the Overworld, I began **sprinting**.

At first, everything looked **normal**. Trees. Tall grass. Hills and mountains, rivers and valleys.

But I soon came across the kind of things I'd hoped I wouldn't see....

As common as the holes left from explosions were the charred remains of many trees.

Within hours,
I found a village—
or what <u>looked like</u> one to me....

Yet blasted crops and scattered rubble were all that I could see.

There were no sounds here beyond the low whistle of the wind.

Even the farm animals had disappeared.

I **sniffed** around every building.

*Not picking up any **villager scent**, I thought. Whatever happened here must have happened **days** or even **weeks** ago.*

Yet, within minutes, I caught **two new scents.** One was **human,** the other **villager.** I soon heard them **approaching** so I hid in some tall grass nearby.

(My Creep ability must have turned me mostly invisible, as they didn't seem to notice me.)

The human had spiked **yellow hair** and brown armor, and he carried **a sword** on his back. The villager had a huge nose and carried **two swords** on his back, one sword slightly smaller than the other.

"I can't **believe** this," the villager said. "It's **just** like the last one I saw."

"**Get used to it,**" the human said. "Every place I've come across has been like this. **Or worse.**"

The villager suddenly seemed so **angry.** His rage quickly subsided, however, and he gazed at the ruins in **sorrow.**

"**C'mon,**" the human said. "Let's look around and see if there's anything we can **salvage.** And stay alert. You wouldn't believe the stuff that's out here."

"I'd believe. I've **fought** a few myself."

"**Really?** Hey. Why are you out here, anyway?"

"I was **exiled.**"

"What'd you do?"

"I made a **wrong** decision. . . . It's a long story."

"They at least gave you a **weapon** or something, right? Some **tools?**"

"**None.** I'd dropped all my stuff earlier. That first night, I was jumped by **ten husks** while trying to dig **an emergency shelter.**"

"**Ouch.** Did you even have a sword at that point?"

"**No.** Just **a wooden shovel.**"

"You fought **ten husks** with a wooden shovel? How'd you manage **that?**"

"I just managed." The villager **paused.** "Why are **you** out here?"

"**Because of this.**" The human withdrew **a piece of paper** from his inventory. "Found it in some **ruins** a few days ago. In a library. It leads to **a cave filled with adamant.**"

"What's **adamant?**"

The human sighed. "I think you've been **holed up** in that village of yours for way too long. Maybe getting **exiled** wasn't such a bad thing, **huh?** Anyway, I'll show you the ropes. Just **stick with me.**" He **drew** his sword.

"Cmon. That cave isn't too far from here. We'll **search this place** first then hit the cave afterward."

"All right," the villager said. "By the way, you never told me **your name**."

"**Just call me S,**" the human said.

"S? That's it?"

"Well, I know my name **starts** with an S. I can't seem to remember the rest, though. Anyway, **let's go**."

They took off.

Of course, I wanted to **reveal** myself and speak with them, but they looked **a little dangerous**.

Once they were **far enough** away, I took out my compass and left the ruins, heading east again. For the rest of the day, the only thing I found of interest was fire. **A forest fire.**

SUNDAY

In my dreams, I heard voices.
The voices of two girls.

"Dude. Scouting is totally **lame**. Nothing has happened for days!"

"It's what we've been **tasked with, Emerald**. It's for the **safety** of our village."

"Yeah. I know. I just miss **hot baths**, y'know? I'm totally caked in grime, these new boots are hurting my feet, and—hey, look! **Over there!**"

"Is that an **ocelot?**"

"Looks like it. What's up with the **blur fur**, though?"

"What were you saying about **nothing interesting** happening?"

"I stand corrected. This is even more interesting than that **human girl** showing up at our village. What's her name again?"

"**ilovedragons1.** Why do some of the humans have such odd names?"

"Who knows. Hey, why isn't this ocelot waking up?!"

Finally, as I felt something nudge me, **my eyes flew open.**

"He's **adorable!**" the girl with greenish-blue hair exclaimed.

"Is that even an ocelot?" the other girl asked. "Looks more like **a monster** to me."

"Whatever he is, I say **we keep him.**"

"Keep him?! **Are you joking?!** I thought you didn't like monsters, **Breeze**."

"Wouldn't a monster be **attacking** us by now?"

"Yeah, I guess."

"It's **strange**, though. I thought ocelots were **afraid** of people? Has he already been **tamed?**" It took a moment for the **realization** to hit. **Breeze?!** The girl on the left is **Breeze?!** Is that some kind of luck or what?!

I rose to all fours and **yawned**. "You don't need to talk as if I **can't understand you.** I'm well versed in **your language.**"

The girls **jumped back.** "**Um**, like, did he just . . ."

"**You can really talk?**" Breeze asked.

"Yeah?"

"Why do I feel things are about to get **crazy** around here again?" Emerald said.

"I've been sent to find **a girl named Breeze,**" I said. "Also, **two boys.** One goes by the name of **Runt.** The other is known as **Pebble.**"

The girls exchanged glances.

"I don't understand," Breeze said. "How do you **know about us?**"

"Through our mutual friend. **Batwing.**"

Her smile **faded.**

Emerald **sighed.** "Um, is he talking about that skeleton you've been **dreaming about?**"

"Yes."

"Right. Shall we head back now and warn the mayor of **impending craziness** the likes of which we've never seen?"

Breeze **slowly nodded** at her, before staring into my eyes. "What's your name?"

"**Eeebs.**"

"**Nice to meet you,** Eeebs. May I ask why you were sent to find us?"

"It's **a long story.**"

"**That's fine.** Would you like to head back to our village with us? You can tell us on the way."

"**Of course,**" I said. "Oh, and now that you mention it, I should say that I've been instructed to **inform you** of something. Regarding your village."

The girls exchanged glances again. "**What is it?**" Breeze asked.

"All of you should leave **before the moon is full**," I said, "and head to **the capital,** as according to **the Prophecy** . . . your village is about to be **annihilated.**"

SUNDAY—UPDATE 1

While searching for the village of **Shadowbrook**, I met **two girls** named **Emerald** and **Breeze**.

I told them about how I was sent to **find them** and how, according to **the Prophecy,** their village would soon be **destroyed**.

Come to find out, I was **never** going to find **Shadowbrook**. It was Breeze's **home village,** and it was completely **wiped out** some time ago. She's one of the **survivors** who fled.

"**Wait**," I said. "Where are you taking me, then?"

"**Villagetown.** We believe it's the last village still standing on this side of the continent."

"Well, **the humans** say it's not really **a village**," Emerald said, "but **a town**. And maybe they're right, y'know? It's changed so much."

"**It has**." Breeze turned away. We were standing on a large hill overlooking a river, and she pointed at something far away. I'd never seen **anything like it** before.

"Is that some kind of tree?" I asked.

Breeze **shook her head**. "It's one of our **watchtowers**. It also functions as a **beacon**. Our builders constructed them around our village to help the **scouts** find their way back."

"All we have to do is head in that direction and we'll be **home**," Emerald said. "**Max** came up with the idea. A friend of ours. Actually, I guess **Runt** should get some credit for—"

I almost **jumped** when she said his name. "**You know Runt?!**"

"**Of course,**" Emerald said. "He's part of our **group.** In fact, he **should** be with us right now."

"Why isn't he?"

"He's currently being **punished.**" To my **blank expression,** Emerald sighed. "We recently graduated from school, and the mayor gave us **one last** little school assignment. We had to write **twenty pages** about our chosen profession. Now, I love my village and all, and I have absolutely **zero regrets** about becoming a **warrior,** but dude

. . . c'mon. Who wants to write twenty pages about **anything?** Luckily, **Runt** thought of a way for us to avoid writing so much without **breaking the rules,** and every other student **copied Runt's idea.** Needless to say, the mayor wasn't too **thrilled** about that. Guess that's why **Runt** is back to crafting **potato-based food items.**"

Resisting the urge to ask, *"What's a potato?"* I **nodded.** "Hmm. Do you think I'll be able to speak with him?"

"Probably," Emerald said. "That is, if the entire village doesn't freak out upon hearing the bad news. By the way, what kind of **dragon** is supposed to attack?"

"I have no idea. **I don't even know what a dragon is.**"

". . ."

SUNDAY—UPDATE II

After the girls took me to their **village,** I was **surrounded** by so many people. No one seemed to be **afraid** of me—not even the children:

"Is that really **an ocelot?**"

"It looks more like **a monster!**"

"**Wow!** Where can I get one of those?!"

I've never been picked up before. Or petted. Or hugged. Or given so much food.

I can get used to this. I **love** Villagetown.

"Thanks for **the fish**," I said, to a human boy named **LazyGiraffe**. "An hour of sprinting can really drain your food bar."

"You can **talk?!**"
"Hey, what's **your name?!**"
"What kind of ocelot **are you**, huh?!"

My introduction to **Villagetown** went pretty much like that.

A girl named **Ophelia** gave Breeze a hug. "**Glad to see you back safely.** What's the deal with this guy?"

"It's **complicated**," Breeze said.

Emerald laughed. "I'll say. Just wait until you hear **the news**." She turned to Ophelia. "**Hey.** Your dad's a **librarian,** right? Ever heard about something called **the Prophecy?**"

"I haven't. Why?"

"Never mind." Emerald glanced farther into the village. "**I'm out.** Time for a bath. See you guys at **the meeting?**"

Ophelia blinked. "**What meeting?**"

But Emerald only winked before taking off.

"Um, **okay?**" The yellow-haired girl turned to Breeze. "What's going on?"

"Seems like this kitten came from **a city of monsters**," Breeze said.

"**Good ones.**" She reached down and **scratched my neck.** "Isn't that right?"

"I don't **consider** myself to be a monster," I said, "**but yes.** You are correct."

"So, why are you here?" Ophelia asked me.

"Have you ever heard of someone known as **a Savior?**"

"No?"

"How about Chosen Ones?"

"Um . . ."

The other villagers looked just **as confused.**

Moments later, a man known as **the mayor** approached, along with many **serious-looking** men in black clothes.

"Breeze? What's **going on** here?! And . . . **what is that?!**"

"We found him **sleeping** under a tree. He has a message **for us.**"

"Right." The mayor stared at me **without blinking** for at least five seconds. "Um. **Good work.**"

One of the men in black robes threw something **around my neck**—I'd later come to learn that it was **a leash.**

I **hissed** and tried **running away,** but whenever I moved more than five blocks away from my captor, I **flew back** toward him.

Breeze moved up to the man. "Father, **stop!**"

He **smiled** slightly. His eyes were **concealed** by these weird-looking black things. "You know **what must be done.**"

SUNDAY—UPDATE III

They **hauled me** away to a small, dark room and asked countless questions. The kind of questions **cautious people** ask when **a blue kitten** suddenly shows up at their village.

"Did Herobrine send you?!"

"Good monsters?! In the Nether?!"

Yes, it's true. And their breath isn't nearly as stinky as yours.

I told them **everything,** but they **didn't believe** a word. No one had heard of **the Prophecy,** and as for **dragons** . . .

"The Overworld hasn't seen **dragons** for over **a thousand years!**" the man named **Brio** shouted. "**One kind of dragon** still lives on, yes, but only in the **third dimension!**"

"**All I know** is what I've been told! **The enderman** gave me this book, and . . ."

After I talked about the book Greyfellow had loaned me, Brio brought in more villagers. They wore **white robes.**

I came to learn that they were **librarians** and had **in-depth knowledge** of this world's history. Yet, none of them could recall ever reading about **the Prophecy.**

"What about these **abilities** you speak of?" the mayor asked. "Care to **demonstrate** them?"

"Sure."

To their **awe,** I **breathed fire,** climbed a nearby cobblestone wall, and turned almost **invisible** when standing still.

"If there was a **pool of lava** nearby," I said, "I could go for a swim. I'm **immune** to fire, just like the monsters that live in the Nether."

Finally, I **summoned my visual enchantment screen.** Brio and the mayor recognized it immediately. Amazingly, they had **visual enchantments** as well. They summoned them using their mind, the same as I had.

"Almost every **living being** has them," Brio said. "Yet, most are **unable** to access them. They must be . . . **unlocked.**"

The two villagers closed their screens, and the mayor looked at mine, which was currently displaying **my enhancements.** "What's **that?**"

"The enderman **enchanted me** somehow," I said, and held up **my purple claws.**

"Did he ask you to step into **a metallic box** of some kind?" Brio asked.

"You mean **a rune chamber?**"

"Yes." Brio turned to the mayor. "Perhaps **he speaks the truth?**"

The mayor nodded. "Listen . . . **Eeebs,** is it? I'm going to call everyone in the village. We're going to have **a meeting.**"

"You'll need to tell **everyone** what you've told us just now," Brio added. For **some reason,** he was smiling again in that strange way. "I suppose we'll soon be making **yet another alliance.**"

The man named **Drill** spoke up. "Tell me **this creature** is joining our army. Please. I want this thing **on the front lines.**"

"Perhaps he will." Brio stopped smiling. "One last thing, **kitten.** Did that book mention the names of the **two Saviors?**"

"Yes. But I **forgot** them. The enderman asked me to remember so many different things. The book said that one of them was a **human.** Does that help?"

"**Not exactly.**"

SUNDAY—UPDATE IV

An hour later, I stood in a **fancy-looking area** of Villagetown. A countless number of villagers had **gathered** before me.

Wait, no. Roughly half of them **weren't** villagers. They looked **different** . . . wore different **clothes.** Perhaps they were **the humans** I'd heard about?

(Now that I think about it, I've seen villagers several times before, back when I was just a normal kitten, but I don't recall ever seeing humans until today. Where'd they come from?)

The mayor eventually **introduced me** and asked me to tell everyone the news.

By "help save the world," the Prophecy actually meant "serve as a messenger."

I suppose it **was strange** for them to hear an animal speak. Stranger still to hear me speak of **a city** filled with **monsters** willing to cooperate.

"The monsters I met know about **magic**," I said. "They're **very smart**. I believe both sides could **help each other**."

Of course, there were many who didn't believe or **trust** me. Such as a young man who **emerged** from the crowd. A human, I think? **He looked up** at the mayor and called out:

"Sir? Do you think it's **a good idea** to work with monsters?"

When I saw him, I could **sense** that there was something **different** about him. It was the **same feeling** I got after meeting **Greyfellow, Batwing, Brio, Breeze, Emerald. . . .**

Still, he was **different** from even them. **Stronger,** maybe? Was the **power** I sensed due to him being higher in level and possessing stronger abilities than the rest? **I'm not sure.**

"You certainly have a point," the mayor said to this human. "We will **discuss** this at length and have a vote."

This caused a **huge commotion.** The crowd only grew louder when the mayor added: "Although it's **hard to imagine,** there may come a time when **monsters live among us** an—"

An old villager man **glared** at me and shouted, "The day I live alongside monsters is the day I **make my own village! I know how to dig!** I'll make an underground house and start a bat farm!"

More villagers joined in:

"I'm with you, **Leaf!**"

"**Me too!** This is madness!"

"No one's even heard of this **Prophecy!**"

"If **a dragon** really does attack, we'll be ready! We've already fended off **thousands of zombies!**"

"Working **with** monsters?! How can anyone **suggest** such a thing?! Do you not remember the attacks?!"

"**No mobs allowed!**" someone screamed.

"Yeah! **No mobs allowed!**"

Roughly half of the crowd began **chanting** this phrase. Then someone **threw a carrot at me.** This was followed by some **seeds,** an apple, and, finally, a loaf of bread.

(I ate the bread, topping off my food bar, so the joke was on them.)

"Stop this **at once!**" the mayor shouted. "We cannot **ignore** what this animal has to say! If there really are **good** monsters out there, we must consider forming **an alliance!**"

He left the raised platform and stood **next to me.** "Even though he is **an animal,** he appears to be quite **intelligent,** and he will be treated with **respect** for as long as he stays here! **Understood?**"

There were many **grumbles,** weak attempts at protest. But just as many people walked up to me. **Including Breeze.**

"I'd like to **take him around** and teach him more about our village," she said to the mayor. "**Is that okay?**"

No, that's not a redstone generator. That's me. Purring.

"Only if Eeebs agrees to it." He sighed. "Kitten, I'm sorry for their outburst. We're a little distrustful of monsters. That being said, do you really wish to stay here for the time being?"

"Why not? I like being held."

"Very well. In the meantime, our librarians will do more research. We'll see if we can shed some light upon this mysterious Prophecy you speak of. And you'll be able to speak with Runt after he's . . . through with his punishment."

"Thank you." I suddenly remembered the human's words. "Sir."

"I'm exhausted," Breeze said to her father. "I'll take him back to our house and show him Villagetown tomorrow."

As she turned around, holding me in her arms, she bumped into another person. A villager in a dark red robe. A bunch of white hair hung from the lower part of his face, and he was wearing a huge red hat and the same black things Breeze's father wore. You couldn't see much of his face.

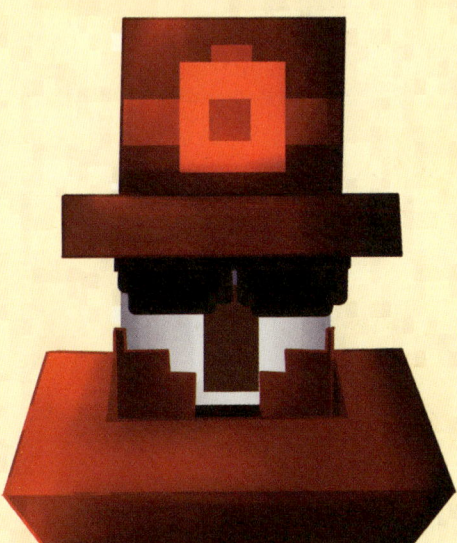

"Sorry," he said. "**Forgive me,** my lady."

She stepped closer to him. "**Hey,** don't I know you?"

"**N-no,** no. I . . . no, I don't believe we've met before. Yes, certainly I'd remember a **damsel** such as yourself!"

"What's your name?"

"**My name?**" He paused. "**Korbius!**" He nodded **profusely.** "Yes, that's my name! **Korbius Wijjibo!**"

"I don't recall ever seeing you in Villagetown before."

"Of course not, for I am . . . **a traveling merchant!** Yes! A merchant who travels! That's **meeee!**" He **bowed.** "Would you like to trade?"

"No thanks." Breeze lingered in front of him for a moment, **her brow furrowed,** then carried me off. It was **strange,** the way she acted.

"What's wrong?" I asked, still purring.

"**Nothing.**" She glanced back at him. "**Guess I'm just paranoid.**"

SUNDAY—UPDATE V

When we entered Breeze's house, I was **shocked** at how **small** it seemed. Compared to Greyfellow's hut, it was **tiny.** Her bedroom was **five blocks wide.**

Emerald said earlier that Breeze's room almost looks like a dungeon. I kinda have to agree.

I **sat down** on the carpet. "Is it really **so hard to believe** that **good monsters** exist?"

"We've been through a lot," she said. "**Monsters attacked** several times already, and some of us were . . . well . . . **we've lost people.**"

"**I'm sorry.** Then I guess I can understand why they're so **distrustful.**"

I **sniffed around** and saw a book lying on top of a raised flat surface. It was **a diary,** just like mine.

Dear Diary,
I miss him.

Where did she learn how to draw like that? I'm so jealous.

She **rushed over** and **closed the diary** before I had a chance to really look at the drawing. Her cheeks were **so red!**

"That's **Runt,** right?"

"Yes. You've . . . seen him before, haven't you?"

"Yeah. **Using one of these.**" I withdrew the **tellstone** from my inventory and told her about it.

"That **explains** a lot," she said. "I was beginning to think **Herobrine** was behind those dreams. Maybe we could **use this** tonight to speak with Runt?"

"Maybe. Batwing said his tellstone didn't always work, though. Tellstones should be able to **communicate** with anyone, sleeping or not. But they're **hard to craft.** The enderman is still working on **perfecting** them."

"Well, if it doesn't work, you can always speak to Runt in person. He'll be **free** in a few days."

"Do they **always** punish him like that?"

"**No,** it's just . . . he's a **captain,** now. **A leader.** Kind of. So the mayor wants him to set **a good example.** A lot of the younger kids **look up to him** now."

"Oh."

Later that night, we **tried using** the tellstone.

I pictured **Runt** in my mind, but nothing appeared. Then, for some reason, I thought of that villager I'd seen yesterday. **The crystal immediately lit up:**

The images **disappeared**. The **purple gleam** returned to the crystal's surface. I pawed the tellstone every which way, but **the images wouldn't return.**

(I'm not positive on this, but I believe he was having a **nightmare** and woke up, which **severed** the tellstone's connection.)

"That was **Pebble**," Breeze said. "So . . . did we just witness **his dreams** or something?"

"I think so."

"Didn't think he was **still alive.**"

"He is," I said. "I saw him yesterday. Before I met you."

"**Where?**"

"In some **ruins.** He was with a human. They were searching around for **a cave.**"

"So, he really did survive. . . ." She said something after this, but **so quietly,** as if speaking to herself. "He must have learned how to use **abilities,** too."

Well, **I think** that's what she said.
Or did I just <u>imagine</u> her saying that?

MONDAY

Breeze gave me a **tour** of the village today.

While we walked through the streets, I noticed these **large pieces of paper** called **"posters."** They were everywhere. Someone must have put them up **last night**.

"Seems like at least a few people haven't forgotten **the meeting**," I said.

"It was **hard enough** getting everyone to agree to let **humans** stay here. I'm not so sure we'll ever be able to form **an alliance** with monsters."

"Well, we've got to **try.** They're really **so nice. You'd like them.**"

We soon forgot about the posters, because **a villager in white robes** ran up to us.

Max. He's a **warrior** like Breeze, but he once had interest in becoming a **librarian.**

"I've read **nearly every book** in the village," he said, "and found nothing relating to **the Prophecy.** However . . ."

He held up a book (History of Minecraftia, Volume II) and turned to somewhere in the middle. "**Look.** Someone **tore out** three pages."

Breeze ran her fingers across the jagged edges. "**Why would they do that?**"

Max shrugged. "Maybe it said something about **the Prophecy?** But who would want to **hide** that? **The mayor?**"

204

"**No,** I don't think so," Breeze said. "Wait. Where did you get this book?"

"**The main library.** I'll go there again tomorrow and double-check for any other books that might have been tampered with. **Wanna join me?**"

"**Sorry.** Today's my only day off this week, and I'm supposed to **show Eeebs around.**"

"It's cool. Emerald's off tomorrow. I'll ask her." He glanced at me. "Really wish you could've brought **that book** you were talking about."

"I could always **go back** for it," I said.

"You might **have to,**" Max said, "if nothing turns up."

Max then took off, and Breeze showed me **so many different places.**

The villagers have this food called "ice cream." Some of it was crafted to look like a creeper's head. Why would they do that? I really don't understand.

It almost felt like someone was watching us. But I didn't see anyone. . . .
One street had something really weird. A villager did something known as a **"farming fail."**

Hours later, as Breeze explained **the combat cave** to me, that **Drill** guy ran up to us.

He **screamed** so loudly, asking Breeze if she was done accompanying **"His Royal Fuzziness"** around. Was he talking about me?!

"You want a little tour of our village, huh?" He pointed down a street. "See all those people **building** and farming!? That's called **hard work!** You'll be **joining them** if you wanna stay here! **Now march!**"

MONDAY—UPDATE I

Drill thinks I need to be **trained.** Long story short, I've been asked to **help out.** If I want to stay here, I must become **a useful member** of the village.

They seem to think I'd make **a great scout.** That means exploring beyond the wall. But scouts should know all the **basics,** such as **mining, crafting,** and **farming.** . . . It's **dangerous,** being a scout. They say the monsters outside are growing stronger. It's an **important** job, too, because scouts are supposed to search for **resources** like iron.

It seems that **iron** is **really important** to these villagers. They use it to make weapons, armor, tools, and even defenses such as doors and gates. The **problem** is that iron comes from the ground, and they've **already mined** most of the ground beneath the village. They say they don't want to go any deeper because it's **too dangerous.**

Food is also a concern. A large number of humans arrived some time ago. The farms here can produce **only so much food.** Right now, people are **consuming more** than can be grown. So they need to make more farms. They've used up almost all the land within the walls, though, which means they must start farming **outside.**

As we followed **Drill** through the streets, he kept yelling at random villagers, telling them to build **faster,** work **harder:**

"You're **lollygagging** like **Stump** in a kitchen! Like **Runt** at the ice cream stand! Like **Emerald** in the Clothing Castle!" In a **much calmer** voice, he said, "In fact, I bet that's where I'll find her. Come on, kitten. Let's go say hello to **your new teacher.**"

I saw **Brio** and **the mayor** at one point. They were **yelling** at workers as well. The word **"efficiency"** was often brought up.

"Build farms on the houses!"

"Don't waste any space!"

Efficient use of space. Proper building techniques. What are they talking about?! I don't even know what a crop is!

Later on, Drill took us to this place called **the Clothing Castle**. Apparently, Emerald really does spend **a lot of time** there.

"Hey, guys! Wanna go shopping with me?"

"Err, I meant trading. I totally wasn't trying to sound like a human. Yeah."

"How did I know I'd find you **here?**" Drill said.

Emerald glanced sideways to the left and right **without moving her head.** "Oh! Are you talking **to me?** Need some **fashion advice,** huh?"

"Hardly. Since Breeze will be **scouting** tomorrow, and since **you're off** tomorrow, you'll be the first one to teach this kitten. **Help him get up to speed.** Show him how to **farm.**"

"**What?** But I was supposed to go fishing and—"

"What's that? You said you're ready to do **five thousand laps** around the combat yard?"

She flashed a smile. A **nervous** one. "Did I say **fishing?!** It's been a long day! What I meant was I'd be **honored** to teach Eeebs! **Where should I begin?**"

TUESDAY

Emerald taught me **how to farm** today.

I personally think it went **very well,** but she seems to think **otherwise.**

Hey, it's not **my fault.** Her instructions weren't very **clear** to me. As if **a kitten** would know anything about **planting seeds!**

Place them on the ground, she said.

That's all I need to do, she said.

'Dude! Don't be in **such a rush!** You need to place seeds in **farmland!'**

She took me to **a grassy area** where she demonstrated how to use this farming tool called a **"hoe."**

Standing on my hind legs again, **I turned three blocks of grass into farmland** and planted some seeds. I felt **so proud** of myself. She didn't, though.

"Farmland should be **close together**," she said. "There's no need to have it all **scattered around** like that."

"Right."

"Okay. I finally got it figured out. Can I go now?"

"Dude? Where's the **water?** You really need to **listen!**"

She told me again about how crops need to be **watered,** or **irrigated.** Otherwise, they won't grow nearly as fast.

I did pretty well, **all things considered.** She gave me a bucket, and **I scooped up some water.** I just forgot about the **"digging a hole for the water"** part.

A minor setback, <u>**nothing more!**</u>

"I've seen a lot of farming fails, but **wow. Just wow.**"

"Isn't diversity a good thing, though?"

All right, I've got this farming stuff figured out. BRB, time to ace the rest and become the ultimate farming champion.

She said I needed to protect my crops. So I did. Not even sunlight will get to them.

"**Come on!** Crops need **light** to grow! You can't just build **a wall** around them!"

"Okay! **Okay!** I'm sorry! I just want to talk to **Runt**, okay? It's part of **my quest!** I can't stop thinking about it!"

"Yeah? Do you have **any idea** what they'll make us do if they catch us sneaking up to him? You'll see **Runt** when he's no longer crafting **baked potatoes,** okay? Just follow **the rules!**"

"Fine!"

Using **a pickaxe,** I began tearing down the wall.

"**Good kitten.** Now, what you should do is build a **fence.** Here, I'll place the crafting table again and . . ."

So I need a fence instead of a cobblestone wall. From here, absolutely nothing else can go wrong. I'm certain of it.

For the first time today, Emerald **smiled.** "Good job."

"How about **a hug,** huh? Or you can just **scratch my chin.** I'm not picky."

"I'll pet you once we're finished. Now listen up. Okay, so, crops need light, **right?** But what happens when the sun goes down? How can you provide light for your crops during the night? **Any ideas?**"

"I **think** so."

According to what she said, with this much light, the crops will grow **ultra fast!**

Emerald **facepalmed.** "We're done for the day. And tomorrow, **Stump** will be teaching you **how to craft**, not me."

"Okay. By the way, **where's my hug?**"

"As if! **Hurmmph!**"

Emerald **stormed off.** Later, a nice girl named **Lola** taught me how to shoot this weapon called a **"bow."**

The other villagers say she used to be very unskilled, but she's recently **shown promise.** She also crafted **a hat** out of a **creeper** she dropped in the wild.

"Told you I'd get better!"

Nessa "Lola" Diamondcube
from **Noob Extraordinaire** to **Scout First Class**.

EXPLORER'S CAP
ARMOR (+2.5)
+ 5% VIEW DISTANCE
+ 10% STEALTH BONUS
+ 3% ACCURACY WITH BOWS
+ 15% CRITICAL DAMAGE BONUS
+ 25% MAP DRAWING ACCURACY

WEDNESDAY

This morning, I met the villager known as **Stump.** One of Runt's **best friends.**

He wasn't **too happy** about having to teach me on his **day off.** Part of the problem was that I kept eating **the crafting ingredients.**

He called me a **walking garbage can,** because according to him, it's not even possible to **eat** some of those ingredients. Our time together can be summarized by **a single picture:**

"Craft something!!"

Notice my blank stare.

(I'd include pictures of my various crafting fails, but at this point, I've become somewhat embarrassed of my complete lack of skill.)

I guess Stump takes his crafting **seriously**—especially **food items** like cakes—so when I basically **decorated** the floor with ingredients, his anger only grew.

Luckily, **Max** interrupted us before long. He just burst through the door, **muttering something** about books and libraries and **the biggest mystery** the village has ever seen.

Seconds later,
<u>we were out the door.</u>

WEDNESDAY—UPDATE I

Max took us to one of Villagetown's **libraries**—the **biggest one** in the village.

"I've been doing **a lot of research** here," he said, leading us past the bookshelves. "I found a book with missing pages in one of the back rooms. . . . But I didn't notice **the carpet** until this morning," he said.

Stump glanced around. "**What's wrong with it?** Besides that **awful** orange color, I mean. **Seriously,** who decorated this place?"

Max walked farther into the room, then stopped. "**Come over here.**"

We followed. As an animal who'd only **just** learned how to farm, I had **no idea** what was going on. But then, I didn't feel too bad, because Stump didn't seem to understand either.

Max pointed at the floor.

Carpeting made from a **sheep's wool** and dyed bright orange.

That should have been nothing more than a decoration, something placed over cobblestone.

"Feels a little **soft**," Stump said, stepping on to one section of the carpet. "**Spongey,** really. Almost like a cake. **What, is there nothing underneath?**"

Max **mined** the carpet up with his bare hands.

He'd discovered a secret.

Max thinks it's been here for **a very long time.**

The ladder led to a secret little chamber.

What sat inside were more bookcases, a chest filled with all kinds of papers and scrolls . . . and **a massive tome,** lying on a table.

Although it looked like nothing more than a large book with a **dark gray cover,** there was **something** about it—the more I stared, the more I sensed **the power** it contained.

Max lifted the tome up in a way that suggested an **immense weight.** *Record of Aetheria* was its name. "It just goes on and on. It's over **five hundred pages** long."

"Five hundred pages?!" Stump moved closer and eyed it suspiciously. "Of what?"

"The history of the world. **The Prophecy,** too. And guess who's name is in here?"

"Breeze?"

"No. **Kolb.**"

I zoomed over to take a better look at the tome. "He's **one of the Saviors,** right?"

"Apparently. I'm wondering why he **never told us?**"

"Maybe he doesn't know?" Stump said.

Max shrugged. "It gets **weirder.** One of the things I've read . . . we're supposedly controlled by some kind of **guiding force** called **AI.**"

"I've heard that before," I said.

Max turned to the first page. "There's also this."

"Whoever wrote this **clearly** didn't want **Herobrine** reading it," Stump said. "That must be why it was **stashed** here. But who wrote it?"

Max turned to the next page.

RECORD OF AETHERIA

ORIGINALLY WRITTEN BY ENTITY303

EDITED BY THE FIVE SCRIBES:
MANGO, IMPULSE75, DIAMOND GIRL, SPARKLE, PHRED13

"We have to ask **Kolb** about this," Stump said. "**He has to know something.**"

Max nodded. "I'll go see if I can find him. You two wait here. **And Eeebs?** Wipe that sugar off your nose. Seriously, man. **Are you a kitten or a pig?**"

WEDNESDAY—UPDATE II

Ten or so minutes later, **Kolb** entered the cramped little room.

"There'd better be **a good reason** for bringing me down here," he said. "**I really—**" He paused when he saw me. "**Oh.** So it's about that. How many have you told, **kitten?**"

"**No one.** I couldn't remember your name."

"So you already **know?**" Max asked.

"**Yeah.**"

"Can you please just tell us what's going on?" Stump asked.

The human sat down on a bookcase. "I can tell you what I know. Of course, **for the safety of your village,** you must **promise never** to tell anyone else. Not even the mayor. **Agreed?**"

Two villagers and a kitten nodded their heads in unison.

Kolb **sighed.** "You know, I used to **laugh at myself** for talking with what I once considered to be NPCs. But now . . . **whatever.** Here it goes."

And so, **he told us his story.**

WEDNESDAY—UPDATE III

The human named Kolb once lived in a world known as **Earth.**

His life was **fairly boring** back then. He went to school, did homework, studied. He also **played games.**

The games he played utilized a **technology** known as **virtual reality.** You threw on a **helmet-like** device, and it seemed like you were in **another world.**

His mom was always working, and he'd **never known** his father, so he often escaped into games to not feel so alone. His favorite place was a virtual reality **Minecraft server** called **Aetheria.**

That world is **this world.** Or used to be.

Max didn't seem to believe him. "You're telling me . . . we're just **game** characters?"

"I don't know," Kolb said. "We still don't know for sure. We've had countless arguments over this, trying to figure it all out."

"Well, what happened?" Stump asked. "You said this game you played was **normal,** right? **Everyone** played it. So **what changed?** Why are all the humans always **freaking out?**"

"Umm . . . it's like this. . . ."

The human then shared more of his story.

It was the year **2039,** and his world was in a similar situation as our own: suffering from **a terrible war.** One day, weapons capable of **unparalleled destruction** were sent through the air, toward his homeland. When this was announced, he was **alone.**

In the eyes of many, **the world was about to end.** So Kolb, wanting to at least see his friends one last time, **entered the virtual reality world of Aetheria.** To say **goodbye.**

There, he met his **best friend, Ione,** as well as one of the game's administrators, **Entity.**

However . . .

With **the world's destruction** just minutes away . . .

"I **blacked out** and woke up still in the game," he said, "**unable** to log out. We call it **the event.** Many of us think there's a **scientific** explanation for what happened. Yet, just as many believe in the **impossible.**"

Max looked up from **the massive tome.** "You mean **magic?**"

"Yeah. I guess so. I've never believed in **that kind of stuff.** Still don't. Yet . . . some humans think Entity is a wizard who whisked them away to safety just before the world ended."

"So that's why you guys have those **arguments,**" Stump said. "Some of you call yourselves **Believers,** and others are **Seekers.** I never understood why until now."

"If we really are **game characters,**" Max said, "does that mean we're **not really alive?** We're just like . . . **golems,** or something? Following **instructions** of some kind?"

The human shrugged. "We've spent days discussing that. In the end, each of you seems **very real,** so . . . it really is like the game **magically came to life."** He sighed. "**Look,** guys. I'm just telling you what I know, and what I know isn't much. It took me a long time to **come to terms** with this. But I've finally accepted it. **It is what it is."**

"I don't meant to interrupt," I said, "but **I'm starving.** Maybe we could talk more over dinner?"

The other three looked at me as if I'd just asked if they wanted to help **build a snow fort** in the Nether.

"It's not even **lunchtime,"** Max said.

"**Oh.** What can I say? I've been living in the Nether. Having no sky kinda messes with your **sense of time."**

Stump retrieved a **strange-looking** item from his inventory and placed it on to one of the bookcases. It had a **familiar** scent. . . .

"Here. Eat this and be quiet. It's delicious. Promise."

"Is that a work of masterful crafting or some kind of giant mutated mushroom?"

—Max

I sniffed again. "What is **that?!**"

"**A stormberry cake,**" Stump said. "**My finest creation.**"

"See, **that's what I don't get,**" Kolb said. "All this new stuff . . . it doesn't make **any sense.**"

"What do you mean?" Stump asked.

"Well . . ."

Kolb went on to explain that the **game server, Aetheria,** was drastically **different** from normal Minecraft.

Minecraft had changed a lot since it was first created—**thirty years and still going strong**—yet, the Aetheria server ran a **mod,** which further **altered the game's rules.**

Stormberries were one of the countless new things **the mod** included. They grew on leaf blocks arranged to resemble bushes. And these **blue** and **yellow berries** could be used to craft a variety of different food items: stormberry cookies, stormberry tea, stormberry rolls and biscuits. . . .

"But **not cakes,**" he said. "That crafting recipe just **wasn't in** the game's **code.** Someone had suggested it on the forums once, but **Entity** never **programmed it in.** Some of us figure that whatever happened during the event not only trapped us inside but also somehow unlocked **a beta version** of the server. **A new update** that Entity **was working on.**"

"You've lost me," Max said. "All right, forget all that. What about you being a **Savior?**"

Kolb took a **deep breath**. "Entity added these things called **quests**. Like, you talk to a villager, and the villager asks you to fetch him some lava or something. **Boom**, you're on **a quest**. So you go scoop up some lava in a bucket, give it to the villager, and he gives you **a reward of some kind**, and the server rewards you with **experience points**, and the quest is complete. Right, anyway, **um**, I guess I was given **a special quest**. Quests come in **three different types**. First, there's your **ordinary quest**. Simple ones like fetching a villager something. Then there are **quest chains**. You complete one quest, it leads to another, which leads to another. Finally, you have **quest trees**. They're more **complicated**, nonlinear. Me being **a Savior** is all part of one **big quest tree**."

"And what are you supposed to do?" I asked.

"I have to **re-forge this**."

He pulled out **a sword** from his inventory. **Its blade seemed to be broken.**

Critbringer

(Keep in mind my poor drawing skill. These paws, you see. His sword looked way cooler than this.)

"I recognize **that metal**," Max said. "That **rainbow** effect . . . that's **adamant,** isn't it?"

"Yeah. This is **Critbringer,** one of the **swords** crafted by **Entity** thousands of years ago. He **gave it to me** in-game before everything went black, said it was **one of the most powerful** quest items **ever made.**"

Stump didn't seem too **impressed:** "If it's **so powerful,** why is it **broken?**"

"It's just part of the **lore.** Entity wrote **detailed history** for the server. According to **the story, Herobrine** tried to **destroy** the blade during **the Second War.** Now, **seven fragments** are supposedly scattered across the world. Shards, they're called. Upon finding one, I can forge it back into the blade by **re-crafting** it. Each shard added will slightly upgrade **the sword's abilities.** Damage and on-hit effects, attack speed, **all that.** The problem is **locating the pieces.**"

"**I saw one!**" I blurted out. "A few days ago. In the Nether."

I told him about **Rarg** and how he had taken **EnderStar's secret treasure horde.**

The human listened intently. "I have to say, I've been too **preoccupied** with the events here. Perhaps I'll pay them **a little visit?**"

Max opened the huge tome again. "You mentioned something about Herobrine trying to **destroy the sword.** Look. It's all right here in this book."

"That's the **lore**." Kolb moved over and flipped through the pages. "But it isn't complete. The full lore is over **one thousand pages long. Entity** wrote this stuff over two years ago. When he became too busy with **programming,** he appointed several players as **scribes** to keep adding to the story."

"But you said Entity **crafted** that sword thousands of years ago," Stump said.

"**Right.** After the event, it's almost like whatever was written down in the lore **became reality** here."

(Um. Wow. Whenever I **level-up,** I really need to put more points into **Higher Intelligence,** because I don't understand much of anything.)

As far as I can grasp:

There was a **virtual reality** game on Earth known as **Minecraft.**

The world was **coming to an end,** so Kolb retreated into the game to say goodbye to his friends.

As their final hour approached, **the event** took place—everyone in the game blacked out and woke up here, and the game mysteriously came to life?

I glanced at the stormberry cake. "**Can I eat now?**"

"Sure." Stump handed me a slice. "**Nothing better** than home-crafted food."

After a cautious **sniff,** I ate the slice in a single bite—and promptly **spit out** crumbs. "Is . . . that . . . really . . . **food?!**"

That was Stump's **tipping point.** He was already in a **bad mood** after I devoured half a stack of his sugar *(sugar he crafted using his mom's special recipe, a family secret passed down through the generations)*, but **insulting his crafting** like that? It was almost as if he was a creeper in a villager costume **ready to explode.**

THURSDAY

This morning, a boy named **Bumbi** taught me **how to build.**

At least, I think.

My goal was to build **a chicken house** behind the school. *(I think it's called a "chicken coop," but Bumbi kept saying "chicken house.")*

It went okay at first.
He gave me some oak blocks.
I placed some oak blocks.
It really did go okay.

Then he **stopped** giving me oak blocks. Because he ran out. *(Is he really a teacher? Shouldn't a teacher be more prepared?)* Luckily, he had some **cobblestone.**

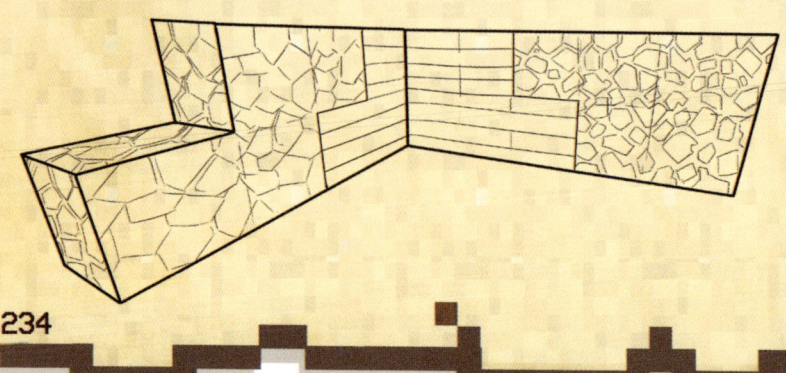

When he ran out of that, he gave me some **gravel.** When he ran out of that, he gave me some **pumpkins.**

And melons.

I'm no expert, but I'm fairly sure this guy didn't know what he was doing.

In Bumbi's world, this is what a chicken house is made of.

> Since he had no more materials left to give me, he decided that I should use sand for the roof. That didn't work out so well.

Oak stairs are **much better** for roof building, he said. And when you run out of stairs, **well . . .** you'd better use fence. **Yeah, that's it.**

I don't like building anymore.

Oh, but wait! Every good chicken house needs a door, **right?**

THURSDAY—UPDATE I

Later on today, I caught up with **Breeze** again.

She could sense that **something** was wrong. She kept asking me what was **on my mind.**

And she knew that it was more than just that **horrible** building experience with Bumbi. She knew it was something **serious.**

I wanted to tell her about what I'd learned yesterday with **Kolb,** but I'd **promised** not to say anything. Are we really living in **a game?** Am I just one of its **characters?**

If I really am just a so-called **NPC,** how am I able to **think** and **feel . . . ?**

And what about my **memories?** My past life? Endless days just being a **playful kitten**—are all of those memories **false?**

I'm **determined** to learn more about **my existence.** I want to know who I am. **What I am.** There must be a reason for all of this. **For this world. For me.**

And suddenly I recalled what **Rarg** had said to me. Sometimes, **he doesn't feel real.** I feel the same way when I'm **tired** or **stressed out.** Could it really be that I'm nothing more than . . . ?

"It's nothing," I said. "Just had a . . . **bad day.**"

"You sure?"

"Yeah."

As we wandered through the streets, I noticed that strange old man again. **Korbius.**

Breeze spotted him, too. It was pretty hard **not** to, honestly. He was just ten blocks away, **hiding behind some flowers.**

Breeze swiftly moved up to the rosebushes. "Why are you **spying** on us?"

The man stepped back, **flustered.** "What? **Me? Spying** on you?! Why no, I was simply . . . **admiring these flowers!** Yes! I **love flowers!** I'm a real connoisseur!"

"**Oh?** Then tell me: What color is **owl's eye?**"

"Well, **hmm** . . . I don't believe I've ever heard of such a flower. Could it be that I've met someone **more knowledgeable** about flowers than even myself? I find that **hard to believe!**"

"Just tell us why you keep **following us,**" Breeze said. "I saw you at the school. **The Clothing Castle,** too."

(Really? She must have fantastic eyesight, because I didn't see him then. Although I did get the feeling that someone **was** watching us.)

"Merely a **coincidence**," he said. "After all, I **am** a traveling merchant. **I'm always moving around!**"

"Whatever. See you around."

When she said this, **Korbius** smiled and said, "Oh, **yes. I will** be seeing you again. **Count on it.**"

Breeze stared at him for a moment, then turned to me. "Come on. **Let's go.**"

"**What's with** that guy?" I asked. "Was he really following us?"

"Yes. **Listen,** I need to go speak with my father. Maybe you can go have a **rest** now that your training is complete. See you back at the house?"

"Okay."

"By the way," she said, "my father agreed to let me **adopt you.**"

"**Adopt?** What is that?"

"It means my house is **your house** now."

"Forever?"

She smiled. "**Forever.**"

THURSDAY—UPDATE II

Last night, I had **horrible nightmares.**

I kept dreaming about what that human had said.

And **Runt.** When will I meet him? **What will happen** once I do?

I woke up in the middle of the night and **tossed and turned** on the carpet of Breeze's room. She was **stirring in her bed,** perhaps having **nightmares** as well.

I'm not sure why, **but . . .** I tried using **the tellstone** again. When I did, a variety of images flashed across the crystal's surface, from many different people, in many different places.

"Look at all these diamonds! They're everywhere!"

"Forget the diamonds for now! Look! See that vein?"

"Yeah. **Wow,** it's . . . what is that, five?"

"Human, sir? We've taken you far enough. You really don't want to go beyond the river."

"Is that biome really haunted?"

"Papa thinks so. Things grow strangely there. The animals act funny. And then . . ."

"Exploring the Overworld is way more fun than tinkering around with redstone circuits all day!"

"Private Lola, reporting for duty!"

"Did you succeed?"

"Yes, master."

"Are we really just NPCs . . . ?"

ABOUT THE AUTHOR

Cube Kid is the pen name of Erik Gunnar Taylor, a writer who has lived in Alaska his whole life. A big fan of video games—especially Minecraft—he discovered early that he also had a passion for writing fan fiction. Cube Kid's unofficial Minecraft fan fiction series, *Diary of a Wimpy Villager*, came out as e-books in 2015 and immediately met with great success in the Minecraft community. They were published in France by 404 éditions in paperback and now return in this same format to Cube Kid's native country under the title *Diary of an 8-Bit Warrior*. When not writing, Cube Kid likes to travel, putter with his car, devour fan fiction, and play his favorite video game.

OTHER BOOKS BY CUBE KID

Diary of an
8-Bit Warrior

Diary of an
8-Bit Warrior:
From Seeds to Swords

Diary of an
8-Bit Warrior:
Crafting Alliances

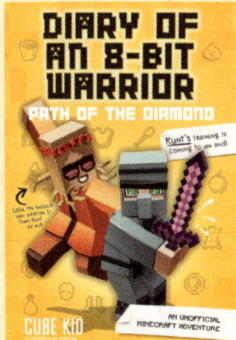

Diary of an
8-Bit Warrior:
Path of the Diamond

Diary of an
8-Bit Warrior:
Quest Mode